Bey Revelations

BOOK ONE: THE TWI-LIGHTERS

DAVID ROCKEFELLER

One Zeus Publishing

'I dedicate this first installment of BEYOND REVELATIONS, 'THE TWI-LIGHTERS' to my wife, Nancy Rockefeller, for without her help, and complete support this first book would've never gotten off the ground.

CONTENTS

INTRODUCTION

The Voice spoke and was heard as always.

The universe moved along as usual, except for a few strange occurrences. Planets orbited their suns; moons orbited their planets, and chaos throughout space continued as normal as normal went. But throughout the furthest reaches of space about twenty stars that had shone throughout most of their life cycles suddenly all at once exploded, creating so many different colors that at least half of them the human eye had never seen before. Then they all just as suddenly went black. This all took about one minute. Our own sun vibrated slightly from within for those sixty odd seconds, but otherwise returned to its normal self.

On Earth nothing physically changed—no earthquakes, no tide or weather changes—but emotional turmoil took place, for that short burst of chaotic time did not go unnoticed. People with strong and updated telescopes around the world saw at least one of these explosions. A few in higher and clearer elevations actually saw at least five, and more importantly, NASA and the numerous space observatories witnessed all of them. Decisions were made, calmly at first, but then as human nature took its natural course, chaos ensued in the realm of the powers that be.

*C*ommander James Johnson sat in-between Sun Ray and Moon Shine, two built-in robots that piloted Mars 2020, a massive spaceship, back to Earth. The ship was already fifty thousand miles into its journey with Mars in its rearview mirror. The rest of the crew, thirty in all, were already in hypersleep. JJ, as he was known by everyone, had just finished checking the controls and the robot's instructions. Everything had checked out perfectly; this was the fourth time this vessel had made this trip, and each time no problems had ever come up, but The Commander was still worried—not worried so much about the ship, but of himself.

He had been in the Mars space program for over twenty years, and The Commander the last five. This was his third trip, and the program wanted him to stay on indefinitely. JJ loved his job, but now he felt that he might be coming down with some sort of space sickness—one that was affecting his mind. He was forty-eight years old, six two, and still muscular. He had lifted weights religiously since he had turned twenty, and it showed. Professionally, he had nerves of steel, and never second guessed his decisions, but what he had seen down in the colony, *that* was what concerned him now—what he at least *thought* he saw. Against all regulations, he had told no one. Not even Co-Commander Dan Hunter, his best friend. And that bothered him as well. Why wouldn't he tell his best friend? They had always confided in each other; it was why these missions had gone on without a hitch, but this time he had stayed quiet. Why? It wasn't all that, or was it?

Two days ago, the mission had been suddenly cut short; NASA

had decided to bring everybody back after the events of the exploding suns, and more importantly, because of the way *our* sun had reacted. *That* should have concerned him; NASA sure was freaking out. But it was what he had seen on Mars's surface that worried him. Maybe the sun events and what he had seen were tied together, but he couldn't help wondering otherwise. He just couldn't help thinking he had "The Sickness." With his right leg slightly shaking, and both hands absentmindedly lightly tapping the silver metal shoulders of the two stoic robots, he looked out the front window of the spaceship, staring out into the dark and cold vastness of space, remembering what he had seen.

It had been three days ago, right after he had talked to communications back at NASA. The conversation had been all about the explosions. On Mars they also had seen the suns blow up, and although all seemed OK after that, the decision was made that *all* personal would come home until further notice. The colony was self-sufficient; the main computer and recently upgraded survival systems had been checked. The backup systems all looked good as well.

The colony was a circular dome-covered structure a mile and quarter in circumference. It was made of flexible glass held up by the artificial oxygen machinery located in the center of the colony. Air was blown out of the massive fans on all sides. This machinery was located inside a two-story structure which also housed the three mechanics that kept the oxygen circulating. They were considered the heart and soul of the colony. The dome was connected to heavy steel fifteen feet squared around the bottom of the dome. Every ten feet posts had been drilled thirty feet into the Mars surface and cemented, holding the whole structure together. Ten buildings of all sizes filled out the dome, housing at least twenty NASA employees at all times. The dome protected its personal from radiation and every type of storm the Red Planet could produce—some quite massive and intense. This would be the first time that it would be empty in its seven years of existence.

The Mars surface around the dome was flat for miles in all directions, with huge, mostly red mountains in the distance. Two cars and one truck were the transportation inside the dome, and three truck-like rovers were housed in a garage-type structure just outside.

As final interior systems were being checked, JJ took one of the rovers out to the eastern mountain range known as Red Hills, where a small gray metal outpost had been built. General tools, oxygen, space suits and various rover parts were stored there, just in case of emergency. He was going to check inventory and bring back the air tanks. Anybody could have done this, for it was definitely beneath his job qualifications, but he liked riding around the surface of the Red Planet. He always witnessed the most amazing views of the mountain range and rock formations. The red colorations were more spectacular than any desert landscapes back on Earth. Plus this was his down time; his place where he could think and meditate in private.

As he reached the storage building he saw the ten-person shuttle take off for Mars 2020, which had been orbiting Mars continuously for the past two months. Don Kingsley, the head mechanic, was also the commander of the shuttle and kept it in perfect working order. Another shuttle was attached to 2020, which JJ controlled when needed. The shuttles had not changed much since NASA first used them back in the days when they only had the space stations that orbited Earth. JJ watched as it rose into the sky. He figured that by the time he got back the shuttle would return, and the last of the NASA employees would be transported.

JJ sighed and shook his head, for he wasn't in agreement in closing the colony down completely. He thought that they were jumping the gun, but realized those decisions were above his pay grade. He knew that NASA was really freaked by the massive rippling effect that had happened even on our own sun, but space on a whole had settled down and seemed normal now. Sure, what had happened was unnerving, unexplainable to say the least, and that unknowing was what had led them quickly to their decision. He could definitely understand their worry. What if it wasn't over? What if it was only the beginning? As far as NASA was concerned, this was a first-time occurrence, so no one knew when it would be over—or what it all meant. Such uncertainty led to the thought, "Let's pull back a bit, and if nothing else happens, then quickly proceed forward and catch up to speed."

JJ loaded the oxygen tanks and was about to lock up when he saw a shadow around a large rock formation about a mile away that he hadn't seen when he had first arrived. He stared hard through his space helmet, and then wiped its glass. Was the shadow moving? No way! But it WAS! His first reaction was to step back, but then he froze. Someone, or something was coming around the formation! The figure was hazy and moving in and out of focus, but he could see that it was definitely walking *toward* him! It looked like a man, a human being, but the figure wasn't wearing any type of space suit. How could that be? He was so shocked that he couldn't move, otherwise he would've run like the devil. And then a dark thought hit him: could this be the devil himself? No space suits. No need for oxygen. No. No, that couldn't be! The figure got to a few hundred yards away before JJ saw it come into complete focus, and he realized his initial fears were wrong. But what he *did* see was just as unbelievable, for the figure he saw looked exactly like Jesus Christ! Twenty more yards, and he was sure of it. It *was* Jesus Christ himself wrapped in an old grayish robe that fell to his feet. He wore tannish sandels and walked slowly towards him, almost as if he had just stepped out of The Bible; and who knows, maybe he had! He was smiling, and then waved. He kept coming until he stood directly in front of JJ, then stopped and nodded.

The Jesus figure put his hand on JJ's shoulder and said, "Peace, love, and good praises to you on your journeys, my brother. You must be strong now, and lead like I know you can." The figure never moved his lips, but JJ heard this all in his mind very clearly; there was no doubt of that. Then the Jesus figure nodded, smiled even more broadly, and abruptly turned around and walked away. After fifty yards he turned around and waved again; still smiling. Then he continued on back to the rock formation and disappeared behind it.

JJ exhaled, and his body relaxed again. He could move. He quickly got into the rover and drove up to the rock formation. He got out and looked behind it. Nothing. No sign of the Jesus figure, no sign of life, no sign of anything, even though behind that rock formation he could see for miles before the mountains grew into the sky. There was no way anyone could have disappeared so quickly, yet the figure had. And yet he was sure that he had just seen, heard, and felt this Jesus look-alike. Had it really been Jesus Christ? It sure looked like him. He looked just like all the photos JJ had ever seen. And in that moment a strange warmth flowed through his complete core, and he knew; he *knew*! In his head, his soul, his *core*, he knew that it had been *Jesus Christ*! He was positive of it, and yet who would believe him? Who? Nobody would. No one! And if he told anyone, even his best friend, then he might begin to doubt it himself. It still didn't feel right, but it was this realization that made him decide to keep it to himself. He had to. He then got back into the rover and drove quickly back to the colony.

Now, as JJ continued to stare out into the vastness of outer space, he shook his head for about the millionth time as he remembered it all over again. Maybe he *was* sick and had imagined it all. Maybe he had "The Space Illness," imagining things, but he didn't want to believe that, though. No, he *wanted* to believe what he had seen—what he had *felt*!

JJ sighed and slapped both robots on their shoulders. They both looked skeletal in nature for dramatic effect, and it worked, for some people never got used to their appearance. Each had different personalities, and spoke in human baritone voices. Sun Ray was more serious and stoic. Moon Shine more human, capable of even joking around with the crew.

"Are you guys cool?" JJ asked, cocking his head. He always made it a point to talk to them as if they were human. It put him at ease, and he hoped that in some small way the robots felt like they were part of the crew.

"Roger that, Commander," Sun Ray responded, turning his head slightly.

"Yeah, boss, we're good," Moon Shine replied, turning to face the commander as well. "You can sleep peacefully this night."

"OK dudes. Just checking. Godspeed."

JJ got up and went to the back of the main deck where his sleep capsule was located. The Commander's module was the only one on the main deck. All others were located on deck two. He got inside and closed the glass lid.

"Sleep time, Moon Shine."

"Roger that, sir." The robot looked to his right panel, which had all passengers' names on it, and pushed the one that read "Commander James Johnson." A thin mist filled JJ's capsule and within twenty seconds he was in hypersleep.

The main deck became quiet again, for the robots never talked to each other, communicating only through the computers and panel boards they were attached to. They both faced straight ahead, staring into the dark void of space, with destination Earth far in the distance. They didn't know it then, but they would never see or communicate with another human being again.

Space as we know it can never be truly defined. Not in our minds, and not in NASA's. You can try to explain this, and try to explain that, but in the end it will somewhere, sometime defy logic. A small example: Venus and Earth are similar in size and are neighbors in our solar system, yet Earth rotates counterclockwise and Venus rotates clockwise. Crazy, but maybe you could somehow accept that, except *all* the other planets rotate like Earth. Venus is the exception, and that's how you have to approach space on a whole. Always expect the exception and know that the exception is the rule. Maybe in a couple of thousand years we will know so much more about the vastness of space, but at present it's an ongoing mystery on many fronts. NASA deals with this every day. They knew that Mars 2020 (the blueprint for the spaceship going to Mars and back was first designed in that year and the name stuck) was on its way back, and even though all seemed OK, they would hold their collective breath until it was safely docked back home. The unexplainable exploding stars and the way our own sun reacted scared the hell out of the higher-ups at NASA, and in Washington. They were basically running around like chickens with their heads cut off, trying to find any data they could on such occurrences, but none were forthcoming. Events that are out of your hands are totally unnerving, and in this instance NASA's nerves were shot. All they could do was cross their fingers and hope nothing else happened, and the spaceship with all souls aboard made it back safely.

But something *did* happen . . .

*M*ars 2020 continued its journey back to Earth. The spaceship was a mile long with six circular wheels that went around its cylindrical center. The wheels turned around the cylinder constantly as the ship moved forward. Inside there were a total of two hundred compartments of all sizes (more than half with windows), plus the main deck. The main cylinder had three levels. As Mars 2020 moved onward, lights blinked on and off inside and outside the ship. From a distance it looked like a Christmas tree on steroids, in stark contrast to the dark space around it.

Twelve hours after JJ Johnson went into hypersleep, NASA's deepest fears surfaced. It was an event of catastrophic conse-quences. Without warning, a large flash washed over the complete universe. Space, which was black and endless, suddenly became complete blinding light. Our sun, and every other star in the universe, went from light to contrasting black. In a millisecond, everything in the universe suddenly became a negative of itself. Comets, moons, planets, and anything else moving around space turned black. Looking at Earth from its satellites and space stations, our world suddenly went dark. Massive amounts of lights seen at night around the planet suddenly disappeared. Earth became a black sphere, third from a now-black sun.

At the same time of the Event, Mars 2020 completely shut down. All its lights turned off, and all engines shut down. The spaceship became powerless, and its speed slowed as its engines stopped working. Inside 2020 all went black. The two robots also shut down, lifelessly sitting at the front of the dark ship. And *that* is how you could describe the entire ship: lifeless, devoid of movement. In an instant, Mars 2020 became a ghost ship. Complete lifelessness . . .

Just over a minute after the first flash, a second flash occurred, and then everything went back to normal. Space became black again, the stars shone as before, the planets went back to their normal colors. The universe was as it was—well, almost. Our sun shined bright, but Earth, although it returned to its mostly blue color, remained powerless and completely dark and lightless. Earth in its half-day state appeared normal, but its night's state remained completely dark.

Orbiting satellites and the space stations of different countries also remained dark—lightless and powerless. They became dark spheres, objects orbiting a dark and powerless planet that slowly but surely were falling back toward Earth's surface.

Mars 2020 also remained dark and lifeless. The robots did not come back to life. Everything inside the vessel remained quiet. Machinery throughout the ship didn't work. Lightless, it continued to slow down on its journey to a now dark planet.

The colony on Mars was completely powerless as well. Its systems remained quiet. The dome was dark. No oxygen circulated. Its temperatures dropped quickly, and machinery froze. It was dying quickly. Within minutes, after ten long years assembling it and keeping it running, it died. The dome imploded, and the buildings began to decay and crumble.

In the next hour, various other stars—some large, some small, some old, some young—began to explode like the others before them. The universe was subtlety changing, yet most of it went back to its normal state. Our sun again shook and vibrated slightly as these new stars exploded, and when the last of the suns had disappeared into darkness, the universe calmed down once again. One might think that our sun was fighting not to explode like the others, and maybe it was . . .

*B*efore this second event took place, in hypersleep, JJ Johnson dreamed. He dreamed a lot. It wasn't unusual to dream, but if JJ hadn't been put into a created state of sleep, he would've woken up screaming many times. He was having nightmare after nightmare. Most of them involved his family. JJ had met his wife Gloria in the space academy. They both became astronauts at the same time and were in many programs together. It took JJ about a week to fall head over heels for her, but almost a month to ask her out. Gloria had been more focused about her dedication to becoming an astronaut, and so she wasn't outwardly aware of anyone else around her. She only focused on the objective: become an astronaut, go out and explore space, get promoted if the circumstances dictated it, and then eventually retire.

JJ loved space, he wanted the same things Gloria did, but he was into having fun at the same time, being more of a free spirit. When he finally asked her out, she said no. JJ didn't give up, getting on special projects with her, on research teams—anything to be near her. After tiring of him asking her out almost daily for a couple of months, she finally agreed to go out on a date—a dinner, but a dinner only. She had way too much studying to do. Everything came easier for JJ; he picked up all programs space quicker than most cadets, and had helped many a student succeed. Gloria had liked this most of all about him. He was a team player and a born leader. Of course, she didn't tell him that at first. She liked JJ, adored just about everything about him; but when it came to love she slowed down that process to a crawl.

Gloria was pretty by most standards: auburn, shoulder-length hair surrounding a roundish cute face, an athletic body with legs that seemed to go on forever. She had been asked out many times, had gone out on a few dates, but nothing serious had ever occurred. No man had ever caused fireworks to go off inside her, and that was perfectly fine because focusing on a career was foremost in her mindset. That blueprint was being followed to the letter until she met JJ.

Against her will, he *did* make her heart skip a beat; he *did* make her want to throw her whole plan away. But somehow, she found the strength to stay her path—at least for a while. They *did* go out to dinner. They *did* go out on dates. And they *did* totally fall in love with each other. They graduated from the academy together, got married, and got jobs on the new space station. JJ quickly rose in ranks, while Gloria found her true place in the space station laboratory. She loved it there, never wanting to leave. At JJ's urging, she did go to Mars on his first trip, but even though it was an amazing overall journey, seeing space and the beauty of the red planet, she yearned for the lab. She enjoyed the exploratory projects they conducted there; it was never boring, and she was *still* in space. And the sights of space, Earth, and the moon were amazing! This place was her calling—at least for the foreseeable future.

While on their trip to Mars together, Eve was conceived. Two years later JJ Junior was added to the family. They both were carbon copies of Gloria, and JJ's friends used to kid him that he couldn't possibly be the father, for neither child looked anything like him. Now they were ten and eight as he slept, the three of them living on the space station. Eventually they all planned on moving to the colony full-time. Future plans were in the works for Gloria to have her own lab and team there, while JJ would work for NASA in its boardroom. They would become full time Martians, hopefully living out their days there, their two children continuing to grow and mature in the Mars colony lifestyle.

In JJ's nightmares, that was never going to happen. They all ended in death—horrible, unspeakable endings. They all centered around a presence that was always just out of view, orchestrating and creating new ways of destroying life on every level. One nightmare intertwined into another to create a hell JJ couldn't escape from until the power went off. Then all went black, flatlining.

*S*pace went back to its chaotic state after the second event took place. No more suns exploded. In our solar system, we still had eight planets plus dwarf rock Pluto, their moons orbiting normally around them. The asteroid belt continued to orbit around the sun in-between Mars and Jupiter; meteors and comets flew in their haphazard directions. No more bright flashes occurred.

*T*he first supernatural event happened just after all power went out. As Mars 2020 lost all power and slowed down, the temperature inside the ship fell quickly. And then somehow stabilized. And then actually rose. The vessel, seen from the outside, still six months away from Earth, seemed to disappear inside an invisible doorway. First the front, then the center, and then the complete ship disappeared from view. Then it slowly reappeared through another doorway directly above Central Park in Manhattan, New York City. It hovered without power as if in suspended animation. It's six circular wheels barely missed the buildings closest to the park. The spaceship then seemed to become part of the Manhattan skyline, unmoving, not unlike its surrounding skyscrapers.

*I*nside the spaceship the temperature climbed to 65 degrees Fahrenheit. It was July in the city, and in the middle of a normal—and perpetually active—summer heat wave. Nothing was different about that; temperatures had averaged 90 degrees during the summer season for the past twenty years, but the last five years the summers had gotten progressively warmer. Global warming was no longer any type of debate; it was a hot grim reality for the most part. Yes, there were still some detractors, but not many. The "Line of Salvation" talked about had come and gone; there was no going back. You could not talk about it enough; Earth was in trouble. Droughts across the United States and beyond were in dangerous states. Heavy rains and thunderstorms caused damaging flash flooding. Hurricanes were on the rise worldwide, many becoming Category 5 monsters. Super storms like the historic Sandy became more commonplace. New diseases cropped up around the world, spread by mosquitos and newer forms of insects, most of them deadly. Vaccines were created to combat the sicknesses they created and spread, but many; young and old still succumbed to them.

This current heat wave had gone over 105 degrees for the past three days in Manhattan. Air conditioning systems had failed throughout the city when the power went off, and they were *all* never coming back on. Another hurricane was forming in the middle of the Atlantic, steamrolling toward the Caribbean Islands; there were three typhoons in the Pacific. Summers overall had become dreaded disasters—hell on Earth. The handwriting was on the wall. NASA knew this and ten years ago had revved up all space and evacuation programs. Construction companies had been created to build walls to hold back the rising water levels around the planet. One had been finished just last year around Manhattan, already saving many areas and buildings around the island. They were made of concrete and stood fifteen feet above hightide at the moment. If water levels increased further, and they would, so too could the height of the walls. Other ideas and projects were in the works worldwide, but the world was fighting a battle Mother Nature and overall weather conditions was going to win eventually; it was now just a matter of how soon.

This was the type of situation Mars 2020 had levitated into. It was one of the biggest reasons the colony on Mars was conceived. Before that it was the new large space station that could house two hundred souls. These projects were just two of the many different endeavors the whole world, working as a team, were feverishly moving forward on.

*a*n hour after Mars 2020 mysteriously appeared over Central Park, JJ Johnson's space capsule's door opened by itself. The light mist that filled the capsule dissipated, and the ship's Commander slowly woke up. The fog behind his eyes slowly cleared, and he gingerly sat up, his hands gripping the sides of the sleep cylinder. He looked over at the robots, and then realized all was not well. Usually there were lights blinking on all the panels—different colored lights surrounding the main board, accompanied by computer noises. Some blinked on and off, and now the main deck was dark and devoid of any semblance of life.

As JJ groggily stood up, he looked past the robots and gasped. "No way, no frigging way!" he said, in total shock. He saw blue—not the darkness of space around the space station, but blue. It was the blue of the sky back on Earth, and that couldn't be. The spaceship just couldn't be in Earth's atmosphere! It wasn't possible! He ran to the front of the deck and stared out the window and was further flabbergasted. He saw New York City, the various-sized high risers staring back at him, and he suddenly felt sick to his stomach. That wasn't *that* unusual after being in hypersleep, but this was different—much different. This was something impossible in every way, shape or form, and would make anybody feel nauseous.

JJ turned around and stared back and forth at both robots incredulously and realized for the first time that they were in "off mode," and powerless—as powerless as the rest of the main deck seemed to be. He fiddled with the main panel, but nothing happened. Dead, dead, all was dead. He stared all around the deck and it was all the same—powerless, all of it.

This has never happened before. What's going on? he thought frantically, feeling faint. He took a few deep breathes to calm himself down.

"What happened to you guys?" he asked out loud, staring back and forth at the two robots. "What the hell happened up here?"

And how in God's name did we end up in New York City? he thought, still not believing any of it. He went to the intercom. "Anybody up? Anybody! Pick up!" And then he felt slightly stupid. Nothing worked. There was no power. *No power!* Of course no one would answer.

JJ sat down in his commander's seat and stared again out at the city. His legs felt like jelly. His stomach continued to churn. He suddenly remembered that he had dreamed some vicious nightmares in hypersleep. Were they connected? At this time those nightmares had been mostly forgotten, and he felt lucky not to have remembered any, for he knew all too well that they had been terrifying. He felt as if he was in one now, too, he reasoned. Somehow, he knew something terrible had happened, something during his induced sleep. He remembered seeing a Jesus Christ figure on his last day on Mars, the exploding suns, the quick exit from the red planet. It all became too much, too coincidental. He suddenly retched forward and vomited on the deck floor.

He gasped and breathed deeply. He had to check on the crew—everyone. He weakly got up and shakily walked toward a circular staircase that descended to the second floor. There were elevators on all three decks, but he knew they wouldn't work without power. He went down the steps, needing the railing to steady himself. Reaching the bottom, he walked down the hall to the large hypersleep area in the center of the ship. Ironically, the doors here opened only manually in case of power failure or emergency.

JJ opened the doors and went inside. He looked around and saw that all the cylinders were still closed, all glass doors locked shut. The cylinders went five high, twenty deep on both sides of the room—more than enough for this Mars journey. He went up to the nearest cylinder, looked inside, and there was no one inside. He went to the next. And the next. They were all empty! He checked every last one of them. All empty!

How could this be? he thought, franticly, looking all around the vast room. The room was eerily quiet. In fact, the whole ship was quiet. Could he . . . could he be alone? It wasn't possible. Where could they be?

He walked out into the hallway and checked every room and area. The labs, sickbay, and the research rooms were all empty. He took the stairs down to the engine room, and *that* was empty as well. Down the hall to the café. Empty. The transporter room. Empty. The crew were all gone. He was alone, alone on this massive vessel. As impossible as it sounded, it appeared to be a true reality.

JJ took further inventory: No power. No energy. No sound. No people. And the spaceship was hovering over New York City, not even in space. Mars 2020 always docked at the space station. It couldn't enter Earth's atmosphere. Yet it had.

He went back up to the main deck and sat back down in his commander's chair. He had to think. He thought of every possibility. Could everybody be off the ship? No. Without power, you wouldn't be able to open the hatch. So then how was *he* going to get off? JJ sighed and shook his head. This was insanity! Crazy! He had to digest all of this before mapping out a plan. And twilight was setting in outside. Further action would wait until morning.

Suddenly he got up and stared outside. New York was dark. There were no lights—no building lights, no lights on the streets or in the distance. Whatever had happened had knocked out the power down there as well, maybe the whole planet. That was a scary thought. He was exhausted, confused, and demoralized. He laid down in his capsule instead of in the commander's quarters. He felt better there. He didn't feel so alone, even though both robots were essentially lifeless. He fell off to sleep almost immediately. He dreamed lightly, if at all. No bad dreams. The nightmares were alive now, in real time, waiting for him to wake up.

J woke up hungry. It was still dark outside, and the inside of the ship was darker still. He walked down to his quarters, mostly feeling his way through the darkness. He went over to his locker and grabbed a handful of protein bars he had stashed there. He hungrily ate two, and then walked back to the main deck.

He stared out the front window and looked east. The sun was about to rise, orange in the distance. He also noticed other oranges eastbound, about ten of them scattered up and down the horizon—fires, large fires, burning brightly in the twilight. Dark smoke was rising into the sky. He should've seen them yesterday and last night, but he guessed that he hadn't because of the shock he was under. That shock was gone now; sleep had done wonders in that department. JJ had time to realize that anything was possible now. New York City did not seem as quiet as he had first thought.

Planes, he thought grimly. Crashing planes when the power went out. Two or three seemed to be where Kennedy Airport would be. If that was the case, there would be a lot of them out there—and unfortunately, a lot of deaths.

The eastern horizon got brighter, and now he could more clearly see dark smoke rising into the air, some going over the spaceship. Flames could now clearly be made out, and they climbed into the sky. JJ assumed buildings were also on fire. The situation seemed worse as the skies brightened. The inside of the spaceship also started to lighten, and that was good. As soon as there was enough light, he would get moving. He had to get off this vessel. He had to find people; he had to know what had happened. It was all such a mystery!

The protein bars also worked wonders; he felt full, and he also felt energized. His stomach had returned to normal, and JJ was ready, as usual, to take on the world.

He watched the sun come up over the horizon, and he saw that the Whitestone Bridge was damaged—no fire or smoke, but severely damaged in the middle. As skies brightened, he saw the back of a plane sticking out of the water below it. It had hit the bridge. Looking over at the Throgs Neck Bridge, it appeared OK.

JJ sighed, left the main deck, and headed down the stairs toward the bottom of the ship. How he would get to the ground he had no idea, but he knew he had to find a way.

J didn't know this, but the hurricane in the Atlantic overnight had grown into another category 5 monster, churning slowly westward towards what was left of the Caribbean Islands. Massive storms over the years had destroyed or swallowed some of them while making others completely uninhabitable, destroying all structures big and small. The three typhoons in the Pacific had also grown into strong Category 5's. Two were headed toward the Philippines, one six hundred miles ahead of the other, and one was headed for Japan. This was the first time in history four Category 5 storms existed at the same time. Disaster on a whole new level seemed to be in the forecast.

Back in New York City, the sun rose against the eastern skyline. The heatwave would see another day, well on its way to over 100 degrees again. Without power, the city and its neighboring boroughs would be in big trouble. The fires still burning weren't going to help lower the soaring temperatures, and the smoke from those fires would make it tough to breathe. Visibility was an issue as well. All and all, it wasn't shaping up to be a good day in Manhattan.

Across the Hudson River in New Jersey, fires were burning as well. Smoke rose into the skies around Newark Airport. Planes had crashed all around the airport area. Smoke could be seen rising far into the blue western skies. It looked like a war zone, and New York and New Jersey didn't seem to be winning.

Various smaller fires burned throughout the city and on the bridges, possibly car accidents. Under the massive spaceship, Central Park seemed to have escaped any damage. The vessel even blocked the sun from blazing down on the park, shading it and keeping it cooler than the rest of Manhattan Island and its surrounding boroughs.

 J reached the engine room and opened a door to one of the rotating wheels that was now stationary. There was a metal ladder that would rotate to the bottom as the wheel turned. Since the wheel was no longer moving, neither did the ladder. The Commander descended the one hundred rungs to the bottom. There was a hatch on the floor, a way out of the spaceship for mechanics fixing an engine due to some malfunction or general maintenance. He hoped that with the ship powerless, the hatch's lock system would be off. It was. He turned a small wheel counterclockwise and the hatch opened. This opened up into a small compartment where another hatch to the outside was located. Again, the locking system was off, and he turned the hatch wheel. He opened this hatch, praying it wouldn't be too far to the ground. His prayers were half answered. The ground was fifteen feet down—not that far, but far enough. There were different assorted steel and rope ladders in the engine room. JJ went back up, found a rope ladder, went back down, and tied it to the hatch. It made it to about a foot off the ground. Perfect. This way he could go in and out of the spaceship if needed. He went down the ladder, jumped off gracefully, and stood on the brownish grass in Central Park.

Even with the shade from the ship, JJ could feel the oncoming heat of the day. It was already brutal. He hadn't felt Earth's summers in quite a while. He wasn't used to them, and immediately started sweating profusely. He would need water quickly—lots of fluids. He should go back for that and more protein bars, but there had to be many stores close by. He needed to see people, see someone—anyone. He looked around and saw and heard nothing—nothing. It was as if the city was on mute. There was no movement, no sounds, no sign of people. He took off eastward toward the first row of buildings.

*a*s JJ walked past 5th Avenue and worked his way eastward toward Madison, the temperature reached 100 degrees for the fourth straight day. The City felt like an oven. The commander looked all around but saw no one. Cars, buses, and trucks flooded the streets; some had crashed into each other, but none moved. A strange thought hit him. Usually it took some time to get used to Earth's gravity, but he was good from the get-go. And then he realized something else, something eerie, something that unnerved him. There were no birds, no dogs, no animals—none. He had been to the city many times, and had always seen many birds flying throughout the streets and Central Park. He had seen many pigeons being fed by people sitting on park benches. Dogs walked by their owners up and down the streets. He saw none of this now, and those facts were added to the impossible situation overall. Life on Manhattan was always crowded, and the traffic chaotic and busy. There was none of that now. It was totally quiet. This *never* happened—day or night! He seriously wondered if he was on Earth at all, for this was all alien in nature. Maybe the spaceship had somehow passed through into another dimension, one with a world without life. This he seemed to dismiss quickly, though, for this *was* Manhattan. It was real. Something had happened while he was in hypersleep; he was sure of it now. He decided to go back to the ship and regroup. Being alone like this felt very strange and unnerving. Something was off and very wrong here. Being back on the ship would put him at ease a bit, even though there was nobody in there either. Sweating profusely, he half ran all the way back to the ship.

J sat eating protein bars and drinking water on the main deck. He stared intently at the robots, hoping against hope they would come back online. They appeared lifeless, in the early stages of decay, and the commander's heart sank a little more. Gathering all information that he knew so far, he assessed the situation. No sign of life on the ship or in the city. No animals. No movement of any kind. No sounds. Extreme heat. A strong heat wave overtaking the city. Fires. Smoke. Moving in the city would be tough. Frustrated, he decided to wait until later in the day, evening even. He had been born in Queens, and his family had moved upstate when he was young. He knew the city well. If there was anybody out there, they might go underground in this heat. But first, he was going to check out the Park Zoo to the south. If people had left the city, they could. The animals couldn't. If the zoo was empty, then he truly was alone. Another uneasy thought: If no one was there, or anywhere else, then what about the space station? His family was there. Could they be gone as well? It was a grim thought—one he didn't want to dwell on. He needed to rest now, recharge his mental mechanisms. He reclined his chair, closed his eyes, and was asleep within minutes.

*a*s planned, JJ left the spaceship later in the day as the sun was falling into the western horizon. He closed the hatch door, keeping the coolness of the vessel inside. It was still hot outside, but the temperature had dropped a bit. JJ figured 85 degrees, less humidity. His plan to wait until now seemed to be the correct one. As he walked south, he discovered a pack of cigarettes and a book of matches on the grass. He didn't smoke, but he tried lighting one of the matches. It lit! Nothing worked, but the match did. He put the matches in his pocket and walked on. None of the flashlights on the ship had worked; maybe all batteries were drained of energy as well. He would light something to see when it got dark. Not far away a bicycle lay on its side, a ten speed. He picked it up, got on, and pedaled south through the park.

*a*s the commander of Mars 2020 bicycled downtown, he noticed many things. One of them, none stranger than the others, was the holes. JJ saw in the grass every now and then various-sized holes; some were deep, some shallow. Some were five feet by three, some two by two. Some were bigger, some smaller. It was a curiosity he would investigate later. For now, though, there were more pressing needs.

A Little Knowledge: Manhattan Island was home to many cemeteries. Some were quite famous, such as New York Marble, Saint Patrick's Cathedral Crypt, and Trinity Church Cemetery Vaults, to name a few. There were also graveyards and single graves that were unmarked. Some cemeteries had been completely moved so the buildings in the city could be built. Protests led nowhere, and the city grew day by day, month by month, year by year. Those protests were slowly forgotten over the years, but the people that had been moved weren't. Their names and history may had been wiped off the face of the Earth, but they were never *really* forgotten, for every life mattered in the end.

Now, in all those cemeteries, the headstones were still there with names—some famous—and dates and quotes, but where dirt, coffins, and bodies should've been only holes remained. In every cemetery, in every grave, only empty dark holes remained. In all mausoleums, remains and their urns were gone. All over the land, over the whole *world*, not one body that had once lived and now deceased and buried was left behind, whether they were ones with tombstones, which were remembered and honored, or those that were cast away like yesterday's garbage—those *dishonored* in the name of progress. And those plots that no one knew about to begin with (right or wrong, desecration or not, in plain sight or forgotten), were all gone now. A few of those forgotten ones were what JJ Johnson passed on his way to the zoo.

ooking Back: One of the nightmares JJ had in hypersleep centered around his mother. Marie Ann Johnson had lived for eighty-two years, all but four of them celebrated. Those other years were her last ones. Cancer had come calling, and slowly but surely beaten her down. When Marie was a newlywed, she was told she couldn't have children, couldn't conceive, but while having a normal physical it was discovered she was pregnant. Marie and JJ's father Robert were elated. They had planned on maybe adopting a child; they wanted a family so badly, and now their prayers had miraculously been answered. The pregnancy was a difficult one, and on the day JJ was born, both he and his mother were almost lost—almost. Marie had complications, but she fought strong and came back stronger. JJ took a little longer. It was touch and go for a while, but Robert and Marie's little child fought hard. He possessed a strong will to survive, the doctors said, and they were right.

After being in a coma for a week, connected to tubes that kept him alive, he came out of it and grew strong. JJ went home a few days later and was never really sick again. A cold now and then, a virus when it went throughout his school class, but that was it. As his early years grew to teenage years, JJ grew stronger than most. All in-between was better than good. JJ studied hard, played on the school baseball and football teams, was popular, and did everything he could to follow his dream of becoming an astronaut. He had exceeded that dream, and his parents could not have been prouder.

Robert died of a massive heart attack when JJ was on his first voyage to Mars. He was seventy. JJ was devastated, but his mother did her best to comfort her son. She told him it was more important to be where he was, helping to advance the space program. He reluctantly agreed, and got through his father's sudden death. When Marie was diagnosed with stomach and liver cancer, she hid it from her son. She knew that if JJ realized she was sick he would not have gone back to Mars. He would've stayed to care for her, put his career on hold, and in her mind that was NOT going to happen. Marie fooled him completely. On video phone she wore a lot of makeup and bulky clothes to hide her skin color and weight loss, and she talked to him only on her good days, which became less and less as the cancer took its toll. When she died, JJ was just docking at the space station on his second return trip from Mars. Again, he was devastated, but he had become more mature and understood why his mother had done what she had. In fact, he loved her even more because of those actions. He realized just how blessed he had been. Having two great parents that had provided a strong foundation, filled with love and devotion, was more than he could've ever asked for. They had passed on so much knowledge to him. He knew that the only way he could repay them was to be the best he could be—be a good husband and treat his children like he had been. He felt that he had done a good job of that, and that had comforted him. He could go on. His life could move forward. They had left him with a happiness that he could pass on to others.

In hypersleep, NASA had created a mist that would normally reduce the risk of bad dreams. You would be put in a relaxed type of sleep, usually preventing nightmares, or what the specialists referred to as "jagged thought processes." Tests had been run for years, the results very positive, but the nightmares had cut right through those preventatives and right into JJ's soul. The NASA mist had failed him completely. On and on they came, driving his subconscious to the brink of insanity. If they had continued on a normal voyage back to Earth, he would have probably woken up completely mad.

This particular dream had JJ sitting in a hospital room watching his mother waste away. She twisted in constant pain, begging for pain meds. The cancer had completely taken its toll. JJ got the nurse to administer another dose of pain medication. As soon as the nurse left and his mother settled down a bit, a dark figure with skeleton-like fingers suddenly appeared and approached his mother. He couldn't see it's face; it was covered by a black hood, but it was filled with many sharp fangs. As JJ sat frozen in his seat, the figure began to eat his mother's face. It ate her eyes first, and then both cheeks. His mother screamed bloody murder. JJ screamed even louder, but he could do nothing. He couldn't move. He watched in horror as the figure ate her complete face down to her skull. Still she screamed, begging for death that didn't come.

The dark creature continued to eat his beloved mother until she was nothing but a skeleton. JJ begged the figure to stop, but the monster just ate faster. With his mother in agony, the creature stood over the screaming skeleton, laughing like a mad hatter, and then suddenly vomited his mother's remains all over her. It molded back over her, but her mouth was in her forehead now, and both her eyes were where her mouth should have been. Her screams of pain were sounds that went beyond agony. JJ was crying uncontrollably, and then the dark figure began eating her all over again. Again, and again this happened; each time her face became more grotesque than the last. It never stopped until the next nightmare began . . .

Weather Update One: The hurricane situation had gotten worse. Two more storms were forming off the African Coast. Both looked formidable. The Category 5 storm in the Atlantic was just northeast of the Caribbean Islands now. The British Virgin Islands were really getting pounded; Puerto Rico was in the bull's-eye next. That storm's strongest winds had reached 190 miles per hour. Destruction on all of the northern islands was a certainty. The hurricane showed no signs of weakening; if anything, it would probably grow bigger and stronger.

One of the Category 5 typhoons was going through the Philippines, destroying a lot of the infrastructure. It had not weakened and would continue westward toward Vietnam. It's twin, five hundred miles to the east, would hit the northern Philippines and then turn north toward Taiwan. It was weakening slightly, but still a Category 5. The third monster was further out in the Pacific and was zeroing in on Japan. This one was the biggest and strongest of the three, and still growing. The strongest winds were two hundred miles per hour at the moment. Japan's immediate future seemed bleak.

GJ reached the Tisch Children's Zoo and bicycled inside. He cycled slowly counterclockwise around the small zoo but saw no animals. He passed the Acorn Theatre, then doubled back. Nothing—just quiet. All exhibits were devoid of life.

He left the children's park and entered the main zoo by the Delacorte Clock. It wasn't working. Shocker there! He rode through the whole zoo. Central Garden—no sea lions. Tropic Zone—empty. The Temperate Territory—the same. No grizzly bears, no penguins or sea birds. Both zoos were deserted. New York City was deserted—an alarming situation to say the least. JJ sat by the Central Garden and shook his head in despair. Was he the only human being left on Earth? In the universe? If so, what then? What *could* he do? Now that the animals were gone as well, the first pangs of loneliness set in. He loved animals; he always had. Growing up he had two dogs. Now he missed them both more than ever. They had truly been best friends. He sighed.

JJ decided to grab as much food from the Dancing Crane Cafe as possible. He grabbed a backpack from the gift shop and went over to the cafe. Chips, candy, and just plain junk food was put in the pack. Something was off, though. There wasn't any meat here—no hot dogs or hamburgers, no chicken, no sausage. He went in the back and checked the freezer. Defrosted rolls, but no meat. Did they run out? What a mystery.

JJ got back on the bike and peddled back to the spaceship. The sun had set. The day had cooled off a bit. He decided to tour the whole city, no matter how long it took. There had to be evidence of what happened here. Tomorrow would be another day. The commander opened the hatch and went inside. Night overtook the city—a city now without lights, movement, or life.

*C*ommander JJ Johnson was on a mission. He would commit to touring the city, trying to find any clue that would explain this strange situation. And when JJ Johnson committed to doing something, his focus and determination was second to none. As he left the spaceship the next day, he decided to check Central Park out entirely. The holes he had seen sporadically on his way to the zoos were of interest, as were abandoned picnic baskets that contained sandwiches without deli meat between bread or heroes. Assorted chips, spoiled potato and macaroni salads in containers were inside the baskets, but all meats were missing-odd clues, but clues none the same.

Untied boats and kayaks floated aimlessly in the lake, probably owned by Loeb Boathouse. He bicycled south, and by Wall Street the mystery of the holes was solved when he passed the Trinity Church Cemetery. Empty plots filled out the entire graveyard, eerily casting odd shadows throughout the grounds. JJ didn't stay long, for this realization blew his mind. Even the deceased were gone. But why—why was *he* still here? He went into a few dark stores, and they had everything but meat. JJ loved steak, but it didn't look like he was going to eat any of that anytime soon! He circled downtown and then bicycled back up the west side of the park. That was day one.

For the next few days JJ got in his exercise. He bicycled all over Manhattan. East one day, west all the way to the George Washington Bridge the next. Whatever he had seen burning on his first night was out now. Museums were searched. Animal remains in there were gone as well. The United Nations took half a day, Rockefeller Center and the Port Authority the other. The third day he climbed the Empire State Building, seeing many fires in every direction burning; some looking like they were out of control.

During these three days the heat wave raged on. It was brutal inside as he climbed the one hundred floors. He was thinking of going into some of the other skyscrapers, but it was way too hot. He drank more fluids than at any time he could remember.

JJ went back inside the spaceship at the end of that third day completely despondent. There were no human beings anywhere, no animals of any kind, and empty plots where the dead should be resting. The never-ending heat wave oppressed him, and the fires and smoke that surrounded him. As he laid down in his capsule, he wished he would disappear before morning. That wouldn't happen; instead, every day after this one would turn JJ's world upside down. By far, his life would never be the same...

*W*eather Update Two: During the last night of JJ's "normal" life the heatwave in New York City broke with a bang. Thunderstorms rumbled throughout Manhattan, and lightning lit up the skies; thunder was so loud one would think it could crack the heavens wide open. It rained extremely hard, three inches by sunrise. Temperatures thankfully dropped 20 degrees. Storms on and off would continue throughout the afternoon. New York and the tri-state area surely needed it; fires were burning everywhere, and the rain was putting a lot of the smaller ones out. The larger ones upstate would continue to burn for a while, but close to the city it became much less dangerous.

General News Information: Fires throughout the United States became widespread. When the power went out, airplanes of all shapes and sizes suddenly fell from the skies and exploded. Fires started everywhere, growing out of control. Some of them crashed into wooded areas or forests themselves. Only nature could put them out, but the United States on a whole was in drought mode. Heavy thunderstorms were the norm now, and they helped contain a lot of the blazes, but still a lot of the country felt its effects. It just wouldn't rain enough in certain parts of the country. Some lakes had already completely dried up, and most reservoirs were way down. Everyone was under restricted water-use rules and regulations and had been for the past ten years or so. Grass turned brown early in the summer season, and a lot of crops didn't stand a chance. Less and less produce arrived at the local supermarkets. Farmers were fighting a losing battle every year. The government helped as much as they could, but the future seemed bleak. The ratio was going in the wrong direction: saltwater levels were rising, and freshwater levels were dropping rapidly.

Weather Update Three: The hurricane situation was off the charts. Three in the Atlantic, one in the Pacific, plus three monster typhoons. Two had formed just off the coast of Africa. One would head northwest into the open waters; it would not be a threat. It had grown into a Category 2 storm, but conditions ahead of it weren't favorable for it to get any stronger. That was the only good news. The other one quickly grew into a Category 3 and was heading due west. Any land in that direction could be in danger. Conditions *were* favorable for it to grow. Hurricane three was a Category 5 and had just passed to the north of Puerto Rico. The island was in shambles; the northern coastline decimated. Next up was the Dominican Republic and Haiti. It was moving northwestward. The Bahamas and the southeast coast of the United States appeared to be in its path as well. Winds at its center approached 180 miles an hour. It would maintain its strength. Another hurricane had formed off the western coast of Mexico and was traveling west. Currently a Category 1 storm, it had plenty of time to grow. Its path was erratic by conditions ahead of it; the Hawaiian Islands couldn't be ruled out.

The three typhoons were true monsters. It was as if nature itself was saying, "Look what I can do!" One had just passed the Philippines, heading west. Total destruction had taken place. Winds topped at 220 miles an hour. Infrastructures were destroyed. A second storm had a path just north of the first. It would then take a sharp turn northward. The Philippines might never recover. Its winds had reached 175 but were down to 145 miles an hour presently. Taiwan was still in its path. The third was making history. It was north of the first two. The winds were presently at 235 miles an hour, and still strengthening! It was still two days away from Japan, so it could still hit the coast as an even stronger monstrosity.

Not to be outdone, Chili, by Santiago had experienced a small earthquake. It was only a 4.0, but who knew if anymore quakes were to follow. The fault line was very unpredictable. Anything could happen.

*a*s the thunderstorms raged outside, JJ had another nightmare. He was stationed at the North Pole. There was a blizzard outside a lonely outpost he had been assigned to.

Communications were out, and again he was alone. There was a knock on the door. JJ opened the station door and a figure stood out in the snow. It wore a large winter coat with a hood. JJ couldn't see its face, but he was so lonely that he motioned the figure inside. The stranger came in and sat down in a chair facing away from him. Every time JJ went around to face the figure, the stranger and the chair moved with him so that the commander was always looking at the back of the visitor's hooded head. "Who are you? What do you want?" JJ asked, puzzled.

The figure didn't answer, but instead started laughing. The laughing turned to cackling. JJ grabbed the chair and turned it around. The figure was faceless, with just a dark shapeless mouth filled with sharp yellowish teeth. A bony, pale skeletal hand held two moving eyeballs in front of him.

"I can see the future, my friend. Yes, I do believe the future I *do* see," It rasped. "Do you recognize your mother's lookers, boy? I do. I know they taste good too. I've eaten them a million times."

With that, the figure put the two eyeballs into its shapeless mouth and crushed them with its razor-sharp teeth. "You taste so good, Mom. You taste *so good*. Oh, and how she screams so delightfully inside me—so delightfully." And then it cackled again, chewing insistently. "Remember me, boy? Remember *me*?" it hissed, swallowing the eyeballs. JJ screamed as the creature laughed hysterically . . .

He woke up sweating and still screaming. He sat up and took deep breaths, grabbing his chest. Why had he dreamed such a nightmare? My God, that was horrible, he thought grimly, shaking his head. He looked past the robots and saw that it was raining hard outside. He could see much lightning in the distance. JJ staggered to his feet and stared out the front window. It's really coming down, he thought. Maybe the heat wave is over. He hoped so. And then something beyond imagination happened.

The rain, which had been falling so hard, began to slow and then stop—suspended in time. Impossible! JJ thought as he stared at the falling rain frozen in place. Above the GW Bridge lightning was also frozen in time. It was as if someone had pushed a stop button; or paused a movie on a DVD player. JJ ran down to the ship's hatch as fast as he could. He climbed down the ladder and walked into the suspended rain. He could feel its wetness on his face. He touched it with his hands. He could actually grab raindrops out of the air! He could *move* the rain, but it couldn't move on its own. Impossible, he thought again, totally amazed. He looked down and saw frozen raindrops splashing off the ground, suspended—no movement. He bent over and grabbed some water out of a puddle, stood up, and then let the rainwater run through his fingers. Only it didn't fall to the ground—it stayed between his fingers. He moved his hand away, but the water from the puddle stayed where it was. It defied logic.

The Commander of Mars 2020 stared mystified at the rain and then saw a large triangular bright white light appear a few yards in front of him. The point of the light was ten feet high and ten feet long at the bottom. Inside the triangle he could see movement, or ripples of darker light vibrating slowly. They changed form, moving like waves on an ocean. Some were bigger and faster than others. One moved ahead of the others and changed shape. The wave formed a perfect circle, and ripples moved slowly inside it. JJ stared open mouthed as this all took place. Nothing seemed real anymore, and he felt as if he had totally lost his mind. Space traveling had finally taken its toll. The other waves also began to form circles but stayed behind the first one. JJ estimated maybe thirty spheres inside the triangular light. They constantly shifted, swaying slightly from side to side, but always staying behind the first one. This circular form stayed still, not swaying like the others. It had more ripples in it, and they began to move in clockwise motion. They began to move faster and faster inside the circular light, and then suddenly disappeared. The circle moved a foot closer to JJ and grew to twice its original size. One ripple appeared across the center of it. It vibrated violently for a few seconds, and then slowed until it floated peacefully inside the bright sphere.

a Memory: When JJ Johnson was about ten, his father took him to a baseball game at Yankee Stadium in the Bronx. They sat in the upper level on the first-base side. JJ's father stated that most of the action took place there. He said that even if a batter hit a ball to an infielder, he still had to run to first base and the fielder had to throw him out. The catcher had to run behind first base to back up a potential bad throw, and the pitcher would have to run to first to receive a throw if the batter hit it to the first baseman. All in all, even on an out there was a lot of action on the first-base side of the ball field; therefore, sitting on that side was the best place to sit. JJ agreed with his father's logic. It made perfect sense.

He loved doing things with his father, and he knew his dad was a good man. He worked two jobs so that JJ had a good childhood, and enough to pay for schooling after high school. He always told JJ that if you wanted two, four, or ten children, you better have enough money to support them properly. That meant that none would be deprived of food, shelter, and anything that was needed during their childhood, or beyond. That also meant that education should be paid for *all* offspring. The addition was simple: if you could only fully provide for two children, then only two you should have. If you made a lot of money, then you could have more children. None should be deprived, not one. Anything less was downright shameful. JJ agreed with that too, always making sure that his children had what they needed. Not spoiled, so to speak—he made them earn what they had—but overall, they wanted for nothing. But the message was clear. Be *respectful* and mature enough not to commit gluttony. It wasn't science, it was math!

Now, as JJ sat with his father at the game, he was grateful. He loved his dad and would run through a brick wall for him. That day he kept his father from getting hurt. JJ had his baseball glove with him, and when a batter hit a long high foul ball right at them, he caught it right in front of his dad's head. His father had been talking to a man sitting next to them about the Yankees, and neither saw the foul ball heading in their direction. JJ had no business being that good at catching foul balls off the bats of major league ballplayers, but he had done it. They even played it on the replay screen. JJ never said anything, but he felt as if something (someone) had guided his glove to the ball and caught it, an invisible presence. It was there, and it had saved his father from injury. He surmised that the presence was good and should not be questioned. JJ didn't, and went on with his life never saying a word to anybody. He thought about it often, and as he stood

outside Mars 2020 in suspended rain staring at this strange triangular phenomenon, he remembered it all vividly.

J moved a step closer, stuck out his hand, and touched the
circular light. It vibrated slightly. He felt a warm, small
shock go through his hand, up his arm, then quickly through the
rest of his body. It didn't harm him—quite the contrary. He felt
calm and relaxed. He stepped back a step, though, and continued
to stare inside the circular light. It seemed to get brighter, and
then the ripples reappeared and began to move counterclockwise
again, only slowly now.

"Hello, James Johnson," It said, sounding like it came from
far away through a transistor radio. There was also static in its
voice. "They call you JJ, correct?"

"Who . . . who are you?" JJ asked, totally shocked.

"We are nomads, spiritual explorers, and we observe and
study. We have been observing your kind since your inception."

JJ took this in, he was trained to access the situation, and this
was a situation. "What are you doing here, and what is going on?
Where is everybody? And why am I still here?"

The ripples moved a little faster and the light inside the circle
got brighter. "We are here to answer those questions, even the
million-dollar ones." JJ raised his eyebrow at that. "Yes, we also
know about your sense of humor. What you are about to hear
might overwhelm, so please try to remain at ease."

"A lot has happened," JJ admitted. "I will try."

"Good. Would you feel better sitting down? We know that your kind likes to do that under stressful situations."

"No, I'm OK. I'm way beyond that line, and still standing. Please just tell me what's going on here."

"We will. It will take a while."

THE EXCLAMATION

"What you call your universe is, in actuality, a chamber," the light presence began. "Your kind is quite intelligent. Your idea of the Big Bang Theory is close to its reality. The Big Bang is the doorway into this chamber. The doorway must remain open for different life forms to survive. The Winds of Time flow through the doorway. These wind currents are the life force that create everything in this chamber. Total creation is constantly ongoing." The circular presence paused.

"What is total creation?" JJ asked. "Is it us?"

"No, total creation is the suns, the planets, moons—non-life formations, many that you know nothing about. It is space dust in its simplest form. It flows into this chamber and beyond. It finds its place in the winds and forms machines for life, machinery meant to keep life going," the presence replied, it's ripples reversing to clockwise motion. "*You*, and all life forms, come directly from The Creator."

"God?"

"That is just a word, a common term. The Creator is called by many names. We don't know what The Creator is, we just know The Creator is there—wherever *there* is. God is just a word your kind made up, but universally it is not the only term used to describe the Ultimate One."

"Does that mean that there are other life forms?' JJ asked excitedly. "We have always wondered that."

The circular presence vibrated violently for a second before calming. "Yes, there are other life forms. In this chamber and in others before it—more than you can count. Intelligent lifeforms always wonder if there are other life forms besides themselves. There is always curiosity about that."

"Did God—The Creator—make them too?"

"The Creator makes most life forms as far as we know . . . it is what The Creator is for."

"Did The Creator make you?"

The presence vibrated violently again before answering. "We do not know the answer to that question. We are ageless. Maybe the answer is yes, or maybe we were created by something else before time began, perhaps another Creator, or another entity."

"Are there more than one Creator?"

"We do not know that either, JJ. Perhaps so. We only know the One. We do not know if there is a need for another Creator."

"Is The Creator good?" It was a question JJ had always wondered about. All life just on this planet alone wasn't nice. Some people were downright bad, and wrong—evil.

"Good is a vast word. The Creator cannot be described in that sense. The Creator is the positive light of all origins, all beginnings, beginnings that we don't know of or understand fully; for there may be no beginnings. It just might have always been." The presence paused. "I know that line of thinking for you is hard to comprehend."

"Yes," JJ agreed, nodding. "It is overwhelming—all of it is. How many chambers are there?"

"An infinite amount. They go on and on, different all. You call them dimensions. That may help you understand better."

"It does," JJ nodded. "But why are you here now? Why is all of this happening?"

The light presence moved yet closer. "Ah, now those truly *are* million-dollar questions."

THE ANSWER

"*T*here is an entity, a dark malignant negative force that The Creator did not seed. It came from a place that only *it* knows."

"The devil," JJ nodded grimly.

"Again, that is only a word that your kind invented. *It* has no name to us, and it is not what you think it is. It is much worse, producing dire ramifications. It affects all. It *infects* all. Without this darkness, there would be no sickness here, no pain, physical or mental. You, and everything in this chamber would never die. There also would be no weather disruptions; every day would proceed calm and clearly. No storms would exist. Species like yours would not kill. There would be no deceit, no selfishness, no fighting, no hating. There would be no wars, and no radical organizations. It paused for a second before adding, I must say, JJ, that some of those extreme religious attacks were grounds to discontinue your species."

"You would kill us?" JJ asked, alarmed.

The presence vibrated, then shuttered. The ripples inside it shook violently. "Sometimes life can be *altered*. Kill is a term we do not use. Termination is a function we can carry out. *We* never have, though. And there are many life forms that are much worse than you. The Creator is the judge, jury, and executioner so far in our timeless tenure. But even The Creator does not act often— only when the situation has gone beyond repair. The Creator does not like to *uncreate*, but sometimes it is done for the greater good. The darkness is always involved in this confusion. *It* is an infection, a cancer, a plague. It's disease flows through the doorway, your Big Bang. Nothing can stop it. Certain species are affected differently. Some are infected *completely*. Those life forms usually become extinct. They do it to themselves. They are driven completely mad and destroy everything that they are. The Creator need not do anything. The species on your planet are mostly only slightly affected. Some more than others, of course, but the darkness affects you all, infiltrates all—even your pets. All animals are The Creator's gifts to humanity, yet you kill them for food supply, or worse yet, for your amusement. They are mistreated by some of your kind as well. The Creator considers *that* a huge sin."

"I love animals, but I eat meat," JJ admitted.

"Yes, the sickness is not total, but all are infected in one way or another. The Creator left many edible vegetation for you to eat, yet your minds have been polluted by the sickness, the infection. Species that live in fresh and saltwater also should not be eaten. Killing living species for survival is one of your worst ignorant sins."

"Now that you say it like that, it makes sense," JJ sighed. "How else are all people supposed to survive, though?"

"The ground grows many things," the light presence replied, its brightness vibrating rapidly. "Many types of healthy vegetables can be grown. Also, your species has reproduced at an alarming rate in the last two hundred Earth years. It has thrown off the balance of life on this planet. Rapid reproduction is the way to destruction on *any* planet. The plague plays a big part in this as well. Selfishness, carelessness, and gluttony levels rise when diseased by the darkness. Many planets suffer this problem. Your species is not the only one when it comes to over reproduction, but this seems to affect your kind more than most. As you can see, JJ, the darkness frustrates true living life on every level."

"This is kind of like the Bible," JJ sighed. "Good and evil against each other. It's like there is always one side, and always the other."

"You are well beyond the end of your religious scripture already," the presence responded. "Your Bible and other religious periodicals in your world are good scripture; they put you on a righteous path, they contain good stories, but they are not the true tale. *That* story would drive you insane and make you scream forever. Your books stop at your comfort level, what you can handle—even with your invented devil throughout its pages. But the truth is much worse than *your* written words. It is. JJ Johnson, I will tell you what I can. And I have more to explain, but one thing is certain: you are living beyond Revelations."

THE REALIZATION

JJ went to his knees, breathing deeply, almost hyperventilating. The circular light dropped to eye level, and both stared at each other.

"I am truly sorry, JJ. All that has happened is overwhelming for you, and the truth is frightening. But I *am* on your side. There is so much I would like to share with you, but time is growing short. So please listen. This is the most important meeting you have ever had—maybe for both of us."

JJ nodded. He sat down cross-legged, and the light presence's ripples calmed. He rocked back and forth to calm his nerves and waited for the light to continue.

"The dark presence has been looking for this chamber for a long time—longer than you can imagine. The Creator has exhausted all distractions, and very soon the plague will find the doorway into this universe. You have been chosen to help oppose this dark sickness. From your birth you were chosen by The Creator who has great faith in you."

"Why me? Why would I be considered worthy?' JJ asked, holding out his hands. His voice sounded tired, and somewhat defeated. "And how could I *possibly* defeat this darkness?"

"The Creator knows the answer—or hopefully the question to the answer, JJ. We do not think you can win either. That thought will not calm you, but that is how we feel," the light presence replied grimly. "We can only tell you what we know, and we will not lie to you. That is against our nature. It goes against the current."

"How could I possibly be successful alone?" JJ asked, aspirated.

"You are *not* alone. There are others. The Creator *has* removed all nonhuman life forces. Animals, birds, sealife, and other types of different DNA have gone back home to Him. The Creator has also brought home most of your fellow human beings. Only a few remain. You are to wait here, and they will find you. You will use your time to supply yourself with whatever you might feel useful."

"What can I use? What . . . what about my family? What about the space station?"

The light presence shook violently for a few seconds. "I am sorry, JJ. The Creator has taken all souls on the space station back home. He has protected them from the Dark Cancer as well. To your comfort, you will know that they have gone safely back home with the others."

JJ moaned, and then began to sob. They were gone. He had thought about this a million times since this whole nightmare had begun. He had always hoped that they were still up at the space station; that he would get to see them again. That hope was gone now. His future was black, bleak. He was staring into darkness, and about to face another darkness that he wanted no part of. This presence was correct: he *was* beyond the end of the Bible—beyond Revelations.

"There are good and bad human beings still here. They *all* will come this way if it is allowed. They will be drawn here by different circumstances. You must know and recognize who is who. The battleground is here and beyond, and life and true death hang in the balance. The infection will have its minions as well. Some you might think are worse than the darkness itself, and they actually might be. Some of the infection the darkness will bring through the doorway with it; others it will find inside this chamber. The exploding suns were destroyed so that severely infected species could not be part of the darkness's insanity. Those abominations were also removed, and put in a separate semi-chamber. If you are not successful in your mission, the darkness will claim those jailed in timeless purgatory. Releasing them will be its prize. Nothing—us or possibly even The Creator—will be safe at that juncture. You have been protected, JJ. The Creator has always directed your safety. From your birth we have been instructed to keep you safe from harm. Think about that as you prepare for conflict."

JJ did his best to digest what he had heard as he watched the light presence back away inside the pyramid light form, joining the others. Different colors fluttered inside, surrounding them.

"Safe travels, JJ," the light form said, sounding further away. "The winds of life will surely be with you."

With that, the pyramid shined brighter and brighter until it's shape no longer could be made out, and then it dissolved more than disappeared into the morning air. JJ continued to stare where the light forms once were, shook his head, and exhaled loudly. All of a sudden the rain began to fall; slowly at first, and then it sped up to normal speed. Thunder rumbled in the distance, along with flashing bolts of lightning. The world seemed to go back to some sort of normalcy, but JJ knew better. If what the light form said was true—and JJ believed it to the deepest depths of his soul—he knew the world he once knew was gone forever. Normal would not be a word spoken now, or in the future. That would be a given. With that, a drenched commander ran back to his ship, climbed the ladder, and closed the hatch behind him.

J sat in his commander's seat on the bridge and stared out at the falling rain. It was still coming down hard. Lightning flashed in the distance. It was still morning, but what a day he had already had. It was all impossible and unbelievable, yet somehow in this new world it had all happened. He had seen rain stop falling, and he had met . . . who? He had never felt threatened, but he had conversed with *something* that wasn't human. Alien. He had spoken with an alien, with more aliens looking on behind its spokesman. And he had been told what was happening, and what *was* to happen—at least a little of what was going on. It could all be lies, but JJ believed the presence. To think the alien was lying was a better road to travel; his family might still be alive up at the space station, and the dark presence (still the devil in his eyes) was just a fable character in the Bible, maybe nothing at all. Before all this, the devil was something that most people HOPED didn't exist—hoped and prayed with all their hearts, JJ one of them. He was religious; he believed in God and heaven, but the devil he could do without.

He knew differently now. He believed the Light Presence. He believed the harder road. And when the alien had said that the truth was just too much to handle, JJ believed even that. Believing that a dark presence was also coming was too much to handle, yet he would have to. His darkest fears were real. They were coming home to roost. And it was all too overwhelming.

He thought about being protected. The presence had told him to think about that. He survived being sick when he was born. He had been told that he was lucky to overcome that. He had, though. Had he been looked after? Had he been saved? Maybe. And then a memory came to him—or something, or *someone* brought it to his attention. This memory had more substance.

JJ had been around ten. It was a gray Saturday morning, and he had gone to the garage to get his bike. He was going to see if his best friend Tommy could come out to play, but his back tire was flat. His father was working and wouldn't be back until the afternoon. He started walking back to the house when he heard this rumbling down the street. There was a farm half a mile away, one with a horse stable. As JJ walked around the corner of his house, he saw about fifteen to twenty horses barreling toward him. They must have gotten loose and were taking advantage of their freedom. They were in full gallop. His mother's car was to his left, and he felt an invisible presence slightly push him toward it. Once he realized the car was there, he jumped on the hood just before the horses ran past him. If the car hadn't been there, he would have been trampled to death for sure. The horses weren't seeing anything but freedom in front of them, and he wouldn't have stood a chance. If something *hadn't* pushed him, got him started, he wouldn't have lived to see Sunday. And as he watched the horses disappear into the neighborhood, he thought of something else: Tommy lived on the other side of that farm, and if he didn't have a flat tire, he would've been riding his bike right into that stampeding herd. He would have been toast. Later that day JJ's dad filled the tire with air. The tire was fine. There was no reason why the tire had been flat in the first place, but it had been. It had also saved JJ from certain harm.

This was proof that some higher force had protected him. Maybe it had been The Creator, or maybe the light presence, but the alien had told him to think about it, so he knew that what had pushed him was probably one of them. He had been saved—protected.

Yes, he reasoned, the visit from the aliens and what he had been told he could totally believe now. He would do as the light presence wanted. He would prepare for what was to come. The alien was right. He knew that now. He was living in a time that the Bible spoke nothing of. He was living in a time that no prophet had ever foreseen. New frontiers lay ahead of him. He was living in a place beyond the end of the Bible. He was living Beyond Revelations!

Book One:

THE TWI-LIGHTERS

Chapter One

STEVEN NASH

S teven Nash bicycled north on the Garden State Parkway in New Jersey until dusk, and then hunkered down inside a rest stop just north of the exit for Atlantic City. The skies were clouding up, and it looked as though thunderstorms were coming at him from the northwest. He hoped so; this heatwave was much hotter than normal, and hopefully the rain would put some of these fires out. The smoke made it hard to breathe in places, and his vision was impaired as well.

It was even hotter inside the rest stop, but he had no choice. It was looking quite mean out there. He sat down at a table with a bottle of water and assorted chips and cookies. Without electricity, all the cold food was spoiled. Canned food would have to do. The first drops of rain began to fall, and thunder could be heard in the distance. Steven was glad for the shelter. There would be many more rest stops as he headed toward Northern New Jersey, and then New York City. That's where he decided he would go. He figured that if people and help existed anywhere, it would be in the city. The clouds moving in were getting seriously darker, bringing night on sooner than usual. Surviving was all he had to hold on to now, and as the rain began to fall steadier he again thought back to what had happened in the last few days—days that seemed filled with a different kind of insanity, a different kind of strange. And *he* was a part of that weirdness. Boy was he. He still couldn't believe how he had gotten to this point. He shook his head, watched as the rain slammed against the glass doors, and again thought about the last few days of his unconventional life.

Steven Nash got on Flight 104 out of Phoenix to Newark, New Jersey. He had been doing this round trip often lately. His elderly parents lived in Scottsdale; they had since Steven's father retired fifteen years ago from the postal system in Paramus, New Jersey. Steven had a condo there, three miles from the house where he grew up, and he *also* worked in the postal system.

Relations between his parents and their only son grew strained early, for Steven knew since he was about fourteen that he was gay. He experimented early and was caught by his mother with another boy in his room after they had smoked a joint—two wrongs, two demerits, one very shocking revelation. Giving oral affections to another teenager and getting caught by one's mother followed by a less than calm conversation at the dinner table when his father got home that night were the beginnings of a friction-packed relationship that only got worse.

Steven had several homosexual relationships throughout his high school days and moved out of his house halfway through his senior year. Tensions had built up and neither parent nor son could live together any longer. Steven moved in with a boyfriend ten years his senior and didn't talk to his parents until his mother called from Scottsdale a year ago to ask him to come out to see his father. He was dying of cancer and wanted to make amends—*both* his parents wanted to make amends. He went out to Arizona and they had held each other, cried, told one another just how much they loved each other, and how sorry they all were. It was late in the game but thank God it wasn't *too* late.

He had made this trip ten times, and his father had actually gotten better. Maybe the reason was better relations, maybe better mental health. Whatever it was, it was working. The cancer treatments had shrunk the tumors in his father's brain, and at eighty-one the new chemo drugs hadn't killed him either. Small miracle or big mirage—it didn't matter. He was doing well. His mother was doing well. The relationship between parents and homosexual son was doing well.

That was what he was thinking about as the plane took off from the 125-degree heat of the airport. His parents had accepted him, he was in a new relationship that was going well and getting very serious, and at the age of forty-five all was looking up—looking up until the power on the plane went out and it began to nosedive. The cabin went dark and people began screaming. Steven looked around and prayed for a quick death, or another miracle. He closed his eyes and pleaded to a God that had made him more different than most, a difference that had made his life harder than most, and a difference that had made love and acceptance harder to find than most. He pleaded for mercy, for release, or a last chance to say goodbye to his parents.

And then as Flight 104 continued to fall like a scud missile, all screaming suddenly stopped. He opened his eyes, looked around, and saw no one. The seats were all empty, all people gone. Impossible. And then *he* started screaming. He screamed because he was alone, and because crashing into the ground was a death his mind just couldn't fathom, a pain he couldn't possibly gauge. The plane fell faster and faster, and then Steven Nash suddenly passed out. His prayers, to some extent, had been answered.

Steven didn't dream. He was in a different state. He wasn't

awake and he wasn't completely asleep. A voice far back in the back of his mind spoke to him, a voice that was loud and clear yet at the same time sounded ageless. It told him that he *didn't* have a choice of who he was. He was gay, and that was all right. He didn't have to pretend to be someone he wasn't.

It said, "Forget the ignorance of all religious books that said homosexual existence was a sin, that being gay was wrong, was *bad*. Just be who you are. You were created to be who you are. Be proud. Stand tall. You are loved no less, no more. The masses are wrong. The pages of prejudices mean nothing. What I say is *truth*—truth. *Rejoice!* NOW AWAKE!"

Steven did, and he remembered what the voice had just told him (which made him feel better), but what he woke up *to* couldn't be real. Flight 104 had indeed crashed. It had landed on the edge of a forest, and part of a large cemetery. The plane had broken up into three parts, and the wooded area was now in flames. Black smoke rose into the sky above him. Steven was still strapped into his seat, but the seat on impact had been ripped from the floor and thrown on a slant against a large tombstone, cracking it. The plane had broken apart right where his seat had been.

He unbuckled his seatbelt, and shakily stood up. He took inventory. He was all right—no broken bones, no blood, no soreness or pain. Impossible! He looked at the large tombstone: "BUCKLEY, JAMES and CLARA." Only James and Clara Buckley weren't there. Only a rectangular hole remained—no coffins, no bodies. He looked around and saw more of the same: tombstones and holes. He walked away from the plane and into the cemetery, away from the growing fire and smoke. The graveyard was huge, but the bodies were gone. Holes were everywhere! Steven wondered what the hell was going on here. Was this another "Night of the Living Dead" spin off? How could he survive a plane crash without a scratch? Or was he dead too? A zombie that didn't know he was a zombie? He slapped his face. No, he felt that. He MUST be alive. But how?

Steven staggered away, moving through the cemetery. Eventually he reached the entrance. A large two-story house stood just inside the front gates. A couple of tractors and three dump trucks were parked out front. Steven went past them to the front door. The inside door was open. The heat was stifling. He opened the screen door and went inside. A large office was to his left, but no one was inside. He called out, but nobody answered. He went throughout the whole house, but no one was inside. He went back outside and walked to the front gates. A main highway was outside. He looked both ways. Cars were scattered up and down the road. A few had crashed into each other, and a few had run off the shoulder of the highway. There were no people, though. He called out as loud as he could, but got no answer.

That was when he knew something was really wrong, different—off. The passengers on the plane had disappeared as it started to descend, and there was no one on the ground here either. Again, he wondered what was going on. He took his cell phone out of his pants pocket. He pushed the on button, but nothing happened. Dead. He knew he had a full charge when the plane first lost power, but it was dead now.

Steven started walking. He would soon discover that he was just outside of Dover, Delaware. There were no people anywhere, no dogs or birds—no life. He opened a few cars. The keys were in each one, but none would start. Not one engine would turn over. He walked onward until he spotted a ten-speed bicycle laying on the shoulder of the road. Steven got on and began pedaling north, eventually going across the Delaware Memorial Bridge, and then continued into New Jersey.

Steven still couldn't believe it all as he watched the rain come down in buckets. Thunder and lightning surrounded him. The heat wave was over. It had already started to get cooler inside the rest stop. Steven was glad. Tomorrow would be a better day. Hopefully he could make it home by the next sunset. He closed his eyes and soon fell into a deep sleep. He slept soundly. He didn't dream. He was lucky.

Chapter Two

JANUS CONNELLY

*J*anus Connolly was in a coma. She had been for the past four years. She was hooked up to life support machines that seemed to have become a part of her—only now they were powerless, dark, and useless. Janus didn't die. She didn't disappear like the rest of the staff and patients in Memorial Presbyterian Hospital in Wichita, Kansas. She began to breathe on her own, but didn't wake up. She remained in a coma. But she was alive! The doctors had almost lost her on numerous occasions in the past, but she had made it through each time. Now the hospital was empty, dark and quiet. There was no one left to save her. But she was still here. And she was still breathing.

Janus, as a high school senior, was at an afterparty following her prom. Along with her date, Thomas Parsons, and other friends and fellow students, they were celebrating a great year and evening. The party was at her friend Marie Saunders's house. It was at the end of a dead-end street with miles of woods behind the Saunders home. Janus went out the back door with a glass of wine to have a cigarette. Going out alone would be a mistake. One too many drinks had clouded her judgement. She was a beautiful brunette with a full figure, and normally never went anywhere alone, but she needed a cigarette badly.

The outside light was on, but tonight that was a bad thing. Four men in their twenties were partying in the woods behind Marie's house, and they were all drunk. They heard the party going on and decided to crash it. Then they saw Janus come outside and decided on something else. They quietly surrounded the backyard, and when Janus stomped out her butt with her shoe, they grabbed her as she turned to go back inside. One put his hand over her mouth while another punched her hard in the stomach twice. She went to her knees gasping for breath, and was punched in the face twice more, knocking her out. They carried her far into the woods, stripped her, blind folded her with her own underwear, and tied her hands behind her back with her blouse. Then one poured a beer over her head, bringing her back to consciousness, and they proceeded to gang rape her for over an hour.

It would have gone on longer, but the people at the party had come out searching for her, and they were getting close. Flashlights could be seen in the distance. One of the four men kicked a sobbing Janus in the gut, and another slammed her head repeatedly against a rock before they all ran off, leaving her unconscious. Her date Thomas was the first to find her motionless body lying in the clearing. The local police and ambulance were called, and the paramedics carried Janus out of the woods.

She had never regained consciousness, and in some way that was a blessing, for Janus had been brutalized during her ordeal. Nobody should've gone through what she had endured—beaten, raped, and left for dead. Being in a coma meant not having to deal with the trauma that she would have to go through, mental or physical. Her family and friends did, though. The story was in the news for weeks. Her parents and siblings needed therapy, and some of her friends needed it as well. The authorities caught the four thugs a few days later; they were arrested and arraigned. All were drifters, and all had rap sheets a mile long. They now were all doing time up at Crawford State Prison. They weren't going to be bothering anybody else anytime soon, but Janus was still in a coma all this time.

Her friends had all moved on, and life on a whole in Wichita had moved on. Even Thomas had moved on. He had truly loved her, and she him. They had dated all through high school, and many had thought they would've married. He had gone off to Arizona State University on a football scholarship. He was doing well and eventually got engaged to one of the team's cheerleaders. He felt guilty; he daily cursed himself for leaving her alone at Marie's, but he slowly but surely moved on. He never forgot her though, sending flowers every month. He wished her well. Her parents and two sisters were left to deal with the memory and trauma, and it had drained them all.

If Janus could've been awake when the power went out, she would've seen her sister Kate sitting in a chair next to her bed, a nurse checking her monitors. She would've seen both disappear as the machines went quiet. She would've screamed.

Chapter Three
THE DARK ENTITY

*T*he door to the chamber (the big bang center) was the size of one hundred billion large suns. The speed of the life force particles that passed through the rip in time moved at two hundred trillion miles per hour. That sounds fast, but when the doorway was first opened the speed was one billion times faster. The current of life that entered the once-empty chamber filled up quickly, and the flow continued to flood in, expanding it indefinitely. If time was to be measured (for humanity was one of only a few life entities that had any kind of time measurement at all), then the doorway was close to sixteen billion Earth years old. It was young or old, depending on one's perspective. It was ancient to humanity, which is only seconds old in the scheme of life inside the chamber's interior.

On this side of the doorway things ran as usual, but on the other side, havoc and chaos were going on. Something was coming, corrupting everything in its path, and coming fast. It still had much distance to travel, but the map to the doorway was now known, the puzzles basically solved. Dimensions, hallways, and mazes lay ahead, but they would be of little consequence. The anti-life force moved with purpose, infecting everything in its wake.

Soon it would reach the doorway, where total infection would take place. The virus embraced its sickness, and it could feel its power metastasizing. It was cunning. It was intelligent. It was insane. It was unstoppable. It was hungry. It was coming—soon.

Chapter Four

PHILLIP HUBBARD

*P*hillip Hubbard had heard the stories. He thought the stories were tales—tall tales. And so, he had taken the bet. That bet was to stay all night at the New London Ledge Lighthouse in Groton, Connecticut, located on the Thames River at the mouth of New London Harbor. It was considered haunted, although nothing could positively be proven. Supposedly a ghost, a former Keeper named Ernie, haunts the lighthouse on a nightly basis. It was rumored that people "back in the day" had tried to stay through an entire night but never made it to dawn in one piece.

Legend had it Ernie had frightened them so badly that surviving individuals ended up in mental institutions, some even declared clinically insane. Others had either shot themselves in the head, or walked calmly and methodically into the Long Island Sound, drowning themselves as if in a trance. Phil believed none of these stories. None of them could be confirmed. And it wasn't as if he didn't do his research. He knew that the state in the past had employed lighthouse keepers on biyearly contracts, and they had left without issue. Johnny Grimes, Phil's friend, disputed those so-called facts and believed each one had gone completely mad, quietly being taken out in straightjackets, which was why they changed keepers so often. He said that Ernie took it easy on them at first because they were all fellow lighthouse keepers, but Phil just shook his head, thinking it was all just a ploy to keep trespassers away.

In 1987 the Lighthouse was automated. The reason: the hauntings had become worse and no keeper considered it safe anymore to stay there. Folklore had it Ernie had decided that all lighthouse keepers needed to stay away, and that *he* alone would man the controls. The last employed keeper, William S. Bentley the Third, had stated that it was "a rock of slow torture." The place was Ernie's domain, William added, and the New London Ledge Lighthouse had become "hell on Earth." Legend also had it that not long after he took his Boston Whaler out to sea, and neither man nor boat had been seen again. The coast guard had searched for weeks but had come up empty. It was assumed that Ernie had consumed both, which was why neither had been found. Phil listened to Johnny tell these stories, laughed, and shook his head.

A Little History: Johnny had lived in New London all his life, working on fishing boats that passed the lighthouse island on a daily basis. He was married with three children and had inherited his parents' house on the Connecticut coastline, which faced the lighthouse island.

Phil Hubbard, on the other hand, had grown up in Albany, New York, and had become a nomad, moving from town to town, job to job. Never being married or having any children, he was able to move around as he chose. Eventually he ended up in New London, working on the same boat as Johnny.

Johnny believed the island folklore he told Phil, but Phil, in all his thirty-three years, had never believed in ghosts, *or* the supernatural. And that included aliens and spaceships. Johnny had also stated that from his home he had seen flying saucers in the star-filled sky at night, flying over the Sound. He claimed they flew in threes, flying together to and from Connecticut and Long Island. Phil laughed until he cried, and now KNEW Johnny was crazy—likable, but madder than a hatter.

Over beers at one bar or another, or at the beach staring out at the lighthouse, these topics had been constantly discussed. Eventually the bet had finally been made while drinking beers down at Coastlines, a restaurant and bar located on the rocky coast two miles west of New London Ledge Lighthouse Island. While watching it's powerful light shine out over the sea, they shook on it.

The Bet: If Phil could make it through one night at the lighthouse, Johnny would give him ten thousand dollars and buy him beer for the next year. Phil never kept much of what he ever made and had never owned his own place. In fact, he was renting a room in Johnny's Uncle Rory's house, and so he had gladly taken the bet. Before Phil would accept the challenge, Johnny would have to come up with the money, which he did.

If Phil *didn't* last the night . . . well, then Ernie would determine his fate! In retrospect, one would think that if a dude was willing to put up ten grand, then maybe there was something to the hauntings and this ghost Ernie, but Phil wasn't buying it, and certainly wasn't about to back out. He just assumed that this would be easy money. To him, there were no such things as ghosts, vampires, werewolves, or zombies.

To make the bet even easier to accept, Johnny even stated

that Phil didn't even have to stay inside the lighthouse; he could stay outside. The place was all locked up; breaking in would be breaking the law, and the bet had to be on the up and up. "Easy money!" Phil exclaimed, grinning from ear to ear. "Not really!" Johnny retorted, and added that Ernie would haunt him anyway, and "scare the living shit out of him; drive him mad, regardless of where he spent the night. Just being on the island would piss Ernie off." Johnny further acknowledged that Ernie might just drown Phil before daybreak. Phil said bullshit to that, and the two friends and coworkers agreed that the bet would start the next afternoon, since both had the next two days off (Wednesdays and Thursdays were considered their weekend; Saturdays and Sundays were always the busiest days of the week during the summer season).

Johnny took Phil out to the Lighthouse in his boat at lunchtime, which just happened to be on the day all the power went out on Earth. Phil had wanted to hang out at the lighthouse for a while during the day before night came on. He was going to enjoy this. This would be easy money. He took BLT sandwiches (his favorite) and a six-pack of beer in a cooler with him. The lighthouse had a cement-like foundation. He climbed the rusted metal ladder to ground level and sat down to eat a sandwich. He downed three beers in the shade of the four-story structure, for, as usual, it was hot as blazes. He became sleepy. He figured he had plenty of time before sunset to explore the outside of the building, so he sat against the foundation and fell asleep almost instantly.

When Phil woke up, it was close to sunset. He had dreamed of his eventual winnings—ten grand, and he had gone on a spending spree. By the time he woke up, the money was gone. He didn't know what he had bought, but it didn't matter. If he had the money, then he had won the bet. It was a good omen, even though he had slept longer than he had intended to. The sun was going down, nothing more now than a bright orange partial ball in the western skies. Night was coming.

He watched the sun disappear before he realized something was wrong, or definitely off. No birds were flying home to their nests. On shore it was completely dark. There were no lights, no movement. The lighthouse light usually came on just before sunset. It was not on now. Phil became a little spooked. He opened another beer, and bit into another BLT, only there was no bacon there. How could that be, he thought. He stood up and looked around. He stared south toward Long Island—no lights, just darkness. Totally freaked now, he quickly downed the rest of his beer nervously. He stared up at the lighthouse and it remained dark and quiet—and imposing!

All of a sudden Phil realized this was the last place he wanted to be. The lighthouse looked spooky. He no longer cared about the money. He climbed down the ladder and sat down next to the water. The tide, and the small waves, were the only movements he saw that night; exposed seaweed all he smelled. He drifted off from time to time, but otherwise he stayed up, shaking, thinking that he had heard noises coming from inside the lighthouse. Time seemed to stop completely, and the quarter-sized moon in the sky seemed to freeze as Phil's heart beat loudly. It was the longest night of Phil's life.

Eventually he saw tints of orange appear in the east. The sun was coming up! No ghost had come for him! Phil had imagined Ernie the Ghost Keeper grabbing him many times during the night, but that was all it was: his imagination. He had made it 'til dawn, but his nerves were completely shot.

As the sun came up completely over the eastern horizon,

turning from orange to yellow, Phil saw one of the three ferries that went back and forth between New London and Orient Point, Long Island, drifting about three miles off to the southeast. It appeared lifeless, dark, and abandoned. A ghost ship! He laughed to himself, shaking his head. As night became day his nerves slowly calmed. He felt somewhat less jittery.

Phil stared at the shoreline but saw no movement—and still no birds. Usually the gulls would be out looking for breakfast, flying around and making loud, angry noises, chasing others away. There was none of that this morning. Maybe there could have been a blackout, or maybe something terrifying had happened on shore, but nothing could stop the seagulls from flying. He scanned everything around him and saw no birds. It was unbelievable, unexplainable.

In the distance, toward New York City, traces of smoke could be seen in many different areas. Another terror attack? Possibly, but why so quiet here? It was baffling.

The ferry was drifting closer, being pulled by the tide. That would be his ticket off this cement block. Even though it was daylight, he wanted away from this place, away from the lighthouse—away from Ernie. He still didn't believe in ghosts, but he wasn't going to take any chances. The ferry kept coming; maybe a mile off now, but it was drifting south of the lighthouse. He put the cooler underneath his stomach, pushed off the cement foundation, and started paddling toward it.

It took Phil about twenty minutes to reach the drifting vessel, and another ten to get to the back of the ferry where the vehicles went on. That area was only five or six feet up, and there were thick ropes located on each end. He yelled for help repeatedly, but got no response. It wouldn't be easy, but he would have to climb up on his own. It took a while, but Phil was eventually able to grab the rope on the right side and pull himself up. He was out of breath by the time he got himself over the side, cursing himself as he banged his knee hard on the metal floor.

He laid on his back for a few minutes, ready to curse the first person he saw for not coming to his assistance. None came, though. The ferry was quiet. The only sound was the water hitting the side. He got up and looked around. The ferry appeared full: cars, trucks, a couple of motorcycles, and even a few bicycles. Where was everyone? No workers, no passengers—nothing.

He walked amongst the vehicles, calling out. Again, there was no response. He walked upstairs and went through the Cross-Island Deli door. No one. He limped over to the cashier area and picked up a couple of bags of chips and a few candy bars. He was about to leave when he noticed a man alone at the back of the sitting area, his back to Phil.

"Hello, sir," Phil said, startled. "Where is everyone? I haven't seen a soul on board?"

The figure was extremely thin with long blonde hair, wearing a gray wrinkly tank top and ruffled black pants which partially covered dirty white sneakers. He didn't respond. He kept hidden hands on top of a small round cafe table. He didn't turn around.

Phil frowned as he stared at the man's bony back. "Hey dude, what's the deal?" He slowly moved toward the stranger. Phil was just about to grab the man's shoulder when the figure turned around. The man's face was nothing but a dirty oil-stained skull, smiling up at Phil with a mouth full of sharp, pointy, yellowish stained teeth.

"What the fuck?!" Phil shouted, backing up, totally shocked. "What the hell are you?"

"Why so unfriendly? Didn't you want to meet me, Phil?" It rasped, standing up. The creature was nothing more than a moving skeleton wearing old clothes. It cocked its head to one side and hissed as it moved toward a completely shocked Phil.

"You hung out at my lighthouse all night, waiting to meet me. I thought you wanted to hang, have a few brews together. Hi, I'm Ernie." And then it held out it's skeletal right hand and started cackling. It continued forward and added, snarling, "And now I'm going to make sure you lose that bet!"

Phil just screamed.

Chapter Five

ELLEN MANSFIELD

Ellen Mansfield worked at the Best Friends Pet Adoption Center in Smyrna, Georgia. She had been there for the past four years, first as a volunteer, and then as a devoted employee. She had gone back to school and was now a veterinarian assistant. She was forty-five years old, married ten years with two girls, seven and five. She loved animals of all kinds and had adopted two dogs and three cats since being employed at Best Friends.

Best Friends had started a trend—a very good one. They never euthanized any of the animals that were up for adoption. This was a righteous act that many other adoption agencies now used. Ellen felt so good going to work. She felt like she was making a difference. She had been involved not just in the health part of the business, but also in finding good homes for all adoptable pets.

Ellen was also involved in other company programs. One was the control of animal reproduction in the city. Anyone bringing in any unowned animal was given a cash amount that was quite substantial, plus a deduction on their taxes. This cut down on strays overall, but it also cut down on the uncontrolled reproduction of those strays, which had always been a major problem throughout civilized times. Less strays on the loose meant less animals to support in the kennels and adoptive agencies. Less strays also meant less new litters. The animal food supply needed for all kennels would be down; health products, which could be quite pricey, were down as well. These new policies and ideas were now being used widespread across the country with positive results. Light could be seen at the end of the tunnel. Ellen went home feeling good every day, with a chance to make things even better tomorrow. For her, when the power went out, life as she knew it changed forever—drastically.

Ellen had taken a late lunch at the local park when the power went off. She was reading a new journal on animal healthcare that had just come out while sitting in her air-conditioned car when her Honda Civic suddenly shut off. She tried turning it on several times without any luck. She was about two miles from work; with this heat too far to walk, so she took her phone out and quickly realized it wasn't working either. Without air conditioning the car was heating up quickly, so she took her bottle of water and stepped outside. Scanning the park, she realized she was alone. There had been various grown-ups and children scattered throughout the park when she had first arrived, but they were gone now. The park was eerily quiet, and she realized why: no sounds of wildlife, no sounds of barking dogs that usually were walked on the various trails, and no sounds of people talking or yelling in the picnic area that surrounded the park pond. There was only silence, utter silence, until she heard a siren-type sound coming from above and behind her.

She turned around and looked up just in time to see a large commercial plane nose-diving at incredible speed right at her. I'm dead, she thought, closing her eyes. The plane crashed just to her left, broke into at least ten pieces that fell all around her. She opened her eyes, saw the different parts of the plane surrounding her, and then she was suddenly thrown about fifty feet. The fuel had ignited and exploded. Flames were everywhere. Ellen caught her breath and crawled more than walked away from the wreckage. At a safe enough distance, she checked herself and realized that she was all right. Shaken, but miraculously OK—not even burned. Just a few scratches. That wasn't possible, she thought as she scrambled farther away from the wreckage and flames. That plane should have crashed right on top of her, but somehow it had broken up all around her. Impossible! But unlike everyone else, it seemed, she was still here.

Ellen started walking through the heat slowly. She eventually made it back to Best Friends. On the way she saw no one. Cars were scattered on the highway, but no people, no animals. Smoke could be seen in every direction, possibly other plane crashes or traffic accidents. When she got back to the kennel, it was empty-no coworkers, and no animals in any of the cages. No dogs. No cats. No sounds. No power. No nothing! A shocked Ellen Mansfield sat down on the floor, shaking. She had become so attached to most of these various pets. A litter of puppies that had just come in three days ago seemed so happy before lunch. The kennel would have no problem finding homes for any of them. Stooges, a ten-year-old retriever mix that had been abandoned two months ago, was going to be adopted tomorrow to one of Ellen's closest friends. She loved that dog, and she knew that Stooges was going to a great home. Now they were all gone. Now that future happiness was murky at best, along with all the other hopeful animals that resided at Best Friends. Ellen shook her head in dismay, and slowly rocked back and forth.

And then she started crying.

Chapter Six

GEORGE SMALLS

From the Journal of George Smalls:

Today I finally decided to do the dirty deed, the deadly sin. Ah, shit—it doesn't matter. Say it out loud. Today, I, George Smalls, after great mental debate, have decided to finally end it all. Yes, commit suicide. There, I said it. Fuck it if I go to hell. It can't be any worse than what I'm living through right now. It just can't. But . . . it didn't happen. Not because I lost my nerve. Not because I didn't have the balls. But because a force beyond my control stopped me. Maybe it was God . . . I don't know. I don't know. But before I forget I got to get the words down before I go completely out of my mind, before the insanity engulfs me and swallows me up. If I skip writing it all down then I won't even believe it myself! I won't. Anybody who reads this won't believe what happened either. Damn it, I can't even get away from this . . . this agony. I . . . I got to write this down. I have to. I. Have. To.

So here goes. This morning I got up and decided that enough was enough. Hell had gotten too hot, so to speak, and the flames had finally started burning the fringes of my soul. Emotions, loss, loneliness, and depression had finally caught up to me. Today, I decided, was going to be my last day. As usual, the first thing I thought about when I woke up was the accident: the loss of life, my wife, my daughter. And the incoming tide of guilt. I knew their deaths weren't my fault, but I was still accountable—very accountable. And, of course, I was still alive. Living with that reality was eating me from the inside out.

But THAT was going to be remedied today. TODAY! The pain was going to end today. I would join my family like I should have a long time ago because I didn't have the nerve. Didn't have the balls. The heat of the day had melted away anything I had left. My plan was simple: drive to the highest point of the Sunshine Skyway Bridge, park, and jump off. Once I was over the side there would be no turning back. I would hit the water like it was concrete. Die instantly. Or drown. What about an overdose of pills, you might ask? Pills wouldn't be the answer. You could always change your mind. Call 911. Today I wasn't taking any chances.

My suicide plan went off without a hitch. I drove onto the bridge, stopped at the highest point, looked around one last time, and then jumped over the side. I fell at a high speed, but I never lost consciousness. I couldn't catch my breath; my heart felt as if it was going to explode inside my chest, and my eyes bulged outward. Otherwise, I was handling it nicely. The day was hot—very hot in fact, but as I fell I felt cool, almost cold. Deep down inside I felt content, calm. I knew then I had made the right choice. My mental anguish was already gone. I'd be closing the door on this world, this life—of what was left of it, anyway. I felt relief.

And then just before I hit the water I saw a flash, and I stopped falling. A foot from impact I completely stopped falling! I defied gravity. A foot above the bay my body was suspended in midair, parallel to the water. And then I slowly began to rise. I began to actually reverse my fall. I felt weightless! I rose higher and higher, watching the water getting further and further away. At one point I thought I must be dead and rising like an angel to my final destination, but somewhere in the back of my mind I knew THAT was only wishful thinking. I WAS rising, but I still felt like myself. The mental pain was back. All my thoughts and memory were intact. I was still ME. I rose over the side of the bridge and landed on my feet next to my car. My weight came back, but my sanity was gone. I hadn't died. I was still here. Impossible!

I felt the heat of the day again. I immediately wondered if any of this was truly real. I looked around and cars and trucks were on the bridge, but not moving. I saw no drivers, no passengers. Everything was quiet. No sounds. No signs of life. There was only me. I started laughing. How ironic. I had wanted to die; leave all signs of life behind, but the complete opposite seemed to have happened. I looked over the side of the bridge, thought about jumping again, but I knew I wouldn't do it. My nerve was gone. Something had stopped me from dying, from killing myself. All of a sudden I felt nauseous and vomited over the side; I watched it fall. It hit the water like I couldn't. I felt weak, so I staggered over to my car, opened the door, and sat down behind the wheel. I sat motionless, staring straight ahead for a long time. Traffic didn't move. Nothing did. I thought about what was to come. The future. The world was a different place. I felt THAT. But the future is what I felt more than anything. What I THOUGHT about. And that was different. I had been living for so long in the past that I had forgotten what the future felt like. Because there wasn't any future. Not for me. Until now.

I tried to start my car, get off that bridge, but the engine was dead. I went to another car, looked inside. The key was in the start position, but the engine was dead. I turned it off, tried it again. Nothing. I realized that I was going to have to walk off that bridge, and so I did. I lived five miles away and made it home by nightfall. On my way I saw many strange and out-of-place things. I'll write them down later. The lights were off; there didn't seem to be power anywhere. In my apartment nothing worked. The future was dark. But was my life still in the dark? I felt enlightened somehow. Everybody else seemed to be gone. There must be some symbolism in that. It was something to think about, contemplate.

Thank God for candles. Thank the Lord for pen and paper. Mission accomplished. It's all written down. My day of impossibility. But that means that it DID happen. It did. It did . . . I'm tired. Drained. The night is half over by my guess. My watch isn't working. Or my cellphone. It's time to lie down. Get some sleep. Get some rest. A voice in the back of my mind tells me I should continue this journal, and so I will. The world has changed somehow, and somebody should record it. Document it. Might as well be me. Might as well be me . . . I'll give it a title. I'll name it "I'm Still Here!"

P.S. One thing I didn't mention. Something I didn't realize until just now, because in this instant I am able to slow it all down. When I stopped falling I told you that I saw a flash. And in that flash I saw much movement, but also something stationary. It was the souls of my wife and daughter. They were transparent, no longer in physical form. They were staring at me, smiling. Bright light illuminated behind them—not just a brightness, but a warmth as well. That whole image is giving me strength to carry on, live another day. I was thankful, and wept for quite some time.

Chapter Seven

ANDREW JONES

*A*ndrew Jones lived in the Bronx. He had lived there all his life. He presently resided in the Executive Towers, top floor, 1020 Grand Concourse, close to Yankee Stadium. Andrew was a major Yankee fan; he had been all his life. Like most people in the area, he followed the team day by day, year to year. Andrew reasoned that if you were a true baseball fan, you followed your team like true religion. You lived and died with every win or loss. He could hear the roar of the crowds from where he lived, yet he had never seen a game at the stadium or on TV. That was because Andrew was blind. He had been since birth.

His mother had been a drug abuser, an addict. She had used drugs of all types all through her pregnancy. The results spoke for themselves. Infections had caused Andrew's blindness; he had been born two months premature and remained in the hospital for three months, hooked up to tubes and machines, but luckily there had been no brain damage or any other physical or mental deficiency. His mother was released from the hospital and never returned to get him. She never knew who the father was, for Dana Smith sold her body for cash, which was how she became pregnant.

Abandoned, he was sent to Catholic Home Bureau, a foster care agency. Andrew was adopted by Harold and Lois Jones three months later. They were the best thing that ever happened to him. They named him, they loved him, they home schooled him, and they raised him. He learned to read Braille and read a book a week from the time he turned seven. Harold was an avid Yankee fan and explained the game of baseball to Andrew. Harold worked in various factories during the day, and also worked part time as an usher and custodian at Yankee Stadium at night.

Lois stayed home and taught Andrew more than most children would ever learn. He was quiet, introverted, and talked only when he had to, but he was a good listener—and being a good listener meant you learned plenty. He soaked up knowledge like a sponge. She taught him how to play the piano. It came easy to him. He practiced and practiced until there wasn't anything he couldn't play, all by ear.

He started writing songs—lots of them. They were pop and R&B related. The right people heard the first few, and he got a record contract. A month before the power went out his first album got released, and people were buying it. Andrew Jones, musician, became quite popular very quickly. He was only fifteen years old, but fans came to visit him on a regular basis, getting his autograph and just shooting the breeze. They left better than when they had come, for Andrew had an enlightening, positive personality.

Another aspect about Andrew was his size. He was six foot six inches tall and weighed 245 pounds. He was naturally muscular, with zero body fat. He also was extremely strong. His hands and fingers were large, but he had no problem playing the piano, or any other keyboard he came in contact with.

Life had treated Andrew well, although it was strangely altered on the day the power went out. He was playing the piano at the time; his mother had gone to the grocery store. His father, as usual, was working. He was alone. His hearing was great; he heard everything acutely: the refrigerator, the clocks, the AC units, the sounds of traffic, the sounds of animals, people talking or just moving around. That all stopped abruptly. Instantly Andrew stopped playing. For a few seconds he stared straight ahead, unmoving. Something was odd, maybe more than odd—more likely downright STRANGE!

He got up and slowly and went to the living room window. He frowned—silence outside. Total silence. A first. He walked through the apartment, out the front door, and took the stairs down to the bottom floor. He did this slowly, holding on to the banister as he descended the steps. Nothing but quiet followed him. He passed no one. He walked outside. It was more than hot, for the heatwave was in full swing. There was a song in there somewhere, he thought absently. He stared all around—silence. Nothing but silence. No movement.

That also was odd, but there was something else that was much odder. For when the power went off, and everybody went *somewhere*, Andrew Jones regained his sight. He began to see!

Chapter Eight

CARRIE WINSTON

C arrie Winston resided at Chicago-Read Mental Health Center. She had been there for thirty years. Chicago-Read is a state run inpatient psychiatric facility with two hundred beds located in the neighborhood of Dunning on the northwest side of Chicago, close to O'Hare Airport in Illinois. The Center had been around since the mid 1850s, and it still being there was a miracle. The Ward had always been run poorly, and it had been on the verge of being closed many times, but somehow it survived. Carrie didn't know any of the history of Chicago-Read, and didn't care. She didn't care about much of anything, or anyone—including herself. Carrie Winston was eighty-five years old, thin and frail, ate little, and as far as anyone that had ever worked on the Ward knew, her mind thought even less. She sat at the same table by the same window trying to put together the same one-thousand-piece puzzle of the Sears Tower. She never got anywhere, but this seemed to keep her busy, so the nurses and aids pretty much left her alone. They would get her up in the morning, dress her, wash her up a little (always less than they should have), sit her at the table, and pretty much leave her to her own demons except to feed and take her to the bathroom. The only unusual thing she did was every day at three o'clock in the afternoon she would get up, stare out the window, and talk lowly in a language only she knew. The Ward had put in time trying to decipher it, but could never relate it to any known language. And who was she speaking to? That was always the question. Carrie never spoke other than at these times. You could talk or ask her anything until your voice got hoarse, and all she would do is look through you as if you weren't there, as if you didn't exist. She wasn't a complete mystery, though. The Ward had a file on her. She had been sent to Chicago-Read after her sister Rita had been killed in a car accident. Rita was ten years older than Carrie, and her only known relative. Neighbors had called the authorities after Rita's sudden death and had told those same people all they knew about Carrie, so at least they had some information on her.

Carrie Banks Winston had been born to Mary and Robert Banks on the south side of Chicago. Besides sister Rita, she also had had an older brother, Mark, who had died of leukemia at fifteen. Carrie had been eight at the time, and it was her first brush with despair. She married John Winston after they both graduated from high school. They had one son, Charles, who at age seven died on Christmas day. He had been diagnosed with lymphoma at five years of age on his birthday. What a birthday present that was . . . He had fought the horrible disease for two hard years before losing his battle. His death devastated Carrie. She never spoke a word of English afterward.

John Winston left soon after his son's death. His and Carrie's marriage had always been turbulent, John being mostly abusive throughout their nine-year union—a union that didn't have anything left after Charles's passing. The police had been called to their two-bedroom apartment often, Carrie wearing various bruises left by their numerous arguments. John had spent many a night in the local jail over his anger issues, and paid many a fine.

Not long after he left, news of his death was delivered to Carrie, who didn't have much reaction. He had been killed by gunshot wounds over another woman. He'd had an affair with a friend's wife and had beaten her during a heated argument. The disrespected associate found out and emptied his gun into John's chest and groin area.

A week after John had left home for good, younger sister went to live with older sister. Rita, being a good sibling, cared for Carrie until her fatal car accident. The two sisters had always been very close, and Rita's death drove Carrie completely over the edge. She withdrew from reality, completely shutting down. Soon after, she had been brought to Chicago-Read with her few clothes and belongings. She gradually regressed, falling further into darkness as the years passed. She used to react when her name was called, but after a few months on the Ward she lived only in a world of her own, reacting to nothing. It was a sad story to a sad life, but it just blended in with the many other lost lives and histories that passed through the front doors of Chicago-Read over the years.

On the day the power went out, a little before three o'clock, Carrie was sitting at her table doing her puzzle when every employee and patient at Chicago-Read suddenly disappeared. Carrie didn't seem to notice. The Ward became hot after the old rattling AC units stopped working. The heat didn't seem to faze her in the least either.

On this different day Carrie did something different as well. She did not stand up at three o'clock and start her odd monologue. Instead, she just continued staring down at her puzzle, oblivious to the changes around her. It was only when the sun began to disappear into the western horizon, and the shadows grew long in the great room, that she showed any reaction. As the first shadows gently touched her thin, frail frame, Carrie Winston suddenly stopped fiddling with her beloved Sears Tower puzzle, got up, walked down the stairs, moved through the lobby to the front doors, and then stepped outside. She looked all around her quiet, hot surroundings, took a deep breath, and began walking eastward. Smoke and the strong smell of jet fuel filled the air as she slowly shuffled forward. She didn't react to that either.

Once Carrie reached the intersection of Sidney and Weaver Streets, Chicago-Read disappeared completely from view. She never looked back at it once, and she would never see the old Ward again.

Chapter Nine

TY WONG

Ty Wong was sitting in McCarran International Airport in Las Vegas, Nevada, waiting on a flight back to Hong Kong when his life turned upside down. He had missed his original flight by thirty minutes, but he didn't care. The business meeting at the Bellagio Hotel had gone better than he had thought. His main business was computer parts for the new systems that were sweeping across the entire globe, but this meeting was where the real money resided—in the underworld, hiding in the shadows. Drugs, new ones—Varrrius and Furrgretion—sex drugs that weren't legal, and never would be because half the ingredients were extremely dangerous when you combined them. Since the drugs had first come out five years ago, many side effects had surfaced. Blindness, cancers of all internal organs, plus nerve and brain damage being the biggest negatives, but there were also reports of rotting genitalia in both males and females as well.

The mindsets of drug users? They usually knew the risks, but they didn't care. They never did. One didn't live forever. One only lived for today. The usual excuse that made them go against logic: the world was a shithole anyway. I'm holding a losing hand, so why did it matter?

And there *were* positives to these new drugs in the short term. They could make you the king or queen of sex—physically and mentally. You could screw your brains out for days without stopping, orgasming strongly like never before. You'd be known as a God and a legend in most parts. You didn't even give a shit if you were banging the opposite sex or your own. One hole just seemed to blend into another. Straight or gay sex was irrelevant—the more the merrier. Morals be damned and thrown out the righteous window!

Also on the negative side was the fact that these drugs were very addictive, and users would do anything to get more. If you were lucky, the authorities caught you and threw you in jail before they killed your insides and destroyed your mind.

Ty had an underground factory back home and had just made a deal here in the City of the Unholy. The details still had to be worked out, but they could easily be worked out quickly by his underlings. His work was big time—literally. He always laughed at this inside joke. It was funny. You could add two to four inches on your Johnson with these drugs. Yes, *big time* was right! He trusted his American counterparts. He did legal business with them and they had both made money, but this new drug business could make them all trillions! More money than any of them could ever spend. It didn't matter that a few degenerates would die or be mangled in the process. The users would have their fun, while Ty and his partners could drown in their wealth. They'd all be happy. Ty made himself believe this as he waited on his flight.

He was staring out at the parked planes on the tarmac in the 125-degree heat when the power went off and the people all around him suddenly disappeared. He didn't have time to think as planes began to crash and explode all around the airport. One crashed into the opposite side of the terminal, rocking the floor beneath him. He started running toward where he thought the exits might be, hoped where they might be. Ty Wong didn't consciously realize it, but as he ran through the airport as fast as he could he was screaming at the top of his lungs. In this sudden chaotic situation, making money on new sex drugs were the last thing on his mind—survival was now number one.

Chapter Ten

THE WISCONSIN CHURCH

*T*here is a small church in Wisconsin, back in the woods, in the middle of nowhere. A small cemetery sits behind it with about twenty ancient-looking headstones. The stones are so old and weather-beaten you can't make out the letters or numbers. A long road through the woods lead to the religious structure, made out of hard dirt. The church has been abandoned at times, but has been used lately. The church has a history of dark folklore, of many haunting stories. They are all true—or *supposedly* true. The congregation that came to Sunday services at 11:00 a.m. and 6:00 p.m. back in the day would tell you that, especially the ones who attended service at 6:00 p.m., when the shadows grew long, distorted, and seemed to dance over the graves of the cemetery. They would tell you the church has always been haunted. They would be pretty sure of that. Which means no one really knows.

The church is actually the Lawrence B. Estonian in Lincoln County. Built way back in the 1900s, it was one of the first Estonian churches built in the United States. The actual beginning of the church congregation dates back some twenty or thirty years before the church's construction, where services were held in private houses and rotated weekly. Like the rest of the population of the United States, the congregation slowly grew, and by 1905 they had enough members to start looking to move services into a church of their own. Funds were collected weekly. The small graveyard was established first. Money from the burials also helped pay for the soon-to-be-built church. Family members were buried five deep on top of each other to save space. Little money was raised in the beginning, but over time enough cashflow was raised to build the original religious structure.

The church was a one story, one-room structure upon completion, made of wood and painted completely white inside and out. A steeple stood above the front door, ten feet higher than the rest of the church. A bell was installed and was rung by a long thick rope. Traditionally, ringing it was usually the pastor's job. Maroon-colored shingles covered the roof and steeple. Enough pews were installed to sit forty parishioners comfortably. A sturdy pulpit had been purchased a month after the church first opened. A large six-foot wooden cross was nailed into the wall behind the pulpit. A small church organ was donated soon after that. Pastor William Pierce gave good sermons. Bible lessons were given during the week on Tuesday and Thursday evenings to better understand the Lord and His Word. The future looked bright. It wasn't.

Around 1920 or so, Pastor Pierce moved into the church, using the small dirt basement as his sleeping quarters. His small cottage had been sold and the money used for church upkeep. It would be the last time any maintenance would be done to the church for many dark years. Three days after Pastor William (the whole congregation called him that) moved in he was found dead behind his pulpit. He was sixty-six years old. Heart attack was written down as cause of death by the local physician, but the members of the church weren't so sure.

When he was first found, he looked like he had been scared

to death by something he had seen. The nights in the woods were darker than dark, filled with all kinds of strange sounds and noises. Your imagination could run amok in those circumstances, no matter how strong your faith was. Also, the large Bible that had always laid open in the pulpit had pages ripped out. The ripped pages were torn out of the back of the Bible roughly, as if done angrily. Those missing pages were the complete Book of Revelations.

That was the first occurrence. There were many more. The missing pages of Pastor William's bible were never found. He was buried behind his church in the small cemetery. Three weeks later someone or something dug up his remains and nailed them to the large cross behind the pulpit. Around his neck hung a sign, its latin letters written in dried animal blood. It was translated soon after, which said, "Worthless Witchdoctor Pig." Pastor William was reburied in a different cemetery somewhere in Minnesota, and his body laid in peace until it returned to The Creator when the power went out.

The church didn't have another service for two months, not until Pastor Ronald Mann was interviewed and hired. In those two months three babies were born, adding to the congregation—two boys and a girl. All three eventually grew up and attended weekly Bible studies. They were all good students. They all were part of the first children's choir that rehearsed every Friday night. They all sang like angels. But when all three turned thirteen years of age, something went wrong—terribly wrong. Pastor Mann didn't live at the church, but on Friday night, on the thirteenth day of June, he didn't return home to his rented room at Peter Barkley's, a long-time parishioner at the church. The three teenagers didn't return home either. The families of the young teens became first nervous, then scared. Around midnight the local constable was contacted. He rounded up two other officers, and then they and the fathers of the three missing children went out to the church. What they found varied in local folklore as the years rolled on, but one thing was certain: hell had entered that church with a vengeance.

The Constable's report read as follows:

Upon entering the church, what we found could only be described as complete evil. Two red candles had been lit and placed on the front pews. Pastor Mann was sloped over his pulpit face down. The children were not in the church, but low giggling could be heard behind the religious structure.

I sent officer Gaunt out to investigate, and the three fathers went with him. Officer Grant and I approached the pastor after getting no response from him. Going around the pulpit we both saw that the minister's pants and underwear were down around his ankles. Dried blood ran down his legs, coming from his backside and from somewhere in front. The pastor was cold to the touch. I lifted his head up and was shocked at what I saw. His eyes were gone, dried blood coming from their empty sockets. His nose was also missing. It appeared as if it had been eaten off his face. His mouth was held open by a large gold cross from a necklace. More dried blood ran over the pastor's lips and chin. Looking further, I discovered that the minister's tongue had been ripped out, along with all his teeth. A pair of pliers lay bloodied on top of the Bible in the pulpit. They must have been pulled out one by one.

It was then, or around that point, that a lot of commotion was heard coming from behind the church. Officer

Grant and I pulled out our firearms and ran outside and around back by the cemetery. What we saw was no stranger or any less evil than what we had witnessed inside the church. Richard Larson, who had died and been buried two months prior, had been dug up, and the three children were hungrily eating his corpse. It was as if they were possessed by demons or something, making animalistic noises and giggling insanely as they ate. Officer Gaunt and the fathers of the three children were screaming, frozen in place. They were just watching the cannibalistic act take place (Officer Gaunt, although under great duress, was suspended without pay for a period of one month afterward). Both I and Officer Grant, one by one, pulled the three teenagers off the corpse and handcuffed them. It was no easy task as all three seemed to possess unusual strength. They yelled and screamed obscenities as they were restrained. Officer Gaunt and the three fathers came out of their trances and helped us pull the children away from the cemetery and church.

It took all night and halfway into the next morning, but we got all three children back to the stationhouse. They were put in separate cells, awaiting examinations. All three continued to act as if possessed, screaming and franticly trying to get out of their cells. All parents waited out in the lobby. They were all understandably traumatized, and awaited examinations themselves. The body of Pastor Ronald Mann was brought to the county morgue along with the corpse of Richard Larson. Until further notice, the church will be closed, and no services will be held. Investigations will take place. Professionals will be brought in.

Constable Jeff Givens was busy for days. Down at the morgue, things got crazy. Complete loss of blood was written down as cause of death for Pastor Ronald Mann. His eyes had been eaten out of his head, as was his nose. His complete genitalia had been ripped off (penis and scrotum) and along with some of his teeth and his tongue had been shoved up his anus. It was determined that he had been conscious when those horrible acts had been performed on him. It must have been a very painful, slow death. Most of this information was hidden from the public, but rumors flew. Stories were told. Some were close to the vest, other tales were off the charts. In some, the pastor's heart had been ripped from his chest, in others he had been beheaded and his limbs sawed off. As time sped by all stories were considered scary campfire folklore.

In the case of Richard Larson's corspe, his face had been eaten off. His heart *had* been ripped from his chest and digested by the children. They had smashed the bones of his legs and arms into many pieces by the shovels that had been used to dig him up. His body was wrapped in clean sheets by the town mortician and quickly reburied in a nameless plot in a different cemetery. The dirt was just filled in at the church cemetery. The headstone with Richard Larson's name on it is still in the small graveyard, but over time, like all the others, the words and dates have faded away, unreadable. This whole procedure was kept under wraps by the authorities. Only a few knew the truth, and that was for the best. The less people knew about this whole situation the better. Stories still circulated, though. Some of them said that Richard Larson's ghost haunted the graveyard and church whenever the moon was full. Foklore by the campfire. There were always new tales to tell.

The three children were quietly moved into the nearest

hospital. They were placed in a separate ward, cut off from all other patients. No one except the police and the children's parents knew where they were. They were too young to be charged with murder. Besides, their mental states remained the same. They were heavily chained to their hospital beds. All they wanted to do was kill, eat their victims, and then repeat the process. They talked in different tongues, in different voices. They were considered possessed by angry demons, addicted to killing everything and everyone in their path. They refused to eat, and their health declined. They vomited dark black bile, and then quickly lapped that up. They lost weight, lost strength; yet day after day they became more and more vicious, screaming and screeching out new and creative ways to kill another human being. All medical experiments failed. Eventually all the doctors and religious heads that had been brought in became totally frustrated. Time was running out. The three children were dying.

A senior priest from Minnesota was brought in. He had supposedly been involved in successful exorcisms. The three families of the three teens were desperate. Their children didn't have much time left. They agreed to let the priest try to not only save their lives, but their souls as well. The priest brought in five other men of five different religions to assist him. The children had become possessed at the church, so the exorcisms would be done there. They would be performed under God's watch, under the church, in the basement. It sounded good, sane even. It wasn't.

The exorcisms were performed, the children chained to the basement ceiling. It went on for five hours. It went wrong. All three children died, exploding from within. Pieces of their bodies spattered everywhere. Insane giggling melted into the basement walls. The religious exorcists survived, but they were scarred for life. None of them would ever perform another exorcism. None of them ever talked about what had happened. All of them thought they were a failure in God's eyes. All of them thought themselves unworthy. All of them spent the rest of their lives in deep depression. None ever dared step foot near the church property again. All of them had the same revelation, seen through a dark dream: if they ever stepped foot inside or near that church again, they not only would lose their sanity, but their souls.

The authorities told the townsfolk the children had been moved to a psychiatric ward up north across the Canadian border. Tall tales. Always more tales to tell. The families of the three teenagers were all moved out of state and were never heard from again.

The church from that point on never officially held weekly services again until many years had passed. The townsfolk again worshipped at home, or just traveled to another church. In that time period they believed the church and its grounds (including the cemetery) were haunted by dark spirits. Maybe the land underneath the church was unhealthy; maybe it was cursed long before man ever walked on this planet. There were a million maybes. It didn't matter. All anybody knew was that two pastors had died terribly on that land only trying to preach The Good Word, trying to show their parishioners the right path.

Stories continued to be told of other hauntings on the land. Most were made up by kids just trying to pass the time of day, but maybe some were true. As time went along the church began to decay, and wildlife became its only parishioners. No one was ever buried in the cemetery again after Pastor Mann was murdered. The road and land around the church became overgrown. New trees grew in the road, and the grass and brush grew out of control. The cemetery suffered the same fate. The grass grew higher than the headstones, and some of them fell over from the shifting ground underneath them. No one from the town dared walk on the grounds. People traveling through sometimes visited the church, took pictures, but that was all.

Then, about twenty years before the power went off, a young pastor traveling through decided to check out the church. He needed a place to spread The Word, and felt like he could make a difference here. All the tall tales he heard from the towns-folk couldn't be true. He decided all they needed was healing. He bought the land, dirt cheap. He cut the grass and trimmed the brush. He took care of the cemetery, uprighting the fallen headstones. He started repairing the church with his own money. Eventually he put up signs all over town saying services would be held every Sunday at noon. The first time only one person showed up. The next four. The one after that six.

The ones that came told others that the sermons were good, and The Lord was back in charge of that ground. More and more began to show up. Soon a small choir was formed. The organ was repaired and played by a student in the local high school. Word got out. People from out of town began to come. They told others. Soon every seat in every pew was filled. Sometimes it was standing room only. Bible lessons were given again on Tuesdays and Thursdays at 6:00 p.m. Those classes were always filled. Stories of Jesus were told. Love and harmony filled the air. Nothing bad ever happened. The haunted tales from the past were forgotten, or at least put on the back burner. A new generation of people now attended the services on Sundays. A new generation learned about the Lord at Bible study. They were happy. They were blessed. They had finally found their way—that is, until the power went out and all the people went back to The Creator, along with all those buried in the cemetery. The congregation suddenly was gone—all gone. They had all gone home. Except for one. One. Pastor Ryan Brookings.

Chapter Eleven

ARLENE DOWD

*I*n Boston, down on Bakers Street, Arlene Dowd sat in her car thinking about her mother. Jeannie Dowd had died suddenly of a heart attack a week ago, and she was laid out at O'Reilly's Funeral Home waiting on some family members to arrive from Ireland. Jeannie had been seventy-eight years old. Up until her last day on Earth, she had been in perfect shape. Other than a cold every now and then, she had never been sick a day in her life. That's how heart attacks go—here one second, going through another day in one's life, and then gone the next in an instant. Like blowing out a candle.

Passing away was great for the one dying—not so great for family and friends left behind. They were usually left in shock, never having the chance to say goodbye. They sometimes feel cheated, cheated meaning that they didn't have time to prepare for a loved one's death. Morbid, but some people need this ritual. In some sudden deaths, the family blames the deceased for dying. The mindset is "How dare you die. How dare you leave me!"

Arlene had none of these feelings or thoughts. She was just kind of relieved that her mother was gone. She felt bad that she felt this way. Arlene was a good, caring person, but her mother had been a strong-minded woman—mean, even. One that had always tried to force her beliefs on Arlene and her two younger brothers, William and Ronald. The Dowd's family life wasn't unusual. Families since the beginning of time were like this. Religious beliefs were just some of the topics parents tried to pass on to their offspring. If your parents believed in God, then they would drive that belief home. If they *didn't* believe in the Lord, then *that* belief would be brainwashed into the children. This went for politics, prejudices, customs, and any other conversations that might take place around the dinner table. Parents wanted their children to believe and think as they did—carbon copies of themselves, so to speak. Sounds good. Sounds right. Sounds *sound*. It's *not*! It's the worst thing you can ever do to your children. That's the way Arlene thought. She believed that *everybody* needed to find their own identity, their own beliefs, their own likes and dislikes—their own *way*. And that way meant questioning everything: everything that your parents, grandparents, various other family members, teachers, religious leaders, books, and various periodicals said. Or preached.

Arlene believed that every little thing should be looked at under your own microscope and analyzed. It should be broken down to its smallest denominator and then put back together from every angle. And that was the magic word: *angle*. Every opinion from any discussion should be looked at from every angle, looked at from everybody's own way of looking at it. Understood from everybody's own way of looking at it. So much could be learned from that. Maybe, she thought, if everybody thought like this, a lot of negatives could be avoided: arguments, fights, even wars. Peace and harmony could reign under this way of thinking. At least then there was a chance.

That was the way Arlene saw things. Her mother thought just the opposite. She always tried to drive her beliefs down your throat. And if you fought her on any of them, then you were in for it. Punishments would be in your future. Hell would have to be paid—paid in full.

One of Jeannie Dowd's deepest beliefs was "there was no God." Her mother had died giving birth to her, therefore there couldn't be a Supreme Being. No God would do that to anybody. Jeannie was resentful, angry. Arlene thought that *that* was understandable; she could understand her mother's feelings. But maybe, just maybe God needed her in heaven, if there was such a place. Maybe she was needed to be with God for a reason no one on Earth could understand. That option would have to be examined, at least, wouldn't it? If, after thoroughly going through all the pros and cons, you still thought that there wasn't a God, then so be it. That would be fine. But why then would you force-feed that belief down your children's throats? We *had* a mother. Our mother *didn't* die giving birth to us. Sure, she wasn't the greatest bargain, but we *still* had her. Wouldn't that mean that there *was* a God? Asking Mom those types of questions meant that hell had to be paid—paid in full.

Arlene believed her mother's belief of no God until she reached her own age of reason, which came around her sixth year on planet Earth. She figured that *that* was when she began to question life in full. And her first question was: if you didn't believe in the Lord, then why would you have any children to begin with? What kind of future, what kind of fate would they have? How dark would their lives be? How desolate? There would be no hope. Death would come, and . . . that would be it! You'd be wiped completely out of existence! No God. No heaven. No hope. And no *sense*!

You could break it all down, put all the pieces back together again and come up with the same conclusion: *It. Made. No. Sense!* And then Arlene came up with the only logical explanation for still having children while not believing in a God: total selfishness while showing no compassion for the child you'd be bringing into this world. It was a brutal conclusion, but one that was true—cold, hard truth. Arlene knew that her mother was better than that. She had compassion. She loved her children. She might have had a strange way of showing it sometimes, but she *did* love her kids. She just happened to be like a lot of other mothers or parents overall; she just hadn't thought it all through. She hadn't examined the topic from every *angle*.

This was just one example of how life existed under the Dowd roof. There were many more. Millions and millions of households were the same way. Some believed this; some believed that. And then those beliefs were pile-driven into their children's brains. Creative minds were not allowed to grow, to think on their own. Personalities were handicapped. Arlene thought it was the biggest type of mental illness circulating throughout most households.

Arlene Dowd was rehashing all this as she reversed her car out of her driveway and drove down to the funeral home to finalize some loose ends. Her brothers were already there. They were more like their mother. They shared her beliefs. They didn't believe in God. Arlene, on the other hand *did* believe in The Lord. She did so with all her heart. She believed in an afterlife. She believed her mother was in a better place, sitting beside a Creator she never believed in. That thought was comforting, and from that thought sprouted hope. Hope for a brighter future.

Arlene had done her math. She had gone through her process. And yet there was another piece of the puzzle that she didn't tell anybody about. She felt no need to tell anyone. Arlene had dreams. Some were the same. Some were very vivid. In them a bright circular light would visit her. It would talk soothingly to her. It was warm. It was spiritual. It would tell her to keep evaluating all things in her way of thinking. It told her that her way was good, that it was the right mental approach, and that approach would always lead down the right path to the truth. "Don't ever let anybody try to change you. Never. You are blessed." And then the light would leave her. She always woke up feeling better whenever she had these dreams, because she knew deep in her heart that they were more than just dreams—they were visions.

Arlene drove into the funeral home parking lot and was about to park when the power went out. The car shut off and stopped just short of the parking spot. She tried turning the key on and off a few times with no results. It was dead. She got out into the heat and quickly walked inside. No lights were on, no air conditioning. Nobody was there to greet her. She walked to the funeral home office. No one was there. She called out—no answer. She walked to the room where her mother was laid out and discovered that not only wasn't her mother there, but neither was her coffin. What was going on? she wondered. She walked back outside. There was a park across the street. No one was there. She looked up and down the street. A few cars were on both sides of the street, but they weren't moving. It was completely quiet until she heard an explosion off to her right. Then another. And another. The smell of fuel began to fill the air, and she could see dark black smoke rising into the sky. Something unusual and different was happening, she thought. Something much different. Another explosion could be heard far off in the distance. There was more smoke.

Arlene Dowd walked back inside O'Reilly's Funeral Home and down to the room where her mother should've been, dropped to her knees, and began to pray. She prayed to a God she not only believed in but now needed—badly.

Chapter Twleve

GRANDPA AND EDWARD

Edward Kennedy was ten years old. He lived in Denver, Colorado, on Senate Drive. He and his mother, Nancy, lived with his grandparents in their home. Home was a two-hundred-year-old, three-story colonial that his grandparents' great grandparents bought when they were first married. It had been in the family ever since. Edward wasn't born here; he lived with his parents two miles away in the Hempstead Apartments for two and a half years. They fought all the time and divorced shortly after Edward's second birthday.

Johnny Devers, Edward's father, left the apartment and moved to Seattle where his parents and other family members lived. Through one of his cousins he met his second wife, Martha. They stayed together five years before that marriage failed. Johnny left town and his whereabouts were unknown.

Edward and his mom finished out the lease on the apartment (with no financial help from his father), and then moved in with the elder Kennedys. Life was good for young Edward. Living with his grandparents was second to none. They were always there for daughter and grandson. Carolyn and Danny Kennedy were the greatest grandparents in Edward's eyes. He could always talk to both of them, for they would always tell him the truth on all subjects. Edward demanded the truth. He didn't want the "untruth" (for his mother didn't lie, she just stretched the truth a little to *protect* him), he wanted the cold hard facts of life, and from his grandparents he got them. He learned more from them than he learned from anybody else. School was good. They helped him with homework; they helped him understand why he was there, and how important it was to go to college and never stop learning. Edward's mom worked hard, working more than one job at times. She wasn't home as much as she wanted to be, but she knew her parents would fill that important void—and that void was family values. She had grown up with them, and now Edward was experiencing life-learning lessons from them as well.

Danny Kennedy was sixty-eight, trim, and in very good shape. He had a full head of white hair, which was shoulder length and kept in a ponytail. He taught Edward sports—not just how to play them, but how to win, and more importantly, how to lose. Gracefully. They went for long walks in the park and through the woods on the outskirts of town. The talked and talked, and Edward gained knowledge way beyond his years. Most importantly, he learned about love and harmony under a family roof. There was nothing better than a positive home life, and Edward had that.

One day when Edward was five years old he caught his grandfather locking the door to the attic. He knew his grandfather went up there often, but he didn't know *what* went on up there. He yearned to know, and wanted to go up there in the worst way. He was curious. If Grandpa went up there, then he wanted to go up there as well. He expressed his feelings about this, and Grandfather agreed to finally show him the attic. And so the next day they walked the steep stairs to the unfinished room above their bedrooms.

To Edward, he walked into wonderland. The room was dis-organized, but the things scattered around were amazing. There were three old ancient television sets. They all still worked. They were all black and white picture screens, no color. They were like the old movies that his mother still watched with *her* mother. His grandfather told him that they were our history, the beginning of amazing improvements to what we had today. There was an old pool table with all the faded colored balls scattered across its also faded felt. A rack and four cue sticks lay on top of the table as well. A folded-up ping-pong table sat against the wall closest to the pool table. There was old furniture. Two old rocking chairs that had belonged to Danny's grandparents sat off to the side. Edward and his grandfather would talk and rock in those chairs for hours in the future. An old hutch sat near the chairs with old china in it. There was an old acoustic guitar, an old drum set, re-cords, and an old record player.

There were a lot of records, maybe three hundred albums, all lined up against the wall. In them there was music from way back: rock music, jazz, traditional, contemporary, classical, coun-try, R & B, and soul. It was all there. The record player worked. Grandfather and grandson would listen to those albums for hours, week after week, enjoying them. Of course, Grandfather had to replay all the ones grandson liked most—maybe more than once. An old furniture piece radio sat next to the records. It still worked as well. They listened to the news and music on FM.

An old bar with two stools was in another corner of the attic. It held old bottles of vodka, whiskey, and scotch. Grandfather said they would have to wait some years before drinking any of those! Edward always remembered his grandfather laughing until his face turned red whenever he said that. An old player piano was there as well. It had a lot of scratches, and its wood frame was chipped in spots, but it still worked and played old tunes.

On top of the piano sat stacks and stacks of old magazines of all sorts: Sports Illustrated, Life, People. Next to the piano sat old newspapers, dating back to the days when Danny Kennedy was a young boy.

But in the farthest corner stood an easel and a canvas. A dark wooden stool sat in front of it. Brushes and paints sat on a small table to the right. None had been opened or used. Behind the easel lined up against the wall were about fifty canvases. They were all blank, including the one on the easel, just ready to be used. Grandfather told grandson that someday someone might become a famous painter and use all of them. Maybe somebody could become another Leonardo Di Vinci. One never knew; anything was possible. Grandfather told grandson that everything up here was part of the past—a good past, but the past nonetheless. The canvases and the paints were different. They were for the future. Edward did not quite understand, but nodded anyway. He knew as soon as he saw those paints . . . he knew that it was all for him. Grandfather smiled as he watched his grandson's face light up. He had done well.

A week after that Edward had a dream—or at least he thought it was a dream. In the dream he woke up and it was dark—and very quiet. He got out of bed and tiptoed down the hall to the attic door. It was unlocked. He knew his grandfather always kept the door locked, but it wasn't now. Odd, but Edward didn't care. Not in his dream he didn't. The night darkness usually frightened him as well, but not now. He rode a warm calmness, a wave that just took him wherever he wanted to go. And where he wanted to go was up those stairs to the world of enchantment—the attic. And that is what he did.

He opened the door and quietly climbed the stairs in the dark. When he got to the top the windows at each end gave him light, the full moon shining in on the east side. There was a lit candle next to the easel. He walked over to it and sat down on the stool. It was then that through the other window he saw a bright light. Still sitting on the stool, it got brighter and brighter. The window opened by itself (that too was always locked) and a very bright white sphere floated inside. It grew and grew until it was six feet in circumference, stopping just below the inclined ceiling. And then (in Edward's mind) a tall alien Being stepped out of it. It was dressed in a white robe that fell to its sandaled feet, which were much larger than human feet. It's six toes were long and bony, but there were no toenails. The creature's hands that protruded from the rope were also large, about twice the size of a normal grown-up's. It's six fingers were also long and bony, with no fingernails. Its head was three times larger than a human head. It was round, and it had three pointy ears on each side. The one closest to its face was the smallest, then the next one in the middle, and then the biggest one in the rear. It had two humanlike dark eyes, a large pointy nose with four nostrils, and a large smiling face. Its mouth had no teeth, and its head no hair, but it was extremely wrinkly. The color of its skin was light gray, darker gray around its wrinkles. Edward should have been scared out of his pajamas, but he wasn't. He felt no fear, only warm calmness.

The creature looked at the empty canvas on the easel, and then at the paints. It cocked its head to one side, and it's smile widened, and then the alien bent down and held Edward's right hand gently. The alien's hand felt warm. Comforting. The tall creature nodded twice, and then Edward's small hand, held by large bony alien hand, picked up a paintbrush and touched it to canvas. The creature then withdrew its hand and stood up straight, waiting patiently. Edward slowly nodded, turned back to the canvas, opened the first bottle of paint, and began painting. His little hand felt funny; it tingled all over, but the paintbrush felt good in it. It felt *right*. It felt as if he had painted many times before, and yet he never had.

He didn't know how long he painted, or what he painted, but by the time it was done the alien was gone, and the window was closed. It was as if he had painted in a trance, and maybe that was the right word. He had been in a zone and was unaware of anything around him as he painted away, possessed. Edward put down the paintbrush and walked over to the window and looked out. Nothing but the moon and stars filled the night sky. He checked the window. It was locked. How could that be? He shrugged, and then walked trancelike to the stairs, down the steps, locked the attic door behind him, and walked down the hallway to his bedroom. He got in bed, pulled the covers over him, and went back to sleep.

The next morning after breakfast Edward told his grandfather about his dream. Intrigued, rubbing his chin, Danny Kennedy took his grandson up to the attic. The attic door was locked. After Danny unlocked it and they entered, they were amazed at what they saw. On the easel sat a canvas, but it was no longer blank. A painting of New York City was on it. It was very good, professional even. The detail and color mix were amazing! It looked as though a professional artist had painted it from the New Jersey side of the Hudson River, and had painted every crevice, every nook and cranny of every building in the city. Grandfather stared at it for a minute, then put his hands on his thighs just above his knees and burst out laughing, shaking his head. Edward stared at him oddly, and then joined him. Still laughing, Danny took the painting and put it off to the side and replaced it with another blank canvas. They then both walked back down the stairs and decided that something amazing had happened. They told no one about the dream or the painting. They decided they would sit back and see if another canvas would be painted. They would only have to wait until the next full moon.

Edward again had the same dream with the alien, only this time the painting was of Interstate 70 just outside of Denver. Again, the painting was very good. Again, Grandfather replaced the painting with another blank canvas.

This happened again and again whenever the moon was full. There were paintings of Kansas City, Indiana, Ohio, Pennsylvania, and New Jersey. The paintings were like a road map heading east, straight toward New York City, the first painting. All were exceptional, detailed. Grandfather and grandson both wondered aloud about who they thought did the paintings. It definitely was a big mystery. In the end Grandfather told Grandson to leave it alone; that all things of all topics would always reveal themselves when the time was right.

When the power went out, twenty paintings sat in the attic. Edward and Danny Kennedy were in the attic listening to some traditional jazz on the old record player. An air-conditioner in the east window was working overtime. They both stopped working at the same time. Grandfather and Grandson both looked at each other. They both figured there had been a power overload. They would discover otherwise. But they were both still here, still together—not alone. And that was a good thing, a comforting feeling. It would be the only time two people would be left together when the rest of life went home. They discovered that Grandmother/wife was gone, and Mother/daughter also. They hugged and cried. And then they pulled themselves together like the team they were.

They discovered what everybody else left on earth found out. They talked. They reminisced about the good times with family that no longer were here. About the dogs that no longer barked, and the birds that no longer flew in the sky. And about the big jet airliners that fell from the sky. They decided that staying in Denver was no longer an option. Denver was like the attic—old history. And so, they decided to leave. They grabbed their bikes out of the garage, filled their backpacks with food and water, and hit the road. They decided to follow the path of the paintings in the attic. They decided to go to New York City, the place of the first painting.

After completing their first day on the road, dodging cars and trucks—some that had crashed into each other—they found an unlocked house and laid down to rest. Edward took the couch, Danny a reclining chair. They were both asleep in seconds.

Edward dreamed. He dreamed of his mother, and of his grandmother. They were smiling at him, standing on a large white cloud. They didn't talk, but he heard their voices inside his mind. They told Edward they loved him—and they always would. They added that he was special, and that Grandpa would protect and see him through. Now go out and paint the world anew! And then they turned into aliens, just like the one he had seen in his dreams in the attic. The cloud turned into a round white sphere, engulfing them, and then it was gone, disappearing into thin air.

Edward woke up and saw his grandfather staring down at him. He was smiling knowingly. Danny told him that they had to go, and so they did, with one difference. Grandfather was now in his true form, his alien form—his *truthful* form. They bicycled down the road as a new day began, and all was right as rain between them, as it should be.

Chapter Thirteen

KELVIN WILLIAMS

Kelvin Williams feared spiders—despised and hated them, couldn't stand the sight of them. He dreamed of them whenever he did something wrong—and boy had he done something wrong *this* time. And he was finally going to get caught. The cops were outside, and it sounded like they had surrounded the Motel 6 he was staying in. He was on the run, and he hadn't gotten far. He thought he could get away and outwit them, but he wasn't that smart. They had figured his shit out. And now they were closing in on him. He was fucked. Totally fucked! He sat against the door, rubbing the sides of his aching head. He thought he saw a couple of large black hairy spiders laughing at him from under the bed. By all accounts, he figured they'd get to him before the cops did. He was sure of it. What a dilemma he was in. How had it gotten to this point? How had he fucked up so badly? He thought back to when it all started to go wrong, and when the spiders had decided to never leave him alone . . .

Kelvin grew up in Houston, Texas. His parents split up, and his mother left him at the doors of the Cantor Brothers Orphanage when he was only two months old. He never knew either of them, and that hurt. It hurt a lot. He grew up withdrawn and quiet—and rejected. Rejected by his own blood. And that hurt a lot too. One day when he was crying, feeling sorry for himself, he saw a small spider scurrying across the floor and Kelvin smashed it with his fist. That night he dreamed of spiders of all shapes and sizes: black ones, brown ones. They crawled into his nose and ears. They worked their way into his brain. And they began to eat. They ate his thoughts. They ate his feelings. And when they worked their way to his eyes and he went blind, he woke up screaming. He checked his ears, nose, and eyes. They adjusted to the dark. He could still see. From that moment on he hated spiders and feared the sight of them.

He didn't dream of spiders again until he punched another boy in the nose for cursing him and calling him a faggot. He broke the boy's nose and was punished. That night the spiders punished him in his nightmares. He came to realize that every time he did something wrong he'd dream of spiders—every time. It didn't keep him from getting in trouble, for doing the deed dirty. But every time? The spiders never gave him a break. And they kept his dreams lively, for the nightmares were always different. Sometimes they entered his mouth. Sometimes the little ones entered through every pore of his body. But they always traveled to his brain. And they always *ate*. They always ate . . .

He bounced around from foster home to foster home, always being sent back to the orphanage for getting in trouble or disrupting family harmony. He grew up angry and vindictive, and always took it out on the family willing to give him a chance. And the spiders always reminded him that *that* was wrong. He was hardheaded; he knew the spiders would come if he was bad or disrespectful, but he just couldn't help himself. And they were all too happy to set his shit straight.

He also had issues at every school he attended. His grades were poor, and as he got older he began to cut classes. He quit when he turned sixteen, and that's when he ran away from the orphanage, the spiders scurrying right beside him. The authorities searched for him half-heartedly for a couple of weeks and then just wrote him off, like so many other delinquents.

Kelvin became a grifter, moving from town to town, doing odd jobs just to keep from starving. He'd sleep wherever he could. Eventually he hitchhiked north into Oklahoma, getting rides here and there until he got caught stealing food in the local food store in Hawthorne, a backwoods town. He was thrown in jail—the wrong jail, with the wrong police chief in charge. At night the chief would berate him to no end, and then come into Kelvin's cell, beat him up, handcuff his hands behind his back, and rape him repeatedly. He was a large man, maybe 350 pounds, Kelvin was short and skinny: no match for the head of police. He would cry himself to sleep every night, wishing that he would die.

After being in jail for a couple of weeks, the chief made a huge mistake. He handcuffed Kelvin's hands in front, put him in his car, and drove them out of town. They turned off onto a long dirt road through dense, thick woods. They came to a small shack that looked like it would implode on itself at any time. As the chief was taking him out of the car, Kelvin, fearing for his life, suddenly kneed him in the groin area hard, twice. As the chief bent over, Kelvin kicked him square in the testicles as hard as he could. The policeman screamed and went to his knees, gasping, and that's when Kelvin went to work on him. He kicked him in the head repeatedly until the policeman was unconscious. The chief's nose had been broken, and it was oozing blood. He kicked the officer in the side many times, breaking a few ribs.

Kelvin found the keys in the chief's front pants pocket and unlocked himself. Breathing hard, he handcuffed the chief's wrists behind his back and slowly dragged him inside the shack—no easy task, but when there's a will there's a way. A single bed was the only piece of furniture inside. It was old and falling apart. Dirty white sheets covered an old worn and dried bloodstained mattress. The steel frame was bent badly in the middle. A few whips and paddles hung on rusty nails on the wall above the bed. He took a paddle off the wall and hit the chief over the head with it numerous times. The chief groaned, and then completely passed out again.

He stripped the chief naked and handcuffed both wrists to the bed frame. He took a thick whip off the wall and viciously whipped the unconscious officer's back and buttocks until he bled. He found a baseball bat in the corner and grabbed it. When the chief groaningly came to, Kelvin began to question him. At first he had to hit him in the back a few times with the bat, but eventually he started talking. He told Kelvin he had raped other men many times before, and when he got tired of them he killed and buried them out in the woods. There were maybe ten or more unmarked graves out there. The men would never be missed, for they were all like Kelvin: strangers passing through. Some had been caught stealing. Some just ended up drunk down at Hot Joe's Bar and Grill and gotten into a fight. They all ended up in one of Hawthorne's jail cells, where Chief Ryan Michaels began to brutalize them. Beat them. Rape them. Punish them with whips and paddles, and eventually choke them to death. The chief admitted that he liked to see the life drain out of his victims' eyes. It turned him on.

What a bastard, Kelvin thought. What a lowlife motherfucker! He lost it. He screamed at the top of his lungs as he broke legs, arms, kneecaps, and finally the officer's back with the bat. The chief was past screaming, past crying and begging for mercy. He was babbling incoherently when Kelvin decided to do something completely out of character. He did what the spiders did. They ate, and so he decided so should he. He bit the police chief's right ear off, and then went for the other.

The chief's screams were more animalistic than human. He struggled, tried to get away, but his back was broken, and so he lay still, realizing his sadistic game was over. He was done. Judgement day had come to claim him. Throughout the night, Kelvin began to eat the chief alive. He bit his nose off and ate his cheeks. He took bites out of his arms, legs, and buttocks. He ate slowly. The chief bled. The sadist bastard finally died, but it took a long time. Kelvin the cannibal made sure of that.

Kelvin stayed out at the shack until the middle of the next morning, eating his Thanksgiving coming out party. When he finally left, there wasn't much left of the police chief. In many places he had been eaten down to the bone. The skin on his face was gone. He was unrecognizable. It was more smashed skull than anything else. His eyes had been eaten. His skull had been cracked open with the bat, and his brain eaten. Kelvin thought the spiders would be proud of that. Before he left, Kelvin took the two hundred dollars that the chief had in his wallet, along with his credit cards. He took his gun, and his handcuffs. He left the policeman's corpse handcuffed to the bed frame. He thought about going back to the jail to shoot and kill the chief's three deputies (they knew what the chief was doing to his prisoners but did nothing to stop him), but he felt the risk of getting caught was too great. He ran through the woods for miles until he hit the highway. He caught a ride from a salesman from Dallas who would never sell anything again.

Eating human flesh was now permanently on Kelvin's menu, and the salesman died before the next sunrise. His remains were thrown in his trunk, and Kelvin drove his car for three days, ending up in Pittsburgh. The spiders kept him company at night, eating away at the rest of his sanity and soul. He pulled into a rundown Motel 6, deciding to stay for a few days before figuring out his next move. He knew the law would find out what he had done, and would be hot on his trail. He was kind of surprised that he had made it this far. He was proud of himself.

A few hours after he checked in a young housekeeper came to see if he needed anything. He said he needed bath towels. She came in and put the towels in the bathroom. Kelvin quietly closed the door behind her and double locked it. She never left. She became victim (or meal) number three. He ate until he was full, and then took a nap. The spiders surrounded him with their sharp little yellowish teeth. He woke up screaming, drenched in sweat. He knew now that they would never leave him alone. He had done enough bad things now to last a lifetime. That was OK because if it got too bad, he would put a bullet in his brain. The spiders couldn't follow him into death. At least he didn't think so. At least he *hoped* not.

Kelvin heard some commotion going on outside. He got out of bed and walked to the window. There were six police cruisers next to the salesman's car, lights flashing everywhere. Damn, he thought, the car. The fucking salesman's car! The salesman had probably been reported missing as well, and *he* had left it right outside. He was caught. He was done. He wouldn't eat another body. The party was over. It was short-lived, he had enjoyed the ride, but it was history. A few officers came out of the motel office with the manager. He pointed at his room. Kelvin ducked down and sat against the door. He made sure the chief's gun was loaded and pointed it at his temple. He couldn't be taken alive. He wouldn't do well in prison. He couldn't deal with getting raped, beaten, or brutalized ever again. He'd wait until the last second, but he would definitely pull the trigger.

He heard them coming closer. He could feel them outside his door. He looked over at his bed. The spiders were still there, staring out at him. There were more of them now, and they seemed to be growing. They could smell his fear, and they were plotting their next move. His enemies were closing in on him from all sides. He was trapped like a rat. He heard his name called from outside, telling him to give up, to come out peacefully. Kelvin giggled hysterically to himself. Why did they always tell you to do the *last* thing you wanted to do? It was funny in an odd sort of way, but his whole life had gone *odd* in the last few days.

All of a sudden the AC unit and his TV stopped working at the same time. He stared at them blankly as he waited for the authorities to break down his door, but nothing happened. He'd wait some more. No one called out to him. It was quiet. He looked over at the bed. The spiders were gone. He looked more closely, but there was nothing under the bed. He slowly got up and peeked outside. Nobody was there. The police cars were still outside, but the flashing lights were off. It was all quiet—eerily quiet. He waited a few more minutes, but nothing. Something strange was happening. He could feel it. On hands and knees he went into the bathroom, and the remains of the housekeeper were gone! The bathtub he had put her in was empty. There had been blood everywhere, but that was gone as well. The bathroom was spotless, spotlessly clean. Hell had gone on in here, God only knew, but all remains of it were wiped away. What had happened?

He waited another half hour, and then he slowly got up enough balls to walk outside. Nobody was there—not the police, not the Motel 6 manager, not any occupants from other rooms. He went to the salesman's car and popped the trunk—nothing inside. He started laughing. The evidence was gone. The police were gone. Maybe even his own *mind* was gone, but he knew one thing: he was alone, all alone. He got into the salesman's car and tried to start it. Nothing. He went over to one of the police cruisers. The keys were in the ignition. He tried turning the engine over. Nothing. He went to another cruiser. Same result. Whatever was going on, whether it was strange or not, was a good thing—a very good thing. He stared at the Motel 6 for a moment, looked around at all the empty police cruisers, and then started walking down the highway. No one bothered him. No one arrested him. No one followed him. He smiled. He was free—or so he thought.

A mile down the road as he was whistling Dixie, Kelvin began hearing clicking—lots of it—on the highway behind him. It had been quiet for the most part, other than seeing a few airplanes fall from the sky and crash, which he regarded as "normal" in this new day, but this was different. Clicking—horrible, horrible clicking! He knew those sounds. They came from his nightmares, but *only* while he was sleeping. Awake he just saw, not *heard*.

Kelvin slowly turned around and hoped against fate. Hope turned to despair, for following not more than twenty yards behind him were many spiders, arachnoids of all shapes and sizes. They all looked mean, and more importantly, *angry*! They went on forever, a countless army of punishers.

Kelvin stopped walking and screamed until his vocal cords gave out. Punishment was about to commence. The day hadn't turned out so well after all.

Chapter Fourteen

SAMUEL EVANS

Samuel Evans got on the new turbo train in Atlantic City. It was one of those models that traveled up to two hundred miles per hour. "Get you there faster," the slogan said. Samuel was seventy-two years old, but looked ten years younger. He walked like somebody thirty years his junior, but today he felt one hundred years old. Today was different, much different, for as he sat in his seat alone he wondered where all the years had gone. And alone was the magic word here. He had just gone to his last company get-together at the Casinos when he had gotten the fateful phone call. It was his oldest son John who had found his mother, Samuel's dear wife Brenda of forty-five years, dead on the kitchen floor. Massive heart attack, he was told. The medics had told John that it was quick; she didn't feel a thing. They always told you that to ease your pain. It never worked, and it wasn't working now. Nobody really knew if anybody felt anything when your heart exploded inside your chest, but just tell them that it was painless. It's what all parties involved could handle.

But there was no handling *it*. Forty-five years doing everything together, never leaving each other's side. Laughing and never letting life get boring was what kept it all together. But always together, always close physically to each other. Doing everything side by side. Now all of that was . . . gone. No, there was no handling it—not in any way, shape, or form. Samuel had just talked to her this morning, saying he missed and loved her. She said the same. Whenever they were apart they told each other this. They meant it, every word.

Samuel and Brenda lived in Port St Lucie. They had for the last twenty years. It was where they were planning on spending the rest of their lives. He had finally decided to stop working completely. He loved his job, but it was time. He had cut his hours but was still at the office a lot. He had worked for Life After Life Magazine for the past thirty years. He was an editor, and a damn good one. Before that he worked for The Daily News in New York. He had had a good career. He had accomplished everything on his checklist, and in the process met the love of his life.

Samuel was on vacation on the beaches of West Hampton on Long Island when he had met Brenda Miles at a cocktail party. They were introduced by a friend of hers. She was the most spirited person at the function—long wavy blond hair, with a figure that wouldn't quit. People said she looked like a movie star, and they were right! How she was available and single was a complete mystery to Samuel. Brenda always said that it was just fate. She had always said that she was just waiting for him to appear— and he almost hadn't. He hadn't planned on going to the cocktail party at all. The original plan was to go across the sound on the ferry to the Mohegan Sun gambling casino with a couple of guys, but that had fallen through. Thank the Lord on that one! And so, Brenda had been right. Fate had intertwined, and forty-five years later here we are . . .

Samuel and Brenda hit it off immediately. They dated, and were married a year later on the same beach. People say some marriages are made in heaven, and their's definitely was! They had four children: two boys and two girls. All four were doing well. John was the only one that lived nearby. He had gone over to check on his mother and had found her on the floor. He was thankfully holding up, he assured his father, and would call his siblings and make all the funeral arrangements. All Samuel had to do was get back home—a tall order when you studied it closer, for all plans for one's twilight years had just changed drastically forever, and not for the better. No, definitely *not* for the better. And so, Samuel had gotten on the train, and had promised to hold up his end of the bargain. Knowing his parents, John knew his father was in bad shape. He was as well, but he would carry the load.

The train wasn't as fast as the plane, but Samuel never liked flying so riding the rail was his best option. Besides, he needed time to think, and reminisce. As the train left the station he thought about their life together. They rarely fought, good times at every turn, four wonderful children. They had so many plans ahead of them: a few vacations, visiting family. Even a cross-country trip. All those plans were history now. Death had taken care of that! That fact was hitting him like a pile of bricks. He fought back the bitterness, because what good would it do? He was alone, and that wasn't changing.

Samuel put his head against the train window and began to cry. He didn't want to go on. He wanted to be with his beloved. He wanted to die. There was nothing left here for him. His children would be fine. Their lives were ahead of them; his definitely behind him now. The train car was half full. Nobody seemed to notice him as he cried silently. If they had they left him alone. That was all right by him. He suddenly felt weak. He had shortness of breath. Tightness in his chest, but it wasn't painful, just a little soreness. He was aware of what was happening. He was slipping away. His heart was broken, and now it was shutting down.

He was calm as he slowly stopped breathing. His heart stopped beating. He smiled contentedly as his head leaned against the window. The last thought he had was that he and his wife were the cardiac kids—heart failure together, dying together. It was meant to be . . .

But he was still here—mentally, spiritually. People always said you rise above yourself as your spirit leaves. The ones that came back to their bodies always told those stories, but not in Samuel's case. His spiritual self was sitting next to his physical body, sharing the train seat. He stared at his slumped body, wondering what was going on. Shouldn't he be rising? Leaving everything behind? He wanted to, but he felt weighed down. He was fighting against an invisible current that was forcing him to sit in the seat.

They say that your life flashes before your eyes when you're dying or in suspended animation like he was now, but none of that was happening. He just felt calm. Almost as if he was just waiting for another type of train, a train with a different destination—heaven, where his wife would be waiting for him at another kind of station.

Suddenly Samuel saw a bright circular light coming toward him from the front of the train car. It stopped right in front of him. He tried to stand but couldn't. Was this his transport, his way to his wife? His true love? His better half? Ripples formed in the sphere and he heard a voice that seemed a long way off. It told him that it wasn't his time just yet; that he had more work to do. That work would find him, and then he would understand. There was a plan for him; he just had to be patient. The wait would be worth it; he would see. It told Samuel it knew he was hurting, and it hurt along with him. It understood. It told him he was not alone; he'd never be. Samuel didn't protest, he didn't complain. Maybe in spiritual form that kind of fight isn't in you. He didn't feel bad; he didn't feel dejected. He only felt warmth and comfort from the sphere, and so he accepted his fate. It wasn't his time; he had a purpose. He knew the light was good. He *felt* it.

The circular light suddenly retreated to the front of the car and disappeared. Samuel felt the weight leave him and his spirit began to move slowly back into his body. He suddenly felt a large current pass him, like a raging, out-of-control freight train. He felt and heard the sounds of many souls, more than he could count or fathom. Souls upon souls passed him at a speed beyond comprehension. And then just as suddenly it was over, quiet again like before. He completed his astral travels and was back inside his body. He began to breathe slowly, and his heart started beating again. His eyes fluttered, and then slowly opened. He remembered it all: his soul sitting beside himself, the sphere, and the voice. And especially what that voice had said. That voice had given him purpose. It gave him hope. Yes, he would miss his wife terribly. He still didn't know how he was going to survive without her, but he would have to learn. All this was going on inside his head as he reentered the physical world. It wasn't the same world he had left, but it was a world he was still a part of.

The train was slowing down. The lights inside the car were out. The passengers were all gone. He was the only one left in the car. He was alone. Fate? He took out his cell phone—dead. He looked outside. He saw smoke in the distance, and then he watched a large airliner crash about a mile from the decelerating turbo train. It burst into flames; black smoke began to rise into the sky. Another crash came from somewhere behind the train. Another minute passed before the train came to a complete stop. Samuel stood up slowly, walked to the car door, opened it manually, and went down the stairs. He stepped off the train onto a field. He walked about ten feet away and looked around. The train seemed fine, but there was no sign of a station in either direction. Samuel figured that the train must have lost all power, for there was no reason for it to have stopped here. He heard another boom a good distance ahead of the train, and more black smoke rose into the sky. Planes were crashing all over. Samuel didn't know what was going on, but he was sure of one thing: he was glad he had taken the train instead of the plane!

Chapter Fifteen

Jason Roberts / Biosphere One

The world holds many secrets. From the beginning of time many questions could have been answered but were blocked because of secrets. In truth, secrets are acts of immaturity and insecurity. Elders will tell you that some secrets must not be known; that they must stay hidden. They will tell you that you need to be protected from certain knowledge. It has been like this since man first walked the Earth. It was a practice employed right up until the power went off, and the people, birds, animals, and sea life all went home. How many secrets went with them? How much knowledge and information were lost? A sinful amount for certain. Over the years as lives and generations passed on, many secrets went with them. They remained secrets forever, and sometimes that was a shame. When NASA landed on Mars and the colony was established, many secrets were kept from mankind back here on Earth. The secrets were so hush-hush that even most of the employees of NASA didn't know them. One of those secrets ended up back here on Earth, in America, in Oracle, Arizona. That secret ended up inside the walls of Biosphere 2.

Biosphere 2 was a series of buildings used for many things

over the years. It originally was used as an artificial closed ecological system. Eight people spent two years within its walls without ever coming out, growing their own food supply. Their interactions were recorded and studied. Those studies were helpful when the colony on Mars was first built and inhabited. Other experiments were conducted over the years. Over time, the Biosphere was purchased by Columbia University until 2005. They used it for experimentation as well. In 2011 the University of Arizona took it over. NASA was the next and present owner. *That* purchase was kept a secret. Only a quiet few knew this information. They were paid off handsomely. Most died with that secret.

When the power went out Jason Richards was living alone inside the Biosphere 2 compound. He was an employee of NASA. He did not go home. He was still part of the remaining population on planet Earth. Here is his story, and more importantly, here is his secret.

Jason Richards had spent the last month quarantined inside the Biosphere alone. Only a few in NASA knew of this. The reason: Jason Richards, NASA scientist, looked more like an alien than a human being. Mars 2020 had been bringing back different types of rocks and soil specimens from the red planet on each trip. They were warehoused in large square metal boxes and locked away in a special room in the back of the cargo area. Tons and tons of specimens over the last ten years had been transported back to Earth and brought by special truck detail to the Biosphere 2 complex to study. Jason headed that study.

Originally ten NASA employees worked at the site alongside him. That total grew to thirty. All of this was kept secret—top secret. Everyone that worked at the site knew this. They were paid handsomely to keep quiet, even from their families. The Biosphere was out in the desert —out of the way, so to speak. It was a perfect place for secrets to be kept. And they were. The tons of soil were put in one area, and the different types of rocks were stored in another and studied.

Certain events could be explained, and some couldn't. Up on Mars, the colony used Mars soil to grow crops. The crops grew at a faster rate on Mars than on Earth, so the food supply was plentiful. One of the studies Jason headed was growing crops in the same Martian soil inside the Arizona site. What made the crops grow faster on Mars? That was the question. It baffled Jason and his two associates. He decided to see what would happen if he mixed Martian soil with Earth soil. He called his superior at NASA, and was told to do the experiment, but to do it in secret.

Secret upon secret was what NASA was all about. Almost everybody was doing secret experimentation on one study or another. That was not unusual, so this wouldn't be either. Jason didn't even bat an eye when he was told to do his experiments in private. He worked at night, and in a restricted area. He mixed the two planet soils together, and planted potatoes and corn. What happened was amazing. Not only did the crops grow twice as fast, they grew bigger. He tested the crops and they seemed normal. He put them in a refrigerator that he had in his quarters, and then grew beans and cabbage with the same results. He kept records, reported back to his superior, and was told to continue his experiments. He added another three large refrigerators to his room and kept all the crops inside.

He grew grapes and strawberries with the same results, but he discovered something else. As weeks went by the crops didn't spoil. None of them went bad. This realization went totally against the grain, but in a positive way. Too much food was thrown away everyday all across the world because it had gone bad. This could be a major breakthrough. Food supply could be managed better on Earth, and Earth soil could be transported to Mars so the same system could be used in the colony.

Half asleep one night he tiredly got up and absentmindedly opened one of the refrigerators and tried a few grapes. Before he realized it, he had swallowed them. He hadn't been given the go-ahead to eat anything yet. Well, he reasoned, it would be *his* secret. He wouldn't eat anything else. He would monitor any digestive changes he might experience. That didn't happen, or anything else. He decided to try a few strawberries. They tasted wonderful, tastier than regular ones. A few days later Jason was cleaning his glasses (he had worn them since he was seven years old) and noticed that without them he could see clearly. He gave himself a few tests, and it was true. He could see perfectly without his glasses! He read a few lines in a book without glasses and had no trouble seeing the words. He was amazed. He was sixty-two years old and all of a sudden he had perfect vision.

He smiled at himself in the mirror, and then frowned. He hadn't shaved in a few days, but he didn't have any hair growth. He felt his skin. It was smooth. That was odd. Sometimes he would shave twice a day, and now his beard wasn't growing at all. Jason grew concerned. Was it the new crops? He decided not to eat any more of them until he conducted more tests.

He woke up the next day standing at the refrigerator eating raw green beans from the new crops. He wondered what was happening. He had never sleepwalked before, and now he had eaten the new beans. They had tasted better than good. He went to brush his teeth and was shocked at what he saw. His ears had changed shape. They were a little larger, and pointy at the top. His hair was falling out—not the normal way where you would lose it on top, but around his enlarged ears and the bottom of his hairline in the back. He was losing hair in reverse!

He checked the rest of his body. He discovered he was losing all his body hair, especially around his groin area. It was almost as if he was shedding. Jason called Tim Delaney, another scientist, and his closest associate. He told him his secret, and of all the tests he had been conducting. He added that he was quarantining himself in his quarters. Tim called a meeting and informed the others inside the Biosphere what was happening. While that was going on, Jason called NASA and spoke to his superior. After discussing the situation, he was told to sit tight and remain quarantined, and that he had done the right thing.

NASA officials showed up later in the day and removed everybody from the biosphere. They were tested and taken away to an unknown location (another secret). NASA doctors with protective suits examined Jason. His vitals were better than good. Jason had long had diabetes, which he had treated with medication, but there was no sign of it now. Overall he seemed in much better health, and he *felt* better than he had in years. His dilemma was all physical.

His head had grown a few centimeters, and so had his hands and feet. He used to wear a size ten shoe; now he was a size twelve. His fingers were longer. His skin had turned a light gray. He had been five foot eleven in height; now he was six foot two. He was hungrier than usual, and had a craving for the new crops. Regular food just didn't taste good anymore. NASA decided to monitor him closely, but from a safe distance. They set up operations right outside the Biosphere. Jason would stay inside alone with his crops. NASA wanted no part of them. Jason would continue to run tests on them until they knew more.

In the next few days Jason changed drastically. He lost the rest of his hair on his body and head. He grew to seven feet tall. His hands and feet doubled in size. So did his head. His forehead was huge. His nose grew and became very pointy. His eyes, once brown, were now red. His ears also continued to grow. They were seven inches from pointy top to rounded bottom. His genitals grew to three times their normal size. His voice deepened. His appetite doubled. He planted more crops and ate the ones he'd grown. His clothes no longer fit, so he wore the largest smock he could find. Jason might not look the same, but he was still himself mentally. His personality and emotional well-being were the same. He still laughed and cried at the same things. He still had that same drive to learn and succeed. He was still *him*. He felt great, and discovered he no longer needed sleep. His energy level soared. He kept in constant contact with the crew stationed outside. They named his situation "Operation Jason Inflight" and kept it under wraps. It was their secret.

Jason didn't know it, but NASA was quite unnerved by what was happening. They eventually contacted Washington and told them of the situation. They, in turn, were also unnerved, and when the government felt that way, anything was possible. They immediately sent people to the Biosphere. Those people talked to and examined Jason, also wearing protective suits. His physical improvements bothered them. How much of a danger could he become? What kind of powers could he acquire? Tensions mounted.

When the power went out and everybody disappeared, the government was leaning toward ending this operation. They planned on killing Jason, and after moving all of the crops, Mars rocks, and soil to a safe quarantined location, blowing up the site. Their stance was that NASA had totally fucked with Mother Nature (and there was a good chance they had), and sweeping everything under the carpet was their best option at the end of the day. But none of that mattered now.

Jason was running tests on the mixed soil when the power went out inside the Biosphere. He tried contacting the NASA people outside, but his cellphone was dead. He walked to the front windows in the lobby but saw no one outside. The tents, trucks, and equipment were all there, but everybody was gone.

Something was wrong, he thought nervously. Why would they leave? All sorts of wild and crazy thoughts went through his mind, and none of them ended up well for him. He went throughout the Biosphere. All power was off. He heard an explosion off to the north. He went back to the front windows and watched in horror as a jet airliner crashed into the desert. He decided that he had to get out of there. Forget the quarantine—something strange was happening.

He packed up as much of the new crops as he could and walked outside. He knew that it was over 100 degrees in the desert, but he didn't feel the heat in the least. He walked over to one of the NASA trucks and looked inside. The keys were in the ignition, but it wouldn't start. He heard another crash off to the north. Smoke was rising into the sky in every direction. He went to one of the tents and grabbed a sheet off one of the beds and wrapped it around himself, including his head. He didn't need it for protection from the sun, but because he was trying to hide his appearance. He walked across the front grounds to the street and started walking north, toward Phoenix.

He saw abandoned cars scattered on both sides of the street but there was no sign of people. In a way that was a godsend, Jason reasoned. Anybody who saw him in his present state would be terrified. They would think an alien invasion was taking place. The further he walked, the more he was convinced he wouldn't meet anybody. He sensed very strongly that he was alone—utterly alone. The quiet was comforting to the new Jason. He felt at ease. For the time being, his secret was still safe.

Chapter Sixteen

GORDON FULTON /
BIOSPHERE TWO

*A*nother secret Biosphere 2 had was the growing of marijuana in Martian soil. That project was headed by Jonas Taylor and Michael Silas, two NASA scientists that Jason Richards knew very well. The growing of the plant wasn't a secret; it was now legal countrywide, but the plants grown in Martian soil were *not* supposed to leave the grounds. The secret was one pound was being sold to the outside world every month. Only Jonas and Michael knew this. They were selling it to a local dealer in Tucson, who was never told that it had been grown in alien soil (the secrets kept coming). They only told the dealer that it was a different type of pot plant, not legal to sell. The rest of the product each month was shipped to NASA for further experimentation. The secret *there* was that some of *that* shipment was also being sold on the sly. Secrets, secrets, secrets . . .

The new strain was sold at twice the amount of regular marijuana because the effects were very different. You smoked less, you only needed to take one toke to get high, and you hallucinated much more. Studies showed that you stayed stoned three times as long, and you felt invincible. There were reports of people jumping off buildings, thinking they could fly (Superman was alive and well). Others claimed to have seen God and the devil, still others said they *were* God and the devil. Reports came in that people were going to the emergency room with bad headaches and double vision problems that would last for days or weeks. The news reported there was a bad crop out there somewhere, and Homeland Security was investigating the situation.

Drs. Jonas Taylor and Michael Silas knew better. Some at NASA knew better also, but the Martian marijuana continued to be sold on the side right up until the power went out. Dirty money was money made just the same. Greed and selfishness to some extent live in us all; so, the bad, unhealthy, and sometimes deadly alien marijuana continued to be distributed and sold. Unlike Jason Richards, those secrets went home with the scientists as none of them remained on Earth. Wyatt Earp would have had a ball trying to unravel this mystery.

Gordon Fulton *did* stay on Earth, and *did* purchase and smoke a lot of the new marijuana. He had a different reaction to the Martian pot, with deadly consequences. Here is his story.

Gordon Gore Fulton lived in Mesa, Arizona. He was a modern-day hippie: skinny and heavily tattooed with hair past his shoulders. He was twenty-eight years old, lived with his parents, and bought two hundred dollars' worth of the Martian pot off a friend from Scottsdale. That friend told him that this grass was super strong, super high grade, from a new vein. Gordon had been smoking regular marijuana ever since he turned fifteen. He started when he stole some of his parent's supply (like a lot of his friends did), but now he was definitely looking for something better. He needed something more powerful; he needed to *graduate*. He had tried snorting heroin and cocaine, but that habit was too expensive.

Gordon worked at Fry's, a local supermarket, stocking shelves and unloading trucks, and that didn't pay enough to achieve the high he was looking for. This new pot, he was told, would solve all his problems. It was exactly what he was looking for. They, of course, were wrong—dead wrong.

Gordon had a different reaction entirely. He smoked the new pot for the first time on the outskirts of Mesa in the desert alone. He had never gotten so stoned. He was flying high in the friendly skies, as the say. He hallucinated—or did he? He believed he saw about twenty bats fly overhead, and that one flew down and bit him on the neck, drawing blood. He believed that he became infected. He felt a strange and foreign strain flowing through his veins.

A few days later, while smoking the new pot, he became convinced he had turned into a full-fledged vampire. In his mind his skin became paler, the pupils of his eyes had a red tinge to them, and he could grow fangs at will. He believed that the light of day would harm or even kill him, and so he changed to working the night shift. During the day he slept, keeping the curtains shut so the light couldn't get in. He ate little. He lost weight. He started craving blood.

During all this time, as his apparent transformation was taking place, he continued to smoke the new marijuana. He smoked every night after work as dawn approached. He kept his job, but became withdrawn. He barely spoke to anybody—only when he had to. He worked in a daze; he moved slower, but somehow the work got done. His cravings for blood skyrocketed. He needed to eat. He needed to *feed*. He became frantic, chaotic, and paranoid.

One day Gordon was suddenly afraid to drive or do any of his other day-to-day duties, so that night for the first time he called in sick and hitchhiked out to the desert to smoke some of his stash. He got a ride from an old man in a pickup truck who told Gordon that he lived in Nogales, which was located near the Mexican border. That was 180 miles away—a long way off in Gordon's fogged mind—so as they left town and entered the desert he suddenly leaned over and bit the old-timer in the neck viciously, severing his jugular. The truck slowed and ran off the highway. Luckily for Gordon, no one was on this stretch of highway at the time. He cared little as he sucked on the man's neck like a rabid dog, drinking his blood. He drank and drank. The blood was like a drug. Its taste exquisite.

When he was finally finished he sat the old man in the passenger seat and drove the truck slowly and unsteadily down a dirt road that led to an old cave that he and friends had found and hung out in. Luckily nobody was out there. He dragged the old man into the cave and sat him up against the wall. And then he smoked much more than he should have.

He heard squeaky noises and saw bats fill the entrance to the cave. He smiled. And then he started laughing. The bats flew into the cave and flew around his head but did not harm him. Gordon felt like he wasn't alone anymore. He had pets. He had friends. He felt like he was one of them. He was home. This cave was *their* haven. Their lair!

He slept all the next day in the cave and the next evening drove the pickup truck fifty miles further south and left it on the shoulder where there was nobody in sight. As he was walking back north (about twenty feet off the side of the highway so he wouldn't be seen) he decided that he no longer needed to work, and so didn't even bother to call in sick. He thought himself above other human beings, and would take what he needed when he needed it. He wouldn't—and *couldn't*—be stopped. He was a higher form of being now, at the top of the food chain. Not *them*. He stopped to smoke.

This stuff was sent from the gods, he reasoned, and laughed as he hurtled further and further into the darkness of his deranged mind. He wondered if it was possible to contact any of his kind, like Dracula. He needed the vampire king's advice. He wanted to change into a bat, and fly from place to place, but didn't know how.

Gordon sensed sunrise was near, so he walked further into the desert away from the highway and camped under a large cactus plant. He covered himself with tumbleweed and slept all day. The next evening he reasoned it was safe to hitchhike, and got a ride with a couple of guys heading to Vegas. They dropped him off in Scottsdale, close to where his friend the dealer lived. He still had plenty of the new strain, but he wanted more—much more, and he would take what he wanted. He felt greedy, but that was of no consequence. He figured nobody alive could stop him when the sun dropped below the horizon.

When Gordon was seated inside John Flood's apartment buying more of the Martian marijuana, he told the drug merchant, while both were sharing a few tokes, that this would be his last day on Earth. He told John that the King of Vampires needed his blood. John laughed hysterically and told Gordon that he had smoked one joint too many. Gordon stood up, smiled, and then with great speed attacked John, taking a large chunk out of his neck. Blood shot out of his severed jugular as the drug dealer fell to the floor. A dark pool of his blood slowly spread around his head, draining the life from his body. His last vision before he died was of Gordon bending down with opened mouth to drink from his damaged throat. His sight was slightly blurred, but he saw one thing clearly: he saw that his friend and murderer had fangs. Vampire fangs! Oh God, he thought as the darkness slowly engulfed him.

Gordon finished feeding, took all of the new strain, and left the apartment. He assumed that John wouldn't be found for days, and he would be long gone by then. He decided to head across the border and continue south into South America. He had to do something first, though. He went home, said hello to his parents watching television in the living room, and went up to his room and packed a bag. He lit up a joint and smoked. When he was done he calmly walked back downstairs and smiled lovingly at his beloved mother and father. He was hungry again. It wasn't long before they were both screaming.

When the power went out Gordon was sleeping under some brush. He was just north of the border. He had killed eight victims along the way. They would be the last human beings he would feast on. When he awoke he encountered no life of any kind. Cars were scattered along the highway, but no one was in any of them. He had an odd feeling that he was alone, totally alone, and that his food supply had been cut off. He was hungry and there were no humans in sight. The bats had deserted him as well. Every night they had kept him company, flying all around him, but not this one. He was in a shitload of trouble. He sat on a rock and stared out into the desert toward Mexico. Hopefully the King of All Vampires was out there somewhere. Gordon needed him badly now. He lit up one joint, then another. He smoked until there was no more.

Chapter Seventeen

GERRY RHODES AND CLAUDE AUSTON

Gerry Rhodes and Claude Auston both had epiphanies one week before the power went out. They didn't know each other, and lived in different parts of the country, but they were connected by a similar vision in a dream. Those visions changed their lives drastically from different sides of the spectrum.

Gerry Rhodes was a fisherman from Lunenburg, Nova Scotia. It is situated on the Province's south shore, located on the Fairhaven Peninsula on the western side of Mahone Bay. His family had been fishermen in Ludenburg for over two hundred years, making a good living and living comfortably. His boat, The Northern Clipper, had been handed down for four generations and was still serving the Rhodes family well. Gerry loved his job, and the two mates he presently had; Jake Langston and George Combs were the best mates he had ever hired. They worked, laughed, ate, and drank down at Giles Tavern together.

Gerry was fifty-five, married with two girls that had both gone off to college in Long Island and presently lived there. He had met his wife Judy at Hutchsons, the country store. Her family had owned it for over fifty years and her father still ran it at seventy-eight years of age. Judy did the books and helped with the hiring and firing. The store would eventually go to her when her father retired—and good luck with that! A good portion of the fish Gerry caught were sold to Hutchsons's seafood section, which consisted mostly of lobsters, Atlantic mackerel, shad, and whitefish. The rest went to the local fish markets, which was still a lot (Judy liked to tell everyone that Gerry caught enough fish to empty the sea ten times over). It was a great family business all around.

Judy was always a supportive wife, one that was constantly upbeat and laughing at home and at the store. Their marriage was a good one and they hoped the girls one day would make them grandparents. Linda lived in Huntington with her husband Frank. She was a nurse and he an electrician. They were trying to start a family and make both sets of parents proud. Gina was also a nurse in Greenport Hospital on the North Fork. She was single and enjoying life in town, where something was always going on, regardless of the season.

On the night he had his vision, he had one of his best fishing days, probably double what he usually brought in, and that was saying something. In his dream a bright circular light came out of the bedroom ceiling, hovering above Gerry and Judy's heads. He tried to shake her awake but all she did was turn her back to him, snoring loudly. Ripples appeared in the light and an old far-off-sounding voice started talking inside his head. It said to stop catching all his fish; that he was killing the Lord's creations. It said the Lord was angry—all sea life was *still* life, should be left alone to live in its liquid world, and by all means should *never* be used for consumption. The voice added that The Lord pleaded for Gerry to comply with His request, for it was still his choice to follow The Lord's plan or continue fishing. But if he stopped now, he would be rewarded with total fulfillment, and possibly more.

The circular light then lowered itself and touched both of Gerry's hands. The light was warm to the touch. It was comforting, soothing. Gerry wondered aloud what he would do if he didn't fish anymore and was told by the light not to worry; he would be cared for. The ripples in the light then seemed to smile at Gerry, and slowly rose and disappeared back into the ceiling. It was then that Gerry woke up, sweating profusely even though the air conditioning was on high.

He went downstairs, grabbed a beer, and sat down at the kitchen table. He remembered everything in the dream, but he decided for the time being to keep it to himself. He felt it would be better to stay quiet until he made this very important decision. And it *was* important! This decision would affect his livelihood, his income. It would affect the family store as well. He wondered how he would live, what he would do, how he would survive— how they *all* would survive. He decided he would think on it, and give his mates the next day off with full pay. He knew that if he decided to stop fishing they would be out of work as well. He went back to bed with a heavy heart, and luckily fell off to sleep almost immediately. He did not dream again that night, sleeping soundly until the alarm woke him up the next morning.

He went to his boat after calling Jake and George and saw a dead shad on the deck. He frowned, for he didn't remember ever forgetting *any* catch on board from the previous day. That would be wasteful, and the Rhodes family had never been wasteful. Every fish mattered; no catch would die in vain. That had been drilled into him from day one, and he had done the same with whoever had been in his employ.

Gerry picked up the dead fish and was about to throw it to the gulls on the dock when it suddenly began moving. It was alive again. It had been out of water on the boat's deck all night, but it was alive and flopping in his hand now. He threw it over the side and it swam away. Had it come back to life after he touched it? Was that "the something more"—a gift of some kind? He decided to go down to Hutchsons and test it out.

When he got there he picked up two mackerel from the previous day's catch that were on ice. They both began moving, coming back to life. There were eight more assorted fish in the ice. He put them all in a bucket and drove down to the docks. When he got there all the fish were flopping around—all had come back to life. He threw them all back into the sea, and then broke down into tears. They were tears of joy, tears of enlightenment and fulfillment. Right then and there he decided that he would comply with The Lord's request. The Lord had blessed him. He had never really been a religious man but that would change. He now knew that The Lord existed. He was convinced that he had been touched by a higher power.

Gerry drove down to the Lutheran Church his family had attended, where he had gone to Sunday School, and sat in the first pew and prayed. He prayed to God for forgiveness for killing so much sea life, for destroying so many of his creations. He promised that he would never fish again; that he would carry the cross of his sins. He would go broke if that's what it took. He promised to find another line of work; his boat would never be used for catching fish again. He felt a hand touch his shoulder from behind, but when he turned around nothing, or no one, was there. He knew it was a response from above. He cried and cried. He had been reborn. Life was anew.

He went home and told Judy what had transpired. For proof, he picked up a dead fish at the store in front of her and it came back to life. She cried as well. They hugged and hugged and cried on each other's shoulder. For the next week he bought fish from all the fish markets, brought them back to life, and threw them back into the ocean, right up until the power went out and all the fish disappeared. Unfortunately, so did Judy, the rest of the people in town, and all animals and all the birds and gulls. He cried about the loss of his wife—he would miss her terribly—and all life in general. He didn't know why he was still here, but he would put his fate in the hands of The Lord. He would carry on and continue The Lord's work, whatever that might be.

Claude Auston was a butcher in the Food Fair Supermarket in Somerset, Kentucky. He was the same age as Gerry Rhodes, also fifty-five years old. He had been a butcher since he graduated from Pulaski High School. In his free time Claude liked to hunt—legally or illegally. He liked to hunt with a bow and arrow. There was a certain talent in using those tools of hunting. Guns, he felt, were unfair and boring. They cut out the *sport* in hunting. Using a bow and arrow leveled the playing field between hunter and prey. Sometimes the prey died slower because he wasn't using a gun, but Claude did his best to put his kill out of its misery as quickly as possible. That was the right thing to do, he reasoned.

He hunted deer, elk, turkey, squirrels, and rabbits. He hunted all year. He wasn't the only one. Many people hunted all year long, hunted illegally at times. Claude was still guilty, though, and he knew it. It didn't excuse him, but there were much worse doings in this world, he reasoned. Killing another human being was much worse. That was ungodly, immoral. Hunting a few squirrels was a lesser of two evils, and he surmised many hunters agreed. Some of his kill he hung on his walls. He had been a bachelor his whole life; he had no children, so he could do that. There was nobody else in the house to protest this action, so elk and deer heads hung on the walls of every room, even his bathroom.

On the same night that Gerry Rhodes had his visionary dream, Claude had his. He was visited by the same circular light, and was told not to hunt the Lord's animals, his creations. He was asked to stop doing his present job, and if he did he also would be taken care of. Claude woke up after the circular light disappeared, and he too seriously thought about his dream.

On his way to work the next day (he hadn't decided to quit his job yet), he came upon a dead deer in the middle of the road. It was dead, bloody, and it's two back legs had been broken. It was stiff, and as Claude grabbed its lifeless head and dragged it to the side of the road, it began moving. Claude dropped the deer's head and watched in astonishment as the deer not only came back to life, but its broken legs healed as well. It momentarily stared at Claude, nodded, and then ran into the woods. Claude, shocked, shook all over. A miracle had just happened. He got back in his truck and *still* continued on to work. As he pulled up to his everyday parking spot he saw a dead squirrel laying in the middle of it. He got out and touched the dead animal. It also began to move and come back to life. It looked at Claude, cocked its head, and then ran off and climbed the nearest tree on the other side of the parking lot. Tears ran down his cheeks.

Claude walked inside the Food Fair where he had worked for over thirty years and quit on the spot. He drove home with the biggest smile on his face. He was happier than he could ever remember. He had lived alone most of his adult life; it had bothered him more than he let on, but even that didn't matter now. Like Gerry, Claude also felt reborn, rejuvenated. He threw away his bow and arrow, vowing never to kill anything again. He also prayed for forgiveness. For the next week he drove around looking for roadkill. He was looking for redemption. He brought back to life more than thirty dead animals: deer, squirrels, dogs, cats, even a few birds.

When the power went out, Claude was in his living room disassembling every weapon he owned. All the heads of his kill on his walls suddenly disappeared. He no longer found any roadkill, or any live animals after that. He discovered that all the people in town had disappeared as well. The world around him became very quiet. He was alone, but, like Gerry, he put his fate in the hands of The Lord. He did not panic. He did not freak out. He would continue to work in the name of the Lord.

There was one other similarity that Gerry Rhodes and Claude Auston had. Every day after they both had their visionary dreams, they both ate only green salads—no meat, and no fish. They ate nothing that the Earth couldn't grow. That, they both reasoned, was what The Lord wanted, and would be proud and happy with.

Chapter Eighteen

REVEREND FRANKLIN LYNDON'S CULT

Selfishness, it was all built on selfishness. Franklin Lyndon started a cult that cut out selfishness of the greatest kind. The self-acclaimed reverend believed that the most selfish act a female could do was give birth to another human being. He reasoned that not one person had ever had the choice to be born, had never been asked to be here. Animals, birds, and sea life didn't have the intelligence to decide whether to reproduce or not, but human beings sure did. Throughout time, he reasoned, married couples had always said, "I want to have a certain variety of children. I want only boys, or girls." The magic two words here were "*I want.*" Whether it was right to bring a child into the world or not didn't matter, because "*I want*" did. And Franklin knew that those two words were completely selfish.

Maybe the soul of that new child was happy where it was, but it didn't matter because "*I want.*" Should a woman who already had five children but could only provide for three be allowed to have more? Where would the food come from to feed this extra child? The money to clothe that child? The revenue to educate that child? And so on and so on, but yet that mother still *wanted* that extra baby. Selfishly she *wanted* that child. "*I want.*"

It didn't seem fair to bring a soul into that sort of situation, yet it happened every day, in every city, in every state, in every country. The difference between human beings and other species on Earth was that humans had a choice. Humans could decide whether to have that child or not. They could make an intelligent decision, a moral one. The abortion laws were passed long ago so the *right* decision could be made. Some still fought against abortion. Those *some* were selfish—very selfish. They *wanted*. That's the way Reverend Franklin Lyndon saw it.

His way of thinking went further. If no one ever had children, never brought any child into this world, then wouldn't every soul remain in heaven with God? Isn't that where we all came from? Isn't that where we all want to end up? In heaven with the Lord? Why would anybody want to take someone out of heaven and bring them into this hell? A *selfish* reason. Oh, Earth isn't the hell that's talked about in the Bible, the opposition might say. Franklin told his flock that anything that isn't heaven *is* hell, because hell had many different realms. One realm might be dying of cancer. Another might be to jump one hundred stories to your death off a building, like the North Tower on 911.

In fact, September 11, 2001, had many realms of hell alone. Being in an airplane, going five hundred miles an hour and stopping on a dime after crashing into a building when your seatbelt is on is one. Being set on fire by jet fuel is another. Dying slowly after inhaling the remains of that disaster while helping humanity clear the debris is another. The realms here on Earth were endless, so yes, you and everybody else are in hell, the reverend proclaimed. And somebody brought everybody, every single soul, into this fire, this realm. Here's another realm: every single mother and father that ever brought a child into this world should have to watch that child also die, and suffer through the way they die, like dying horribly of cancer over a long period of time. Those parents just might decide *not* to have that child if they knew how they'd end up. Maybe they wouldn't be so selfish—maybe, possibly. One thing you could be sure of in this world: you had to die to get out of it.

Reverend Franklin remembered going on vacation and watching a baby seagull crying for food in front of its mother. The newborn would not leave the mother alone. The elder seagull would regurgitate its own food to feed its young. But that wouldn't last forever. There would come a time, a *day*, when that mother wouldn't feed that baby anymore. Nature would take its course, and then it would be every seagull for itself. *Selfishness*—but they didn't know any better. Studies show that 90 percent of all seagulls die in their first year of existence. Not only is that sad, but it's unfair. The baby seagull was crying for food, thinking, I never asked to be here, and now I'm hungry. Now that's hell. A different realm, coming at you from a different angle.

Lower forms of life don't decide to reproduce, they just do. They have no choice. Humans do. Little babies cry for their bottles. They are hungry too. They also never asked to be here, and that hunger follows you until the day you die. Over and over, day after day, that realm of hell comes for you. There is no way of stopping that tide. "I never asked to be here, and now I'm hungry."

Franklin never received a message from God on his mission, but that is what he was on. Not a cult, per se, but a mission. He was born in San Diego. He had a normal childhood. He didn't want for anything; his parents were hard-working and loving people who were always upbeat. He had two brothers and three sisters who all grew up happy and lived productive lives. Everybody got along. Everybody spent a lot of time surfing off the sandy beaches in better-than-good weather. Nothing traumatic ever took place.

No, Franklin Lyndon brought his mission into this world with him. It spoke to him even before he uttered his first word. But he always *knew*. He always felt where his future lied. He knew that the road he was on was not popular; it went against the grain, it went against religious beliefs. His road was rocky, and a lot of people spoke out against him as he grew older. Some called him crazy; some called him insane. Some even thought he was evil. He wasn't. He knew that. God never spoke to him in his dreams or when he was alone. He didn't even know if God even existed. He thought that if God *did* exist, then he had turned his back on the many that had come this way.

Franklin stayed his course, though. He found a dollar on the sidewalk, played the lotto and won 250 million dollars. Maybe God hadn't turned his back on him afterall. Maybe a higher power had intervened. Or maybe it was just plain luck. Whatever it was, he now had the funds for the mission to become a reality. He bought a 150-acre ranch in Bozeman, Montana, and plans began to materialize. Flyers were sent out. He traveled cross-country. His *word* got out. It made sense to some. Couples began to show up at the ranch wanting to know more. He led them into his house and told them everything he felt. He preached his mission. He preached his *sermon*. Heaven was within reach. Houses went up on his estate. Couples moved in; they believed in his message, his cause. All the women had tubal ligation; the men vasectomies. Their children would remain in heaven, their souls saved.

When the power went out, 867 couples had moved onto the ranch. They grew their own food and worked as one family unit. They were all happy and content. They all went home to The Creator feeling that way—all except Franklin. He was taking a nap when everybody disappeared. He woke up abruptly when he heard a plane crash off to the south. He searched the compound and found no one—no followers, no pets. No birds flew in the air. It was then that God spoke to Franklin for the first time. He heard The Creator's voice from deep inside his own mind. God told Franklin that he hadn't turned his back on him, and that he had done well. This mission that he had carried into this world was complete, but his work on Earth wasn't done. He had more to do. The voice told Franklin he should search his mind and he would know what to do. And then the voice was gone, replaced by the sound of another plane crashing, this time off to the north.

Franklin smiled, nodded, and stared into the smoke-filled sky. He had a purpose, and God had spoken to him, telling him that he had done well. What else could be better than that? He began to cry uncontrollably. They were tears of joy.

Chapter Nineteen

THE CURSE OF THE SILVER

We will now switch gears.

Let us now go back in time to when Jesus Christ was crucified. That is where this series of stories begin. Judas Iscariot received thirty pieces of silver for betraying Jesus Christ, the Messiah. Judas repented; he threw the bag of silver back at the priests, the powers that be. That we believe to be true. After that, the stories about Judas gets foggy. There were no newspapers or periodicals back then, so nobody could be blamed for not telling the exact story of what really happened to him. Some said that he hung himself; some said that he was gutted. Still others said that he died in an accident and bled to death. What is closer to the truth will be talked about later on in these journals. The storyline here is about the pieces of silver—the so-called blood money. The silver was worthless to the priests after the betrayal. Potter's Field was supposedly bought with the blood money, with Judas being buried there, but that would contradict the fact that the money was worthless.

No, in fact it was the *silver* that was buried in the place called Potters Field. The dirt around the blood money turned crimson red, a darker red than the red clay that covered the land. Judas's body was never found; again, this will be talked about later. After

Jesus was resurrected, the silver was dug up and stolen. Once it was gone the crimson red dirt returned to its original dull red clay color. Potter's Field no longer plays a part in these journals. The tales go where the silver ends up.

Judas did repent, but he was a pawn in the greater scheme of things. He *was* forgiven, but his thirty pieces of silver became cursed for all time. They traveled further than most cash ever does, in the strangest of ways, and anybody who ever possessed even one of those thirty pieces was doomed to damnation. The ironic part was that most of the unfortunate souls that came into contact with the blood money didn't even know where it came from. They were unaware that they came from Judas Iscariot, traitor to the King of Kings. Nor were they aware that they were about to be cursed and damned to horrible fates They did not know that it was part of a payment to betray the Son of God, but they soon found out that owning a piece of that silver would bring them luck much worse than bad—much, much worse.

It was not God's wish for this to happen, but sometimes bad things happened to objects of horrible occurrences, infected by evil entities of unknown origin. That is what happened here. Let us start at the beginning of the blood money's travels.

Jonas of Aaron was a stable hand. He grew up poor and lived a pauper's life. He married a woman, Clara, twice his age whose husband was killed in a knife fight. He hoped that she had at least a little money. She didn't. She was left with nothing; her dead husband had been nothing but a worthless nonworking drunk, but at least Jonas had a place to stay. It wasn't much, little more than a shack, but he had been sleeping in alleyways for a long time, so it was still an upgrade.

To survive, Clara had been selling her body to keep whatever she owned. She was close to fifty, but still appealing, which meant she had three sexual entrances and she whored herself using all of them. Jonas had been a buyer. He had paid for her services. They hit it off and secretly got married.

Clara continued to whore herself and Jonas took care of the horses like before. They still lived only a step above starvation after the taxes were paid, so Jonas continued to live as a predator, stealing whatever he could: food, clothes, even a little money whenever the opportunity arose. He had been lucky so far, never getting caught. He had become a pretty good thief.

When the priests buried the 30 pieces of silver late at night Jonas just happened to be in Potters Field getting oral sex from Clara's best friend. Adultery wasn't a word in his vocabulary; he took whatever good cheer he could find and hoped for better times tomorrow. He was a survivor, and Clara's friend was a helping to that end.

Jonas stared intently at the priests, wondering what they were doing. He was glad that Sara was facing away from what was taking place. When she was finished he quietly guided her in the opposite direction and walked her home, then returned to the fields. The priests were gone, but he discovered they had buried something. He decided to be patient, lay low for a bit, but he was going to dig up whatever they had buried. It could be valuable—if not to him, then maybe to someone else. He would wait to see if anybody came back. He knew havoc was going on in the city with this Jesus situation. Jonas didn't give one iota about this Son of God rhetoric; he just figured that living this poorly surely meant there wasn't a God here, there, or anywhere else. So for the next few days he watched the field, and it remained quiet.

On the following moonless night he crept into the field and started digging. He had to dig three feet before he hit pay dirt.

He carefully dug around an object that turned out to be an old wooden box. Its size was a foot squared. It had a lid, and inside he found some old papers, but nothing else. He couldn't read; he had no idea what the papers said. (Maybe if he had, he would have reburied the box and gone home, forgetting this whole mess. But he didn't, and that's what matters here). Jonas figured they might be valuable, so he closed the lid, filled in the hole, and tiptoed out of the field carrying the box. He went home, moving in the darkest of shadows, where "only the goblins dared to venture." Clara was sleeping when he got in, snoring loudly. He hid the wooden box under his clothes and quickly fell off to sleep.

The next night after work Jonas copied what the priests had written on parchment paper and buried the box in a wooded area close by. He never saw the box again, and he never knew there were thirty pieces of silver hidden underneath the papers in a secret compartment, because he finally got caught stealing some fruit and vegetables by a shopkeeper the next day. Jonas was fast, but on this fateful day an invisible hand grabbed his ankle and he fell to the ground.

This time he had picked the wrong person to steal from. He was a large and heavily muscled man who caught up to Jonas as he was picking himself up. That happened in a dark and empty alleyway, where no one was around. The shopkeeper beat Jonas into unconsciousness, breaking his jaw and three ribs in the process. The man was beyond being angry and irate, for people had been stealing from him on a daily basis. Murphy's Law, or was the curse starting its work?

Jonas woke up hog-tied in the back of a horse-driven wagon. The shopkeeper told him he would pay dearly for what he had done. He told Jonas that he hadn't been the first person to steal from him, but he would make sure Jonas never stole from him again. Jonas was then hit over the head with a piece of wood, driving him into unconsciousness again.

They traveled for days until they hit the shores of the Dead Sea. A cousin of the shopkeeper hung out there. He was in a gang of hoodlums, and the Dead Sea was a good place to get rid of some unwanted problems—and Jonas was one of them. The shopkeeper knew his cousin had a small boat hidden in the brush by the Western shoreline. He roughly pulled Jonas out of the wagon and proceeded to beat him almost to death before throwing him in the boat, still hogtied. Jonas had no will left to fight; he knew that he had internal injuries and would probably die. He had lost some fights in the past, getting drunk and cursing the wrong patron sitting next to him, but he had never been beaten like this.

The shopkeeper rowed far out into the sea, tied large rocks to a begging Jonas with heavy chains, and then dropped him overboard. He dropped a hundred feet to the bottom of the sea, drowning horribly. Jonas never knew that he was doomed from the moment he dug up that box. He never knew that he was in possession of Judas's blood money. That didn't matter now. He was dead. And then the curse of the thirty pieces of silver really began to work its dark magic.

Yes, Jonas was dead, but not totally. He did not die and go to heaven or hell. He did not fall into unconsciousness. He was floating a foot or two above the floor of the sea, hog-tied and held down by the rocks and chains the shopkeeper had expertly tied him to. Yes, the heavily salted water had rushed into his lungs, choking him and cutting off his air supply, but he was still conscious of where he was and all his surroundings. He had not gone anywhere. He hurt all over and couldn't breathe—his lungs burned indescribably—but he was conscious of it all. All his nerve endings sent bolts of extreme pain screaming to his suffering brain.

Maybe this was hell. No, Jonas reasoned, this was worse than hell. It had to be, because he was in a perpetual state of dying, in a suspended state of agony. If he could have screamed, he would have loudly. He had entered into a fateful realm worse than he could ever have imagined. He didn't know it, but the curse of Judas's blood money had entered his agonized insides and was keeping him right where he was, physically and spiritually. His soul was lost to damnation. This he realized pitifully as he gasped for air that wasn't there and struggled mightily in the murky depths of the Dead Sea. As his eyes bulged outward and his nerves stretched beyond their means, Jonas of Aaron understood the full meaning of a fate worse than death. God help me! he thought despairingly as a darkness grew inside him, consuming his complete inner core.

Even though he was in the depths of the Dead Sea and anything he possibly could've heard would have been completely muffled, he heard the distinct sound of coins jingling in his mind, over and over and over. As he slowly drowned repeatedly, the pain becoming more acute with every repetition, he prayed for mercy. None came.

When Jesus Christ was being crucified just outside Jerusalem in a place called Golgotha ("place of the skull" in Aramaic), Judas tried to hang himself close by in Potters Field where the chief priests ended up burying the cursed thirty pieces of silver. He should have been successful, but he wasn't. He struggled, choked, and gagged for fifteen minutes before the branch of the tree snapped and he fell to the ground gasping. He had repented of his crime against Jesus of Nazareth, so the curse of his decrepit purse was removed from his soul, but what would happen to Jonas of

Aaron also applied to him. He could not fully die. He looked to the heavens for answers but received no reply.

He sat down next to the tree and cried until he had no more tears left. He wiped his swollen red eyes and saw a white circular light appear in front of him. A person, or humanlike being, came out of the light and held its hand out to Judas. To Judas, this presence looked like it was right out of the future. It had short hair and was beardless, totally unlike all the men Judas had ever met. Its face looked foreign, as if from an alien land. Its eyes were a light shade of blue. He was taller than most men, standing maybe six and a half feet. He wore a robe the likes of which Judas had never seen before. The material was foreign, the style as well. It wore no sandals on its feet, which were bigger than any in these parts. Judas didn't know what to do, so he shakily took the hand offered to him. The hand was warm to the touch, and a voice spoke to him, yet the being's lips never moved. It said, "Judas, you have done your work well; now it is time to come home. The Father is waiting to greet you in the House of Finality. He will welcome you at the front gates. Come . . ." Judas stood up as if in a trance and followed the being into the circular light. He felt relieved and happy for the first time in a very long time. He felt worthy.

He smiled warmly as he passed through the light with the strange being, and then they both, along with the circular light, disappeared. The field was quiet, and then one by one all the leaves fell from the hangman's tree. Judas was never seen again, and the tree never grew another leaf, except for the branch that he tried to hang himself with. It never lost its leaves. It was the only part of the tree that lived, and nothing could kill it. Birds built nests in the branch and new life was born for years afterward. For some unknown reason, no one ever touched the branch that had snapped and fallen to the ground. It lay at the base of the leafless tree for many years, producing new life every new spring season. No one ever climbed the petrified leafless hangman's tree, but if they did, they would've seen two words carved into its tallest branch. Those two words were "Judas repented."

It is not documented anywhere in any scripture, or in any ancient folklore, but there were many terminally infected people at Jesus's crucifixion. Even though the true sickness was many, many years away from inhabiting this universe, its infection was already making its effect felt. Many reveled in what was happening to the three men on the crosses. They cared little for what they were going through. They LOVED what was going on. They loved nails through skin and bones. They lusted after the blood and pain displayed before them. Hell's fires were growing; hate was metastasizing. The Earth seemed desolate.

It seemed destined for failure yet hope still lived in the crowd. Many people cried as they watched the sad way these men were put to death, especially the one called Jesus in the middle. He seemed to have a halo of light around him that no one could explain. They knew a man with that kind of aura shouldn't be treated like this. It was an abomination.

Yet others felt totally the opposite. An unsettled balance was being established. The hearts of demons were being born in the crowd; their souls grew dark, and their seeds would be planted in many future generations to come. That tide could and would not be stopped. Somewhere in a dying realm a darkened presence laughed hysterically about that fact. It knew. It *knew*.

The blood money, the thirty pieces of silver, remained buried for almost two thousand years, but their power remained strong. The curse was patient. It was waiting.

The more things change, the more they stay the same. People are born, live, and then die. That never changes, no matter where you live on this planet. The difference in this equation is the "live" part. *Sometimes* you live. You grow up, get a job, and make enough money to eat and have a home, marry, and start a family. You have some entertainment, grow old if you're lucky, and then die. Sometimes that death process is quick like a heart attack, or the process is slow, like dealing with cancer, which eats away at you slowly. Those are just two examples of death. There are many others—way too many others. And then sometimes you don't really live; you *survive*. Sometimes you are born into horrific circumstances where you have to beg, steal, or kill for your next meal. You could have been born back when Jesus Christ walked the Earth, or it could be present day, but one thing never changes: we all don't come into this world *equally*. We don't all start life's race at the same starting line. It is reality, and depending on who you are and who you aren't, you may live comfortably, or you may live as a predator. It is unfair, but that is how it is. That is life in a nutshell, no matter where you live on this Earth. It is a grim and dark reality, but a reality just the same. As life goes on improvements are made, health care improves, the industrial age takes place, technology moves forward, etc., etc., etc. This is all part of the "live" part.

As all of these changes are and aren't taking place the blood money laid dormant in the ground, and the only way that would change is *change* itself. And that is what happened. The area where Jonas of Aaron buried the thirty pieces of silver began to die. The grass, the surrounding trees, even the ground itself began to decay. The dirt turned crimson red in color and crumbled to the touch. That's because in the immediate area water (or moisture) did not exist. If it rained, the water just seemed to flow away from the dying grounds. These were the effects of the land around the buried silver. The future spelled death.

Eventually it was decided that the area would be used as a cemetery for the poor and homeless, those unfortunate souls without the funds for a proper burial. There would be no headstones and no markings. A wooden stake might be used, but little else. They would be buried in the cheapest of coffins, by the cheapest of means. There would be little or no fanfare of a funeral, no religious service or a traditional sendoff. They would be basically dumped into the ground, and their lives mostly forgotten. The cemetery would be called "Paupers Pit"—a fitting name for the poor souls that would be buried there.

This happened in the summer of 1862, and that was when accidentally the wooden box with the hidden thirty pieces of silver were dug up. Amazingly, the wood that made up the box was in the same condition as when Jonas of Aaron dug the hole and buried it so many years before. That was because it had a mission, and that mission was to house the cursed thirty pieces of silver until somebody possessed them again. Sometimes evil cannot be destroyed. The blood money was a perfect example.

How's this for luck: Daniel Sandberg dug his first grave in Paupers Pit and uncovered the box that contained Judas's unwanted payment. It was the biggest mistake of his life. The curse would continue on its deadly path. Progress would continue to move forward. Time's clock would continue to tick to the next tock. The more things change, the more they stay the same.

Daniel Sandberg had put the box in the back of his cart and started for home when the pains in his chest started. He took a few more steps before collapsing at the cemetery entrance. He stopped breathing completely a minute later. He was twenty-eight years old. It was after sunset before his boss found him. His wife was notified, and he was buried the next afternoon, ironically, in Paupers Pit. He had little money, and his wife spent most of it on his funeral. A small wooden cross with his name on it was put in the ground.

As soon as everybody had left the cemetery and his crying wife was led away, six feet below the dirt in a cheap wooden coffin Daniel Sandberg opened his eyes, gasped, and started breathing again. His chest was still in the pained-filled state it had been in when he collapsed and found it extremely hard to breathe, but he would not stop breathing and die. He was in a perpetual state of having a heart attack, locked in a cheap wooden coffin six feet underground. He banged on the sides of the coffin and clutched his throbbing chest. He struggled to breathe air that wasn't there. He screamed as best he could but the pain in his chest restricted almost all his physical movements. In the back of his mind he knew that he had been buried alive (or half alive), but the intense agony that felt like his heart exploding kept most of his brain busy.

Above the ground it was getting dark, another day was coming to a close. Paupers Pit was quiet; Daniel's gasping wails could not be heard. He never knew that the wooden box he had dug up contained Judas's cursed thirty pieces of silver. He never knew that he had been cursed, but he was aware that a horrid kind of hell had come calling, and it was not leaving anytime soon. It was pitch black inside the coffin and he couldn't see a thing, but every beyond-hurting second it became darker and darker, and his condemned soul and spirit fell further and further into an abyss that had no bottom. The curse moved on.

Jacob Walden was Daniel Sandberg's boss. He found the

wooden box in his worker's cart after they removed Daniel's body and he took it home. After the funeral he dismantled it and was the first soul to actually find the thirty pieces of silver. He had been feeling bad about Daniel; Jacob thought he was a nice man, and his death sure as hell was a shock to say the least, but now he felt as though he had found the pot of gold at the end of the rainbow. He didn't really care where these silver pieces came from. Maybe they were Daniel's, but Daniel was dead. If they were his dead worker's silver, then why would they be in the cart? It was all so confusing, and so for the time being he decided to keep it all hush-hush. He let the silver pieces fall through his fingers. He felt their texture, their warmth. They had to be worth a lot, and compared to yesterday he was going to be quite rich, and that meant leverage, power.

Jacob thought about Daniel's wife Matty. She was a beautiful woman, but a woman that was now a widow without any money. He had always lusted after her, had always wanted her for his own. He had always been jealous of Daniel, but Daniel was dead now, lying in the earth and gone forever. He was sorry about Daniel's plight, but life went on, didn't it? If he could benefit by his death, then so be it. His plan would be to promise to share the silver with Matty if she would become his wife, his bride. They could both come out well on this arrangement. Jacob was a lonely and homely man that nobody would marry, but that was because he wasn't wealthy. Now he would be.

He got drunk that night and masturbated repeatedly about the pretty widow that was probably crying herself to sleep that very night. Well, that would change, he thought happily as he drunkenly laughed out loud and grabbed his growing penis in his hand. Yes, that would change. The blood money vibrated on the table nearby, waiting.

The next morning a hungover Jacob, looking worse for wear,

went to see Matty, and she rebuffed him until he showed her the pieces of silver. Then she reluctantly changed her mind. She was so poor and her future so bleak that she decided to marry him. At least she would have some financial stability.

There was much talk in the town, some heavy gossip, but neither of them cared. He was desperate for a woman, and she wanted to live, not just survive. They married one week after Daniel had been buried. Their fate was sealed. On their celebrated wedding night during their first time as man and wife, they both suffered similar heart attacks to Daniel's and stopped breathing. They were both found in their wedding bed with their arms wrapped around each other by the local constable the next afternoon—two more dead because of the curse. The count was up to four. Jacob was forty-one years old, Matty just twenty-three. They were both buried next to Daniel Sandberg.

Johnathon James, another gravedigger, shakily walked home after shoveling in the last bit a dirt. He was spooked, because even though he never told a soul, he would've bet his life that he had heard some sort of gasping sound coming through the dirt on Daniel's side. He knew it couldn't be Daniel; he had seen the dead man himself. But still . . . could some rodent already be inside his coffin? He shivered at the thought. He was so traumatized that he quit his job and left town soon after. He had the eeriest feeling that if he stayed, he would die horribly. He eventually ended up in New York digging graves in New York City's Marble Cemetery. He made friends and worked there until he retired. He ate and drank with them, but he never mentioned Daniel Sandberg or the sounds coming from his grave. He somehow knew not to.

Jacob Walden and Matty Sandberg-Walden both woke up in their coffins like Daniel had. They both were in the same perpetual state as Daniel, both gasping for breath while their hearts felt as though they were about to burst inside their agonized chests. As if things couldn't get any worse, all three could hear each other's gasps, each other's pain. They were all buried that close together. All three knew they were damned. All three prayed for mercy. None came.

A day before the wedding Jacob had buried the thirty pieces of silver under his woodpile. He never told Matty, because he felt that she might take it and leave him. He was right, because that was *exactly* what she was planning on doing. None of that mattered now, and if the truth be known, some might think that they got what they rightfully deserved. Over time folklore had it that Jacob, Matty, and Daniel had been cursed. They didn't know how right they were.

The curse of the thirty pieces of silver would be hidden again for many more years. Nobody in town would buy Jacob Walden's land. Buyers were scared off after hearing the story of the three puzzling deaths. They didn't know how right they were *not* to buy his land.

The brush around his property grew wild and out of control. Because of the local folklore it remained vacant right up until the power went off. The blood money did not stay under the woodpile, though. It was found in the fall of 1960, by accident. The curse again had laid in wait. And again, it remained patient.

Marijuana became big in the area, a drug of choice. A local teenager, Michael Bernstein, saw Jacob Walden's vacant lot on the outskirts of town and decided to become Johnny Appleseed—which meant he began growing pot in the backyard. There was a small stream that ran beyond the backyard that Michael used to water his growing plants. Over time Jacob Walden's woodpile completely fell apart and the bag of silver became exposed, the dirt washed away from all the storms over the years. Michael was with three other friends smoking reefer by the pot garden when he saw the top of the bag. High as a kite he picked up the worn, dirty bag, opened it, and discovered the thirty pieces of silver. Jason Rye, Izzy Brand, and George Hyman were Michael's friends, and they split up the blood money. They all claimed possession of the silver—a bad and deadly decision. Fates were sealed. Michael took nine pieces, and the other three took seven each.

Michael went to the library and did some research. He was the first person to figure out that the silver was probably Judas Iscariot's traitorous payment from the high priests. He went home and called the other three friends to tell them his findings but got no answer each time. He didn't know it but all three were already dead. This news Michael would never know. His parents went out for dinner, so he lit up a joint and laid down on his bed, staring up at the ceiling. He passed out with the joint still lit. The bedspread caught on fire, and the flames spread quickly. Michael normally would have woken up, but the curse was taking hold, keeping him asleep.

Within fifteen minutes the house was in flames, Michael included. By the time neighbors called the fire department and the first truck arrived the whole residence was engulfed. Witnesses reported that they saw the face of the devil or a demon in those flames, but those visions were quickly dismissed.

Michael Bernstein was burned beyond recognition. His remains resembled a blackened skeleton for the most part. Amazingly his eyes appeared unburned, but they looked like they had seen something more than unsettling. Maybe as he burned to death he woke up and saw the same face of the devil that the witnesses had seen. His burnt body was wrapped in cool cloth before being put in his coffin. Both his parents had to be sedated before and after the funeral. They would never be the same. Both would be committed to the mental ward within the next year. They never left. Michael Bernstein, pothead and dead before his life really even started, was seventeen years old.

Once everyone had left the cemetery and his grave was filled in, Michael's eyes moved in the cloth and he became aware of every fiber of his being, every nerve ending, which were screaming in burning agony. Suddenly flames appeared and they burned the cloth before engulfing what was left of Michael Bernstein. The coffin wasn't affected, for the flames refused to burn its wood. Only Michael was in flames, and he felt their every touch, their every caress. He silently screamed in agony, for he no longer had vocal cords. His eyes somehow remained unburned; he could see even though they felt as if they were burning as well as the rest of his body. He saw what appeared to be a demon formed by separate orange-blue flames smirking back at him. Michael burned and burned again, hour after hour, day after day. The demon laughed and laughed at the burning teenager; its cackles heard deep inside Michael's screaming mind. The curse had waited and awakened with a vengeance. Michael Bernstein, condemned to an eternity of unrelenting burning agony, listening to constant demented laughter, was the last to get the joke.

Before Michael suffered his deadly fate, his friends experienced the curse as well. Jason Rye, Izzy Brand, and George Hyman all went over to Jason's house to listen to some of Israel's popular music. They went there because his mother was the only one that worked. Everybody else's mother would be home *all* day. Houses that had mothers home all day were taboo. Nobody was hanging out at those residences. You wouldn't be able to do what you wanted, and that was to mostly party. Jason's father had died in a car crash when he was five, so his mother had gotten a job at the local food market and was gone all day.

The three friends lit up a joint, passed around some local liquor, and listened to Galey Tsahal, the IDF radio station which played local popular songs. Music and cheer filled the room. All of a sudden, the music increased in volume all by itself. The boys liked loud music, but this became earth shattering. Jason tried turning down the volume, but it just kept getting louder and louder. All three tried leaving the room but the door wouldn't open. They tried the bedroom window, but it wouldn't budge. Jason threw a chair at it, but it just bounced off the glass.

Something was way wrong here, they all thought at once, totally freaked. They were trapped, and the volume just kept going up. Blood began coming out of their ears and all three began screaming. A moment later all of their eardrums violently exploded but they still heard the volume increasing. Blood began flowing out of their ears at an alarming rate. Their heads suddenly began to hurt badly. Blood began to run out of their noses, then their eyes. Their brains were hemorrhaging. The pressure inside their heads grew and grew. The volume of the music just kept getting louder and louder. Suddenly their eyes exploded outward, blood pouring out. All three teenagers screamed one last time and then collapsed on the bedroom floor, shaking uncontrollably. All the blood in their bodies flowed quickly out of their ears, eyes, noses, and mouths, running all over the floor. They all turned completely white and were dead in seconds. The music suddenly stopped, and the bedroom door slowly opened by itself. The scene was completely gruesome.

Later, Jason's mother Florence came home from work and found the three boys dead on the floor. There was blood everywhere, and six eyeballs moved slightly in its flow. She screamed at the top of her lungs and fainted, falling loudly on the blood-soaked bedroom floor. Her screams were so loud that the next-door neighbors came running. They found what they would later call total carnage. They shivered uncontrollably every time they remembered what they had seen. No one could figure out exactly what had happened, and the autopsies offered few explanations. No one remembered hearing any loud music that might have explained their blown eardrums. Their deaths went down as total mysteries. Four separate funerals were held the next day, in different parts of Givat Shaul cemetery. It was one of the saddest days imaginable.

The families of the deceased were completely in shock and inconsolable. Jason's mother had to be hospitalized and mercifully missed her son's funeral. She never visited her son's grave, and never stepped foot inside the cemetery for the rest of her life, which only lasted a year. The doctors would only say that she had probably died of a broken heart. She remained despondent until she went into cardiac arrest, never recovering from what she had witnessed. She was buried in a different cemetery in an unmarked grave. Those were her wishes, and they were reluctantly carried out by her family.

The families of the other two boys both moved away and were never seen again. It was reported that they had both moved to different countries; Izzy Brand's family moved to Chicago in the United States, and George Hyman's family to Great Britain. All of them spent the rest of their lives complaining of hearing *everything* way too loud, music included. They all lived into their nineties, but all went deaf by the time they had reached their eightieth birthday. Even though they couldn't hear a thing, they *still* complained of hearing all sounds way too loud. The curse knew no bounds.

After the sad funerals were over and everybody had left the

cemetery, all three boys woke up in their coffins hearing the music they had been listening to at its loudest and their brains, eyes, and eardrums began to explode again and again, minute after minute, hour after hour, day after day. Hell came at them in waves, and the tide just kept coming in. The curse of the blood money committed them to damnation. No one could hear their relentless screams over the screeching sound of the music only they could hear. The curse of Judas's traitorous payment smiled in satisfaction, dancing gleefully to the sound of hells bells.

Life after the four boys were laid to rest became very somber. Massive amounts of flowers were laid on their graves for days after their burial. The whole area was in a dark state of depression. People would be walking down the street and just start crying. "Why them, why the young?" they'd ask, shaking their heads in despair. "Why would anybody have to die that way?" People's faith was tested; many people stayed home on Saturdays, not going to the synagogues for worship. Rabbis began circulating in the neighborhoods, trying to calm the masses. In the beginning they weren't too successful, but time heals most wounds. The distressed began to see the light again as life calmed to some sort of normalcy. The good side of life uses time to heal, but so does the bad. The curse still lived; it had lived much longer than anyone alive on Earth, and it remained strong. And when it was forced to be, it lay dormant.

Nine pieces of silver were somewhere in the burned rumble of Michael Bernstein's house, hiding in the burnt rubble. The cleanup would be a slow go; the house had burned completely and most of what was left had fallen into the cellar and foundation. An investigation was taking place, but it was being done with respect. So far, the silver had not been discovered. Progress would be tedious at best. The three boys that had gone to Jason Rye's house must have hidden their silver somewhere between

Jacob Walden's vacant residence and the Rye's. When the authorities investigated and cleaned up Jason's bedroom no silver had been found. No clues were found to explain the three deaths. The investigation was left open, all possibilities being looked into.

The question could be asked: Why did this curse have to exist? Why did people, good or bad, have to suffer its power and intensity? It seemed inhumane in so many ways. We know that Judas Iscariot had betrayed Jesus Christ. We know that Jesus suffered immensely on the cross. We know that he died horribly. But when and where would the curse end? Could it end? Good questions for thought. Praying might help. Repenting like Judas might help. Only time would tell.

Across the street from the burnt remains of the Bernstein's residence at midnight, a dark hooded figure stared intently where Michael Bernstein's bedroom would have been. Its face was hidden by the darkness of the night. It stared as if searching for something, something important. The figure didn't move until the full moon emerged from behind storm clouds, lighting up the street. The figure disappeared as the moonlight touched its silhouette. Loud thunder could be heard far off in the distance, moving away. The rest of the night was quiet and uneventful.

The next day, Saturday, while everyone was at temple, a stranger walked up to the Bernstein house and jumped into the cellar. His name was Father Tom O'Brien. He had heard about the boy's deaths. He knew something was wrong, and that the answers to that wrongness lay at the bottom of the foundation.

He moved burnt pieces of wood, and in the right corner of the basement he found what he was looking for. He knew where to look, because he saw it in a dream. He picked up the nine pieces of silver and left the foundation quickly. He knew he didn't have much time.

Down the street he got in his car and drove to the woods by Jacob Walden's house. He parked the car and walked quickly into the woods. He began to feel sick to his stomach; his insides felt like they were turning to mush, and he vomited violently. His vomit was laced with blood and dark bile. He doubled over, went down to one knee, but never let go of the silver.

A circular light suddenly appeared in front of him. Father O'Brien felt a large lighted hand come out of the sphere and grab him by his collar. The hand pulled him quickly inside, and then it disappeared. The ground around Father Tom's vomit turned bright red. It was warm to the touch. A cold wind blew through the trees for about thirty seconds, before calming down. The bright red dirt returned to its normal dark brown, and then all was quiet. Father Tom O'Brien was reported missing but was never found. The nine pieces of silver were gone as well, and would never curse another human being, but there were still twenty-one pieces out there.

That night the dark figure returned and stood in the same spot, staring menacingly at the Bernstein residence. The moon came up over the trees and lit up the neighborhood. It also shone its moonlight on the hooded figure. What's important here is that the light shone on the figure's face. It was skeletal in nature, with two red, piercing eyes. Raw hate and anger filled those eyes. The creature began to growl—a deep, low growl that came from deep within its dark soul, sensing that what it was staring at the night before was no longer there. The frustrated figure suddenly appeared to vanish into thin air, and never returned to what was left of the Bernstein house.

Father Tom O'Brien had been a priest in the Dominus Flevit Church, a Roman Catholic Church located on the Mount of Olives, opposite the walls of the Old City of Jerusalem. He had preached there for two years. He had heard about the four unfortunate dead boys and had prayed for their souls. On the day he found the nine pieces of silver at the Bernstein's residence and disappeared, he left a letter in his bedchambers. It was discovered later that evening by Father James McMann.

The letter read as follows:

To my best friend James,

Last night I had a visionary dream—a very different kind of dream. It was one that I remembered fully when I woke. It was one that I hoped I would remember nothing of, but because I did, I fear now that this will be my last day on this beloved Earth. If it IS God's will, his wish is my command. I know that you will search for me, but I fear that I will be gone by the time you read this. I have immensely enjoyed my time at Dominus Flevit. I love our flock, and I love and cherish all the times we've had. Our path to righteousness has been my pleasure. The souls we've reached together goes beyond blissfulness and gratefulness. But here is what transpired.

Before I fell asleep last night, I prayed as always. I felt happy and fulfilled as always. Then I fell asleep, and the "as always" part ended. In my dream I am in these woods behind this house, and this round circular light appears. I am not afraid, even though I probably should be. A circular smaller light appears and comes out and floats in front of my face. Wrinkles appear in the light. A voice speaks to me. It tells me to go to Michael Bernstein's house, the poor boy that burned to death inside his house last week. It tells me that I must find nine pieces of silver in the right corner of the basement underneath the burnt wood that has fallen over them. The silver will be in a small old grey bag. The bag is ancient. Yes, I know what you are thinking. Could these pieces of silver be part of Judas Iscariot's blood money? Well, maybe they are and maybe they aren't, but what is important, the light says, is that I must find the silver in the morning and bring them back here to these woods. I'm told that the silver is evil, cursed. It will condemn whoever owns it. The light says that I must move fast when I find the bag—very fast. It tells me that The Lord wants this to be my ultimate mission, my reason for being, even though the silver will probably kill me. It is important that I find the silver when I wake, for another force is looking for the silver as well, and that malignancy is close by. It will infect a polluted mind to acquire the silver, because that force wants the curse to continue. It cannot. The curse MUST stay in a dormant state. The light tells me to bring the silver to it; that is

The Word of The Lord. The light then retreats inside the larger circular light and disappears. The directions to these woods are spoken to me over and over again inside my head, inside my dream. Then I wake up and remember everything like I stated earlier. I debate whether to do what I must, but I KNOW that I must follow these instructions given to me. There is no choice. It is The Word of The Lord. He has spoken to me through this dream and the light. I hope that I succeed; I hope I survive. I hope.

Again, I love and will miss you all! Pray for me. God watch over me.

Your true friend,
Tom

Father James went to the Bernstein residence the next morning. He didn't expect to find Father Tom there. He didn't, but he felt his friend's spirit in the air. Above him a breeze began to blow, and the birds chirped in the tree branches in the next yard. They voiced life and hope to the crestfallen priest. He smiled as the tears began to flow. He believed in Father Tom's dream. He believed and trusted in The Lord. In his prayers each night thereafter he would pray for his best friend, for his soul. But right now, he would go to the authorities and report Father Tom O'Brien missing. Father James didn't expect them to find him, for in his heart he knew he was gone. He would hide his friend's letter in his room and read it often. It is what Father Tom O'Brien would want. God bless his soul!

When the three boys were lying on the floor dying in a pool of their own blood, a robed, hooded figure opened the locked door and glided more than walked inside. The figure was skeletal in face, hands, and feet. It went to each boy, grabbed each of their heads in its skeleton-like hands, and stared into their beyond-traumatized faces with its piercing, crimson, lifeless eyes. Each boy slowly and shakily reached into their pockets and handed the creature their seven pieces of cursed silver, as if hypnotized. Just before everything in their heads exploded outward; even though they couldn't see, think, or comprehend, they all seemed to *feel* what the creature was there for, what it *wanted*. Putting all twenty-one pieces of silver in its robed pocket, it left the bedroom, walked down the hall to a full-length mirror, and stepped inside it. The mirror, for a few moments, became a liquid doorway. On the other side the hooded figure got into a small gondola on a dark, deserted shore, and with one long oar rowed out into an unknown, motionless sea. It disappeared into a dense fog, and then the mirror became itself again. In its reflection was Jason Rye's slightly ajar bedroom door. Beyond that door death had approached and had partially claimed its own, but the cursed twenty-one pieces of silver were in the possession of a different kind of darkness; one that could spread a different kind of lifelessness. Twenty-one out of thirty pieces of Judas Iscariot's silver was on the move. The curse was still alive and kicking. God help its next victim or victims.

Evil has bred in different places and in different objects since the beginning of time—long before this chamber was opened and used. Judas Iscariot's blood money was an evil created by a traitorous deed—not Judas himself, not anybody that nailed Jesus Christ on that cross that deadly day to die horribly. Just the deed. That can grow like a deadly, diabolical cancer cell that just keeps multiplying. It gets caught up in a dark current that is hard to stop. The skeletal, hooded figure was attracted to the pure evil of the blood money and wanted to keep that evil alive and infecting those it touched. We will understand a little more about this dark figure in the next few stanzas. I'm sure you will find him interesting. Evil breeds in different places. And in different *things*.

THE HOODED FIGURE

When Jesus Christ was beaten nearly to death, and then nailed to His cross, two other men where crucified as well, one on each side of the Messiah. One of the two men repented his sins to Jesus as he was dying. Titus, he will be called. He was rewarded by The Lord when he died and went home without conflict. He was a simple thief who stole from the wrong person. He shouldn't have been crucified in the first place, but a lot of the people (powerful and common) back then were souls of true savagery, and demanded to see a condemned man suffer immensely before death set in. The crowd was bloodthirsty in nature, and seeing a crucifixion was just another day in a life to them. Early man was ruthless, but you can still see his roots in man today. That dark part of man's soul is still strong, and sometimes it can't be subdued.

The other man was the only one that truly deserved to be crucified, if, in fact, someone ever should die in that manner. His name was Helishious, and he was truly a bad seed. He grew up poor in the lawless lands in the hills, and he blamed his parents for his struggling survival situation. He went hungry most of the time and had little or no clothes. He was made fun of by the other children that had more, and he more than once wanted to kill each one of them in very sadistic ways. Anger and hate grew strong in his darkening soul, and he dreamed of murder and retaliation.

When he turned twelve, he knifed both his parents to death after he was beaten by his father for beating another boy half to death for ridiculing him. Sticking a large knife into both their chests wasn't enough. He cut out both their tongues, cooked them both over an open fire, ate them, and then he gouged out both their eyes and stuffed them into their mouths to take the place of their tongues. He then set them both on fire and watched them burn to black coal cinders, cursing them until what was left of them had cooled.

He continued killing people here and there, always being cunning enough to escape capture. He raped women wherever he went, killing most of them after he was tired of having forced sex with them. He was finally caught and sentenced to bare the cross after killing a married middle-aged couple and their young son and daughter. The authorities found him having sex with the dead corpse of the wife, the mother of the family, lost in his demented lust. He did not repent like Titus. He cursed Jesus as he weakened, even as he stood on the top step of death's door.

When the three crucified men were all dead and everyone present had had their fill, they were buried. Jesus was buried in a tomb by a man named Joseph of Arimathea. He wanted to make sure he was buried in accordance with Jewish law. He was a good man. Titus and Helishious were buried in unmarked graves in an unknown area.

During a strong storm lightning hit the grave that housed the body of Helishious, and his corpse came back to life. He dug himself out of the dirt and screamed insanely as he looked around the area of his gravesite. He walked the land as not much more than a skeleton. He stole a robe with a hood, slitting the frightened man's throat in the process, and walked aimlessly, still carrying his anger and rage. He went back into the hills where he was born, hiding in the shadows, moving only at night, and waited for a sign. He knew who he had been when he was alive, and he still recalled all of the memories of what he had done. He knew he was a dead man walking and waited patiently in seclusion for his reason for still being here in this wretched land.

The storm that brought him back happened many years after he had been crucified. During that time his body lay decaying in his grave. Jesus had been resurrected and gone home. Judas Iscariot had repented and gone home as well. The cursed blood money had made its mark on a few.

One day while he was waiting in the hills, a voice spoke to him during another bad rainstorm. A bolt of lightning struck some bushes and started a fire. A distorted, crimson face appeared in the fire and told him about the thirty pieces of silver. It told Helishious what he wanted him to do. He now had purpose, and a mission that involved evil. Evil was what he was, and the face in the fire knew that. The voice explained how Helishious could pass through dimensions by passing through anything that reflected his image.

Back in those days large gold pieces were polished so you could see yourself in them. They were the first real mirrors of our times. Helishious used these primitive mirrors to travel into places he wanted to go. His adventures will be explained in detail later. They go beyond what most creative minds can envision.

You can guess what Helishious's mission was: find, possess,

protect, and keep the curse going strong. The thirty pieces of silver were pure evil; there was much for them to do. The voice in the fire said there was one problem: Helishious was condemned and could not take the blood money himself. A human being must give the silver to him, someone among the living. It was the only way.

By the time Helishious caught up to the exact whereabouts of the thirty pieces of silver, life had completely changed. It had become civilized, advanced, lawful. He didn't like any of it, and he certainly couldn't relate to any of it, but over the years he had learned to tolerate many things that he couldn't deal with while he was alive. He had grown mature, even though the evil that coursed through his bones burned hotter than the heat of the sun itself. He willed the three young boys to hand over the silver they possessed. They were long lost to the curse by that time. He had a craving lust inside him to dismember them further, but the greater mission was to possess the blood money and spread its evil—nothing more. He lost out on the other pieces, and he raged inside like never before, but he still had more than half. He would wreak havoc on this world; he definitely didn't like what humans had become, and he knew just where to go with the silver: The New Land, America, the United States.

The Western World did not exist when he was alive, and he was glad of that. He hated everything about the States. They had rules and regulations, they were prim and proper, they were way too civilized. Men, in these times, were not true men. Man and woman had somehow melted into one equal being. Helishious couldn't stomach that, and he *had* no stomach!

He rowed on The Sea of Sorrows until he reached the dark, lifeless shore and passed through a full-length mirror. He was in an apartment in Manhattan, New York City. It was midnight, quiet. He dropped one piece of silver in front of the front door.

Then he passed through the mirror again and was gone. He did this again and again throughout the country, dropping one piece of silver in various states in various homes where the occupants could easily find them.

This activity did not go unnoticed by the circular light. As each piece of silver was being placed in a home, it followed and appeared close enough so that a human hand could come out of the light and grab each one. You couldn't tell whose hand it was, but it *was* human. In the scheme of things (possibly to be explained later), it *had* to be human. The light followed Helishious until all the silver had been recovered. When the sun came up the next morning, all thirty pieces of silver had been recovered and Earth was safe from the curse. Hopefully and thankfully, it was over!

When Helishiuos found out by retracing his steps he went into a major rage, but he had enough restraint to return to the dark shores of the Sea of Nothingness to express his displeasure. Gray skies and thunder crackled overhead, and the voice told Helishious to be patient, and wait in the shadows. It told the skeletal being that something big was about to happen, and his services would be needed again, and this time the outcome would be different—very different.

And so ends the chronicles of Judas Iscariot's cursed thirty pieces of silver at this time, at least for the time being. It could have been much, much worse, especially if the silver had circulated around the United States. America never knew how lucky it had been, how much grief it had been spared. One could only imagine how dire the situation could have been if not for the circular light and those that assisted it. Maybe that human hand had been the hand of Father Tom O'Brien, maybe someone else. That information might be revealed at another time. Regardless, this time, the curse, and the evil of Helishious, had been thwarted—this time. The skeletal creature was still lurking in the shadows, and still extremely dangerous. Hopefully he was being closely monitored—hopefully.

Chapter Twenty

ELISA

We now return to Present Day.

Elisa was employed by the Palmers in Boulder, Colorado, a college town. She did the house cleaning and the cooking. She had also taken care of Mrs. Palmer, Helen, who had stage 4 liver cancer and been bedridden on the first floor. A hospital bed had been put in the living room and Elisa had spent all her time keeping her employer as comfortable as possible—had. *Had*. Helen Palmer had died five months before the power went out. All these years with improving treatments still couldn't stop the relentless tide of death; still couldn't stop Helen from dying.

After the funeral Elisa went back to cooking and cleaning and taking care of Mr. Palmer and the twin girls, who had just turned ten. Helen had only been thirty-eight—way too young to die. Elisa missed her. She had *cared* for her dearly. She shouldn't have felt that way. She shouldn't have cared in any way. That was because Elisa was an android, Model ROBO142. She was one of the first of her kind. Her model so far had been a pleasant success. The company, ROBOHLP, was planning on sending advanced models of her kind to Mars to work in the colony. That *had* been the plan, anyway.

Elisa looked like any thirty-year-old woman; she resembled a young Sally Field, an actress back in the Twentieth Century, but she moved much slower and stiffer. She wasn't supposed to have feelings, she wasn't supposed to miss anybody, and she certainly wasn't supposed to ask questions about life, and death—especially about death. But she *had* wanted to know everything about it and wanted to know all those stories about where you went after you died—all those stories in that Bible book, the ones about heaven. Elisa wanted to know where Helen *went*, and where she was now. She wanted to go there one day if that was possible, but she was an android and didn't know if her kind went there or anywhere at all. It was all so confusing, so *grey*. The whole life and death thing just seemed *wrong* to her. There was something imperfect about this whole complete full circle of life thing—this *thing*! Another emotion came over her that she wasn't supposed to have: anger. Another was grief.

After the funeral the rest of the family went into a funk, a dark and deep depression, and Elisa had helped them in any way she could; but she was also experiencing those same feelings, feelings she was telling no one about. She thought that if anyone knew then they might send her away, back to the company she had come from. Her thoughts were in turmoil all the time now. Question after question about her feelings went through her memory banks, but no answers were answering back. There was nothing strange about that. That was because she wasn't supposed to be asking these questions to begin with. It was amazing that she was functioning properly at all, but somehow, she managed to maintain.

When the power went out and the planes fell out of the sky, Elisa didn't power down. Everything inside her continued to function normally. She was the only android that kept running; and also, the only one remaining in her household. Without direction, she walked around town but saw no one. Everything was still. Everything was quiet. She was alone—utterly alone. She walked to the cemetery where Helen had been buried and found her and everybody else in the graveyard missing. There was nothing but empty holes in the ground. Elisa found this very odd. A shift in the world had definitely occurred, and she didn't know what to do, where to go. She stood in the cemetery by Helen's empty grave for three days, crying tears that she didn't have. She missed her family, and everybody else as well. Elisa was somehow grieving. She also should have shut down but didn't. When everybody went to sleep at night, she usually plugged herself into her recharger. A full charge would usually last thirty hours or so. As she was feeling the emotion of loss, Elisa had wanted to power off when she came out here, but she was still powered on—and on full charge, no less. She would have no relief, no release from these feelings. She would have to go on; she would have no other choice.

Elisa stayed at the gravesite for another hour, and then went back to the Palmer house, where she had spent the last five years (her whole existence, in fact), silently said a prayer ("Wait, where did that come from?" her memory banks asked), packed a small suitcase of all her belongings, and then walked down the street. A voice (God?) that was not her own spoke to her from the back of her memory banks and told her to go to a place she had never been before. The voice told her there was a place waiting for her, a city—a big city. New York City.

Chapter Twenty-One
WENDI BEALS

*W*endi Beals didn't believe in God—never really did. To her, religion was one of those things that just didn't add up. When she was young her mother *made* her go to church and Sunday school, every Sunday, without fail. In Wichita, Kansas, you got homework from the Sunday School lessons every week, so she forgot more than most people ever knew about The Bible. Yet bad luck seemed to follow Wendi wherever she went. It was Murphy's law at its best.

When she was ten years old her father left for work and never returned for reasons only he knew. He said goodbye, smiled, and gave his wife a peck on her cheek like always, but that was the last time his family ever saw him. That was hard. Wendi's mother Sue, her brother Sam, and her sister Rhonda all blamed themselves to some extent for his unexpected departure. Wendi could never understand why you would ever desert your family. How could you leave your wife and children—be a minister, and leave your family? How? How could you preach the ways of The Lord and still throw away your family like yesterday's garbage? That just didn't add up.

Then two years later her older sister Rhonda was raped,

murdered, and left in a ditch less than three miles from their house. How could you go to church every Sunday, praise Jesus and His Word, and then have this happen to your sister? Wendi had been told that Rhonda had been beaten so badly that her face was unrecognizable. Cause of death was strangulation, but that was just the end of what Rhonda had been through. It had been a closed-casket funeral. She was just seventeen. The family was devastated. It just didn't add up. The pieces of the puzzle just didn't fit. Wendi reasoned that religion was a farce. There couldn't be a God.

Things went from bad to worse. Six months later younger brother Sam was out riding his bike with two other friends when a car careened out of control and killed all three boys. The driver had been drinking and driving too fast. They were all just thirteen, just starting life. This time the whole town was devastated. Wendi and her mother Jennifer both needed therapy after that loss. They still went to church every Sunday; her mother Sue's faith stayed strong, but not Wendi. She had lost faith, faith that she never really had to begin with. Her life was godless. It just didn't add up.

A year later Sue had a massive heart attack, dying instantly. She was forty-seven. Wendi was seventeen, and now her whole family was gone. After the funeral, Wendi never stepped into a church again… until the day before the power went out. That was four years later. Wendi finished high school while living with her Aunt Mae who lived a few blocks away. Her family's house was sold, and the money was put in a trust.

Wendi moved to Los Angles and worked as a secretary in Hollywood. Things were looking up. She had some cash flow; she started going out with a guy she thought could be the one, and she loved her job. And then she saw the dead deer on her way home out by the hills. Wendi pulled over and slowly got out of her car. There were three of them, a mother and her two fawns. Babies! Dead on the side of the road. Dried blood covered all three. Wendi finally broke, went to her knees and cried until she had no more tears left. She had cried for all of her family; she missed them all terribly, but she had held her own. She had taken it and had remained standing tall—until now. For some reason, seeing this family of deer laying helplessly on the side of the road with nobody caring for them just broke her heart. She had had enough. She looked to the sky and yelled "Why?" shaking her fist in the air. She screamed and screamed, letting it all go. And then it happened. She got a reply.

A circular light appeared and engulfed the three deer, and then they all slowly came back to life. The light then just as quickly disappeared, and all three deer walked slowly up to Wendi and rubbed their heads against her. They were not afraid. It was as if they all they shared a sacred bond. Then they ran off into the woods, but before they did all three turned around and stared back at Wendi with the knowingness of a love shared between close new friends. Wendi laughed with joy, got back into her car, and stopped at the first church she came to. She went inside, and while sitting in the front pew stared up at Jesus Christ on the cross and began to weep. A priest walked up and asked if she was all right, and she smiled and said she was fine—that she had finally found God. He nodded, smiled knowingly, and walked away.

Soon after, when the power went off and she was still there all by herself, Wendi knew that God had chosen her for something—maybe something important. She was now one of his flock. It finally all added up.

Chapter Twenty-Two

THE BABY

*J*n Portland, Oregon, Robert and Jacklyn Rubin were expecting their first child when the power went out. They were eight months pregnant, and it was a girl. It had been the best of times, being happily married for two and a half years and then taking the pregnancy test and discovering that you were going to have a baby, start a family. They had talked about having children, maybe three or four if things went right, and maybe more than that. Having a big family was not out of the question; only money issues could prevent that. The pregnancy had gone well until the day of the power event, when during a normal exam their doctor had found some problems—big problems that somehow had evaded him.

The baby's heartbeat was different. It was beating twice as fast as normal. Tests were taken, and then retaken. That was because they showed that the baby no longer had a brain, or any other organ in her body. In fact, those tests showed that the inside of the baby's body was pretty much hollow, empty. There was no heart, but the machines showed that something *was* beating inside the fetus. There were no veins, arteries, or blood flowing through the unborn child, yet the baby was still alive. Other doctors were called in to run more tests, but the results were all the same. This was a first in the medical world, and as anybody could imagine, all the doctors were completely baffled. They kept the Rubin's at the hospital to run more tests, but they never got the chance. The power went out and everybody disappeared, all except the baby. Jacklyn was lying on a hospital bed when she, Robert, the nurses, and the doctors all vanished into thin air. Now only the baby remained. It had no brain, no heart, no anything, yet it was alive, and was still there. For the first time it was out of its womb, out of its safe cocoon. It looked like a normal fetus of eight months, but its face had no eyes. In its place were just two dark holes that went to a brain that wasn't there. The baby girl moved its head back and forth, and its little arms and legs twitched every few seconds, as if spasming. The hospital room was completely quiet when the round circular light appeared in the doorway. It glided slowly toward the baby and stopped once it had totally engulfed the child. The light became brighter until the baby completely disappeared inside it, and then it too disappeared, taking the newborn child with it.

Chapter Twenty-Three

THE GHOSTS OF DAVIS HOUSE

There is an old two-story house that sits on a cliff. It overlooks the Atlantic Ocean in Newport, Rhode Island. It is over 350 years old and was moved here by the water over 200 years ago. It used to be on an estate about ten miles inland. It housed servants back then. Things happened in that house that not many people know about—many things. Some were very bad things, and because of those incidents the house remains haunted, or inhabited. It has been that way since the day it was moved off the Marlow Estate to where it sits now. The people that were victims in the house are still there, ghosts trapped in a timeless dimension of despair.

Mr. Eric Davis owns the house now. He owned it right up until the power went out. He did not go home with everybody else, so I guess you can say that he owns it still. His grandparents bought the house when his father Ben turned ten years of age. It had been rented for years during the summer season, and Ed and Martha Davis bought it after renting it for three straight Labor Day holiday weeks in a row. Afterward they used it as a summer house, opening it up every year on Easter and closing it after Halloween and the pumpkin season. The family lived in

Bridgeport, Connecticut, during the cold winters. Eric was raised by his grandparents. His parents died in a plane crash coming home from a wedding anniversary vacation in Punta Cana in the Dominican Republic when he was twelve, two days short of becoming a teenager for the first time. The plane plunged into the ocean off the coast of North Carolina. The cause of the disaster was never uncovered, and Eric's parents' bodies were recovered on his birthday. What a present!

It was hard for a while, but he still had his grandparents to lean on. They were solid; they were rocks. They both kept Eric grounded. Life went on, it always does. Eric went to school in Bridgeport and spent the summers in Newport. It was a good life. He had friends at school and friends in Newport. He was never lonely. After opening the house on Easter weekend when Eric was seventeen his grandfather had a massive heart attack and died instantly while he slept in his bed. All the bedrooms were upstairs, along with the only bathroom. Eric had always felt eyes on him whenever he went upstairs to the bathroom or to his bedroom, but after his grandfather's funeral those feelings of not being alone intensified. He knew something was there. He could feel it all around him. He asked his grandmother if she felt these feelings of not being alone when she went to bed, but she said she didn't. He didn't know if he believed her or not, but she was the rock of the family now—his rock. He had to believe her, and if she wasn't telling the truth he knew that she would never let anything happen to him, supernatural or not.

Eric married Jane Hopkins and didn't spend as much time at the summer home as before. Work back in Bridgeport kept them both busy. That was OK, because Grandma was strong and could stay by herself. She spent a lot of her last years alone at the house during the summer. She had a few good friends and neighbors, but times were never as good as when her husband and Eric brought joy to the house. She began to live in the past, a death sentence for someone moving swiftly through the years. Martha eventually died at the ripe old age of ninety-eight. She died on her birthday in Bridgeport General Hospital during one of the worst snowstorms in modern history. She had had a good long life—a life that Eric could celebrate. He and Jane separated not long after his grandmother's death. They were only married for eight years, but they fought enough for fifty. Eric was so traumatized that he swore that he would never get married again. He was true to his word.

After the divorce was finalized, Eric decided that he needed a change. He quit his accounting job at the local firm, O'Donahue and O'Donahue, and moved permanently into the Newport house, working odd jobs and doing people's taxes during tax season. He built an extension, adding a bedroom and a bathroom on the ground floor. He still felt a presence in the house but downstairs it was bearable. He never went upstairs again, closing it off. He had a door installed at the bottom of the stairs and kept it double locked.

Eric never knew of the things that had happened in the house so many years before. He didn't know of the tales and the secrets of the Marlow Estate. It was probably better that way. Some stories are better left untold, but for you, dear reader, here they are.

The Marlow family was rich—filthy rich. The main family lived in London and Wales, but some of the family resided in the colonies in New England. They made their money in trade. They owned twenty ships that went back and forth across the Atlantic. Their cargo included sugar, tobacco, and tropical groceries. Also on those ships were black slaves from Africa. They worked on the tobacco, rice, and sugar plantations. They also worked on the estates of the rich. The Marlow family on both shores of the Atlantic owned many African slaves.

When John Marlow moved to Rhode Island from Wales he took ten of his personal slaves with him. He and his wife Becky moved into a fifteen-acre estate in North Kingstown, Rhode Island. The estate was partially wooded, with a small pond. A small cemetery was created in the west corner. The mansion itself was a three-story brick building in the shape of the letter *U*. The driveway ran up and inside the *U* itself. There were two front rooms that were used for entertaining, two large kitchens, two large dining rooms that sat twenty people each, five newly styled bathrooms and fourteen bedchambers. The master bedchamber was bigger than most houses in the area. It had two bathrooms, one for the lady of the house and one for the master. The whole bedroom was probably 2,200 square feet. A large barn sat to the right side of the mansion, which housed ten horses and five carriages. The slaves spent a lot of time in there since at that time horse and buggy were the main type of transportation used.

John ran the American family trade business from the estate. The Marlow's also owned property and docks in Newport as well, and John traveled back and forth between the estate and the docks twice weekly. The slaves resided in the servant house that Eric Davis now owned. It was made mostly of wood with a foundation made of bricks. The first floor had a small kitchen, dining area, and front room. The steep stairs to the upper floor consisted of four various sized bedrooms and an updated bathroom. Most of the townsfolk only had outhouses, and to have an indoor modern bathroom was a big delicacy. The slaves were honored and appreciative, and treated Master John with the utmost respect. Business boomed. John and Becky had two sons and a daughter.

Life was rosy until one cold December night. An event took

place that could not be explained in any kind of sane conversation. Becky and daughter Virginia went missing. Nobody knew of their whereabouts. All John knew was that the two of them were upstairs getting ready to go to a Christmas party and never came back down the stairs. They searched the estate but found nothing. A search party was assembled; they went out into the surrounding establishments but produced no leads or clues as to what had happened to the two Marlow women.

A drained and dejected John came home at dawn to freshen up and check on his two sons, John Junior and Adam. They were both asleep in their beds, two slave women keeping watch by their sides. He went into his bed chambers and stopped short. An old woman that looked like she was one hundred years old was lying on his wife's side of the bed. Her hair was pure white and disheveled. Wrinkles completely covered her tired face; her mouth turned down on the right side as if she was recovering from a stroke. She was still. John rushed to her and screamed. The old woman was clearly dead, but what made John cry out was that the woman looked exactly like his wife, only much older, and she was wearing the night clothes his wife had worn to bed just last night when she was young and vibrant. That was impossible! Both John and Becky were only thirty-five, so logically it couldn't be his wife; yet he knew in his heart that it was.

A shrill piercing scream came from the hallway. It was one of the female slaves, Jessica. John ran out into the hallway and saw her staring into Virginia's bedroom, shocked. As he frantically entered the room, he saw that in Virginia's bed was another old woman. She had the same disheveled white hair, wrinkles, and stroke-contorted, parched lips. John ran to her and screamed again. She looked like his daughter! The old woman wore his daughter's night clothes. Again, it was impossible. A doctor was called in. He examined both and concluded that both women had died of old age, natural causes. Scars and other basic tests were run, and it was determined that the two women were, in fact, both his wife and daughter. But how could that be? John thought. Becky was in her prime and Virginia was only thirteen. It was unexplainable, but the unimaginable had clearly happened.

Arrangements were made. The usual strange funeral rituals were performed. As was always the case, the surviving family members were left numb and emotionally overwhelmed. Deep down John didn't know where to go from there. Both women were buried on the estate three days after their (untimely?) deaths. John and his boys were grief-stricken. The slaves from the servant house helped as much as they could, but they, too, were shocked and hurting. They had all been treated well by their owners, and they felt grief just as much as if they had lost a member of their own family. John was never the same after the funeral. He would visit the graves every day and stay there for hours, just staring at the new headstones, crying. He aged ten years overnight, losing weight and looking gaunt.

Work suffered; the family took action and sent John's brother James over from Wales to pick up the slack. He was two years younger than John, but a different individual entirely. He was a bachelor and known for living his life after midnight—which meant that he loved his drink and women. He did what he had to for his older brother, keeping the trade business moving, until John committed suicide. That happened four months later. There was an old oak out by the graves of his wife and daughter, and John hung himself on a Monday night in early spring. A second funeral and third gravestone joined the other two.

James took over the estate and the business full time, and the slave women took care of the two Marlow sons until they were shipped off to Wales to go to private school. The family would make sure they would be well taken care of, and their careers in the Marlow industry would be formulated. Everything in the business was calculated.

There was another reason why the boys were sent away, and that was because after John's funeral James became the real James, and the family knew that relations could get tense. He would always make sure that business was taken care of, but Family Marlow knew that James had a dark side, one that must be fed. Keeping John's sons on site would not be a healthy proposition under any circumstances.

Once they were gone James began to drink heavily in the evenings, and began to eye the house slave Jessica. The female slave was twenty-seven, and a real looker. She had curves on top of curves, and James fantasied about her constantly. She was married to Daniel, a muscular man that stood six and a half feet tall, but submissive and obedient to a fault. He was a gentle giant who worked hard on the grounds. They had two twin boys, Robert and William, both five years of age, who helped their father in any way that was needed.

All the slaves knew a storm was brewing with this new master. He was not like Master John, who had treated them with respect. No, Master James drove them hard and without emotion. He was heartless and possessed a bad temper. They all hoped they would survive the dark and grey clouds that began to hover above the Kingstown Estate. One day three new men appeared on the grounds. The slaves were told the men were employees of the Marlow Company and that they were to be obeyed at all times— or else. The storm was growing and moving closer. The three new men were as heartless as Master James, if not more so.

Every night the four boss men drank heavily and made a lot of noise. The slaves shook with fear, wondering if they would ever feel safe at night again. So far so good, but for how long could that last? White drunk boss men and defenseless black slaves just didn't mix. That was a true concoction for disaster. The future looked bleak as the storm moved closer.

The dark storm finally hit home one night when a drunken Master James, along with all three of his cronies, staggered into the servant house with guns drawn. They loudly marched up the stairs to the second floor, summoning everyone out of their bedrooms. It was after midnight and all the slaves sleepily came out, shaking with fear. They had known a night like this was probably going to happen, but they had always hoped against hope. The servant house housed three separate families. There was Daniel, Jessica, and their two young boys; Charles and wife Tonya; and Robert, wife Jenny, and their three children Robert Junior, Diane, and baby Jane. The men were only interested in Daniel and Jessica—or more directly, Master James was interested in Jessica. She and Daniel were ordered into their bedroom by James and his main boss man Clay Lennon, a mean individual if there ever was one, and the rest of the slaves were paraded downstairs and into the kitchen by the other two boss men, William Bosworth and Michael Robbins. They were told to sit at the kitchen table and not move if they knew what was good for them. Upstairs, hell was taking place. While James pointed the gun at Daniel, Clay hog-tied him with two sets of handcuffs. He was then punched several times in the face and stomach and told to stay still. Then the two men stripped a screaming Jessica naked, threw her on the bed, tied both her wrists and ankles to its four corners, and began to gang rape her repeatedly for over two hours. They took turns on her while the other kept a gun on a crying Daniel who screamed in frustrated agony. He fought to get to his feet a few times and had to be pistol-whipped into semi-consciousness. By the time the two men had finished their disgusting act his face was a bloody mess. Both slaves had cried all night: Jessica from the constant assault, and Daniel from witnessing the whole despicable event. It's one thing to know that your wife had been raped, and another to have witnessed it and not been able to do anything about it.

Before James and Clay left the bedroom and threw the key to the handcuffs at a released Jessica, Master James told them both that if they didn't do what they normally did in the morning, or if they showed retaliation of any kind, he would kill their two boys slowly, and in front of them. They agreed to do as he said; they knew they had no choice. They knew that James was heartless and would definitely follow through on his threat, and if they retaliated and tried to harm or even kill their evil owner then they would probably be put to death as well.

The next several days were tense to say the least. The boss men were even harder on the male slaves. Robert stood his ground while being berated for moving too slow and was stripped naked, tied to a post, and bullwhipped by Clay. His back and buttocks were a bloody mess by the time he was released and carried into the servant house. He was bedridden for three days and his wrists handcuffed behind his back as he lay in agony on his stomach. This warning message was received, and the rest of the slaves became docile and submissive thereafter. They were in a no-win situation, and they all prayed to God for their hell to end. It *did* end, but not in a way the slaves would have wanted.

A few nights later the storm turned into a hurricane. After drinking heavily again the four men invaded the servant house and repeated the rape performance, only this time Daniel and Jessica's two young boys were brought into the bedroom to watch Master James and Clay rape their mother repeatedly. They were handcuffed to their father and forced to witness an assault no child should ever see, especially since the victim was their mother. They screamed, cried, and begged for it to be over, but it went on and on. Daniel couldn't do anything, his children handcuffed to each of his wrists. Even though he was hog-tied, he was so incensed that he knew he could have broken free and killed these monsters, but thinking about his children's welfare prevented him from following through. He was emotionally beaten, yet he still had to keep it together and console his boys.

James, on the other hand, knew that what was happening here was completely heartless and soulless, but he totally got off on having this twisted kind of audience. Imagine raping a fine-looking woman and having her family be forced to watch those proceedings. It was too good to be true. To him, there was no better high. He had absolutely no feelings for these slaves or the ramifications of what these acts could cause. James just thought it was funny—and just. He laughed and laughed as they cried and cried, pleading for mercy. Inwardly he hated slaves and loved to belittle them. He kept them at gunpoint at all times, and when Clay was thrusting away, he put his gun to Jessica's head and made her tell the boss man that she liked the way he was "making love" to her. He made her moan and beg for more. He put the gun against her children's temples and threatened to kill them if her and Daniel didn't treat tomorrow like any other normal day. They had to promise Master James and promise hard. Just to be sure, when the two rapists left the bedroom, they took the two boys with them as hostages. Jessica and Daniel pleaded and begged with their owner not to take their young twins but take them they did. They were told that if they played well the boys would be returned to them eventually, but eventually was not going to be tonight. After the men had left with the boys all the slaves hugged and cried and promised to be good like the master asked. It was the only thing they could do.

The next morning, they all got to work like any normal day, but they did it with tears in their eyes. How could a God make monsters like these men? How could they treat them so badly, worse than vermin? The two boys sat on the front porch all day, a boss man sitting with them with his gun cocked and ready. The women worked in the house and were harassed verbally and physically, but thankfully were not raped. They prayed to The Lord that it stayed that way, hoped that He would hear their pleas.

That night Master James had the local constable over for dinner. He was a large, middle-aged man who had a mean look about him. Jessica, Tonya, and Jenny served them. They shared drinks and laughs over dessert. They shook hands heartily with the policeman before the man left. Another dinner was planned for later in the week. The women heard the invite, for it was said purposely in front of them. A message had been sent. The master was going to make the officer his friend, his confidante. Another ray of hope would become another dead end. Hope was becoming a word without meaning. Marlow Estate was turning into hell on Earth.

Daniel tried his hardest, but he couldn't take it anymore. His will to live had gone on permanent vacation; hope had died along with his broken heart. He hung himself in the servant house bathroom. At that time the ceiling was unfinished, so he looped a rope over one of the framework beams and tied it off. Charles found him just before noon. He cried his eyes out as he cut the rope and lowered his good friend to the floor. When he told Jessica, she walked up to the bathroom, emotionlessly, trancelike, and hung herself as well. Charles walked and pleaded with her to think it all through, but there was no turning back, and he reluctantly agreed with her. She made him promise that he would look after her boys, but she could bear no more. She had been stripped of all her dignity, like her husband, and needed to be with him. Hopefully, the Lord would be there to comfort both of them as they entered the pearly gates. Charles cried his eyes out as he watched her take her last breath on Earth, then cut her down and slowly walked outside and went back to work as if nothing had happened.

He was doing some weeding when Master James, snarling, asked where Daniel and Jessica were. With lightning speed, Charles grabbed his shovel and swiftly hit his owner over the head repeatedly, killing him. Clay ran up and shot Charles right between the eyes three times. The two dead men lay almost side by side, but only one of them was smiling, knowing that the worst of the vicious storm had finally passed. When the constable arrived, he quarantined the remaining slaves in the servant house until further notice.

The Marlow family was contacted and told of what happened. The remaining slaves were sent back to Wales on the next ship after being interviewed by a Marlow employee who was in charge of the Newport Docks. Clay Lennon, William Bosworth, and Michael Robbins were also on that ship and told to keep the slaves in line. The three boss men and the surviving slaves never made it to the distant England shoreline. Halfway across the Atlantic the crew overpowered them all, shackling them one by one every few feet to a thick chain that was connected to a four-hundred-pound anchor and thrown overboard. They all traveled into the cold dark depths of the ocean and drowned together. The cover-up was complete; the family name was cleared of conspiracy.

The Marlow Estate stayed empty for a month until John and James's father Gregory came to stay. He was nearing retirement and had decided to take over the business on this side of the ocean that his two sons had so totally screwed up. On his voyage to the colonies he brought back to Marlow Estate his two grandsons. He hoped to tutor them in the family business and leave it in their hands. That was the plan. Also accompanying them were fifteen new slaves.

Gregory Marlow was seventy years old when he docked in Newport Harbor with his grandsons and took over the Marlow Estate in North Kingstown. The first thing he did was visit the cemetery where his two sons now resided. He cried for them, and he cried for their souls. Things have a way of balancing out, and boy had they for the elder Marlow. His wife Belinda had died horribly from cancer three years prior. He watched her deteriorate down to nothing. He felt her pain, her agony. All the money he had ever made couldn't bring her back. They had had a good marriage, had good times and fond memories, and her dying and his being left alone had balanced the books.

A year later his daughter Susan, twenty-one years old and a beautiful woman who had her whole life in front of her, was shot in the forehead by a disgruntled Marlow Company employee. The employee, Joshua Johnson, then shot himself dead on the front steps of Gregory's estate. All the money he had ever made couldn't bring Susan back either. He had memories of her life, all the good times with her, watching her grow up full of love and thoughtfulness. She had brought him so much joy. The books had been balanced further. His two sons were now dead as well, buried below his feet. He was finally here in America with his two grandsons because of that. Those books had also been balanced. He vowed to do right by them and do right for their futures. He hoped that the books this time would balance in their favor. He was wrong, dead wrong. He lived a few more years, dying suddenly of a massive heart attack. He died inside the servant house on the second floor looking for a slave named Angela. What he saw on that second floor was the cause of his exploding heart. After all that he had done for the company, some good and some bad, justice had finally come knocking. The book on his life had finally been balanced completely.

A Bit Of History: When Gregory Marlow died Abraham Lincoln was running for president in 1860. Running against him was John Bell, a Constitutional Union Candidate, John C. Breckinridge, a southern Democrat, and Stephen Douglas, a northern Democrat. He won, and became the first Republican Party President, and major changes were about to happen in the United States. The Civil War took place, the North won, and slavery was abolished. In April of 1865 President Lincoln was assassinated. The country mourned a great leader, yet when he died, he left a country still divided. Racial issues continued to be a problem after the War, mostly in the South.

In the North, in Kingstown, Rhode Island, on the Marlow Estate, those issues didn't exist. John Junior Marlow was twenty-five years old and Adam was two years younger. Their grandfather had raised them not to be prejudged against the black slaves that worked the land. Relations between the new, rich white owners and black slaves couldn't have been better. When they were freed John Junior had the servant house moved to Newport near the docks, and the male slaves became employees who worked the Marlow Docks. The movement of the house was quite extensive, and very tedious. It was literally taken apart piece by piece, transported by horse and wagon, and reconstructed on the Newport property. This process took about three months, and by the time the whole operation was finished, the house looked exactly the same as when it had been first built on the Marlow estate. The women still worked inside the Marlow mansion, traveling back and forth on horseback every day from the servant house in Newport, only now they were paid—and paid well.

In fact, they were better off than most of the townsfolk, and that didn't sit too well with them. What also didn't sit well with them was that the two young Marlow brothers were having relations with two of the now freed black female slaves. They would have been married if it would have been permitted, but they carried on out in the open just the same. Tensions began to build. The Marlow brothers hired more freed slaves from the surrounding neighborhoods to work the docks, and the white dockworkers that were considered lazy were either laid off for a period of time to get their act together or fired outright. That definitely didn't sit well with those who had worked the docks for the Marlow business for years, and tensions built further.

In early 1865 John Junior and Rosetta had a baby boy. Rich white men had impregnated black slave women in the past, but those offspring were still considered slaves. They were treated like all other black babies. That was considered plantation thinking. If a baby had only 1 percent negro in its DNA, then the newborn was considered black. It was a slave. This time it was different. This baby was free. This baby would live better than most of the townspeople. This baby was a Marlow. This baby had a royal bloodline. Tensions boiled over.

Two weeks after John the Third was born they had a celebration party at the servant house. Everyone that worked on the Marlow docks attended. Everyone that lived in the servant house was there. John Junior and Adam Marlow were there. They celebrated the birth of a new Marlow son. The celebration went long into the night, but none of them were alive when the sun came up the next morning.

While the celebration was going on, a thunderstorm blew through. Lightning filled the air, and the roar of thunder shook the ground. A little while later another storm approached, this one quiet, and deadly. A group of seven hooded dark figures moved in the darkest shadows up to the servant house, carrying loaded guns. They walked into the house, not bothering to knock. All the noise of the celebrating residents suddenly stopped. A few tension-filled quiet moments followed, and then the gunshots started. A few screams could be heard for a time, but the sound of those guns were loud and mean. They went on and on. They might've been heard a long way off, but when the residents of Newport were asked about it the next day, not one person said that they had heard a thing.

What *had* happened was that the constable, two deputies, and four townsmen went into that servant house and shot everyone inside to death—the Marlow's, the black dockworkers, and the freed black families that lived in the servant house, including all their children. Dead too, was the newborn baby, John Marlow the Third. When the last shot was fired, and the hooded figures stared emotionlessly at their motionless victims, a tall English gentleman that stood well over six feet wearing a black suit and matching high-heeled shiny black boots walked into the house behind them. He towered over everyone in the house. He was from Wales. His name was Arnold Marlow, a cousin to John and James Marlow, a nephew to Gregory Marlow, and an uncle to the now dead John Junior and Adam Marlow. Oh, and a second cousin to John Marlow the Third, the newborn baby whose whole life had just passed through this world in mere days.

Arnold handed the constable letters of money and instructed him to put all the bodies on his vessel, which had docked in the harbor three hours prior. Using five wagons, they transported the bodies to the docks, and two hours later that ship left port, carrying all the victims, a crew of twelve, and the tall man, Arnold Marlow. All of them and that ship were never seen in these parts again. Two days later, far out in the Atlantic, all the bodies were dumped overboard inside burlap bags tied to heavy anchors. By that time search parties back in Newport were looking for people they knew they would never find.

History will say that all of these murders never happened, but it was just one of many defiant stances taken against the freedom of slaves. None of these horrific tales would be found in any history books or periodicals. Those acts of vile violence were wiped clean and never talked about again—ever. Not even in any bedtime stories.

Arnold Marlow had many black slaves back in Wales. Well,

they weren't actually slaves; they were paid apprentices that, unlike John Junior's freed slaves, were paid minimal wages. *That* kept them where they were, so they weren't actually free. Sure, they could've left Arnold and *tried* to get different employment, but very rarely did different companies hire black help from *other* companies. They were trapped between a rock and a hard place. That wouldn't last, though, Arnold knew that. Times were changing, and he knew the days of all types of slavery were coming to an end. He didn't have to like it, and he didn't, but what he had orchestrated back in Newport had to be done. He was running the Marlow business in the old country, and he had decided to move the American part of the business to the docks of New York. More money could be made there—much more than in Newport. That was the main reason he had everybody killed in the servant house: money, greed, selfishness. Oh sure, he hated the fact that black slaves had been freed in America, but all that did was make his decision to kill everyone easier. The reason why the townsfolk in Newport agreed to kill everyone in the servant house *was* because they hated black slaves being free, and they hated anyone white who agreed with good ol' President Abraham Lincoln that all slaves should *go* free.

Arnold sold the Marlow Estate in Kingstown, the servant house, and the docks in Newport and put that cash to good use in New York City. The servant house was rented to summer folks until Ed and Martha Davis loved it so much that they bought it. None of the renters ever knew what had happened there, the Davis family included. Again, like in so many instances all around the world, it was better that they didn't know. Sometimes the truth about a situation *should* remain secret.

In conclusion, Arnold Marlow *did* make a lot of money running the family business. It was a great decision to move the American side of the business to New York. He, on the other hand, didn't live very long to enjoy it. On the same day that President Abraham Lincoln was shot dead by John Wilkes Booth on April 14, 1865, while watching a play in Ford's Theatre in Washington, DC, Arnold Marlow died in his bed back in Wales. A former black slave woman who had slept with him the night before found him dead when she woke up next to him that fateful morning. The cause of death was written down as a heart attack, but the look on his frozen face said that he had been scared half-way to hell and back. He was fifty-six years old, the same age as President Lincoln. How ironic!

When the power went out Eric Davis was sleeping in his bed. He hadn't felt good that morning. He thought maybe he was coming down with a summer cold. He woke up and discovered that nothing worked: not the electric, the appliances, his car or truck. He walked all over town and discovered everyone gone. He discovered that all the gulls were gone as well. He realized that having a summer cold didn't matter anymore. He admitted to himself that he didn't like this quiet. Not hearing the seagulls talk to each other was major. That quiet alone made him feel totally uneasy. As he walked back home, he had another feeling, a very different feeling about his house. He unlocked the door at the bottom of the stairs for the first time since his grandmother had died and slowly climbed them to the second floor. He walked from room to room, looking all around each. There was nothing there. There was no presence. It, or they, were gone. Whatever Eric had felt up here was no longer in the house. It had gone away like everything else. As he went back down the stairs, he looked at the big cowbell that was nailed to the wall. It was very loud and had always been used to call everyone to dinner. Scribbled white painted words suddenly appeared above it. They read, "Go to New York City." He sat out on his back porch for a while looking out at the blue sea, thinking about what he should do. Suddenly he got up, walked inside, packed a sports bag, and walked down the front path to the street. He looked back at his house and thought about all the good times he had had there, all the fond memories. He thought about his grandparents, his parents, his wife, and his friends. They were all gone now but this house still stood tall by his side. Tears began to fall. He turned away and walked down the street, crying. He had a feeling that he would never see his house again. He didn't.

The story of Noah and his ark are somewhat relevant here. The story was written in the book of Genesis. God told Noah to build an ark before a catastrophic flood event would take place. He told Noah to get two of each animal and put them on the Ark. They, foremost in this writer's opinion, are the primary ones that are to be saved. God told Noah that he and his family would be the only humans spared in this flood, that every other human being would die in the rising tide. The world would be cleansed and reset. The reasons why God wanted this to happen differ in different versions, which means that nothing can be certain about this tale. One version states that humankind had become more evil than good and needed be taken out of the equation. Another says the flood was to kill most of the humans to curb an overpopulated world. In this writer's opinion, both are probably correct to some extent.

In relation to this chapter, the way black people from Africa were captured and sold for slavery was wrong. The way slaves were mostly treated, and the way most slave owners *felt* about them is even worse. It is a sin to feel that certain races of people aren't as equal as oneself. To this day, there are problems between black and white people. Those issues need to be eliminated completely. In 1865 American slavery was abolished, but that didn't solve the race issues that existed, or exist even to this day. (That balance needs to be restored.)

Animals, in relation to Noah, are yet another issue. Some religious people believe that animals don't have souls, that only humans do. Remember, Noah built his ark to save the animals first, not us homo sapiens. When the power went out and most life went back home to The Creator, even though it all happened in a split second, the animals went first, before the humans. We think that we are supreme—the top of the food chain, so to speak. And then some cultures and genres think that they are better than others. This way of thinking never stops. Prejudges are created, and hell's fires are relit (and then balance must be restored). In the case of animals, they DO have souls just like we do. They prove it every day. Their love is pure. We, the humans, do not have purity. We are polluted by the force that is about to come into this chamber, whether we want to believe it or not. Since some Humans think they are a higher form of life, a supreme species, they sometimes think they have the right to treat animals badly. The ones that have and are reading these pages know who they are. If they can truly remember how they felt when they mistreated those gifts God gave to this world, then they remember feeling a cancer racing through their veins, infecting their soul, darkening it.

Noah knew The Lord felt betrayed, and so the ark was built. The flood waters raced in and killed most of mankind. The love in the world that remained was purer and prejudices almost completely destroyed. Man was not completely wiped out and began to repopulate the Earth. This time reproduction grew out of control, at least until the power went out. Selfishness and greed again metastasized—prejudices too. Wars created by hate were fought, again, and again. Stories like the ones in the servant house happened daily, repeatedly, all over the world. (Balance must be restored.) Some of those stories will be discussed in future pages. Remember this: we all need to treat everything with respect. Respect others—all others—and wars, fighting, hate, selfishness, greed, and prejudices go away. When you separate a baby animal from its mother, or if you mistreat or abandon them out in the cold, think about what you are doing first. Noah tried to do right by God; he will be remembered for that. Is another flood on its way? Food for thought.

The tale of the two Marlow women that aged a lifetime overnight is a different kind of bedtime story. It involves an old friend, Helishious. As we left him, he had just failed trying to spread the curse of Judas Iscariot's pieces of silver. Before and after those diabolical times he spent years walking on the endless dark Shores of Nothingness or rowing out into the Sea of Sorrows in his gondola-type looking boat, meditating and waiting for the presence that was coming. It got boring, though. Living (if that is what you called it) all those years could get to anybody, especially when you were alone.

This place of timeless eternal gray twilight was what was left of a former chamber. It used to be full of life with spectrums of brilliant colors. Now the skies were full of storm clouds where thunder rumbled and lightning crackled, though there was no wind or breeze. The Sea of Sorrows did not have a ripple or tide. It was lifeless, and nothing lived in its depths. A light mist floated above its surface, completing a mysterious ambiance. There were islands far out in the sea made of burnt, black rocks that were chilly to the touch. Back on land the Shores of Nothingness went on endlessly. Black sulfur-like sand made up the substance of the large beaches where total lifelessness sunbathed. Beyond the beaches, immense, pure, black-colored mountains rose higher than some of the storm clouds themselves. They were made of freezing stone, crystalizing at the top. There were no suns in this forgotten chamber, no stars above those mammoth structures. Clouds of all shades of grey filled the sky, but there were no lights or beacons beyond them. It was a world and universe that had died a long time ago, yet it was a perfect environment for the man made of moving bones. The temperature was a constant 60 degrees, even though without a sun this place should have been as cold as space itself. The Sea of Sorrows was even warmer, about 75 degrees Fahrenheit. The waters were the same temperature as when suns warmed this chamber when it was alive and vibrant.

None of this mattered to the dead man himself; he didn't feel anything. Not having nerves limited him. He felt neither hot or cold, nor the feeling of touch. He still, personality-wise, was himself, and he thought with an invisible brain that got more intelligent with age. He *felt* loneliness, though. It raged within the marrow that was still left inside his decrepit bones. His connection with Becky and Virginia Marlow's disappearance is a strange and scary bedtime story, but one that must be told. Pull the bedcovers up around your face and get ready to shiver, unless your nerves are as dead as those of Helishious.

Helishious could do one thing that nobody else could do: he could move through anything that reflected his skeletal form. That included the Sea of Sorrows in the dead chamber. In the living chamber it could mean any body of water, objects, and especially mirrors; as we have read.

When Becky and her daughter Virginia were getting ready for that Christmas party upstairs, they were looking at a large bedroom mirror together, putting on their faces, so to speak. Their makeup was the best, and most expensive. Nothing was too good for a Marlow woman. They were making small talk and laughing when, in a flash, two skeletal hands came through the mirror, grabbed the throat of each woman, and pulled them through it before they had a chance to scream for help. Passing through dimensions from one chamber to another temporarily knocks every human out for a few minutes, and when the two completely startled women came to, they realized they were laying on a black sand beach.

They looked all around the dead chamber, too shocked to say a thing. Then they saw a boat coming out of the mist. Someone was rowing slowly toward them. The figure wore a long robe, and it had a hood that covered most of its head. The boat reached the Shore of Nothingness, and it was then that they saw the skeletal face, hands, and feet of Helishious. They both screamed and passed out again. Helishious laughed at the two unconscious women as he walked onshore. This happened every time he brought a woman through the doorway to his lifeless world and they saw him for the first time. He had done this many times before over the centuries. He liked company, and it was always a woman (men he had no use for).

He meant no real harm. He just liked to talk to his visitors, catch up on their, and the new world's, current events, and if they became completely unglued, then *that* was a bonus. Being rewarded with that extra pot of gold at the end of his colorless rainbow happened 100 percent of the time. He never got tired of their frightful expressions, and he took great pride in calming them down and taking control of their emotions. When they all came to, he would talk in a soothing voice for a while about life in their chamber, and then offer them an ultimatum. They would have to choose. Their choice was completely up to them, and they always chose the same.

The two women came to, and Helishious told them where they were, and why they were here. He informed both that he was lonely, and would not harm them. He told them to just stay calm, and everything would be all right. They were, of course, completely afraid and uncertain, but then the calmness in this creature's voice soothed them some. Their nerves settled, and all three sat on the beach and talked about life in the modern world. Helishious wanted to know how life was changing; he needed to keep up on the current events. It never ceased to amaze him how life in the new world was evolving, moving forward. New inventions were being made, things he just couldn't fathom. He began to think man was capable of creating anything he wanted. Helishious figured he would use those creations to his advantage when the time was right.

When he had finished learning everything he could from them, he gave them his ultimatum: They could stay here with him in this world and learn about his lifeless chamber and all his worldly travels, or they could go back through the mirror to their own world. He laughed heartily when they both quickly chose to go back to their own chamber and life. He told them they would have to take a ride in his boat to a certain spot, look at their reflections, and dive into them. They readily agreed, and so all three got into his boat and rowed with his long oar about a mile out into the Sea of Sorrows. The women saw many small islands in the distance, and they asked what was on those islands. Ah, he told them, shaking a skeletal finger playfully at them, if they wanted to know what was on those islands, then they would have to stay. They didn't, of course, and he laughed some more. He rowed a little further, and then told them to look over the side. They did, and then so did he. All three of their reflections now looked back at them. Helishious then quickly grabbed them both by the back of their necks and dove over the side, taking them with him. They both screamed and passed out again after they hit the water, but they were, in reality, passing through the large mirror in the master bedroom in the Marlow mansion. Helishious released his hold on their necks, and then he quickly went back through the mirror without even looking back at them. They had used up their usefulness.

The two women came to a few minutes later. They didn't look at each other. They moved as if in a trance. Becky got into her bedclothes, got into her bed, and was asleep in seconds. Virginia walked slowly and quietly down the hall to her bedroom and did the same. Nobody saw or heard them. Within the next ten minutes they both began to age very quickly, until they looked like the figures that John Marlow found dreaming in eternal sleep. Helishious went back to his world and rowed back to shore laughing. The joke was on them. If they had decided to stay here with him, they would have lived forever, never aging a day. What they didn't know was that once they entered this lifeless chamber and went back to their own world, they would age rapidly in minutes. He didn't know why they aged, but they always did. He guessed that it maybe had something to do with the doorway, but he wasn't sure. Maybe all the days and years from the old chamber were added to their young ages in their own one. Anything was possible. The presence that was on the way might be able to give him an answer, so he would wait patiently. The joke was definitely on them, though. It always was. Helishious began to walk the beach of the dead and think about what he had learned.

On a starless night after Becky and Virginia Marlow were

buried, Helishious came to visit them to make sure that they had, indeed, died. He always needed to bear witness to his dark and sinister deeds. He used the reflection of the small pond on the estate as a doorway. He almost felt regret for their demise. He had liked both of them more than most. He could only talk to all of his visitors in his present physical state, and this time it was a good thing, because if he was human form he would have raped them both repeatedly before catching up on the evolving world of the living.

He was staring at the two headstones when he heard a noise. A man was walking slowly toward him. He was carrying something. As the man got closer Helishious realized it was John Marlow. Helishious hid in the shadows and watched in fascination as the master of this land threw a rope over a large branch of an old tree near the headstones and hung himself. He watched as the man struggled, and Helishious moved in front of him, staring up into the man's condemned eyes. John Marlow stared back at the skeletal figure in disbelief as he gasped for air. He saw the hooded figure smirk up at him and whisper loud enough to hear, "They are dead because of me. Because of meeeee."

John Marlow stopped breathing, and his body slowly relaxed. His eyes froze in place, and his body became still. He had released himself from his tormented agony, but the vision of the skeleton man still silhouetted behind his pupils. He took the snarl of Helishious's hooded skeletal face to his grave. John's last thought as he left this world was, "God help me."

Helishious visited the Marlow Estate on a few occasions. Something drew him to the place, and after Daniel and Jessica hung themselves in the servant bathroom he knew why. Their spirits were trapped inside the house that housed the black slaves. Helishious could see them as they floated around the second floor aimlessly. They saw him but weren't repulsed by him in any way.

They just smiled and kept on moving. Helishious thought they were probably constantly looking for a way out. Helishious knew better. They were here until a higher power decided to release them. He thought hard and telepathically asked them what had happened to them. Telepathically they answered back and told him. He nodded and left.

He came back after a time and the servant ghost house was no longer there. It was somewhere; he could feel their spirits in the distance, and if anything, their presence felt stronger. Something had changed. He followed it until he found the house by the sea, only when he entered there were many more ghosts floating around, including Marlow people and children. They told him their story. He nodded and left. He somehow felt pity for the ghosts, and he pitied no one.

Helishious went to the constable's house late at night while the policeman was sleeping and put his right skeletal hand on his forehead. Helishious had many talents. He could read thoughts of others while they were sleeping by way of touch. He found out everything—what had happened and who was responsible. Helishious smiled, nodded, and then put both his index fingers to each ear and pushed them all the way in, piercing the man's brain. He snapped those skeleton fingers off and left them inside the Constable's ears. That kept the blood from running out of them. A little blood ran out of the man's nose, but that wouldn't matter. The policeman's brain was hemorrhaging, and he was dying slowly. He would be dead by morning but until then he would dream hideous and constant nightmares. Two new index fingers grew back in seconds, and the dead man left the bedroom. Justice for the ghosts had been done here.

A new constable would have to be elected; the old one had gone sour. Helishious appeared in Arnold Marlow's mansion and woke up the top man of the family. Arnold tried to scream but

Helishious had put his middle skeletal finger to his lips, freezing his face and vocal cords. He told Arnold that he was going to die slowly and painfully. Helishious smiled menacingly down at the petrified man and stuck his left skeletal hand (as if it was transparent) inside Arnold's chest. He broke the hand off at the wrist with a sickening snap, and then another skeletal hand began to grow. The hand inside Arnold began to squeeze his heart, causing him excruciating pain. The hand then released its grip, and the pain stopped. But that was only for a moment, for the hand began to squeeze again, only a little harder. The pain was greater as well. This went on for hours, and when the sun began to rise the hand finally squeezed hard enough to stop Arnold's agonized heart completely. Helishious's hand dissolved into Arnold's heart and disappeared forever.

Helishious himself stood off to the side and watched the painful torture take place. He loved every minute of this. He was a born sadist of the worst kind. He couldn't be reasoned with; he just got off on torture and pain—life-ending pain, such as with Arnold. Every so often he would bend over and whisper in Arnold's ear that when he finally died, he was going to the fires of hell, and new and exotic pain would replace the agony he was feeling now. Helishious didn't know if that was true or not, but the effect of his words hit home hard. Arnold was actually beyond hell by the time he died, and Helishious thought it poetic justice.

He went back to the servant house and told the ghosts what he had done. They were all still trapped in the structure and didn't seem to care. They just wanted release from this purgatory. They had been robbed of their lives and forbidden to follow a path home to the next realm. Helishious understood and went back to his lifeless world. He never visited the ghosts of the servant house again and didn't know they had been released until the power went out. Helishious did not care, for he had new and more important business to attend to.

So now more light has been shone on the mysterious skeletal Helishious, and the lifeless and dead world he calls his domain. His character is complex to say the least, and his talents seem to be endless, given to him by an unknown dark force that he was still to meet—but that would come.

So, dear reader, beware whenever you are looking at yourself in a mirror; remember he may be looking back at you on the other side. He might want to ask you some questions and spend some time, time that will end up being very short for you, unless you decide to stay with him in his forgotten chamber. My advice to you is don't choose to stay. It might be a fate much worse than death itself. It might be, but that is your choice. So now this bedtime story at this time is over, and if you can, I hope you have pleasant dreams. That is, if you can sleep at all.

Chapter Twenty-Four

THE EGG

*B*ronson Island is a small, rectangular, two-mile radius, man-made island off the coast of Southern California that at one time was used for oil drilling. The island is built on a large sandbar five miles off the coast of Santa Barbara and up until the power went off was used for something else. That something else had been kept secret for five years. The U.S. Government owned the island, and a secret scientific operations team was stationed there. Also, on the island was U.S. Military personnel, and for good reason. Something on that island demanded security, and constant attention. The island was surrounded by three U.S. Military ships. They were there in case the situation went south, and as one day followed another that could have become a realistic possibility. Tension filled the region, for everyone there was in unchartered waters, no pun intended. Here is that island's story.

For years Bronson Oil had been drilling off the Pacific Coastline on a man-made island the company created. The island itself was rectangular in shape and built on pilings that went down about fifty feet. Large inflated floats surrounded the island to hold it steady. Dead palm trees also surrounded the island, creating a wall around the complete complex, going down from ten to fifteen feet. They protected the structure and the five buildings from turbulent seas. Floats were positioned underneath the trees and anchored to the ocean floor.

The buildings were one story structures made of solid concrete. They were square shaped, with small windows on each side. All the drilling apparatus was located in the middle until the drilling was stopped and the government took over. Docks were built on the complete east side of the island next to the buildings, where five military boats were moored.

On the day that the drilling stopped for good a small earthquake measuring 4.5 struck the coastline, and the ocean floor thirty feet around the drill collapsed and fell another twenty feet. Cameras showed something circular and white in color in the fallen ocean rock and sand floor. The object was estimated to be about the size of a basketball, and egg shaped. Government officials were alerted, and divers deployed. The object was put in a large metal box and brought to the surface. As soon as the box was out of the ocean it began to get warm. In a couple of minutes, it was too hot to handle. The metal began to melt until it liquified! The egg-shaped object was left but it had turned fire orange in color, and everybody warily moved away from it. It lay on dirt so nothing else burned or melted, but it could not be touched.

It stayed that way for two months, and in that time period all the Bronson employees were removed, with the scientific government team replacing them. A glass structure was constructed around the egg, and even though none of the team thought they could contain it, an alarm system was installed in the glass and would warn the team if anything changed. The structure itself was ten feet squared and five feet high. Twenty cameras were placed around the object, and it was monitored constantly. Security was set on high alert, and the egg became the biggest secret of the day. Everyone that knew about the object that worked for Bronson Oil was quarantined back in Santa Barbara with no communication with their families. They were kept in a secret bunker right up until the power went out. They never saw their families or anybody else again. Back on the island the egg became a complete mystery.

The glass structure had a six-by-three-foot door, and a primitive robot with a protective suit went inside to conduct experiments, but as soon as it got close to the egg it began to heat up. It became so hot that part of the robot's suit and hand melted away and had to be replaced. The robot was forced to keep its distance after that, and the research limited. The team became frustrated, but the government became edgy and highly nervous, which meant that they would become unpredictable. Three military vessels surrounded the island and the team was told to further proceed with much caution. Central intelligence was smart enough to know that things could go very wrong at any moment, the plug would be pulled, and the situation rectified. In the worst-case scenario, the scientific team would become collateral damage—expendable pieces of a chess game they weren't sure they could win, or worse, finish.

One day the head of the team, Dr. Charles Gathers, was walking outside the glass enclosure. The egg was pulsating like a human heart. It had started doing that when the robot first entered the enclosure. He stared at it intently when it suddenly spoke to him.

"Hello, Dr. Gathers," It said in a low, deep, hollow voice. "Thank you for freeing me from my dilemma down in your ocean. I am very grateful. I was down there a long time."

A marine walked by and nodded at the doctor and kept on going. He never even gave the object a second look.

"No, Dr. Gathers, he can't hear me. Only you can. I am projecting my voice only to you. I would have talked to you sooner, but I had to learn your language first. For that I am sorry, for I know you are curious about me."

Dr. Gathers looked around nervously. The marine that had passed him stood off to the side, staring at the object. He lit a cigarette and inhaled deeply. Another soldier stood on the other side of the enclosure. He smiled and nodded at him, and then looked off into the ocean. The sun was setting, and another great sunset was about to occur. This marine hadn't heard the object speak, either. The egg had spoken loud enough for both men to hear, yet they never reacted to it.

"Please believe me, Dr. Gathers, I only wish to talk to you. The others will act irrationally, and then I would be forced to disable them, and I do not wish to react in that manner."

"Who . . . who are you?" Dr. Gathers asked nervously, his hands beginning to shake. He looked around but the marines still didn't react, not even to him talking.

"You don't realize it, but you are talking to me telepathically, just like I am to you," It replied. "You are speaking to me without moving your lips, even though you think you are talking normally. To your question, I am from another place in another time. I am the last of my species. I do not know what I am, but we called ourselves Durontuerals. The closest word in your language with which I can describe myself to you is 'brain.' I am a brain, but I am much more. Your Einstein in your history books was called a genius, but he would be considered retarded, or mindless, to my kind."

"Do you mean to harm us in any way?"

"No, but I will protect myself. I will not be touched. We trusted before and now only I am left," It replied sadly. "We experienced what you call evil, it was cunning, and unbelievably outthought us. We did not think that possible, but it destroyed everyone except me. I do not know why I was spared and was able to escape through the great divide, but I did and ended up here."

"How long have you been here?" Dr. Gathers asked, digesting what this creature was telling him. He had no reason to, but he believed what it was telling him. He also believed that this creature could wipe them all out if it wanted to, and it hadn't so far.

"I am timeless, Dr. Gathers. I do not know how to answer this question," It replied, sounding tired and fatigued. "I can only tell you that I am older than this chamber, or what you call your universe. In my journey of escapement, I lost most of my powers and energies, and that is why I was entrapped in your sea. I do not know if I will regain them."

"But why here? Why, out of all the places you could go, why did you end up here?"

"I do not know," It replied, sounding somewhat frustrated. The object became still. "But coming here was beyond my control. Something brought me here; I do not know what. I am tired now. Talking telepathically drains what I have left. We will talk again."

"Please wait, I have more questions—many more, in fact."

"In time, Dr. Gathers, in time."

"OK, OK. What should I call you? Do you have a name?"

The object was quiet for a moment, and then it replied, "Call me Future, Dr. Gathers. I live for what's in front of me, so it is logical to be called that. Now I must rejuvenate, Doctor. We will talk again."

And then the aura changed. The air became lighter, and the scientist's ears painlessly popped. Dr. Gathers nodded at the two marines, who appeared oblivious to any type of conversing between he, and what would now be referred to as Future, and he went back to his office. The sun had set, and stars began to fill the sky. The moon slowly rose in the east as a new day rapidly approached—a day that would be very different than all others.

During that night Dr. Gathers dreamed a lot. He tossed and turned, and moaned "No, no" over and over. The reason: the object known as Future entered his head and showed him visions. From where Future physically was in the glass enclosure, large veins pulsated wildly. The guards watching it at night noticed what was happening but were frozen in place. They couldn't move a muscle and couldn't yell out to anybody. They watched on helplessly as the object continued to spasm. The veins seemed to change colors of all shades as they bulged in and out. It looked like a small Christmas tree, with its lights blinking on and off on a rhythmically constant basis.

As Dr. Charles Gathers slept, Future's world was shown to him, as well as what happened. It was a reddish planet that looked a lot like Mars, yet completely different. In the sky there were five suns that radiated orange and red rays that warmed the planet. It had rivers of yellow liquid that flowed through a desert of lifeless desolation.

In Future's visions, Doctor Gathers was shown a large shadow moving with purpose toward large mountains in the distance. The object that made the shadow was flying high above him. He couldn't make out what it was, but the doctor could feel it vibrating high in the sky over his head. It was huge and menacing. Future told him in his subconscious mind that this presence had murdered all of his kind in a matter of seconds! The doctor understood that Future had luckily been underground in the northern caves when the creature invaded its world. Future distinctly heard a voice in its mind telling him to remain motionless. The others were then shown to the doctor. They were objects that looked similar to Future, scattered across the landscape. A few were whole, but most had been torn to pieces. Those pieces seemed to go on forever, and Future told the doctor that there were many more of its kind on its planet than there were humans beings here on Earth. Future informed the doctor that its planet had been twice the size of Jupiter in this current solar system, yet life of all kind was wiped out so quickly that Future was scared for the first time in its existance. Being afraid had never been experienced by any of his kind. They lived in a peaceful environment, a kind of utopia. Violence was not present in any form. Bliss, peace, and actual love filled its community, yet this presence had quickly taken all of that away.

The next vision that the scientist was shown was an angry electrical storm that seemed to follow in the wake of the large shadow. The landscape began to crumble and fall away quickly. Future told the doctor that his planet was being totally destroyed by this storm. The ground around Future fell away, and it began to fall into nothingness. Future then drifted out into a dark space that had once housed many suns. They were all gone in an instant, but Future could feel the presence everywhere around it. It felt like sickness, or disease, a terminal infection. Future felt the presence move toward it, closing in. It knew Future was near. Future saw physical tentacles move toward him—slippery, humungous appendages that housed cancers that could not even begin to be cured. Just before they reached Future a strong current took it into another space, another universe. Future showed the doctor the planets in this solar system as it sped by.

Future crashed violently into the ground that would one day be called California and was buried in Earth's inner solid-rock core. It couldn't move or see anything around it, but it heard fluids move above. Future told the doctor that time passed slowly, but every now and then the rock around it would shake, shift, and move. Future was still trapped, but it moved much distance in the rock over time. Future felt no life around it for many years, but eventually it sensed movement on this planet. That movement built and built until this moment, or "The Now." And then it told Dr. Gathers something that the scientist did *not* want to hear: as soon as Future was brought out of the ocean and onto this landmass, it felt the presence that had destroyed Future's world and its surroundings. It was very far away but it was definitely coming closer; Future could sense it.

The doctor woke up shaking and sweating profusely. He looked at his watch and it said one o'clock in the afternoon! How could that be? That was impossible! He never slept past six in the morning, yet he had. He felt a quietness around him—there was no power. All electrical equipment in his room was dark. Puzzled, he quickly dressed in shorts and a T-shirt and walked outside. Nobody was walking around; nobody could be seen. No birds flew above his head, and they were *always* up there, crying out as they fought for scraps, huddled around the garbage area. He wasn't alone, though. Future was still behind the glass structure, vibrating wildly.

"Yes, Dr. Gathers, I am still here," Future said evenly. "But everyone and everything else around this land mass is gone."

"What . . . what happened?"

"I do not know." Future replied. "I was in your dreams, yet I saw and felt everything leave. Your power supply is off as well. There is no current here."

Dr. Gathers frantically looked all around and realized Future was right. He looked at his watch and it still said one o'clock. It had stopped! He searched the entire island but there was no sign of life. He looked out into the Pacific and all three military ships had floated many miles away from the island. He was alone, totally alone—with Future.

He went back to the creature and stared as the glass enclosure fell away and Future began to grow legs like a spider, ten in all.

Each were about two feet long, one foot thick, and flexible, each ending in a sharp point. It moved over the glass and stopped two feet in front of the scientist. The doctor couldn't move or speak; he was frozen in place. His nerves were working, though, and he was frightened beyond belief. He silently prayed for his life and soul, for he felt he might lose both.

"I have paralyzed you until we talk, Dr. Gathers," Future said, pulsating again. Its legs twitched with their new growth and ability to walk. "I will not harm you, but I know I frighten you, and I don't want you to act irrationally. Before I release you, you need to be calm. This is how my species looked back on my planet. If it helps, your appearance scares me just as much as I frighten you. That glass enclosure helped both of us in the same manner. We both fear each other's appearances, but I don't fear you any longer. I now only want to survive with you. We are on the same side. Are we . . . cool?"

"Yes, Future," Dr. Gathers replied. The scientist knew he had no choice, but those leg appendages definitely unnerved him.

"Good, I am glad. I like you and want to trust you. Can I release you now? Will you stay calm?"

"Ye . . . yes. I'm OK, or as good as I'm going to be."

The doctor felt himself being released. He slumped to the ground and breathed heavily, staring at what now looked like a spiderlike creature. He knew he really didn't have a choice, anyway. He just hoped that Future was telling the truth.

The sun was setting, and lights could be seen on the mainland. They had power. Maybe people, too.

"Yes, Dr. Gathers, they have power, but not for long. My presence effects time to some degree. Here on this island we are seven Earth days ahead of everywhere else, but they will catch up to us quickly now," Future said calmly. "Something has happened that has never happened before. In three of your twenty-four-hour days the same thing will happen everywhere else. Nothing will stop it. We must stay here until it does; then we can decide to leave."

"OK, Future," Dr Gathers replied, nodding and staring at the mainland. "OK. I will do as you ask."

And that is what they did. Future and Dr. Gathers talked for the next three days, getting comfortable with one another. They talked about the future and the past. They talked about Future's fateful world, and the dark presence that Future still felt. The lights on the mainland finally went out on the third day, and the two of them got into a lifeboat and Dr. Gathers rowed toward shore. Thankfully the waters were calm, and the tide was in their favor.

Chapter Twenty-Five

GENERAL SHERMAN

There is a tree called General Sherman located in the giant forest of Sequoia National Park in Tulare County, California. It is the largest single-stem tree on Earth. It is close to 350 feet tall, the girth at breast height is over 90 feet and 135 feet near the ground. It is also one of the oldest trees as well, possibly over three thousand years old. The tree is named after General William Tecumseh Sherman of the Civil War. It has weathered the test of time, standing tall even before Jesus Christ walked the Earth. It was here before Christopher Columbus discovered America and the United States established. It is older than all the Western history of its country, but when the power went out, without a sound, it disappeared like so many people and animals that went home. Where it went no one knows, but it was the only tree that disappeared during the Event. A large hole remained in its place, surrounded by fellow giant Sequoia trees that had been its neighbors for many, many years.

Chapter Twenty-Six

THE MUSICAL BOX ONE

*L*et's retreat into the past once again.

In the mid 1800s there was a small village in western Pennsylvania called Utopiaville. It lay in a heavily wooded area, off the beaten path, and was not located on any map. Ten families lived there, forty-five souls in all. They were peaceful people who went to worship in the small church in the center of town every day at noon. They were not religious fanatics but loved to praise Jesus Christ daily and reconnect with His Word. They were self-sufficient and stayed to themselves, only using the next town's mail post for mail and packages, most of them religious.

They made no enemies and were friendly with anyone and everyone they encountered. They grew vegetables and potatoes and stored enough of them in the one barn they built together to survive the cold winters. They were vegetarians who didn't believe in killing animals for consumption, or for any other reason. They valued all life and felt that by consuming any wildlife would make their souls and physical bodies impure. They were ahead of their time, which meant everyone else thought they were odd at best. They weren't a cult, just offering a different lifestyle, complete with new ideas and values. Their goal was to find the spiritual road to complete righteous salvation and to rid themselves of hate, selfishness, gluttony, or any other negative force that tried to block that positive religious journey.

On June 6 of 1866 they were all found dead by the local constable and his two deputies. No one ever found out what really happened, or whatever folklore was believable, but mass suicide was ruled out. No one ever lived there again, and trees and brush eventually overtook the entire village. The buildings and cabins have decayed over the years, and the church completely fell apart.

Something bad happened there, bad enough for others to avoid and abandon a village that was built on love, peace, devotion, and harmony. Here is that community's story.

In the fall of 1865 in late October Robert Silas did what he always did. After the noon church service, he rode his horse Dillion five miles to the mail post in Mittletown. He loved picking up the mail; it was his "me" time, and he and Dillion could ride like the wind, which the horse seemed to love just as much. Robert also loved talking and meeting new townsfolk once he got into town. He was an extrovert, young and full of life. At twenty-five years of age with Jesus Christ on his side, the sun shined on even the gloomiest of days—not this one, though.

This glorious day it was unseasonably warm, almost like August. He rode into town and picked up the mail, which consisted of only a few thin pamphlets (today's junk mail), and a rectangular box the size of a shoebox wrapped in brown paper. It was addressed to Father John Browne. Nothing unusual, but if Robert had looked more closely, he would have noticed that there was a stamp on the package that was foreign to normal American postage, maybe to any country's postage.

As he left town a figure watched him until he disappeared down the dirt road. He was a tall, muscular man with a full beard and long wavy black hair that fell to his broad shoulders. Once Robert was completely out of sight, he mounted a black horse and rode out of town in the opposite direction. As he rode past the last building in Mittletown he was smiling, and as his horse galloped toward the dense, dark woodlands he was laughing.

Robert gave the package and pamphlets to Father Browne and sat down in the front pew. He was curious and watched intently as the minister unwrapped the box and opened it. It was a musical box.

Music boxes were new at that time, invented thirty years prior to this date, but this one looked extremely old—ancient, even. It was gold in color, and had flowers engraved around its lid. Those designs look old as well.

Father Browne opened the music box and it played a tune neither of them knew, but they both agreed it seemed ancient in sound and texture. Father John closed the lid and put it on the top shelf inside the pulpit, along with the pamphlets. He studied the handwriting on the brown paper and frowned. The style was unusual, the ink a reddish color he had never seen before. He wondered who would send this to him, so the next day he went to the Mittletown mail post himself to investigate, but the postmaster had no idea where the package had come from.

Father John frowned as he stood outside. He rarely left Utopiaville; he felt out of place whenever he was outside its boundaries, and for valid reasons. The people here didn't see to smile very much, and they didn't seem all that happy. They didn't radiate spiritual purity, so they seemed dark and totally alien to him. This musical box, he figured, came from someone like them, and that was bad karma, so when he got back to Utopiaville he put it in his church office closet on the top shelf. There was something unsettling about it and the tune it played, so keeping it away from his flock would be best for all concerned—out of sight, out of mind. That decision ended up being the worst of his life, and the beginning of the end for the small village.

Father John Browne was fifty-four years old, one of the elders who lived in Utopiaville. He had started this little community with lifelong friend Michael Brookens twenty years prior, with the idea to congregate with people who believed in the Lord Jesus Christ and wanted to live a positive, loving lifestyle. They bought forty acres of woodland and cleared half of it for a church and surrounding buildings and cabins, all made out of the trees that had been cut down. Nothing ever went to waste, and these fallen trees would house his followers and hopefully their descendants for years to come. His motto was: "Always move things forward, and never look back or live in the past, unless it is beneficial."

Little by little the community grew, working together like a perfectly oiled machine. They were an extended family, they were happy, and all the negative aspects of life were kept out of their little world. It *was* Utopia, or as close to it as it could be. People still died, that was inevitable, and Michael Brookens unfortunately was one of them. In 1858, he had a massive heart attack while dining with Father Browne on Easter Sunday, and was buried in the small cemetery behind the cabins. Fifteen people were buried there when the musical box entered Utopiaville, and more deaths would follow—many more.

Father John had a wife, Joan. They had met in Utopiaville and had been married in a small ceremony ten years before the musical box came to visit. She was fifteen years younger than the pastor, but they were best friends and very much in love. She was very beautiful, had long blonde hair, and full figured. Father John considered himself very lucky. He prayed every night, telling the Lord how grateful he was, usually with tears in his eyes.

They went to bed on the night the musical box was put on the shelf and slept peacefully until 3:00 a.m. That was when the lid on the relic opened and it began to play its haunting tune, over and over, for an hour. Then it stopped playing and the lid slowly closed. That would've been fine except for two things.

The first was when the musical box opened many small, dark gray, wormlike creatures with heads like dragons, possessing sharp, vicious-looking teeth and blood-red, menacing eyes moved around and caressed the casing of the relic. Maybe they were dancing to the music, or maybe they were moved by the haunting tune, but they never stopped moving around the box until its music ended, and then they went back inside before the lid closed.

The second was when the music started playing in the middle of the night Father John Browne began to dream. They weren't normal nightmares, just grusome and horrifying, and he experienced them until the music stopped playing and the worm-like creatures crawled back inside the relic, the lid closing shut behind them.

At 4:00 a.m. when the musical box stopped playing Father John woke up screaming. His wife woke with a start and stared at her husband, grabbing his shoulders. He looked back in horror and held her tight, the two of them rocking back and forth. When he calmed down he told her about his nightmares, and neither one of them slept a wink for the rest of the night.

When the sun came up Father Browne went into the church office, and with pen and paper in hand, decided to write down what he'd dreamt. He felt that it might be important to do so. Below is the first of his Periodicals.

October 31, 1865

I, Father John Browne, am writing this journal

for positive use only. The Lord Jesus Christ will hopefully oversee these words I write and help me in all ways. Last night I had some terrible nightmares, and in my opinion, they were all considered totally evil visions. In our community we preach all good and positive thoughts, so having dreams of such wrongness went against the grain of Utopiaville. In my dreams I saw great fires burning the woods around us, entrapping us. I called out to my flock, but no one was there. I ran from cabin to cabin but found not one brother or sister. Then I heard noises coming from the church and ran inside. What I saw went beyond comprehension. All the townsfolk were gathered around the pulpit, moaning and groaning. They were all without clothes and lustfully intertwined, in orgy fashion. What I saw went beyond total lewdness. There were men on women, men on men, women on women, even men and women with children coupling by the altar. I was frozen in place, and watched as they continually changed partners. I called out for them to stop but they completely ignored me. I looked around for my dear wife Joan but could not find her at first, but then she appeared in the pulpit. She was without clothes as well, and was screaming, for behind her stood an unknown tall man, and he was whipping her extremely hard with a thick whip. She was yelling for more and he hit her harder and harder. I again yelled for everyone to stop but they continued to ignore me.

Suddenly from behind me large hideous snakes and pythons encircled my legs, curling up and embracing my complete body. They ate my clothes off and then beyond my control I slowly moved toward the orgy, insanely screaming. My hands had changed to large knives, and I began slicing my devoted flock to pieces. Blood ran everywhere, and my congregation began to drink their blood and become whole again. I repeated my slicing of their bodies and they drank again. I looked up and saw my wife being taken sexually from behind by the tall stranger whose face remained hidden. Their coupling and moans of passion drove me to new heights of madness. I again began driving my sword hands into the faces of my flock. Meanwhile, the fires from the woods caressed the church walls and entered into its sanctuary. My wife began screaming as the fires engulfed her and the tall man, and then they disappeared inside the flames. Their moans didn't stop though; in fact, if anything, their groans of passion intensified. The fires surrounded and engulfed us all before I woke up screaming.

As you can imagine, my wife was awakened immediately and consoled me until I calmed. She told me that it was all a bad nightmare, and I should pray to God on it. As soon as I finish putting down these words that's exactly what I'll do. Jesus, I pray please be with me in these trials and tribulations of darkness and viciousness. In God I trust.

Father John Browne, faithful spiritual leader of Utopiaville

A week went by without incident, and like all dreams and nightmares the ones that Father John had began to fade away and become somewhat forgotten. They were still on paper in a journal in his office desk, and he would never forget them, but they weren't reality; they were all in his mind and not real. That was the main thing. Life continued in the community as usual, and positiveness reigned throughout the village, so Father John pushed his dreams back into their own infected darkness. That didn't last for long, though.

Sundays were always considered the Lord's day in Utopiaville, and different types of church services were held all day long. Sunday school was held from ten to eleven thirty in the morning for all children. The main service went from noon to two, where Father John gave his weekly hour-long sermon. A community lunch was held between two thirty to three thirty, where the main sermon was discussed and dissected, and then adult Sunday School concluded the spiritual sabbath, from four to five thirty. After that groups split up for Sunday dinner and relaxation. Just about the whole community took part in these Sunday marathons, so you can just imagine how exhausted they were by the time the sun disappeared behind the western tree line, Father John included. Normally candles in all the cabins were all out by ten o'clock on the sabbath. They all agreed a good night's sleep prepared them for a brand new week of productive work and service.

Father John kissed his wife good night and they were both asleep within minutes. He had a peaceful night until—you guessed it—3:00 a.m., when the musical box opened and began playing its sinister tune. The wormlike creatures again slithered out and did their caressing dance around the box casing, only now they had many little legs on each side that helped them move faster. They also now had five distinct segmented parts that pulsated to the beat of the musical box's song.

NARRATIVE NOTES: If one could witness this all take place, one would be driven into complete madness. We all talk about the supernatural; authors write books, directors make movies, and there are programs on science fiction channels today but in the end we all discard it as creative fallacy. It's not real, it's not reality, we've never seen such creatures, therefore they can't exist. We would be wrong, of course, and that was what was happening here. The supernatural exists in the shadows of the shadows and in dark, vacant desolate zones in most cases. That is why we subconsciously fear the night and dark places, like one's cold damp basement. Unknown and unseen species live and survive there, only sometimes some are more severe—or worse, dangerous. This was such the case in Utopiaville, in the church's office closet, and now these lifeforms were growing. Angry storm clouds were swirling into place above the small spiritual community, and no one on the right side of God could see them, but they were beginning to *feel* them.

The dreams Father John had this time were different, but they produced the same shocking effects. His screams were coated with despair, for he thought that his nightmares of wrongness would not return, and now he knew that he had been wrong—oh, so wrong. His wife again had to comfort him until he calmed down, and again neither one of them could get back to sleep for the rest of the night.

Let us return to the pastor's journal for more information on his interrupted nocturnal slumber. His handwriting would became shakier as time went on, and his thoughts become more manic and desperate as one day wove into another.

November 10, 1865, and after...

My nightmares returned last night with a vengeance. I do not know how so many wrong and negative thoughts could reside inside the bowels of my mind, but they obviously do. I somehow must cleanse my spirit and soul, so I no longer have such vulgar visions. I must search for the light beams for assistance to keep the darkness from invading my thoughts. God, I pray for your help on this matter. Please hear my plea.

My nightmares begin with my good and best friend, Michael Brookens. A lot of the ideas and plans for Utopiaville came from him. I was the spiritual part of the plan, but he was the brains. His creative force powered this place; he is more Utopiaville than anybody, me included. I was thinking of renaming the village to Brookens in his memory and name (and I had a lot of support from the community on that idea), but then I remembered Michael never liked to take any credit for anything he did, so in his memory I DIDN'T go through on the name change. God rest his soul. His spirit is still here, but not in this dream.

In this nightmare he dug his way out of his grave and knocked on my door. I opened it and Michael stood there grinning—or should I say what was left of him. He was mostly skeletal in appearance, and his left eye was missing, but he was still wearing the clothes he was buried in. They were dirty now, and chunks of mud hung from the dark blue suit that he had worn every Sunday at church. In his bony hand he held a large live rat, and it was franticly trying to get free from my good friend's grip. Michael brought the rodent to his mouth and bit into its belly. He chewed and swallowed it, and skin began to grow on my dead friend. The rat squealed and squealed in shocked pain. Michael took another bite, and then another. The rat fought to the end, but it eventually stopped moving. It hung loosely in my best friend's skeletal hand, and then Michael Brookens gobbled down the rest of his ghoulish meal, bones and all. My best friend grew more skin and muscle and looked like his old self again, but I could sense something different about him, something out of place. I know my friend, and he would never in a million years eat meat of any kind, yet here I had watched in horror as he ate a live rodent.

I heard a noise behind him and noticed for the first time that there was a trail of white maggots following him, and beyond that I saw my complete flock lying dead on the ground. They had been eaten, their blood and insides lay everywhere. It was a horrible scene, especially when it involves your devoted parishioners, and it turned and twisted my insides.

Michael laughed insanely as he told me that human flesh was the best tasting meat. I tried to scream, for this creature was nothing like the good, honest, and pure man I knew, but again, I was frozen in place, unable to move. He moved toward me and bit into my cheek, ripping it off. I don't know if you can actually feel pain in a dream, but in this abomination, I felt agony. Michael acted like a deranged savage, biting into me again and again, literally eating me alive, like he had with everyone else in the village. Maggots began to crawl through my exposed bones, tendons, and nerves, and they felt like burning poison ivy that itched badly.

A tall dark figure with no face appeared behind Michael, and its presence had an aura of terminal, diseased infection, tenfold worse than what I envisioned cancer to be. This presence radiated death, and it terrified me. Michael then ate both my eyes, and I saw no more. I was in total darkness, but I was still able to feel, although I wish I was unable to possess that sense. As Michael continued to devour me, I could feel the dark presence move inside my bones and caress my soul, darkening it. I was suddenly able to see again, but I was looking through eyes that weren't my own. My body turned around and those foreign eyes saw my wife standing there, smiling. "Eat me," she said passionately, taking off her clothes. All over her torso maggots started coming out of her pores, and they all hissed at my remains. I was revolted at the sight of her, but I still moved toward her and began to eat; with each bite I craved eating more and more of her, and so I ate. I knew I was not myself anymore, I was part of the polluted disease that had invaded me. I heard a cracking sound above me and felt another Being approaching. What I saw through those alien eyes fractured my soul . . . and that was when I woke up. I cannot put down in words what I thought I saw, but I know that if I tried to, I would be condemned to damnation for all of eternity. God help me!

The sun came up like it always does, but my mind was completely clouded over. My wife tried to console me, but I felted violated emotionally; I felt spiritually exposed and used. At the noon service at best I went through the motions, feeling unfo-cused and somewhat distracted, and my flock could clearly see that something was bothering me. After the service a few of them asked if I was OK, and I replied that it wasn't anything I couldn't work myself through. Inside, I wasn't so sure. My positiveness was being chipped away at, piece by piece. I prayed to The Lord for guidance and assistance.

I had no dreams that next night, but as I was in my church office the next morning Clyde and Emma Ross, a couple that had joined the community five years ago came to see me for help and spiritual guidance. They both had experienced bad nightmares and I clearly could see that they were badly shaken, not unlike myself. We huddled by the front pew and talked. They both had dreamed of demons from depths below even hell itself that had made them kill each other by cutting off their limbs and sexual parts. The limbless couple were both then raped by the perverted demons repeatedly, and unbelievably they liked it and begged for more. They had become something other than themselves. They cried, and I cried along with them. They were two of the happiest people that lived in Utopiaville, and here they were lost in a violent sea of dark despair. We prayed together, and we had them and their two young sons over for dinner that evening. I did not want them to be alone when the sun went down, and the nightmare goblins woke up from their sleazy slumber; I didn't want the unsettled couple to question their sanity or goodness.

That night I had Robert Silas, a single man that beamed with sunshine in his soul stay with the Ross family . He is my right-hand man in most matters, and he had no problem helping out. God Bless him. He slept in a chair outside their bedroom, but they did not have a repeat performance of the night before. They seemed better the next day, but I wondered what was going on here. An invisible negative force had stumbled into our community, and I was nervous and even a little afraid. I prayed more than I usually do. I hoped to the heavens above that my prayers would be answered. November otherwise was quiet on the dream front. The Rosses seemed fine, and I was better as well. We had an Indian summer that continued past our Thanksgiving festivities, and all seemed well; there were smiles all around. The community worked together with a renewed intensity; smiles and laughter filled the warm, mild air. God seemed to have answered my pleas. I was grateful.

But I was wrong—oh, so wrong. Halfway through December the weather took a turn southward, the temperatures dropping like a freezing stone. I wasn't sure if it was the cold temperatures or not, but I began to see some despondent faces during the noon services and the Sunday get-togethers. I did not see the normal happy faces that I was accustomed to, especially with the festive Christmas season upon us, one of the most joyous times of the year. Usually I would hear people singing religious Christmas songs as they moved about, but not so much this year. Whatever I did hear seemed to be strained and joyless, if anything. I asked a few of my flock if anything was wrong, but all they would do was shake their heads, say God was good, and their prayers would be answered. I'd nod and smile. I didn't press them on it. The Ross family was fine, but I knew that they would never forget what they had dreamed. I wouldn't forget my nightmares either.

Thankfully Christmas and the New Year went off without a hitch, but on the sixth day of January, the dark storm came back—literally. Strong winds began blowing from the northwest in the morning and the snow began falling after another lifeless noon service. It fell and fell, right through the night and into the next morning. I got dressed, pushed my front door open, and realized the snow was up to my waist—two feet at least. Our simple shovels were all we had, and we dug out that whole next day. Simple paths were dug throughout the village as usual, and of course going into town was out of the question for a while.

As I shoveled away, I noticed how quiet everybody was. Usually people would call out to each other, laugh and make fun of our snowbound predicament, always keeping things light, but not this day. The wind was still howling, it felt below zero, but still no one seemed quite right. The normal paths were shoveled, but the pep and normal happy chatter were missing. People dug listlessly at best, and as I watched them, I noticed that each shovelful seemed to be a strained chore. They seemed off-kilter, and I knew. I knew!

That night we held a late service, which was usual after a snowstorm or any other act of God. Usually when I spoke the congregation looked at me intently, trying their best to digest my spiritual message, but not this evening. Many stared into their laps or looked this way or that. Something was heavy in their hearts and thoughts, and so I asked if anybody needed to talk to me after service. Many nodded and raised their hand. Excusing the children with their mothers, we gathered together in the front pews. Good Christian men told me they were having bad dreams: evil nightmares and horrible thoughts. They were afraid to talk about them, for they were filled with "the devil's tales." One by one the men replayed their dark dreams, shivering uncontrollably as they told them.

Clive Barron was first. Everybody is afraid of things that might crawl into their ears while they are sleeping, such as ants, spiders, and the such. He was having nightmares of those things and more COMING OUT of his ears, nose, and mouth. They grew tenfold as they fell to the floor, scuttled over to his wife Mary and daughter Samantha, and began to eat them as they slept. It was horrifying at first, but by the time they were unrecognizable, Clive reluctantly admitted he was glad they were dead and laughed hysterically. (He, of course, was ashamed to admit these feelings and we prayed together, asking The Lord for forgiveness on such thoughts, and he felt a heavy weight leave him immediately.)

In turn, Clive informed me that his wife had dreamed of going into Mittleton, and there was nothing but evil demons and ugly minions running through the streets. They looked like goblins with large hands, feet, and genitalia, for they were not wearing any clothes. They were covered with thick, course black hair that wasn't exactly hair, but wormlike parasites that moved back and forth like seaweed under the sea. At the end of each hair follicle was an evil-looking mouth with tiny sharp teeth, opening and closing spasmodically. Mary told Clive that she was appalled and afraid to death at the sight of them, but as they closed in around her, she began to actually get aroused. (This he also was ashamed to tell me, as she was ashamed to tell him.) The evil creatures told her if she played right, she could claim a seat next to their all-powerful master and live eternally. She didn't need that incentive, she told them, they were all turning her on like her husband never could, so she began to give them all oral sex, their organs growing to such size that her teeth all cracked and her tongue hemorrhaged and bled as they orgasmed red hot steaming thick fluid down her burning throat, which she hungrily swallowed. All her body parts repaired themselves before the next genitalia was used.

She worked in a crazed ecstasy, and when she was finished, she was led into a tunnel that spiraled downward into a damp darkness, blinding her. That was all right, though, for the goblins said they could see clearly and would make sure she was headed in the right direction. They felt her body from head to toe as they moved on, and she climaxed repeatedly (this again she was ashamed to tell) until they approached two lit candles that burned at eye level on both sides of a bright red door. One of the demons opened the door and Mary looked inside and immediately started screaming at the top of her lungs. What she saw she immediately forgot, her mind and memories defensively shutting down, otherwise she felt her soul would have been lost forever. She remembered enough to know that what she had seen was beyond pure evil—of that she was quite sure.

The next day I prayed with Mary, and she thanked me repeatedly, but I was afraid. That presence at the end of her nightmare I could relate to. It was the opposite of our God, possibly possessing even more power and energy than our Lord, if that could be imagined. It was one that was completely negative in nature, a darkness that could blind any positive force in existence, and that was very scary.

Darryl Miller was next. His nightmare was quite different. He had been married to his wife Ruth for twenty years and been part of Utopiaville for ten of those years. Before they moved to the community, they had lost a son, Edward, to leukemia at the age of two. Horrible—no parent should ever have to lose a child. Just my opinion here, but one most God-loving people would agree with. They were devastated, and moving to Upotiaville was great therapy for both of them. Neither one of them wanted to chance having another child, so they became the greatest aunt and uncle to all the other children of our small village. They are two of my favorite people—always positive, always smiling. Darryl wasn't smiling now, though.

In his dream his son Edward, now twelve years of age, walked into town, only the leukemia was still alive and devouring un-infected cells. He looked at Darryl and said, "Look what you've done to me. I can't get away from this disease, my body refuses to die, and I'm in complete agony. Hells bells are ringing in every one of my nerve endings. You will pay dearly for this; my Lord has informed me. Yes, you will surely pay!" All of sudden Ruth appeared next to Darryl and took all her clothes off as if she was in a trance. Darryl was paralyzed in place and could not stop her from disrobing, looking on helplessly as she took off her under-garments. Her face was emotionless as she beckoned her son to come to her. He did, moving slowly and groaningly with every step.

When he reached her, she laid down on the ground and spread her legs as wide as possible, and then her son widely spread her vagina and worked his way back inside her. Darryl looked on in horror, and then Ruth began to look ill. Her skin turned pale white, her eyes became bloodshot, and her skeletal frame began to implode in on itself. She looked up at her husband, in obvi-ous pain, and said that he should've never forced himself on her (Darryl told me he didn't, which she confirmed later), otherwise their son would've been fine. She continued to look worse and worse; the cancer took her over like a deadly bacterium, and then like an overpowering tide, Darryl moved toward her opening as well and was unbelievably sucked inside her distended vagina. Inside he saw the cancer cells move toward him; they all had mouths full of razor-sharp teeth that opened and closed spasmodically. He then screamed and woke up.

Darryl was crying, and we all moved to him, comforting him. He was racked with sobs, and I silently prayed to The Lord for answers to these mind-boggling nightmares. How could a mind imagine such insidious thoughts? I know how bad he feels about his deceased son, and even though I can't imagine how badly he feels, I know he's hurting badly. I'm beginning to understand why the community has been emotionally detached lately; myself included. How can this cloud above us be dealt with? I prayed with all my soul for an answer, and I wished I didn't have to hear any more, but the others who were waiting to tell me their nightmares were looking at me pleadingly, hoping that telling their dreams would help them with their pain. God, I pray.

Allen Hines was next. He was in his bed when he was young, and his father came into his room. He was petrified, for his father Earl used to sexually abuse Allen and his two brothers, Justin and Tyler, sodomizing and beating them all on a regular basis. His wife, who also felt his wrath, finally turned him in. He went to jail and was stabbed to death by fellow inmates when they found out why he was sharing space with them: even THEY had limits. But that was in the past, and in Allen's dream he was back again, smiling evilly. He took off his clothes and beat Allen with a switch before raping him again. That was bad enough, but then Allen began liking it and begged his father for more. He was obsessed with homosexual tendencies in his dream. He cried and cried when he woke up, and he told us he felt so dirty, for he wasn't that way at all. He loved his wife Lady, and he hated what happened to him back then. He told us he felt so much better being here in this community, and he had no idea why he had dreamed something so filthy. Surely God would turn him away when his soul knocked on the gates of St. Peter. I told him that wasn't true, God loved him, but I could tell that this weight he was carrying wasn't getting much lighter.

Daniel Sayers dreamed that he was on the cross, being crucified next to Jesus Christ. He could feel the pain from the nails that were driven through his hands and feet. He and Jesus talked while they were dying, and the Son of God told him a secret. He told Daniel that there was no heaven, only hell, and that they were all headed there on a hellhound train. He said that the Bible was all a lie, and the joke was on all who believed. This demented Jesus began laughing hysterically as fires began to burn underneath their nailed ankles and bleeding feet. The flames climbed up their crosses and engulfed them as a train whistle blew in the distance. Daniel awoke screaming, and his first thoughts were to start doubting his love and devotion for God and Jesus Christ. I told him that it was all a bad dream, his nightmare was nothing but a big lie, and we would talk further on it. He nodded and told me he believed with all his heart in The Lord and Jesus Christ, but the dream had struck a chord—an out of tune chord.

Michael Murphy dreamed of being in another world that he somehow knew was dead. He had been part of a bad, devious magic trick, being locked behind a door in a big wooden box. When the door to the box reopened by itself, it opened into this dead world. He seemed to be alone, but he somehow knew he wasn't. Something lived here, and he sensed he was alone with it. This world was colored with different shades of grey without a shining sun. He was in a dark gray sand desert that went on endlessly in every direction, and the wind was howling. The wind blew the sand all around, making it hard to see very far. All of a sudden, he saw a tall dark figure moving toward him. The figure didn't move its legs but seemed to smoothly glide across the gray and desolate landscape. It was the magician who had locked him into the box in the first place, and he was smiling. He told Michael that he had run out of tricks, he couldn't take him back to Earth, and that he would be stuck in this dark, dank world. Michael became frantic, and then the world he was standing in began to fall away. There were no sounds, no cracking, no nothing. Michael fell away with the rest of the world, spiraling out of control.

He finally stopped in a darkness where he couldn't see, hear, feel, or move. And then he heard a voice in the back of his head say, "This is what death is—pitch black darkness. Silence. Your world has fallen away, and now you are underground in your new home for eternity. I believe you call it a coffin. Enjoy!" That was when Michael woke up screaming. He said he knew death would come for us all, it was unchartered territory, but now he feared it more. And now he THOUGHT about it more. That was worse. He knew death was in the back of his mind, but now it was in the front of every thought he had. He shook his head and began to weep. I put my arm around him and told him we would pray on it with The Lord. He nodded but still shook with fear.

Benjamin Drake and Donald Smith both dreamed of demigods that made them murder everyone in Utopiaville and have sex with all of the corpses. Now they felt unclean, and unholy. They thought themselves the devil's children. Even though it was only nightmares, they thought they had soiled their souls for all of eternity. I, of course, brought them both back to reality. I told them that they were good, God-abiding citizens supporting the good cause. They did not murder, and they were not necrophiliacs in any way. Council with these two would be a must.

Robert Silas was the last to speak. He bit his bottom lip nervously and looked me right in the eye. "We're all going to die soon," he said sadly, not losing eye connect. His nightmare shook me the most. He dreamed that everybody in Utopiaville was hung on various tree branches that surrounded the village. Everyone. Our hands were tied behind our backs, and we all fought and convulsed until all the life was drained from our bodies, and then became still. It didn't end there, though. Our souls were swallowed up by a darkness that radiated sickness and disease. It took us to a light, but not the kind we all hoped for. No, this light was a mean-looking orange fire that raged and shook us as our souls moved closer to it. We began to hear screams, moans, and horrid sounding screeches as the fires began to surround us. It hurdled toward us, and eventually overtook us. The burning, Robert recalled, was worse than any pain imaginable, and our screams joined many others. "This is your reward," a loud voice bellowed beyond the flames. The voice was deep and laced with malice. Robert then, of course, woke up bathed in sweat while hyperventilating. He said it seemed so real, he could still feel the agonizing burning pain and emotional hate and evil in that voice. He would never forget that! I told Robert and the rest of them that we would pray on these nightmares and do everything we humanly could to stop them. God would deliver us from this state, and we would be grateful.

Before we left the church, we prayed for a ray of hope out of this bad situation, but it didn't exactly work out that way. The nightmares did seem to subside some, but their blue mood didn't. I talked with my whole flock, and they all felt the same: violated and dirty. Despite our clouded spirits, we made it through another brutal winter and worked hard through the spring, and God was good. The weight of the storm cloud seemed to have lessened. Lord, I pray.

That was the end of Father John Browne's journal. Although the dreams and nightmares seemed to affect the community greatly, nothing in the notes pointed toward mass suicide or any murdering suspects. In fact, if anything, the writings at the end of the diary seemed to point toward life getting better; the positiveness seemed to be returning. Below are the Constable's notes from the ongoing investigation, under the heading "UTPA 101."

I sent deputy Josh Hardwick out to check on the souls of Utopiaville. I found it strange that no one had been into town or to the mail post in quite a while—maybe two weeks. I am no different than any other constable or law officer: I felt something wrong about the community lately, about the way Robert Silas had acted the last month and a half. Before he had always seemed upbeat and happy, but lately he seemed distressed about something. He didn't smile much or speak to any of the townsfolk like he usually did. That was odd, but I initially dismissed it. I thought that maybe he wasn't feeling well, or maybe a love interest had fallen apart, something to that effect. I asked him in late May if all was all right out at the community and he replied that God was taking care of them, but I still felt something out of whack, unGODlike. That was why on June 6 I sent the deputy out to see what might be out of sorts. Well, "out of sorts" was definitely an understatement!

Officer Hardwick rode back to my office and informed me that everyone in Utopiaville was dead. He was so shaken he couldn't tell me what had happened, so I called for Officer

Benjamin Winters and we both rode out to the community after leaving Officer Hardwick with Dr. Feldman. The two of us rode into Utopiaville and couldn't believe what we saw. There were upside-down crosses made of trees planted in the ground all over the tiny village and nailed to each was an upside-down body, bodies that were naked and bleeding from odd bite marks. Everybody had been beheaded, and their heads were nailed to the top of the upside-down cross their body was nailed to. Their eyes had all been removed from their sockets and were placed in their opened mouths, mouths that looked as if they had seen the devil himself. With what I was seeing here, maybe the devil's chariot had rode through the small village. All men, women, and children were in this condition. Even a newborn hung from an upside-down cross, which really turned my stomach. Its small head nailed to the top made me shutter to no end. I wondered who could do this to a life so new—so innocent.

Officer Winters was on his knees, and his lunch of sweet meats and bread was on the dirt ground in front of him. Father John Browne's body was found inside the church. He was nailed to the large cross that had hung in the front of the religious structure since it had been built, but now it hung upside down like the others outside. His head had also been cut off but was facing away from me, facing the wall. His body had been mutilated the worst. The odd bite marks covered his nude body, but his hands and feet had also been sawed off. His eyes, ears, and tongue as well. They all laid on top of the pulpit, and when I moved them into an evidence bag there was a message written in blood on the open pages of the large black Bible. It read: "Balance Has Been Restored Here."

It took six days to take all the bodies down, examine them for evidence, and then bury them. The small cemetery did not have enough room for all the residents of Utopiaville, so some of them were laid to rest in the middle of the village in front of the church and cabins. Father Alfred Smith from town held a private service for the lost souls, and then the road was roped off. No one was to enter the village limits except for law enforcement. Whoever did this unbelievable act of violence has not yet been found, even though different sanctions have examined the clues and evidence of the murders. All involved will not rest until the murderers have been rounded up and captured. Until then, I will pray to The Lord for the residents of Utopiaville. They did not deserve this; they were good people— God-loving, Christian people. God rest their souls.

I also found and read Father John Browne's journal on events that may or may not have been connected to these butcherings. I'm inclined to believe that something sinister happened in this good community. Dark forces hide and appear in strange places in this world, and only God knows the reason why. I have an open mind to the cause of these despicable acts taken upon this poor town. I can believe or disbelieve almost anything, and that is what makes me a more than an adequate constable. I will NOT give up until I find the culprits.

God Bless us all.

Constable James Bedford

At 3 a.m. in the early morning of June 7, 1866, a tall figure with long, shoulder-length hair and an unkept beard walked into the quiet and dark Utopiaville Church from a back door and tiptoed into the church office and moved to Father John Browne's closet. He was wearing gloves even though the night was warm. He picked up the musical box that was still on the top shelf and quietly retraced his steps out of the church and out of the community through the thick wooded forest on the west end of the village.

Nobody saw him, for it was a moonless night, and the investigation had been halted until morning. The deceased had all been taken down from the crosses and were covered by sheets. A guard watched over the bodies but did not see or hear the figure enter the religious structure from the rear. After the tall man moved a mile into the woods, he met another dark figure and handed the individual the strange musical box that had so unnerved the minister of this poor establishment, and then the two of them disappeared into the darkness.

Chapter Twenty-Seven

THE MUSICAL BOX TWO

We continue to talk about the demise and horrific events that took place in Utopiaville before we leave this sad and abandoned village. When the power went out the town was completely overgrown and forgotten; it was hallowed ground where life no longer existed. Even wildlife and animals stayed away from the area, avoiding walking on the land at all, sensing that something bad still resided there. Ghosts of despair were even felt in the air above the community, for assorted birdlife refused to fly over the area. They veered one way or the other, flying away from the airspace over the village.

Little change would have been noticed after the Event took place, other than the empty holes of the many graves that suddenly littered the center of the small township and the forgotten, overgrown cemetery beyond the trees. Some brush and young trees fell into the empty graves when the coffins and remains inside disappeared, but there was nobody there to see or hear it take place. There *were* two lifeforms from those sad events in history that still walked the Earth after the power went off, and this chapter is about them and their histories. One was the tall dark figure that removed the strange musical box from the deceased town once called Utopiaville, and the other was the figure that waited for him in the dark woods outside of town.

The tall man with the long shaggy hair and the unkept beard is named Thorzeous Mongolas. To the human eye, he appears to be in the thirty- to forty-year range with a tinge of gray in his beard that covers a face without any wrinkles or scars. He is seven foot, two inches tall, and underneath his full-length black cloak he is heavily muscled, much stronger than any man on Earth, and that is because he is *not* from this world, nor this chamber. He did not come through the Big Bang life-force doorway, but by ancient magic—very ancient magic, for Thorzeous Mongolas is a warlock that has passed through many chambers over hundreds of millions of universal lifetimes. His ultimate objective is to worship and work for a presence he has never met physically but has connected with telepathically. He is extremely intelligent, which makes him extremely dangerous. The musical box belongs to him, and it holds a kind of magic that comes at you from many different angles. It worked its powers in the little village of Utopiaville, and it waits to perform again, and then again.

Not long after the power went out and most people had gone home to The Creator, Thorzeous suddenly appeared in the thick overgrown brush in the center of Utopiaville and stared intently at the empty graves in front of him. He slightly frowned as he surveyed the entire forgotten establishment (he did this by rising a foot into the air and rotating counterclockwise without moving a single muscle), and then he looked down at his right hand. That hand held the ancient musical box, and it began to play. Thorzeous listened to its eerie tune and began to smile.

The other figure that Thorzeous handed the musical box to in the dark western woods was his wife of many millennia. She is a witch that can cast many spells, and she *has*, but only when her husband allows her to. She is devoted to her spouse, and more importantly, to his cause in all things past and present. She can take on many forms, but when the power went out, she was a beautiful brunette, full figured at five foot six inches tall and quite irresistible. She didn't need to cast a spell to get you to want her, and she didn't when she walked into Utopiaville to destroy a righteous, just cause. The name she used back then was Joan Winters, who became the wife of the leader of Utopiaville, Father John Browne. As Thorzeous smiled down at the musical box, his wife suddenly appeared (she was wearing a full-length black gown that fit tightly, showing off her desirable charms) next to him and held his left hand. She also smiled.

The last entry of Constable James Bedford, dated June 28, 1866, concerning the Utopiaville investigation before he was removed from the case and replaced by government investigators:

> All deceased individuals of Utopiaville have been buried and blessed by Father Alfred Smith. All except one: Joan Browne, the wife of Father John Browne. Maybe she was abducted, maybe she was involved, but she is the focal point in our investigations. We will diligently pursue all avenues to find her, for WE believe she holds all the answers to what happened in Utopiaville. God, I pray, please help us on our mission to solve these senseless and horrifying murders of this good community.

Joan Browne, of course, was never found, and the murders of Utopiaville were never solved. The investigation remained opened, but no further clues or leads ever came in. Eventually the case was put on the back burner and forgotten, as frustrating as that might seem. Joan's real name was Rutherynna, and she was almost as ancient as her husband. She didn't have the telepathic connections to the underworld that Thorzeous had, but she was no less dangerous—maybe more so when she was angry.

History notes that turmoil was happening in the country's capital. President Abraham Lincoln had just been shot dead; America was reeling and mourning the loss of a great leader. Tensions were high all over; slaves were freed and roamed the land looking for work to survive. The country was divided, but the little town called Utopiaville stood above it all. That infuriated the warlock and the witch. They were furious, which made them very dangerous. Below are the accounts of what happened in Western Pennsylvania back in the mid 1800s.

The ideas and concepts that made up Utopiaville were ahead of their time, as stated earlier. There had been foundational ideas of peace, harmony, religion, and value-of-life concepts before, but the pieces had never quite fit as well as they did in western Pennsylvania. The situation there was pure positiveness that kept building on itself day after day, year after year. If left alone it might have grown into the model used for today's society. Its concepts concentrated on suffocating out the negatives of day-to-day existence, making life more like the Lord meant it to be—heaven on Earth, so to speak. There would be no selfishness, no greediness, no hatred, no conniving, no jealousy, no lying or taking advantage of any situation concerning your brothers or sisters of all races and creeds. Your neighbors' beliefs in all things should be respected and honored. How many wars after this time (1866) could have been prevented if this community had been allowed to grow, and its word spread across the land? How much better would we all treat each other, working as a cohesive unit toward a common goal? How many souls would've been saved from disgrace and damnation? How many? Probably an insurmountable amount, and with the various evil and dark forces moving amongst them in the shadows, this could not stand. If allowed to continue, righteousness and goodness would prevail and reign in the future, so steps had to be taken to stop this tide from rising.

Enter Thorzeous Mongolas, and his wife Rutherynna. They were the tools used to put a wrench into a well-greased machine, and as we all know, destroying a situation compared to building one is much easier to succeed at. Unfortunately, this is the reality we are all faced with every minute of every day, so the blueprint was drawn up by the dark couple to topple and destroy this growing community on orders sent telepathically from the higher presence.

When Rutherynna walked down the narrow dirt road into Utopiaville as Joan Winters looking for a new way of life, she was accepted immediately. Father John and Michael Brookens were both immediately smitten with her, for she had put a spell on each when they had interviewed her, hoping that the two top men of the community would fight for her (maybe even *kill* for her), chipping away at their positiveness, but Michael bowed out in favor of his best friend before that negativity could take place. He loved and craved her to the day he died, but his friendship with John mattered more.

John married Rutherynna as Joan, with Michael the best man, but she despised and never forgave him. It wasn't in her DNA. Soon after the wedding Rutherynna killed Michael for being weak and submissive to John, summoning up a spell that made his heart literally explode inside his chest cavity. Everybody mourned Michael, but Rutherynna hated him and spit on his grave whenever the situation presented itself. She was happy he was dead; he had ruined her initial plan. In the long run he was one of the lucky ones, though.

She became the good wife and laid in wait. Though she inwardly hated every moment of that abbreviated liaison with the religious leader, she understood and knew what the final outcome would be. She went to all the church services and became the perfect wife of a minister, but when everybody was asleep, she secretly worshipped the rightful lord of the underworld, cleansing herself of the Christian pigs that surrounded her and their pitiful God that they prayed to.

Thorzeous, meanwhile, was involved in other matters that will be discussed later, but when he returned he affected the township with a vengeance. He mailed one of his magical tools, the musical box, to his fill-in husband, and watched as it was taken back to Utopiaville. It was ageless and had been constructed by Thorzeous in another chamber which housed all sorts of horrors. The odd thing about the musical box, though, was that it had to be carried in and out of the small village, for the powerful Warlock couldn't make it appear and disappear inside the boundaries of the small town. That was a first, and it showed Thorzeous just how powerful this spiritual positiveness was. He knew that he had to be careful, but he also knew that if he *was,* this would all go down easy peasy. Magic was magic, and his was the best in this universe. That was fact, not bragging. The warlock was way beyond that petty bullshit.

The musical box had been used many times before in different solar systems, galaxies, and chambers, and in each case the warlock presented the ancient casing with gifts that were eventually turned into the wormlike serpents that were talked about earlier. Inside, the musical box opened up into a chamber of its own, a universe without borders. Tortured moans, groans, screams, and loud screeching reverberated constantly inside the confines of the box, intensifying whenever its tune filled the air, releasing its physical minions. Father John Browne was correct to feel uneasy about it, but he had no idea just how evil a heirloom he had sitting on the top shelf of his church office closet.

Thorzeous and Rutherynna both worked their magic and created the nightmares the community started having, starting with Father John and working their way through the rest of the villagers. The main idea behind those horrible dreams was to create doubt in their God and the positiveness and goodness in themselves, and it worked to perfection. Even though they talked their way through those dreams and still had faith in their Lord, the doubt in all their goodness and sanity remained. That cancer would continue to grow, and as they had more and more nightmares over the coming weeks that disease metastasized. The townsfolk smiled less, their minds polluted with evil and distressful thoughts, and eventually in all those nightmares they began to *enjoy* all the bad things they were doing. They didn't know it, but they were being brainwashed from a different-angled prism. That was phase one.

Phase two was physical and more intense, and it involved stronger magic. As stated in Father John Browne's journal, when spring arrived the situation seemed to get better. Anything but that was the truth. In reality, in early May the pastor tried to write that the situation was continuing to deteriorate badly, but he found his hand paralyzed every time he tried to move his pen. His hand shook uncontrollably, but he could not write down one word.

As if hypnotized, Father John suddenly dropped his pen and sleepwalked back to his cabin. When he got there his wife was in bed, but she was not alone. Thorzeous was lying next to her. They were both nude, and they smilingly beckoned him to join them. Father John methodically took off his clothes and got into bed next to them, and they remained in there all day and straight through the next night. They made the pastor of Utopiaville do things that he would never imagine doing, sexual acts that were done with both women and men, and he absolutely loved it. Hour after hour passed, and his lustfulness intensified beyond his wildest dreams. Without question he did everything asked of him, and then without coaxing he went beyond even that.

You might ask, "What about the noon church service?" It didn't take place, for when Father John got into his bed with the warlock and his witch, everybody in town suddenly froze in place. Robert was two steps from the church when he suddenly stopped moving until just before the sun came up the next morning. Darryl Miller was working on the crops when he froze; Allen Hines in the barn tending to the few horses when he stopped moving. And on and on it went. If anyone had entered town, they would have found it almost amusing, but definitely eerie, odd, and strange.

When Father John passed out from exhaustion just before the next sunrise, Thorzeous walked outside and touched everyone in town on the forehead, and when he did, they all trancelike walked back to their beds and slept the whole day until the following morning. There was a reason for that, for when the warlock returned to his wife's lair he snapped his fingers and Father John woke up suddenly, hornier than ever. He had no idea why he was feeling this way, and because of raw basic animal instincts he didn't care. All he was sure of was that he wanted more sexual relations—much more.

Rutherynna was behind the pastor, and she reached over and started masturbating him until he orgasmed yet again, only this time it was much more intense. A minute later he again was completely aroused, and that was when Thorzeous told Father John that if he didn't denounce his alliance with his inferior Lord and worship the true master, then this soulful *enjoyment* would end, and he would remain uncontrollably frustrated until the end of his days. Now Father John Browne had faith that would rival any devoted Christian, but being helplessly under this strange magic spell he didn't stand a ghost of a chance. He mentally fought against the warlock's ultimatum and his insistent urges for an hour and a half before he reluctantly gave in to his strong lustful urges.

He already knew that he had gone against the Good Book and the Lord by experiencing homosexual sex, and he would have been forgiven of this sin if he had repented his lewd actions, but he now wanted sex with men even more than he wanted the love of a woman, such as his beautiful wife. Father John did not know what had come over him. All he knew for sure was that he was lost—lost in a sea of lustful deceit—and so he finally reluctantly succumbed to the mighty warlock's demands. He loudly, with tears in his eyes, proclaimed his faith for the dark king that would become his master, screaming in sexual agony to become a faithful slave to the dark forces of the universe. Thorzeous smiled triumphantly, touched Father John's forehead with his thumb, and the minister of Utopiaville laid down on his bed and began masturbating repeatedly, fantasizing about every kind of homosexual act imaginable from the receiving end. The pastor knew that his once-pure soul was lost to totally polluted damnation, yet he didn't care—in fact, he didn't have the *fight* in him to care. He was drowning in lustful violations of his own rightful causes without a fight, and that disgusted him. He wasn't worthy of the good God he had always worshipped and adored, and he now felt that he should burn in the fires of hell for it.

Thorzeous and Rutherynna watched the actions of the tormented pastor for a few amusing minutes, and then they moved on to the next occupant in the small ambushed township— Robert Silas. The evil couple walked into his cabin, and the warlock woke him up with a touch to his forehead. In a trancelike voice Robert begged to be whipped and punished. He told them he had an uncontrollable urge to feel pain and suffering. The warlock told him to strip naked, and then his hands were tied tightly to the beams in the cabin ceiling. They then both whipped him to shreds with whips, straps, and bamboo canes that were dipped in brine until he was within an inch from death. Thorzeous touched his forehead, and he magically healed quickly, and then they repeated the process. He begged for more; he *craved* more, but the warlock wouldn't comply until Robert denounced his God like Father John had. He succumbed quickly. They beat him yet again as he screamed in painful ecstasy, then he was healed again and told to go to Father John's cabin and do whatever the pastor commanded him to do. Needless to say, you can only imagine what happened once he entered the minister's lair, and they stayed at it for days without taking a break.

The warlock and the witch moved from one person to the next, granting them their desperate pleas after disconnecting themselves from their beliefs and righteous ways, until there was no one left.

Benjamin Drake and Donald Smith killed all the children in town with knifes, swords, and assorted tools like hammers and saws, then had varied sex with all their corpses. They were then brought back to life and the acts repeated. Darryl and Ruth Miller joined them, and then on and on it went until everyone had succumbed to Thorzeous' demands.

By this time spring had turned to early June. The dreams still invaded their minds as they acted out damnation acts of evil, but they were no longer nightmares. They were abominable fantasies the townsfolk were then able to act out in real time, and they became worse as the days moved toward summer.

From the moment Father John Browne was overtaken by the evil magic of Thorzeous Mongolas, the musical box was open, playing its strange tune constantly, the wormlike creatures moving around its casing like maggots, dancing to the murky sounds of shadows.

Phase Three began when the clock struck doom at midnight on June 6, 1866. The evil warlock went into the church closet and spoke a foreign language that only the wormlike serpents understood. The music changed, becoming higher in pitch and intensity, and the worms moved down to the floor and followed Thorzeous out of the church and into the main square. All the townsfolk were standing there nude and trancelike, swaying from side to side. There must have been thousands of the wormlike maggots. They were an inch long in length, and as thin as a pen with angry serpent mouths filled with sharp pointy teeth that opened and closed constantly. They moved up and into every orifice of every member of the community: mouths, noses, ears, vaginas, and anuses were invaded by the wormlike maggots, and then they began eating. They ate the citizens of Utopiaville from the inside out, leaving only the skin and various muscles to keep the bodies intact. At the end of their meal they ate straight through every neck of the community, detaching the head from each body.

Screams and horrible moaning could be heard as the souls of every member of the small village moved on a strong diseased current inside the church and into the open musical box. When all the souls were inside the lid closed, trapping the condemned spirits of every resident of Utopiaville. The magic now completely withdrawing from them, the Utopiaville residents met the condemned souls of other victims from different worlds and realized their dreadful fate. Hate and evil swirled all around them, crushing and immobilizing their infected souls.

Imaginary burning fires burned around and through them, and even though they were dead and had no physical bodies, they all felt the intense heat burning through their spirits. They screeched in constant agony with no relief in sight along with the other lost souls from other worlds.

Hell comes in different realms and levels. Some are worse than others. This hell was worse than any level written about in any religious periodical here on Earth. The residents of Utopiaville realized this, understood their grave fate, and that realization made their situation even worse. No one would have signed up for this. Overtaken by a magic that had completely overpowered them, those spells now left them. Their ecstasies quickly disappeared and there was no more pleasure, only unimaginable pain and suffering.

Back in the physical world, through the magic of the powerful warlock, the dead, headless bodies with the maggots still inside them built the upside-down crosses. When that job was completed, the wormlike maggots exited the bodies and swarmed around Thorzeous and Rutherynna as if in a frenzy, wanting to see more. The warlock didn't disappoint; he spoke again in that foreign tongue, and then the lifeless bodies moved by themselves into place on the inverted crosses. Raising his large hands high above his head large nails came out of nowhere and shot through each body, holding them in place. The maggots then carried each severed head up the crucified carcasses and sat them on top of the crosses. Larger nails shot down from the sky and through the center of each head, impaling them onto the crosses. The maggots returned to the foot of the evil couple, screeching madly with glee. They then carried the body and head of Father John Browne into the church and repeated the process of impaling him onto the large cross at the head of the religious structure after it had been turned upside down.

Their work done, the maggots moved back to the musical box, the lid opened to receive them, and then closed again. The lost souls of Utopiaville thought they had been placed in the worst hell imaginable, but that realm was nothing once the wormlike serpents reentered the box and began to swarm their slimy essences around them. All the residents of the community realized that true hell had no boundaries; it could always get worse, and it did.

Thorzeous and Rutherynna surveyed their masterpiece. The warlock wrote in blood his message about "balance" before they walked westward into the thick woodlands. They had to leave the musical box stationary for a few hours while the universal hell inside it metastasized, thrusting the souls inside into new depths of sorrowful agonies.

As written earlier, it was reclaimed later, and then the warlock, his witch, and the musical box returned to their lair in an empty chamber on the edge of total hopelessness until needed further. In their evilness they reasoned that true balance had been restored.

Chapter Twenty-Eight

RORY SNYDER

*R*ory Snyder played baseball for the San Francisco Giants. They were on a roll, winning the last two World Series, and were twelve games ahead in the National League West so far this year. Rory had been a big part of that success, winning the last two Most Valuable Player awards in the National League *and* the World Series. Without him the Giants might not even have made the playoffs—that's how important he was. He batted fourth (cleanup) and played right field. In his tenth season, even though he had a long way to go, the sports media was talking about him possibly having the most lifetime home runs by the end of his career. He had 387 so far, and a lot of them had been massive moon shots of 400 feet or more. He wasn't all that physically imposing, six feet three inches tall and 220 pounds, but he had a compact swing, and he had an amazing eye, not swinging at many pitches out of the strike zone.

When the power went off, he was in the bathroom after just hitting his thirty-third homer of the year with two men on in the first inning. It was a day game and the sky was bright and sunny, 83 degrees—perfect for a baseball game, and perfect for Rory Snyder. He loved day games. He always said that he saw the baseball more clearly in the day compared to night games. He was an enigma: he was a switch hitter (which meant he batted both right and left), but when called on he could also pitch in relief. He was drafted as a pitcher (but of course he was switched to the outfield when the organization realized he could hit) and could throw one hundred miles an hour. It was the only pitch he really had, but he could locate that pitch well, almost to perfection, and he had successfully been used in the majors in the later innings from time to time. There was one more thing: he was ambidextrous. He could throw that fastball equally with both hands. He was one of a kind, and the Giants had signed him to a seven-year contract over the winter that was the richest contract ever signed.

When he went down the tunnel to the bathroom after hitting that home run, the crowd went crazy. They were besides themselves, for they knew they had the best player in all of baseball, and they were winning with that player. They chanted "Babe, Babe" over and over, their nickname for him because he was constantly compared to the immortal Babe Ruth, who had started his career as a pitcher but then had gone to the outfield. He had hit 714 home runs and won the World Series with both the Boston Red Sox and the New York Yankees, where he had become a legend. To the fans, Rory was a legend in his own time just like "the Babe," and he seemed to add to that legend daily.

He was drying his hands under the hand dryer when the bathroom shook a little. Earthquake? he thought, knowing that this was an area where earthquakes were common, being close to the Andreas fault line. A World Series had to be postponed a week back in 1989 because of a strong earthquake that killed many (one was too much), and did damage to various structures, including the Golden Gate Bridge. The hand dryer stopped, the lights went out, and Rory noticed that all had gone quiet—no crowd noise, no field or stadium noises, nothing. He started back up the tunnel to the dugout and saw no one. No one was in the dugout, no one on the field, and no one in the stands. It was impossible, but somehow, he was alone. A minute ago, a baseball game had been going on, and now no one was here. How could that be, and more importantly, how *physically* could that be? He checked the TV monitor, and it was out. He picked up the dugout phones, and they were dead as well. He took out his cellphone, and that wasn't working either.

He walked out onto the field until he reached second base, and then scanned the complete stadium. The stands were empty, and so were the dugouts as well as the bullpens. He yelled out "Hello!" a few times in each direction, but got no replies. He took his hat off and scratched his head. He could smell the food (hot dogs, fries, various sandwiches, burritos, tacos, and such) coming from the mezzanine, but there was no one there to cook or eat them.

Rory walked back to the dugout, jumped over the railing, and walked up the box-seat aisle. It was funny, he thought, he had really never been in the stands much. It felt strange, but this situation *completely* felt strange. He walked up to the food zones, and he was right. No one was there to buy anything, and no one was behind the counters to sell or cook everything Rory was smelling. That was something people had asked him over the years: "How can you play baseball when you smell all this food circulating around the ballpark?" It was a good question, and he had always answered it the same way: "I just block it all out, just like I block out the noise of all you fans when you are screaming for me to get a hit."

He now looked at where all the hot dogs were cooked, and even though Rory could still smell them, he saw no sign of any hot dogs or any other meat products. The hot dog buns were still there, french fries as well, but no meats of any kind. All the power was off up here as well.

Rory was on his way to another eatery when he heard a large splash coming from the Bay, and then he heard a loud crash coming from the opposite direction toward the city. He ran down the hallway on the first base side and could see a large plane in the Bay that had broken into four large pieces. They were bobbing up and down in the water, and then another large plane suddenly crashed through the stadium structure on the third base side. The nose rested halfway up the third base line. It loudly exploded, and fires started to burn on the field and behind the damaged ballpark. Rory went down the steps and made it out of the ballpark as fast as possible. He stood by the Willie Mays Statue in front of the stadium and surveyed the situation. He saw smoke in five other spots rising in the distance. More planes must've crashed, he thought nervously. He kept his eyes on the sky for about ten minutes before he felt comfortable that no more planes would fall near the ballpark. He walked around to the third base side and saw that fires were burning.

Rory walked back around to the front of the ballpark and thought of a plan. He went back inside, quickly went to the Giant's locker room, changed into a sweat suit, grabbed his duffle bag filled with toiletries, grabbed as much food (minus missing meats) as he could with another bag, and then left the ballpark. As he was leaving, he saw a poster telling everyone that the Giants were going to New York to play the Yankees after this series. Rory had been looking forward to that trip. He had grown up in northern New Jersey, and his wife and three young daughters lived in Englewood Cliffs just outside New York City, and that was where he was headed. He hoped and prayed to God that they were OK and would be there to greet him when he got home. As he walked away from the ballpark, he realized life as he had known it had changed forever, and baseball didn't seem very important anymore.

Chapter Twenty-Nine

THE EXPERIMENTAL SPACE MISSION

*W*hat would you do if you had the chance to go on a mission into the vastness of space to witness and study planets, moons, comets, asteroids, etc., in our solar system and beyond? Would you go? And what if you knew it was a one-way ticket, and you'd never come back to Earth? Would you still go? These were tough questions some NASA astronauts had to ask themselves, for the agency was planning a highly secret mission to do just this. The magnificent beauty of space and the mystery of what might happen from one day to the next would be your reward if you went, but you'd be leaving everything else behind if you did go. You'd never see your family and friends ever again. That might mean your wife or husband, and even your children. Parents, siblings, and various relatives would also be on that list. Just leaving Earth itself might be hard. It *is* home, the only planet you have ever known, and it is relatively safe compared to what you would be traveling into. Most of what would be in the distance is *not* humanly friendly. You could at least see and talk to your family, but you would never physically see them ever again.

It was a lot to think about, but the astronauts asked to take on such a mission all decided to go (several family members vehemently disagreed with their decision, and there was a lot of infighting, or internal duress), which wasn't much of a surprise to NASA officials. The six astronauts accepted for the mission were trained and prepped for two years, and they were called "The Rover Explorers." The spaceship, named Pioneer One, was small and compact, seventy feet long, twenty feet wide, and fifteen feet in height. The vessel was made up of three sections. The front section consisted of all piloting equipment, computers, communications, etc. The middle section was the living and kitchen area. This was the largest section, consisting of six small bedrooms with baths, cooking, and lounging space. If the astronauts weren't in hypersleep, most of the time would be spent here. The back section was the science and general warehouse area. This was called the life support zone. Back there they would sustain themselves by growing their own food in a small hot house and recycle their water supply using their own urine.

When they took off, they were loaded with supplies, seeds, and supplements that would last decades, so they had a good head start. The crew would go into hypersleep in three-month-long shifts of two (the pods were used as their beds as well) while the other four crewmen worked in the hothouse and monitored their life-support systems. All six were trained to do each specific job needed for survival. This included flying the vessel, preparing and growing crops, and general maintenance. Three were physicians, and the other three were in training. This was a dangerous mission, and the situation could go south at any time, so all on board needed to be as diversified as possible. Predicting when problems might occur was optimum for general survival.

So, when would this mission take flight? Surprise, it already had—five years ago! Ship and crew had just passed Jupiter and its many moons, sending all information back to Earth, when the power went out. All systems shut down, and like Mars 2020 it slipped through a rip in time (going in the complete opposite direction), and amazingly came out next to the Colorado River at the bottom of the Grand Canyon on the Northern side near Phantom Ranch, a historic oasis, and next to Bright Angel Creek.

Pioneer One hovered two feet above the ground, and it held one survivor: Dr. Janice Seymour. She had been in hypersleep and slowly woke up, realizing like JJ Johnson on Mars 2020 that everyone on board was gone, and all systems down. She moved to the front of the vessel and looked outside. She saw the Canyon and the Colorado river and couldn't believe her eyes. She was back on Earth, and that was an impossibility! Yet here she was. How could that be? she thought, shaking her head in disbelief. Dr. Janice moved to the back of the ship and saw that its rear door was open. Her spirits rose, hoping and praying that the rest of the crew had left the ship to explore their surroundings, explaining why they weren't here, why she was alone.

She was doing the slow freak, her emotions all over the board, and there was good reason for that, for you see, dear reader, the whole crew of Pioneer One ended up being one family.

Not a NASA family, a single working unit, but a *real* family! Pioneer One consisted of Doctor Seymour's parents, Dr. Carl and Lisa Seymour; her husband Dr. Tom Gordon; and their two teen-aged twin girls, Carol and Marylyn, both eighteen. NASA had decided that sending one family would be better than parts of six different units. The space officials had argued long and hard on all fronts and angles, but at the end of the day decided to go the one family route.

Needless to say, the Seymour clan couldn't have been happier. They were one of five families considered and were deemed all around more complete than the others. The difference was the children, the gifted twins. Both had trained with their parents as they grew up and went to school in the NASA facility. They were both in great physical shape, and intellectually excelled beyond college-level capacity.

Dr. Janice thought about how well they all worked together as she slowly stepped outside (for she still wasn't sure if this *was* Earth). She looked all around as she breathed in the Canyon air and heard the moving river but nothing else—no wildlife, no birds or hawks, nothing. She called out but got no response. Something was obviously wrong here, and she wondered if she was in an alternate universe, or something of that nature.

All of a sudden, she saw a few empty rafts pass by. They were loaded down with gear, and the oars skirted on each side, but there were no people. A dark realization set in. She had to face the possibility that she was alone, and her family gone with the rest. Something had happened to change everything, and her survival mode kicked in. She ran over to the river and waited five minutes before another three empty rafts approached, also devoid of people. Quickly she wadded into the river where there were no rapids and was able to pull two of them to shore. They were both loaded with equipment and food—things needed for survival. She grabbed a peanut butter and jelly sandwich out of a cooler and wolfed it down with a bottle of water, then went back to the ship and closed the rear door.

It was hot, hotter than blazes out here, and she wanted to keep the vessel as cool as possible. She called out again, screaming at the top of her lungs, but all she heard was the echo of her own voice bouncing off the canyon walls. Nothing else. She was alone, maybe the last human being on Earth. She trembled slightly and then suddenly broke down, crying and laughing all at the same time. A cruel joke was being played on her, and it was sad and funny all at the same time. NASA didn't want to break up a family for this mission, didn't want to separate them, and yet here she was, back on Earth, alone and without her family. How ironic!

Chapter Thirty

WE ARE BUILDERS

A Narrative Story

We are builders.

The human race, since the beginning of our existence, has built things to make living life easier. We build houses of all types and sizes to live in, depending on how big a family is or how much space we would like to have. Those structures protect us from the elements of nature (hot and cold, snow or rain), and other countries, groups, or individuals that might want to harm or steal from us. It protects us from the increasingly more severe elements from Mother Nature: hurricanes, tornados, torrential rains that produce damaging floods, including some that destroy our infrastructure, such as roads, bridges, or even dams.

We are builders.

The human race builds buildings of all sizes, some that even touch the sky. They are called skyscrapers, and they are being built higher and higher each and every year. Construction never stops. That is *our* nature. Put enough of these amazing structures together side by side, and they become cities. Human beings go to work in most of these, spending a good part of their day there. We never seem to have enough buildings, and yet overall there is so much real estate where we have yet to leave our mark. But give us time, give us time . . .

We run the world from these places and give them all the comforts of our homes, if not more so. We have built cities that go on for miles. Some cover complete islands, such as Manhattan Island in New York. Why? Because we can't stop building; we never stop improving on what we already have.

New types of architecture infiltrate the continuing building process on a daily basis. New structures of all shapes and sizes are erected that satisfy improved compliance procedures.

We are builders.

The human race has built different types of transportation: cars, buses, trains, airplanes, boats, ships, and spaceships, etc. They are all made to get us from one place to another much faster than walking or running. Spaceships help us even leave the planet, sometimes to visit neighboring planets, such as Mars.

We are builders.

We human beings love what we build, or what others have built for us. We fall in love with them, and sometimes treat them even better than our fellow men. That is understandable from certain types of view, but short sighted. They are structures made out of wood, steel, bricks, and other items that man has produced. They are inanimate and considered nonlife. They should not be treated better than any fellow human being, and yet they occasionally are. Sometimes the things we build are even worshipped like gods. We worship God inside churches, other structures that we built, but some people step over a moral line. Sometimes we lose perspective of the way we feel about the structures we build, and cry about their losses. Homes are destroyed by Mother Nature—floods, hurricanes, tornadoes to name a few. The rising sea levels around our cities threatens *their* futures. As we have read, strong, enforced, tall walls have been built, and many parts of those cities have needed to be altered or destroyed because of our growing changes in climate control.

Homes built near some of our beaches have been destroyed as the changing water levels rise and cannot be rebuilt on the same land as the tides keep moving closer and closer to them. Storms, such as nor'easters on the East Coast, destroy what we build. Some face destruction by man himself. The Twin Towers in New York City come to mind.

And yet, when the power went off, and most went back to The Creator, they still sat, quiet and empty. A few questions come to mind. Do those structures, those built by us, miss us at all? Are they lonely because most of mankind is no longer here? In most cases probably not, and most people would consider those questions quite silly, or outrageous!

Perspective from many different angles: we cry over losing our homes, either by financial means or by Mother Nature, and yet when *we* die, they seem to go on without emotion.

We are builders.

The things we build usually have longer life spans than us. That is logical. New York City, for example, was first built in the 1700s, and a lot of those buildings are still there, standing tall. Some bridges decay badly and are replaced, yet others grow old, are maintained on a constant basis, and will continue to help us cross growing waterways.

Life goes on, and these buildings, bridges, and other structures serve new generations of people as the years roll on. Do they love, or miss us? Do they miss the people who built them? Different perspectives must be used while answering these different types of questions. Something to think about.

The story in this chapter centers around an extremely decayed neighborhood. It involves a destructive force of nature, a woman, and a mysterious pet. Hopefully it puts our questions into perspective and answers them to some extent.

We are builders.

We rebuild what is sometimes damaged or destroyed.

And sometimes we don't.

Perspective.

Amanda Primrose was fifty-five years old. She grew up in Green Bay, Wisconsin, one of ten children to William and Laura Primrose, who grew up poor and wondering when their next meal would appear on their old dining room table. Amanda was the youngest, and most of her older siblings had already left home long before she became a teenager. Most were never heard from again; some the young Primrose girl had hardly known. Sad, but Amanda Primrose had never shed a tear over them. Why? Because she grew up in a perpetual state of anger, where little love lived.

Little money and nourishment had a lot to do with that as well. Her two parents rarely kept a job for long, mostly because they had an affliction with the bottle. These were the memories that Amanda remembered about her early life, and no matter how hard she tried to force them to the back of her mind, they were always *right* there, pounding at her temples, giving her migraines. They kept reminding her of what she continued to struggle with, as over time she never owned much, if anything.

Here's perspective for you. The Primroses lived on a road with much decay and potholes the size of small canyons. They lived in a small, dilapidated little house that only had three small bedrooms, plumbing that never worked very well, a roof that leaked in many spots, and heat and electricity that had been turned off many times because of unpaid bills. Eventually, when Amanda turned twelve, her parents lost the house. As with many others in the dying neighborhood, it went into foreclosure, and that was when the family broke up for good.

At the time Amanda and her brother Simon were the only siblings still living home. He was a year older than her, and the authorities were forced to put both of them in separate childcare facilities. Why separate? They were considered irritations of the State, the bottom of the barrel. Heartless? Yes. Out of the ordinary? No, for there were many poor children going through the same situation as the youngest Primrose children, their families basically abandoning them. And yet when Amanda (and Simon to a lesser extent), found out that they would have to leave their house, their home, they cried. Even under the conditions in which they had to live (or survive), they *loved* their home, their house—their structure.

(We are builders, and we love what we build . . . Ah, but do they love us back?)

Amanda never forgot her home, and she continued to cry every so often whenever past memories came back to haunt her. Perspective. Amanda never saw her parents, Simon, or *any* of her other siblings ever again, but did she cry over that? No. Not even a tear. Perspective seen through different feelings of emotion.

Once Amanda turned sixteen, she was adapted by Raymond and Lizzy Lowery. They had no children; Lizzy couldn't conceive no matter how hard they tried, and so they took a chance on Amanda. They were a wonderful couple and gave the teenager whatever she needed. It turned out to be the best few years of her life. She had three meals a day, heat when it got cold, air condition when the days got hot, a home with two bathrooms where the toilets always flushed, a shower that always worked, and more importantly, one that spouted hot water. And yet, no matter how wonderful it was, it wasn't the creaky little home she had grown up in that housed so many issues and problems.

We are builders, and yet we think homes will be there forever . . .

No, not Amanda's old house, but her adopted parents' home. It happened when Amanda was in school, and her adopted parents were home. They were packing for a vacation that the three of them would take to Disney World in Florida, but disaster took place. Something went wrong with the furnace, and it blew up. The house quickly went up in flames, and her parents didn't survive. They had both been knocked unconscious by the blast, and by the time the first fire trucks had arrived, they had succumbed to smoke inhalation before the first flames had a chance to caress their lifeless bodies.

At their funerals, Amanda cried, for loss had found her again. She cried for the loss of her foster parents, their home, and the love they had shared. The whole tragedy brought back memories of the home she grew up in, and Amanda cried some more.

(I cry for you as well . . .)

Amanda was sent back to the orphanage after the funerals. Contractors rebuilt the Lowery house, and a new family, the Reillys, moved in. They lived in the new house on Gilbert Street right up until the power went out and they returned to The Creator. The house was empty and quiet for the first time since it had been rebuilt, for the Reillys had three young children who played throughout the home, making noise like happy young ones do, and now they were gone; never to return.

(Did the house miss them once they went back to The Creator? Hard to tell, since no one was around to tell one way or the other.)

One Note Of Interest: shortly after the Event took place, a jet airliner crashed into a house two streets over from the Reillys, and five homes burned to the ground before the flames were extinguished by the heavy thunderstorms that passed throughout the neighborhood. No one was around to rebuild those structures as their remains sat alone during the following days and endured complete darkness throughout the following nights. That was sad in an abstract sort of way, but did those burned structures care in any way? Did they *feel*? Was someone, or anything watching over them?

(No one around to rebuild us . . .)

Amanda had left the Smithsonian Orphanage a few months after she returned, running away from almost everything in her life: the facility she had been returned to and its unloving ways; the memories of the Lowery's, the love they had shared; the poverty of her early life, which began at her earliest memories; and the total uncaring ways of her parents, most of her siblings, and the local school system on a whole. There, the teachers made her feel invisible; her classmates teased and made fun of her, in class and out; and the hall monitors and security officers berated her as she passed by.

The only memory she cherished was her home, her house growing up on Johnson Street. There was some sort of spirituality there, something intangible—Some *THING*.

(Come visit me . . .)

And so, Amanda did that for a while. She would walk down her street and meditate on her home, hoping the house would communicate in some telepathic way. In the beginning, this became an everyday exercise, but when the house didn't outwardly respond, her visits became less and less. Otherwise she hung out in shopping centers or the Exodus Mall during the day, just to be around people (even though day by day she became more and more withdrawn, a true definition of what you'd call "a loner"). She would hang out at the food courts and beg for cash so she could eat. She didn't need much; Amanda "ate like a bird," and spent most of the money on fluids. Sometimes she'd run into people she knew; they'd feel sorry for her and buy her a meal. Some would actually sit down with her and shoot the breeze, and then walk away, thankful that they weren't in Amanda's situation.

Amanda would always say a prayer before eating. (It was something she had learned to do while living with the Lowery's. It was something she appreciated, and her one connection to a God that she always thought didn't like her. The prayer always ended with, "I'll try to be better, just so that I may one day have what others take for granted.") She would hold her hands together and silently word her thanks, regardless of who might be watching her. Thank God for the mall, Amanda would think as she watched the people go this way and that.

(Keep visiting me . . .)

At night she would sleep in a wooded area down the street from her house. Amanda always wondered if they would tear it down and rebuild it, but they hadn't as yet, and so she prayed every night that it would never happen. It was so run down. There was no paint left on the shingles; the old gutters had fallen off and were completely rusted, and most of the windows had been broken, probably by the local kids who had nothing better to do. The grass was thigh high, the grounds unkept, but it was still there, and that's what mattered.

(I'm fine; it is you that I worry about . . .)

Once fall rolled around that first year, Amanda took to the road, hitchhiking south where the weather wasn't so cold. She thought that she'd be back in the spring, but she never made it back until a year before the power went off and most went back to The Creator. During that time, she worked odd jobs, mostly waitressing in out of the way diners where only enough customers to pay the bills ate. The tips were bad, but she always bartered for free food and a place to sleep during her time of employment. The food was rarely edible, and the coffee almost made her vomit the nourishment she had consumed, and she wondered how she managed to keep it down, but it kept her going, and "going" was all that Amanda focused on. "Thank God for the fuel and roof over my head," she'd say as she laid down on a makeshift bed made out of anything that felt comfortable.

(I am here for you; you could stay as long as you'd like . . .)

Amanda would heed that message and stay until the diner she was working in usually went out of business or couldn't afford to pay her. She'd contemplate going back up north each time her last job ended, but then she'd hop a bus heading to nowhere, and stay on until the next town, city, or state, or more likely, the last stop. During those interludes on the buses she'd meet a lot of different people, and she found out that a lot of them were in the same situation she was: just wandering around the country with all they owned sitting next to them. "The country's gone to hell for most of us good people," they'd say grimly, staring at Amanda sadly, "and it's never coming back!" Amanda would shake her head in agreement, and stare out the window, hoping something better would pop up down the road. That "something better" never materialized; in fact, the future and everything in it seemed to get more dire as one day greeted the next one.

And so, Amanda mostly traveled either further south or west, until one day her stomach started hurting and most of what she ingested wouldn't stay down. She went to a clinic in San Antonio (this last time she took a bus back east), and they told her, without fanfare or emotion, that she had "The Big C" in its later stage and should get her affairs in order. Affairs. *Affairs!* What affairs? Amanda had always found that term terminally funny, and now it was being said to her directly, in terminal terms. Amanda rarely laughed, but she did that day as the shocked clinic doctor and nurse watched her walk out into the parking lot.

(Come home, Amanda. It's time to come home . . .)

This was what Amanda heard outside the clinic that day, clear as rain, and it was the first time the voice at the back of her mind had called her by her Christian name, and that made her feel warm and loved. Without delay or thinking otherwise, Amanda hopped a bus heading north for the first time, even though winter was setting in, and the days were getting colder. Snow was forecasted at the northern border of Wisconsin in the next few days, but Amanda didn't care. If she was dying, then she was going home, and "damn the torpedoes!"

Thirty-five odd years had gone by in a blur, and as Amanda reflected on them, she shed a few tears as the Greyhound bus headed for Green Bay. As she boarded the double-decker, Amanda was one of only five passengers, each alone and scattered throughout the first level, but by the time the bus passed the Texas/Oklahoma state lines, all of them had moved closer to each other, shooting the breeze. Amanda, as usual, did more listening than talking as she thought about the present times, the past, and her future.

She reflected on how fast life flew, and how a person's days could get caught up in its strong, forward motion, wondering where life could've gone. She thought about how life's different highways dictated how they lived, and how changing lanes brought them either happiness or grief. She wondered how some became rich and lived in mansions, while others struggled to keep a dry roof over their heads. She had been neither, living just below the poverty level, popping her head up just long enough above its surface to make it through another day. Someone a few seats in front of her said that when they were young, the general consensus was that times would get better, but they only seemed to be getting worse from their perspective. Amanda nodded in agreement and frowned. Perspective.

Depending on whose perspective you were talking about, life was either worth living, or you hoped the next realm would look kindlier on you, and others like you. And through it all, with all the negativity, and the endless foreclosures, the buildings kept going up, and the ones already there in every city kept adding more and more floors, slowly disappearing into the low-lying gray storm clouds that dominated the approaching spiritual horizon.

We are builders.
And we never stop.
We build to the heavens.
And the gears of construction continue to turn and churn.

(But come back to me Amanda, for I will protect you.)

Amanda heard the voice and thought that it couldn't be. Her old little house must have been torn down years ago to make room for new construction—either large housing or company buildings. Certainly, it would have imploded even on its own if it had gone completely ignored.

(Come back, for I wait for you.)

That last comment brought on fresh tears, and Amanda hoped and prayed that it was true. Throughout all the years and the lost memories of times since, she never let a day go by without thinking about the Primrose residence. All these years later, she still loved it, if not more so. All these years later her memories of that place were clear in her mind, as if they had just happened, while others not so far removed had mostly disappeared into the misty fog of yesteryears.

(I'm still there . . .)

Hours later, as some got off at their stops, waving goodbyes with bright smiles, and others boarded for destinations possibly beyond hers, Amanda concentrated on her family as a whole. There had been absolutely no contact between *any* of them over the years, which she found completely astounding. Were her parents still alive? Had any of her siblings passed away? Had any of them defied the odds and become successful? And how much bigger had the Primrose family grown on a whole? These, and other questions flooded her mind as the bus rolled into Green Bay and it's less than busy bus depot.

As Amanda grabbed her bag and said her own goodbyes (she was the only passenger getting off), she realized she'd never really given these questions much thought. She loved her family, even if not much love had ever been shown her way; but that was all right. She knew that the focus of survival had gotten in the way and diverted their overall attention. And yet never a day went by, no matter how bad it had turned out, without her thinking about her house—her home.

(I'm waiting.)

True to the weather reports that day in early November, it was cold, gray, and dreary as early afternoon set in. Amanda flagged a cab and took the four-mile trek to Johnson Street as the first few flurries began to fall. The taxi dropped her off at the top of the street (the driver said that this part of town had been vacant for the last fifteen years or so), and she started walking. If her house was still standing, it was half a mile away. The road was uncared for; large potholes littered every part of the street, and in other places large pieces of asphalt had broken off from the rest of it, some sticking straight up into the air. No wonder the taxi let her out where he did, Amanda thought sadly, as she stared at the first few homes that had once housed families of all sizes.

They were in bad shape, and definitely unlivable. They consisted of roofs with half their shingles. Windows were broken and doors either missing or hanging off rusting hinges. Paint peeled off wooden shingles. And inside each one there was nothing but darkness. On the left side of the street telephone poles with wires were still there, but each house Amanda came to was lightless, and lifeless. Uncut grass and unkept shrubs, which looked like they had grown out of control for years, lay to one side for the season. A few trees had fallen on some properties as well; one even had fallen halfway across the road.

Amanda gingerly walked around it, and then she saw it. Her house! Her home! (Hello!) It was still standing, or at least most of it was. She picked up her pace to a jog, her bag bouncing off her hip as she went, and stopped in front of it. (Welcome home.) Tears welled up in her eyes, and her love for this forgotten little home instantly doubled. The roof was more gone than there; large holes littered here and there, and all the windows, at least in the front, were either completely gone or mostly broken. Their shutters, which had no paint on them, hung from rusted hinges at odd angles. The front door was gone, with only darkness beyond its entrance. The chimney to the side of the house had half collapsed, with damaged and cracked bricks scattered about.

(I'm still alive and kicking . . .)

Amanda walked across the unkept front lawn; the driveway and walkway were completely gone, and she noticed something in the doorway. As she got closer, she saw that it was a small mangy mutt of a dog, and it's left hind leg was severely broken, sticking out at an odd angle. It whimpered in pain but wagged its tail as Amanda came closer.

"Who are you?" She asked as she bent down cautiously to pet its shaking head. (A friend.) The dog tried to stand but cried out in pain, and lay back down, shaking all over. "How long have you been here?" Amanda asked, examining its broken leg. The dog wagged its tail in response and rolled on its side. "It's a good thing I came along when I did," she added, turning around to look at the falling snow. The wind had picked up and was blowing snow into her face. "Let's get you inside and see what we can do to protect us from the storm." She carefully put her arms underneath the dog; it whimpered once but seemed to understand what Amanda wanted to do and endured whatever discomfort it was feeling. Amanda felt it go limp, relaxing in her arms, and they went inside. "We'll be OK," Amanda assured her injured companion, even though she was far from sure of that.

(A friend in need, is a friend indeed!)

What happened next defied logic. As soon as Amanda stepped completely inside the house a front door materialized in its rightful place, new windows replaced old and broken ones, the roof repaired itself, and the freezing interior of the front room quickly warmed to a comfortable 70 degrees. That was because a fire suddenly burned in the old fireplace, with many pieces of firewood stacked in front of it. Lights from three furniture lamps flicked on by themselves, each sitting on an end table. New furniture—a couch and two recliners—were situated in the places where Amanda remembered them being, and a large smart television attached to the far wall came to life, showing the news. A weatherman was on the screen, telling everyone that the snowstorm would rage throughout the night, dumping over a foot and a half of snow—the first of the season.

An area rug was laid out in front of the fireplace, and Amanda carefully put the dog down on it, and gasped. The dog's leg was no longer broken, no longer sticking out at an odd angle, and didn't it look as if the stray had just come back from the groomers? It wagged its tail and cocked its head as it looked happily up at the astonished woman. It suddenly sat up, and began licking

Amanda's face enthusiastically, and she laughed so hard she fell backward. The dog stood up as if nothing was wrong with it, and happily barked once, snuggling up and down Amanda's side.

Amanda happily stood up and shook her head as the dog jumped up and down by her feet and went into the small kitchen. With a happy mongrel following close behind her, the overhead light immediately came on, and the refrigerator came to life, humming loudly like it always had in the past. She opened it, and at this point was only mildly surprised to find that it was filled with salad greens, garden vegetables, bottles of water, condiments, and bread. Amanda opened the freezer, and it was filled as well with assorted frozen cheese pizzas, dinners, butter, and frozen vegetables. On one side of the counter sat four five-pound bags of potatoes, a large wooden bowl filled with yams and sweet potatoes, and next to that sat five cans of organic vegetarian dog food—high quality stuff—and a twenty-five-pound bag of dry organic food.

The same small round table with four chairs sat against the wall, and Amanda sat down in her favorite chair and started to cry—not from grief, but from joy. How was any of this happening?

(You are protected here . . .)

She looked out the kitchen window, and in the fading twilight Amanda could see that the snow was really coming down, and the wind had picked up. Blizzard conditions, Amanda thought grimly, and yet it was warm and cozy here inside the kitchen. The dog nuzzled up against her leg, and she petted its head affectionately. She wondered what its name was, what happened to it, and how it ended up here.

(All in due time . . .)

Amanda fed them both, and then they both sat down on the couch to watch the news, the dog actually jumping up onto it! Amanda herself amazingly felt better and realized that her appetite was back. The cramps had subsided somewhat, but she still felt extremely tired, and before you could count to ten, both of them were fast asleep. The fire in the fireplace continued to burn, keeping them warm as the storm raged outside. As soon as they were in deep slumber, the television set showed only snow, its volume turned down to zero, and the lamps dimmed. Only the sound of crackling wood in the fire could be heard.

Perspectives, from different angles—we glance through different-colored glass prisms.

We now go across the street to where the Cranstons used to live. At one time five noisy kids used to play outside here, and their father Lloyd could routinely be seen working on his rebuilt cars in a driveway that is no longer there. His wife, Mary Anne, would belt out orders to her flock throughout the day, just in case any of them forgot who was in charge. The house is only half there now, as if a bomb had gone off inside it. Even the ghosts of their memories have dispersed, finding other places to live now, as this, and all other homes on this street continue to *un*build. In this moment where spiritual clocks silently *un*tick, increasing wind and snow blow into it, creating loud wailing noises that sound like distorted cries of dismaying agony. Overall, this whole neighborhood is deserted, discarded, and abandoned, and nothing really moves or changes here but the weather. Only the laws of gravity live here, dragging down pieces of what is left: shingles, rotting wood and drywall from disintegrating exterior and interior walls, pieces of severely cracked siding falling to the unmanicured lawns in this timeless part of town.

There are many neighborhoods like this one scattered all across this country as the growing cancer of poverty spreads (even as new neighborhoods of the rich spring up in a never-ending cycle of building bigger), but let us now turn the colorful prism of perspective around, and look at the Primrose residence across a damaged street during this growing snowstorm. You would think that in the whiteout this house would be a beacon of light and hope in this desolate landscape, but it is anything but. It is what it has always been—another house in decay, much more than halfway through its life cycle of disintegration. It is dark and lifeless, snow and wind blowing through large holes in the sagging roof, and broken windows that could not prevent the intrusion of the weather at hand. Another rotted beam on the right side of the roof breaks off and falls into its interior as a strong gust of wind pummels the structure, and it moans defeatedly, waiting for the next wave of destruction to damage it further.

Perspective. From a different lens, and a different eye. Plus, a different reality. A miracle, really, for at the same time a house *un*builds, it *re*builds, and protects two souls from an unrelenting storm.

Perspective. For yes, Amanda Primrose and her new friend are still safe and warm from a fire burning in a fireplace only they can see, and a home that is coming back to life that only they can experience. As the prism of light turns back around, let us go back into the house, back into its safety as the elements of nature rage outside it's *re*built walls, unable to penetrate its regeneration.

We are builders.
Others *un*build, and *re*build.
And the cycles of construction move along and can't be stopped.

Let's delve deeper into the moments after Amanda and her new friend fall into slumber and look into yet another side of the prism of light—one we have yet to see through.

Five minutes after the television began showing nothing but snow, it turned off completely. Instantly the mongrel woke up and sat up, staring at the blank screen. It barked once, and a picture appeared inside the television's frame. It moved as if in real time, but it is not. The dog knew this, and many other things that none of us human beings have an inkling about. That is all right, for that is the way in these matters—secrets to most, known facts to a special few. The dog's overall knowledge was beyond our basic concepts, but it was patient, for it knew it must be. That was the way of the machine's gears and must not be questioned. A bright white beam of light suddenly shone down onto the couch as two souls—one awake, the other in deep slumber—existed upon it.

We are builders.
We build in a physical realm.
Others build spiritually.
And the cycles of total construction move along and *won't* be stopped . . .

The picture on the television screen showed a cave with a large entrance. Besides it, on the right side, sat a large boulder. It was big enough to block the entrance, and it *has*, but now it had been rolled away so that *others* can move in and out of the cave if need be, for whatever reason. Many reasons exist, but we will only need to know one of them at this time. The prism of light slightly shifted, and the picture on the screen began to change. The interior of the cave, dark at the outset, now showed a light presence, and then more lighted presences could be seen behind the first, but not as bright as the one in front. All the lighted figures were mostly shapeless, and yet *had* shape—the shape of clouds that change the longer you stare at, or *into* them. Looking more like ghosts, they hover, all staring through the television screen.

The prism of light shifted a tad more, and the dog barked happily at the television screen once, loudly. Tears ran down its face, wetting its now-clean coat—its now *healthy* coat. It knew what was there, what was *through the now*, and cried tears of joy, for another meeting was about to take place.

We are builders.
We build in a physical realm.
Others build spiritually, creating love and understanding.
And the cycles of total construction move along; along in its rightful path . . .

"Hello, Righteousness, how are you this stormy evening?" The lighted presence in front asked in a calm tone.

The question was rhetorical; Righteousness knew this, and

wagging its tail, barked at the television screen once more. It stood up on all four legs without pain next to the sleeping figure named Amanda Primrose, and continued to whine and cry uncontrollably. The tears were necessary, for they cleansed the dog's matted coat. Within seconds the mongrel looked completely groomed, and ready to claim first place in any dog show competition.

(We *all* build . . .)

"Another phase is upon us, Righteousness, and time is short. Realization shows us that we are strong, and the storm cannot threaten you. Are you ready to protect the one chosen?"

Righteousness barked again, twice this time, and laid back down, placing its snout on top of Amanda's left calf, right above her ankle.

"Good. Communication between us will not be needed for a while, as you well know. Carry on as planned. Any questions?"

Righteousness barked once, and an understanding had been established.

The bright, lighted presence in front and the many others that followed it moved forward and out of the picture, leaving the cave, it's entrance, and the boulder behind. They are no longer needed, and so the television set returned to snow, and Righteousness closed his eyes and rested. A wind gust blew hard against every wall of the house, but did not enter; it *could not enter,* and that was good.

We are builders.

We build in a physical realm.

Others beyond our comprehension build spiritually, spreading love, understanding, and tranquility throughout all fragmented time and space.

And the cycles of total construction move along in a meaningful purpose, their tides unrelenting and unstoppable in their present and future form . . .

The colorful prism shifted a little more, and Amanda rested in deep slumber. She'd had quite a day—in fact, she struggled through quite a life. Throughout the realms, this fact is known. As stated, she was one of the chosen, another valuable piece on an abstract chess board that harbors beings from many parts of the present chamber and beyond. This information was also known by Righteousness, the strange new canine friend who slept alongside Amanda at the moment. The prism stopped and glistened, showing many illuminating bright new colors—many that have never been seen before by any human eye. They were beyond beautiful and radiated complete positiveness. Let us delve deeper now and see where this chapter turns next . . .

Once Amanda fell asleep, she began to dream of her past, and what she had been through. Memories flooded her thoughts, and her soul cried out, for she suddenly realized just how much she had missed her entire family, even though most of the time they had treated her with coldness. To her, that was quite OK, for survival comes before love or emotion, and their focus had to remain on that. She didn't know that every one of them had passed away, either quietly, or violently.

As she fell deeper into slumber, Amanda began to see the bright colors of the shifting prism, and felt a calmness flow over and through her inner core. A bright light began to materialize in front of her in the shape of a star. This star had ten points—twice as many as a normal one. Behind it, many more different shades of lighted stars materialized as well, and the sleeping woman knew by feel that they were many. These presences also radiated calmness, and so Amanda let herself float freely in the many colors of the prism as they closed in and felt their essences as they joined with her spirit.

The ten-pointed star floated closer to her, and Amanda felt blissful love mix with her spirit. She felt a different type of warmth embrace her, comforting her. A voice from inside the star spoke to her, telling her many things. This interaction lasted for several moments. At the end of the conversation, and after Amanda had asked the presence many questions, the voice gave her a mission, which she gladly accepted. Then the bright star, and the others behind it, completely disappeared, leaving her floating alone in the prism's colors. Left behind inside her soul was the blissful love the stars had brought along with them, and it felt good—*right.*

As the lighted prism began to shift in the opposite direction, Amanda fell back into her sleeping body and began to stir. Righteousness opened his eyes and sat up on the couch, watching the youngest sibling of the Primrose family wake up.

Amanda opened her eyes, saw the dog looking at her, and smiled. "Hello, Righteousness, how are you? I'm so glad that you are here."

The dog barked once, and Amanda nodded. They both stared at each other a moment longer, a common knowledge passing between them, and then Amanda hugged her new companion. Righteousness licked her face affectionately, making Amanda laugh.

"All right, boy, let's go get something to eat, for we have work to do," Amanda announced, getting up off the couch. She started for the kitchen with Righteousness right behind her, tail wagging.

Looking down at the dog, she added, "I now know why there is no meat in the refrigerator or the freezer, and I understand fully. What wonders there are in this new knowledge, and I fully embrace what I've learned." Newfound love, warmth, and calmness swirled within her soul, and Amanda realized that Righteousness had those attributes as well. Their souls were interlocked, and Amanda smiled in blissful peacefulness.

Amanda stared out the kitchen window, saw that it was still snowing, but it had let up quite a bit. The wind was still howling, but the skies were brightening, letting everyone know that the worst was over. By the looks of it, a foot of snow had fallen. The going would be tough, but Amanda knew exactly where she had to go today, and it wasn't too far.

The duo ate breakfast—Amanda Oatmeal, and Righteousness dry dog food—and then they prepared to leave. Amanda put on the coat she had worn all the way from Texas (gloves in pockets), and Righteousness wore what he came into this world with. They both stood by the door, listening to the wind for a second, and then Amanda opened it and they both stepped outside. The house immediately went back to its decayed condition, and Amanda and Righteousness were out in the elements, unprotected.

(I'm still here to serve . . .)

Amanda looked quickly down at Righteousness as a dreadful thought entered her mind. Would the dog go back to being injured, close to death? Her fears were put to rest, as Righteousness was as he had been inside the house: fine and uninjured. He barked once, and then they were off, heading toward the railroad tracks, which were even further from the living, and mainstream society.

We are builders, but sometimes structures *un*build.

Sometimes realms interact and defy logic.

While others build spiritually and share precious knowledge.

And the cycles of complete construction move along in abstract directions, it's gears moving this way and that.

And then all that changes . . .

Perspective—two souls moved toward an objective. Others might suggest the opposite, depending on where one stands. The prism shifted once again, and the light from its essence shined a strong, bright beam through both determined spirits as they moved further into the distance toward a deserted railway station.

Trudging through the first snow of the season was slow going, and Righteousness needed to jump instead of walk to make any headway. Amanda offers to carry the small-sized dog in her arms, but the canine barked once in defiance and increased its speed, moving many feet ahead of the Primrose woman. Amanda shook her head in amazement, for the dog seemed to have limitless energy; and besides, its hind leg had been broken and mangled just a day ago. But it was all taken in stride, for Amanda had begun to believe in miracles; God only knew what she had experienced in such a short time since returning to Johnson Street.

As she moved slowly forward, Amanda realized something else: her stomach had stopped hurting completely, and she hadn't experienced a cramp since waking up this morning. She didn't dare question it, and she discarded that knowledge as best she could, tucking it into the back of her thought processes.

Righteousness suddenly stopped and turned around, barking once. The dog was now ten paces in front of Amanda, even though the fifty-year-old woman was moving like someone ten years younger. She looked up and could see the unused train station in the distance. It too had fallen into decay, but not as bad as her own home and others on Johnson Street had. Amanda could see that the roof was still intact—at least the side she could see. The wall facing them, which had once been dark green, was in fairly good condition and only needed a fresh coat or two of paint. The two windows on this side had been broken, but at least they had been boarded up with new plywood. Yes, it had definitely been ignored by the mainstream system of day-to-day life, but Amanda knew that others used this facility for shelter—namely the homeless. This information had been relayed to her during her time of slumber, along with many other topics, including Righteousness's name. The dog retreated to where she was, and then maintained her pace as they made their way over the snow-covered tracks that separated them from the abandoned station.

Amanda and Righteousness moved around the side of the station where the front entrance was and tried the rusted metal door, which was locked from the inside. A rustling could be heard inside, and then Amanda could hear shuffling footsteps come to the other side of the door. A silence followed, and then muffled whispering could be heard. Amanda estimated that at least five to ten people were involved in this quiet conversation, and then shuffling could be heard again. A lock was unlocked, and then the door slowly opened a foot or two. An old man, possibly one who had lived through at least eighty winter cycles, looked shockingly into Amanda's smiling face.

"Who . . . who are you?" The old man asked through a toothless mouth.

His head was bald and shiny, and his face on the thinnish side. Pronounced wrinkles overwhelmed his face, and he wore a black eye patch over his left eye. His right eye was bloodshot, and looked dark and sickly. His nose was pushed in, as if he had lost at least a few fights where it had been broken. His lips were parched, dehydrated. Scars were everywhere, ones of all sizes. He wore an old Green Bay Packer winter coat that had seen better days, and black gloves that had holes in them. He wore black boots without laces. He looked cold. He appeared stressed, but glad to see her.

"I am Amanda Primrose, and this here is Righteousness, my new friend."

Amanda scanned the room and saw at least twenty souls, none doing better than the old man. It was hard to see who they were, for they were all bundled up, most wearing ski masks. A small fire was going out near a broken window that hadn't been boarded up, and smoke from the dying flames were carried outside by the wind. The interior of the station was in pretty good shape. Graffiti filled its wooden walls, but otherwise it seemed very sturdy. There was makeshift furniture made out of just about everything imaginable, and old mattresses littered the room. They all looked uncomfortable and damaged. Old and dirty sheets and blankets covered them, providing enough warmth to stop death from claiming each and every soul.

"It's her!" someone shockingly stated, pointing with a gray gloved finger.

"You weren't lying, Joe," said another man who sat on the closest mattress.

"God's eyes, it is her," echoed another.

Amanda looked quizzically at the shocked group, and then back at the old man. "What are you talking about? I only got back into town yesterday, just before the storm got serious."

The old man slowly held out his hand, and Amanda shook it. "I'm Joe Kellerman. These people behind me are my friends. We all . . . well, all of us have seen you in our dreams almost nightly for quite some time. Your dog too. We've had discussions about you for months. We gave it serious thought, because all of our dreams have been the same."

"Dreams?"

"Yes. In them you are in a diner serving food, and each one of us come in and you serve us. When it's time to pay the bill you say, 'You have paid enough, and now it is time for me to help you.' And then you disappear into thin air, replaced by a bright star for a few seconds, and then we leave."

"I *have* worked in diners—many times."

"God's at work here," a female voice interjected. "Maybe we have not been forgotten. Bless you child—bless you!"

"But...."

"But nothing," Joe said, holding up his gloved hand. "When it comes to The Lord, you don't question it. You just *go* with it. I've said that many times."

"I guess . . ." Amanda admitted, nodding. "I guess you're right."

"Why are you here this morning, Amanda?" Joe asked, smiling. "It's brutal out there. Do you need shelter?"

Amanda shook her head and frowned. "No, I am here to get you good people. I have better shelter than this, and through a dream of my own last night I was asked by someone, or some-*THING*, to help you."

"Another dream," another female voice said.

"Lord's at work here," the other female added.

"Yep," echoed a few others.

"What's wrong with *this* place?" another asked. "It's been good to us for years, and the police don't bother us, just as long as we don't start trouble."

"It's OK, but another storm is on the way, one worse than the one last night," Amanda replied, frowning. "You will not be safe here. Don't ask me how I know, but I do."

It was quiet for a few moments, and then Joe said, "I think we should go. We've all had the dreams. We've all seen Amanda in 'em. I say we go."

The whole group muttered under their breathes for a few moments, and then they all agreed to go with "the one in their dreams."

"Where do you want us to go?" Joe asked.

"Johnson Street."

"That's over in the ruins."

"The ruins?"

"That's what they named that neighborhood after everyone lost their homes and they went into foreclosure," Joe replied. "It became a place where only ghosts exist now. I remember that time well. One day that part of town was alive and well, and the next it was quiet and lifeless. It was depressing and sad, to put it mildly, but then again, a lot of us fell into that bottomless pit."

"That's for sure," a few of the group added.

"But what could you offer us there?" someone asked. "Ruins is the right word for that place. I feel that it's better here. Besides, it's too far. None of us would make it, especially in this snow. At best, half of us are on the way out anyway."

"All of you are," Amanda stated, moving past Joe and look-ing at everyone. "That is why I am here. I think all of you know that deep down in your souls, for I'm in the same situation as you good people. But I have hope. Please, just try to think outside the box. Remember the dreams."

"I'm going, "Joe said, sounding definite.

"I know," Amanda said, turning around and smiling at him. "That's why I walked past you. I didn't have to convince you. Please convince them."

"I will."

And he did. It took a while, for they were now living their

lives in a different realm, one that the lighted prism had altered ever so slightly. And again, these people were homeless and unwell, surviving as best they could instead of living the end of their lives in homes of their own, protected from the elements and outside forces of the world.

Most of these older folks could never travel the distance to Johnson Street under normal circumstances, never mind trudging through a foot of new snow. Amanda knew this and told everyone to form a single line and hold hands, which they did.

As the group left the train station, headed by Amanda Primrose and Righteousness, the prism of light shifted once again around them, stretching "The Now Realm" even further. Newfound energy from years past entered each of the homeless people's interior cores, and with each new step they took through the snow, not only did they not become tired, but the opposite effect took place. New energy revitalized their old and broken bodies, and they moved at an increasingly quicker pace as the wind and snow blew around them.

The group could not see through different realms, but Amanda and Righteousness were able to. Dark shapes took physical form, materializing around the group. The two beams of light from the prism intensified on Amanda and the canine, and a few strange things happened.

These two beams of light also could only be seen by Amanda and Righteousness, and not the homeless group. The newly revitalized homeless group also did not see what happened next.

As the group moved forward, and the dark figures moved in around them, Amanda transformed into a completely white and yellow light. Her physical form remained intact, but she shone like a star. Righteousness grew to twice the size of Amanda, turning into a vicious canine that looked more like a giant German shepherd. The dog snarled and showed its sharp teeth as it stared angrily at the imposing presences. As they came closer their shapes could be seen more clearly. Though hidden, they looked human-like, but their frames were covered with hooded robes that fell below their feet—if, indeed, they had them. They levitated a foot above the snow and floated instead of walked toward the homeless line of spirits.

Righteousness ran around the hand-holding single line of homeless souls, barking and snapping its giant jaws at the incoming dark tide. They immediately stopped in their tracks as the group continued to relentlessly move forward. As the massive, imposing canine continued to circle the group, the dark hooded figures came no closer. In fact, if anything, they retreated a few feet. They did not leave, though, and moved along with the homeless group, remaining the same distance away from them until they reached Johnson Street, and the neighborhood where the Primrose family had once lived. Then they dissolved into the cold, crisp air.

As soon as that happened, Amanda went back to her original physical form, and Righteousness did the same. The canine barked once more at that area where they had been, and then returned to Amanda's side and moved forward with her, as if nothing had happened. The two beams of light from the colorful prism also disappeared at the same time the dark figures dissolved into thin air.

During this time, as stated before, the group did not see what had just taken place. They saw Amanda only in her physical form during their whole trek toward the abandoned neighborhood and Johnson Street. They did, in fact, see Righteousness (in his regular physical form) leave Amanda's side and circle the group constantly until they reached the neighborhood. They also saw the canine bark and show its teeth as if something was moving in. They did not see any of the dark hooded figures, though—only cold, crisp air on a day that was rapidly clearing, the sun breaking through gray storm clouds. What is noted here for the first time, which only the single-lined homeless group heard inside their heads, was a whispering voice telling them to continue walking, never mind Righteousness and his frantic antics; everything was all right. This message was repeated constantly until the group entered the neighborhood where Johnson Street awaited. These whispered, insistent words were obeyed by the group, and as they gained strength with every step they took, they *spiritually* became stronger as well. They didn't glow brightly like Amanda did physically, but the group did inwardly, and the discouraged dark hooded figures saw that, and scowled. This also, along with the protective actions of a transformed Righteousness, kept those insidious entities away—and make no mistake, they were negative and disruptive in every way possible.

The group approached the south end of Johnson Street, and Amanda told the group to rest. It was the first time they had stopped since leaving the train station, which covered several miles. Through foot-high snow, and at advanced ages, that was quite a feat. In fact, if the truth be known, the group wasn't even breathing hard—another amazing feat.

Johnson Street Itself was a half-mile long; there were twenty-five houses on the left, and thirty-one on the right. At one time many children played on this lively street (it was not a main vein), and in family backyards. Playful noise heard from young lungs, and life at its richest and happiest, once lived on this strip for many years, and to see it now in this state, as well as many other streets in many different neighborhoods all across a new America, was sad to see. A new aura had materialized and dropped over many parts of the States, with each area showing its own "Identity Crisis Depression and Decay."

As the homeless group stared down the street and saw the

conditions of the homes, they regressed and began to grumble and voice their displeasure. Joe, who walked just behind Amanda, turned to stare at his train station roommates, and held up his hands.

"Folks," he said, "look at how different this one day has been for us so far. We all have dreamed and talked about this woman and her dog for some time—*all* of us have—so please give her a chance. I doubt she would bring us all out here to prank us. That would be a bad joke, and I, for one, don't believe she has that darkness in her."

More grumblings persisted, but then they eventually settled down. Joe was obviously the spokesman and leader of the group, and it didn't take a rocket scientist to realize they respected him.

Once the group became quiet, Joe continued. "Amanda, what exactly is your plan, because we *are* in the Ruins, and I can't see an endgame here."

Amanda smiled at Joe, and then at the others. During the group's back and forth, she had remained silent. Over her years working in diners, she realized that listening to others was her best attribute. She had heard many customers argue in the past and found it better not to interject herself into the fray. If a customer wanted her opinion, she would wait until she was asked. In this case, Joe was that person. He was the opening she was waiting for, and she held up her hands as all eyes looked upon her.

"You are about to see some miracles, folks," Amanda started, smiling. "All of you will be cared for by some*one*, or *something* that believes that *all* lives matter. You people, like so many, myself included, have been discarded by society to some extent. That is a sin. That is wrong. Today justice in this part of the world will be served. Today justice will be handed out *rightfully*, and the ledger balanced properly. *Spiritually*, we are all the same, and should be treated, and *respected* just like everyone else. Most in this neighborhood lost their jobs and livelihoods unjustly, and then were treated sinfully. Some of you have gone through the same mistreatment. It is unjust. It is wrong, and a higher power frowns down on such insidious sentences." She paused. "You have all dreamed of me. Before today I did not know that you had. As you have journeyed from the train station to this blessed place, outside dark forces have tried to stop us. They have tried to stop this mission. Thanks to all of you, Righteousness, hopefully myself, and The Lord above they have failed this day. But tomorrow is a different day, and one fast approaching. Darkness in physical and spiritual forms will always be among us, but we will fight them with everything we've got. Please give me the chance to show you how justice will be served on this delightful day."

And she did. The group talked amongst each other, and all agreed that everything Amanda had just said was true. They all knew *something* had happened on their way over here, and they *felt* it as well, and so they all agreed to see this day through. They would not be disappointed.

Amanda led the group down the street to the Primrose residence. First, she took Joe across the street and led him inside the Cranston residence. The rest of the group looked on with puzzled expressions, for all they could see was the Primrose woman and Joe talking. Eventually Joe hugged her and started to cry. He backed up, and Amanda handed him a package of tissues to wipe the tears that had run down his battle scarred face. It appears to all outside that the woman they have all dreamed of, and Joe, have walked into a house that is way beyond repair. And yet their leader is seen crying, but also smiling. He is crying tears of joy, yet no evidence has been shown as to why. To this end, they all individually keep an open mind. (Give it a chance . . .) And they do.

Amanda walked out alone and did the same with the rest of the group. Some were left in groups, others preferred their privacy, for they have been deprived of that dignity for so long—something most of us take for granted.

When everyone had taken possession of their new residences, three houses on each side of the Primrose residence, and two houses on each side of the Cranston household, all of the homeless group disappeared inside badly decaying houses. Had the Event taken place? Had the power gone off? Had all animals and most people gone back to The Creator? No, for that would not happen for many months. Let's delve into what took place and see if justice had been served like Amanda Primrose stated it would be.

When Amanda walked Joe Kellerman across the street to the Cranston residence and went inside, the leader of the homeless community saw the house come back to life and instantaneously rebuild itself around him. The furnace started up, filling the home with warmth, the electricity turned on all lights, and a television set came on, showing the midday news. The weatherman, meteorologist James Frances, was on, showing that, indeed, a new storm was on the way for the following evening. This one would produce strong blizzard-force winds and drop one to two feet of snow on top of what had already fallen. Amanda told Joe that food would be in the refrigerator, which *would* be working, and it would replenish itself whenever the food supply got low. Joe began crying, and hugged Amanda, who hugged him back.

She asked him how his health was, and he told her he didn't know; he hadn't seen a doctor in years. His head hurt often though, as well as his stomach. He confided to her that some days he hurt worse than bad, and he had prayed for death on more than one occasion. Amanda nodded, and asked him how he felt now. He thought for a few moments, and then replied that he felt fine—in fact, he had felt good ever since he had woken up that morning, and he informed her that he'd had a bad night, vomiting twice while cramps wracked his midsection. Amanda told him that a presence in her dream had told her that he had cancer, first starting in his stomach, and then traveling to his brain. She quickly added that the presence had taken his sickness away, and he no longer had cancer.

Joe kept his emotions in check, for this was too much to believe, but he *did* feel better. He wanted to believe; he wanted to feel good. He was sick (no pun intended) of feeling pain, and of seeing a desolate darkness in his future. But this revelation must be questioned. Amanda realized his confusion, agreed with his assumptions, but told him to keep an open mind, and wait and see. He agreed, and then she said her goodbyes. Before Amanda left Joe agreed to come for dinner that evening, and she told him he was welcome anytime he needed her. He said thanks and wiped away tears with a handkerchief that Amanda handed him.

She did the same with the rest, and by late afternoon the complete group of homeless people were homeless no longer; in fact, they were in a better place than most of humanity that day, and the days that followed, right up until the power went off and they went back to The Creator.

Good to her word, Joe felt better, and never experienced any symptoms of cancer again. Was it gone? Had he even *had* cancer? Debatable, for he had never gone to a doctor's office and got conformation on his condition, but he *did* feel twenty years younger than his eighty-two years, and so he didn't push fate. He came over for dinner that evening, and many more afterward.

The same went for the other people in the group. Paul and Maureen Brown moved into the house next to Joe. They were the only ones married, both seventy-six years old, and both dying. Paul had pancreatic cancer, but had yet to feel any symptoms.

He also needed hip replacement and felt pain with every step he took. Amazingly he had walked from the train station without much effort and continued to get better in that area. Maureen had lung cancer. Almost immediately, she was moving around without labored breathing, and within a few days both felt completely healed—which they were.

The rest of the group felt rejuvenated as well. All their ailments healed and disappeared, and they lived healthy lives right up until the Event took place. All of them interacted with each other, having lunch or dinner together, playing cards or other games they found littered around their new homes, and watched the news and other programs with each other.

The day after all of them had moved into their new homes, it did, indeed, snow. It was thought by most to be the biggest blizzard in "a dog's age," and Weatherman Frances even said so on the news. It dropped twenty-eight inches in the Green Bay area alone! As fate would have it, the old roof of the train station fell inward, due to its decay, and the weight of the two back-to-back snowstorms. That became a topic of discussion all that winter. Just think, they all marveled, one more day and that roof would've come down on them. They couldn't thank Amanda enough for saving them, for surely disaster would have taken place if she hadn't come to rescue them when she had. Just one more day! It became the group's motto.

Every few days part of the group went with Amanda and Righteousness to other out-of-the way areas whenever each of them dreamed of others in need. In each dream the rock would roll away from the cave, and the faces of those who needed to be saved would appear from inside. A bright glow would form around those individuals, and then the voice (further on back into the cave) would tell them where they were, and how to get there. Once awake, those that had the dream (Amanda was always one of them) would venture out and bring each new member of the community back to Johnson Street and give them their own residence. They did this until every house on the street was filled, and then they all became one big happy family as winter turned into spring, then early summer.

Another miracle: you might wonder why the authorities never bothered the new residents of Johnson Street, never chased them out of the decaying neighborhood. That was because whenever one of the groups left their homes, they became transparent to everyone other than themselves. Yes, the area was periodically patrolled by the police, but never once did they ever see any of the new residents of Johnson Street walking back and forth to each other's homes, nor whenever they went out looking for more people to save. Just like the first time in what became a regular ritual, they would always walk back to Johnson Street holding hands, becoming invisible to the rest of society forever thereafter. At times the police *felt* as if some*thing* was amiss, and even physically patrolled the area, walking the complete length of Johnson Street from time to time, but never did they ever see any of the group. Some even walked alongside the patrolmen as they searched the area. The group had a good laugh more than once over that, some laughing until they cried. The prism of altered light was working completely in their favor; they knew it, and they took full advantage of that.

A thanksgiving: Each day, usually after breakfast, "The Johnson Community" as it was now called, instead of a homeless group, gathered together inside the Primrose residence for up to an hour to say a few prayers of thankfulness to The Lord. They were all grateful and appreciated what they had been given. They reasoned that so many take for granted the priceless little gifts they don't consciously think about, but not this community. Precious little things in their life became bigger than most will ever consider, and so during this spiritual time many tears were shed. Each day one person would talk, telling the rest of the flock their story—their hardships before ending up on Johnson Street. Most had lost their faith during their dark days (if they had had any religious beliefs in the first place) and refound it tenfold here. Afterward they would recite The Lord's Prayer, hug each other, tell each member that they loved them, and then go about their day as they pleased without worries or cares. Wouldn't we all like to live our lives as such!

A supernatural occurrence: during these morning times of spirituality and togetherness, lit candles of all colors magically appeared around the Primrose living room, and the windows became stained glassed, like in churches. The room became a sanctuary—a place (or house) of worship. That was the balance on the positive side. On the negative side of the ledger, once everyone was inside Amanda Primrose's sanctuary, it became totally dark outside. A black presence swirled around the home like an evil entity, which it was. The blinding essence was like a fog, where visibility was zero. This negative entity did not come without dire consequences.

Early on, as the community first became aware of this phenomenon, Joe opened the front door, his curiosity getting the best of him. He quickly slammed the door shut and started screaming in pain. His right arm, which he had stuck outside, had cracked at the elbow, frozen solid. It turned completely black, broke off, and fell to the floor, breaking into many pieces. What looked like little termites with sharp red teeth came out of these fragments and ate them within seconds. Then they just as fast died on the welcome mat, becoming first motionless, and then completely disappearing. Within minutes, as others looked on, Joe grew back his forearm and hand as if nothing had happened, but two things were clear: whatever swirled outside the house during their time of worship was cruel and deadly. The same went for the darkness if it entered the Primrose living room, and whatever was inside it, like the termite things. Joe told the group that he sensed other things out there as well: dangerous creatures with very bad intentions. Evil intents. This insidious phenomenon completely disappeared as soon as they ended their spiritual worship, and they were allowed to leave. At that point, nature, and the prism of light, returned to normal and the worshippers walked out of the Primrose residence after service untouched and unharmed.

Another strange occurrence that the whole group noticed: even though it was completely black outside during this hour of Thanksgiving, the stained-glass windows glowed, and their magnificence filled the room, spreading the positive rays of the sun throughout the makeshift sanctuary. This was an example of the prism of light on full display.

Overall, though, justice had been served, but not without dealing with the swirling darkness and other outside forces. Shocker there! Each time another homeless member was brought back to Johnson Street, the dark hooded figures appeared, and Righteousness had to drive them all away in his altered physical transformation. Amanda never knew who they were, or why they wanted to prevent them from bringing in new members to the Johnson Street Community—not until much later.

On the day of the Event, everyone on Johnson Street went back to The Creator except Amanda Primrose. Even Righteousness went back, but not instantaneously. First let us go back to the exact moment of the Event, and see how it differed from previous chapters, and yet to be told stories.

Amanda and Joe were in the Primrose kitchen, talking about

having a barbecue, Righteousness sitting by their side, when simultaneously Joe disappeared, all power ceased to work, and it became extremely quiet. The Primrose house went back in time to its decayed form, looking just like it had when Amanda had first come back, just before the area's first snowstorm back in the fall.

Shocked, Amanda looked down and stared at Righteousness. He was staring back up at her, wagging his tail. He suddenly transformed into what Amanda had begun calling his protective mode, and lovingly licked her face. There were no words between them, there never had been, but they'd had many spiritual conversations, and they were having one now. He was saying goodbye. Maybe not forever, but for now—and that hurt enough. She felt her heart breaking, and so he licked her face harder, and faster. And then Righteousness began to fade; slowly at first, but then it accelerated. He disappeared completely while still licking her face, and Amanda could still feel him doing that long after she could no longer see him.

Amanda, trancelike, walked outside and looked around. What is happening? she thought, sitting down on the front lawn. Why is everyone gone? She had been told that something was coming, but this? It didn't make sense, but then, did any of it? Yes, this last half year had been spiritually uplifting, and it all worked in her favor, but did it really make sense? Was this real—had *any* of it been? She buried her head in her hands and burst out in tears.

All of a sudden she heard three loud crashes in succession, and then saw black smoke rise into the air. A breeze began blowing, and Amanda smelled jet fuel. It was strong. It was close. It smelled extremely unhealthy. (Planes with no power . . .) Fires slowly rose high into the sky, and she realized that they were in the neighborhoods beyond the tracks where the well-to-do people lived—or *had* lived, if, indeed, *they* were still there. How ironic, she thought, somewhat bitterly. The people who always wanted possessions, and then still weren't satisfied, craving more and more, were losing everything now. Whatever event had taken place was now destroying their neighborhood—up in smoke, *unbuilt!* (Unbuild, uninstall, yes, but Amanda, please look into your heart . . .) And so, she did.

Amanda suddenly thought that if anybody *was* still over there, they'd be in trouble. (Now your heart is beating straight, my child.) She started running down Johnson Street, in the direction of "the other side of the tracks," and suddenly stopped.

(It won't matter . . .)

Introspection: in this situation, it wouldn't, but Amanda instantly thought back across the years to when it *could've* mattered. We all have done that, haven't we? Could've helped, but didn't? If I had only acted differently; if I had only *cared* a little more . . . Some examples: helped someone that was being bullied, but didn't. Offered to financially help out a friend, or even a complete stranger, but didn't. Given your leftovers to a hungry homeless person sitting on the side of the street, but didn't, and then ended up throwing them away when hunger didn't come calling again that day. That's what Amanda was thinking about as she started toward the fires. Could I? Could I possibly help someone in need, in danger, in peril? Maybe even save someone's *life*.

That line of thought was interrupted when an invisible force grabbed her by the shoulders, holding her back like a racehorse, and told her in no uncertain terms, *"It won't matter!"* The presence also added two more lines of raw reality. "You have done enough, my child. It is time to think about *yourself* now!"

Amanda, unlike us, dear readers, was not privy to the knowledge of the Event, and so she couldn't have known that no human soul was over in the danger zone across the tracks to save—no one anywhere in her vicinity. And yet she stopped to listen to the voice, and stared west, where changes were happening . . .

Dark storm clouds appeared on the western horizon, and loud thunder and lightning could be heard. The fires blazed and grew, and Amanda suddenly heard two more crashes behind her, possibly no more than a few miles away. Fires sprung up in that direction as well as more jet fuel could be smelled. Nature took its course, though—this time extremely violently. Amanda stood underneath a partial roof as it began to rain. Within seconds, it was raining cats and dogs, to put it mildly. Amanda would later look back on the changing weather in reflection, *knowing* that she had never seen nature unleash just violence in her life. Never had she seen it rain so hard, and with such intensity, and never had she heard thunder so loud, and so close to the ground. Never had she seen so much lightning, shooting through the dark clouds and hitting the ground in so many places. Never had she heard so many trees falling all around her. Never had she felt the wind pick up like it did. Never had she . . . Amanda feared for her life and began praying.

(Fear not, my child . . .)

Amanda went into the house's basement and huddled in a corner. A minute later she heard a roar and realized the worst-case scenario was happening: a tornado had formed and was churning, moving in her direction. She knew this, for she had witnessed a few of them while living in Texas. She shook with fear and began crying.

(Fear not, my child, for *un*construction must take place . . .)

Amanda prayed out loud, for the rumbling could now be heard all around her. Never had she feared for her life like she did now. Please, she thought frantically, no more nevers.

(You're back in Kansas-land now. But no need to tap your heels three times . . .)

The decaying house above her cracked and split, and then was ripped from its foundation, and some of the floorboards went with it. Wind and rain came in through many openings, and water began filling the basement. The tornado slowly moved away, but it still wasn't safe to leave; the winds were still too strong. Amanda would be forced to soon, though, for the water level in the house's foundation was rising quickly.

More loud and angry roaring could be heard south of her, and she wondered if another tornado had formed. If it had, she would drown, for the water level was five feet deep already. Amanda huddled near the top of the basement steps as heavy rain pelted her face. It hit her at angles that seemed to defy the laws of gravity, but nothing was normal now. As the water level reached her feet (six feet and climbing), everything began to calm down. She still heard roaring off to her south, but it was moving away, not toward her.

"Thank you," she said out loud as the rain and wind let up.

Amanda climbed the few steps to the first level and couldn't believe what she saw. In proportion to where she stood, she saw things that yesterday she thought would have been impossible. No houses could be seen in any direction; they had all been ripped from their foundations and lay splintered everywhere. All except one—hers! The famous Primrose residence. It was still in its decayed condition, but it stood alone, defiant.

(We build, we unbuild, and sometimes we stay the same . . .)

Way in the distance Amanda could see three massive tornados heading east, destroying everything in their path. There were possibly more than three, but that was all Amanda could see. Big parts of airplanes could be seen over the landscape, laying this way and that. She could still smell jet fuel, but the rains had dilated it, weakening the strong odor. No fires burned, all extinguished by nature's overpowering fury.

Shaking her head in amazement, Amanda walked gingerly through the wreckage back to her house. Watching out for nails and sharp pieces of splintered wood, she could still hear the rumbling of thunder in the distance. Large puddles of water were everywhere, and rainwater dripped from everything above the ground, but otherwise the quiet eventually overtook the area, and Amanda felt utterly alone once again—and this time it was welcomed.

Another miracle: as Amanda walked into her house it became whole again. The power didn't work, including the refrigerator, but the leftovers from last night's dinner were still cool, and so Amanda ate the remains of her greens and potato salad, and lay down on her couch, totally exhausted. With no television to keep her company, she drifted off rather quickly, snoring loudly. If anybody had been around, her snores were the only sounds to be heard as twilight set in.

This night Amanda dreamed, or became part of her own subterranean thoughts. She found herself in front of the cave with the rock in front of it she had dreamed of so many times before, only this time the perspective was different. Always in the past she had seen this scene as if through a television set or on a movie screen, but now she was part of the landscape herself, standing on a dirt path with plant life growing wildly on each side. They were like no other shrublike growth that Amanda had ever seen before. Multicolored and vibrant, they seemed to be alive and breathing, inhaling and exhaling constantly. They were also growing at an accelerated rate. As Amanda looked around her, they grew from waist high to three times over her head, with no indication of stopping. She walked up to the rock, which was dark in color, and felt it. To the touch it felt cool, almost cold. It suddenly rolled to the right, and Amanda had to shield her eyes, for the brilliant light she saw inside the cave was extremely bright.

"Hello, my child," Amanda heard from somewhere inside the light. The voice was low in tone, but peaceful and calm. "I have brought you here to bring you news of what is to come. There is a midsized rock to the right of the cave that you can sit on. Then I will fill you in on certain details you need to know."

And the voice did just that. Amanda listened, and learned much. By the time the voice stopped talking Amanda felt herself get sleepy, as if drugged. She wanted to ask many more questions, but she couldn't talk or move. It wasn't as if she was paralyzed or anything, she just felt as if she was *dissolving* somehow. It felt as if every atom of her being was separating and fading away. Suddenly her mind and memories flatlined, and the next thing she remembered was waking up on her couch. She glanced by her feet, hoping to see Righteousness laying there, but he was gone, and she missed him terribly. Tears welled up again, and she quickly wiped them away. No time for things I can't control, Amanda thought, getting up off the couch. There are things to do, places to go! This she knew, and she also knew that she must start out alone; for she *was* alone. There were others; this she now knew, but she had been told that she would be alone for a while. She would travel alone, and without Righteousness, her closest friend. She remembered being told that he wasn't *allowed* here anymore; the situation would become too unstable. The voice had told her many things, but not all was understood. Through the realms of different time zones language had changed, and so she had been told information in an ancient tongue. It would make total sense eventually as the gears of time ticked away.

Amanda spent the next two days packing an overnight bag filled with a change of clothes and food, and then rested up for her journey. During the daylight hours she sat outside her house and scanned the wreckage that the storms had produced. She wondered where they had ended up, and what damage they had done.

A timeline on climate change: weather overall in these times had changed drastically, deadly. Tornados were more common and widespread. Severe thunderstorms were almost a daily occurrence during the increasingly warmer summers. Flooding was an issue everywhere as rivers and streams overflowed their banks almost weekly. Those who had predicted these changes sat back and said grimly, "I told you so." Most of these early meteorologists and scientists were long gone by the time the Event took place, but they knew, they knew. Those who choose a different stance, mostly due to political differences, still shook their heads in defiance, but that side of the ongoing debate had less and less data to show in their defense. Most were considered fools, and kept their conversation amongst themselves, embarrassed to say anything in the social realms of the country.

Amanda thought about these changes, and other more concerning situations as well. As stated, she was alone, but still not alone. The black hooded figures were still around, standing in front of her to the east. They floated above the wreckage at the end of what was left of Johnson Street, but came no closer. One thing had changed about them. Still faceless, each one of them now sported two red eyes that stared intently on the Primrose woman. Amanda was nervous and scared, for a chilling metamorphosis had taken place and Righteousness was no longer around to protect her. She took a few steps toward them, and felt the air go from cool to cold. They, in turn did not waver, instead stood their ground in defiance, and continued to follow her movements with their red eyes. They shifted slightly with every step Amanda took before she retreated into her house.

Instantly she felt extremely exhausted, and Amanda lay down on her couch; trembling, and feeling weak. Who are these creatures? she asked herself in fear. How will I . . .

Be able to travel? she finished the thought after falling into deep slumber and waking up in front of the cave again. The rock had been rolled away, but there was no light inside, only darkness. Amanda walked down the path and looked inside. It felt barren, empty. She turned around and saw someone moving down the path toward her. He had long shoulder-length brown hair that was thick and wavy. He sported a well-kept beard. He wore a white rope with sandals. Tears welled up in her eyes, for she recognized him as he came closer. It couldn't be, and yet it is, she thought in amazement. As the figure came closer Amanda felt an aura of love and fulfillment surround her, and her spirit filled with bliss.

"Hello, my child," the figure said, giving Amanda a warm hug. "You have done well and pleased many."

"Jesus? Is that you?" she asked, hugging the figure back. A bright light surrounded them, and Amanda had never felt so protected, so *engulfed!*

"I am who you say I am," Jesus replied, releasing her and stepping back. He held her shoulders loosely, and an electrical current flowed into her through his hands. "I brought you back here to let you know that the desolate ones will be harmless now. I have given you a little bit of the light to ward them off."

"The desolate ones?"

"Yes, the dark hooded figures. They are lost souls of the unholy and should be taken seriously."

"Yes, I thought so. Righteousness kept them at bay, but he is no longer with me, which is why I am so afraid."

"You need not fear them now, my child. They will now fear *you*, for you have the spirit of Righteousness inside you. You now have the light of a thousand angels to complete your journey. Leave tomorrow with confidence and follow that light. It will safely guide you."

"Thank you, Jesus. Thank you so much. I—"

"You need not say anything more, my child. Just be you. That is enough."

Jesus then disappeared, and Amanda fell back into deep slumber before waking up on the couch. She opened her eyes and smiled as she stared up at the ceiling. She hugged herself, for all was good; all felt *right*. Amanda felt the electric current flowing through her spirit, enlightening her soul, empowering her. How blessed she was! To Meet *him*! The *son*! How many . . .

(More than you think.)

Amanda shook her head, for she still couldn't believe it. These last nine months! Righteousness. The rebuilding houses. The people we helped! The people *themselves*! It was truly an astounding journey that she had been on—was *still* on. Like anyone else, Amanda had, and continued to ask herself, "Why me?" The answer she always got back, either through her dreams or a voice in the back of her mind, replied, "Why *not* you?"

Amanda closed her eyes, and somehow fell asleep once again. This time she did not dream and slept straight through the rest of the night. The electric current grew inside her soul during that time, now known as "The Righteous Gift." It altered her essence, both spiritually and physically. Amanda still looked the same as a bright sun came up over the eastern horizon that morning, but she possessed much more than when the sun had set the previous evening.

We are builders
Some build physically.
Some build spiritually.
And some build in both realms, becoming something new.

Around ten thirty that morning, as a hot sun rose high into a cloudless and bright blue sky, Amanda left her home—one she had loved so dearly. Fresh tears welled up in her eyes as she turned around at the edge of the lawn to look at it for the last time. Possibly for her eyes only, Amanda saw her house in one piece, with no decay. This was the first time this had happened, and she reasoned it was for her benefit. Memories, not all good, flashed through her mind. That didn't matter. It was her first protector, her first *love*. And it was still protecting her, looking out for her overall well-being. Even now! Yes, even as she was about to leave it for the last time it would not let the last image of it be one of decay—only welcoming and strong.

The sun rose higher into a cloudless blue sky. The air was still and calm, a complete contrast from the violent weather a few days ago. A beam of light appeared and continued east down what was left of Johnson Street.

(Follow it; it will lead the way.)

Amanda nodded, exhaled, blew a goodbye kiss at her home, then turned around and started walking. The beam was ten feet wide, but for how long it went Amanda had no idea. It disappeared over a damaged, or completely destroyed, eastern horizon.

In the distance, on both sides of the beam, Amanda could see the lost souls of the unholy beginning to unite. They were many, darkening both sides of the lighted beam. Many red lights from their eye slits could be seen, and they continued over the eastern horizon.

Amanda could feel the electric current surge through her entire being, and she bravely marched forward. As she passed by the first dark-hooded lost souls, tortured screams of agony could be heard inside their crowded darkness. They were terrifying and intimidating in tone, and Amanda started to shake with fear.

(Disregard those failing tactics.)

And Amanda did. Defiantly she never wavered after that as she disappeared over the eastern horizon. Inside her head she was determined to journey onward, and so she did. Two words repeated inside her head as she took each step: *go east.*

Eventually the screaming inside the lost souls of the unholy faded away, and then so did the lost souls themselves—first their piercing red eyes, and then their hooded darkness. This all happened after Amanda's first ten miles. Once they no longer stood on each side of the beam she breathed a sigh of relief but knew full well they could return at any time. She felt blessed and loved. She smiled, held her head high, and continued onward.

Back on Johnson Street, the Primrose household stood proudly alone among the debris. But as soon as the last of the lost souls of the unholy disappeared in frustration it first returned itself into its decayed condition, and then crumbled to the ground. Within seconds after its remains settled and became quiet, they disappeared, leaving nothing behind—not even its foundation.

We are builders.
Some build physically.

Some build spiritually.
We are builders.
And sometimes we *un*build.
And sometimes we remove . . .

A controversial point of view: controversial yes, but this topic must be brought to the surface. Probably more than a few people believe that inserting Jesus Christ into a storyline, and the cave in which his body was laid to rest in, would be considered blasphemy. I do not. Why? Because I believe that I was meant to write this story just as it's printed—plain and simple. I believe that people need to see life through different eyes, seeing all things from different perspectives, or through the prism of light. The cave is symbolic and used in a completely positive light. That's my opinion, but you may disagree, and that's fine too. We all have the right to think a certain way. Can't we just agree to disagree? Isn't that a better way to settle all different points of view?

Chapter Thirty-One

THE CONGERRIANS
AND THE SICKNESS

Pyramids are located all over the world. Their structures have outer surfaces that are triangular in shape and converge in a single point at the top. Some pyramid bases can be trilateral, quadrilateral, or any polygon shape. They have at least three outer triangular surfaces (at least four faces including the base). A common pyramid is the square kind, which consists of four triangular outer surfaces. For thousands of years they were the largest structures on Earth, and in this chapter we will be concentrating on three of them. Over the years they have sunk at least thirty meters into the planet's surface, but are still equivalent in size to the Great Pyramid of Cholula, in the Mexican State of Puebla, and two structures in Egypt: the Red Pyramid in the Dasher Necropolis, and the Great Pyramid of Khufu, the latter being one of the Seven Wonders of the Ancient World that still remains. It is made of limestone and is considered an architectural masterpiece. It contains over two million blocks ranging from 5,500 to 33,000 pounds. The base covers thirteen acres and its original height was 488 feet. Today its height is down to 455 feet because of the theft of the fine quality white Tura limestone encasing the stones, but it still remains the tallest pyramid.

One wonders why early man built pyramids. History shows two reasons, both philosophical and architectural. Philosophically, as man evolved from animals, he got his early knowledge from nature (fire, rain, wind, etc.). As civilizations developed, so did religions. Man began worshiping nature's elements like water, wind, rain, the sun, etc., and each had a god attached to it. Many religions still worship these gods today. The ideas to build pyramids came from the physical presence of mountains. Since prehistoric times human beings have wondered about them. They are huge, especially compared to mankind. They are physically imposing, and we have always yearned to climb them. Even though the risks are great, we still today attempt to climb the biggest and tallest of them, like Mt. Everest. These humungous natural structures contain numerous treasures in the form of fruits, vegetation, flora and fauna, various sized caves, and waterfalls. Their natural beauty (slopes and shapes) are breathtaking. Early man was able to survive many times over because of what mountains had to offer. In short, it was a survival haven. Mountains simple vastness in size have left a great impression on mankind on a whole since it's dawn. The numeral myths and legends associated with pyramids are the testimony of this. Many civilizations thought that the souls of their ancestors resided in mountains, as well as gods. Mountains were also closer to the heavens than any one physical form, therefore they must be spiritual presences—a gateway to the home of the gods. The shape of a pyramid resembles "all ways of life" leading to one goal: nirvana; merging with the almighty, the afterlife theory.

If there is a pyramid, it is assumed, then there is an inverted pyramid as well. The inverted pyramid represents knowledge gained by one individual and his sharing of that information to others, causing it to spread amongst all men (this sharing happens less and less today, for then that individual no longer seems so special or important). Physically, pyramids are basically simple: the base is wide, and the top is narrow. The entire weight of the large structure is vastly distributed on the large base. This gives more durability and strength to the pyramid over millennia. Case in point, if the World Trade Center had been built in the shape of a pyramid, it probably would not have collapsed as it did. (Then again, nobody in their right mind would have thought that some-one would purposely fly jet airliners into them, killing themselves in the process.) Due to the slopes on the three or four sides of the pyramid it is protected against erosion and heavy winds (such as a sandstorm). It is also protected against rainwater, for it just runs down the slope and cannot log up anywhere.

There is a third reason why early man built pyramids. Before life began, beings from foreign planets visited Earth for various purposes. As man evolved he would claim to see these triangular spaceships either landing or taking off out of valleys and canyons. Since humanity had never seen such technology, these alien ves-sels were considered godlike in their eyes. On one such journey these aliens landed on Earth with prisoners on board from a dif-ferent solar system, and something went terribly wrong. Here is what happened.

For centuries, a race called the Congerrians regularly visited Earth, mainly for its water supply. They didn't need it for survival themselves, per se, but they knew other races across this Galaxy did, and so they would load up their tanks and barter their goods to other species that lived in different parts of the universe, al-ways getting the better of the bargain. They were an advanced race that possessed the best machinery as well, such as spacecrafts, weapons, etc., and always invested in improvements from their riches. Those are their positives. Their negatives more than out-numbered their attributes, by far.

Before we delve into them; know this: their planet was in one of the solar systems where a sun had been destroyed, killing off everything in that sector, including their entire race. Once it ex-ploded, the planets that orbited that star careened out of control, creating complete chaos on the satellite's surfaces. Parts of the sun hit the planets like spears, splitting them into many pieces. That shouldn't have been possible, but what this solar system was ex-periencing went way beyond normal logic. When that happened, all occupants perished quite quickly in that trauma, most being thrown into the atmosphere and into the vacuum of space. The others burned into gray ash in seconds and were no more, their screams lasting longer than their physical forms.

That was mere days before the power went off on Earth, and most of all life went back to The Creator. As all of this was go-ing on, all but one of the Congerrian spacecrafts were in their home Dock, and were completely destroyed. The spacecraft that survived wasn't many light years away, but they were far enough away to survive. It was one of a few spaceships that had visited Earth on many occasions but hadn't been back there for quite some time. The story behind that will be told in the lines below, but let's do things in order, and let patience be the virtue.

The Congerrians were evil-minded vampires. Any race that had ever encountered them knew that to be fact. They were con-sidered the bullies of the universe, and most species quivered in their wake, ready to do anything to survive their unsettling visits.

Physically, they were between eight to ten feet tall, and most weighed more than four hundred pounds. Here was the strange thing about them. They looked more similar to human beings than any other race in the chamber as far as body structure was concerned, but otherwise they were completely different.

They possessed a head with reddish wavy hair that fell halfway down their backs. Their faces looked human: two eyes, a nose in-between, two ears, and a mouth, but when they opened that oral cavity most races recoiled in terror-filled fear. Three red pointy tongues, each stacked on top of each other, moved like spasming tentacles in and out between purplish thin lips that seemed to constantly grin, as if the creature knew a secret that no one else had an inkling about. All its many whitish teeth were sharply fanged, and were capable of cutting through almost anything, or any*body*. Its neck was thick and veined, and blood could be seen running through those enhanced arteries, black in color.

From their shoulders down to their feet, Congerrians were extremely heavily muscled, and they were as strong as they looked. Unlike human beings, they had larger hands and feet—maybe twice as big in proportion to their frames, and had one extra finger and toe on each. They dressed in armored tank top upper-body ware, complete with two-inch sharp silver spikes across their chest area, black in color. They hugged the Congerrian muscular body, making their torsos look even more pronounced and impressive. They wore tight armored black shorts that fell to their knees, hugging their sculptured, large upper thighs. They wore sandaled footwear that exposed most of their feet, which were partially webbed, but that didn't stop the vampires from running as fast as the wind, able to run down inferior prey easily and quickly. Their finger and toenails were long and pointed, and cut like knives. Their skin was pure white, which made their red hair, eyes, and tongues even more prominent and imposing.

They carried large ten-foot black pointy spears that they could throw up to three hundred feet, and up to a hundred miles per hour, killing or mortally wounding a victim upon impact. Like vampires in storied novels and movies, they drank the blood of others, although they rarely stopped drinking until they had completely emptied the lifeline of those victims at a very quick rate. Once that happened, their victims didn't die, or become vampires in their own right. No, they became robotic slaves, used for all purposes, including sexual pleasures. Yes, Congerrians had an extremely high sex drive, and they were vicious during their couplings. They possessed large penal-shaped appendages that measured fifteen inches in length, and were five inches thick upon arousal. If the recipient wasn't already devoid of their life force (blood), they would have, for the most part, died during the sexual assault they were forced to endure. Instead the bloodless victims would wear their wounds in agony, and eventually heal within a few hours, wherein they might be taken violently again.

Congerrians loved to inflict pain and were considered the ultimate sadists of the central sector. They whipped and beat partners they wanted to keep, but they cut, stabbed, bit uncontrollably, and chopped up the ones they didn't, and threw them away like yesterday's garbage. Either way, they loved to hear the sounds of pain and anguish, and the drawn-out screams of agony as victims begged, pleaded, and cried for their lives. Most of the time those pleas fell on deaf ears, for the Congerrians had little respect for life overall. In their history they fought few battles or wars, for their adversaries were usually totally overmatched and beaten soundly long before a conflict be considered a war. Let's delve further.

The Congerrians' planet and solar system was located very close to the door of this chamber, and it defied logic. Why? Because as everything (quasars, galaxies, stars, solar systems, planets, etc.) continually moved away and outward from the doorway, riding the current of life, this one didn't. It stayed stationary, and it had since the doorway was first opened. Space is chaotic, and doesn't follow logic (at least *our* logic), but this defied much more. There is no reasoning for this phenomenon, other than the fact that a higher force might be fudging the books for some unknown reason.

It wasn't as if this solar system physically stood out; it didn't. Yes, they are all different in one way or another, but there was nothing keeping it from moving away from the doorway like the others, and so it remained a mystery. It supported the largest sun in the entire universe, making our star look like a small speck in comparison. It burned at 50,000 degrees Fahrenheit, or about five times that of our own sun. Eight planets rotated around it; most were gas giants the size of Jupiter (which, ironically they all resembled for the most part, even sporting rings), and three were completely solid like Earth, but devoid of water. At one time or another all satellites supported different types of life, but the Congerrians had wiped them completely out before most of them even got started.

Two planets were a mixture of gas and rock, unlike any satellite here in our solar system. One, the second closest to the enormous star, was devoid of life at any time, except for a primitive insectile species that looked a lot like a fly and mosquito mix. They had no wings to speak of, and so they couldn't fly, which were needed to find a food source, and so they only lived long enough to lay their microscopic eggs under rock fragments scattered about the surface. The process would then repeat itself, never progressing past it's primitive state. Maybe they eventually would have evolved, but the vampires set up a few outposts on the planet and wiped the species out completely without even realizing it. They sprayed the surfaces of the satellite with a heavier gas they had created to change the atmosphere to suit themselves, and it killed the eggs throughout the land masses very quickly, making the insectile species extinct. Who knows what they might have become, but even if they had evolved into something more advanced, I'm sure the Congerrians would have wiped them out—maybe even just for sport.

The other planet was the closest to the sun, and was where the Congerrians migrated from. They called their planet Culeagulars, and it was only two million miles from its large and powerful sun. Its outer shell consisted of gases, and its inner core was solid for the most part, but there were a lot of areas where the surfaces were liquified, which sported the highest temperatures on the planet. That hot, unstable molasses-type substance was the life force of the planet, and the food and nectar of its powerful inhabitants. In its beginning phases many different species lived on the surface, and even some survived in the gases above, but the Congerrians wiped them all out, selfishly wanting all of the life force for themselves.

And what was the life force? The planet's circulatory system. Yes, the planet was alive and growing, and in the center of its core a heart shaped organ beat constantly, circulating its blood supply throughout its many interior arteries. At various points wounds opened up, and fluid rose to the surface, giving life to its various parasites—the strongest and most intellectual of those being the Congerrians. It also produced many toxic gases that surrounded the inner core, becoming so thick that a human being would not be able to fall through it. (Of course, our species wouldn't last a millisecond on Culeagulars, our complete essence burning up immediately, but you get the idea.) Around all of these, fires burned for many miles, constantly producing new strains of new gases, mixing with the old, making the planet grow. Culeagulars was red, orange, and crimson in color, the many thick rings orbiting its vastness actually visibly emitting gases of their own, and from a distance the complete satellite appeared as if it was on fire, burning out of control like it's giant sun. To us human beings, it would resemble one thing: hell.

In a far-off galaxy, many light years away from Culeagulars, another solar system existed, and it couldn't have been more different than where the Congerrians came from. It possessed five small bluish-colored Suns, and six similar-sized planets that all orbited each other. From afar it looked like a single atom in full swing, and then some. In reality, none of the suns or the planets ever came closer than 135 trillion miles of each other, and so the solar system overall was quite large. Each planet had many colorful rings that orbited them, the suns glittered and sparkled like no other stars, and so the solar system was quite colorful and unique for the most part. One would say that it was decorated like Christmas at all times, but the species that occupied each planet were anything but what this place in space portrayed from afar.

They were nocturnal creatures for the most part; vampirism in nature, but there was one major difference between these suns and all others. Back on Culeagular, the Congerrians could only come out at night, otherwise they would burn up and turn to ash in seconds, but none of the five suns here radiated enough heat or gamma rays to prohibit these vampires from moving around during the daytime hours. They radiated a tint of blue around the outer layers of the atmosphere, a sort of cooling system, and so all of the occupants could operate and function during the day as well as night. Most planets spent at least 75 percent during one rotation in the dark, because they constantly rotated away from each sun rapidly, while each satellite also blocked sunlight from each other. And it wasn't light all the time during one orbit cycle, either. The 25 percent daylight time during one circuit was sporadically segmented. To our measuring system, one rotation of each planet lasted about forty-five hours, seventeen minutes. Daylight hours? About ten hours, and each segment of light lasted roughly two hours, followed by three hours of darkness.

Still, a lot could be accomplished during their short daylight times, and the vampires worked diligently without rest from the various sunrises to sunsets. Unfortunately for them, once the Congerrians arrived they found out that they themselves could walk these surfaces during the daytime hours, and they found it quite enjoyable for the most part, spending much downtime on them before leaving for further business operations. It was a different experience for the Congerrians, and they found it quite exhilarating to exist under a star. The bluish rays from those suns actually gave them a feeling of euphoria, but that didn't, in any manner, alter their dominating attitudes of destruction whenever they landed on each of these planets. And let's leave no doubt: the Congerrians visited all five satellites and returned to them sporadically for both pleasure and business. Let's zoom into the chaotic movement of these five satellites and delve a little into their histories and find out where their connections with the Congerrians lie.

All inhabitants of this solar system had one thing in common with the Congerrians: they all survived on the life force that circulated throughout living bodies, and the planets themselves, like Culeagular. Many gushing nourishment oases existed around each of the five planets, but if punishment was ever dealt out on one of these satellites, the worst verdict handed down could be the draining of one's life force, literally killing the defendant, who was drank by the leaders or judges of their emotional courts. These beings were not violent in nature for the most part, but they could be heartless in their rulings, and extremely strict in their laws. They also looked similarly physically to the Congerrians, only somewhat smaller, and not as powerful as far as muscle mass was concerned, but how could that be? How could two species that existed so far away from each other look so much alike? It was because in the beginning, in the early stages of this chamber construction, these two solar systems sat right next to each other, but as with every other one besides Culeagular, they began to flow away on the life current, eventually disappearing completely from view. But they knew each other well and had quite an eventful history while they were still relatively close to each other.

Digging deeper, each of their planets were similar in size (about the size of Uranus), and in the beginning of their existence, before anything existed on them, they were filled with massive oceans that covered at least 80 percent of their surfaces. The fluid from these seas was crimson in color, and created and maintained life on all five planets, which were eerily similar to each other. Their names were Mammalaqua, Borberettra, Danmurra, Ramnamberri, and Salamonfer. Once species began to swim, fly, and walk upon them, their oceans slowly began to dry up, and by the time all went back to The Creator, each satellite's oceans covered less than 20 percent of the surfaces, much less than needed for all life on the planets to survive. Most life, especially sea life on all five planets, became extinct, either by natural causes, battles of annihilation, or deprivation, leaving only the most advanced species trying to survive their eventual, inevitable demises. What happened? Read below.

As was stated earlier, the Congerrians were much more advanced than most species, and were the first to fly, not only through space, but they also learned ways to bend it to their advantage as well. Their spaceships looked like prisms, or were diamond shaped. They traveled with one point facing forward, constantly moving in a corkscrew motion. They had a large fleet, close to five hundred in all, which traveled throughout the universe, Earth included—but again, let's leave that part of the story for later.

When the two solar systems were next to each other, the Congerrians worked together with the vampires of the five planets, trading goods, life forces (while ingesting one of the other's blood, they achieved a high they couldn't get anywhere else, plus their sex drives went off the charts), and slaves (their own species, plus lesser ones). The bartering system worked for centuries, but like most species over time, one got selfish and greedy, wanting the whole bag of riches. Sharing was forced to take a back seat, and the Congerrians, being the stronger race, started an 'aggression,' killing almost everyone and everything on the five satellites.

They took slaves (most of them consisted of the leaders, scientists, and researchers—ones that could benefit them the most) back to Culeagular, and kept enough on their spacecrafts for themselves, slowly draining the life forces completely from their bodies and discarding their remains into the vastness of space. Before that occurred, they made them reproduce sporadically so that they would never run out of new life force fluids.

Before the Congerrians left the five planets, they polluted and poisoned the vast oceans on each satellite, throwing the ecosystems completely off kilter. The lesser species that lived in the oceans (Over time, they almost completely lost their vibrant crimson colors, replaced by first a yellowish sickly mixture of slimy fluid, and then a dark grayness that appeared devoid of life. Only specs of red remained, but they were mostly hidden by the growing cancer that now ruled the satellites.) withered and died, which created even more toxic bacteria in the fluid. Along with the rest of the poisons, they evaporated into the atmospheres, creating massive storms not unlike hurricanes and tornadoes combined, only millions of times stronger. They lasted for centuries, killing off almost everything left on the planets, and for a long time afterward the planets continued on their interlocking orbits quietly, with little to no signs of life moving either on the lands or seas. New life did, indeed, begin again, primitive at best, but that was only because the old worlds were slowly dying, and going through an extremely slow rebirth.

Because of the devastating storms that raged around the planets, the seas were contaminated, and the life force that kept the oceans alive and vibrant began to die themselves. Between the evaporation and toxins, their substances receded, and much more land (dry, cracked, hardened soil) covered their surfaces. As crazy as it may seem, it was in these new land masses where new life began, for nutrients in the dry dirt produced spores that hatched new microorganisms. The hard soil protected these small cell life forces from the outside world, and they slowly grew in solitude and peace. They wouldn't need water or fluids to survive, since the five planets were losing those attributes anyway. Life has a funny way of adapting to its environment, and it was being done here. Alas, they would never obtain full potential, for the Event took place, and like almost everyone on Earth, they all went back to The Creator, riding the current like so many others.

As this part of the chamber was dying, looking at the solar system from afar, the bright and vibrant colors from the rotating planets slowly disappeared, and were replaced by lifeless grayness of all shades. They slowly blended in with the darkness of space, seen only at close range when they crossed paths with the five small suns, which still shined brightly. It was sad to see, considering how vibrant this part of the solar system had once appeared before the Congerrians had come to wreak havoc on it, and its innocent occupants.

Getting back to the history of the Congerrians, their space fleet never wavered in their approach to other parts of the chamber. They remained aggressive in their pursuit to visit new random planets, looking for resources, riches, and life force fluid of the inhabitants. Most were overtaken and annihilated, and their wealth confiscated before heading on to the next unsuspecting satellites. In most cases, these species were mentally, as well as physically, ripped to shreds, and their circulating life force drained from their bodies. What made things worse, the shackled prisoners of the five suns, also needing this bloodlike nourishment, were allowed to join in the slaughter, even though they didn't want to morally. Like all races that need nourishment and become hungry, they did things that went against all their laws and morals.

During these times they were kept in a weakened state in their holding cells on the spaceships, and when given the chance, the crazed, starved slaves of the Five Stars were just as savage in their killing as their controlling masters, who immensely enjoyed hearing the screams and moans of the inhabitant victims as their prisoners became part of the fray. Some of the inhabitants of these new planets were taken on board the Congerrian space crafts, and used either as a continuing food supply, or for remedial slave duties as the endless journey through space continued. Sometimes they were even used for bait on other new planets, and died horribly, sometimes being eaten by unsuspecting vicious cannibal-like species while the Congerrians sneak attacked them from the darkest of shadows. Those consumed were the lucky ones, for if they could have been interviewed, they would have only described their suffering existence until they were completely used up as quite simply, "Hell."

The Congerrian race was vicious, to say the least, and was feared throughout the galaxy. They were highly intelligent, though, which is always dangerous when it comes to any attacking, aggressive species. This vampire gender became even more deadly when they learned how to bend and fold space through new machinery. A main theme of the crews was if they could travel to all points of the chamber quicker, more riches could be acquired, as well as obtaining many more slaves for various uses. They had scientists working day and night on continuing advancements, all for the betterment of "the Cause." These destructible nomads were unrivaled in so many ways, and once they discovered how to ride the folded waves of the deep ocean of space (even finding secret wormholes in the process), three of the Congerrian fleet inadvertently came across our solar system. All planets throughout the universe in their path were generally inspected briefly by the vampire conglomerate, taking inventory, and they would have continued onward, but Earth intrigued them. Surprised?

Sure, our neighboring planets each have their own beautiful aspects, but as we all know, Earth is different. It stands out like a bright blue jewel in the middle of vast darkness, and so, the Congerrian vessels veered toward it like they were magnetized to it and orbited our satellite and moon twice before landing on its surface. They examined its riches all around the globe on its computer screens and checked it off to return on a regular basis to extract whatever it had to offer. All three spaceships took samples of both fresh and saltwater back with them to run various tests to see if it was worth selling. After further inquiries, it was deemed valuable to regular trading partners back toward Culeagular, and so over the years they went back many times, taking large doses of not only the different types of fluid, but also large chunks of the gigantic glaciers at both the North and South Poles. That was their one mistake, when you broke it all down. Thank God things went south, for if the Congerrians blueprint had been successfully carried out to the fullest, Earth would have been left completely barren like many other unfortunate satellites before it. Let's delve deeper.

When the Congerrians first landed on Earth, primitive life only existed in the deep depths of the oceans that surrounded its fewer land surfaces. The powerful vampires mostly ignored these early life specimens, vowing to focus on them later when they advanced in intelligence and physical attributes. They knew that life always worked that way and could judge just when a species was about to jump forward in its advancements. On return trips they took some of these primitive species, especially if they showed any promise. Some were kept, but most were either sold off as trading chips or left on other planets to see if they could adapt to other atmospheres. Few rarely did, and so the Congerrians dismissed life on Earth as primitive and as something that wouldn't ever amount to much. They would be wrong on many fronts, but one such strain ended up destroying all aboard the three prism space crafts, both friend and foe.

As stated earlier, the Congerrians were intrigued by the massive ice glaciers, and so they took large chunks of it firsthand before extracting water and other elements of the planet that would one day be named Earth. At first, all went well with their visits, but on their last trip into our solar system the three vampire vessels cut large chunks containing foreign undetectable bacteria that would soon come into play. After loading the ice into the spacious cargo bays, two of the ships flew off to what would become the Sahara Desert in the Middle East. At that time an ocean dominated the area before moving in many directions in what would eventually become the Atlantic Ocean, the Pursian Gulf, plus the Mediterranean and Red Seas. These two vessels would hover above the water and drop large tanks into the ocean, collecting large samples to sell to those that would use it to bolster their life force, sometimes for outright survival. These species paid a terrible price for this salt and fresh water, selling some of their own species, even some of their own *families*, to help save a society!

As the saying goes, when the glacier ice was loaded onto the Congerrian space crafts with bacteria buried in the frozen water, the chickens had finally come home to roost. In a short amount of time, all three Culeagular spaceships—one in Mexico, the other two in what became the Sahara Desert—lay vacant with no sign of life whatsoever. After all, the evil deeds these vicious vampires had done over time finally came back to haunt them with no quarter given. Poetic justice in a way, only it took the lives of every other species on board as well (some innocent, some not), leaving behind three empty ghost ships I fondly reference as "Flying Dutchmen." How could this have happened to such a strong and powerful race? What could have transpired? Well, dear readers, I have the answers to those questions, and possibly a few more, and you will read about those events below.

Another few questions you might ask: Did God have something to do with it? Did The Lord finally put a stop to this powerful vampire conglomerate? Quite possibly, but as time has gone by, and I have hopefully gained important knowledge myself along the way, I believe that God has pretty much had a hand in just about *everything*. It might seem at times that He has turned his back and let havoc create it's special kind of unrelenting chaos, maybe more times than not, but think about it this way: sometimes to achieve the end result you have to take a step backward to eventually take two steps forward. That's just my opinion. All opinions matter, though, no matter how different. Sometimes if you take all different opinions, put them all together and shake them all up, they might point to the true answers that we are looking for, a common acceptance. Will that question be answered along with the others about the Congerrian's demise? That's left up for your own interpretation as each and every one of you take a little trip into the grey.

When the Congerrians first discovered and removed a chunk of the glacier ice at the poles, they didn't sell all of it. No, they kept about half, for they found through experimentation that it served many purposes. In fact, when you look at them more closely, you'd wonder to yourself why they would part with any of it at all! Greed, probably, and maybe they realized that they could get even more riches by trading away at least some of it. Whatever the case, it was beneficial to the advanced vampire race, and until that fateful last visit they reaped many more riches through trade with it than with any other cargo they had in their warehouse bays.

First off, they found out that the glacier ice on this planet, when induced orally, enhanced the strength of their life force energy and overall mental health thought processes unlike frozen ice from other planets, moons, or other satellites such as comets and asteroids. There never was a reason found as to why that was, for the Congerrians had sampled many different frozen ice materials from all over the universe, but there was something about Earth's supply that created a different effect.

In the rear of the spacecrafts, current and added supplies of blood types were kept in a cold environment and used as needed. Unlike the vampires like Dracula and the such in horror novels we have read, this vampire nation controlled their intake of various life force bloods, and never over indulged. They always seemed to know when enough was enough and left nothing to waste. Whether they were just sufficient in their feeding, or frugal to a fault, they never overindulged.

This feeding fluid was kept in large tanks and drank in rooms not unlike bars here on Earth. All life force blood supplies were not equal, and so the better fluids went to those with higher ranks within the crews. Leaders received the best, and the grunt workers drank the lower-quality blood, or even unstable or infected fluids. Sound familiar? Anyway, the glacier ice was put in a device not unlike an air-conditioning mechanism, and a mist was lightly sprayed throughout the large warehouse area, keeping the life force at optimum quality.

When Earth glacier ice was used, the life force gave the Congerrians a high they had never experienced before, yet they were still capable of carrying out their duties. This high level of euphoria lasted for hours, and sometimes if they were lucky, days. New Congerrian ideas and advancements accelerated while under this intoxicating blood fluid. Ways of improving space travel, outsmarting other inferior races in trade proceedings, new ways of eliminating those species if need be—those types of things.

Also, those vampires lucky enough to sample the glacier ice had their sexual appetites and abilities reach new heights. Length of session, intensity of orgasm, new creative ways of mixing violent lewdness in evolving sadists acts were born, and then improved upon. Some of these resulted in horrible deaths, and the victims' carcasses were fed to lesser life forms, an act known to most species as one of the biggest insults known to Congerrian life on a whole.

These were some of the differences while using Earth glacier ice. It's no wonder Earth was visited more often than any other planet, moon, or satellite in any other solar system. It brought back in trade more than any other water supply in any form, even though those enhancements didn't have the same effects as when the Congerrians used it. Hope filtered through those other races, almost *praying* for the same highs the vampires achieved.

THE DEMISE OF THE TWO CONGERRIAN
SPACESHIPS OVER THE OCEAN

Once the infected glacier ice was loaded into the cargo bins, the upper-level vampires on the two spaceships over the ocean, being the selfish breed they were, immediately began feeding— and let's just say that since this was special life force fluid, they drank a little extra, possibly ingesting an added shot. This was unusual, for that type of action went against their ways, as stated earlier, but maybe the bacteria had something to do with that. At first they felt the amazing euphoria they always felt and began to immediately mate with their partners and others, some being prisoners from the Five Star planets.

But before they had finished, they all unexpectedly stopped, and trancelike walked to the many exits on the space crafts. They ordered the guards to open the doors, and then without emotion or fear, went outside. Now you have to understand that it was daylight where these spaceships were—afternoon in the Middle East, and early morning in Mexico. May I remind everyone reading this that we are talking about vampires here, a species that needed to stay away from the rays of a shining star. The guards that were ordered to open the doors knew this but could be beheaded and fed to inferior races if they disobeyed or questioned an order, and so they did not hesitate when their superiors commanded them to unlock the exit hatches and move aside.

Those leaders levitated above the vast ocean below them. They were instantly consumed by flames; yet as they burned slowly and eventually turned to gray ash, they did not utter a single scream, even though they felt fire just like us human beings do. The guards and the lower level Congerrians stared on in amazement more than horror, for the vampires were cold hearted and emotionless under normal situations and knew that this was their only a chance to move up the food chain. Yes, this was how members of this superior race reacted toward each other.

Each space craft roughly housed one thousand Congerrians, plus another two hundred slaves and prisoners. Out of that total, one hundred were upper-level management types, vampires that ruled with iron fists and gave no quarter. They were mostly *hated* by everyone below them in rank, but they didn't care. They had supreme power, and that's all that mattered. Feelings of any kind had no business playing any part in the Congerrian blueprint, those leaders surmised, and that way of thinking would always be. So, as those leaders calmly walked outside and dissolved into thick flames and smoke, sly smiles were shared all around as the lower levels went to inform others that worked on the main decks of what had just transpired.

By that time, *those* Congerrians had just finished feeding on the new glacier ice, and the infection was starting to show. Most of them grouchily dismissed the news blowers with a wave of their hand, basically ignoring the horrifying news, and went to find a sexual partner for the foreseeable future, their sexual hormones raging wildly. Most of *those* sessions ended badly, actually having a reverse effect. Many of them were unable to perform for the first time, and, understandably, took it out on their devoted sex partners, some even murdering them by ripping their hearts out, or by beheading them with swords.

That first night much bloodshed was splattered throughout the ship, but eventually those who had not yet fed on the new glacier ice restored some sort of order. By then, besides the leaders who had calmly walked outside to burn, others had brutalized and murdered fellow Congerrians for what they thought to be minor infractions, along with many slaves, some of them from the Five Suns. But then they too began to feed.

Just what was going on here? The plain answer was that the

bacteria in the new glacier ice chunks had somehow driven the vampires out of their minds in contrasting ways. It attacked their nervous systems from every angle, creating much discomfort in their heads and their infected minds. It was, basically, an *invasion*! Some even killed themselves with large knives through their hearts, or through their brains.

Once the last of the Congerrians drank the life force, *they* too became infected and experienced similar symptoms. Crazed with agonized blinding pain behind their eye sockets, they mindlessly released all the prisoners on the lower decks, some of them the vampires from the Five Star solar system, by pushing the release buttons.

The released prisoners, which consisted of many races, went throughout the spacecrafts looking for nourishment, since the Congerrians kept them in a state just above starvation. Only the slaves kept for sexual interactions were allowed adequate nourishment, and other than the prisoners from the Five Star district, which were vampires themselves, the others had to learn to survive on tainted life force liquid that kept most of them in a weak and sickened state. Once they found and ingested the new life force fluid they had all heard about, they all turned on each other, fighting inside and outside the ship.

Most of those that chose to exit the spaceship fought and drowned in the ocean, unable either to swim or maintain enough energy to stay above the surface. Their lifeless bodies filled with saltwater and descended to the ocean floor, eventually being covered up by sand and vegetation as they decomposed over time. The vampires of the Five Star solar system either burned up like the Congerrians by going outside, or went completely mad inside the twin vessels, killing off all of the lesser species before murdering themselves. Life force blood was splattered throughout the space crafts, and with no one left on board, the vessels eventually ran out of power and sank to the ocean floor. They became completely covered by the sands of what would eventually become known as the Sahara Desert.

One spaceship, while descending to the ocean floor, drifted many miles to the north, possibly over twenty miles, and eventually rose to the surface with the ocean floor as the oceans shifted to different areas. One quarter of the ship was visible above the sandy surface and sat alone for thousands of years until man eventually walked the surface of the Earth and discovered it, making many more in its honor. Primitive man did not find any blood life force on board, and much of the interior of the vessel had deteriorated to the point where nothing but crumbling dust and debris remained. Evidence of alien life was completely destroyed, but what *was* left was worshipped like a powerful God when primitive religion was first born. The other space craft was never uncovered and remained miles below the Sahara Desert's surface when the power went off and most went back to The Creator.

Whenever a Congerrian space craft landed on solid ground, half of the prism-shaped vessel burrowed deep into the earth. The main deck, or frontal control room, pointed straight up in the air, as if to punctuate just where the spaceship would be headed next. While docking took place, dark shields lowered over the large rectangular-shaped main deck windows, a glass-like material, to protect the vampires from the sun rays during the daylight hours. During the sun ray time, most of the crew either slept in their coffin-shaped beds, or worked in the lower decks— those that were below ground level and protected from the sun. Work in these many lower levels never ceased.

Grunt workers, slaves, or prisoners worked in long, coordinated shifts, moving about as they completed various duties. Scientists and architects worked in the decks above them, experimenting with gathered samples of soil, rock, and of course the new large chunks of glacier ice. The only personnel that moved in the levels above ground were guards and security units, constantly surveying the desert during both day and night (the awake) hours. The spaceship flying maintenance crews worked on the main decks, getting the ship ready for "Deep Star Drive"—mechanisms that forced space to bend and fold to their pleasure. Galaxies could be traveled across in a few years' time, where before it took eons longer. The ship's operators worked with these crews, improving the gears and machines that defied logic. From a distance the spaceship looked like a large pyramid, towering fifty stories above ground level. Tannish, or light gray in color, it stood tall, strong, and intimidating, even though there was no life yet on Earth to see it. The planet was theirs for the taking, and take it they would, but this time they took something they should've left alone and buried—glacier ice, and the virus housed inside it.

THE DEMISE OF THE THIRD CONGERRIAN SPACESHIP IN WHAT WOULD BECOME MEXICO

Maybe it was a fateful omen of sorts. Many times before the Congerrians had come to Earth, during all seasons, with the weather for the most part usually calm and surreal, yet this time many storms were raging around the blue-tinted sphere, one of which was headed toward the vampire vessel in what would one day be called Mexico. Not that it really mattered, because the ship was well built and could withstand much more than bad weather here on Earth, but this storm would one day be called a hurricane, or typhoon, depending on where you lived. This approaching one would be considered strong, maybe a Category 4, and the security units watched with mild amazement as its rain and wind raged throughout the massive desert.

A few crews were even sent outside to collect water samples from the heavy rains. The winds were blowing at over 125 miles an hour, yet the powerful vampires walked around as if they were taking a stroll around the park. They laughed at an inside joke, one where there was enough cloud cover to protect them from the sun's dangerous light, and rays. The Congerrians took great joy in nature's way of protecting them against their number one enemy: stars.

They didn't believe in gods, since they considered themselves beings on the same level as such, and so they thought their ancestors were looking over them, protecting them from the afterworld, a realm they rationalized as a dimension just a ripple away from the one they existed in. It was a different sort of religion, or spiritual interaction, but this time they would be wrong in their assumptions—dead wrong—for as the hurricane with no name roared past them, the first glacier ice was being ingested by the top ranks of the ship, and deadly spores that somehow weren't detected by the experienced scientists on board began to work their dark magic on the vampires' physical internal systems.

The effects on the creatures of the night created somewhat different symptoms here. Possibly it was a different strain, but it affected the vampires in a different way, even though the end result was the same. Right after the next sunrise they would all be dead and gone, and not even the spirits of their ancestors could save them. If their beliefs about the afterworld were correct, they had all gone to join their brethren, with no one left here to protect and look after. The bacteria that claimed all the vampires was, in reality, a greater god than the Congerrians, and so the end joke was on them. If they had been here to hear it, they wouldn't have laughed.

Surprisingly, unlike the two Congerrian space craft hovering above the ocean in the east, all levels of the vampire space crew ingested the new glacier ice with little effect. Things seemed normal, and business went on as usual, at least until the hurricane passed by them, and the weather began to calm down. The first sign of dysfunction happened right after sunset. Higher-ups working in the holding cell area, trancelike, unlocked all the slaves and prisoners, including the vampires that came from the Five Suns, and walked them outside and into the desert, leaving them there and returning to the ship and their posts in the holding cells.

As they passed various Congerrian personnel during this trek no one seemed to notice this mass exodus as it was happening. They acted as if they either didn't care that all prisoners were being set free, or were just blind to it. Under normal circumstances, they definitely would have questioned the endeavor taking place, or at least abused the slaves or lower-level species as they passed by. They did neither, only nodding at the guards and continuing on to their next destination of business. Those slaves working throughout the space craft were also led out of the massive vessel, meeting the rest of the prisoners just outside the spaceship.

Later, the Congerrians would have no memory of how all the prisoners had escaped, for that's what they thought had happened. They were furious, for how could that have happened? Too many levels of defense would have to be outmaneuvered, and that just wasn't possible—or *tolerated!* That situation could have gotten pretty dicey, for the vampires had very bad tempers when things didn't go their way, taking it out many times on lower-ranking officials, and blood usually flowed during those tense moments, but the spores from the bacteria had begun an overall infection.

Headaches, which turned from bad to skull splitting, overtook all of them, and the life force flowing through their systems slowed in speed and changed color from crimson red to a dark,

sickly yellow, zapping them of most of their energy and enthusiasm. A lot of them vomited up blackish bile that smelled like
contaminated waste. Painful moaning was heard throughout the
whole ship, and all working personnel suddenly stopped what
they were doing and held their heads with shaky hands, trying to
rid themselves of the mounting agony that was surrounding their
brains like a military ground attack. The last rational thought the
higher-ups had was that they would have to set up search parties
to round up the escapees, but that could wait . . . yes, that could
wait.

Meanwhile, the prisoners were completely puzzled at this
whole exercise, but what really threw them off was that before the
guards left them out in the desert, they unemotionally handed
the vampires from the Five Suns all their weapons and communication devices. They were stunned, for the guards, under normal
circumstances, carried the most weapons, and so they were left
with a lot of fire power—enough to maybe put up a tough fight if
need be. They watched in shocked silence as all the guards, maybe
twenty-five in all, peacefully and calmly walked back to the spaceship in silence, which was odd as well. One characteristic about
the Congerrians that all other species knew: they loved to talk and
joke with each other (yes, they did *have* emotions), and the slaves
sometimes wondered if they would *ever* shut up. None of that was
happening now, but this new phenomenon was working in their
favor, and so they all turned and ran from the ship as fast as they
could. They found some large hills with dark, narrow caves, and
hid in their shadows. By sunrise they had worked their way to the
back of them, maybe a mile in, and faced all entrances, weapons
drawn. They could hear the wind still howling outside, but it was
starting to lose its luster as the storm slowly faded behind the
western mountains. Not much was said, and the air was tense,
but they knew one thing: they had been given an ace card in the

deck that had always been stacked against them in the past, and they would use it if they had to.

By early morning, most of the Congerrians couldn't take the growing virus inside their systems any longer, and walked outside, screaming, as part of the sun could be seen behind a few lingering storm clouds in the eastern skies. Like their brethren overseas, they became engulfed in flames and turned to ash, their cries of agony fading into thin air. The ones that remained in the ship suffered mightily, their brains turning to mushy jelly. Their last thoughts were of amazement, of how could this have ever happened to them! They lay scattered throughout the ship, their twitching, dying bodies slowly becoming still, and then they were no more. The bacteria ate their lifeless bodies from the inside out, leaving nothing behind, including their clothing.

Since the Congerrians had been attacked so viciously and violently by the glacier spores, they didn't even realize that all operating systems had been attacked and no longer worked as well, including their communication systems. It would take many millennia before they'd be missed, and before the Culeagular Space Force would send another vessel to Earth. By then, life on Earth had taken hold, including early man, and land masses and oceans had long since shifted, but let's not write out of order. Patience will set all time passages in correct order, so let's not disrupt that normal process.

For many days the released vampires from the Five Star solar system and the other species hid in the caves and waited for the Congerrians to send out forces to retrieve them. The slaves and prisoners, after further review, knew that they had no real chance of mounting a serious attack against their captors, even with all their newfound weaponry, and so their in-house conversations centered around whether or not they wanted to either surrender, go down fighting, or take their own lives, ending the hell that had engulfed them for what seemed like eternities.

As the days passed by, many of them discussed their dismal life on the spacecraft, what they had already gone through, and what new ways of punishment they would probably experience once they were back inside the vessel and under Congerrian rule. Many shuttered and nervously moved about the caves as the hours slowly passed, but eventually they began to wonder if the Congerrians would ever attack. Many left the caves long enough to see if anyone was coming but saw no sign of life anywhere in the vastness of the hot desert. A few ventured close enough to see the spaceship but saw no movement there either. They began to wonder if something terrible had happened and discussed mounting an attack of their own on the vessel. Maybe, just maybe something had gone terribly wrong, and the powerful vampires might be vulnerable. Sickness, insanity, or infighting might be occurring within the ranks. Nothing was off the table when it came to those evil beings, and as the slaves remained hopeful, yet cautious, they began making plans to sneak back inside the vessel and take whoever might still be in the spaceship by surprise. A scout had noted that the front doors were still wide open, even though no guards were present. Still, they were wary, and held back, afraid to make a move. They silently and outwardly cursed themselves for being such cowards, but still remained inside the protective caves.

What finally pushed the slaves into action was hunger. They needed nourishment—life force fluid—and there was none of that in the caves. The spaceship had plenty, and you know what happens when that feeling of emptiness drives you over the edge— you do things that you wouldn't do under normal circumstances.

So on the seventh night of their short time of freedom, all the prisoners bravely left the safety of the caves and approached the front doors of the Congerrian space craft, their weapons drawn.

Looking inside the ship, there were no lights or power on, and the interior was pitch black. That was all right, for the vampires of the Five Star solar system could see perfectly well in sightless environments, and so they all went inside first. The others waited patiently but were getting hungrier by the second. They waited for an eventual attack by their mighty masters, which never came. All remained quiet inside the vessel until the Five Star vampire species returned, and then they all entered the ship. The good news: there was no sign of any Congerrians on board. None! The bad news: there was no power on the spaceship, and so getting to any food supply would be no easy task.

All of the slaves had only been fed low-end scraps of nourishment during their time of imprisonment, and so none of them knew where the food supply was kept. That was just a small part of the genius while discussing the Congerrians—even if the possibility existed that they could be overtaken, their life force fluids would stay hidden. The only species on board that could see through the heavy twilight was the Five Star vampires, and so they took off again in search of nourishment for all. Eventually they found it, breaking through many doorways in the lower decks, but in the long run, even though they all would've died slowly in the caves if they had stayed there, that would've been a better fate compared to what transpired over the following few days.

The vampires of the Five Star Solar System found life force nourishment in some of the Congerrian vampire quarters, and after drinking their fill they took a good amount back to the rest of the prisoners. It was enough to satisfy them all, but more importantly, it helped rejuvenate their weakened bodies to functioning levels. Still, while the fluids rushed through their arteries and circulatory systems, it put them all into deep slumber—a much-needed rest period where they basically lay dead to the world. They were dreamless slumbers, but that was a good thing, because that would change over the following days. The Five Star vampires never found any of the high-quality glacier ice, but that didn't matter. The bacteria spores were loose and had gone airborne inside the vessel. As the survivors slept, they inhaled the alien sickness, and by the time all of the slaves had awoken, things had changed, and not for the better.

During the time the Five Star vampires slept, the sickness worked its way through their cores, and even though they didn't experience explosively painful headaches like the Congerrians had, major changes had happened to their bodies. They actually felt fine, but their physical frames had aged drastically. While most of the vampire species didn't age beyond middle age, they now looked ancient and in death mode. Their bodies had completely shriveled and pruned, leaving only bone and skin behind. That outer covering turned a sickish pale gray in color, almost sticking to protruding bone structure and bloated arteries that continued to circulate now-infected bluish blood fluids that moved much slower than usual. Their teeth had all fallen out of their mouths, and their eyes turned a sickly yellow. The rest of the other species looked on in horror, but so far they all woke up in the same condition as when they had fallen asleep. That wouldn't last.

The Five Star vampires looked at themselves, and instead of being terrorized, began laughing hysterically. Not because they thought they looked funny, but because they had lost their minds, which were ingested by the invading spores. Personalities and memories were replaced by raging madness, yet that insanity was completely under control and thinking clearly. Total possession had taken place, and so even though their forthcoming actions stunned the others, who were frozen in shocked terror, the bacteria knew exactly what it was doing.

All at once, the vampires, who never stopped laughing, slowly stood on wobbly legs, walked over to a slanted wall, and dissolved into it, disappearing completely. To the rest of the slaves it was too much to contemplate and handle, and so they all got up and started running for the open doorway, which closed shut just before they got there, leaving them in total darkness.

That lasted only seconds, for all of a sudden a humming noise could be heard, followed by red illuminating light, which filled the corridors and levels of the complete vessel. The slaves, now prisoners of the spacecraft once again, huddled close together, frantically looking all around them, wondering what was going on. They knew that the Congerrians were nowhere to be found, so who, or what, was doing this?

They didn't have to wait long, for the Five Star vampires slowly reappeared out of the wall again, levitating three feet above the floor. Each of them was attached to a large cross made out of a black metal material in crucification manner, even though that type of punishment had never been seen before. Large stakes went through wrists, arms, shoulders, thighs, and ankles. One larger stake went through their chest cavity, where the vampires' heart-pumping systems were, yet the Five Star beings still lived and moved and were in no apparent pain. They were no longer laughing but frowning as they looked down at the rest of the frightened slaves.

After a few seconds of uneasiness (especially on the slave side), the crosses holding the vampires slowly rotated upside down. The vampires all at once said something in a foreign language, just a few spoken syllables, ones that the prisoners had never heard before, yet they somehow *knew* what they meant. What did they say? "Wake up now." All the slaves digested that message, and then all their thoughts and memories faded into a dark abyss in which their personalities would never return. Like the Five Star vampires, they were already dead, and their bodies used as puppets.

The bacteria spores took over all mental controls, and then the fun began. The doors of the spaceship reopened, and all the slaves methodically walked outside, faced each other, and began a killing spree that any warmonger would have been proud of. Ray guns, spears, knives of all sizes, and outright physical combat took place. One by one, species were wiped out, leaving the stronger or smarter ones to continue the onslaught. During the first few hours of carnage, the crosses holding the Five Star vampires floated just outside the spacecraft, turned rightsized up, and then the crosses corkscrewed themselves into the desert soil, and they watched the bloodthirsty show.

They were laughing again, but there was no sanity in that cackling, and green bile began to drool out of their toothless mouths. Every so often some of the combatants strolled up to them and slashed at their bodies, cutting them to shreds, exposing bones that broke easily. This made them laugh even louder, even though their strength and life force were leaving them. The attackers attached their oral openings to the vampire's wounds and sucked out whatever life force fluids they could swallow. This made them stronger, and better equipped to continue fighting—helping them in their will to survive. Copycatting ensued, and others drank from wounds they inflicted. Eventually the Five Star vampires hung lifeless, but their laughter had mentally transported to their attackers, and the battles raged on.

Over the next few hours, the fighting never stopped. Blood of all colors painted the hot sands of the smoldering desert, and one by one the combatants dwindled in numbers. In the end, five beings of different origins faced off against each other, and they fought like never before. They shot, slashed, and tortured each other to the point that even the eventual winner wouldn't survive. That ended up being a serpentlike creature who staggered back into the spaceship and collapsed ten feet from the doorway. Eventually the doors closed again on their own, and no evidence of what had happened could be seen either inside or outside the vessel.

Over the many years that followed, sparse vegetation grew around the pyramid, roots growing up the sides. This was how the next Congerrian spacecraft found their brethren's vessel. We will discuss what happened as they investigated their fallen comrades' spaceship, but let's first delve into the history of the bacteria spores. Once you discover what they are (or were?), you may never go near a pyramid again—let alone go *inside* one!

The bacteria spores are really not defined as a foreign virus that infects its victims. No, it more or less infiltrates and possesses its prey as it cocoons into one's physical form, attacking one's mind, body, and spirit. Even the Congerrians, who never knew what hit them, were no match for these glacier cells of destruction. These powerful vampires who had wiped out species after species as they stole their wealth and natural resources fell by the wayside as they became hosts of decay.

THE ORIGIN OF PURE SICKNESS

The infectious bacteria of the North Pole glacier ice are fragments of one central being that was fractured so far back in time that it cannot be measured in any amount of years or millennia. For us human beings, it can be only be measured in chambers rather than in centuries, or any other form of backward passage.

Since there is no apparent beginning, or at least we can't envision one, this fragmented being might actually go back far enough where there might have been no materialized *anythings*—no chambers, no stars, no satellites, or anything else we see in the skies today. No alien species that might exist in the various solar systems, galaxies, and quasars in this chamber—nothing! Maybe it existed when creation was in its possible beginning phase, and possibly only gods of positive and negative energies floated in early molecules of black nothingness. What we need to understand and comprehend here is that it is extremely ancient. It still lives, and it somehow ended up on Earth, of all places, in glacier ice, and when a selfish, greedy species (the Congerrians) took some of it from its frozen cocoon, it became unleashed.

When it was one complete entity it was given a name: Blarmusimuss. We will revisit fragments of its history, or as much as I want to reveal at this point in time. Most of what will be discussed is when it existed here in this chamber, or entered it. I did say *most* of it, but to some the *least* of it might be more interesting. Only the following lines and words will determine that. Enjoy.

When Blarmusimuss was whole, it lived in a realm of its own, one that was much bigger than this chamber, or our universe is. It had a kingdom, but not like the one you might envision. It was dark and dreary; it had no structures like a castle with a moat around it, and it had no one to converse with, or slaves to work for it. It had nothing to harm, nothing to love, nothing to hate. And *that* was how Blarmusimuss liked it. Loneliness is only a word when its definition is all you know, and so as the saying goes: you never miss what you never had, only in this case this creature *liked* to be alone. Why? Because it had what you could call multiple personalities—only in Blarmusimuss's case, it had many thinking, tentacled organisms, or what we would call brains. Yes—*brains!* How did it possess so many physical thinking mechanisms? It didn't know for quite some time, but eventually something happened, something that became an awakening of sorts.

Blarmusimuss floated through darkness, never seeing, never hearing, never *feeling*. It did not know its origin, but that was just fine as far as it was concerned. Its world was endless, and its journeys went on indefinitely. Time didn't exist or matter, for no clocks ticked away anything it could lose. Nothing mattered. It knew no issues, no pain or anguish to feel (it was, in fact, numb), and so it basically had no *problems*, living an existence of extreme low maintenance. It just . . . *was*.

That was, until something entered its world and changed its perspective forever. That *something* was a presence that felt completely different than it in every way, and yet it was connected to it in many ways as well. The foreign entity had a conversation with Blarmusimuss, and that was all it took. It's funny in a way. Life can go on without change or interruption for ages, never expecting any diversions, and then having one conversation with someone can *alter* your existence and outlook forever.

Some examples, first in a good way. You want to become a doctor, a lawyer, a teacher, even a man of the cloth, but you don't have the funds. Then you meet somebody, maybe someone out of the blue, who bumps into you and tells you that he has put millions into an account for your education, just because you deserve it. Oh, you will pay it back, but at least you will become what you wanted. Farfetched? Probably, and usually this only happens in your wildest dreams, but you get my drift.

OK, here's another, and probably more realistic. As a young child, your parents sit you down for a little chat. There's something you should know. They tell you there is a higher being that has created us, plus everything around you, and his name is God. He is considered the highest form of existence, and he controls all. Now maybe you are three, or even four years of age, but as long as you could process thoughts you had a completely different idea of what this thing called life was all about. For instance, you might have thought your parents were that higher life force, and that they were there to "arrange" how life would go. Now, after this "little talk," things have changed, whether it's for good, or bad. Before this conversation the equation was different. It was you and your parents. Now it also includes this unseen higher being called God.

And then you begin to wonder; what else is different than what you thought before this conversation began? Before you just *were*, and now you are thinking—thinking a lot. New roads are there to travel, ones that were hidden before, and you didn't think existed. They lead to different destinations. That could be for the good. It's just changed you and your life forever. Imagine that— all those added equations with just one little talk!

Another example, this one pointing in a different direction. You have never really been sick before, but during a normal yearly physical it is discovered that you have a brain tumor which your doctor explains to you is inoperable. Now you have to consider options that you didn't have to deal with before. Life has suddenly taken a different route, and a darker path may have to be followed. It was an instance like this that took Blarmusimuss into a different level of consciousness; one that it didn't know existed. Think about that: before this presence entered into its world, Blarmusimuss just *was*. Life was life as it knew it, but after one interaction—one—for the first time, things had changed forever.

And what did that conversation consist of? For one, that there *was* life other than itself, and that it had a name. It would answer to that name, and follow messages given to it telepathically. Who was the presence that had entered into its world? Blarmusimuss was told that it was to be known only as "The Father." It didn't know what that meant, but it was told that it would know in time. It was also told that it was time for it to move outside its comfort zone, its tranquil realm, and begin its foretold mission. And so, it did. It went with The Father, and learned many things as they weaved in and out of many corridors, passing many different-shaped doorways. It developed a unique personality as it learned it's mission in full. The Father told Blarmusimuss that "The Mission" could be done quicker by being in many different places at one time, à la legion, and so it was separated into many different parts. How many? An infinite amount, and then some. Each segmented fragment then had its own mission, but they all knew that they were all part of the whole. It was an evolution of a different kind—one that never stopped adapting to any physical or mental distraction.

And so, it began. It aggressively started devouring life in many different realms and places, with new thinking mechanisms growing in even newer parts of itself, and even more vicious personalities entered into the equation. Blarmusimuss became hungrier and hungrier as time went on and felt The Father lurking in the shadows at every turn. Eventually, after wreaking havoc again and again through the doorways of many past chambers, it was told to enter into this current realm, and so it flowed through the doorway on the life force currents and spread itself throughout space and the universe, which included Earth.

We now travel to Earth and will soon learn of the unison between Blarmusimuss and our beautiful blue life-filled planet.

By the time Blarmusimuss passed through the doorway, it was famished for new species to attack, just like it had felt many times before. Yes, it had developed a predator-type attitude; mix that with a raging anger that was almost uncontrollable, and you had quite a force to deal with. It had developed that anger-type emotion since it's new inception, for it still missed (and always would) it's tranquil atmosphere before The Father came along to disrupt its nonevolving existence. From its mindless state to its awareness now, hate and tantrums filled its many brains and thought processes. The Father was way too strong to attack, and so it invaded and destroyed everything, and anything else that breathed any type of life in its path. Besides, The Father coaxed it on, telling it new methods and new ways to overtake its prey, so each time it entered a new chamber it was angrier and more dangerous than the time previous. Another emotion had begun to grow subconsciously inside it's ever changing mindset: evilness—hateful, spiteful evilness! With dark fuel filling it's disgruntled mind, it became a raging uncontrollable freight train of uncaring hurt.

And what was Blarmusimuss exactly? Sickness—pure, ever-evolving sickness. That is how it started out. It was created by The Father, kept in a dark realm until different types of life began to blossom and grow, and then unleashed to disrupt and destroy the positiveness of creation. It was groomed to become more powerful and relentless as time ticked along, which was exactly what took place. It was avoided at all costs by all life that could sense its presence, and overtaken by those that were helpless against it.

Blarmusimuss was like an army. It had its generals, captains, privates, and everything you could imagine in-between. Its weaker fragments created all regular sicknesses: colds, viruses, and various disruptions that most life recovered from. They created disruption and sent warnings to most life that experienced terror throughout its life force that infection could get worse, which of course, was true. Those feared fragments, as we here on Earth know all too well, were much more dangerous. They created cancers, heart failure, blood disorders—diseases that slowly broke down life mechanisms until death took over and life ceased to exist.

And then there was the most dangerous, and cankerous parts of Blarmusimuss. Those strong fragments swarmed in the innermost core of the infectious abomination and were saved for special times. They didn't make news headlines, because usually no one was left alive to report the disaster. They wiped entire species off the map of life, and those deadly fragments had done it many times since the beginning of their union. The Father directed Blarmusimuss during those times, orchestrating the fragments like an extremely experienced Philharmonic conductor. Not only did they destroy life's creations, they evilly abducted their essences and swallowed their spirits, eventually infecting them as well. There was no exorcism blueprint to use during these situations for the most part, but like all sicknesses, they didn't always win.

The exceptions were rare, but Blarmusimuss's fragments *did*, indeed, lose occasionally, which only maddened its anger and hatred. Earth, and it's constantly improving methods, rivaled the sickness more than any other species at any other time, both mentally as well as physically. Still, death eventually happened to all things, and Blarmusimuss had still not lost a conflict during a final battle. Each win enhanced its superiority, strength, hatefulness, and evilness, which was extremely scary for those few beings that knew its most intimate characteristics.

Once Blarmusimuss knew part of it was to travel to Earth, it quickly rode the currents of black space toward the tiny blue planet. It didn't know why Earth was the destination, but it also didn't care. It never questioned the commands of The Father; it never thought that far. Its thought process only reasoned that if

the blue jewel in the middle of nowhere was to be the new promised land where the infection would become something *different*,
then so be it. The Father had never failed the fragments throughout their travels through different realms and chambers before in
the endgame, and so it went. What was so unusual was when it
finally arrived, the satellite was still in creation mode, and so no
life existed anywhere on the planet.

Through it's unusual use of mental communication, it expressed complete confusion in its message to The Father. The
Father responded by telling it to "lie in wait," a term meaning to
stay patient. Blarmusimuss expressed feelings of revulsion with
this orbiting rock. It had beauty and radiated positiveness and
warmth—characteristics the sickness felt scorn for. These were
aspects the fragments knew were the complete opposite of its own
characteristics. It wondered why these topics of discussion even
existed—why everything wasn't like *it*! That was how it was in
the beginning before The Father arrived; why couldn't it be that
way now?

For the first time it felt an unease about its surroundings,
yet the infection refused to let the emotion of fear enter into its
realm, even though Blarmusimuss was childlike in many ways.
The Father understood, and directed it to the polar north, where
fluids froze in freezing temperatures. It needed to rest and wait
for The Father's word. Blarmusimuss understood and traveled to
one of the coldness parts of this world. It settled in a desolate
location, one it felt most comfortable in, and went into semi-consciousness—it's favorite state. It was aware yet remained strong as
its other, less-powerful fragmented brained tentacles continued
to attack growing life in the vastness of this new chamber. That
was good. If one brain was satisfied with an infection, then every
other brain felt that contentment as well. Sickness was strong,
and sickness would grow and survive. New infections would be

created, bringing new agonies in response, and so the strongest fragments could lie in wait for an infinite amount of time. And that is what they did.

Over time new ice formed, covering the strong nucleus part of Blarmusimuss completely. The cold felt pleasant, comforting. More and more ice formed around the fragments, shielding it as the sickness patiently waited. It knew that in a different situation more diseases could have been spread, but weaker parts of the whole were working its magic throughout the universe, and that would have to be good enough. Besides, it reasoned, The Father knew best, and Blarmusimuss knew all too well that some things were worth waiting for.

As time went by, life's seeds found their way to Earth, and very quickly the little blue planet became extremely populated, somewhat like so many others. Yes, other satellites had produced many new forms of life in the past, but nothing like what was happening here on this smallish rock, especially in the warmer climate areas of the planet. The smaller fragments of Blarmusimuss followed those life spores to Earth and fragmented even more as many species began to inhabit the satellite. It rested in contentment and began to understand the reasoning of The Father. The more species, the better—more to attack, more heartache to spread. What could be better? A calm came over Blarmusimuss, and if it could smile, it was doing that now. It rested, and thought over and over again, What could be better?

Earth was different than every other plant in the chamber in this manner. It possessed many more species than any other satellite by a large margin. Life in the seas, life on land, and life in the air continued to multiply right up until the power went out and most went back to The Creator. Many of the species throughout the history of Earth became extinct and replaced by even more new ones. Sickness and death ran rampant each and every day, but new births still outnumbered the outgoing souls. The smaller fragments of Blarmusimuss had a field day twenty-four hours a day and were rewarded with new life and brand-new species, many of them never getting off the ground, being extinguished before they even had a chance to survive. The sickness was content and relayed that message to The Father.

Sickness and eventual death followed the domino effect of life, in which Blarmusimuss became the final part of the equation. On some other planets, the fragments actually annihilated complete inhabitants of those satellites—not on Earth, though. Yes, some species became extinct, but others thrived under all kinds of circumstances.

Blarmusimuss was a lethal infection that attacked not just life, but objects not considered alive to the human eye and mind as well. They were, and *are*, pulsating and breathing entities in much different ways. Stars (suns), planets, moons, comets, quasars, meteors, and other such satellites die as well, although it takes much longer to suck the life force out of them, but eventually they all succumb to the relentless attacking fragments. Because of Blarmusimuss, everything dies. Everything ceases to exist—even empty and discarded chambers, which have the longest life spans to date. Only a few of the oldest ones have imploded and fallen into a black abyss, ending up Lord knows where.

All of this was known only to beings that came before man, and that is quite interesting to this author. Space is chaotic, which is nothing new to us. Over time, throughout many chambers in the past—including this one—suns, planets, moons, and other spheres have collided with each other, with destruction, sometimes total, happening in their wake. Comets and meteors collide with larger objects and much more, crashing into surfaces throughout the universe as we have seen here on Earth, and especially our own moon. Craters cover much of the surface of it, creating large canyons and valleys of all sizes. Meteors have crashed into Earth's surfaces as well, creating the same different-sized divots as our moon. We know that. We also know the dinosaurs were wiped out by one of these objects, probably by a meteor that crashed into Mexico (not hitting the Congerrian pyramid spacecraft, of course).

But what we don't know was that a supernatural occurrence took place just seconds before the meteor fell through our ozone layer. Time temporarily froze, but life on Earth didn't. Let me explain: for a period of time, all the inanimate objects—including the sun, all the planets and their satellites, plus our destructive meteor—froze in suspended animation. The dinosaurs didn't, though, and even as they sensed that something had changed, they didn't know what. They soon would. As soon as everything came to a complete stop, a dark swarm came out of the Congerrian spacecraft. It appeared like an army of locusts, or something similar, and physically attacked the shaken Vulcan giants, devouring almost half of them in mere minutes.

They never knew what hit them as the nearly invisible fragments of Blarmusimuss began taking large chunks out of them at an alarming rate, infecting them instantly. Shocked, afraid, and in severe pain, they cried out in agony as they were eaten until they were no more. Not even their skeletal structures remained! Their last thoughts were of various terminal sicknesses that ran throughout whatever remained of their massive forms, until that part of them was quickly devoured as well. Yet some reptiles not mentioned in any science journals from the pterosaur family were spared. They flew through the air and looked similar to dragons and serpents with large webbed wings. They were dark grey in color, and fully scaled. Their three square eyes were blood red, located just above a large snout filled with large, sharp, and deadly teeth. For all intended purposes we will call the dragons the Dronasauorus, and the serpents Gronasauorus.

They were two species that didn't produce many of their kind. Why? Because both of these Vulcan monsters ate most of their young, acquiring a taste for mostly their own species. Fully grown members of these reptiles fought to the death in the air and ate their defeated combatants. These surviving monsters, numbering in the hundreds, were herded by the fragments of Blarmusimuss into the darkness of space, where they completely disappeared from view. Where did they go? No one on this side of sanity knows, but eventually we might all find out.

Once the feast was complete, all the fragments returned from all around the world to the Congerrian spaceship and laid in wait once again. It was one of the only times that they left the ship, but once again they left much death and despair in their wake. And then when all of the swarm had returned to the bowels of the spaceship, suspended animation ended, and the meteor struck the Earth, killing off the rest of the dinosaurs. Of course, that occurrence was never recorded in any periodicals, since there weren't any in existence at that time, so you are hearing about it for the first time here. Breaking News!

This is quite a revelation, and one that no one could confirm or deny except those involved in that event, and they can't relay the tale. The dinosaurs certainly didn't survive to mandate any details that might have been left out of this story, and Blarmusimuss is in hiding, lying in wait. It raises questions about what had happened, ones that we might or might not eventually get the answers to. Why did Blarmusimuss attack these massive creatures, and why were the Dronasauorus and Gronasauorus taken away? Did the fragments get permission from The Father, and if so, why? These are just a few of the questions that might be asked, but we do know that no evidence of this vicious attack was left behind to be found, and there is no evidence that the Dronasauorus and Gronasauorus even existed! Why is that? Maybe the answers to this, and our other questions, will be answered in the not-too-distant future. Only time will tell. Now let's get back to our main story.

When the Congerrian vampire spaceships first landed in Mexico, and just above the oceans in what would become the deserts of the Middle East, Blarmusimuss felt their movements. It was hungry, and it wanted to attack, but after conversing with The Father, still communicating through many mirrored realms, the fragments were told to remain where they were; that it was way too soon to follow the ancient protocol that had been drawn up long before. Blarmusimuss reluctantly relaxed and continued to lie in wait, but monitored the aliens closely as they visited the planet at various times afterward. Each time they returned, Blarmusimuss wanted desperately to attack and destroy (it's main mission in life, death, and everything in-between), but was calmly corralled and put at ease by The Father.

Once the Congerrians started chopping into the glacier ice and getting closer to the fragment bacteria, The Father ad-libbed and changed protocol. Adapting to new circumstances were paramount as far as The Father was concerned, and he relayed that important message to Blarmusimuss in no uncertain terms. If and when these alien vampires "rubbed cheek to cheek" with the fragments, then they should be punished properly, The Father reasoned sternly. Yes, these aggressively murderous beings existed on the right side of the ledger, being darker in nature than most species, but suffer they must. There must be no quarter.

This was all Blarmusimuss needed to hear, and The Father added that it could unleash any and all of its vileness on this disruptive force. They must be taught not to meddle in higher forms of existence's plans, and so let the chips fall where they may. Changes in protocol could, and would be made, but the end result would not change no matter what route was taken. And so, as was written earlier in this chapter, it was done.

Afterward, Blarmusimuss was advised to lie in wait in the depths of the Congerrian spaceship in Mexico. That location would be the best place to lurk. It would be dark and unwelcoming, and hopefully would not be bothered further. The fragments of the other two space craft in the Middle East traveled through invisible currents and rejoined their brethren in the spaceship in Mexico. That area would be acceptable as far as The Father was concerned, and even though conditions were completely different than inside the glacier ice to the north, the mission should eventually meet with the same results. For the time being, Blarmusimuss's hunger had been satisfied, and so the new conditions could be tolerated.

During the following waiting period, life exploded on Earth, and man began walking the surface of an ever-growing and changing planet. As human beings evolved, they encountered the two above-ground pyramid spacecrafts and began erecting similar structures in their honor. Copycatting the design of the Congerrian spaceships, outside and in, many more structures were built in their image. In early man's mind, these two pyramids were considered vessels of the gods and should be respected and worshipped at all costs. Any desecration to these massive structures would be met with severe punishments, some even leading to death, and those paths leading up to their demises would be paths filled with blood, torture, and beheadings. Man, like his unknowing predecessors from other planets long before him, was beginning to walk the same balance between good and bad—and sometimes downright evil. The pyramids, if they had been a living entity, would have seen this. One living entity did witness many atrocities over time but held no prejudices to any living organism, peaceful or barbaric, friend or foe: the sickness, the virus, the fragments—Blarmusimuss.

THE FOURTH CONGERRIAN SPACECRAFT

One such incident that became a tale of local Mexican folklore happened many years ago as early Spanish tribes wandered through the vast hot deserts searching for natural resources such as water and food. The story goes that they first encountered the immense pyramid (the Congerrian spaceship) sitting alone in the sand and set up camp around it. They kept their distance, never going inside, and began worshipping the large structure, praying for water and food and anything else they might need for survival. As they were chanting, they heard a loud roar coming from the heavens above them, and shockingly saw a large spacecraft descending from the clouds. It looked very similar to the pyramid structure on the ground, and it landed just outside the tribal camp, about a mile away. It sat for a while, giving the tribe a chance to pack up and run away in the opposite direction. Eventually a door opened, and ten large godlike beings (Congerrians) exited the vessel.

Now in the tribe's mind, they described these beings as twenty feet tall dressed in reddish robes. They stared intently at the tribe for a few minutes, which made them retreat even further. The aliens stayed just inside the doorway of their spacecraft until the sun set, and then, ignoring the tribe completely, they walked quickly toward the pyramid structure and entered it. Eventually only half of them ran out, but before they could get back to their spacecraft the door was shut, keeping them outside. They carried strange lights in their hands, shaking them up and down. They roared in hateful anger and banged on the closed door. Suddenly the vessel roared and blasted back up into the star-filled sky at unbelievable speed until it disappeared completely from view. The remaining beings screamed in obvious frustration and ran off toward the hills to the west.

The amazed tribal people watched in shock as this all took place; they huddled together and slept in shifts until dawn. In their tales they all admitted that it was the longest night of their lives, and they were never so fearful. The next morning, they gingerly walked back to camp, but found no signs of whatever had happened the previous day. The five beings left behind were never found, and so the tribal heads reasoned that they had disappeared into thin air and returned to the land of the gods. They told tales of gods running at great speeds through the moonlit desert night and flying up into the darkness, past the moon and beyond. Of course, they didn't call it the moon yet—just the round ball of fire that traveled across the night sky on most nights.

It was after these tales were told to others that early man began worshipping the skies as well. They thought that these flying ships traveled to a place beyond their means, to a realm all of them yearned to go. A place that would eventually be called heaven, where all gods lived. And so the spaceship was worshipped, and those inside were considered the highest form of life. Gods all! The pyramid was worshipped as well, for some of these beings had remained behind, living inside it. Again, it was reasoned that this large, massive, pointed triangular structure was a place of spiritual housing, or sanctuary, and was not to be disturbed, and so it wasn't.

The tribe eventually moved its camp to places far away and left the gods in peace, considering it sacred ground. They never returned but continued to pray to the heavens and skies above, and then relayed their tales of the incident until they had passed on. Over time the stories changed, as most tales do, but one part of them never wavered: the gods existed, higher beings from higher places living in rich kingdoms, and they controlled everything in the skies and on land. The tribesmen figured that anything that could fly into the unknown must possess that great power, and so they were worshipped and prayed to every night.

From a different perspective, the five Congerrians that escaped from their comrades' spacecraft ran into the same caves the vampires from the Five Star solar system and the other slaves had when they were unceremoniously and mysteriously released by their captors. Going back to before the rescue spaceship had entered the Earth's atmosphere, the Congerrian leaders on that vessel had held serious discussions that something had probably gone terribly wrong with the three ships that had visited Earth on a semiregular basis, and so they used great caution when they landed next to the Nexusian, their comrades' spaceship. Ten, mostly lower-level guards were issued the mission to explore and search the vessel for what might have happened to the crew, and if nothing was learned, they would move on to the other deserts in the east to search for the other two. This one was the senior vessel, with the most valuables on board, and so logically it would be "visited" first. If nothing was found, the valuables would be confiscated, and then they would move on to the other two spaceships for any other answers to their comrades' demise.

Defense procedures were set up for the worst-case scenario,

and so they were more than ready when they heard screaming and mass confusion coming from the communication devices of the lower-end guards sent in to investigate. Below is what was heard on those devices by those inside the Mother Ship, and what drove them to close the spaceship doors before the five soldiers were able to reenter the vessel, translated into English.

"We are entering Nexusian, with Rondu Unit leading fifteen meters in front. It is completely dark, no power evident. That, of course is not possible, but everything is dead. I feel no evidence of life on board, either friend or foe. So far, so—

At this point the Rondu Unit had suddenly stopped moving forward, grabbed their heads, and started screaming. They spasmodically fell to their knees, and small blackish spots surrounded them like angry and hungry mosquitoes, appearing to bounce repeatedly off every part of their bodies.

"General, we are under attack by an unknown enemy. Unit Rondu is down! We are returning instead of assisting, due to circumstances overall. I repeat, we are under attack . . . tack . . . returning to ship—"

The five Congerrians turned and ran as the last transmission was heard. Retreat was not a term that was used often, for usually the powerful vampire race was always on the offensive. Once retreat was spoken, the captain inside the vessel motioned to his next in charge, and the doors were closed quickly, just before the remaining five reached the doorway. No communication was relayed from inside the Mother Ship at any time, for there was no need. Survival on every front was paramount, and so that blueprint was followed without delay as those inside the ship prepared to leave. Those that had left the spaceship were essentially considered collateral damage and would be left behind. An infection of any kind would not be let inside the vessel. Every action to blast off was done in silence, for useless communication would only delay the real-time mission, and as stated, survival was paramount.

"General, let us in, we are OK. Do not leave us."

Loud screaming could be heard from behind that plea, coming from inside the Nexusian. The sounds were ones of complete agony, which further sealed the fate of the five left outside.

Engines started up, and the Mother Ship began its ascent, moving, to us human beings, at unheard-of speed. The five moved quickly away from the ship and shockingly stared up at it as it rose into the sky.

"You—" the words are not translatable, but were references used in anger, and then were followed by roars of rage from all five left behind.

Communication devices were turned off inside the spaceship, and so no more was heard. By the order of logic, the units left behind were immediately forgotten, and what lay in front (the future) was all that mattered. Space was bent hurriedly, and the Mother Ship disappeared into a universe many millions of light years away. This process was repeated five times, until the general felt comfortable about survival mode, and then transmissions were sent back to Culeagular about what had transpired, and their losses. In this message a memo is sent:"Do not send any more vessels to visited planet—now, or in the future. An unknown dangerous and deadly enemy resides there, one that we cannot compete with. Treasures in that part of the dark (space) should be forgotten, and we should not return to that sector ever again."

Eventually a return transmission came through, regretfully agreeing with that final assessment, since the Congerrians *never* liked to admit defeat to any alien force—plus they absolutely *never* liked to lose out on any riches. Subsequent warning transmissions were sent out to the rest of the fleet, and Earth and its magical glacier ice were forgotten for the time being. Ships were redirected to different parts of the chamber, avoiding that sector. Defeat was a terrible pill to swallow, but one that needed to be taken, and the Congerrian Empire, after all the computerized data was read and analyzed, knew when to cut bait.

Once the five Congerrian vampires entered the dark and long-veined caves, they huddled together and watched their number one enemy, the sun, come up over the horizon. They all felt an emotion that was kind of new to them: fear—nervous, deep-rooted fear. Usually they created this emotion of despair in their foes, but now they knew that feeling as well, and they didn't like it. They could see the Nexusian in the distance, and they all decided that there wasn't enough distance between *it* and *them*, and so they all agreed when the shadows became long to move further west when the sun descended behind the hills that evening. It was a good plan, and a smart one, but they didn't live long enough to see it through.

You see, when the Rondu Unit (the first five Congerrians that entered the Nexusian) moved cautiously down the corridor to the main operations area, they began to feel increasingly weak, their massive muscular arms and legs becoming extremely heavy and numb, their vision blurred, and everything they could see was only in black and white, devoid of color. A migraine-type of pain attacked their temples, but it was a vision that materialized in front of them that really shocked and unnerved them.

In their past histories, one of the tales told to them by their ancient ancestors was one of a fire god, one that was completely ruthless, heartless, hateful, and evil. The story goes that with one look at this fearful creature you would turn to stone, and everything inside you would begin to crack and fall apart, turning you completely to dust. During this transformation, unheard of pain would rack your inner core, and your spirit, personality, and essence would be pulled from your body and stolen by the dark presence, with no way back. The tale got worse. Once your spirit was inside the creature, your memories of the past would burn away, and you would be left with only insane thoughts where you would experience endless deaths involving new and excruciating agonies.

Most young Congerrians scoffed at those stories when they were told, but that didn't matter now, because all five saw the face of this presence in front of them, smiling wickedly. The creature was crimson and bright red in color, with orange fire surrounding it. All that could be made out were two dark eye slits, a large pointy nose, and a wide grinning mouth filled with sharp, menacing, yellowish teeth. A forked reddish tongue flicked in and out, long enough to brush up against all five of the shocked vampires. One touch of that serpent-like digit produced excruciating heat that began to burn the five Congerrian's insides, especially inside their heads. Their eyesight burned with red hot flames, which was the last thing they saw before their pupils burned to a crisp. They felt a strong current start to suck their essence through those flames, and then they knew no more except for the burning agony that never left whatever remained of their memories. Before total awareness completely deserted them, they all realized grimly that those tales of old folklore were sadly all too true. Indirectly, while their minds were burning in eternal flames, they subconsciously felt tiny beings eating at their cores, physically as well as spiritually. They screamed but were unaware of doing so.

They traveled downward into a melting fire that only intensified and became part of the presence that had so quickly claimed them. Their DNA remained just a tad different than the fires, and that part never stopped screaming.

As twilight fell on the desert, the five remaining Congerrian vampires, after resting, got up to travel in the shadows of the sun. They weren't yet in need of nourishment (they could go days, or even a week before needing life force liquids), but besides getting away from the spacecraft, they needed to at least start searching for their next food supply. Life of all kinds had been detected on the blue planet, and they would be examined to see which ones would be most suitable. That part of their mission became mute quite quickly, for as they walked toward the cave entrance they saw the same evil face the Rondu Unit had.

It blocked the cave entrance and was surrounded by flames. Before they knew it, the same fate befell four of the Congerrian vampires, but the fifth, the leader of the unit and the one that had communicated with the Mother Ship, was spared by the fragments. His name was Zennetto, and he was a mighty warrior who had led many comrades into slaughtering battles over the years, claiming many souls. He had relentlessly and tirelessly helped conquer many species and taken them prisoners. Some of those victims were vampires from the Five Star solar system, but his overall usefulness had run its course. A younger warrior, Justituas, had become more valuable and number one in the Congerrian military's eyes, overshadowing the older warrior's exploits. Zennetto, over the course of the last few millennia, had become expendable, but had survived up until now.

This mission, the military leaders had surmised, might be the perfect time to rid themselves of the old warrior once and for all, who had become a nagging nuisance to his current superiors. Why? Because his overall body of work had become sloppy, and he had murdered a few fellow Congerrians that the military had deemed valuable. He had also frequently bedded female vampires that belonged to others—a few even owned by Congerrians higher up on the depth chart than himself. Those females, who knew they were committing punishable sins but couldn't help themselves, since the famous Zennetto was still a mighty warrior who was well en-dowed, met with horrible fates, and discarded without emotion.

Zennetto didn't seem to care, for he was still the strongest warrior on the Mother Ship, and routinely challenged all comers if confronted. Few did, but those that had tried failed in their attempts, and were tortured and killed by him in the end. Still, when he was asked to head this possible dangerous search team, he knew that it might be a setup, but Zennetto couldn't help himself. No one could beat him in his mind; he mistakenly thought himself too valuable to lose, and so his bravado had gotten him in the end. Still, he was still alive, even though his comrades lay scattered around him, lifeless, quickly turning to grayish stone. He stared intently at the face in the flames, growled viciously, and stood defiant. If he was going to die, he would not go down quietly.

The presence in the flames stared at the mighty warrior, and smirked. "So, you are the great warrior of Culeagular, Zennetto."

The voice that spoke in the Congerrian vampire tongue was baritone, and sounded very far away. The voice was stern and powerful; it's tone confident. A slight echo could be heard behind every word it spoke, as if they were bouncing off the halls of many realms. It was a voice to be reckoned with, and so Zennetto decided to give it respect. Life was balancing on a tightrope, but he was still alive, still surviving and standing upright. That meant something.

"Who are you?"

"If you want to survive, your master."

Zennetto stared hard at the presence, showed his fanged teeth, and hissed.

"That's the spirit," the presence said, chuckling. The flames spread further into the cave, closer to the Congerrian. "That's why I picked you. I knew out of all your race, you would never lose that."

"What do you want with me?" Zennetto, asked, relaxing. He had shown his bravery, even though whatever this *thing* was, it was way beyond whatever he had ever encountered before.

"Not much. I want you to be what you are and do what you do."

"That's it?"

"Yes."

"And?"

"And I will enhance your gifts.

"And?"

"You will become a devoted servant."

Zennetto snarled and bared his teeth again. He didn't like the sound of that. He didn't bow to anyone.

"You will to me, but the choice is ultimately yours," the presence said, obviously reading the Congerrian's mind.

The fires grew on the ceiling of the cave, just above the warrior vampire. Heat filled the damp cavern, much warmer than the heat of the day outside. Zennetto felt its power like few ever had. Even though his personality went completely against being the submissive spirit he must become, this new strain of strength was intoxicating. The mighty Congerrian went to his knees and nodded.

"Say it."

"Master, I am your devoted slave and servant."

"Then it is done."

And with that, the flames fell from the cave ceiling and consumed the giant Congerrian vampire. For one split second he screamed in extreme agony before becoming completely silent. Zennetto could not be seen inside the flames as they burned out of control. They spread throughout the entire cave and into its deepest arteries for about five minutes, and then the complete fire turned to little black ink spots, fluttering in the air like dust particles. There were many more surrounding Zennetto, outlining his complete muscular frame, yet he still couldn't be seen. A strong invisible current took the rest of the fragments back to the front of the cave, and they, too, surrounded the Congerrian vampire, as if he was a magnet of some kind.

A minute later the black particles began to disappear and Zennetto could be seen. He stood erect with his eyes completely shut as if he was in a trance, swaying slightly from side to side. The presence still blocked the cave entrance, but there were no more flames surrounding its face. Zennetto slowly opened his eyes while every muscle in his body began to double in size. The Congerrian vampire was large to begin with, but now he looked like an award-winning body builder. His clothes shredded in places as his enlarged muscles ripped through them, and his hands and feet grew as well. His footwear ripped apart, and he looked to the heavens and let out a powerful war cry like never before, beating his massive chest with his fists. His hair grew to chest level, and his eyes became so bright that they beamed like red headlights. His fangs grew to twice their normal size, and his crimson tongue licked his enlarged lips, which had become quite parched.

Zennetto stared at the face at the cave entrance and asked in a slightly deeper voice, "Thank you, Master."

The presence slowly nodded, its face emotionless. "No need for pleasantries—you made the decision at the crossroads for yourself."

"Still—why? Who *are* you?"

"I am the sickness."

Zennetto looked confused as he cocked his head and flexed his new bulging muscles.

"My name is Blarmusimuss, and we both now serve the same Lord. If you follow direction, you will sit in a good place when the game is over and reap the benefits."

"But—"

"Do not question me before the answer is ready to be delivered, Zennetto," Blarmusimuss cut in sternly, a distant thunder bellowing inside the Congerrian vampire's head. "All information will be given to you at the appropriate time. Now listen to the guidelines I have set up for you. They must be followed to the letter."

Zennetto nodded, listened intently, and then turned completely around and walked further into the cave until he no longer could be seen. Once he was out of view, the presence slowly faded away, it's face first turning to tiny black particles that momentarily floated in the cooling air before disappearing completely.

Blarmusimuss returned to the depths of the giant Congerrian space craft and continued to lie in wait. The fragments watched intently over time as primitive man improved in every faucet of progression, completely engrossed. Its weaker particles continued to circulate throughout the complete chamber, wreaking havoc in every direction.

Returning to real time, not all of early man's plans went as planned, which should not come as a shock to any of us. Being so close to Blarmusimuss, many workers near the Congerrian spaceship either met with horrible fates or came down with new various illnesses that had no apparent cures. Average life expectancy dropped drastically in this region, and so the copycatting pyramids took even longer to build as they were erected nearby.

Man, being curious and venturing into places it maybe should avoid, sent brave and adventurist scouts deep into the Congerrian spaceship in the beginning. Not shockingly, none of them ever returned, and so it became off limits. Early man assumed that the gods had become angry and killed everyone that had descended into the dark depths of the pyramid—their domain.

Much later, others ventured into the darkness, mostly in the last few hundred years. Some returned, but they brought back even more fear with them. Some were covered from head to toe with sores and boils, babbling about evil and ugly demons that had touched and caressed them all over, creating the ugly open wounds they sported. They talked of a human boneyard in which some of the remains had been crucified against the walls of the different levels of the pyramid. They talked of strange writings on the dark and dank corridors accompanied with constant moaning and loud screeching screams from far below, echoing off the walls. None of those poor souls lasted very long; their wounds burned deep, with fatal infections setting in which none of their primitive medicines could help. They died horribly, and even when they were fortunate enough to lose consciousness, they awoke screaming from horrible nightmares of an Armageddon where pain and deceit reigned, where evil alien beings ruled with complete and total terror.

Some awoke saying that they had conversations with demons, warlocks, and witches. They held jobs, positions in high places. They changed the laws and regulations of society, where evil ruled over good. Fires burned eternal everywhere, and the climate was stifling hot. They spoke of a future, man's future—*our* futures. Those messages were followed by screams, and then those new leaders went to work. These were just a few of the nightmares the patients experienced. They awoke returning to their pains in the awake world. Agony continued. They begged to be put out of their miseries. Some of those requests were granted, not just for the patients, but for those that listened while trying to heal those deadly infections that just ate deeper and deeper. The doctors and their assistants tried to deny it even to themselves, but they just couldn't hear any more of those dreams (visions?) and *see* any more of the human-eating infections.

In some cases, those that walked out of the pyramid with no apparent marks had their eyes explode outward once they hit the sunlight, and black maggots came out of their slits. Most of them were smashed and killed by the guards or physicians looking after their patients, but some of them scurried away, hiding in the dark. Those wormlike survivors then at night creeped into rooms that housed either doctors, assistants, or the guards, and the maggots entered into their heads through their ears. Before dawn each and every one of them had the insides of their heads either partially or mostly eaten, experiencing horrible agonizing pain before eventually hemorrhaging to death. They half awoke between worlds and were aware of what was happening to them, feeling the tiny creatures moving and devouring more and more of their brains. They were completely paralyzed, not able to move or even scream for help.

But even that was not the worst of it. As more and more of their brains were devoured, the victims felt their minds being transferred into the thinking mechanisms of their attackers, and then they knew their true adversary. Inside the maggots, they silently screamed in horror as they realized that even though their physical bodies no longer existed, their thoughts and spirits were trapped inside the black creatures from the depths of the pyramid. The fragments of sickness had become their wardens, and before the sun completely rose in the east they had scurried back into the pyramid and descended into the deepest levels of the vessel. From there we can only imagine what happened to those that only wanted to help those in despair.

After those early dreadful events occurred, cement walls were erected to not only prevent anyone else from venturing into the lower levels of the pyramid, but to keep anything down in those depths from coming up and causing more pain and despair. The assumptions of who was responsible for this went from the gods in the skies above to the devil below and his henchmen. Who was correct in their thinking? That didn't matter, for cement walls five feet thick were erected in the corridors leading below, and thereafter the pyramid was pronounced completely off limits, guarded constantly by the military. Anyone trying to get anywhere near the massive structure was either arrested, chased away, punished in the public squares, or in more extreme cases, shot and killed. It worked for the most part, but every so often some venturing soul, or souls, would try to bypass the walls. These individual's curiosity overcame the barriers, and some even found hidden doorways that led to a hell that even those with the most creative minds could not imagine. In every case before their minds and bodies were overtaken, they wished that they had never been born.

When the power went off and most went back to The Creator, Blarmusimuss stirred, feeling a drastic change in the winds. In the darkness the fragments completely awoke from their semi-slumber and listened intently for a sign. It came soon after, as current events were relayed to it. "The time is almost upon us, Son," The Father said, with more emotion than Blarmusimuss could ever remember. The fragments didn't know this new vocal tone, for it didn't deal with such things like other life forms did, but it was passion—pure, unadulterated passion. The voice also sounded a lot closer, as if less realms and barriers now stood between them. "The patience you have shown will soon be rewarded, and the forces that stand by us will soon be completely unleashed, and we shall have it all!"

If sickness could smile, Blarmusimuss was beaming with erotic glee. New and dangerous viruses and diseases bubbled and boiled inside new created fragments of the whole, and a screeching sound never heard before echoed throughout the depths of the Congerrian spaceship, cracking the walls of the lower levels of the vessel. The cemented walls that early man erected in the corridors crumbled into dust particles, and yet the fragments of the whole stayed where they were and did not venture outward.

"Patience," Blarmusimuss murmured over and over again as its strongest fragments began circulating haphazardly throughout the bowels of the Congerrian vampire spaceship. "Patience."

The fragments of sickness, Blarmusimuss, was, by no accord of its own, a destroyer of life and creation on a whole. It liked its power and played with its victims as we have seen with the Congerrians, and those that dared venture near its core inside the massive spaceship. And yet as man evolved into what we are today, doctors, specialists, scientists, etc. were able to combat "the virus" on at least some levels. An invisible balance and line was drawn in a different type of sand, swaying back and forth as a backroom brawl constantly took place. Yes, if Blarmusimuss's strongest fragments had constantly attacked all life on Earth, we wouldn't have stood a chance against the infection, but we could stand up to its weaker particles and bounce back.

On other worlds and satellites those weaker fragments were sometimes more than enough to wipe out complete civilizations without any problems—but not here, not with human beings. Why was that? Maybe The Creator had something to do with that, or maybe we were just plain lucky. Some say we are created in God's image, and if that is true, will we then be able to overcome and defeat Blarmusimuss in the end and become gods ourselves? Will we one day be able to conquer all sicknesses? Who knows, and those are questions that each and every one of us might have to face one day as mortality stares glaringly back at us.

Some say we live many lives, returning from death to live again until we get it right. Some people have claimed to remember past lives, if, indeed, they have lived here before. Déjà vu, it is called. Let's just say that this is the case, the *truth*. Would Blarmusimuss know this, and would it get frustrated knowing that we keep coming back in new and improved bodies? I would, but maybe the fragments wait for The Father, who might be able to fix that possible situation. One thing is true, though, whether folks of every opinion want to believe it or not: human beings are constantly evolving and improving with each new generation. Physically we are getting faster and stronger. Sports athletes break old records on a regular basis. Researchers and scientists find more and more remedies to ward off disease. Improved surgical procedures save more lives. We are living longer; statistics prove that. Quality of live is better overall. Gods one day? We are certainly headed in that direction. If anything, these questions, and many more like them, are food for thought.

Ever since life of any kind existed on Earth, Blarmusimuss has gone to work trying to destroy it. Many species before human beings were wiped out early on, and who knows, maybe some would have gone on to be even more advanced than man himself, but we will never know since we weren't around to witness or record it, but it was going on. Different diseases and plagues were used to do this by the fragments without thought or emotion. Below are some of the major diseases that have attacked man that *have* been recorded and documented. They have killed many, but it is important to point out that we, as human beings, have survived somehow, and we have advanced enough to combat or conquer these sicknesses and diseases and have continued on as a species.

It is also important to note that our battles and wars with Blarmusimuss are the biggest conflicts we have ever had to face to date. These tug of wars never end, and we continue to fight each and every day to survive against this massive destructive presence. It is the only way a species can survive and move on into the future, continuing to evolve.

430 B.C.: Smallpox

This disease is caused by the variola virus, which spreads through skin to skin contact, through the air, or by bodily fluids. During this ancient time period, smallpox killed more than thirty thousand people in Athens, Greece, reducing the city's population by at least 20 percent, and probably more. Yes, mankind lost many battles fighting this disease, yet we survived.

541 A.D.: The Plague of Justinian

This sickness with no real name killed more than fifty million people in the Middle East, Asia, and the Mediterranean Basin, according to primitive estimates, for over two hundred years. During that time, it would subside for a short period before rearing its ugly head again and killing many. This plague is caused by bacteria that is spread by rodents bitten by infected fleas. This sickness used two different species to attack mankind—a tag team conglomerate, so to speak—and the disease had a sick sense of humor because just when man thought it had defeated the plague, it resurfaced with renewed vigor.

1334 A.D.: THE GREAT PLAGUE OF LONDON

This sickness actually started in China during this time period and tragically spread throughout trade routes, wiping out entire towns and settlements. Florence, Italy, alone lost around one third of its ninety thousand residents in the first six months! Overall, Europe lost approximately twenty-five million people. It was referred to as "The Black Death," and was one of the most devastating pandemics in human history. It was also caused by ground rodents in Central Asia, and preexisting conditions such as war, famine, and weather contributed to the severity of this horrible killer.

1519 A.D.: SMALLPOX EPIDEMIC

When Hernando Cortez arrived in what is now called Mexico in 1519, it had a population of around twenty-five million. A smallpox epidemic resurfaced and killed between five and eight million of its native population during the following two years—almost a third of its citizens. During the next century less than two million souls would survive this sickness and other communicable diseases brought over by European Explorers.

1633 A.D.: SMALLPOX

This deadly disease reached Massachusetts during this time period, brought over by settlers from France, Great Britain, and the Netherlands. Like before, this sickness quickly spread to the native American population, which up until now had been free of this communicable killer. It is estimated that possibly over twenty million souls perished after the Europeans landed.

1793 A.D.: Yellow Fever

In Philadelphia, Pennsylvania, during this time period a yellow fever epidemic killed a tenth of the city's forty-five thousand people. This is a viral infection spread by a particular species of mosquito. In the spring of that year, a contradiction occurred. Spring usually brings new life, but not this time. It brought the opposite. Blarmusimuss's bad joke? Maybe, but only the fragments were laughing. During that deadly season, French refugees, some with slaves (there's that ugly term again), arrived from Cap-Français, Saint-Domingue. These two thousand immigrants were fleeing the slave revolution on the north side of that Caribbean island. They crowded the port of Philadelphia, bringing the deadly virus with them.

1860 A.D.: The Modern Plague

This plague in the modern era killed more than twelve million people in China, Hong Kong, and India. It wasn't until thirty years later that people figured out how the bacteria was being spread and a vaccine was created. This bubonic plague was spread all over the world. It was considered active until 1960, when worldwide casualties fell to two hundred cases per year.

1901 A.D.: Smallpox

Another smallpox epidemic broke out in Boston and infected almost 1,600 people, killing 270 patients. During a three-year period, most of the deaths occurred within a week or two of being infected, while recovery time took much longer.

1910 A.D.: The Great Pneumonic Plague

This plague was the largest outbreak in the twentieth century, which occurred in Manchuria. In just over two years, approximately sixty thousand people died. Manchuria was a political mess during this period of time, and so information on this plague was sparsely recorded, and is foggy at best. Scattered reports were sent that the plague had appeared along the railway, but concern was slow in coming. Many died quickly in towns along the rail line, but the virus never ventured far from the tracks. This plague *still* occasionally causes small outbreaks in parts of sub-Saharan Africa.

1918 A.D.: The Great Flu Pandemic

In just two years this epidemic killed between thirty to fifty million worldwide, among them almost seven hundred thousand Americans. Historians have suggested that this Spanish influenza mutated and became most deadly in the spring of 1918 (spring again, and again, a bad joke), spreading from Europe to ports as far as Boston and Freetown, Sierra Leone. The archival records suggest that this pandemic may have originated with transported Chinese laborers, but no one knows for sure. This global flu outbreak was one of the deadliest epidemics in modern history.

1952 A.D.: Polio

Polio peaked in the United States during this year. Nearly sixty thousand children were infected, with three thousand recorded deaths. By 1955 a vaccination was created, which began to prevent further infection. Man is the only natural host for polio. This virus enters the mouth and multiplies in lymphoid tissues in the throat and intestine. Some of the virus can enter the blood and go to other sites where it can multiply more extensively, creating more havoc. Another round can infect the central nervous system (CNS), the spinal cord and brain.

1984 A.D.: AIDS.

In this year, scientists identified the human immunodeficiency virus, or HIV, as the cause of AIDS. In 1984 this disease killed more than 5,500 people in the United States alone. HIV infection is spread by human body fluids—including blood, semen, fluids from the vagina, or even breast milk—getting into another person's blood. That can occur through broken skin, or the linings in your mouth, penis, vagina, and anus. Having unprotected sex with an infected partner is usually how this virus is spread. Better treatments, and all-round preventative information are battling this virus, but it remains active.

2003 A.D.: SARS

Severe acute respiratory syndrome was first identified in 2003 in China. In this virus's first six months, more than 8,000 cases were reported, with over 770 cases succumbing to the disease. This virus is a serious form of pneumonia but is treatable if addressed in its early stages. It is believed to have started when the virus spread from small mammals in China.

2009 A.D.: H1N1 FLU

The global H1N1 flu pandemic may have killed as many as 575,000 people, though only 18,500 deaths were actually confirmed. This H1N1 virus is a type of swine flu, a respiratory disease of pigs caused by the type A influenza virus. Initially called an "outbreak," this infection was first recognized in the state of

Veracruz, Mexico. As the virus spread, now called an epidemic, the Mexican Government closed most of Mexico City's public and private facilities in an attempt to contain H1N1. The attempt failed, it spread globally, and eventually was called a pandemic. It is spread by respiratory droplets, person to person, and symptoms usually last for four to six days. Antivirals were recommended for those with more severe symptoms, or in an at -risk group.

2010 A.D.: HAITIAN CHOLERA

After a deadly earthquake that paralyzed the nation, an epidemic of cholera killed at least ten thousand people in Haiti. This outbreak hampered the country's rebuilding process. The United Nations would later apologize for initially denying claims that Nepalese peacekeepers brought the deadly disease to Haiti after the quake. This earthquake severely damaged a public sanitation system that was marginal at best before the 7.0 earthquake struck, creating ideal conditions for infectious diseases.

2014 A.D.: EBOLA VIRUS

This West African Ebola outbreak was the largest on record. It killed more than 11,300 people during its attack on humanity. The Ebola virus causes severe bleeding and organ failure, spread by animals or insects.

2016 A.D.: ZIKA VIRUS

The Zika virus is spread through mosquito bites. It is the first mosquito-borne disease to cause birth defects. It is also associated with stillbirth, miscarriage, and neurological deficits. While it is not a killer virus like other epidemics, there is a big impact on population growth, as couples are afraid of the virus and decide to either abort a pregnancy or not have children at all because of it.

2019 A.D.: COVID-19

This is a respiratory virus that at the time of this writing is currently at its zenith. It is a coronavirus that most likely started in China and spread quickly throughout the holidays and the 2020 New Year by human-to-human contact. It has moved so fast that people all over the world have had to shelter inside their homes to help combat it, since no vaccine exists (hopefully by the time *you* read this one has been created). All world events have been put on hold, while crippling its overall economy, with many losing their jobs. Physically it affects people differently, which is part of its genius and deviousness. Its most diabolical aspect is that it hides, sometimes spreading in people that show no symptoms whatsoever (asymptomatic), or not until they *begin* to show them. It viciously attacks the elderly, or those with preexisting conditions. It has been a completely different type of pandemic virus than those of the past, and has killed many worldwide in a short amount of time.

As stated above, this coronavirus, known as COVID-19 (not the nineteenth coronavirus of our history, but named after its birth in the year of our God 2019) has shown that it hides in the darkest of shadows, and attacks those unsuspecting humans that cannot see it. But the virus has been aided, for others have helped it hide! Who? Those it attacks—human beings!

Diabolically, world leaders either hid its existence or used diversions to downplay its lethalness, and by the time all COVID-19's cards were placed on the table, it was too late to stop its deadly effectiveness. That is sinful, plain and simple.

Introspective: COVID-19 has brought to light many aspects

of life that we either take for granted, or only think of subliminally. Our grandparents, who lived through the pandemic of 1918, could attest to this, and possibly could've helped us now in our time of duress. Sadly, they are no longer with us to assist in our time of need. Let's delve deeper into this subject.

Freedoms: we are being sheltered in our homes, unable to move about freely in our neighborhoods and establishments, visiting friends and relatives, either in social environments, in hospitals, churches, or God forbid, funerals. Before this invisible bacterial enemy invaded our airspace to take these interactions away, we took them all for granted. Sports, a major outlet to take us away from our stressful day-to-day lives, can no longer take place on a normal basis, because of restrictions put in place for overall survival. The same goes for concerts, plays, going to the movies. It goes on and on.

Food Supply: how we get our fuel for survival, and the places we get it. As an individual, I would watch as people moved in and out of our supermarkets, and couldn't help wondering how desensitized we human beings have become. We never stop to realize and *understand* what procedures take place before you grab that package of ground beef in the meat section. COVID-19 breaks it down even further. It creates everything from restrictions on entering a supermarket to how much you can buy. In the beginning (depending on one's point of view), as the diversion, the *deceitfulness* of the virus in the United States was eventually exposed, people ran to supermarkets to buy up everything in sight—not unlike what happens when a snowstorm or a hurricane is about to hit. Selfishness and gluttony usually take place, and because those frantic actions were taken during this pandemic strict rules and regulations had to be implemented so that *all people* could share in what we, as human beings, need to survive.

These are just a few examples of what takes place when

infectious diseases enter our airspace to create chaos. While they can bring out the best in some (healthcare frontliners, etc.), they bring out the worst in others. While some help those in need, others hoard everything for themselves. It is the normal balance of mankind, and the line between right and wrong. And remember one very important ingredient of the overall equation during times like these: *you can never lie when it comes down to sickness. Never!* That foolishness will always be exposed eventually, and people will see it for what it truly is: an act of evil. Amen.

(This is the only section in this book where current events are ongoing.)

These are just a few examples over time of where Blarmusimuss's tentacles were quite busy. While its innermost powerful core lied in wait for The Father, its lesser fragments still worked tirelessly, even using one or more species against one another. Quite devious and diabolical!

In conclusion, Blarmusimuss brings death instead of life. It brings separation instead of togetherness. It brings chaos instead of calmness. It brings sadness instead of happiness. It brings tears of loss instead of laughter among loved ones. It brings pain and grief, instead of healthy feelings of contentment. It is disruption. It is diabolical. It is a murderer. It is everything negative to all things positive, and so over time mankind has been forced to fight back with different remedies and serums and will continue to do so as long as disease and sickness exists. This author simply refers to the fragments as the ANTI-LIFE.

Here is another line of thought to ponder: even when life loses its battle with the fragments, the general concession states that our souls (most of the time) go back to The Creator, and the Kingdom of Heaven. That bit of information might not be known to a presence such as Blarmusimuss, but somehow I don't think it evades The Father.

Narrative Note: Eating a healthy diet and commiting to routine exorcise puts you in a better position to fight off any sickness or virus, such as COVID19. This can never be said enough. Give yourself an edge, and do what you can. It may help in the long run.

Chapter Thirty-Two

PRESIDENT WILLIAM BURBERRY

Former President William Burberry sat down in his favorite lawn chair early in the morning and looked out at the Atlantic Ocean on the morning when the power went off and most of the people went back to The Creator. This looks like it will be quite a day! he thought as he watched the sun come up over the horizon. It had the color of bright orange and he knew instantly it was going to be extra hot in a few hours. He could almost see the flames coming off it, he mused, smiling. To him, this was the best time of the day—a new day, a new beginning, the start of new creative textures, and what could possibly beat that?!

President William was now eighty-seven years old, widowed and alone, yet not alone. He and the love of his life had never had any children, all by design. Business and politics were a twenty-four-hour-a-day job, and if you wanted to do it correctly, he reasoned, you could have no distractions. Still, that wasn't the main reason, he knew, because if he *had* fathered a child, he would've been a fraud, a hypocrite.

His campaign had been run on the problem of overpopulation of the planet; he felt and knew that reproduction was a star in the sky. Every point, which represented every problem, all eventually pointed to the overcrowded countries around the world. He had made his case and shown his evidence; the people had listened and reacted, for the population had finally leveled off in the past decade, and he had been given credit for it by the tabloids and news broadcasts. Oh, it certainly wasn't the only case he brought to the American public, but we are getting ahead of ourselves.

As was stated, William was widowed; he had lost his wife Debra to Alzheimer's disease. She battled it bravely for five long years, him with her every single day fighting it along with her. The day she died he felt as if he had lost a war—and in fact, in many ways, he had. He considered death a brutal, unstoppable force without feelings or emotion, and he could see it clearly in his not too distant future. Sure, former presidents received the best treatments that weren't available to the general public, and even though he didn't necessarily agree with that arrangement— he reasoned that *all* people should have the same available drugs and procedures to survive—he knew that the authorities would keep him alive as long as was humanly possible.

As was stated earlier, he was alone, but never alone. Secret service was with him twenty-four hours a day, never too far from his side. As president, he was extremely popular for many reasons, yet two assassination attempts had been made on his life. Both times they had failed miserably; both times the men involved had been shot dead without mercy, which meant that he knew their deaths could have been avoided, but the government lately wasn't taking any prisoners, and the money that it would take to keep them alive and pay for their trials could be used elsewhere. His retirement estate sat on a high cliff in northern Maine in a town that had been renamed in his honor.

Williams, formerly known as Ellsworth, was as scenic as it got. Islands filled the ocean, and on a clear day like today, you could see for miles, admiring God's creations. President Burberry's estate was located on twenty acres of mostly woods. A quarter-mile driveway weaved around the trees until the last five acres, which were cleared for his retirement home. It had fifteen bedrooms, now mostly used by the secret service and estate staff, a country kitchen that seemed to go on for miles, a large dining room, twelve bathrooms, and a living room with his office facing the cliffs and the front of the mansion. A length-long deck ran along the ocean side of the mansion, which was where William spent most of his time these days (or at least when the weather was good), staring out at the ocean, reminiscing about the "good old days."

Yes, he admitted, he was mostly living in the past. Tears welled up as he remembered the days when this place was filled with friends, relatives, colleagues, and of course his lovely, beloved wife, running the show and giving orders to anyone in earshot. Those memories would also make him laugh, watching everyone running away from her. She had a good heart, though, and she always treated the staff fairly. Today though, he vowed, was too nice a day to dwell on the past—yet as usual he started thinking about the times he had resided in the White House.

That had been twenty years ago, and he had been the first president elected who didn't belong to a party. He had won handily too, losing only two states. The country had been in turmoil in his earlier days when he was a democrat senator from Maine, and he set out to destroy the two-party system before he ran for the highest office. That was the master plan, and America seemed more than ready for a major change. One side had always resisted the other, and year after year nothing really got done, and the country paid the price for this insidious insanity.

The market continued to slide, 401s lost money, jobs continued to disappear, etc., etc., etc. On and on it went. Only the space program prospered, and that was only because the Mars program *had* to keep going because *someone* had to survive this madness.

Thank God the colony had been a success, even though with the distant suns exploding they were temporarily shutting the project down.

That concerned him, on both fronts. The suns had to be a sign for something, and he never would have agreed to shut down the Mars colony program in any way, shape or form, but that decision wasn't his to make anymore. When he left office, he had done well to improve the whole political system. There was less infighting, the best decisions and ideas were passed and used, and *things got done!* There was no us-against-them syndrome anymore, or at least not much of it, and an overall positiveness reigned across Washington, which spread across all the states.

Times were still hard—they would always be trying—but you could feel and sense a difference in the air. Countries still argued and fought against each other, terrorists still struck innocent cities—America included—and the warming of the Earth was creating issues everywhere, but he kept things moving forward as best he could for his eight years in office. He left with the highest job rating of any president. He was very proud of that; he had remained extremely popular in his retirement, and was constantly kept in the loop. The drastic changes in government policies he had introduced were being built upon, and he hoped that the two-party system would be gone forever. History has a way of repeating itself, though, so you never knew for sure. He hoped and prayed every day for an improving country, one that would prosper long after he was gone.

President Burberry stayed on his deck until noon, when suddenly he heard gunfire coming from the woods. He was immediately herded inside the house and into his office, which was the safest room in the mansion. It was built like a bomb shelter, a place no one could get to him. The walls had been restructured with steel, and the windows bulletproof.

He watched in horror and fascination as a tall man in a long black cloak walked purposely up the driveway, raised his hands toward approaching gun-firing secret servicemen, and set each one on fire, their bullets having no effect on him. There were always ten men in the house at one time, and they were scrambling this way and that, taking up positions as they realized this intruder was different and extremely dangerous. The man walked up to the front door and it exploded, and gunfire could be heard again, followed by horrific screaming.

President William said a prayer, for this intruder seemed unstoppable and supernatural in nature. None of the secret service were having any success, and they were dying like flies. Suddenly the office door (which was also made of steel) became unhinged and fell to the floor, and the tall man stepped over it, entering the room. The remaining secret servicemen fired everything they had at the intruder, having no effect, and when the tall man raised his hands this time, all the remaining men's heads suddenly exploded, blood spraying everywhere. He seemed to notice none of this, only keeping his gaze on the former president.

The man had to be seven feet tall if he was an inch, and he had long, wavy, black hair. If he seems familiar to you, dear readers, he is. It was Thorzeous Mongolas, the warlock that owned the musical box and destroyed the town of Utopiaville so many, many years ago. He grinned viciously at William, showing a mouthful of fangs, and was about to raise his hand again when a round circular light suddenly appeared behind the former president. A transparent hand came out of it and quickly pulled him inside, and then the light disappeared before the warlock could react. Thorzeous screamed in frustration, dropped his arms to his sides, balled his large hands into fists, and then suddenly the whole estate was on fire.

The evil warlock walked through the flames and back down

the driveway, and by the time Thorzeous left the estate grounds the whole mansion had completely burned to a crisp in record time. Not even any smoke was rising from the ruins, it had burned that quickly. The warlock turned around, stared back at the Burberry estate in disgust, and growled his displeasure at what had just happened a few minutes prior. Something had saved that minion, and he had failed in his efforts to enslave him. He had lost this time, and the warlock was furious, for he was used to having his way. He couldn't just appear inside the boundaries of this estate; something had prevented him from doing so, and it had cost him dearly. He screeched again as he looked up at the sky. Dark, menacing storm clouds suddenly appeared as his rage echoed throughout the woods, and then he suddenly disappeared.

A few local policemen drove past the estate a few minutes later, and even though they should have seen the roof of the burnt mansion in the distance and some of the burnt remains of the secret servicemen, something clouded their vision and minds, and so they drove on slowly without stopping, writing down in their police log that everything was A OK up at the Burberry estate. Thorzeous Mongolas might have had a little something to do with that, but in a few short hours none of that would matter anyway. Yes, the former president had been right: it had and would continue to be *quite* a day, a day that would change the future for all in so many ways. The warlock might have known this day was coming and had decided to attack the compound and possess William Burberry before he went back to The Creator. We don't know at this moment if this theory is correct, but maybe in time we'll find out.

Chapter Thirty-Three

THE SOLDIERS THAT REFUSED TO DIE

*P*ain and suffering, suffering and pain—there are many realms of both, and they seem to go hand in hand. People experience pain and suffering every day to some extent: losing a loved one, being let go from a job, feeling betrayed or jealous, being bullied. You experience pain and suffering when you get sick with a disease that might kill you, like various forms of cancer, or even ones that are temporary, like a cold or allergy, or ones that will take time to heal, like a mild heart attack, stomach, or intestinal issues. Even losing a game in any sport such as baseball or football are part of these experiences. Regardless of the problem, pain and suffering are right there to keep you company, just to remind you of where you are or what you are in for. It's all part of the cycle of life.

Here, we are going to talk about the pain and suffering of three different men from three different times, yet all were remarkably alive in this world when the power went out. Their pain and suffering reached impossible heights that are hard to believe, yet this suffering did happen. At this time, if they could, they would gladly sit down with you and discuss them, if only to save what was left of their sanity, but those conversations will have to wait for now. Below are the chronicles that explain each man's plight. If you are human, you will surely feel for each. Here are their stories.

John Jeffries fought in the Civil War for the South. He didn't want to fight (like many on both sides) for many reasons. For one, he didn't like violence; he got along with everyone he met, and John hadn't even experienced a fistfight growing up, even though he was the youngest of eight brothers and sisters who fought all day long. He came from Atlanta, Georgia, which at that time was quite peaceful compared to other cities and states of the Deep South. He hated no one and was even sympathetic to the northern cause of freeing the black slaves (of course this he told no one). He was eighteen years old, skinny as a rail at an even six feet, but could eat with the best of them (if there was enough food), and had just been engaged to his lifelong sweetheart, who he had fallen in love with in the second grade. Her name was Sarah Saunders, and she was a cute petite blonde girl that had always been very popular growing up. The future was theirs for the taking, and then "The Cause" and the demigods of war had come calling for him.

Reluctantly he answered their calling and went with his fellow soldiers to fight in the Battle of Antietam, which was known as the battle of Sharpsburg. Most of his service time was spent in camp trying to avoid sickness and disease, but unfortunately he was on the front lines for this battle. It didn't take long before he was shot twice in the chest, three times in the stomach, and once in the groin. He died slowly and painfully, bleeding out as he waited for a medic that beyond his knowledge had been shot dead not more than thirty yards away. Once John's body was recovered, it eventually was shipped back home to Atlanta.

He didn't die alone, though. This battle was the first army-level engagement in the Eastern Theater to take place on Union soil and was the bloodiest single-day battle in American history, with a combined tally of over twenty-two thousand either dead, wounded, or missing.

During that one-week period, between when he took his last breath and his family burying him in one of the family plots back in Atlanta, John Jeffries's soul did not go to heaven or hell, or anywhere else in-between. No, it went inside a man who had just been shot in the face in the Revolutionary War in the battle of Bunker Hill. In this man's broken body, he instinctively slowly rose to his feet and blindly began moving toward intense gunfire. He had no ambitions of shooting anyone at this point; he was just trying to get away from the intense pain he was feeling on the right side of his head. One of his eyeballs had been shot out, exploding back inside his head, and blood was pouring quickly into his good one. Part of his skull on the right was missing as well, fragments cutting into his partially exposed brain. The pain he was feeling was beyond description, and he quickly fell to his knees with its intensity, dropping his bayonet in the process. Within seconds mercifully three more shots hit him in the chest. Down he went face first like a sack of potatoes on top of another dead American comrade that, of course, he didn't know, and John died shortly thereafter.

Did he stay dead and go to heaven this time? Absolutely not. Instead, his soul went directly into a man that was hanging by his arms from a ceiling beam in a dark, dank basement, maybe not too far away from the Sharpsburg battle, because he could still hear insistent gunshots in the distance. His wrists were bloody from rope that was tied way too tight, and his arms had lost all feeling, as he didn't know how long he had been hanging from the rafters. He had no idea why he was tied up, but he soon found out.

Two men dressed in overalls came downstairs and began punching him in the face and in the stomach, wanting to know where the gold was. He had no idea what they were talking about and told them so; they of course didn't believe him and beat him some more before asking him again. He swore that he didn't know where this treasure was; he hadn't a clue, so they beat him some more. By his own estimation most of his ribs had been broken, he was bleeding internally, and maybe his lung had been punctured, for he was coughing up dark thick blood and it hurt horribly to breathe. His nose had been fractured and most of his teeth had been knocked out. He moved his jaw and realized that was broken as well. That part of him might have hurt the most, but he couldn't tell for sure, for one pain point melted into another one.

John was in bad shape and didn't know if he would survive if he didn't get medical help in the very near future, but that wasn't going to matter because the real pain was about to begin. The men came back down the stairs and without a word began dousing him with gasoline and set him on fire. He screamed and screamed as he burned to a crisp; it was the worse pain he had ever experienced. There was no mercy in this realm of suffering, no passing out from the agony. As he continued to burn in the deepest pits of hell, a voice in his head told him he would have to endure some more—maybe much more—but the tone of that voice was somewhat soothing, in an odd sort of way. For some reason this horrifying news of reality had a reverse effect on him. Even though he could still feel intense pain, he was able to somehow deal with this ongoing torture.

Gratefully he died soon after and entered a long, winding,

dark, segmented tunnel or wormhole that seemed to go on forever. He twisted and cartwheeled to-and-fro as he sped uncontrollably through this hollow, strange structure. Eventually he slowed down and found himself in a seat in a flying machine. He knew this because he was sitting by a window, and as he glanced outside he could see a large river and a big city about a mile below. He thought it was New York City and the Hudson River, but he wasn't sure because here there were buildings much too big for what he had heard about the famous metropolis. This was only a fleeting thought, though, and he only had time to glance outside because havoc was going on inside this flying structure. Men up in front were holding knifes and yelling at the seated people that were staring back at them. Men, women, and children were either screaming, yelling, or crying. John wanted to do all of these things as well, but for different reasons.

John didn't know what this flying thing was, but what he *did* know was that something very bad was going on here, and the vibes he felt were very similar to the hate he felt between the North and the South during the Civil War. Still, this somehow felt more vicious, more rabid, and that scared him, because nothing ever went right when people felt this way about each other. The men up front had that look, that determination that he had only seen on the battlefield. They snarled at the seated passengers and spoke in an accent and language that was strange to John, and he could feel the hatred radiating off them. He didn't know it, but he was on American Flight 11, which was seconds away from crashing into the North Tower of the World Trade Center. John, of course, didn't know the history of these attacks, and that he was about to fly into a building that his mind could never fathom, but all of a sudden he saw a flash, and then his mind saw part of the letter *S* in stop, and then—nothing.

There was another flash, accompanied by many screams, and

then John was back in the wormhole, moving forward again. In no time he appeared in a strange suit standing in an office hallway in a windowed building. He thought that he was moving or somewhat drunk, for the floor seemed to sway. Other people didn't seem to notice him or the movement of the floor as they hurriedly passed him by, but then something crashed underneath them, and then *he*, as well as everyone else, fell to the floor. The building seemed to be swaying back and forth like a palm tree. Within seconds he could smell gasoline, and then he saw dark, thick smoke. Some windows had broken inward into many pieces, and a few people were bleeding from flying glass.

People came out of offices and ran to-and-fro, some moving to the glassless windows. He ran with those businessmen, looked outside, and couldn't believe what he saw. He was in a building that was as high as the flying machine he had just been in, something had exploded just below them, and fires were beginning to burn. John immediately began shaking, for he had a brand new fear of how much pain and suffering it could bring. People began hanging out of the windows, waving their hands and objects, screaming for help. The steel of the building was heating up quickly, and the smoke and fire was growing out of control. Strange twisting sounds (almost groans) were coming out of the steel structure; people heard it and freaked out even more.

John couldn't believe what was going on, and if he knew what was going to happening in the next hour or so, he would have believed it even less. John didn't know it, he couldn't have, but he was on the one hundredth floor of the North Tower of the World Trade Center on September 11, 2001, and the plane he had just been in had crashed into the building just a few floors below him. As time went on it became much hotter, and people began to lose hope. There comes a time in your mind when you accept your fate, and that was beginning to happen here. He could see

it in the faces around him—that look of total despair and desolate acceptance. They knew they were about to die; there was no
help coming. People actually began to calm down, even though
this situation was just becoming worse and worse, the heat building and building, and then John saw something he thought in a
million years he'd never see: people began letting go, either consciously or unconsciously. They began jumping out of the building, falling a quarter of a mile to their deaths. John watched them
go, and before he knew it he was doing the same. It was the only
way out, and burning to death again was completely out of the
question. He stood on the ledge with suitcase in hand and without stopping jumped away from the burning steel. He fell and
fell, flailing his arms spastically, and then—he was back in the
wormhole, but again not for long.

John found himself in another flying machine, with yet more
Middle Eastern people threatening seated passengers. Again, he
was by a window, and he looked in horror as he saw two large
buildings, one of them with a big hole in it; fire and massive
amounts of thick black smoke poured out of it into a bright blue
sky. It was quite a contrast. Sitting here this time he realized that
he had probably already died twice on this day, and maybe he was
about to die again. "Why are you doing this to me"? he asked The
Good Lord above. "Why?"

John glanced to his right across a narrow aisle and saw his
grandmother, his father's mother, sitting in a seat, knitting as
if nothing was wrong. She looked the same as on that day her
heart had suddenly stopped while she was knitting in her favorite
chair. Her white hair was tied up in a bun, and she was wearing
dark gray-rimmed glasses that always slipped halfway down her
pointed nose as she subconsciously knitted away. She was wearing
that same blue, faded polka-dotted dress that went down to her
stocking ankles and those black, thick, high-heeled shoes. Seeing

her made John realize just how much he loved this woman. Tears began running down his cheeks, blurring his vision.

"Grandma?" he asked, wiping as many of the tears away as he could, but more replaced them, if not more than before. "Is that you? What are you doing here?"

At first she didn't reply, just kept knitting, and then she suddenly cocked her head, looked her grandson's way, and replied in that voice he would never forget, "Don't worry, Johnny. You were *made* for this. You'll be just fine. Whatever *does* kill you makes you stronger than anything—*anything*." She paused another second, and then added, "I love you Johnny. I love you so much!" And then she disappeared and the seat was empty again.

He wiped more tears away and glanced back out the window. The flying machine had started to change direction. This is insanity, he thought wildly. His grandmother had died ten years earlier, and she had been his favorite. They had had many conversations about life in general, and he had walked away from each talk better for them. Grandma knew about many things and was preparing him for the future. Was it *this* future? Maybe . . . just maybe. "I love you too, Grandma," he said out loud, staring out at the burning building. He slumped back in his seat and whispered, "Thank you, God. Thank you for letting me see her one more time."

The flying machine curved around the buildings and headed straight toward the one that wasn't on fire. He wanted to close his eyes and wait for the impact, but he couldn't do it. He felt this flying structure speed up, heard people screaming as the men up front yelled out something, and then . . . darkness again.

For the longest time he seemed to float in suspended animation, as if he was in outer space itself, only there were no stars or planets to look at, only the black presence of nothingness. He thought about all the deaths he had been through, all the physical, mental pain and suffering he had experienced, and he realized he couldn't take anymore; he was at the end of the line.

"Please God, no more—no more," John pleaded in the darkness, and then suddenly he was back in the wormhole again. He moved slowly down the tunnel for a long time, moving in every direction imaginable. He wondered if he was on his way to hell itself, and then he wondered why he might be headed there in the first place. He had always done what he had been told. He was a good son and brother, he had always thought of others, he was a good student, had gone to church with his family, and had been true to the love of his life. Why would he be forgotten and put through such agony? He didn't hate; he loved. It just didn't make any sense.

He suddenly came to a stop, and it was pitch black all around him again. He heard distant, muffled voices that slowly got closer and louder. Somebody was talking about him, saying his name. He suddenly recognized that it was the voice of his pastor, the Reverend Alfred B. Reeves. He could make out his words—he was giving John's eulogy. He could hear weeping in the distance, which sounded like his mother and sisters, and maybe his girlfriend. God, he missed them! He missed his life, and he missed his fiancé and family, especially his beloved grandmother. He missed his friends, and even the people he didn't much care for. He realized that all the anger, hate, jealousy, and any other negative energy used in this world were wasted emotions that meant nothing. Only love mattered, and wasn't it a pity that it took until his funeral to realize this valuable pearl? He felt like crying for all the life he would miss, for all the love he wouldn't experience. The voices slowly faded away, and then he heard a voice in the back of his head say "Go to sleep," and so, he did.

When the power went out so many years in the future he suddenly appeared and woke up on a beach in Myrtle Beach, South

Carolina, dressed in the gray military uniform he had been buried in. In his mind he had been asleep only one night, and he had no idea of how much time had passed or how he had ended up here. He remembered everything about what he had gone through— all his deaths, all his pain and suffering—but somehow he was still alive and here on this beach. It was beautiful, and a perfectly warm, sunny day, but something was very wrong, for it was way too quiet.

He had gone to the beach with his family when he was young, and he had remembered that it was filled with people laughing and talking, children expressing their joy of such a wonderland, dogs barking as they ran with their masters up and down the beach, and of course the seagulls. Them most of all. They always seemed to be everywhere, flying overhead, grubbing for scraps, or fighting with each other. None of that was happening now, just the sound of the waves hitting the shoreline, and that seemed strange. He stood up unsteadily, and exhaled. "What the hell is happening here?" he asked himself, shaking his head, frowning. No one answered him.

Lawrence Heston shivered along with his fellow soldiers as their boat approached the beaches of Normandy, on June 6, 1944, during World War II. Normandy was located on the northern coast of France, and this was the biggest amphibious invasion in history by the Western Allies. The attack on Normandy began with overnight parachute and glider landings and massive air attacks and naval bombardments, but that didn't matter when it came to the morale of Lawrence and his companions. Most of them were either vomiting up their last meal (some called it their last supper, remembering Jesus Christ's last meal before he was crucified), praying to God, trying to find a way out of this insane strategy, or emptying their bowels literally in their uniforms. None that actually survived this attack were proud of how they reacted, but who could blame them. Who could really blame *them,* the ones who thought that they were probably condemned to die way too young, and way too innocent? Who? Why, dead men walking—that's who!

Here was the plan: get to shore, run like a maniac onto the beach, make it to any kind of cover, and then attack the enemy, who was behind cover and taking target practice on the Allied Forces. Even though those odds seemed way out of whack, somehow those Allied Forces were successful, but that's all in how you define the word. To most of us, being successful means you achieve your goal without losing anything—especially any souls, which meant this tactic in this case was a total failure. I believe (like many others, although few voiced their opinion) that if all the government officials, their wives, and their children were involved in this attack, it would've never gone down. They would've ripped up the blueprints, and possibly fired some of the higher-ups for suggesting such an outrageous plan. You hear all the time that if you die in honor, in honor of your country, then you died for the greater good—and to that I say *bullshit!* It sounds good, but all it is really is good brainwashing. Now remember this: every soul is worth more than anything, anywhere! Every soul is worth more than any country, any planet, any universe. If more people believed this, I believe many wars could, and could've been avoided, and different ways of solving different issues would be used. Going to war on any side is a complete negative, and should never happen.

Unfortunately, we are human beings, and have all the flawed characteristics (hate, anger, jealousy, bigotry, selfishness, etc.) to lead us all down the road to destruction. War is at the end of that destination, and we have repeated it again and again. Throughout the history of our existence people have gone to war, even though many people die every time! That is always the answer to that equation, no matter which way you attack the problem. Think about that. Every time we go to war people either die, come back maimed (without limbs or various other parts of their anatomies), or are mentally damaged, sometimes beyond repair. Sometimes I wonder if the ones that die quickly in war aren't the lucky ones. At least there is no more pain, and hopefully gone back to The Lord where they will be taken care of, where their souls would actually *mean* something.

Being disabled either physically or mentally doesn't seem to work out that well either. Many varied disabled military personal who return are either forgotten or discarded. That might seem harsh, and it is. Ask any soldier who has returned from war in this manner and they will tell you that many times, if not every time, this is true. The country that these soldiers have put their lives on the line for would love to sweep these injured warriors under the rug and hope they are never heard from again. Wow! And so how do these war pigs of destruction worship their God on their holy day, their Sabbath? It is fraudulent to say the least, and it happens again and again, war after war.

Of course, there are good Samaritan stories to tell, tales that will bring tears to your eyes, but if that tally doesn't add up to 100 percent.......... All veterans should be taken care of before others. They are the ones that put their lives on the line, but make no mistake: all people should get the best care available. Every soul is worth the same; nobody is better than anybody else, but try explaining this to the heads of state, political heads, or your normal owners and managers on any job in the world. That ideology doesn't hold water, to use one expression, which will probably lead to another war, and another one after that. History repeats itself, and war is hell.

At least it was on June 6, 1944, for Lawrence Heston and his fellow combatants. They knew they were headed straight into the devil's pit, and if Satan had met them on the beach with some suntan lotion they wouldn't have been surprised. The dark one wasn't there, though another demon was waiting with guns and firepower to cut them down, and many of them were.

One of them was Lawrence Heston from Pittsburgh, Pennsylvania, but he didn't die right away. He reached the beach and was hit in the right shoulder. He fired off rounds of ammunition blindly at the cliffs where the Germans were, but he hit no one. During the whole attack he never saw one of the enemy-not one German! After that he was hit in the stomach and went to his knees, and another round hit him in the neck, just about finishing him off. He lay on the beach, which was becoming bloodier and bloodier by the second, gasping for air. He knew he was done, and as he took inventory of himself he knew that the bleeding was beyond stopping, his neck beyond repair. As he was starting to lose consciousness, a medic momentarily stopped by him, shook his head absentmindedly, and moved on. That was all Lawrence needed to know. He prayed to The Lord and prayed for his soul. His life might have passed before his eyes, but he was beyond looking at it. He took his last breath, and then joined the many others that had lost their lives on that fateful day. Unlike them, though, but like John Jeffries before him, his soul didn't go to heaven or hell—but let's not get ahead of ourselves.

Let us go back in time in reverse for a second. Lawrence Heston had died on the beach of Normandy, but what he had witnessed just before that would've driven most people completely over the edge. As his boat approached the beach, three soldiers were shot in the head just to his left (he had just switched places with one of them), so besides seeing parts of their heads laying at his feet, he immediately felt guilty as well. "What if I hadn't switch positions? What if I had done this, what if I had done that?" ran through his brain like an out-of-control freight train, giving him an instant headache—more than the one he was carrying to the shore to begin with—and the images of his dead companions with their fragmented skulls didn't help.

They reached the shore, the boat doors opened, and lines of soldiers stormed the beach. He was in the third line, but he might as well have been in the first, for every one of the soldiers in front of him were shot down almost immediately. Lawrence ran into the water and up the beach with tears in his eyes, knowing . . . knowing. And *that* was the worst of it, knowing that this was the end—his last day and moments on Earth. He knew before, but now he was certain of it: he and his fellow soldiers had been led into slaughter. Some would live, of course, but it wouldn't be him. He was scheduled to be in the first line of boats that reached shore, so the handwriting was on the wall. He ran with his troops and before he was hit the first time, he watched quite a few soldiers from his boat cut down. Blood was beginning to run everywhere, and he hoped and prayed this would be the worst of it, that it would end quickly. He was wrong on both counts.

Lawrence had been drafted into the army in August 1941. On September 16, 1940, the United States instituted the Selective Training and Service Act, which required all men between the ages of twenty-one and forty-five to register for the draft. This was the first peacetime draft in United States history. It was put into effect to fill vacancies in the military that could not be filled through voluntary means. It was used until 1973, when the United States Armed Forces moved to an all-volunteer military force. There is no known count of the people lost because of this draft; certainly no one was proud of its amount. The wars or conflicts that followed World War II during this draft included the Korean War (1950–1953), Cuba (1961), Vietnam (1961–1973), and the Dominican Republic (1965). Lawrence was one of the first to serve, but like many before and after him he never got to finish his commitment to the armed forces. His name joins many on the imaginary wall of shame of unnecessary deaths due to the idiocy of war in worldwide history. New names continue to join the old as history repeats itself while new wars increase instead of decrease.

Side Note: All men and women who have fought for any cause are still the true heroes of everyone's societies. They give up their lives for their countries, and they can never be repaid. If I ever meet their souls in heaven, I will salute them for their service, and I will be forever in their debt. God bless their souls; I openly cry for their spirits, and the lives they should have been allowed to live.

Lawrence Heston grew up the first of nine children of Michael and Carolyn Hester. There were five boys and four girls who fought for what was put on the table every evening, and they grew up tough. Michael worked in the steel mill by day and hardware store in the evening. He worked hard for his family, setting a good example for his flock. Carolyn cleaned houses when she could, especially when Lawrence and his sister Peg got older and could watch their younger siblings. Nothing came easy for the Heston's, but they always somehow got by. Lawrence sacrificed throughout his teenage years, but he loved his family.

He loved sports and was good at them but couldn't join the school teams. Besides taking care of his younger brothers and sisters, he also worked at the local grocery store to help make ends meet. He was known as a good kid, and when he was drafted he had high hopes of serving his country well. He didn't like war, and he certainly didn't want to fight in one, but he went into the army without any complaints. It should've ended better for him, but you play the hand you are dealt. Lawrence made many friends during his military training, and some of them he saw die first-hand that fateful day on the beach. The visions of their remains stayed with him for the last few seconds of his life, and the time afterward. Like many soldiers who have gone into combat before him, he was scarred for life. This was the history of the second man that would have to deal with pain and suffering beyond normal standards.

After Lawrence Heston died, he entered the same wormhole John Jeffries had many years previously, and he materialized on a large, clear, grassy plain that stretched many miles in each direction before he saw forests and mountainous regions on each side. It was a battlefield, and he knew this very quickly because he saw massive armies of men to his north and south charging at each other, yelling war cries and raising swords in the air. Guns didn't seem to be in the equation; maybe they hadn't been invented yet. He could sense the heavy aura of hate and anger closing in around him, for he had felt that heaviness before. Both sides were in armor and helmeted head gear, their long wavy hair flowing out over their large straining shoulders, bouncing up and down haphazardly.

Lawrence took inventory of himself, and he was still dressed in his World War II army uniform, looking completely out of place except for the dried blood that covered it. He wanted no part of this battle, so he took off as fast as he could toward the east end of the battlefield where the woodlands were the thickest, but as he closed in on what he thought was good cover Lawrence realized there was another group of men waiting there. These warriors were like none other he had ever seen before. They were all on large white horses, and wore no armor. They instead wore caped robes that were dark in color, and as he got closer this army seemed to be grinning hungrily at him. They didn't move until he reached them, and then he realized that he had run in the wrong direction, for these were not normal men, not human beings in any true sense, but some sort of alien species. He stopped just in front of them, and to his horror he realized they weren't grinning at him, but salivating.

They all had fangs, and their faces were pale white, like ghosts. Their eyes were blood red, filled with hunger, and Lawrence knew that he had just run into an army of dangerous vampires— people always swore that these beings were only a legend, but here they were! The one leader in front got off his horse and slowly started walking quickly toward him. He wore pointy black boots with shiny gold buckles that surrounded the ankle area and clicked with every step. Lawrence, petrified, turned to run, but the creature held up his right hand, which was abnormally large with equally large bony fingers and long pointy fingernails and he suddenly was frozen in place.

A moment later the creature reached him, and Lawrence realized that he was at least seven feet tall and extremely muscular. He grabbed Lawrence around the throat and picked him up as if he was as light as a feather, and bit viciously into his throat. He felt his blood being drained out of his jugular very quickly, like powerful rapids moving in a river after a heavy rainfall, and he quickly became weak and faint. He was turned around by the large vampire and witnessed the two armies fighting fiercely, swords wielding and blood flowing everywhere.

Many men on both sides were already dead, or lay dying, but he didn't really care about them now, because he was in the throes of a much more dangerous group of soldiers. He suddenly felt a long wooden stake, maybe seven feet tall from top to bottom and razor sharp on both ends, enter him from the bottom of his neck and through his open mouth, then the end of it was thrust mightily into the ground, and he was left there to hang, dying. He was choking and gagging, and before he took his last breath and died he saw the army of alien vampires ride past him toward the battling armies and savagely butcher whoever was left. Both armies were no match for these creatures, and they began to end up like he was, staked in the ground. Lawrence died on his, the life drained from his body, and he ended up back in the wormhole, moving at speeds he could not fathom.

Finally, after a long period of time he found himself in a hospital bed, attached to many tubes and machines, most of them making various types of sounds that no one sick would want to hear. He was in a quarantined area, because doctors and nurses were moving to and fro in white spaceman-looking suits, covering their entire bodies. He could see their faces through a clear rectangular shaped area, and they all looked very concerned. Large plastic sheets covered the walls on each side, and he wondered what kind of hell he had dropped into now. He tried to talk and move but he was paralyzed; only his eyes could dart to-and-fro.

He noticed that there were other patients just like him on either side of his hospital bed, strapped down around their chests and abdomen, and one of them suddenly went into convulsions, his arms and legs flapping up and down. The man had dark red blotches on his face and arms, and other parts of his body that were covered by a hospital bed sheet, and something was moving inside those areas. Suddenly his eyes exploded outward, and tiny, mean-looking, spiderlike creatures began to crawl out of the patient's eye sockets. The doctors and nurses sprayed a substance on the tiny creatures, and they stopped moving—dead on arrival, so to speak. Obviously they knew what they were dealing and battling with, and the patient was wheeled away quickly on a gurney. A few of the creatures that were still slightly moving were put in a large bottle and taken away. He realized that he had dropped into another type of war, this one maybe interstellar, and this one seemingly much more dangerous.

Up to this point Lawrence had felt nothing, but now he suddenly felt something alien moving inside his body. His insides felt as if he had a bad case of poison ivy that was spreading rapidly, and he felt like screaming. His insides felt as if they were melting, and he could feel something popping all over. He watched in horror as his own red blotches opened up and the same hideous tiny creatures started exiting his body. Many others were still inside him, and they were eating him hungrily from the inside out. The pain was excruciating, and he watched as the doctors sprayed him like the other patient, but the creatures that were still inside him continued to eat, biting viciously through unprotected body tissue.

He was quickly wheeled away, spasming in convulsed agony, pain that he couldn't begin to describe, suffering he wouldn't wish on his worst enemy. He was rushed down a long white hallway that was also covered with plastic and wheeled into a room that had a large dark gray tank. A thick, heavy door was opened slowly by a protective-suited man, and inside a large fire was burning. In his head he was screaming, "No! No!" over and over, but he was, without emotion, thrown inside by the spacemen and the door closed.

He burned and burned, but he never lost consciousness. More spidery creatures began to exit his body rapidly, trying to flee from every orifice he had, but they all failed and quickly burned to a crisp, their bodies popping and sizzling until their ashes floated into the air. That didn't happen to Lawrence, though. He was *still* alive and aware of his feelings and surroundings as he was pulled from the oven-like structure, every nerve ending was screaming in unrelenting agony. Then he was placed in a freezer of some kind. The throbbing pain began to numb, but to his horror his body began to heal itself, and within no time he was back to his own self, his organs, tissue and skin back to normal. But that was the worst-case scenario because he began to feel the creatures inside him begin to move again, cocooning inside his organs, laying eggs inside his heart, liver, stomach, and intestines. The itching started again, and the red blotches began to reappear.

Inside his head Lawrence began to scream—not just from the intense itching, but from the fact that he could not die (at least the doctors had not discovered a way to end his agony yet), and he was being hooked up to tubes and experimented on again. The doctors poked and probed, but every time he was touched, his nerve endings screamed in agony. Maybe the creatures inside him had set up a defensive-type device to keep the doctors away. Lawrence didn't know that for sure, but what he had become was a vessel of pain and suffering, and he screamed until he could scream no more.

Then he was thankfully back inside the dark wormhole, moving slowly. The pain was gone, the creatures inside his ravaged body gone as well, but the memories remained. As he traveled through the wormhole he wondered just what was happening to him. Where was he? Was this his final fate? Why was he enduring this pain and suffering? His questions went on and on, and he prayed to God for it to end, but his prayers fell on deaf ears, for suddenly Lawrence found himself inside the Naval Base in Pearl Harbor, Hawaii.

He was on guard duty with other soldiers at eight o'clock in the morning on December 7, 1941, when the first Japanese fighter planes attacked the military base. The barrage lasted just over two hours, but its effects were devastating. By the time it was over, twenty naval vessels, including eight enormous battleships and three hundred airplanes were destroyed. At least two thousand American soldiers were killed, and another one thousand were wounded. The day after the attacks President Franklin D. Roosevelt asked Congress to declare war on Japan, and they approved. Three days later, Japan's allies Germany and Italy also declared war on the United States, who then declared war on them as well. Two years after the conflict began, the United States entered what became World War II.

Lawrence Heston knew this all too well as he was shot in various parts of his body. He was hit in his stomach, chest, and shoulder. He began bleeding badly and slumped to the ground. Others around him were hit as well, some not as badly, but others were lying on the ground, motionless. He could hear soldiers crying out for help, and others, like him, screaming out in pain. How ironic, he thought grimly, holding his stomach as blood ran from his various wounds, I died on the beaches of Normandy, and now I'm going to die again at the beginning of the war when I was first drafted. When will this hell I'm in end?

Other military personal moved chaotically back and forth around him, and a military doctor suddenly appeared and bent down to examine him. This navy medic also shook his head sadly, and quickly moved on. Soon after Lawrence Heston took his last breath, dying for the second time in the same war. He ended up back in the wormhole, and like John Jeffries before him, heard his eulogy read by his minister, Pastor Kevin Porter. Lawrence also experienced the same feelings of missing his family, and the deep definitions of life and love. He too was told to go to sleep, and he woke up a mile and a half north of John Jeffries on the coast of Myrtle Beach. He was the second man that was dead before the power went out and came back alive afterward. Pain and suffering, suffering and pain—when would it end?

Donald Summers was born on March 13, 1947, to George and Cindy Summers in Ozone Park, Queens, just outside New York City. He was the second of four sons. The family joined a mass exodus out of the borough with many other families, moving to Rockland County in southern New York State, which was still considered upstate to those that still lived in the city. It was a place where new infrastructure was taking place, and a three-mile bridge, The Tappan Zee (since torn down and replaced with The Mario Cuomo Bridge), was being built across the famed Hudson River, connecting the county to Westchester. As many immigrant families moved into the four boroughs surrounding New York City in Manhattan, families like the Summers moved north to this new suburban countryside. It was only a half-hour drive outside the City where many people could still work, commuting daily, yet far enough away for them to distance themselves from the old homesteads they were trying to get away from.

Crime had always existed in the five boroughs, but now that activity was escalating rapidly. Families that had lived there for decades became nervous and anxious, afraid of the new people who were walking up and down the streets in front of their houses. They wanted to find a more laid-back way of life in a more rural area. No more did they want to be surrounded by endless concrete and the loud noises created by mass transit. No more did they want to constantly worry about the increasing muggings and robberies that were on the rise. The murder rate was also going up, and many senseless funerals were taking place. Too many good people were saying goodbye to loved ones, and too many young people took the wrong fork in the road and ended up in prison.

On the job front, populations were growing, and a lot of families had five or more children, which meant that not having enough to eat was becoming a reality. Livelihoods were getting harder to come by, even though work at that time was still plentiful. It was just that stealing and robbing people in the neighborhood was easier than working a normal job or having to look for a second one. The elderly were easy targets, women and children as well, but if you moved throughout the neighborhood in a gang then no one was off limits. Those hoodlums all carried sharp knives and handguns. A lot of innocent people either ended up in the hospital or in the morgue if they fought back.

The days of not locking your front door became a thing of the past. The days of walking alone were over. People needed an escape; families needed to keep the lifestyle they were always accustomed to. People needed an answer to the problems they voiced to their closest friends. Upstate New York became the solution to their unstable situation.

The Summers family moved into a development in West Nyack, a hamlet of Clarkstown. It was a quaint little town, quiet and friendly. As other families moved in, new friendships and relationships were made. They began to congregate, going to the same churches, shopping at the same stores, celebrating holidays with block parties, and even carpooling into the city or just outside the city limits. They all had children, a lot of them around the same age, who went to school together and became fast friends. All and all it became a tight-knit community as the infrastructure grew quickly all around them. This all happened around the mid 1950s, ten years after the end of World War II, and just before the 1960s began and a young new President took office, John F. Kennedy.

As the new decade was ushered in, it is worth noting that it was the beginning of a new age. Life as an American citizen had changed forever. A fresh new face took control of the President's office. New music of all kinds exploded onto the scene, a lot of it coming from England. Young people began to fight the system like never before, protesting in Washington and around the country whenever something bad happened. Bigotry was still alive and well, but now people were fighting back. Senseless murders of black people were still being committed, but people of all colors and cultures were gathering and protesting, fighting for unity. Four men of note were assassinated in the United States during the 1960s, fueling unrest.

On Friday, November 22, 1963 at 12:30 p.m. in the afternoon in Dallas, Texas, John F. Kennedy, the thirty-fifth President of the United States was shot and killed by Lee Harvey Oswald, who two days later was shot and killed by Jack Ruby. Oswald was an American former Marine who was honorably discharged and defected to the Soviet Union. He was first arrested for shooting a policeman thirty minutes after the assassination of the President, and later charged with that killing as well. There were questions whether Oswald was a lone killer, or whether others were involved. These chains of events created great unrest in the country and took a lot of air out of the balloon. John F. Kennedy represented new hope for the future of a government that was no longer trusted, and his death brought on more unrest than ever before. It wasn't the only reason for distrust, but let's not get ahead of ourselves. People of all ways of life wondered if our own government was involved in the assassination. Nothing concrete was ever found, but suspicions have circulated ever since. A further divide in the nation was created.

If anyone else *was* involved in that assassination (anyone in the government, other agencies, groups, or organizations), then most of them took that knowledge to their graves with them. They would have to answer to a higher power to be judged, and that court played no games. The loss of President Kennedy was a great loss for the country. He was a positive force, and things would have gone down a different way if he would've lived. God bless his soul.

Malcolm X was an African American Muslim minister and human rights activist. He was shot twenty-one times in the chest, left shoulder, arms, and legs on February 19, 1965, in Manhattan's Audubon Ballroom. He was pronounced dead at 3:30 p.m. on that fateful afternoon. Three men were charged with his murder. He was called one of the greatest and most influential African Americans in history. Malcolm X was thirty-nine years old. In his wake the divide grew.

Martin Luther King Jr. was an American Baptist minister and activist who became the most visible spokesperson and leader in the civil rights movement. He preached nonviolence in trying to move the country forward on race relations. On October 14, 1964, he received the Nobel Peace Prize for combating racial inequality through nonviolent resistance. On April 4, 1968, he was planning a national occupation of Washington, DC, to be called the Poor Peoples Campaign when he was assassinated in Memphis, Tennessee, by James Earl Ray. Ray fled the country and was arrested two months later at London Heathrow Airport, sentenced to ninety-nine years in prison, and died in 1998 while serving his sentence. After the assassination many riots occurred across the country, wounding a nation. Eventually a national holiday on the third Monday of January (Close to Martin Luther King's birthday, which is January 15) was observed, but it took some time, and a few states fought against having it. At the time of his death Martin Luther King Jr. was only thirty-nine years old, ironically the same age as Malcolm X. As a nation mourned his death, the divide widened.

Robert Kennedy was an American politician and lawyer from Massachusetts. He served as the United States junior senator from New York for over three years until he was assassinated. Before that he was the sixty-fourth U.S. Attorney General for three and a half years under his brother, President John F. Kennedy, and his successor, President Lyndon B. Johnson. In 1968 he was a leading candidate for the Democratic party for the presidency of the United States. He appealed mostly to African Americans, Hispanic, Catholic, and young voters. Back again was that fresh new idealism for a new beginning, a chance for the public to trust the future of government policies and actions, but unfortunately, on June 5, 1968, at the Ambassador Hotel in Los Angeles, California, he was shot three times by Sirhan Bishara Sirhan and died in the Good Samaritan Hospital in Los Angeles the next day. Robert Kennedy was forty-two years old. He had a very good chance of becoming the next President, but those hopes were extinguished when he was suddenly cut down. Richard Nixon ended up becoming the thirty-seventh President of the United States, was forced out of his second term because of Watergate, and so basically government went on as before. Add that all up, and the nation's divide was basically complete.

A DECADE REVIEW AND BEYOND

People have asked what happened in the sixties to change society, and there are many reasons. Assassinations were committed, four of them, and one of them was a president with fresh ideas— ideas the country was ready to embrace. Two of them were African American activists, and their murders hurt the movement toward ending bigotry. The fourth was a presidential hopeful who also wanted to end the race problems in the United States and bring equality into the equation. All four victims brought hope to the table, and all four were killed in cold blood in an attempt to stop their progress.

What bothered society the most was that it was rumored that the government, or people employed by it, might be involved in some if not *all* of these murders, trying to keep progress from moving forward. Young people started talking about a revolution, but it never really materialized. They acted out in several ways, though, trying to get their messages across. Music exploded, some of it taking on the government, singing about distrust and free-doms they thought should be instituted. Free love spread like wildfire, the idea that love should be exercised, not war. Males of all ages started growing their hair long. Some grew beards, some started wearing earrings. Both sexes began wearing different types of clothes; many wore tie-dyed T-shirts with peace signs on the front, and massive drug use overtook the country. Grass, hash, pills, acid, cocaine, and heroin were sold in large quantities across the nation to people of all ages, sometimes with tragic results.

Still, there was another story that shook the nation to its core, something that dominated the headlines in every newspaper across the country and beyond: the Vietnam War. The war started in the fifties between North and South Vietnam, and the United States got involved in the early sixties, sending troops over there until 1973. During the 1960s it was at its worst, and many American soldiers lost their lives. The draft was in full swing during this decade, and people who refused to go ran across the borders or tried in many ways to get out of serving. A lot of Americans didn't believe in the war, and when survivors came home they were not treated well. This treatment was a serious injustice to the men and women who had served to protect a country that didn't seem to appreciate them, and it came from all sides. This war (which wasn't even considered a war, but a conflict) divided a country for more than ten years, almost fracturing a nation.

Our last person of interest here is Donald Summers from Rockland County, New York. He wasn't drafted, he enlisted, but like many others like him, they had no idea what they were getting into. Soldiers that came home, some whole and some not, were affected in one way or another, and they told stories filled with horror and contempt. War is hell, it always has been and always will be, but this conflict was more publicized than others, and the publicity was mostly negative. Trust in the government was at an all-time low. Everything that happened in the 1960s was an old fashioned bitch's brew, and when you stirred all those components together it created a brand-new era, which brought on a brand-new society, one that was smarter and started asking questions when situations didn't seem kosher. The days of the 1950s and before were gone forever. It was truly the end of the age of innocence.

Donald Summers grew up like most children in the suburbs, going to school and church, making friends, raising hell and having fun. Life was good, even though the war was ramping up and the draft was claiming souls. Moving upstate seemed to be a good idea for the Summers family, for they smiled and laughed a whole lot more than they cried. That ended on December 2, 1964. That was the day George Summers, good husband and father, suffered a massive heart attack at work in the city and died on the spot.

Gone was the head of the family. Gone was his job, and gone were the good old days.

Some families fall apart when something of this magnitude happens, and some pick themselves up and get back to living. Cindy Summers buried her husband, the only love of her life, and then got a job in a local factory making peanuts compared to her husband, but that didn't stop her. She got a second job with an agency cleaning offices part time. In between those jobs she went home and made supper for the boys, who now had to look out for themselves a lot of the time. On and off she worked a third job on the weekends at the local law office, working the books. Between all that she was able to pay the bills, keep clothes on her boys, and stay healthy enough to get up each day and do it all over again.

She and the boys went to church every Sunday and thanked God for what they had. They prayed for their husband/father, and hoped that he had found peace in heaven . Cindy Summers was a marvel, and a good example to look up to. She was proud, never asked for a handout, and brought her boys up to be the same. She lived to see her family have productive lives and lived to the ripe old age of ninety-three. She died in her sleep with a smile on her face, for she had done what she had for her family, and now it was time to join her husband who was taken from her so many years prior.

The oldest boy, Jason, was a good boy who took over his father's duties. He watched over his younger brothers, got a part-time job at the local supermarket, and gave most of what he made to his mother. With the rest he bought groceries for the family, for that's what big brothers did in the Summers household. After high school he enlisted in the marines and did his tour in Vietnam, coming home without carrying many physical or mental scars. He was tough at home, and tough in war. He beat that overall hell overseas, came back home, and continued his life.

He went into the marines because there was no money in the Summers bank account for college, which was one way you could beat the draft. He got married later on, had four children of his own, moved to Maine and lived a good long life.

The two youngest boys, John and Danny, opened up a body shop and gas station and raised their families well. All their children were able to go to college and have more than their fathers had. Mom Summers had raised them well—a good example for all. Her motto was if life threw you a curveball, you got back up, dusted yourself off, and swung hard at the next pitch.

That didn't happen for Donald, though. No, life threw him more than a curve—much more. He never made it back home, but before he died he sent home his memoirs of what happened overseas. A lot of it was hard to read; it was what war was in its purest form. His mother and the family read it and cried until they had no more tears, and then moved on. Those memoirs were a big curveball, but not big enough to stop going on.

Cindy Summers went to work the day after the funeral, working even harder than before. Her co-workers couldn't believe that she had returned to the job so quickly, but there were bills to be paid, and a household to maintain. She had now lost her husband, plus one of her sons. The dominos had fallen in a certain direction that didn't favor the Summers, but that could never stop her or her family. Below are the memoirs that Donald Summers sent home. They show just how cruel war really is, and the effects it has on its participants. It is full of pain and suffering, and may be hard to digest. Reader beware.

To my family back home. I love you and God Bless you all.
I am writing this while I can. I say that because I have already

died twice, and I don't know if I have any lives left. I hope not . . . no, I hope not, even though I really *will* be dead then. I know I sound crazy, but I don't think that I am. You all know me, you know that I've always had a good head on my shoulders, and even though what you will read here will sound utterly insane, and it is, I came through it somehow. Jason will understand. What I will tell you will be hell—total hell. War is hell—utterly burning, fires-out-of-control hell. I think if you asked any soldier that has been in combat, they would tell you the same. War is hell—there is no other way to describe it. Saying this repeatedly keeps me sane, for knowing that war is hell is spoken by someone with a clear head.

Over here in Nam, I think it is worse than any time before. I say that because even though I haven't seen the devil, I know he's close—real close. I can feel his bad breath on my neck, and it is evil and vile. God is nowhere to be found, so Satan can do as he wants, and here in the jungle he works his magic to a T. It's even hotter than hell here. Every day it seems to get hotter by the second, and so it's the perfect climate for the dark angel from down under to work his magician's tricks.

Mom , I'm sorry, I should have taken out a hefty loan and gone to college or gone into the ministry. If I had the chance to do it all over again I would've chosen one of the two. I know that now—oh, do I know that now, but it's water under the bridge. You can't go back in time. Don't cry for me, though, Mom, and I know you won't. You've always been so tough in every way, and I have been following in your footsteps ever since I've been here, so don't worry. I'm in control—at least I think I am. Any who, I guess I better start telling you what's been going on over here before I die again, because that is entirely possible at any moment. Oh, and Mom, let me warn you before I forget: beware the preacher who tells you he holds the keys to the pearly gates so your soul can enter. That's bullshit, it always has been, but I'm getting a little ahead of myself, even for me.

God, I wish I was back home; everybody here feels that way. The government has some nerve getting involved in this jungle bungle, believe you me! But that news headline is getting out fast, if you haven't read it already. OK, OK, OK! I'm babbling. Without delay, here we go!

The first time I died was during the battle of Dak To, in the central highlands. We were moving through the thick jungle, and we came upon a graveyard in the sky. You might think I'm crazy, but I'm not. There were thirty or forty men, some South Vietnamese and some American soldiers, and they had been hung by the neck in the trees. They were all naked, and they were all missing both their eyes and all of their reproductive parts. That's the best way I can say it for you, Mom.

Blood was still coming out of all those areas, so we knew that this hadn't been done too long ago. God only knows just what these poor souls had gone through, just how much pain and suffering they had endured. I had heard that the Viet Cong soldiers did this to prisoners—tortured them, sometimes for days, and then watched them die slowly. I had always thought that it was just propaganda, things said to scare the shit out of you. Well, it did that but when you actually saw proof of it, you just . . . lost it. You lost your last meal, you lost faith in The Lord above, you lost hope for a better world, and you lost a little bit of your soul and mind forever. It took us a full day to cut them down and give them a proper burial. We were supposed to move on, but none of us were in any mood to see what was up ahead of us, and during this process we cried and wept at what else we discovered. All of their genitalia had been stuffed up their anuses, and a small thin tube had been rammed up the urethra of each of their penises, probably done before being cut off from their tortured bodies.

This was another torture we had heard of, a hideous, sadist act. The torturer stimulates the prisoner's penis to hardness, and then a small tube is pushed inside the pee hole and broken off, and then the captive is made to drink fluids (water, clean or swampy, poison that will burn your insides to mush, or urine either from the captive or the capturer) until he is filled to the brim. He cannot urinate, and so the slow torture begins. Eventually the captive's bladder bursts, and he dies inside from uremic poisoning. It is very painful, and very slow. Imagine when you drink a few beers and you got to go to the bathroom, and you can't. Hells bells begin to ring in a new year, and you celebrate in complete agony. God have mercy!

The devil had his hands all over this dead zone of searing pain and agony. All of their eyeballs had been poked out and put in their mouths, and then they were sewn shut with thin, sharp needles. Hate covered these actions with vengeful anger, you were completely brought back to the reality of this hopeless situation, and you shuttered. After the painful burials we drank ourselves sober, and we hugged and cried ourselves to sleep. When we woke up the next morning, we all had changed mentally. We all harbored new docked anger—anger we didn't know existed inside us. Gone was the little piece of peace we had left in our hearts. I think that we all became true gladiators that day—soldiers without emotion.

We trudged on for two days, wallowing in our own dark thoughts of rage. Moving through the jungle was hard, what with the swamps and heavy rains that never seemed to end. On the third day toward evening we heard voices faintly in the distance—voices of the enemy, voices of the Cong. We moved closer and saw ten of them around a campfire. They were eating, drinking and laughing, but not for long—oh no, not for long. Ten of them, twenty of us, and we had the jump on them. We snuck up and ambushed them, knifing five to death before they knew what hit them. They were the lucky ones. God, Mom, were any of us lucky over here? No, but at least they died quickly.

The other five weren't so lucky. Forgive me, Mom, that cloud of hateful revenge that was with us that day has passed into the distance now, but it was directly overhead then. I've prayed for forgiveness to The Lord over and over, but we did what we did that fateful evening. We can't take it back; it's too late. They are the enemy; they are why we're here in the first place. That's what we told ourselves, but we held them down and cut their tongues out and scalped every one of them. They screamed and screamed as we stabbed them again and again. Blood ran everywhere as we cut their throats. We screamed our outrage at them, and that was the last thing their dying eyes saw.

Once it was over, we left quickly, leaving their carcasses to rot. Maybe they were the ones that had done that to our soldiers, maybe they weren't, but it didn't matter. Someone was going to pay, and we knew that if we weren't as barbaric as them, then we wouldn't survive. We didn't anyway. Our whole band of brothers didn't live to see another day. We were ambushed later that afternoon. I don't think we got off many rounds. I was shot many times; I felt like a pin cushion, and took my last breath before the sun set in the west, but something strange happened. I ended up in some tunnel and moved in it on an invisible current. All of a sudden I was in another part of the jungle. I was still in country, for as I staggered along I saw dead from all sides. Bodies littered the ground, and I had to fight the urge to vomit, the smell was that bad. I checked my image in a puddle, and to my surprise, I was still me. I knew that I had been fatally shot a few minutes ago, yet here I was, now without a single mark.

I suddenly came upon a small clearing, and in the middle of it

I saw a small circular hut made of straw. It was makeshift at best and held together by bamboo and tree limbs. There didn't seem to be anyone about, but I was taking no chances. I hid around a tree until dusk, and then I crept up on it. As I got closer I saw that the hut actually had an old wooden door that was circular at the top. I pushed it inward and it moved freely. I peeked around the door and couldn't believe what I saw. Mom, this is no lie— I wasn't smoking no dope (at least that day)—but as I peeked around the door I saw a long hallway that went on further than I could see.

The hallway was seven feet high, and about five feet across. The floor, ceiling, and walls were all painted in different shades of white. I noticed old wooden doors (just like the one I had just entered) on each side of the hall, about twenty feet apart. Unbelievably it was air conditioned inside and it felt really good. I dismissed the insanity of it all, since it was close to 100 degrees beyond the door, which I closed behind me quickly. It felt good too, because I know we couldn't afford one back home; we had to swelter every summer. But Mom, if I ever make it back home somehow I will buy you one; you deserve it.

Anyway, I slowly walked down the never-ending hall for about a half a mile until I encountered an open door. I glanced inside and saw what I should've seen when I opened up the hut door: the inside of a small hut, and an old woman stood in the center of the room, her back to me. She was dressed in an old dirty black house dress that went down to her bony white ankles, and she wore black pointy shoes that sparkled continuously. Her white hair was in a bun, tied at the back of her head. Her arms and hands were in front of her, as if she was holding something. I stood there staring at her, not knowing what to say. I could see through the straw walls, and the jungle outside. It was also hot in there, not like in the air-conditioned hallway. How could this be? There was no explanation for any of this, including how I was standing there after I had just been shot and killed.

All of a sudden the old woman turned around, but she didn't turn by moving her feet. No, she raised slightly above the ground and turned to face me without moving any part of her body. She was holding a bright red cereal bowl in her bony hands with fingers that had long, pointy, yellowed fingernails. They were chipped and dirty, but that wasn't what shook me. *She had* no face! I'm not hallucinating here, but other than a million wrinkles she had no eyes, nose, or mouth. We faced (?) each other, not speaking—her because she didn't have a mouth, and me because I was shocked beyond words.

She held out the bowl for me, gesturing for me to take it. I took it from her, her hands lightly touched mine, and they were freezing to the touch. The bowl was filled with liquid of some kind, and I stared into it. I saw myself sleeping on a beach I didn't know. I was dressed in my uniform, but I had the strangest feeling that it was in a different time, maybe even another world. The old woman pointed her finger at the doorway behind me and gestured for me to leave. She took the bowl out of my hands and turned her back to me again in the same way she had moved to face me before. I stood there for a few uncomfortable moments, and then walked back into the hallway, shutting the door behind me. I continued walking further on and came upon another open doorway on the other side of the hallway and again glanced inside.

Again, I was inside the hut; the old woman was there, but this time she was facing me, and now she actually had a face. She wore large glasses with dark pools for eyes, her nose long and pointy, her teeth were half missing, rotting, and yellowed. She looked American, definitely not from this region of the world, and she was stirring a large pot of liquid brew that sat in-between us. She motioned with a nod to again look into the pot, and I saw a dead soldier lying on the jungle ground. His head was turned away from me, so I couldn't see who it was. Suddenly I saw movement from the dead man's chest, and then large, black, spiderlike creatures started breaking through his chest and began eating him. They even started eating his uniform. The creatures moved up to the soldier's head and moved it towards me, and the face was mine!

I yelled, stepped back, and suddenly I felt a burning sensation and movement in my chest. I watched in horror as these same spiderlike creatures started eating through my chest and moved quickly to my face. I screamed, and then I heard the old woman yell in a man's baritone voice, "Get out of the hut!" I moved backward, back into the hallway, and the creatures were suddenly gone. I hadn't closed the door, and as I looked inside the room was black, total blackness, yet I felt that something was in there, moving, crawling . . . slithering. I quickly closed the door, and that creepy feeling went away. I gasped, checking my chest again, but nothing was there. I looked ahead and behind me, and the hallway looked like it went on forever in both directions. I felt trapped, trapped in this hell. Could it be that I *was* in hell? Could hell look like *this*?

Questions kept creeping into my mind when a door suddenly opened and a lot of Vietnamese soldiers came out and started charging toward me. They had guns, and when they saw me they pointed them in my direction. I took off in the direction I had come from, and a door up ahead opened and large serpent-like snakes came out and started toward me. They were grayish in color, covered by large sharp scales. Their heads were twice the size of mine, each with a mouthful of razor-sharp teeth. Their eyes were blood red and looked hateful. Their bodies were over ten feet long, and about three feet around. They slithered toward me, making sloppy sounds on the floor.

I turned back around, and the Vietnamese soldiers were gone, but a monk stood in the hallway with a large gold key in his right hand. He held up his left hand, and the serpent-like creatures froze in place. The monk wore a large light brown cloak with a hood, and his face had all these cauliflower-like knots all over, distorting his facial features. His mouth was curled in a half smile on one end and a frown on the other. One eye was pointing skyward, while the other was staring at the hallway wall. He held up the large gold key, and then opened up a door to his right.

He brought the key back in front of his face and said in a muffled, low voice, "Never trust a religious man who says he has the key to get you into heaven. He's a liar, a liar that isn't really a religious man at all." He started chuckling, and then he disappeared into thin air. That unfroze the serpent creatures and they again started slithering toward me. I ran to the door the monk had opened with the key, went inside without looking, and closed the door quickly behind me.

I turned around to see what was in this room and found myself on another planet, a planet that looked dead or discarded in every way. It was black and gray, but otherwise colorless. The sky was covered in angry storm clouds, and thunder and lightning crackled above; otherwise this place was quiet and unmoving—dead. It seemed that dying was the only thing I couldn't do, but here I had found myself in a place that seemed dead in almost every way. I looked back, but the door I had come from was no longer there. I realized I was trapped here on this foreign planet; there was no way out.

The monk was right; never trust a religious man who says he has the key to your heaven. This was definitely not heaven; this was more like purgatory. Maybe I deserved this, maybe this was my fate. Maybe. I looked around and saw a body of water in the distance and started toward it. The water was completely still, and the beach sand was coal black. There were islands in the distance, and I could see lightning hitting the top of one of them. As I approached the shoreline I saw a dark figure in a gondola out by the island closest to the beach. He had one large oar, and after spotting me, started rowing towards me. He reached the beach a hundred yards north and beckoned me to come to him. I thought I was alone here, and even though I was apprehensive of his presence I started toward him. As I got closer, to my horror I realized the figure's face was skeletal, wearing a black cloak with a hood. His fingers were also skeletal and devoid of tissue and skin.

Still, even though many different kinds of thoughts were racing through my mind (most of them bad), I continued walking toward him. He wasn't attacking me in any way; all he wanted was for me to come to him. Maybe he was lonely; totally alone here. I didn't know, but if I didn't go to him I'd never know. Besides, what else was I going to do? Where was I going to go? I stopped by his vessel, and he suddenly reached out with amazing speed, grabbed my arm, and pulled me into the gondola roughly with incredible strength.

I tried to pull away, but I couldn't move. I was suddenly paralyzed, unable to get away from this creature. He sat me down on the boat seat and began rowing out into the still waters. He stopped about thirty feet out, looked at me oddly, cocking his hooded skeletal head to one side, and said, "You must go back. You don't belong here," and then without fanfare picked me up and dumped me over the side. I was still paralyzed, so I started dropping to the bottom. I couldn't breathe, couldn't struggle, and then for some strange reason I felt like laughing because ironically, I couldn't die either. Right? Yes, right as rain.

I passed out, and when I came to, I was back in the Vietnamese jungle, in a swamp. A Viet Cong soldier was pointing a gun at me and fired; and then all went black. It took a few seconds, but then

I was back in that strange tunnel, moving to-and-fro. I slowed down and then passed out again. I woke up and found myself just outside of base camp, back with my platoon. I staggered into camp, and a few soldiers ran to assist me. They couldn't believe I was alive. They had bombed the area we had been killed in, and no survivors had been found. I was interviewed by the superior officer in camp and deemed mentally and physically unfit to serve further. I would be honorably discharged. At this time, I am awaiting papers that will send me home, so that is why I have the time to write these memoirs. I hope to see you all soon. This place is one hell zone nobody should be sent to. This part of the world is primal, and some strange things are happening here. If any outside forces are in the area working under the radar, I wouldn't be surprised. I believe they exist; I believe they are here. I believe I experienced their presence. God help anyone that is sent to this part of the world.

Love always,
Donald

P.S. I believe what I saw was real. I do not believe I am mentally ill. I believe that there is life and places that exist in the shadows of our world, or underworlds.

Donald Summers mailed off his memoirs and spent the next two weeks either being interrogated further, or in the medical facility answering questions about his strange experiences. No one could explain how he was still alive, or how he had returned to base camp, but stranger things had happened in this world. The military decided to keep a watch on one Private Donald

Summers, see if anything, or anyone else came in contact with him. See if anything else that was considered strange would happen around him. He had become a person of interest—serious interest. Unfortunately, something did happen. After all he had said about not being able to die, on the day he was set to leave he was found dead in his bunk. After examinations were completed, the cause of death was written down as a heart attack, but what they actually found they kept to themselves, and his body was sent back to his family. He was buried a week later, and once his body was safely in the ground, the military felt much better. Secrets had to be kept, and the armed forces were just as good at doing that as the rest of the government. They would keep an eye on anything else that might be considered out of the ordinary, but the book on Donald Summers was closed as far as they were concerned.

After the power went out, Donald Summers materialized on Myrtle Beach a mile north of where Lawrence Hester was. He woke up and stared out at the ocean, then up and down the beach, and then he knew. He knew that all he had been through was real: the deaths, the hut, and the infinite hallway with its many doors and what lay inside them. He knew because he had seen himself on this beach in the bowl the faceless old lady had showed him. She had shown him a piece of his future, and he shuttered at that thought. It might be hot as blazes on this beach, but he was shivering all over.

It was all too much to comprehend, too much to take in. The last thing he had remembered was being over in Vietnam, getting ready to come home. Now he was here, wherever that was, and he was still in his uniform. He began to weep. After a while he got up to leave, but a voice in the back of his head said, "Wait!," and so he did, sitting back down and taking note of his surroundings. There was no life and no sounds, just the waves hitting the shore, massaging the sand. He felt alone, alone in his private universe. He had died again and appeared on this quiet beach. He looked south and eventually saw movement, maybe someone on the beach coming toward him. He stood up and shaded his eyes. A few seconds later he made out two figures—ones with military uniforms on. He recognized both; one was wearing a gray southern Civil War outfit, the other a World War II one. He suddenly fell to his knees and started crying, crying for him and for the men walking toward him. He knew, just *knew*, that they had endured some of the same pain and suffering he had. They were all brothers in arms, and if by any chance they'd have to go through, any more distress, they would now go through it together. He looked to the sky and said out loud, "Thank you, Lord, thank you."

When Helishious had seen Donald Summers walking toward the shoreline, he knew that something had gone astray. After he had returned the military man back to the world of the living, he knew he had to do something. Nobody was supposed to be in his world unless he, Helishious, had brought that person here himself—yet here the military man was. He used the swamplands near Donald Summer's base camp to study the situation and saw that not only was the military man still alive, but he hadn't aged a day! Impossible! This could not stand on all counts as far as Helishious was concerned. On the night before the soldier was to go home to the United States, the dark skeletal dead man entered Donald Summer's barracks.

General James Watkins studied the medical report he had been handed on Donald Summers. It was just as strange as the man's crazy tales he had babbled about after he had staggered back into base camp. That was OK, though, because he was finally dead to all concerned. He would tell no more tales, and that was good. Less information was always more when it came to war. It was simpler to say, "Sorry, your son died defending his country," than to say, "Sorry, we screwed it all to hell by sending troops into the wrong sector, and then covered it all up by bombing the whole area, yet still had a man from that fuck-up walk back into basecamp with all kinds of crazy stories to tell." Now he was dead, and dead men tell no tales—or in this case, no *more* tales. He was considered crazy as a hatter, and that assumption would now live in infamy.

It had been determined that if Private Donald Summers *had* gone home and continued his rantings, forces back home would have "taken care of business." Now none of that was necessary. The general glanced at the report and whispered, "Jesus Christ" for the umpteenth time, for after an autopsy examination had been completed it was found that Donald Summer's heart was no longer inside his chest cavity. It had been removed, but in a way the medical doctor couldn't explain. It was just gone. He had not been opened up, and his skin and chest cavity had not been disturbed—at least not until the autopsy had been performed. He was sewn back up with someone else's heart and shipped back to the States. Once he was buried in his grave his strange bedtime stories would be put to bed with him, and that would be good. Coverup number whatever was completed. General Watkins then, on instructions from his superior, lit a cigarette, set the medical report on fire, and watched it burn until it became nothing more than cold gray cinders. "Boo-yah," he whispered out loud as he lit another cigarette.

One Last Note Of Interest: When General Watkins set Donald Summer's medical report on fire, he also did the same thing to his memoirs, and yet they still made it back to Donald's home address in Blauvelt, New York, and his mother and family read them. How was that possible, for the General had watched them burn completely? Eventually that question might be answered, but for now we'll just let it rest in peace. All I can say at this time is that even though some stories must stay secret, others must be told—and were.

Chapter Thirty-Four

PLEASURES

*R*eader's Warning: these next two chapters are sexually oriented and might be a little too straight forward for some folks. The sexual content is written in graphic detail to some extent, and if you feel that you would rather skip them, then please go ahead. I wouldn't, though. I would just put myself in the mindset to learn more about sex on a whole, and its various participants—keep an open mind, so to speak. I know there are a lot of puritans out there, but there are still parts in these chapters that will intrigue you—I know they will. And I also know that some readers will get into these next few pages more than others, and some might not admit they *will* be interested, but those individuals can't be blamed. There are forces all around us, those that like to control us and try to beat various types of sex out of our minds, saying they are evil. Those folks would be wrong—totally wrong. They will say sex is quite dirty and give that word on a whole a bad name. That will be talked about in further pages throughout this manuscript, but that's just the way it is. Everyone thinks differently, and so I have red tagged these two chapters in respect to all. Again, kind readers, I repeat: *beware*!

There is an island named Pleasure off the coast of Oregon that multimillionaire Marlo Freeman bought for her own lewd vices, as well of those of others. The island was formerly called Eagle's Rock, and she pulled a few strings and bought it from the state. Marlo was a beautiful tall brunette who was considered an Amazon, standing an even six feet and weighing 180 pounds of curves and muscle, devoid of any body fat. She worked out with weights every day, did aerobics three times a week, and watched what she ate. She also worked her midsection at least forty-five minutes each day, usually in the morning. She didn't have a six-pack, no, she had an eight-pack!

She could kick most men's butts by herself on brute strength alone, but she also possessed karate and boxing skills. Her face was movie-star quality, and she had breasts that were on the large side and an ass that men *and* women admired and craved. She was thirty-six years old, but by all accounts she was just hitting her prime. She had many clients that visited her island on a regular basis, and they all went home satisfied—that is, *if* they were going home at all, and that *did* happen on occasion. Marlo had twenty employees, and they were all devoted to her beyond a shadow of a doubt.

A castle made out of mostly stone had been partially constructed fifty years ago by the state and sat on the highest point of Pleasure. Marlo had it completed once she took ownership, and the finished product more than satisfied her needs. It had two lookout towers that were manned by hired security twenty-four hours a day. One faced the open sea and the other faced the coastline. She figured that danger of all kinds could approach from any direction, so she had to be ready if the shit hit the fan. Not everything that happened on the island was legal by any means, so these security towers were very important.

The structure featured twenty-five suites that all contained a large heart-shaped bed, a hot tub, and a large playroom that had chains of all kinds hanging from the ceilings. They also had a urinal and a regular toilet out in the open that was part of the playroom. Any person, or persons, using the suite would have to relieve themselves in front of whoever else might be there with them. No, no secrets or hang-ups on Pleasure. Sometimes removing that private privilege was part of the game being played. Pleasure was completely behind the notion that relieving yourself in front of others was a way of bettering yourself on a whole. They figured that it was just another part of the overall brainwashing conundrum of society that was being torn down. It was good argument banter, and always unnerved those that couldn't get past it..

The castle also had a dungeon which was used for various tastes—sometimes extreme tastes, illegal tastes. While someone was either being straight-out trained or trying to complete a certain successful fantasy that seemed just out of reach, they might be sent 'downstairs.' Punishment was sometimes required to give a certain client a jump-start to get them moving forward, and many methods were used on them. It was mostly used as a positive tool, and many former clients had said afterward that even though it was painful both physically as well as mentally, they were better off for it.

Others just wanted pain, and they were taken to the lower bowels of the castle. There they would get what they paid for, and possibly a little more. That was classic masochistic behavior. They were never satisfied with what *they* wanted or could stand. What they never voiced was that they needed to go where they had never gone before, and that was pain beyond comfortable or bearable. Pleasure understood this mindset fully, and they never failed in their efforts to satisfy these exquisite needs.

A week before the power went out Marlo Freeman was arrested along with three other close associates for murder. They were being held in Portland. Each had been interrogated since their incarceration and had told the authorities many stories about Pleasure and other murders that had occurred on the island. Each was looking for a deal. Each was in big trouble. Here are their stories and the murders that they were involved in.

Carl Rosen was a body builder. He had lifted weights since the age of fifteen. He had jet black curly thick hair that the girls went crazy over. His dark complexion also made him popular with the female gender, and he usually got his way with all the ones he dated. Always a strong boy, not many schoolmates picked a fight with him, and those that did took a beating that took days, if not weeks to recover from. In his immaturity he could be a bully when the situation called for it, but he had mostly outgrown those childish characteristics. He stood six foot two inches and weighed 250 pounds. He was quite imposing, and had played linebacker on the first-string school football team all four years, knocking out quite a few opponents in the process. If he was on the left side before a play, the other team changed the play and ran away from him. He was that dominant. He might've gone all the way to the pros, but a career-ending knee injury in his last game in school changed all that. Still, he was given a tryout years later with the professional Seattle franchise, but it was obvious that he wasn't fast enough. He convinced himself that he probably never was fast enough, and so he moved on, satisfied that he had at least tried.

He bounced around after that, until ten years prior when he caught a break and got a job as a security guard at Pleasure. He did well, and within five years had worked his way up to chief of security on the island. He knew of all activities that were taking place on the premises at all times. It was his job to know so, he was briefed daily on all new clients and schedules and reaped from the fringe benefits he was thrown. He did his job so well that Pleasure had no idea that he was working undercover for the government. He was a mole. The problem mixed in with it all was that Carl was having an affair with Marlo, and that made the cases he brought up against Pleasure iffy at best. Would he ever reveal all information, or would he hide and destroy evidence like he had in the past? He was a live wire at best, but they had no one else, and the authorities had invested quite a bit in him, but trust was not high on the list of Carl's attributes.

Jason Miller was a stud. He could be sexually active with ten different clients in one day—women or men. It didn't matter. Having sex with either gender was just a job to him. He was always the dominant, though. He gave all the time. Sometimes it was part of his job to give against a person's will. Either they paid for it, or someone who had a grievance against a certain client had them kidnapped, "date raped" as the staff at Pleasure called it, and then punished in many different ways. Nothing was off the table, and Jason was on the books for at least fifteen suspected murders. Each case would be brought up and reviewed before the state went to trial. If he cooperated and told the authorities all he knew, the government might show leniency. He would have to tell a lot, though, and turn in others. They needed him to help shut down Pleasure for good. They needed him to help them put Marlo behind bars for the rest of her life.

Jason was only five ten, blonde and regular in build, but he was large where it counted. He was not much longer than most average men, seven and a half inches, but where he was different was the circumference of his penis. It was over two inches, and the head of his organ was extremely large and thick—two and a half inches around. If someone wanted to try a little (?) sodomy, or payback was in the cards, Jason was asked for. That was his game. He resided in room number one.

Wendy Haas was thirty-two years old, and she had worked for Marlo for half of those years. She was a runaway from New York City. Her parents had been quite wealthy, but she couldn't get along with them. They had been members of some weird religious cult, but both had been assassinated by the State. They were deemed extremely dangerous, possibly homegrown terrorists, and everybody knew what they did to those kinds of people in these dangerous times. Wendy didn't miss them, for she didn't believe in their beliefs. The day she set out on her own she found them sitting at the kitchen table facing each other, a bullet through each of their brains. She had been on her way home from school, and after she found them she packed a knapsack and took off for different parts of the country, always heading west. She sold her body to stay alive, but that was OK, for she was as tough as they came. She learned to love sex, and took full advantage of it.

There wasn't anything she wouldn't do, except one thing. You had to take that approach when you walked the busy concrete street corners, but she knew full well that the stranger the request, the more money she could make. She was a pretty girl: blonde, full figured since she was a young girl, and extremely street smart. She took her trick's money, then stole the rest in their wallets when they turned their backs on her. Once she got caught, somewhere in northern Idaho, and the trick had raped her repeatedly for three days before she turned the tables after hitting him in the head with a frying pan. He was making her cook for him inbetween the forced sex, and she surprised him with a roundhouse right. Wham! The pan had been red hot, just off the stove, and he screamed bloody murder before he was hit twice more, knocking him unconscious.

Before he came to she had tied him to his bed face down, his wrists and ankles tied to each bedpost, and then whipped repeatedly with his belt on his back and butt. She made him beg for mercy by the hour, and just when he thought she would release him, she whipped him some more. Payback was a bitch. It was her first taste of experiencing sadism. She found that she liked the feeling of beating someone to a pulp and taking control of them. Getting even with a scumbag felt good too. Since this trick had kept her a captive for three days, she kept him *her* captive for six. He had taken her without consent roughly, so she did the same and more.

Wendy had proved to herself more than once that she was no one to be fucked with, and whatever happened in the future would be OK. *She* would be OK. What she did in retaliation was pure genius. Every hour as the clock chimed she greased and regreased his distended anus and fisted his rectum while she masturbated herself to orgasm. When she had finished and gained control of herself, she roughly ripped her fist out of his ass and waited for the next hour to come. The trick's screams never really stopped, they only lessened in intensity. He cried pitifully, but Wendy felt nothing for him, just like he hadn't when he stuck his dirty tool up *her* backside repeatedly and came. She had been virgin there, but no more. She had already cried enough tears over that reality before she reversed this sorry situation. She thought about it right to the end, when she treated his head like a spike, hitting it repeatedly with a sledgehammer until it was recognizable no more.

She stole his car, dumping his remains in the trunk, and continued west. She met Marlo in a diner in Portland, and the two became fast friends. Wendy had to confide in somebody, for eventually she had to get rid of the body. It was beginning to smell really bad. Marlo knew a good desolate place to bury her problem, so she took the younger woman home, seducing her in the process. She respected Wendy; Marlo thought she had bigger balls than most men. The part of the story that drove her over the edge was when Wendy told her that she wasn't completely un-humane, for to keep the man from starving and being thirsty she forced fed him his feces and urine. That was way too heady, and Marlo satisfied her new lover until she could orgasm no more. Their bond had been strong from that day forward.

When Marlo bought Pleasure Island, Wendy became her first employee. She went to work as a dominatrix, a true sadist. She punished a special clientele that had a special taste for pain and suffering. Whippings, beatings, spankings, and bitch slapping were only a part of her job. Sometimes she worked in extremes, and body parts were sometimes damaged or broken. It was amazing how many submissive people were out there. They came for release in droves. Men and women, boyfriends and girlfriends, husbands and wives, or slaves brought in by their masters or mistresses. When they all left, their itch had been scratched; they never went away dissatisfied. Three times she had gone too far, though…

Marlo had taken care of those mishaps as well, and Wendy was forever grateful. She was devoted to her queen, whom she had fallen in love with on the day they had met. They still had sex from time to time when it was convenient, and it was always breathtaking. After what had happened, she could never make love with another man again. She became a full-time bull dyke, bringing girls home to her suite from time to time, having intense lesbian sex, and then sometimes sexually whipping them until they told her they loved her. She would be a hard nut to crack, the authorities surmised. She was in room number two.

Alfred Altman and Marlo Freeman grew up together. They both came from wealthy families, grew up completely spoiled, went to school and got high together, even having a sexual relationship during their senior year. It was volatile, it was vicious, it was love/hate. Both fought with each other often, which usually ended with black eyes or bruises. Both sets of parents were very happy when they eventually broke up, but the breakup wasn't like most. Neither one of them walked away with a broken heart, but both knew that if they didn't stay away from each other, one or both of them would end up dead. They both left their destructive relationship with a mutual respect for each other, and set each other up with victims they could eat alive.

Alfred was a monster in every way. He was six foot six, 270 pounds dripping wet with little body fat, and worked out regularly with Carl Rosen, one of the few people in Alfred's world he got along with. He kept his hair in a crewcut and had a rugged rough look about him, but it was his eyes that scared most people he came into contact with. They were dark, mean, and they burned a hole right through your soul. You didn't want to get into a staring match with this brute, and you wanted to avoid getting in his way at any cost. He was involved with Pleasure

Island for three reasons: money, sex, and forced muscle. He had inherited millions from his parents, who both died young: his father from cancer, and his mother in a car accident. Some thought Alfred might've had something to do with that, the authorities included, for he was an only child that stood to gain everything they had, but those thoughts for the most part stayed in the shadows and remained hush-hush. Questions about that accident *this* time would be brought up by the authorities. Whatever edge they could use they would; nothing was off limits.

Alfred had poured some of that cash into Marlo's business, and they became partners. Marlo was always the boss, though. Seventy/thirty was the cut, and Marlo owned the whole estate and island. They both made millions, and as stated before, they both respected each other. When Marlo and Alfred had had sex in the past, they learned a lot about each other. He was another machine; he could go all day and night. Marlo had always said that Alfred was the best lover she ever had, and *that* was saying something. It could get rough at times, and that was good, but Alfred could make Marlo orgasm like no other. They still got together every now and then whenever the timing was right, and the sex was just as intense as when they were in high school. Marlo knew he would be good for clientele too, and his vicious attitude came in handy consistently when rough sex was asked for. Sometimes he and Wendy worked together, even though the dominatrix couldn't stand anything about him. She felt that he was everything she hated in men on a whole, but boy could they coordinate together when dealing with a client.

The third, and final reason why Alfred was a major plus was obvious: he kept everybody in line. And I mean *everybody!* If a client got out of hand and didn't follow the rules, most of the time they left the facility damaged, and in much pain. This included both men and women. Alfred had no qualms about beating a woman into submission; in fact, they usually left in worse shape than the poor men that were dumb enough to challenge his wrath. Fellow employees also needed to be straightened out once in a while. Sometimes they overstepped their bounds; it happens in every business to some extent, but the punishment would definitely end up harsher here. If a person was fired on Pleasure (and that didn't happen often), they might end up in the hospital along with their last paycheck, and if they said a word about what had just happened to them, they very well could end up in the nameless boneyard out at sea.

Alfred intimidated everyone that walked into the castle, but he *was* afraid of one person, and that individual was known only to him. He could never talk to anybody about this person; he knew this because he had tried. Once, in a panic, he had tried to tell Marlo, but his vocal cords had mysteriously stopped working. He couldn't sound out one word, and then he had paid dearly for that indiscretion. After that experience he had learned his lesson and kept his big trap shut to keep their secret alliance safe. He knew he'd be done in every way if he tried to open his mouth again; he had in no uncertain words been told that. Alfred was in room number three.

THE WITCH AND THE DEMON

The only individual that was able to keep Alfred Altman in line was named Glorifinia. Just Glorifinia—she didn't have a last name; there was no need for one. She was a witch from the thickest jungles of Central Africa, and she had been working her magic since the beginning of the fifth Century. At the time of this bedtime story, she was an eighteen-year-old black woman with a short afro, a pretty face, large breasts, and an even larger behind. She, along with the rest of her tribe, wore very little, only some sort of skimpy garment around her middle. Her breasts were constantly bare, and she was considered one of the better-looking girls in the tribe. Her parents were hard workers who searched for food and planted primitive seeds that produced vegetation. She was promised to the chief's son when they both turned twenty, which was a regular ritual that had been established generations before. The chief's son was a homely looking boy, thin and unmuscular, unlike his father, but he was to be the next leader of the tribe, and that would make her the next queen. There were a lot of perks that went along with that, and that beat working in the soil and river.

Legend had it (and she had told Alfred Altman the same tale) that a demon named Lazerious had kidnapped her during a bad rainstorm and raped her in every orifice repeatedly for three whole days, impregnating her. Lazerious was very ugly and evil looking, and he wore no clothes. His skin was light greenish gray in color, and he was short, just five feet tall with a large misshapen and mostly bald head. He had large, beady, dark eyes that bore a hole right through your soul, a short fat nose, and a large mouth that housed a long, pointy tongue with only two front yellowish teeth. His belly stuck out as if *he* was nine months pregnant. His hands were large and knotty, and his fingers fat and nail-less. His feet were large and knotty as well, but what stuck out the most was his genitalia. His fat penis and grossly oversized scrotum hung down almost to his knees, and Lazerious played absentmindedly with them constantly. He was vulgar to say the least, and evil-minded right down to his demented core. After his sizzling seed had been planted inside Glorifinia's burning belly, the demon vomited up a sticky reddish substance and made her eat it repeatedly over the next seven days before taking her orally with his gnarled long penis after each of her meals.

Her pregnancy sped up and she painfully gave birth after only two weeks' time. The child was a half breed: half demon and half human. It looked more like Lazerious, weighed fifteen pounds, and it hissed and growled as proud parents (sic) stared down at it. The demon chuckled down at his spawn, and then, without a hint of any emotion, grabbed the creature, stuck a long sharp bit deep into the newborn's body, and cooked the offspring over an open fire. After it had stopped screeching and its skin had turned completely black, the two parents ate it down to the bone. Glorifinia told Alfred that she had never been so hungry, and nothing had ever tasted so good. Ten minutes later she experienced horrible stomach cramps and defecated right in front of Lazerious. He pointed at her multicolored, smelly waste and laughed at her startled and ashamed face, and then she gave in and started laughing too. She cackled insanely until she cried.

She changed after that, mentally as well as physically. She began craving live flesh, and also became, in her own words, hornier than an insane demented witch in heat. Her nose grew pointy and long, along with her hands and feet. Her fingernails and toenails grew as well, becoming very pointy and razor sharp. Her hair turned fire red, and her ears became long and pointy at the top. Her breasts grew to twice their normal size, and a red, thick liquid oozed from her nipples, running down her still-distended stomach. She begged the demon to fuck her wildly, and so he did until she bled from every one of her entrances. He mounted her in every position and she strongly climaxed many times over.

She couldn't get enough, but after a few days the demon got tired of her and cut her off. He put his hand on her forehead, and his hand slowly melted into her skull, his fingers wiggling wildly as they disappeared into her. Lazerious pulled his wrist back, and another hand quickly grew in its place. Glorifinia could feel his original hand in her head, moving all around massaging her infected brain and mind. Eventually she felt as if her head was about to explode; the pain became extremely intense, ten times worse than a damaging migraine, and then she screamed until she passed out.

Later, when she awoke, her headache was gone, and so was the movement inside her skull, but the demon was nowhere to be found. Her horniness was gone as well, and so after waiting a few hopeful days to see if Lazerious would return, she dejectedly staggered back to her village. The villagers, as well as her family, saw her physical changes and banished her from the tribe. She frightened them. They claimed she was possessed by the devil himself, was now his concubine to take care of, and she had to leave immediately. Her future husband spit in her face, and he looked at her in disgust as it ran into her mouth. She spat right back at him, hitting him square in the face, and hate grew like deadly cancer in her heart as it turned icy cold.

"You will pay for this!" she screeched as she looked around at all of them, and then turned away and walked bravely back into the jungle, never looking back. She survived on live insects and rodents and found a cave that was covered with thick vines. She told Alfred that she still lived there, for it went deep into the ground until the air turned hot, and fires roared all around her.

A month later Lazerious visited her one more time just after dusk, waking her up and coupled with her until dawn. He gave his permission for her to start eating live human beings whenever she became hungry. He said that she had a strong, expanding power growing deep inside her core, a gift from him, and that turning cannibal would make it grow stronger and stronger. He also told her that he would never return again; he had other more important affairs to attend to. She cried and cried, begging the demon to stay with her. He immediately became incensed and raised his right hand and made a fist.

His original hand inside her head began to scratch at her brain, and she screamed for him to stop. Somewhere in her agonizing pain she heard him tell her that begging was a sign of weakness, and was unacceptable. He told her that if she showed any sign of that again the hand would squeeze her brain until it turned to mush, and she would feel constant pain for the rest of eternity. Hell would become her constant companion, and she would go completely mad with agonizing pain that would grow by the second, and her torture would go on unchained. He told Glorifinia that he had no more use for her; to him she was yesterday's useless defecation. He then held her chin tightly and stared into her wild, hurtful eyes. He grinned, winked, and told her she had a large food supply back at her own village. He then disappeared into thin air, his laughter echoing off the dark walls of the dark cavern.

He was true to his word; she never saw him again. Glorifinia told Alfred that Lazerious had been her first and one true love.

As time went on, one by one she kidnapped half the people of her village, taking her family first, and then the rest based on how she felt. Some of them were able to run away to other villages, and the evil tales of Glorifinia were born. Warriors surrounded villages, providing a defense just in case the dark witch attacked, and yet other tribes in the area didn't take the chance and slowly moved out of the region. She could have the jungle—her fire, they reasoned. They hoped and prayed that she'd burn in her own juices and be banished to the heated fires of hell.

As she explored her new home, Glorifinia found a large pot in the back of the cave. Where it came from she didn't know, and she began cooking her victims in it. When their screams began to subside, she pulled them out and ate them before they took their last breath. They died slowly and painfully, and as they were consumed by the hateful witch they wished for death to take them to the next realm, but that wish never came fast enough. Glorifinia knew how to prolong their souls from leaving their dying bodies too quickly.

She cauterized their fateful wounds to stop the bleeding. She ate their eyes first, so they wouldn't know where she would strike next. She saved their still-beating hearts for last, for they tasted the best. She especially enjoyed eating and torturing Jaris, the chief's son she was to wed. She took her time and relished his screams, which quickly became primal. It was sweet music to her ears, and she kept his screeching going for twice the amount of time as the other villagers.

When there was no more human flesh to eat in the village, Lazerious spoke to her from the back of her increasingly darkening mind. He whispered a spell to her, a spell that would allow her to disappear into an invisible wormhole that would transport her to far distances in a short amount of time.

Years later she eventually stumbled upon Alfred Altman on Pleasure Island, transforming herself back into the beautiful black woman she had once been. He was perfect in every way as far as she was concerned. He was strong and good looking, he loved sex, and he had a mean streak that turned her on. He made love to her all night, but by morning, after tying his wrists and ankles to each corner of the bed, Glorifinia showed him what she really looked like. He screamed and screamed for help, but nobody came to save him. She told him they were all frozen in suspended animation and would remain that way until she left. She told Alfred that unless he did as he was told, he would confront a horrible fate.

Alfred flatly replied that he would never do that; that he would fight her to the death. She laughed at him and put her hand on his sweating forehead. Her hand, like Lazerious's hand, melted into the captive's head and worked it's painful magic. Her hand scratched his brain, and he screeched in pain. Somewhere through his tortured agony he heard her tell him what Lazerious had told her. She then disappeared, and the bonds holding the big man down disappeared as well.

Glorifinia returned every so often and told Alfred what she wanted. She wanted sex and a warm body (preferably a beautiful young woman) to take back with her. He reluctantly did what she wanted, and she made him repeatedly admit he was now her slave, brainwashing his infected mind. He knew he never wanted to experience her pain again, so he complied with her requests, although he still defied her that once. That was his nature; he couldn't help himself. She made him pay even though she wasn't there physically. The hand in his head squeezed his brain repeatedly, and his insides felt as if they were on fire. This lasted far longer than he could stand, and he passed out. When he came to Glorifinia was on top of him, glaring down at his frightened face. She viciously grabbed his penis and ripped it off. He screamed in agony, both from the pain and from the loss of his manhood. She then said something in a foreign language, held his penis against his groin, and it reconnected. The pain of the experience remained until she told him if he ever tried this infraction again, there would be no mercy. After that, he never tried to tell anyone about her again.

He always knew when she was about to come, for the hand in his head would begin to vibrate, reminding him of the pain he might experience if he didn't do as she asked. He would tie up one of the erased clients (people who came willingly to Pleasure to become slaves to the island masters, their past lives given up and their whereabouts unknown) and stuff them in his bedroom closet, locking them in. God help them, he thought grimly, when Glorifinia took them away. And God help me! Sometimes the witch only came to him every three months or so, but she always came. She always came...........

The charge against Marlo Freeman, Alfred Altman, Jason Miller, and Wendy Haas was murders in the first degree of Michael and Susan MacDonald. All four suspects were arrested by FBI agents David Rivers, John Jarvis, Kathy Morrison, and Anthony Santana. They all had been watching the goings-on of Pleasure Island for a few years now but had never had enough evidence on the Freeman/Altman group to bring them to justice. Now they did, and the birds were singing. Carl Rosen had many reports on many cases, but this was the first time that Pleasure had screwed up—and had screwed up badly. Carl had always claimed that Alfred was the wild card, and so had stayed close to the big man, watching him constantly. They lifted heavy weights together, hung out together, and drank together. Alfred was not an easy individual to get along with, and he trusted almost no one, but Carl had somehow broken through. He knew that the big man was going through something; he seemed aloft at times, and so Carl stayed even closer. Alfred lately was drinking more, and he told Carl more than he should have. On file were fifty-five misplaced clients (inventoried people that were missing from the dungeons but no one in society had reported them), thirty people who never returned home and *were* reported missing by their families, and various other infractions, most of them due to misconduct: clients who ended up in the doctor's office or the hospital (cases that were always settled by the client and Marlo Freeman).

They were the most frustrating. Clients would rather keep their fetishes quiet, their reputations intact, so they always took the deal Marlo gave them—and some even went back to Pleasure afterward for more! It was confounding, to say the least. Numerous times the FBI and local authorities got warrants to search for the missing people that had been reported, but no clues of their disappearances had ever turned up. It was as if they had vanished into thin air, and even with Carl working in the shadows they came up with nothing. The agency *knew* they had been murdered; there was no question about that. It was just that there wasn't enough proof to bring them in, not until the MacDonald case.

It still was frustrating because all of a sudden Carl seemed to go dumb. It didn't really matter; they had the bodies of the couple, one without a head (which had never been found), and each suspect was blaming the other. Someone was going down; they just needed a little more information and evidence than they had to get them all. Below are the details and scant interviews that took place just before the power went out.

The MacDonalds were no saints. Under different circumstances they would be part of the accused, but this time they had "stepped in the shit," as the saying goes. Michael and Susan MacDonald were both forty-two years old at the time of their murders. Michael was a lawyer who snorted way too much cocaine with just about anybody—especially if *you* had some. He was five ten in height and weighed an even 180 pounds. He was average in looks, but nobody would give him the time of day if he didn't make so much money. He defended murderers, rapists, and he even defended Pleasure in a civil suit, which became the genesis in this case. The people that knew him would consider him a pompous asshole who was selfish, greedy, and creepy.

By looking at him you knew he was into something; you just didn't know what. He lived just under the radar, and people who lived in the shadows usually were a little more than shifty. He came from a family of lawyers who drank way too much and dabbled in various recreational drugs from time to time, so Michael wasn't very creative either, for he did just what his parents and other family members had done. He had a stash of drugs hidden in a secret compartment in his basement. Even his wife didn't know of this secret hiding place, *or* the drugs. She would've been extremely pissed if she had known, though, for he had sworn to her that he had given them all up, including coke. She'd had it with his lies, and with just about everything else.

Michael thought he was a great lover, but he was anything but. His wife would second that, for he didn't seem to want her at all, and when he did, he seemed like he was just going through the motions.

He had a younger brother, Sam, who worked the other side of the coin. He couldn't keep a steady job (he never finished high school), he drank and smoked pot from morning until night and sometimes during the "witching hour" (the early hours before the sunrise). He was almost completely worthless in the eyes of the people who knew him. He did do one thing better than his established older brother, though: he could fuck. He had a bigger-than-average penis, and he had no trouble "getting it up" for the occasion, something Michael couldn't say.

Three years before the murders, he began having an affair with Susan MacDonald, which meant they tore each other's clothes off and pounded into each other as if possessed, cursing like troopers as they screwed through the morning and afternoons, stopping only for lunch. By three in the afternoon they would both be thoroughly exhausted, worthless for the rest of the day. Sam would stagger home to his apartment, light a joint, look around his cluttered "suite," and decide that today wasn't the day to clean up. He looked like his brother, but disheveled, and yet Susan liked him a whole lot more than her husband, and on more than one occasion she had told him his dick was twice the size of Michael's. That always brought a smile to his face, and he felt like he was worth a million bucks, even though he definitely wasn't.

Susan MacDonald was still a looker: blonde with pretty features and a cute, curvy figure. Some would call her pretty, and she definitely turned a few heads, but her soul was as black as coal. She was heartless and cold, and the biggest reason she cheated on her husband with Sam was because she knew that when he found out it would destroy him emotionally. She hated him, and that was why she stayed with him. The longer they stayed together, the more pain he'd feel. She enjoyed making him suffer, making him hurt. Oh, there was love once, but that emotion had withered many moons ago.

Whatever feelings she had left ended when Michael first went to Pleasure to satisfy his urges. That was the day the love in their marriage completely ended, and the fires of hell took over. Susan started going to Pleasure as well, for she had urges just like her husband. Those urges were awakened when she stepped onto that rock out in the sea. Below is their history with Pleasure Island.

Michael MacDonald had defended Pleasure in a case that was eventually settled out of court. Everyone that entered into the Pleasure realm signed contracts protecting the ownership, and those documents were definitely kosher, but sometimes things went over the edge—over the line, so the saying goes. Marlo could have paid out her ass, but Michael had negotiated shrewdly, and she went home feeling as if she had actually won. She would've paid twice the amount to get this out of the way, so she told the lawyer he could have a session or two for free if he so desired. He could consider it a bonus on top of what he was paid.

Michael thought about it, and the two of them met in her office the next day. Marlo had thought that he would want to take her to bed, have a little straight harmless sex, and that would be that. He wasn't unappealing; he seemed pretty proper and upstanding, but what he wanted surprised her. It shouldn't have; people came to Pleasure and asked for all sorts of outrageous requests, but it still blindsided her. What he wanted was three sessions with Jason Miller! He explained that even though he was married to a beautiful woman and had cheated on her with other women throughout their marriage, something in the back of his mind had always nagged at him. He had always been able to keep those lewd and against-the-grain thoughts at bay, and he would have continued to go on as before, but this offer had broken through his defenses. Marlo told him to go home and think about it for a week's time, and if he still wanted to go through with his request regarding Jason, then she would set something up pronto. Marlo told him she didn't want him to rush into anything he'd regret later, for she was always looking to do right by her clients—especially the lawyer who had just saved her a lot of money.

Michael thanked her and thought on it for seven days, but he knew right away that he would go through with it, because now that he'd voiced his desires to someone of Marlo's stature, he now *craved* acting out his unusual fantasies. To each his own, he had no problem with that, but what he craved went completely against the norm, against the morals he had grown up with, and definitely against his religious background and the church he had been brought up in. Maybe that was part of the reason *why* he wanted to do this, but he knew that if he believed that he would only be fooling himself. He *wanted* to have sex with a man, and he *craved* a man treating him like a woman in heat—or an outright whore. He wanted to experience sexual relations from the other side of the coin, and if he liked homosexual sex like he thought he would, he could definitely go over to the other side completely.

Damn Susan, he thought; he was sick of all her bullshit. They fought more and had sex less. It was mostly a chore now, something to put him to sleep faster, where he dreamed of being with men of all types. He would wake up in a cold sweat, tip toe downstairs, masturbate wildly, and then sneak back to bed, feeling dirty. And it wasn't the homosexual thoughts that he thought were dirty, it was the sneaking downstairs—the sneaking! It made him feel unclean, and unfulfilled.

Part of the case against Pleasure involved Jason Miller, and Michael was attracted to him immediately. In the file, it was mentioned that Jason had sessions with both sexes, and when Michael learned that, his head started spinning. He had met and talked to Jason during the pretrial proceedings, and inwardly was totally smitten. He kept it in tow, but now he wouldn't have to. He figured Marlo was about to give him the best Christmas present he could've ever asked for, and for the next five days he masturbated about the Pleasure stud every chance he got. Michael knew he was lost to his lustful desires, but he didn't care. Before he had even had a session with Jason, he knew he was already hopelessly in love.

Marlo, on the other hand, had really only suggested Michael take a week to think about it so that she could choreograph what would go down with Jason. She already knew that the lawyer wouldn't change his mind; the look in his eye told her he was in too deep already, and so she devised a plan to make back all the trial money she had just lost on this case. She told Jason to completely overwhelm the defense attorney—pull out all the stops. He smiled, nodded, and understood. Situations like this one had happened many times before and would occur again many times in the future. The complete staff at Pleasure more than knew that defiant sexual taboo desires were stronger than any drug known to mankind. The magnetic pull of these emotions could—and would—make men and women of all ages, cultures, and creeds lose their ability to think logically and slow down their ability to think about the right decisions to make. Pleasure would, during this time, take over those rational decisions for them, and then the client was hooked—hooked like a fish on the end of the line, and as they were being pulled up and out of the water into the boat, or in this case, Pleasure Island, their banks accounts would begin to dwindle due to the constant massaging of their different sexual urges.

NARRATIVE NOTES: If you, dear reader, think you are different, you'd be wrong. You might not act out on your urges, you might have the emotional strength to fight them off if that makes you feel better, but you still have them, and that's the most important thing. God still knows about your dark, hidden sexual desires, but contrary to what you've been brainwashed to believe by everything and everybody in your cozy little comfortable life (parents, friends, siblings, schools, organizations, governments, and churches, etc.), he doesn't *care!* The forces of life that try to control and stifle your existence and joyful passions constantly *are* what concerns The Creator. They are the ones that should be worried and confess their indiscretions. One of the Ten Commandments in the Bible states that thou shall not kill. In that statement the dimensions are vast. It doesn't just mean that you shouldn't kill another human being. It also means you shouldn't *kill* another person's joy or passion (sexual or other), as well. Think about that as we journey forward in life on a whole; stop before you try to destroy another person's happiness and likes. You might not agree, you might not share in their desires, but take a little advice and move away from them and concentrate on yourself. You might find many more treasures at the end of your own rainbow. God Bless you in all your travels—sexual or not.

When Michael called Marlo that morning to say he would be going through with his date with destiny, she immediately told him to show up that evening at 7:00 p.m. They would talk one more time, and then he would be ushered on to Jason, who would be waiting patiently in his quarters—or, if Michael preferred, his lair. Michael laughed nervously, but he was in fevered turmoil mode, and he relished the sound of that. His lair. Jason's lair. It would be there that he could finally find out about himself, and act out on his hidden, forbidden desires. Maybe a whole new life awaited him after this evening, a whole new beginning. (In reality, he wasn't too far from the truth). He cancelled his afternoon and the next day's appointments due to imaginary illness; he knew he'd never be able to concentrate on his current cases, and you never knew what tomorrow would bring. He was a smart man, unlike his younger brother, and his assumptions about his evening at Pleasure might bring great promise. No, he wouldn't be working tomorrow; and no, dear reader, he wouldn't be murdered this evening either. That would happen and be discussed later on in the pages that follow.

That evening after sitting down opposite Marlo in her office, she once again wanted to know if he was sure he wanted to go through with his request, and once again replied that he did. Marlo then had Michael sign the proper documentation before leading him down the hall and up a flight of stairs. Jason's quarters were high up on the right side of the castle, facing west toward the Pacific Ocean. Michael's heart was racing as he was reintroduced to his masturbating fantasy lover of the past week, his fevered pitch on high. Marlo winked at Michael as she left the bedroom, and then the night began, per Jason's instructions.

What happened that night turned out to be pure magical ecstasy. When Michael entered the room, it was filled with scented red candles. Jason's quarters were the size of three master bedrooms, the walls and ceiling painted in light blue. The bed was king size and heart shaped and placed in the center of the massive room. A fireplace sat off to the side, and it was burning three logs, warming the room on the chilly, moonlit evening.

We won't go into the details of the encounter between the two men (although some of you might really want to know—and maybe more than some), but we will know that Jason did something different. He undressed Michael slowly, feeling him up in intimate places as he went. He then made the lawyer watch as he undressed himself, trying to turn him on completely. He did, for Michael's eyes widened in lewd fascination as he saw Jason's large member, almost drooling on himself. Jason then gently guided him belly down onto the bed, spreading his legs wide apart, and prepared him with lubricant, then mounted and entered him slowly in what was soon to become an all-nighter. It wasn't supposed to go past midnight, but it went straight through to the next evening! Fireworks and magic exploded all around them, both never expected what eventually transpired, because by the time they both dressed and left the room they had both fallen madly in love with each other.

In Michael's estimation, the session had gone way past its expectations. His assumptions about himself were totally correct, and he now knew where he stood sexually. He still liked women to some extent, but he now knew that he enjoyed sex with men a lot more—at least when it came down to Jason. He had been much bigger than Michael had expected, and he was extremely sore when the marathon encounter was over, but he couldn't get enough of the Pleasure employee.

Jason, on the other hand, had started out treating this session like all his others, just another trick, but soon realized he was breaking the first law of Marlo Freeman's handbook. He had, without fair warning, fallen head over heels in love with the lawyer. He liked Michael's enthusiasm toward following his every command, he more than once suggested Jason go further in what he was doing at the time, and the lawyer either called him sir, or more stirring—master! That suggested to Jason that he could be drawn into that kind of sinister world as well. Jason himself didn't really get into that kind of physical kink, but he knew that before this encounter was over he would put the lawyer over his knee and spank him hard until he begged for more. He felt a certain power and high in overtaking him, and he liked it. This lover had inadvertently helped him realize that, and that fact broke him. Jason intensified his actions above the sweating lawyer as the evening progressed, falling helplessly in love himself!

This shift in Jason's feelings took less than two days, and it shook him to his core. In his life he had only fallen in love once, and that was with his mother's younger sister, Doreen. Doreen was fifteen years older than Jason, but she was a beauty queen. Standing just under five feet, she was petit in stature but had all the curves to drive a man mad. Her brunette hair fell halfway down her sensual back, her face was beautiful, and her smile would always lighten up a room. Her breasts were small, as was her backside, but both were very shapely. Men would watch that ass until it moved completely out of sight, and Jason on more than one occasion had done exactly that. He admired his aunt; she was outgoing, friendly, and extremely adventurous.

A few days after he had turned fifteen, Doreen took him to the movies, only this movie wasn't the normal action one he was used to seeing. No, this one was pornographic in nature. It had many sexual scenes of every kind of sex, and he became completely aroused. Doreen felt his erection through his jeans and told him this was normal, and not to be ashamed. She whispered in his ear that she thought he was hot, and that she wanted to do these types of sexual things with him. She further told him that it would be his extra birthday present. He was surprised but became even more aroused.

She led him like a little puppy dog back to her apartment, and thus started a relationship that went on until his eighteenth birthday, when she suddenly, without warning, disappeared. Jason's family put out a missing person's report on her, but nothing ever came of it. It was as if she had fallen off the face of the Earth, and maybe she had.

Jason had fallen for her hard; he missed her greatly when she was gone, but while she had been there she had taken her favorite nephew down a lewd road of sexual ecstasy. To him, she was a goddess, and he would do anything for her. That had sometimes become a problem to some extent. Doreen had taken him further into the sexual realm by introducing him to some of her playmates. She got him into trying three ways with some of her girlfriends, which were all good in his opinion (they were all beautiful in their own right), but she had also gotten him to try homosexual sex with a man friend of hers as well. That made him feel guilty and dirty, and he told her so. She just told him to grow up and enjoy the different types of fruit out there; there was nothing wrong with any type of sex. He was slowly won over, and with her in total control continued down that road of wild and lewd madness.

Jason had taken that mindset into his job here at Pleasure, and he was one of the highest-paid employees because of it. He had sex with quite a few men who wanted to dabble in the heady nature of it all, but Michael was different. He knew that you could never question why you were attracted to this person or that, but the attraction here, this time, was strong, and growing by the second. By the time the lawyer left and set up his next appointment the following week, they both had told the other that they loved each other deeply, and that this had been the best night of both their lives. Maybe Doreen knew something about him all those years ago that he didn't know himself, or maybe these were feelings that had been lying dormant; he just didn't fully know. But what he *did* know was that he was deeply head over heels with someone that looked quite ordinary, but was mentally very appealing, and physically overwhelming.

Something disturbing ate at him as he lay in his bed alone the following night. Jason had always been the top, which meant that he was the giver, not the receiver. Even the man Doreen had introduced to him sexually had been the bottom. But as he thought back on the last twenty-four hours, he realized that he had lost all control and had begged Michael to assume the reins, and so they had reversed roles. Jason discovered that the sex was just as good this way—maybe even more so. Those memories of the night before refused to leave, and so he feverishly masturbated three times before he was able to fall off to sleep, dreaming further about Michael and the sex they had had, and more importantly, the sex they would have in the future. He woke up sweating and gasping for air at about five in the morning and masturbated yet again. What is happening to me? he thought tiredly as he slowly drifted off again. This time his sleep was deep, and he had no more dreams.

When Susan MacDonald handed in her husband's dry cleaning a few days after his and Jason's first time on Pleasure Island, she was in a funk. Michael had disappeared for two days, and when she had questioned him on it he just shrugged and said he had stayed at the office, going over some paperwork on his current case. Bullshit! He seemed indifferent, but happy. Was he having another affair? She smelled his clothes, but no perfume was evident. Even though she was screwing his brother, she still didn't want to be cheated on herself. She was quite selfish, kind of what she thought of her husband, but in her opinion what was good for the goose *wasn't* good for the gander. Before handing over his suits to the clerk she checked his pockets and discovered a receipt from Pleasure.

"That motherfucker," she fumed, knowing all about what went on out there. Everybody knew, but more than 75 percent of the clientele were out-of-towners, or out-of-staters. Nobody close to the island wanted to be seen there, but Michael, who had done a lot of business down in that area, had not cared, obviously. The time to tell that stupid asshole about me and his brother is soon approaching, she mused, driving home.

When Susan got comfortable back at their lonely homestead and fixed herself a stiff drink, she thought further. So, he had been out at Pleasure, had he? Well, two can play that game! Susan took out her phone, looked up Pleasure's number, and called. She was transferred to a Marlo Freeman, and told the woman she was thinking about visiting and finding out about herself.

Marlo set up an interview for the following evening, for

Michael's wife seemed extremely anxious. Marlo new why; Michael wasn't thinking clearly, and he had probably left a trail that followed straight back to Pleasure, and in her crystal ball she could see another client being added to the mix. She smiled to herself as the next afternoon ticked away, knowing the woman was probably stewing in her own juices. She wasn't wrong, for Susan paced the floors all afternoon, wondering what woman Michael had been with.

Pleasure had a parking lot on the mainland, and a helicopter took her out to the island. It was the only way to get there, for the island had thirty-foot cliffs on each side. That wasn't exactly true, though. The dungeons built under the castle had a few secret walkways that went down to the waterline, and a speedboat was anchored to a dock behind a hidden doorway that led into a large cavern. Many souls had been disposed of by using that speedboat at night, burying them out in the biggest cemetery only a few knew anything about.

When Susan entered Marlo's office she immediately confronted the woman about her husband. Marlo admitted Michael had been there, but after engaging the scorned woman further while succeeding to calm her down, she suggested a free session on the house. She couldn't give out any details on Michael, he had certain rights, but so would Susan if she wanted to accept a Pleasure session. Susan, wanting to get even more than anything else, readily accepted. Marlo explained what the island was all about, including a few details Susan hadn't known. She told the upset housewife all about the different satisfying fantasies, but if she just wanted regular sex that would be all right too. Everything was possible; anything was on the table, and Susan had one free ticket to ride. The hook had been dangled, and Marlo knew just how to bait it.

Marlo led Susan into what she called a waiting suite and told her to think on it. There was a bar inside; Marlo made her a stiff highball, and then she left. On the far wall there were three large TV screens playing different porno movies, and various forms of sex were going on in each one. Susan watched each one intently, but she already knew what fantasy she wanted to act out on. Still, she also needed some time to calm herself down. What was she really doing here? Did she really want to go down this dark road? Did she really want to do this just to get back at Michael? Did she . . . did she . . . did . . . she? Yes! Yes, she did. She really did! It was way past the time to know if she still felt physically excited about the thoughts that kept creeping out of her mind's creaky closet at night (or day) and traveled down to her horny womb. Even though she masturbated every so often to these unrelenting strong urges, she still thought back on her past, just to make sure.

Susan grew up the third daughter of John and Millie Stansfield. They had ten children total: five daughters and five sons. They were raised in Portland, so Susan had never really left home. She was the only one in her family that didn't, though, and that was because every one of her siblings died before the age of twenty— every one of them. They had left Earth, and hopefully were with God in heaven.

John Junior, the oldest, died of leukemia. He lived the longest, but had the deadly disease since birth and spent almost half his shortened life in a hospital bed. He was twenty.

James, eighteen, died by choking on a piece of meat on his birthday. Steak had been his favorite, but it was deadly on this night.

Sarah, nineteen, Bobbi, sixteen, and Billy, fifteen, died in a head-on car accident, all three dying instantly. Sarah was driving, and it was deemed her fault. The old couple that were driving in the other car survived, receiving only a few scratches.

Ronald, thirteen, died pitching for the Gulls baseball team when the opposing batter hit a line drive off his forehead. The baseball was hit so hard it ricocheted into the Gulls' dugout up the first base line. He managed to survive in the hospital for two days, and at one point looked to be on the mend. He was sitting up in bed talking to his parents when all of a sudden he stopped talking, looked to the right corner of the ceiling, and said in a much deeper voice, "Yes, Lord," and then lost consciousness, slumping down on the bed. He never woke up and became the first Portland little leaguer to lose his life on a baseball diamond.

Daisy was a swimmer on the high school team. She had a good chance to win in the finals and had visions of trying out for the Olympics. She was found face down in the school pool after going in at six in the morning to practice on the day of the final meet. There was no foul play involved, yet no explanation as to why she drowned. She was eighteen.

Janet was only seven years old when she passed away. She was climbing the big oak tree in the backyard when she fell and broke her neck. She died instantly.

Larry died in the hospital—cause of death, unknown. He just stopped breathing as his family looked on. He was only one day old. Crib death, they called it. Nine dead.

Susan was the only child left. Her parents were still alive, but they both resided in Happy Pines, a psychiatric hospital build twenty years ago just outside of the city. No one could blame them for trying to forget their past. No one could blame them for checking out on reality. Losing nine children was no small thing. Burying nine children in Portland Cemetery, visiting them every Sunday after church could do that. They spiraled downward until

Susan graduated high school and moved out.

Shortly afterward the neighbors found them sitting at the kitchen table. They were both staring up at the ceiling, as if in a trance. They were both taken to the hospital, and neither one of them ever said another word again. After being sent to Happy Pines, Susan visited them every so often, and every time she found them the same way: sitting in wheelchairs looking upward.

Eventually Susan never went back, and she also stopped going to the cemetery to pay her respects to her siblings. It was all becoming too much to take. Sometimes she thought that her soul had cracked, she felt so alone and depressed. She turned to drugs and started turning tricks to survive. She did them both in the cemetery her brothers and sisters were in, but on the other side where there were fewer headstones. She never visited them on those occasions. She felt unworthy, and sometimes felt that she should be dead too. Why had she avoided death so far? Why had she been spared?

As fate would have it, she was arrested one day by an undercover police officer, and was defended by a young lawyer just starting out named Michael MacDonald—like the hamburger joint. He got her off and asked her out. The rest is history—maybe rocky history, but history just the same. Susan had demons, though. During the days she was a hooker, she almost always had straight, normal sex. Wham, bam, thank you ma'am. But there was that one time . . .

And it was that one time that always crept back into Susan's head, and its memory always pulled at her deepest emotions. What was different about that time? Because it was a woman, a beautiful sensuous woman around thirty or thirty-five, and she had bought Susan's services. When this beauty, named Joan, first propositioned her, Susan said she didn't do that kind of thing;

that she only did men. She appreciated a woman's beauty, her curves, but she had no desire to couple with the same sex. A lesbian she was *not!* Joan kept at her, eventually willing to triple the money she would have to pay.

Susan finally relented, and they went to Joan's apartment, which was just outside the city limits. The tryst lasted for five days. What went on Susan wasn't proud of later on, but she had to admit that it had been the best sex of her life, by far! They went around the world, orbiting every lesbian fantasy they could act on. Joan paid her ten times what she said she would pay and told Susan she had had fun.

Susan never saw Joan again, but it wasn't as if she didn't try. She went back to the apartment and knocked on the door. The neighbor next door told Susan that nobody lived there, not for the last six months or so. Susan told the neighbor that was impossible; she had been there just last week. She left and tried to forget about Joan, but that wasn't so easy. You just didn't forget a woman like Joan, and the way she handled herself (and Susan) in bed. Their coupling had been special—very special.

She went back to the streets until she was hauled in and met Michael. He swept her off her feet and they got married five months later. She forgot about Joan to some extent, but her presence was never too far away. The beautiful trick had crept back into her fantasy thoughts every time she had sex with Michael, and then with his brother. Every time!

It was funny! Michael thought he was the greatest lover, for Susan orgasmed every time they made love; but it wasn't because of him. It was Joan—all Joan. Joan made her orgasm hard. In reality, it was the memories of her lesbian lover during those five exciting days and nights that made her reach orgasm quickly, and repeatedly—not Michael, not Sam. Joan. Eventually she realized it was Joan she was in love with, not her husband. Their marriage was never the same after that realization, and it showed. They argued more, and when they weren't doing that, they moved about each other in uneasy silence.

She began to dislike Michael. The dislike turned to disgust, and then to hate. He was here, and Joan wasn't. Susan was frustrated—totally, sexually frustrated. She knew it wasn't Michael's fault, but she didn't care (her selfishness coming to the surface), plus he didn't help matters either. He continued to act distant, becoming despondent and depressed around her, unlike a real man. Susan hated him more for that, and so she turned to his brother. He was better in bed, but Joan still entered Susan's lewd thoughts when Sam made love to her. She wished so badly she could find Joan, but now, as she sat in this wonderful suite on the island of Pleasure, maybe there was hope for her after all—maybe, just maybe. She decided to act out on a fantasy that had been burning inside the deepest parts of her soul. When Marlo came back she would tell her what she wanted—what she *craved!* She hoped Marlo could comply with her needs.

A half hour after Marlo had left Susan in the waiting suite to contemplate her desires, the owner of Pleasure returned. Susan was nervous and anxious all at the same time, and so she came right out with it. She told Marlo that she wanted to have lesbian sex with her. She explained that she had all these urges that kept wanting to come out. She told Marlo that she thought she was beautiful; she had a fantastic figure, and she could easily see herself worshipping the owner of Pleasure Island. To prove her point, she got down on her knees in front of Marlo, bent over, and began licking her shiny, black high-heeled boots. When she stopped a few minutes later, the owner said sharply, "Who told you to stop!" and so she continued licking her mistress's heels, redoubling her efforts plus kissing each one from time to time, moaning her submissiveness, completely embracing her heightened emotions. Her nerve endings tingled uncontrollably from head to toe.

When Susan was talked to sharply like Marlo had just done, it was all over; she was in sexual heaven. To her, there wasn't a better high in the world. Eventually, maybe five minutes later, Marlo commanded Susan to return to her chair. "Is there anything else?" Marlo asked sharply, looking deep into the submissive's eyes. Marlo knew people on a whole, and she knew this kind. There was always one more thing, always more to ask for. They had the chocolate layer cake, but they wanted the ice cream too. And then the cherry. Enough was *never* enough. They were like little children, and this one was spoiled rotten to the core, but Marlo would surely remedy that!

"Yes, Marlo—"

"Yes, *Mistress!*" she corrected Susan loudly, almost screaming in rage. "For a pure submissive, you sure need a lot of training. That will take many sessions. That will take a lot of your money, and your full attention. Are you willing to go where I *need* you to go?"

"Yes . . . yes, Mistress, I am willing," came the reply. Susan lowered her head in shame. "I'm so sorry. I will try to be better. I truly want to please you. It is what I live for now, and I will never forget to call you Mistress again."

"You better believe you won't forget again, or else I'll whip the skin off your fantastic ass!" Marlo saw the woman quiver when she said "whip," and she instantly knew Susan wanted that as well. "Now tell me what else you want."

And Susan did, never forgetting to call her Mistress at each interval. As she poured her heart and soul out to the owner of Pleasure, she realized just how much her insides ached from keeping it all bottled up for so long. She had become unnecessarily angry and vindictive. She told Marlo that deep down she really disliked all men, especially her smug, uncaring husband, who she felt thought he was better than her. She told her about his brother Sam, and how she was screwing him aggressively to get back at Michael. She, in detail, told her mistress about her time with Joan, and how the disappearing woman had affected her; how she had awakened hidden feelings and changed her sexually forever. Susan told Marlo that she needed to be dominated by a woman; she was a closet submissive, and lesbian. And finally, she told the owner of Pleasure that she wanted to beat a man's ass with a cane to get back at that whole gender. Joan had used one on her behind until her ass felt like raw hamburger, trying to correct her deficiencies, and it had hurt like hell. Just once—just once—she would like to do that to a male—one who thought he was better than any woman, or at least her. She would do anything for that!

"And anything you will," Marlo told Susan, pacing back and forth in front of her new project. She bent over and looked her new client directly in the eyes, speaking softly but demandingly. "You belong to me now. You must surrender yourself fully to me—your body, mind, and soul."

"Yes, Mistress, I will. I promise you I will," Susan said sincerely, nodding, never breaking eye contact.

"Your promises better be truthful, otherwise I'll throw you off this rock, and you'll never be able to return here again."

"They will be, Mistress. I confess wholeheartedly that I no longer can live without you."

And so it began.

Marlo reasoned that both MacDonalds were going to be part of Pleasure for a long time. They'd become the next cash cow, for she had done her homework, and knew that Michael was pulling in at least a million plus per year. She told her new slave to undress quickly and get down on her knees. A collar was fastened around Susan's neck, and on all fours she was led down the hall to her mistress's lair. That night became a blur to Susan as she thought back on it. Just when she thought Marlo had run her through all that she knew, Susan was put through even more paces. It was amazing! The sex and her mistress's creativity were amazing! She couldn't believe her good fortune.

Just having a mistress was exhilarating, and she pledged her devotion again and again throughout the night. By the time she left the island the next morning at sunrise, she had become a new and different woman—a sore one, with a brand-new attitude and a new respect for everyone around her. She promised her mistress that she would treat her husband better, and break up with Sam immediately. Marlo promised that if the worthless piece of shit brother-in-law started anything he would be dealt with severely. Whatever Marlo wanted she would do now, and that was good, because she wouldn't have to think for herself anymore. She hated making decisions (Michael usually handled that department), and so she had completely surrendered ownership of herself over to her Mistress.

Marlo now possessed her—body and soul—and Susan knew she would be disciplined by her mistress whenever it was needed, or for no reason whatsoever! She had needed to be punished many times on her first night at Pleasure, and she sported many angry red whip marks all over her body as Marlo French-kissed her goodbye. She was to return in one week's time, even though she begged beyond shaming herself to come back sooner.

One other thing: all through the night Susan didn't see or fantasize about Joan, but she still felt the woman's presence in Marlo's chambers, as if she was lurking behind her, just out of view. She loved her new mistress, but she still couldn't shake her first one. She would just have to deal with that, she mused, as she drove home.

All that next week she treated her husband better, and they even had sex (Susan had called Marlo to make sure that it was alright) once midway through her waiting time. She thought about both her mistresses during their coupling. They were both judging her sternly, and as Michael thought he was stimulating her as usual, she fantasized about having sex and being dominated by both of them at the same time. What a high *that* was! She orgasmed hard just before her husband did, but little did she know that Michael was fantasizing about someone else as well. He was thinking of coupling with Jason, being taken repeatedly by his new homosexual lover, and he came just as hard as his wife. Homosexual . . . the word alone just got him going. Admitting to himself that he was at least mostly gay was a big relief, a giant weight removed from his sagging shoulders.

This policy of making love in marriages was nothing new. Most couples, whether they wanted to admit it or not, fantasize about someone else when they are in bed together making love. There is nothing wrong with that; in fact, it is quite healthy, both physically and mentally. This alternate behavior forces your body and mind to be more creative, and both parties are usually better off for it. Whatever floats your boat, as the saying goes. Michael and Susan MacDonald *were* better off, and it made married life more bearable, even though their love lives were heading in completely different directions. Does any of this sound familiar to any of you readers?

The main blueprint drawn up by Marlo and Pleasure had the

couple staying together yet venturing out into different galaxies sexually. Eventually, they would intertwine with each other's tastes, becoming a part of the other's pleasures and desires. For example, Susan would lie down in front of Michael, receiving oral sex from her husband as Jason was sodomizing him from behind. Or on the flipside, Susan would be double teamed by her husband and her mistress, the wife riding the husband vaginally while her mistress was sodomizing her anus from behind with a strap-on dildo. Those choreographed scenarios would come later, though, when both were mature enough to deal with those lewd and heady situations.

While those sexual liaisons were in the not too distant future, Marlo had gotten together with Jason and Wendy Haas, planning on what would transpire later in the week. All agreed it would be quite a show, and hopefully everyone, including the MacDonalds, would enjoy it immensely. Everyone from all sides couldn't wait for the end of the week, even though the MacDonalds didn't know what was going to happen. They were running strictly on raging hormones and sexual desires, while the crew at Pleasure were running on acting out different scenarios. Even sex can become boring when you do it the same way every time, so Marlo and the gang were constantly changing it up, using all of their creative juices.

Eventually the end of the week came, and Michael was instructed to arrive at Pleasure two hours before Susan. Neither one of them knew the other was headed for the same destination; they were both sworn to secrecy. Besides, Michael didn't even know that Susan had had any interaction with Pleasure at all, and Susan didn't know what kind of lover her husband was into. What a surprise that would be! All was going as planned.

When a person decides to enter into a world such as Pleasure, achieving your goal can be difficult, and you might have to endure certain situations that are touchy to deal with. A lot of people have to experience emotions that are completely the opposite of what they want, just to know why they want those desires to begin with. When people such as the MacDonalds were interviewed, these concepts and concerns were explained in full to them. Still, even though they might get hurt, physically as well as physiologically, 99.9 percent still ventured into the island's strong magnetic realm, searching for their true self. They gamble on their feelings and emotions and damn the consequences. I believe in their decisions to plow forward through the unknown, for isn't that the truest, *purest* essence of life: having no idea what may happen? If you already know, then life would begin to get boring quite quickly. I would rather trudge forward into the grey fog that lies between the known black and white sidelines. Wouldn't you? I hope after reading this and truly thinking it over, you, too, reader, will feel like I do.

The MacDonalds thought that way. Here is what happened on that fateful night—their last night. It didn't go as planned for them, or the people who work at Pleasure, but sometimes that's the way it works out. When you gamble, you either win or lose, but for some people that doesn't even matter. It's the thrill of the game that matters; that's the true satisfaction. The *thrills!* If you don't want or *need* that thrill, stop reading and move on to the next chapter right now. But if you do: enjoy. You've come this far, so I'm betting that you'll venture onward. It will be worth it; the treasures at the end of the rainbow will be great, one way or the other, for the endgame here will certainly surprise you.

One other situation was taken care of during that week of excruciating waiting. Susan had called Sam MacDonald and told him that their fling was over. She told him that she felt so guilty, and wanted to make amends with her husband. Sam would hear none of it and had started screaming and threatened to tell Michael everything if she didn't keep the tryst going. When she further tried to explain her stance, Sam belittled her and called her every name in the book. He had, in that instant, proved himself to Susan to be a total scumbag. Marlo had thought he would react in this manner, and so she had instructed her obedient new slave to then relent and tell Sam to come over to Susan's house in an hour. Through further instructions, she then called her mistress, who then said she would take care of the situation pronto.

When Sam knocked on his brother's front door, it wasn't his cheating wife who answered it. No, it was a security employee of Pleasure who did, and after he had been roughly grabbed and pulled inside his brother's house and the door closed behind them, he was punished with a beating he had never experienced before. He was unconscious when it was finally over, but he had endured much pain before mercilessly passing out. He was professionally hog-tied and thrown into the trunk of the employee's truck and taken to Pleasure. Once he was inside the castle and taken to the deepest dungeons, he was untied and beaten again by Alfred Altman. This beating was even worse than the first one, and much more sadistic. By the time it was over, three ribs had been broken, his nose fractured, and more than half his body sported bruises that would take weeks to heal. He was stripped naked, and his wrists were shackled to chains that hung from the dungeon ceiling. His legs were left free of chains, for they wanted to see him struggle in his bonds.

They left him alone for a complete day, wallowing in his suffering, before Alfred, Marlo, and Wendy walked into the cool chamber the next morning. Sam was crying and begging to be let free. He was told, in no uncertain terms, that *that* was never going to happen. He would remain a prisoner of theirs for the rest of his miserable life, which, if he didn't obey them all properly, wouldn't last too long. He cried like a baby as Wendy came up behind him with a huge greased anal plug and rammed it up his shocked rectum. The pain was immense, and he screamed at the top of his lungs, his cries bouncing off the stone walls, but they were heard by no one that wasn't in the room. Wendy then took her favorite paddle off the wall (a two-inch-thick wooden paddle with a long handle) and began spanking his bare ass with it. Each shot to his ass sounded like gunshot going off, followed by incredible animalistic screaming. When each scream subsided, another shot of the paddle was administered until he finally passed out. Alfred waited a few minutes, and then bitch slapped Sam awake, loosening a few teeth in the process. He moaned in pain, but was told that his punishment was just beginning. He was too defeated to do anything but hang his head and groan incoherently. Marlo was next. She picked up a three-inch strap and slowly and methodically whipped his back, ass, and thighs with it, increasing the speed with each new blow. Skin wise, it didn't do too much damage, but the pain he felt was intense. Again, the blows didn't stop until he passed out.

When he came to again he had been taken down and tied to what the people at Pleasure called "the sexual seat." It was made of hard plastic, and black in color. It looked like a horse saddle, and the person was laid belly down over it, the individual's backside positioned high in the air. It had straps on all four sides that were fastened around both elbows and both knees, rendering the participant completely helpless. They could struggle somewhat, but that was part of the seat's ambience. Legs were fastened just wide enough apart for their genitals to be showing, along with their anus. Sam struggled in his bonds when he came to, and he begged beyond begging to be freed. He was ignored as they watched him twist and turn in his entrapment, and then he was finally told why he had been kidnapped and brought into this dungeon.

He was informed that he was a total worthless piece of shit and didn't belong out in free society. Not only had he mistreated his beautiful sister-in-law, but he had threatened and frightened her as well. He was told that his brother enjoyed the company of men, enjoyed a good thick dick up his horny ass, and maybe, just maybe, that 'afternoon delight' ran in the family. Marlo then roughly removed the thick anal plug from his rear, twisting it back and forth as it was pulled from his distended anus. He screamed, his head bucking from side to side, trying to rid his backside from the pain it was feeling. The security guard that he had encountered at his brother's house entered the room and smiled evilly down at Sam. He was a big man, standing six and a half feet tall. He weighed close to three hundred pounds, most of it muscle, yet he wouldn't stand a chance against Alfred Altman in one on one combat-but that wouldn't enter into the equation here because they were all part of a tight, cohesive team. Marlo, Wendy, and Alfred quietly left the room and closed the door behind them. The big man locked the heavy wooden door and turned back to face Sam. Removing his clothes slowly, he told the condemned captive that his name was Ross Remington, and he was a full-blown practicing bisexual.

Sam struggled when he heard that, and as he looked back he started screaming wildly, for the man sported the biggest penis he could ever imagine seeing. It was at least ten inches long, and over two inches thick. It looked angry, hungry, and it was ragingly hard. Ross chuckled as he got down on his knees behind Michael's brother. He greased his giant member, and slowly entered the condemned man's asshole, taking his forbidden cherry in the process. All night long the two got closely acquainted, and when Ross unlocked the door and passed Marlo and Wendy on the way out, Sam confessed his sins and life to the eternally damned. He cried and cried, and Marlo told him his punishment was now for the moment complete. His future life would consist of living here in the castle as a pleasure slave. He was told that Ross liked him, liked him a lot, and would desire his presence again tonight in his private chambers. He was broken and nodded in defeat, accepting his fate.

Sam was found hanging by his wrists in the adjacent chamber next to the dead MacDonalds by the FBI. He had been whipped, beaten, spanked, ridiculed, and sodomized by many in his short stay on the island of Pleasure. He was a changed man, if he was still a man at all, and he told the authorities all he had been through. He was a wild card in these investigations, and by the time the power went out, every employee had been arrested, jailed, and charged with various crimes. They all went back to The Creator, all except one—but let's not ruin this chapter. That person will be revealed shortly.

When Michael MacDonald arrived at the castle, he was immediately ushered down to Jason's bedroom suite. Jason met him at the door; they embraced, tore off their clothes, and stumbled toward the heart-shaped bed, which now was covered in bright Valentine-red silk sheets. They broke off their kiss to fall into what would become their most used position on the bed: Jason on top of Michael, belly down in the reverse missionary position. Unbeknownst to Michael, they were being filmed from eight different angles, and their actions didn't disappoint. Their movements and their moans of raw emotion were intense, and Marlo would sell the footage to the porn industry company she dealt with down in Los Angeles. Both men's faces would be doctored to protect the participants, and only Jason would see any dividends from the lewd homosexual action. It was just another way Pleasure made money, and those roses smelled of millions for the high-rise sex rock that lay just off the coast of the mainland.

After their first go around, Jason whispered in Michael's ear. The lawyer was told that their relationship would constantly move forward to the next level, and that the defense attorney's dedication would always be challenged, making the relationship and bond between the two lovers that much stronger. One of those challenges was about to happen, and they would have to leave the bedroom for a while. Michael nodded, and then he let Jason put a collar around his neck attached to a short chain dog leash. He led him out of the room and down the hallway, both of them still naked. Sounds of lust and groans of pleasure were heard as they moved past closed doors, which only intensified the two men's lust for each other. Michael wondered and fantasized about what might be going on in those rooms. Were they satisfying their lusts like he was? He hoped so.

They moved onward, Jason leading the docile, obedient lawyer behind him. Michael didn't know where he was being led, but he didn't care. He also didn't care that he was completely naked and being led around on a chain like a common sex slave, and that anyone could see him. He didn't care that he sported a massive hard-on made of granite, or that his lover in front of him possessed one as well. He only knew that he was releasing emotions that had been suppressed inside the deepest regresses of his mind, ridding himself all of the hang-ups that surrounded those true feelings. He had broken down those walls of control that he had grown up with. He had rid himself of all that constant brainwashing his parents, the church, and the rest of society had burdened him with, and that felt good. And it felt *right!* And so, it was.

Susan helicoptered over to the Island two hours later, around eight, and Marlo met her in the lobby of the castle. The castle seemed much more vibrant and alive on this darkening evening. The sun was changing from a bright yellow to a light orange, and it would only deepen in color as it set into the blue Pacific. Marlo kissed Susan deeply, and then commanded the housewife to strip completely and get on her hands and knees. She did so quickly, becoming more turned on by the moment. Old feelings returned as she realized they had never really deserted her.

Deep down inside she felt totally submissive and became hotter with every command given to her. Marlo understood this classic submissive behaviour, and smiled in total exhilaration as she led her crawling docile new slave down to her quarters. This is the greatest job in the world, she thought happily as they entered her lair. Money and pleasure, pleasure and money.

Marlo told Susan to get into a black leather outfit that lay on her bed. The outfit covered her complete midsection and half of her swelling breasts. It cut deeply between her love slit and the cheeks of her shapely ass. Knee-high black leather high-heeled boots were put on next, and then she put on elbow-length black leather gloves. Marlo handed Susan a whalebone cane, led her out of the room and further into the core of the castle, roughly tugging on her leash whenever she lagged behind, for her boots were hard to walk in. The Portland housewife loved to be treated in this manner, and she tried her best to keep up. Susan loved rough treatment, and knew that she would pay dearly for it later, but she was beyond caring. Like her husband, she was hurtling forward into a dark abyss, one where they could both act out and enjoy their darkest fantasies. The night was young, only just beginning, and for the two MacDonalds they thought that they were in for an evening of total bliss. They were only half right, for this evening was all they had left.

Marlo led Susan down three flights of stairs to one of the dungeons. The walls, as well as the steps, were made of stones the color of many shades of gray. They were lit by torches that hung on the walls every ten feet or so, giving the stairway a medieval ambience. All the castles' stairways were narrow in nature and seemed to close up completely (an optical illusion) behind them. The temperature dipped 10 degrees before they reached their destination, and Susan shivered. She shivered not only from the coolness and dampness of the air, but from the anticipation of what was to happen next. There is no amount of money that could pay for all this, she thought feverishly as she was led into an open chamber. She *would* remember to thank her mistress properly at the end of the night, or whenever her dominant owner wanted her to.

The chamber was round in shape, and it also was made of large, rectangular, gray stones. The walls were covered in hanging whips, crops, straps, and paddles, waiting to be chosen and used. Various chains hung from the ceiling and lay scattered on the basement floor, but what Susan concentrated on were the two figures in the center of the basement room. One was chained to the ceiling and floor, his wrists and ankles spread as wide as possible so he couldn't move. He was naked and shook with wanton anticipation, wondering what was going to happen next. His back was to the two women, but Susan quickly realized that he was her beloved husband. Michael, in all his courtroom glory, was chained like a prisoner in the bowels of Pleasure Island, totally submissive, just like his wife, who stood next to her dominant mistress, subconsciously drooling at the sight. That sight was completed by what the other man was doing. That man, Jason Miller, was fondling every part of Michael's body—his privates in front, his quivering buttocks, his back, and his chest as he was being seriously soul kissed. Moans and groans came from the two men as they were wrapped in total rapture, unaware of the two women looking on. One was shocked; the other expectant.

"Yes, Susan, your husband came here to act out on his fantasies," Marlo lamented loudly. "He, in reality, is a full-blown homosexual, and likes a man to use him like a wife most of the time, which means that he likes it up the ass. Jason, on the other hand, is an employee of Pleasure Island, but he has committed the number one sin in our established Castle Handbook. He has fallen in love with your husband—hard! Michael has also fallen in love, but that was what we expected him to do." Her voice raised in volume, but not in an angry way. "Jason will have a session with my righthand man, and he will be corrected, beaten severely until he surrenders his emotions for your husband. If not . . ." she trailed off, never taking her eyes off the two engaged male lovers.

Neither man seemed to hear, know, or care that the women had entered the chamber, and continued what they were doing. Michael knew that somehow his wife was in the chamber with him with Marlo, but right now he didn't care. He would try to explain his way out later, but right now he didn't want to interrupt this sexual bliss he was feeling. Jason's hands and fingers massaged between the cheeks of Michael's ass, and he moaned louder inside his lover's kissing mouth. Susan gasped at the sight. She had never realized that Michael felt this way toward his own sex, but she had never let on of how she really felt either. She now knew why her marriage had fractured over time. Neither one of them had been truthful with the other, maybe even themselves. Maybe it wasn't too late for them to repair what they still had left, but she also knew that she would never give up her new mistress, her new owner.

She pledged to herself that she would stay married to Michael and try to understand him better. She would allow him to keep coming here to Pleasure Island, or to have other homosexual affairs whenever he wanted. She would also continue to worship her lesbian owner, and never live without a mistress again. If Marlo ever wanted her to leave Michael for whatever reason, she would do so without question. He did not own her; he never did, but her mistress did. The math was easy. She loved, then hated, and now again liked her husband to some extent, but she worshiped her mistress, which went way beyond being in love. Susan turned and faced her Mistress, went quickly to her knees, bent over, dismissing the pain of her outfit which was pulled even deeper between her legs and ass crack, and began licking the dominant's black boots and losing herself in her powerful emotions.

Wendy Haas quietly entered the chamber, saw Susan busy at her mistress's boots, and tapped the island's owner on the shoulder. Marlo had never stopped watching the two men; she was mesmerized, for she never tired of studying the act of lovemaking. She was a voyeur as well as everything else when it came down to raw human encounters, and she was enjoying this one on many different fronts. She made it a point to watch these two in action in close vicinity. Soon—very soon.

The owner of Pleasure glanced over at Wendy, who was dressed similarly as Susan, nodded, looked back at the two men, and said, "Jason, move away so we can further Michael's sexual journey. He has a lot of mileage to travel on this night."

Jason quickly stopped what he had been doing, even though he was caught up in total rapture, and reluctantly moved away from his chained, yet unchained lover. He shuffled over to the other side of the chamber, almost pouting. From all the making out he was out of breath, and tried his best to calm himself down. He didn't want to leave Michael in the center of the chamber, at this point in time he *never* wanted to leave him alone again, but it was in the blueprint drawn out for this evening. If he valued his job, and he did, then he would follow it to a T. He also knew that he had fucked up big time, yet he didn't care in the least. He also knew that Alfred would beat the living shit out of him, and this night might end up with him hooked up to too many machines in the part of the castle that was used as a hospital. His best friend tonight might be Dr. Levers, and even though she was a beautiful piece of ass and Jason had always wanted to fuck her in every way imaginable, he had no taste for seeing her anytime soon. He was condemned, though, and he still didn't care. Love had a way of doing that to you. God help him, and God *damn* him for falling in love with Michael.

Aunt Doreen would be smiling and nodding in acknowledgment of how his behavior had betrayed him in this homosexual tryst. She had witnessed how enthused and excited he became when he sodomized that football player. She had seen where he couldn't, and she had exposed feelings he didn't know he possessed. Now that he looked back on those times, he realized that he *had* enjoyed the tightness of anal sex with that man. He had tried to get his aunt to try it with him, but all she did was smile and shake her head no. Later on, she had explained that watching him enjoy a homosexual high was what made the scene so heady and worthwhile, and so she had made him do it again and again. He never refused, and now he knew why. He liked fucking men. He liked fucking that giant football player's ass. And he *loved* fucking Michael's lovely tight channel best of all. Damn Aunt Doreen! She knew. She knew . . .

Jason continued to curse himself opposite the three women, but at the same time he couldn't wait to see what would happen next. Even though it would be painful to watch, and painful for his new lover, he knew that Michael would be the better off for it. Before the end of the night he would move on to the next phase of his treatment—treatment that would make him a better and happier man. And that was Pleasure. No matter what you thought of the business, and what you thought of different sexual variations, you had to give the island that. Whenever you walked through the castle's doors, you walked out a better person. That was the main objective. No matter what you were doing there, no matter what deviancy you were into, that was always the objective. That was positive, and that was good.

His thoughts suddenly turned to his aunt, his first true love. He didn't know where she had gone, but he suddenly missed her deeply. He wished that she could tie him up like she had done in the past and make him do things he would never do without her direction. She had broadened his horizons, and he needed her now to show him even more. He wanted her to meet Michael and watch them make love. He wanted her to masturbate over them like she had when he had explosively orgasmed inside the tight regions of the football player. He almost came in front of the three women on the other side of the chamber, thinking about what she had commanded him to do over time, but he knew he would have to hold off. Soon he would be asked to sodomize Michael in front of his wife for a long period, just the three of them in this circular basement, and he didn't want to blow that. If he did, Alfred would surely kill him and throw him out in the watery boneyard in the ocean. That scenario he would try to prevent at all costs, and he hoped in the future that would never happen, but in his not too distant future he was sure that he would be seeing Dr. Levers, and he would be seeing her beautiful face and body in too much pain to satisfy himself with her. In fact, having sex with *anyone* at that time, even Michael, would be the furthest thing from his mind. A prophet he sometimes was . . .

Wendy had a short black strap in her right hand, about twelve inches long and an inch and a half wide, and she slowly and methodically circled the chained Michael MacDonald. Every so often she reached in and carefully felt his aroused bobbing penis and his tight scrotum below. She went around behind him and massaged and squeezed the lawyer's ass cheeks sensually, running her long, manicured fingernails gently down his man crack, stopping at his puckered, moist anus. She quickly and viciously rammed her middle finger into his rectum and began wiggling it back and forth at various speeds. That had its effects, it always did, for Michael started moaning in sadistic pain and pleasure, and pushed back as best he could toward the dominant, squeezing and unsqueezing his aroused anus, like he had been taught by Jason.

"That's good, slave Michael," Wendy cooed in his ear, her warm breath blowing through his earhole to his sexually infected brain. She bit his earlobe lightly, but enough to make him wince, and whispered, "From this moment on you will treat all women with total respect, even though you prefer sex with men." He nodded in acknowledgment and promised he would. She also told him that he would from this day forward treat his wife like a queen, even though she now belonged to her new mistress, and that compared to her, he was nothing. He nodded again, and then she drove the nail all the way in. "Also, from now on you must ask Mistress Marlo anytime you might want to have sex with your wife. You no longer are spiritually married to her, and from now on you will always be second fiddle to her. She loves and craves her new owner much more than she even remotely wants *you!*" This she said so everybody could hear, and to emphasize that, she turned to Susan and asked the island's new slave, "Isn't that true, slave Susan?"

"Yes," Susan replied, bowing her head toward this new dominant. She realized that this woman was as beautiful as her owner, and she was becoming moist between her legs. This new woman was also turning her on strongly, and she hoped that Mistress Marlo would lend her to Wendy at some future time.

Wendy stared at Susan as if she couldn't believe what she had just heard. "Yes *what?*" she challenged, raising her voice.

"Yes, Mistress," Susan quickly corrected herself meekly. She bowed her head in embarrassment.

"That's right, slave," Wendy hissed, shooting daggers through the female submissive. "Every woman employed by your owner is your mistress, and every man employed here is your master, and you shall address them as such. And as long as you are physically on this island, you will be used sexually in any way they want to exploit you. Do you understand, slave?"

"Ye . . . yes, mistress," she stammered. "I understand."

And then Wendy, who is and always would be a perfect dominant sadist, pushed the final nail in. "And do you realize that *that* could include your perfectly shaped sweet ass, slave Susan?" she asked, making sure that the female slave knew that Wendy was talking directly to her. It was a tactful way to drive a certain topic home, and the female dominant used it whenever the situation required it. She studied the new client as she spoke. She *was* cute, and she had all the right curves. She wasn't young, but she was seasoned. She had a perfectly shaped behind, and amazingly toned upper thighs. She would sample this slave at the right appointed time, and would give that ass all the attention it needed. Wendy thought of something devious, and so she smiled wickedly before Susan could respond, and asked slowly in a lowered tone, "Have you ever been fucked up the ass, slave Susan?"

Susan thought about this question before answering, for the question was tricky to some extent. Her mistress had used a strap-on dildo on her anus quite a bit on their first encounter, but even *that* wasn't the first time. Joan had also used her in that manner countless times. Not only had she quickly learned to love it, but it made her feel more owned as each thrust was made. It was heady, completely over her sexual ledge, and she swore to Joan that Michael and all others would never invade her mistress's cherry. That was hers alone, her owner's command, but she had new owners now, and she knew she'd now have to change her stance on the matter.

"Only by my mistress," she finally replied, nodding at Marlo. "Mistress Marlo knows all about it."

Michael turned his head at that, and then quickly turned back around and looked down at the floor, defeated and hurt. He had tried to do that for years, and Marlo had been able to do it right away. He now knew where he stood. He had Jason, and it had felt wonderful when he had sodomized his tight back passage, but it still hurt, though. Reality hurt, and the actual act reminded you time and time again. He listened intently as this dominant continued.

Wendy turned to witness Michael's shocked reaction, and as she saw him drop his head, she pushed further. This nail needed to be hammered straight into both their fractured souls. "But have you ever been fucked up your tight asshole by a man?"

Susan quickly shook her head, and replied, "No, Mistress."

"No, Mistress, what?"

"No, Mistress, I have never been fucked up my tight asshole by a man. Never, not even my husband, even though he has asked me to let him do that many times."

Wendy smiled triumphantly as the slave confessed. They had her now, and Pleasure would take her down roads she had never traveled. Their options were infinite, and the company would use each and every one of them on this female submissive and get rich in the process.

"But you will now, slave Susan," and this time it wasn't a question, but a factual command. "Before the end of your venture here on Pleasure Island, I will personally make sure that every male employee gets the chance to fuck you in your sweet shapely ass, and it will be filmed and filed away for our viewing in our archives. You might have your own fantasies to live out, but that works both ways. We have them also, and we act on ours as well. We all benefit from them in the end, and are all better human beings for it in the process. Answer truthfully, slave Susan, do you have any problem with the men here using you in this manner?"

"N . . . no, mistress, I don't. I don't really want to, but I know I no longer control my life, and I will do anything that my owners ask of me. I will do anything to prevent losing her—or you."

"Good," Wendy said evenly. She looked over at Marlo and stated, "I think we have the right confession and answers we want out of her for the time being." She looked back at Susan and lowered her voice, "Slave Susan, let me tell you a final bit of information that concerns your immediate future. Before the end of the night a male employee or a person of our choice will deflower your precious tight asshole—maybe more than once—and myself and your new owner will witness it. Do you understand me?"

Susan shook all over but nodded her head. "Y . . . yes, mistress, I understand. I understand fully. And . . . and I will try my best to enjoy it, if it pleases you and Mistress."

"Good!" Wendy said happily, but then added, "Oh, and by the way, and I think your new owner will agree with me. Your husband Michael will also fuck your beautiful ass, but only if he asks Mistress Marlo nicely. In fact, I think he will sodomize you more than anybody else in the future. That will be your punishment for not being a proper wife. A woman married to a man should never stop her beloved husband from using all avenues of sexual fulfillment. A woman who acts like that should be skinned alive and thrown out of her home to the wolves waiting outside. What a bitch you are, you righteous cunt. You'll learn, and learn in a hurry, and be better for it."

Susan wanted to explain that she wanted to keep her promise to Joan but decided against that. Joan was in the past, and Marlo was her future. She would *not* lose a mistress again, for she now knew she could never live another day without one. She hung her head in shame, for she had, indeed, been shamed, stripped of her pride in every way. This new mistress was extremely good at her job, and Susan would do whatever the dominant said, but Mistress Marlo, her owner, could never be topped. Susan took pride in that, that the owner of Pleasure was her first choice—her ONLY choice, really, and that could never be changed.

Michael hung from his chains, hearing what was transpiring between this new dominant and his wife, and he couldn't believe how his—their—lives had been changed by this place already. He couldn't thank them enough. So many people go through their entire lives not being themselves, living lives *others* wanted for you—for *them*. For them . . . It takes a brave person to live your life for you, especially when you have different needs than the norm—needs people say are wrong. Michael reasoned that they are only wrong when it doesn't justify the lives *they* believe in.

Michael knew that he was different longer than he could remember. He grew up in a strict Catholic family. He had two older sisters that both married young and moved away from their parents because they wouldn't let them live as they pleased. If the church said you should live a certain way, you did. There was no grey, only black and white. And that is always the magic word, isn't it? Grey. The grey. The space between constants. The church says you should go to service every Sunday. You should worship God. You should follow the ten commandments to the letter. You should . . . not be gay. Not be homosexual. The outlooks on that had somewhat changed, but . . . Michael had had those thoughts from the time he turned nine, or maybe before that. People that belonged to the church said that if you *were* gay, you'd go to hell. They said you had a *choice*. A choice—really?!

He had these thoughts, these desires, and he was *forced* to suppress them. Was that right? Was that humane? Should he suppress who he was? God had made him who he was, and it wasn't what the church had said he should be. Who was right, and who was wrong? It remained a dilemma until he realized it didn't matter if it was right or wrong. He had to take himself out of the black and white zone and move into the grey realm. He had to move away from what other people *wanted* him to be and jump into the current that went another way. When he, by accident really, defended a client from a situation at Pleasure Island, a door had been opened to him, and he had bravely walked through it. He decided to see if they were the answer, and they were. They almost made it too easy. He talked about how he felt, and nobody was shocked—nobody thought he was evil and condemned to the endless fires of hell. They didn't think in black and white; they thought that he should be himself, and that was beautiful. They told him it was OK to be straight, it was OK to be gay—it was OK to be *different*. It was . . . *enlightening!*

Michael began to weep as he first stared over at Jason, and then looked over his shoulder at his wife, the life that was mostly a lie. Yes, he still and would always love her, but look at her now. Her life had been a lie as well, but now she was happy. She was content! Even as she was physiologically brought to her knees. She was so beautiful, but there was a new light shining in her eyes, and even though that dominant had made her be who she *needed* to be, and it hurt, it needed to be said, and it needed to be done. Plus, on a selfish note, he would get to do the one thing he had never been able to do. And that would be good too—for both of them, hopefully.

Wendy Haas came up behind Michael with the strap and brought it down hard across his defenseless backside. An angry red welt suddenly appeared, and he didn't hide his feelings as he received more shots to his reddening behind. He screamed for mercy that even *he* knew wasn't coming. He was told he was being punished for not being the man he should've been—for himself and for his wife. He was told that he would receive more of the same in the future if he didn't improve at every level. Just when Michael thought he couldn't take any more, Wendy stopped and stepped back until she tapped Susan on the shoulder and nodded toward her husband. Susan smiled weakly at the dominant, and then stepped behind her husband. She saw the angry welts, and even though she felt sorry for him, she knew he had needed them. He could've and should've treated her better. She would make sure he didn't repeat his mistake in the future, and she vocally told him so as she reigned down shots of brutality across his already battered rump. The whalebone cane bit into his meaty cheeks, and they shook with each atomic shot, bringing new feelings of agony which went way beyond what Michael could take.

He screamed and begged and begged and screamed. He told his wife that he would learn, and never repeat his mistakes. He told her he would treat her like a queen and respect her like the royalty she was. It was only when he hung his head and passed out that she stopped hitting him. She was screaming herself, screaming her hurt. Marlo came up and put her arms around her slave until she quieted, and then guided her property back to where Wendy was smiling. They all stared at Michael's ass, and it was severely damaged. Blood ran from many cuts, and if a few of them turned to scars, then he would wear them proudly as a sign of becoming a better man and husband. Jason, on the other hand, was openly crying. He knew that Michael needed this, but it still hurt. He wanted to go to his lover, but Marlo had told him hours before in her office not to assist him in any way. It was her slave's husband's cross to bear, and he would carry it alone.

THE SUPERNATURAL JOINS THE GROUP

It happened when Wendy started toward Michael. He was just regaining consciousness, and she froze in place against her will. So did Jason, Marlo, and even Michael. Only Susan could move, think, and hear—and *see*. She heard distant footsteps coming down the castle steps slowly. A shadow entered the chamber before the person, and that person was Joan! Joan from her past, the dominant she had missed and loved so dearly; the one she thought about every time she had sex. Joan looked the same, yet completely different. Now she looked very angry, and betrayed. She was dressed in a black dress that hugged her curves, and what sweet curves they were.

"There you are, my little slave," Joan said softly, but there was malice behind that voice. "Come to me and worship your true mistress."

Susan immediately scurried over to Joan, got down on her knees, and began kissing her dominant's hand, which was offered to her. "You've been a bad little, girl, haven't you?" Joan asked, looking down at her slave. "And you've broken your vow to stay virgin."

Susan shuttered, for she knew what she was talking about, and so she intensified her kissing. She knew her mistress was right, right to be angry, but how could she have known. It was a chaotic conundrum—one that had dead ends in every direction. She felt terrible, though. Now that Joan was actually here, she realized that Marlo meant nothing to her, as well as Michael, or any of the others. Tears streamed down her face, as she slowly looked up into the beautiful majestic face she loved so much. "I'm so sorry, Mistress. I thought that you would never return, but I love you so much; I've never stopped loving you. I'll do anything you want to make up for my disgraces, but please forgive me."

"You're damn right you'll do anything," Joan screeched, her anger echoing off the dungeon's stone walls. Susan shuttered as Joan walked away from her and moved over to the stationary Marlo. "And you threw it all away for . . . this! Susan, she's nothing but a harlot, a fake. And you let her use my *entrance!* You will pay for that!" And then she kissed Marlo on the lips and fondled her body. Susan crawled to them, jealousy raging through her soul. She cried as she licked her mistress's boots.

"Jealous, are you, my little slut?"

Joan raised her right hand, and then Jason suddenly moved toward Michael, who came back to life. Joan became a puppeteer, and Jason and Michael became the puppets. The Pleasure trainer got down on his knees and began giving oral to the lawyer. He moaned and groaned until he orgasmed heavily into Jason's sucking mouth. Jason then got up and went around behind Michael and entered his anus roughly. The lawyer yelped; his backside in agony, but he could put up with that as long as his lover was inside his stretched rectum. Susan watched as they moved in unison and listened to their moans of pleasure. When Jason orgasmed, he screamed at the top of his lungs, looking up at the chamber ceiling. When he had finished, like a robot he withdrew himself from Michael, went back across the room, and froze in place again.

Susan felt a little jealous, but nothing compared to when Joan kissed a stationary Marlo. That was much worse. She could never imagine seeing her mistress with anybody else—no matter *who* they were. Joan snapped her fingers, and Wendy walked behind the lawyer and began whipping Michael again with her strap. She hit him hard, again and again, and this time she also included his whole back and thighs. He screamed and screamed in terminal agony, but the dominatrix just kept hitting him. This time Michael was *not* allowed to pass out, and his suffering was great, his screams echoing off the dungeon's walls. Joan finally snapped her fingers, and Wendy stopped mid-whip, stepped back, and froze. Michael didn't, though. He continued screaming as blood ran down his body. It fell to the floor, creating a small puddle.

Joan abruptly went to him, slapped his backside hard several times, and told him to shut up. He screamed even louder when she spanked his ass, and so she grabbed his head with both hands and twisted it viciously until it completely ripped off his neck, severing every artery. Susan screamed in horror as blood flew in a torrent out of his neck, the rest of his body hanging limply, lifeless. Joan threw her husband's head viciously against the wall, and it was only then that the lawyer stopped screaming. Joan then came back to Susan, glaring down at her cheating property.

"On your feet, bitch!" she screamed, and Susan stood up quickly, crying, screaming, and becoming aroused all at the same time. "And shut your stupid, gutless mouth, you cheating whore! I have things to tell you, and you must hear them."

Susan stopped screaming instantly. Did I have the power to stop screaming so suddenly, or did Joan do it? Who *is* Joan? What *is* this woman? she asked herself, staring submissively up at her mistress.

"What I am, you ask?" Joan replied, obviously hearing Susan's thoughts. "I am a witch named Rutherynna. I have lived for countless centuries—more than you can fathom. I am married to a warlock named Thorzeous, and we take souls in our wake. Yours is next. I took all of your family's souls as well just before we murdered them. Your parents lost them to me in a bet they shouldn't have made. It was a very stupid bet, and your last thoughts should be ones of *hate* for them. They are the ones responsible for all your family's suffering. One by one I killed your siblings off and received my payment. What a stupid, self-centered bitch you grew up to be. I never loved you, I just fed you lies to continue my game, and you swallowed them all up without even thinking. I guess the saying you humans made up is correct: the apple doesn't fall too far from the tree. But let me remind you that I *don't* love you; I hate you. I always have. I want you to know that. I wanted to steal away your love first, before I finished the job, you worthless piece of excrement. You make me sick; you are a stinking piece of shit! Now, finally, it is your turn."

With that said, Susan froze in place, but she was still aware—very much aware. She saw a very tall man in a long, black, hooded cloak suddenly appear in the dungeon next to his witch wife, and he was carrying a musical box that looked very old—ancient, even. He handed the box to Rutherynna, and she opened it. A strange tune began playing, and then Susan felt her soul and her essence slowly leave her body and move toward the sinister sounds coming out of it. She tried her hardest to fight it, but she was powerless to stop it. She saw her body receding behind her, still frozen in place. It now looked like a ghost ship. Nobody was on board; it had become a Flying Dutchman, a vessel in legend lore that floated listlessly over the oceans of time with no real purpose.

Susan continued traveling on the strong current, and just before her soul entered the musical box she saw the eyes of many centipede-type beings waiting just inside its darkness. She automatically knew they were waiting for her, for they silently called her name passively over and over again, as if they had known long ago that she had been promised to them, and that's when she finally realized her fate was sealed. Her traveling soul completely entered the box and the lid slowly closed shut. Darkness completely surrounded her, but that was not the only thing that did. She screamed and screamed as she suddenly heard the distant screams of others, some she even recognized.

Thorzeous and Rutherynna walked around the dank dungeon, touching each of the Pleasure employees on the forehead. Then Thorzeous picked up the head of Michael MacDonald by the hair and looked into his eyes, which were unbelievably open and seeing. Michael stared back in horror, for he was still aware and alive. He couldn't move, his body was no longer there, but he could think, see, hear, and worst of all, feel. He felt the pain where his head had been severed from the rest of his body, and that pain was intense. It burned, it stung, and it *raged!* His mouth screamed in silence, for he no longer possessed vocal cords. They had been left behind in his lifeless neck, atop a body that felt so very far away now. He looked into the red piercing eyes of the evil looking warlock, and knew his future and fate would not be pleasant.

"Oh, if you only knew," the Warlock voiced out loud, smirking, obviously hearing his thoughts. "If you only knew…" And then the married couple suddenly disappeared, along with the lawyer's living, severed head.

As their travels began through the couple's wormhole passageway and into their personal realm, Michael saw many things—things that would drive most completely mad. If he could, he would only explain it this way: "It was horror beyond horror." He no longer cared about what he wanted, or who he was. He no longer cared about his love for Jason, or the future they might've shared together. He cared about nothing but pain and despair, and the inhumanities he had already seen, plus the ones that lay ahead. He silently continued to scream, and realized that this hell was much worse than the one described in the Bible—and that wasn't to say that *that* hell didn't exist as well. It probably did, and it was possibly even worse than this one. "Oh, it does exist," Thorzeous said absentmindedly, still listening to the condemned lawyer's thoughts. "And no court can get you out of this sentence, *boy!*"

The warlock and the witch moved onward slowly. They didn't move by walking or running. No, their legs remained completely still while they angled slightly forward and rode the current of a motionless wind. Rutherynna, holding the old musical box, opened it and listened to its eerie song. The tune had changed ever so slightly. It always did whenever another soul was added to its count. Now there was only a few more things to do before this chapter in their long existence was complete. Rutheryanna and her devoted husband Thorzeous would certainly relish in that conclusion. The evil married couple looked at each other as they passed through new caverns of despair and smiled wickedly. Yes, they surely would.

After Thorzeous and Rutherynna had left the dungeon, Marlo, Jason, and Wendy slowly unfroze. When they saw the beheaded body of Michael MacDonald and the slumped-over body of Susan MacDonald laying in the corner, they did 'the slow freak'. Thorzeous had touched their foreheads, making them believe they had murdered the MacDonald's. They were hypnotized even now, and in a daze Marlo dialed 911. She told them there had been two murders out at Pleasure, and that Marlo, Jason, Wendy, and Alfred Altman had been responsible. The authorities helicoptered out, saw the two dead bodies, and arrested them all.

Alfred had been doing some paperwork when all this was happening, and he, too, had frozen in place. When the FBI found him, they had to shake him to get him moving. He was also hypnotized, and he told them outright that he had murdered at least twenty-five people in the last twelve months before he could even think about what he was saying. Carl Rosen was the only one who hadn't been affected, but he didn't know of any of what had gone down.

They were all held in custody, and confessed to every person the FBI was looking for. Marlo told the authorities that she had all the evidence they would need in her safe room, a room behind a bookcase in her private suite. There were computers, laptops, and piles of paperwork describing various missing people, what had been done to them, and where they'd been disposed of. The water boneyard was found, and divers found many body parts of the victims.

Still, there were many loose ends plus other cases left unsolved when the power went out. When that happened, Marlo Freeman was the only one who didn't go back to The Creator. She was in a cell in the county jail, waiting for sentencing. She completely came out of her hypnotic state, totally confused. The last thing she remembered was being in Dungeon Three with the MacDonalds. How did she end up in a jail cell? She yelled out, but nobody answered back. The lights were out, and as day became night the shadows disappeared into the darkness. It was quiet—too quiet for Marlo. She began yelling, but still no one came. She shook the cell door in frustration, and then sat down. She was frightened. What if something *had* happened, and she was here alone? How would she get out? She laid down on the cell cot and dosed off. The dreams she had did not put her at ease.

After Sam MacDonald was released and taken home after being interviewed by the authorities, he for once cleaned up his rented room. Why? Because he had been trained to. Part of his job as a Pleasure slave was cleaning up, not just after himself, but others as well. He had to wear a little French maid outfit while doing so, which showed off half his rear cheeks. This also served another purpose, which was to embarrass him. They were successful on that front, for whenever he passed somebody in the hallway he lowered his head in shame. People, employees as well as clients giggled as they passed, and all he wanted to do was disappear.

When he was finished straightening out his living area, he dressed in a nice sweat suit, shaved, called a cab, and was dropped off at The Golden Goose, a Bar located at the end of South Main. He went inside and ordered a gin and tonic at the end of the bar. As he sat there, Sam reminisced about his wild and crazy ride out at Pleasure Island. Some thoughts were good—most bad. He did realize that he came out of it all a better person. He now cared and respected everyone he met, and he felt happier. He hadn't been too happy about Pleasure's methods, but they had certainly worked.

As he was halfway through his second drink, a bald black man sat down next to him and ordered a beer. He said hello, and they began talking. The talking turned to laughter, and all memories of Pleasure faded into the background, forgotten for the time being. Eventually they left together, and the man, whose name was Juan Perez (at least that's what he told Sam) drove him to his apartment, and they had a few more drinks. It got quiet, and then Juan grabbed Sam's hand and led him into his bedroom without saying a word. As you can surmise they didn't sleep much, and in the morning Sam was extremely sore. He felt wonderful, though, and he whistled as he went into the kitchen, made breakfast for the two of them, and took it back to the bedroom, closing the door behind him. That door didn't open again until the sun was going down, and the shadows became long.

When the power went out, Glorifinia was in the wormhole on her way to Pleasure Island to visit her good friend Alfred Altman. She was hungry for both nourishment and sex, two things she craved desperately. Her master had enslaved and imprisoned her in so many ways. Sometimes she wished for her past life, but had she really wanted that life? If she answered honestly, it would be no. She never really even *liked* the boy she was to marry in her tribe, and that was why when it came down to it, she made him suffer the worst. Even after all these many years, his screams were what she remembered most about her tribe's demise. Oh, how he had suffered and paid for spitting in her face! He was practically nothing but bones and a beating heart before he finally left this world. No, the more she thought about her past life, the meaner and angrier she became. Would she take it out on Alfred, or the sacrifice he'd have waiting for her in his closet? Maybe this time it would be both.

Alfred was quite a gem. He ruled and bullied the humans that existed around him, and she took great pleasure in making him beg like a little bitch for the smallest of things, like his life. She would threaten to eat him alive just to see the fright behind those beady little eyes of his. He got a good dose of his own medicine, and she reveled in it. She even made him pay during their sexual romps. Sometimes she would act so docile and proper, and give him oral better than he'd ever had it, and then bite his penis off just before he ejaculated. Oh, how sweet the music sounded with his various-pitched screams before she worked her magic and re-attached his traumatized member. She laughed at his shocked expression, and then threatened him with a repeat performance if he didn't do as she said and be a submissive little meek slave. He'd kiss and lick her dirty bare feet and promise to be a good little bitch for all time. What a high that was! No, this time she would let him off easy, but he better give it to her good, and follow her every direction, or he'd be sorry. Boy, would he! Maybe this time she would *only* threaten to eat his eyes and leave him blind. You had to keep them on their toes, you know!

As Glorifinia appeared inside his Pleasure suite, Alfred wasn't there. That never happened. Something was different, she could sense it. She went to the closet and ripped the door from its hinges, but there was no nourishment there, either. Just the ropes lying on the floor that he used to tie them up with. Now she definitely knew something was adrift. She had scratched his brain days ago to let him know she was on her way, and now nothing was here. She listened intently, and realized that she didn't hear animal, wildlife, or insect life either. Now she became uneasy, frightened even. Something major had happened in this part of the world, and she didn't like or understand it. Glorifinia walked out of the suite and down the hallway to the window that faced the sea. The movement of the ocean remained the same, and the sky looked normal. She sniffed the air, and suddenly smelled normal flesh. It was off to the north, she was sure of it. Flesh in all its glory, and it was alive.

The air in front of her rippled, and she reentered the wormhole and sped toward the northern airwaves in front of her. She materialized inside a jailhouse and quickly looked all around, expecting just about anything, but it was empty. No one was here, and there was the same absence of wildlife banter. She listened intently, and then heard movement in the last cell. It sounded like the snore of a sleeping body. She quietly walked to the front of the cell and saw a woman, a very beautiful woman. As her eyes adjusted to the darkness, she saw the face she'd seen before. It was the owner of Pleasure Island, Marlo Freeman! She had heard all about this pristine bitch from Alfred. What was she doing here? Rhetorical question, for it didn't matter. All she knew was that it was the only thing living in these parts. She murmured a few foreign words in front of the cell door, and it slowly opened on its own.

As Marlo slowly awoke she foggily saw the outline of a person moving into the cell. And was it just her imagination, or was the figure slowly gliding towards her a foot above the floor? Her first thought was that she was finally saved. Her second was that she was totally wrong, for as she was about to speak, she heard a hungry voice cackle, "Wakey, wakey, eggs and bakey." A few moments later the screaming started. They were pitiful sounds, which changed in pitch to indescribable agony. They lasted a long time—a very long time.

A short time after Rutherynna and Thorzeous left Pleasure Island (the Warlock still holding Michael MacDonald's head by his hair), they all materialized inside a large room filled with senior citizens. "An old folks' home," the couple both said to him telepathically at the same time. "Happy Pines, it's called, but that's a joke. Nobody here is really happy; they're old and fearful of death, which could happen at any moment. Now mind your manners, for you're about to meet your wife's parents. We hope you like them . . ." Their thoughts trailed off as they glided toward an old couple sitting in the corner. Michael stared at them and couldn't believe that these people were Susan's parents. Grandparents, yes, but not mother and father! They were both dressed in old, wrinkled, faded-blue sweat suits, and cheap white sneakers. Both had hair that was thinning and completely white. John Stansfield wore thick black glasses that made his eyes seem twice as large, and his face was completely wrinkled. He had sores on his parched dry lips, and had no teeth. He looked ready to celebrate his one hundredth birthday, but one he wouldn't be aware of.

Millie wasn't much better. You could tell she had been a very pretty woman at one time, but by the wrinkles she sported now that appeared to be a very long time ago. Her nose was crooked, as if it might've been broken at one time or another, and one lazy eye sagged lower than the other. She was also missing teeth, and her tongue lifelessly hung to one side. They both stared up at the ceiling, their mouths hanging open as if in wonder, looking at something that didn't seem to be there. "Oh, it's there, cupcake, it's there," the evil couple responded, stopping in front of them. "What they are looking at is a poker hand," they told him. "A losing hand—one that cost them their whole family. Now watch what happens . . ."

The warlock let go of Michael's hair, and his head suddenly was thrust back into the dim, dank wormhole tunnel. His head twisted and churned through its pipe-like structure, and he tele-pathically was told by the evil couple that he was traveling back through time. As the clock's hands moved backward he re-aquired his body and became whole again. Eventually he slowed to a stop, and he physically found himself in a smoke-filled room standing behind a card game in Las Vegas. He didn't know what hotel it was, but it was in a back room, private and quiet.

Four people sat at a table in the middle of the room. A dim light shined overhead, and the light bulb blinked on and off every so often. The rest of the room was bare, except for a small bar over by a closed door, and a small lamp on each end shined brightly. The walls and ceiling were white, and the floor was tiled dark blue. The two men were smoking thick cigars, and both women were passing a joint back and forth. Glasses of scotch and ice sat next to each individual, and all four seemed to be enjoying each other's company, even though you could tell they were playing high-stakes hands. Michael recognized two of them immediately: Thorzeous and Rutherynna. He knew their names well now; in fact, he knew *too* much about them. Telepathically they were all connected, their brainwaves inter-twined. The other two looked familiar, but he wasn't sure if they were Susan's parents or not.

The Thorzeous that sat at the card table put his cards down, looked directly at Michael, and said out loud, "They are your wife Susan's parents back on their honeymoon night, many years ago. They are young, they love to gamble, and they are quite stupid. Playing cards with them is like taking candy from a baby. And really, what kind of person would want to gamble instead of soiling his new wife's body in a heart-shaped bed? Think about it, Michael. Millie, in all her glory, is there for the taking on her first night as a married woman, more than she ever will be. She is not a virgin, not by any means, but she is ready to be defiled in so many different types of ways. *We* know that, but her husband is oblivious to her needs and only wants to gamble. He is a slave to the cards, and so she says nothing, even though she is dripping wet between the legs. That is unacceptable on every level, and so they both deserved to be dealt with—no pun intended."

The Warlock then turned back to face the Stansfield's, and picked up his cards, smiling. Susan's parents don't appear to hear him speak, and so they continue playing the hand.

Rutherynna looked at Michael, adding, "They really suck at cards. Usually we dismiss people like this; we only go after the goody two-shoes, but these two stick out, and totally disgust us. They are both good looking and sexy, as you can see," she states, holding out her hand to them, "but they must be taught a lesson and be punished severely."

Michael looked at the couple, and they *did* look good. John Stansfield was handsome enough to be a movie star, a lead-role type of actor. He had jet black, wavy hair that was thicker than thick—an Elvis Presley look-alike, just perfect for this city. A man that looked like he did was made for this town, the condemned lawyer thought. Maybe they're just--

"Jealous?" Thorzeous asked, finishing the thought and turning to face Michael again. "Maybe just a little, or maybe I just didn't like his face. It doesn't matter; he's still going to lose this hand." Turning back to his cards, he said, "Give me two, John, and make 'em good." The two men laugh, one nervously, and the women giggled as they passed their joint back and forth.

Michael looked over at them, at Millie, really, and saw Susan in her. God, they looked alike. The same colored hair, the same face. Even her body looked like his wife's—

"And that *great ass*," Rutherynna finished, inhaling and handing the joint back to his mother-in-law. "She had that same great backside." She grabbed Millie's right ass cheek, and they both smiled warmly at each other. "I gotta tell you, Michael, I enjoyed this ass just as much as I enjoyed your wife's. Goddamn Susan . . . she could've been a star." The witch bore a hole through Michael's soul when she said, "Your wonderful wife begged me to fuck her ass 'til the end of time, just like her mommy did." Both women laughed, and then soul kissed while the men got down to the nitty gritty.

Cutting to the chase, John, of course, lost. He had two pair, two kings and two jacks, but Thorzeous had four queens. "Fuck me, Freddie!" John yelled, slamming down his fist on the table. "Double or nothing!"

Thorzeous stood up and shook his head. He grabbed the money on the table and handed it to Rutherynna. "No sir, you have no more cash, and I'm not going to let you lose everything you own. That, my good friend, can be very unsettling."

"Please, please," John countered, begging. "That was all the cash we had—all our honeymoon money. We can't leave this way. What else could we bet to make you play one more hand?" Michael's father-in-law desperately grabbed Thorzeous's wrist.

The warlock looked down at his held wrist, and John quickly let go. The big man scratched his beard and thought. He looked at them all, and then bent over and whispered something in his wife's ear.

Don't do it! Michael thought frantically, making two fists. Please don't do it!

"Don't do what?" Rutherynna asked, nodding at her husband. Then she looked at Michael with a wicked smile. "We have to give them a chance, little butt-boy, otherwise they won't have a bed to debase themselves in. We like to help the worthless!" And then the evil duo laughed sadistically. Rutherynna grabbed Millie's shapely ass again, and the lawyer knew that ass would be in the wager. "Oh yeah, it will be in there somewhere," the witch answered, nodding. "It's just too perfect not to own."

Millie either didn't hear or mind what the witch was saying, but Michael sure agreed with her. Mother and daughter had the same perfect ass, and if only Susan would've—

"That was not yours to take!" Rutherynna screamed, and the lawyer felt two imaginary hands close around his throat and start to choke the life out of him. He was lifted a foot into the air, and his vision quickly started to go black. "That was my property!" The Witch was livid, and Michael would've been a goner for sure if not for the warlock quickly going to his wife and calming her.

"Shhhh, Rutherynna," he whispered in her ear. "Remember, we have other plans for him. Besides, he needs to see all of this."

"But!"

"But nothing! Relax. Relax, my love."

And then Michael felt the choke hold loosening. His vision returned, and he fell to the floor in a heap. He struggled to his feet, gasping for air. "I'm . . . I'm sorry. I was—"

"You were trying to take something that was not yours," the witch interrupted, snarling at him. "You tried to be a thief in the night, just like that bitch Marlo! You better watch your thoughts, cock lover, and mind your manners. You hear me?"

"Yes, Rutherynna."

"Yes, Mistress. We are not equals by any stretch of the imagination."

"Yes, Mistress. I'm sorry; I won't disrespect you again."

The witch just nodded, and then went back to fondling Millie's rear cheeks with both hands, and his mother-in-law sighed happily. Thorzeous coughed, and then Rutherynna smiled meekly, and then turned to face the two men. "How badly do you want to win back your money, John?"

Rutherynna held up her hand, and the newlyweds froze. She turned and faced Michael again, taking a serious tone. "John and Millie Stansfield: you met them, and you know how they are, or appear to be. They are good Christian people who go to church every Sunday and say prayers to God before every meal. They raised their children to be good Christians as well. They were all good in school, and stayed out of trouble, all except your wife. Susan was a little different. She was a rebel, and sometimes she took those characteristics to new levels. She was also the prettiest of the girls—a carbon copy of her mother. But her parents weren't all what they appeared to be. They both had a big gambling problem, and they had different types of sexual tastes, which they both found out about themselves early on in their relationship. They kept those tastes under wraps, but we exploited them as they proudly entered the realm of the city that never sleeps.

"They got to Las Vegas as the sun was setting, lost some of their spending money, and then went on the prowl. They hired a female hooker down at the new meat pound joint, but she never made it to their honeymoon suite. We intercepted her and her bodyguard and paid them twice the amount just to find out what they were into; then sent them away without any memory of us or the Stansfields. The prostitute knew plenty about them; clients needed to tell the staff what they were into so they could send the right trick to their room for their pleasures.

"What we found out was shocking! They were both huge submissives and wanted to be punished with various whips and straps, plus they were into being spanked over a lap. Punish was the magic word here. They needed to be punished so God would forgive them their lewd sins. They both liked to be sodomized by either a man or woman, but preferred a woman with a large strap-on. They were basic sex slaves who were constantly looking for a dominant to discipline them. Well, they were going to get what they paid for, and more.

"While Thorzeous went to handle some other business down on The Strip, the Stansfields were going to encounter me. I didn't disappoint. They let me in, and let me tell you, they were even further down the road to shame than first thought. I gave them what they wanted, and much more. I won't go into details, but by the time I left their suite they would do anything for me—and later on, they did. I gave them an address and they came to our room in old Las Vegas. They met Thorzeous, who I said was my boyfriend, and we partied and gambled until dawn. By the end of the night they had lost everything, and John was desperate.

"Millie was so taken with me that even though she had just gotten married, she would've left John in a second if I told her to. I was quite smitten as well, but my feelings were totally under control. She had that great ass, though, and it could be intoxicating. Anyway, here is what they bet in that last hand. They both thought it was a no-lose gamble, but they were both terribly wrong. Now watch."

Rutherynna put her hand down, and the Stansfield's unfroze again. "I want to win it back bad," John replied desperately. "We won't be able to stay for our honeymoon if I don't get to at least play."

"What else could you bet, then?"

"All we have is ourselves," John said dejectedly, holding out his hands. "Only ourselves."

Rutherynna stared at him for a moment, and then said, "Give us a minute," and then motioned Thorzeous over to the bar. They conversed quietly for a few minutes, and then came back to the card table. The warlock sat back down opposite John and stared hard at him. Rutherynna went over to Millie and put her arm around her waist and lightly squeezed her right ass cheek. The warlock told John, "My friend, here is the deal. I don't want to ruin your honeymoon, and I refuse to. But I will play one more hand. Are you ready to hear my bet?"

"Yes! Yes!" John excitedly replied. He took another swig of his drink and relit his cigar.

"OK then," the warlock continued, puffing on his own cigar. "This is what I propose. If you win, John, you win all your money back and we will all go our separate ways, but if I win, you two will *still* get all your money back, but then we own you both. Now before you go crazy, let me tell you what that would entail. For the rest of your stay here we would have a foursome, and every so often after that we would visit you to collect interest on your payment. Now Rutherynna told me about your tryst and your desires. It doesn't sound too bad, does it?"

John looked at Millie, who was enjoying Rutherynna's hand massaging her ass, and she readily nodded. "OK, OK, we're good."

"Are you sure?"

"Yes, yes, we're sure."

That was the worst decision they could have made. Of course Thorzeous beat John, and their lives slowly deteriorated. For the next three days the evil couple ran the couple through their paces, and *that* sex was great. During that time Millie was taken by Rutherynna into a separate suite the dominant couple had reserved down the hall and was overwhelmed repeatedly. The newlywed wife fell further in love with the witch, just like her daughter Susan would years later.

On the last night, John and Millie were positioned on their sides, facing each other. Thorzeous positioned himself behind John, Rutherynna behind Millie. They told the newlyweds to start soul kissing and wrap their arms around each other, and when they did the warlock and the witch melted inside them, possessing them totally. They made love while the actual couple were asleep at the wheel, so to speak, and their first child was conceived. This conception was not done in the normal way. Thorzeous as John Stansfield sodomized Rutherynna (as Millie) repeatedly, while a full moon shined high above the lewd city, and didn't stop until the first tinges of orange began to show in the Eastern horizon.

Thorzeous's seed traveled into her rectum again and again, burning through membranes until it rested in the womb of the newlywed. The seed was planted, and the Stansfield's went back home pregnant beyond their knowledge. Michael watched all this action, and of course he became aroused. The evil couple didn't seem to mind; he was sexually unchained, and began masturbating wildly. They were watching him, though, and inwardly they smiled.

As both couples bid each other goodbye, Michael was thrust back inside the tunnel-like structure, and little by little lost his body again. Once he was nothing but a head again, he flew out of the wormhole and back into Thorzeous's right hand in Happy Pines. His head and partial neck ached again, and he realized that *his* own honeymoon was over.

"Yes, it is definitely over," The Warlock added, menacingly. "Now listen to Rutherynna."

"Every so often we visited the Stansfield's," the witch said, pointing at the old couple. Michael still couldn't believe it was them. "You will when you hear me out, you pathetic man lover! Stop thinking and just listen. We melted into them again, and their next child would be conceived—our children. That was their payment to us, their *interest*. We took their souls, and their lives were short. As expected, because of that John and Millie's lives went beyond the confines of normal hell. They began to age faster than the normal human being, because they weren't living, they were *dying!* And isn't that what people do when they lose a loved one? They die just a little bit faster. Now imagine parents losing nine of their own children. That would be beyond surviving. We eventually froze their minds like you see now, and all they saw was that last losing hand, reminding them of what they had done to themselves all those years ago. I used to visit Millie alone from time to time, and she became a very obedient slave. We had intense sex, and at one point she begged me to take her away, but I told her that would never happen.

The last time I saw her, just before her aging accelerated, I told her we had taken all of her children—mind, body and soul—and she screamed maddeningly. When I disappeared she was still screaming, falling to the floor and holding herself. She finally understood that love, hate, despair, and depression could all melt together to make one tasty bitch's brew. Now watch, Michael, watch closely as Thorzeous unfreezes their pathetic minds."

The warlock snapped his fingers, and the Stansfield's both slowly woke up and became aware. They lowered their heads and looked over at the dominant couple and both immediately began screaming. All the memories of all their children's deaths came flooding back. All the heartache, all the crying and feelings of despair, all of that had been created by the couple now in front of them. They had gambled, and lost—lost so much. It had all looked so good in the beginning, but they slowly saw it all spiral into the depths of hell. They both silently prayed to God for forgiveness as they both watched in horror as their owners approached them.

"Your God cannot save you now, my little minions," Rutherynna said, smirking, cocking her head to one side and opening the musical box. "Listen to the pretty music, my little pretties. It is now time to come home."

Michael saw both their souls begin to leave their bodies and move toward the musical box. In his head he could hear their desperate screams for mercy, but there was none coming. They pleaded to be saved, but it was too late. Their essence disappeared inside the box, and the lid close. Michael was then told the whole story of the musical box, what lay inside, and *who* was inside. He was told that hell was just a hop, skip, and a jump away, and that it was finally his turn.

Thorzeous, holding his head, brought it up close to the open musical box, and Michael could see the hungry centipedes crawling just inside. He saw their sharp little teeth and evil red eyes. Behind them he saw other horrors, and wondered who created them.

"Certainly not your God," he was told by Rutherynna, speaking telepathically again. "But that doesn't matter. Meet your new friends, Michael. They're not as nice as your friends on Pleasure island, but they will have to do."

"But why? Why me?" he asked as his head touched the musical box. He could feel the centipedes crawling all over his face, and they began to eat. There was nothing he could do to ward them off, and so he did the only thing he could do: scream. And scream he did. In the back of those screams he heard the witch tell him that this was his fate because he had married Susan, and that she wasn't his to take. Rutherynna wondered in his thoughts how he could marry such a beautiful piece of ass when all he wanted was to take it up the ass himself? The witch added that she would scratch his itch for him, because he was about to receive the biggest ass fuck of all time! Both Thorzeous and Rutherynna laughed at that. How ironic!

After a long period of time, accompanied by much screaming and pain, the lawyer's head was completely consumed. Even his skull had been chipped away at until there was nothing left. He had been totally aware of what was happening to him right to the end, when the last of his brain was eaten.

When there was nothing left for the centipedes to eat, his thoughts and memories all exploded outward, and were pulled back magnetically inside his spirit, and was swallowed up by the strange and dangerous musical box, its lid closing behind him. He found himself in total darkness, but he knew he wasn't alone. He could hear and feel things moving around him before they decided to attack. He heard sounds of agony and despair in the distance as something pierced his essence. He felt another piercing needle enter his soul, and then another, entrapping his core. Other damnations began to circle him, each one deadlier than the last. He felt his spirit splitting apart, and he experienced a million deaths repeatedly. He could never really die, just like every other soul that had entered into this realm, and so he experienced pain in every way imaginable, over and over. Just before he ended one hell and started another, something powerfully evil crawled into his last conscious thoughts, showing him horrors beyond his wildest imagination, and before he knew it, whatever was left of his splintered soul was filled with agonizing screams again, and God (or something else) only knew if they ever stopped.

Chapter Thirty-Five

LAZERIOUS

The disappearance of Doreen Masterson, Jason Miller's aunt and lover, did not happen of her own accord. Most of the family knew that she was "out there," and they figured she had run off to explore her multitude of desires and would come crawling home to rebuild herself, restarting the whole pathetic process all over again. That was not the case this time, but again, dear reader, let's not get ahead of ourselves.

Doreen was wild, completely different than her older sister Meg, Jason's mother. No, while Meg had grown up on the straight and narrow, getting good marks in school and doing what her elders told her to do, Doreen was just the opposite. She fought the law of all things, and their foundations. She was forever getting into trouble, at home and at school; her parents had both punished her repeatedly, even spanking her over their knee, but it did no good. In fact, in confidence she told Meg that she liked the spankings, they woke up strange and forbidden sexual feelings in her boiling loins. Meg had thought her crazy, had laughed it off, but Doreen was driven to find out more about her desires, which were vast.

She had lost her virginity at eleven with the father of her best friend, Candy, and after they had done it three times she begged the man to spank her hard over his lap. Candy's father, Frank, had gladly complied, and then every so often they got together to do it all again until she eventually got tired of him.

She then seduced Candy into having lesbian sex, exploring all new realms of emotional and physical pleasures. Doreen had even told Candy's father that she had broken up with him because of her desires for his daughter, but if he ever said anything she would tell the authorities all about *them*. She also told him that she would *consider* fucking him again if he behaved and kept his mouth shut. He reluctantly agreed; he knew he had screwed up royally and was behind the eight ball, and besides, he had fallen madly in love with Doreen. He was true to his word, and so she gave him "a piece of ass" every once in a while, just to keep him honest. She even let Candy watch from the bedroom closet as she screwed her father silly, making him beg for sex like a pathetic little boy.

Candy, like Doreen, was a little dementedly slanted as well, and so she enjoyed the forbidden sex show. Maybe Doreen had helped her down that dark, lustful road, acquiring sadistic tastes, but all Doreen knew was that she had gotten a big thrill out of being watched, and by who was doing the watching. That whole scene had been quite heady and exhilarating, and she began fantasizing about seducing the mother and wife as well (which she reluctantly had not acted on). But what floated her boat the most was control: total control. Controlling people that she knew intimately was powerful, and a massive, powerful high.

That high had first been experienced at home. She was the youngest child in the family (that meant the most spoiled, as in most households), and even though she was always in hot water, she was still the baby, and she usually got her way, to the dismay of her older sister. She wanted—and knew *how*—to control every situation; that was what mattered. Crying, stomping your feet, throwing a temper tantrum, etc., were ways most children learned to get what they wanted. Some were better at it than others, and Doreen was a pro; it didn't matter how many people she left in her wake. Getting your way and gaining control was an art; it had to be done right, and Doreen had the right blueprint for its success.

She smoked dope and other recreational drugs from time to time, and drank her parents' liquor whenever they weren't around. Doreen always had boyfriends, and a few girlfriends as well; she knew early on she was bisexual, but she never got emotionally involved with any of them. Maybe she was incapable of truly loving somebody, or maybe she was just afraid of falling into somebody else's web, but she avoided falling in love at all expense. All her lovers, on the other hand, always fell for Doreen hard—and then she had them.

She would have her control in full, and she used it to manipulate their feelings, as well as everyone else's inside her circle of casual acquaintances. She would always dump her lovers when she knew they were in over their heads emotionally, and reveled in their despair when she left them in shambles. Sometimes she would continue the relationship after the breakup, only to break it off again when they were further controlled or damaged. She was a first-class bitch if there ever was one, someone all people should always avoid coming into contact with. That was hard, though, because she was beautiful, popular, and witty—all the components of a dangerous bitch's brew, and she stirred it to perfection.

When she seduced her nephew, it opened up a whole new avenue to explore. It was pure incest, it was taboo, it was forbidden, but it was exhilarating! She shared her lusts and fantasies with the handsome teenager, and she taught him everything she knew. She also made him do things he wasn't ready for, maybe would never be ready for, but getting someone to do something they didn't want to do was a strong form of control, and as we all know, that was her favorite drug of choice. She could never get enough of it. She laughed to herself on many occasions, for how ironic was it that control was the only thing that could control *her?* That question was rhetorical, for the two of them would be in bed together for the rest of their lives—or so she thought. Getting back to Jason, she loved him like any aunt would, but she also needed to control him; and so, she had. She had many deviant plans for her new lover and nephew, but she didn't get to see them all come to fruition.

On the day she disappeared, she took Robert Fleming, the man Jason had had sex with, up to the family cabin just outside Portland. She had taken lovers up there before, even Jason, but she had gotten her greatest thrills of control with Robert, a former football star at USC and in the Canadian Football League. He was the same age as Doreen, had had a productive career in Canada, gone into real estate back in his hometown, got married to a high school sweetheart, and had two beautiful children.

His fall from glory started when he met Doreen in a bar on the main drag after he had taken her to see a townhouse. She never had any intention of buying the bi-level; all she knew was that she wanted the former football player for herself, and would do anything to get him under her spell. She seduced him easily with her good looks and seductive charms, but not in the normal way. She decided to sexually use him in a different way—a diabolical, sadistic way. After getting him drunk and giving him oral sex behind the bar, she took him home to her lair. He expected normal sex, but she had other plans—much different, forbidden plans. She told him if he wanted to go further with her beyond tonight, then he would have to do as she said.

He readily agreed; he was already lost in lust. It felt totally violating to him, but she reversed their sexual rolls. He was made to get on his hands and knees, and then receive anal sex from Doreen, who was wearing a large strap-on dildo. She took him repeatedly throughout the night, and then as the sun rose slowly over the tree line, she let him have her normally. She snickered as he exploded inside her, for she knew that this would be the only time they would ever have vaginal sex. They continued in their reversed sexual roles until Robert admitted to Doreen that he at least liked the anal intercourse she gave him, and then she knew she had him! She then began bringing other boyfriends in to use the big football jock both anally as well as orally. He cried like a big baby at first, unable to comprehend what he had just done, but then he accepted his darkened fate and continued to be a main character in Doreen's lustful desires. She controlled him in a way that was totally on the other side of the fence, and she reveled in her success and powerful feelings.

When she brought Jason in to use the hulking former football star, it was just too much. She loved watching two men get it on, much more than watching lesbian trysts (which she had manipulated in the past as well). She loved that the top, her nephew, was half the age and size as the bottom, the big football player. She loved the fact that she had made Robert go over to the other side, for even though he would still do anything for her without question, he was really now only interested in having homosexual sex. He now confided to his mistress that he loved being with men, and if she desired it, she should find even more men to fuck him on a regular basis. Doreen knew he was lost, had even encouraged him to find a boyfriend, and he had. In fact, he had found two.

His wife eventually found out, and he was in the middle of a messy divorce, as well as dealing with a damaged reputation, but he didn't care. Robert told Doreen that after all he was about to lose, he still had her, and he still had his gay lovers to fall back on. His boyfriends couldn't compare to her, but at least he wasn't left out in the cold. How wrong he would be. When Doreen heard him say that, she knew that she had him: hook, line, and sinker.

On the night they *both* disappeared, she planned on screwing him throughout the night, giving him the best sex of his life, and then dumping him. That never happened. What she got, some might say, she definitely deserved, but Robert didn't. He was a fly caught in her fatal web, and would've probably lived a long and normal life if he had never met the lustful sex queen, and so he continued to be a victim right to the end—and beyond. At one point as he fell into a fate no one knew existed, he prayed fearfully for his soul, and even though Doreen was the cause of it all, he prayed for hers as well. No one deserved what they got. Here is what happened on that fateful night.

Doreen and Robert entered the cabin, which consisted of a front room with kitchen, two large bedrooms, and a bath, and toasted their evening with a couple of shots of whiskey and a large joint. Then, after getting naked, they basically ran into the master bedroom and got down to business. Doreen had bought a new strap-on with a bigger, fatter dildo attachment, and the session immediately became intense, with moans and groans echoing off the log cabin walls. At the halfway point of their evening, Robert cried tears of joy and told Doreen he loved her more than life, and pledged complete submission and devotion to her. She smiled evilly, for she couldn't wait to see the look on his face when she told him this unusual affair was over. Oh sure, she would contin-ue to ass-fuck his brains out from time to time, just to continue being in control of his sorry existence, maintaining her mistress status with him, but he had basically worn out his usefulness as far as she was concerned. It was time to move on.

This was what always happened when you hung out with Doreen Masterson. She always got tired of her lovers, no matter how long their relationships lasted, and now her main concentration was going to be focused on her nephew Jason. He was hot, he was sexy, he was pretty good in bed, and she had big plans for him. One of those plans was diabolical, to say the least! She planned on trying to seduce her own sister, and then watch Jason fuck his own mother in every way imaginable, watching her guarded sister lose all control of her feelings. What a head trip that would be! Her goody two-shoes sister falling down a dark, lustful rabbit hole along with her son. It was just too much. She would secretly film them and control their lives with family blackmail. What a scandal that would be if the news ever got out! Oh, it might seem like that at first, but she had no doubt that the two of them would love screwing each other's brains out, and then they would be hers—her personal slaves for all time!

One way or the other, the future held no bounds, but none of that ever happened. As they were about to start the second half of their evening, they both heard movement from the living room. They stared at the open doorway and watched in unbelievable horror as the demon Lazerious entered Doreen's bedroom. He smiled wickedly and held up his right hand as the utterly surprised couple tried to get up and run, and they froze in place. The demon grabbed each one and tied them face down over the bed, their behinds raised high in the air as he thrust two pillows under their waistlines. Lazerious levitated two feet in the air behind them and sodomized both for three whole days without any interlude. He orgasmed repeatedly inside their bowels, and his steaming semen melted through their insides, turning their organs into steaming mush. A hideous smell of burning flesh filled the bedroom, and in response the lights in the house flickered on and off repeatedly. Amazingly the two captives didn't die, but they screamed constantly in tormented, twisted agony.

During their marathon raping the demon telepathically told them that he was their new master, that they now belonged to him until he tired of them, and if he did tire of them, then their eventual fate would become much worse. The message was sent to keep their master happy or else, and it was repeated over and over again during the three-day sex session. By the end they were both screaming constantly in agony, their insides on high blaze. They could feel the demon's seed burning completely through to their souls. Through those screams Lazerious told them more of the same was in their future, along with some new twists and turns. He asked them if they were ready to behave and become his devoted slaves. They both readily agreed that they would be good servants and keep their master happy.

"How ironic, Doreen," Lazerious mused out loud as he pounded into her burning backside viciously, "You love being in control, and now I control you. I will make you pay for being a total cunt again and again. And you, Robert," he chuckled as he switched partners and rammed his raging thick penis inside the man's ravished bowels, "You are mine because you are stupid and uncaring, carrying on with this bitch and her brew. Didn't you know that she was going to dump you after this evening of lust, you pathetic asshole? You disgust me to the core, so here's something for yours," he said as he roared his powerful orgasm, shooting bolts of burning pain into Robert's sizzling innards. The big man screamed until he passed out, and then the demon angrily came around, viciously slapped his face, and peed on it until the former football player came to. He groaned in pain as he was released from his bonds.

"Fuck her ass," Lazerious screamed at the condemned big

man. Robert's pain dulled, and his penis unbelievably swelled. He moved behind Doreen and rammed inside her distended backside, cursing her silently for the position she had put him in. The demon pushed his cock inside Doreen's screaming mouth, muffling her agony. They both finished at the same time, and then Lazerious untied her bonds. She slumped to the floor, crying, moaning, and groaning all at the same time. She was mentally and physically defeated, drained of all her spiciness and vinegar. She was a willing slave now, trying to avoid this monster's pain no matter what she had to endure. She conceded to herself miserably that her past life was over, over much too soon.

The demon told them it was time to go to their new home. He put his arms around them both, and then they began to melt into the demon's body. They screamed like never before as their bodies melted inside their master until they completely disappeared. For Doreen and Robert, all became dark as their bodies melted away to nothing, leaving only their souls inside their dominating new owner. They couldn't see, but they could feel and hear. They were not alone. They heard others groaning and crying all around them, and eventually realized they were doing the same. They subconsciously joined the choir of painful sorrows, and those dark tunes never ended. Their hymns were sounds of total despair, echoing off the demon's insides, which seemed vast in distance. Their whole beings (or what was left of them) ached constantly. Their souls darkened, infected by the demon's fever. Every so often both of them were defecated out of their master's backside and materialized again into human form, and then their rape was replayed, along with renewed intense pain.

"Please me, slaves," Lazerious commanded loudly, standing behind Doreen and pushing inside her anus savagely, beginning the rape process all over again. "Please me or I'll show you that my hell has no boundaries." They moved with renewed enthusiasm on their hands and knees, told the demon with passion that they loved him, and swore he was their Lord and Savior for all time.

As Lazerious was using Doreen he laughed inside her head, remarking, "Isn't it ironic, cunt, that I was the one that finally popped your treasured anal cherry. You tried every kind of sex there is, but you were too much of a bitch to try the ultimate satisfaction." She replied by screaming and screaming as he pounded into her damaged backside again and again, brutally punishing her ravaged insides for what seemed like days. Then they were both put back inside the demon's insides, painfully melting away physically until they were needed again—and again.

Some say that history repeats itself, but so too, does hell. Sometimes they were brought out together, sometimes they were brought out with others, and then sometimes Doreen was brought out alone. For her, those were the worst times—times the demon thought she justly deserved. By the time Lazerious was finished with her on those one on one sessions, Doreen was reduced to a mass of painful mush, fucked and beaten so badly no one would recognize her, inside or out.

On occasion Robert was brought out with another male, and Lazerious enjoyed watching the two of them together before ravaging both of their outrageously distended bowels. It didn't really matter in the endgame; their fate was sealed. Each time they sizzled back inside their all-commanding master they lost a little bit more of their sanity, and a little bit more of their soul. They were being slowly consumed and devoured, losing themselves wholly. Before they completely lost their memories, minds, and souls, they silently prayed to God to save them. Either The Creator didn't hear their plea, or there was nothing he could do to save them. They now both knew the real definition of being condemned to damnation—until they knew no more.

Chapter Thirty-Six

TIMOTHY MANSON AND REX

*T*imothy Manson was a twelve-year-old boy that had just buried his best friend, Rex, with his father, James, out in the back yard just outside the city of Gatlinburg, Tennessee. You weren't supposed to do that, for health and environmental concerns, such as soil and water contamination. In a lot of areas, you weren't supposed to bury *any* animal, but Rex had been different—much different. Even his father realized that, which was why they took two shovels out of the garage shortly after the sun sank into the western sky and buried their ten-year-old German shepard in the fading twilight.

James Manson, a dentist who had an office in town, had bought Rex as a puppy from a patient whose dog had just given birth to a litter of five, when Timothy turned two, and they had both grown up together. They would be best friends for life (forever even, the son thought), only their lives didn't run parallel with each other. That was a lesson Timothy learned the hard way. While he grew from a baby into a growing adolescent boy, Rex grew to full maturity much quicker, and then got old just as fast.

German shepherds, like most large dogs, have a shorter life span than smaller dogs, averaging between eight and twelve years.

Sounds like a short time, and it is, as far as a human beings are concerned. "It just doesn't seem fair," Timothy told his mother Mary, a pretty little petite blond who seemed much more attentive during these emotional conversations. James, a tall, extremely skinny man, just said it was the way of the world, and was not meant to question. He added that God meant for dogs to have shorter lives, and we shouldn't in any way question the Lord. But Timothy, inwardly and outwardly, *did* question such things. When the best part of your day is spent playing, talking, eating, and just plain exploring with your best friend, you shouldn't have to lose him. That just wasn't right, the young boy reasoned.

Timothy questioned why one day, after having a yearly checkup down at Doctor Abbott's (the town's veterinarian), he discovered that Rex had a serious heart ailment, one that was slowing him down permanently—which was why he didn't run as fast as he used to. Oh, he'd look at Timothy, and at least *want* to run like before, wagging his tail at full throttle, but his body said something else entirely, something the young boy couldn't possibly relate to. It's hard to rationalize when one's life is on the "upside," and the other's is on the "downside."

Rex understood, and even though he tried in his own way to tell Timothy that his time was on the short side, he could see the hurt in the boy's eyes as the running turned into trotting, then eventually to walking, walking with a limp, and then just laying down, just about refusing to move. The usual afternoon entertainment, which had gone on the same way for years, slowed to a crawl, even though Timothy wanted to run like never before, but best friends understood each other begrudgingly, and as far as Timothy was concerned, that just wasn't acceptable.

It was a few days after Easter Sunday that the two of them had gone to sleep like any other night on Timothy's bed, (Timothy, for the past year, had had to help his best friend up onto the end of the bed because of hind leg arthritis, even with the new and improved medications available), but only one of them had woken up. As you could imagine, that ended up being one hell of a day, to say the least. It could have been worse, though. Timothy was a notorious late sleeper, a hard-to-rise young man, and so James had always come in quietly to take Rex out for his first walk of the day to do his business. And so it was he that discovered that Rex had moved on to "The Happy Hunting Ground," a place that father told son was created by God, where dogs could chase rabbits and other small animals all day to their hearts' content. So luckily, before Timothy had slowly rubbed the cobwebs out of his eyes, James had carried the body of the German shepherd out to the garage and covered him with a large tarp.

Breakfast that morning, as you can imagine, was filled with many tears as parents told son that Rex had moved on to that magical land of eternal youth, that he could now run as fast as he did when Timothy had first started school, and was happy to boot! It was a good tale, and maybe it was true when you broke it all down, but it was still a loss, a *big* loss, and Timothy knew that it was going to take a very long time to get over—if *ever!* And why was that? Because everything you did was now done without your best friend, the one you had shared everything with since you could first remember.

After the burial, parents told son that it would get better over time, but that seemed like a little white lie to Timothy. As the next few weeks excruciatingly crawled by, things *didn't* get better; in fact, they got worse. He couldn't stop crying, because everything he did, he now did alone, and now that he had more time to think about things on a whole, the memories flooded in, and the tears would begin anew. At school he couldn't concentrate, and his grades suffered. He'd sit in class and stare into space, hearing, but not comprehending what Mrs. Comstock taught.

His parents had a teacher/parent conference meeting with her, and informed the soon-to-be-retired schoolmarm what had happened with Rex. The teacher nodded and understood, recalling to the depressed parents that she herself had gone through a similar situation when she was growing up. She told them the story of losing her cat of sixteen years, when she, herself, was only ten. That was a traumatic time in her early youth, and the teacher suggested getting Timothy another dog to replace the old one. The parents had mixed feelings on that, but they told Mrs. Comstock that they would consider it wholeheartedly.

That night Timothy decided to pray extra hard to The Lord, begging Him to send Rex back to him, saying that he missed him so much. He cried himself to sleep that night, and Timothy dreamed of himself and Rex running as fast as they could through the fields behind the house. All was good, all was right with the world, until he woke up again, and the nightmare of reality began all over.

Mrs. Comstock took a different approach to her teaching ways with Timothy after meeting with his parents, and his grades began to slowly improve. She talked to him alone on many occasions, telling him that she understood his loss, and that it would get better. Still, he remained in a depressive funk, and spent a good amount of his free time alone walking in the fields, crying, and calling out Rex's name, hoping against hope that he'd come running through the high grass that had just started to grow again in the early spring air. Rex didn't come, of course, and Timothy cried some more as he dejectedly trudged home. He prayed to God again that night, and the night after that.

He prayed each night all the way to the end of the school year and into the first days of another hot summer. Timothy passed all his final exams and ended up with a B average. When June turned into July, early one morning a large crate was delivered and dropped off at the Manson's front door. The doorbell rang, and Timothy answered it. Nobody was there; only the crate. It was made out of old weather-beaten plywood and framed and nailed shut by two-by-fours. It was about five feet square in size, but there was no packing list attached to it, or returning mailing address. No nothing, but here it was.

The new Defensive Blueprint Operation had been put into effect. Terrorism stilled reigned like terminal cancer throughout the world, no country exempt. James called the alternate 911 number, an eight-digit number that everyone knew, and the special authorities were called in, properly named "Internal Connective Services." The outside of the crate was scanned, examined, and then carefully opened out by the street. Inside something was tightly wrapped in bubble wrap. Scanners ran across it with no explosives found. Still, they proceeded with caution. The bubble wrap was carefully removed, and what remained was a statue of a German shepherd dog that looked just like Rex. Attached to its tail was a packet inside a plastic bag. The paper appeared very old and worn, the edges frayed in places, yellowish in color. It was a letter written in English, but the lettering was different. They were much more artistic in nature, as if each individual letter had been carefully penned to paper, a separate portrait unto itself. Captain Donald Tillman carefully unfolded it and read it out loud. It said:

To Mr. Timothy Manson:

This is a gift from an admirer. I cannot say from who, for reasons beyond your concern. What you have demonstrated is true and pure love, something your world needs much more of.

Your light shines bright, and let it continue to

do so. This gift will enhance the brilliance of that shine. Enjoy it, as it will enjoy you. You are a person that understood just what a gift you had in your dog and best friend, Rex. Let me put you at ease and let you know that he is happy where he is, and will always remember the love you shared. That love is what will allow both of you to carry on along your separate journeys, and even though you do have them, they will just run parallel to each other. This special gift is also named Rex, and he doesn't need batteries, nor does he have an on or off switch. To activate him, just say, "Rex, wake up!" and he will come "online." That's it, and he will stay with you always, and never age or pass on. That's why I said that he is "special." He is the exception to the rule. So, in closing, again, enjoy your gift, and continue to let the love inside you grow to bounds unchained. Bless you and Rex always,

From a concerned friend who cares

P.S. You will discover a secret when Rex is activated which I think you will find enjoyable. It is a little something special "extra" that I think that you deserve. Love to you, and everyone you touch as you continue on your important future journey.

P.S.S. Sometimes prayers ARE answered in special ways.

When Captain Tillman finished reading, he continued to stare down at the words he had just read, his eyes slightly reddening.

Timothy had tears running down his face. In his mind he didn't think he had any tears left, but he always seemed to have a fresh supply on hand when it came down to the subject of Rex, and the loss of him. The young boy looked around and was shocked at what he saw. Everyone, Captain Tillman, his men, and his parents were also crying, overwhelmed with emotion. They all understood all too well what was happening here, for they all were remembering similar instances of loss—losing a loved one, a close friend, or even an animal of their own.

Memories like these, no matter how far we try to push them back into the recesses of our overall thoughts, never fail to come rushing back when the situation arises. No matter how big of a mental wall we try to build to keep the tidal wave of emotions in check, it's never high enough. Loss—if you live long enough, and that usually doesn't take too long as a human life takes shape, you experience the emotions associated with that small but expansive word. Everyone on the Manson's front yard understood this, and after hearing the words to this letter could relate to what Timothy was going through. Your first reaction is to help a young boy in obvious need, but that help was possibly right *here* in front of them in the form of this caricature of a dog.

Even though everyone was crying (some more than others), they were all smiling through their tears. They were tears of joy, a pot of riches found at the end of a very special rainbow. Through all this the young boy was discovering some of life's strange contradictions, but in this case it was all good. Timothy, as young as he was, automatically no longer felt alone in this. Sure, his parents shared in his loss, but this was different; it *felt* different. It was good to see others show remorse, and cry along *with* him. He looked up at the clear and deep blue sky to see if anything seemed out of place, but everything seemed normal. Still, Timothy thought, this all just might be a bad trick. He went over to the stationary dog; it felt hard, like solid metal or something of that nature. He wondered how this could replace Rex. Even the dog's fur felt like metal. Timothy was aware of eyes on him, and as he looked around he saw that they were all waiting to see what he'd do. They were all curious to see what would happen; they all had never seen anything like this. No company made anything like this metal dog, and they all wanted to see what would go down.

"Go ahead," James finally said through his own tears, speaking for all of them. "Let's see what this thing will do." The authorities put their hands on their holsters, taking no chances, and then Timothy nodded, and said the magic words. "Rex, wake up!" Nothing happened for a second or two, and then a miracle occurred—or at least that's what everybody there told their families when they went home that evening.

What happened was this: the metal that composed this version of Rex crackled and melted, transposing into skin and real fur. Rex's eyes came to life first, blinking, and then seeing. Slowly but surely the dog's body parts began to move, as if they were becoming unfrozen. As this was happening, Rex began to pant and smile warmly. His eyes stared, and then registered who stood in front of him, and he suddenly ran to Timothy's open arms, whining. Timothy hugged the uncontrollably happy dog, and the boy became overwhelmed as well. The German shepherd was jumping all around in Timothy's arms, and the boy was laughing loudly, and it appeared on the surface as if the passing of Rex had never happened. Everyone watched in total amazement as they shed many more tears, and they all knew that this was one day they'd never forget.

Eventually the new Rex was thoroughly examined by a state veterinarian called to the Manson's residence, x-rayed by the task force, and deemed harmless by the middle of the afternoon. Faiths were reaffirmed or altered on that hot, early summer day, and all those in attendance went on in the days ahead equipped with heavy hearts and big smiles, brightening up the days of everyone they came in contact with. The authorities continued to monitor and examine Rex from time to time right up until the power went off and most went back to The Creator, but the results all came up positive.

After the authorities left on that special and unusual day, convinced that all would be all right, Timothy and Rex ran off for the fields behind his house, his parents happily watching them go. And yes, Rex ran like the wind, just like he had when he was young—when Timothy was just starting school and the German shepherd used to mock his young master with his speed, circling him repeatedly. When they reached the wooded area before town, they stopped by the large gray rock they had always rested on. Timothy was gasping for breath, but it was all good. Good, because he was no longer alone, but back again with what at least looked like his best friend, and to him, that was good enough. Rex, of course, was not out of breath, didn't even look as if he had been running as he sat down on his hind legs, like any other normal dog. He stared back at Timothy, as if waiting for something.

"I don't know who you really are, boy, but you look so much like Rex," Timothy said, gasping. "Amazing!"

Rex cocked his head and then asked in a deep, manly voice, "Do I look that much like him?' The color suddenly drained out of Timothy's face as he stared back at the German shepherd. His mouth froze mid-gasp, as if time had seemingly stopped. The boy felt suddenly numb, his blood freezing in place. Rex cocked his head the other way and broke the silence.

"Yes, Timothy, that is the secret that was talked about in your letter. I can talk. I can do that because we can then discus things as they occur—things that are necessary."

"What . . . what *are* you?" Timothy asked, all systems moving again. He clenched and unclenched his fists, feeling blood pumping excitedly. The temperature seemed to rise 5 degrees as the sun moved from behind the trees. The air, which seemed so heavy a second ago, began to move in a light warm breeze, as if a weight had been removed from it.

"I am a gift from an unknown giver," the German shepherd replied, standing up and moving directly in front of the shocked boy. "I am here to bring you joy and happiness, and to protect. I am not a robot, but I am not like any dog living here on Earth. I will never age, never fall ill, and I don't even need your oxygen to breathe. I do have a heart, though, even though it doesn't pump blood throughout my body like yours or any other type of life on this planet, but I do feel, I do love, and I love you just as much as Rex did."

Timothy hugged Rex tightly as fresh tears rolled down his face. He sniffled, released his hold, and then looked directly into the dog's eyes. "I believe you, Rex, but who is the giver? Is it God?"

"I don't know who God is. I just know that I'm supposed to be here with you. And that's all I want to do."

"Wow! Really?"

"Really, but we can't let anyone know that I can talk. That I do know. Otherwise, I think like a dog, and know what a dog knows. You will teach me more, just by being you. That is how pets like me learn. We watch."

Timothy grinned, for he knew that to be true. This Rex thought just like a dog—*his* dog. The only difference was that this version could talk. He liked that. "OK, Rex, I understand. I love you too. All I know is that I feel better than I have since I lost Rex Number One. That sounds funny. Does that make you Rex Number Two?"

Rex cocked his head before answering. "If that's what you

want me to be; otherwise I'm cool with just Rex."

"Just Rex, boy," Timothy said laughing, patting the dog on the head. "Just my number one friend, 'til the end of time. Let's go, boy! Let's boogie!" And then they both ran off, back into the fields.

That was three weeks before the power went out. During that time the two of them were having the best summer of their lives, even though it was Rex Number Two's first one. They'd play in the fields until Timothy got tired, and then they'd talk for hours, both learning from each other, and growing increasingly closer. The boy let the memory of Rex Number One retreat into the back of his mind, and from time to time he felt guilty about that. Rex Number Two told him not to think that way; all dogs just wanted their masters to be happy, for they knew what was written on the wall of time. He told the boy that Rex Number One was well taken care of, and he would be happy that Rex Number Two was down here with his master, living *life* again!

When the power went off and most of the people went back to The Creator, the two of them were out in the fields running for glory. Timothy kept on running, not knowing what happened, but Rex felt something shift that only animals could sense. He stopped running and looked around, looking for anything that would back his suspicions. He stared into the sky, sniffed the air, felt that something had changed, and then he knew! There were no birds, no sounds of life, no sounds of the many different species that made sounds only an animal with acute hearing could detect.

Timothy saw the dog cocking his head to one side and asked him what was wrong. Rex said he didn't rightly know, but he felt that something *big* had just transpired. Rex told Timothy his suspicions as they slowly walked back across the fields, and then heard loud crashes in the distance. Again, and again they heard them, followed by dark grey smoke that rose high into the sky. Soon after they smelled what would be the fumes of the numerous crashing planes that were dropping from the sky. The two of them ran back home, Timothy frightened like never before. Rex nuzzled him constantly, letting the young boy know that he was here, but the German shepherd was quite unnerved himself. They ran into an empty house, and began to discover what everybody else still on Earth was realizing.

Soon after, heavy thunderstorms with torrential downpours tore through the area. Those storms put out the numerous fires started by the falling airplanes, saving many wooded areas, neighborhoods, and overall infrastructure throughout the city. After the storms had passed, the two of them both walked throughout town, calling out for any other signs of life, knocking on doors in the neighborhood, but they both came to the same conclusion that others had. They were alone—utterly alone. They both felt the loss of family and fellow human beings, and many tears were shed.

During many conversations afterward, and a dream that Timothy had about New York City, they both decided they couldn't stay here any longer; they needed to find other people—if other people still existed—and move east. And that's what they did. Three days after the Event they left town and headed toward the big city. They surmised that if anybody else was still on Earth, they would go there. The dream had told Timothy exactly that. It was a sign possibly sent to them by God. Ever since Rex had been delivered, each night he would lie at the foot of Timothy's bed, watching over his master. Every evening before turning in, they both would pray to The Lord for bringing them together.

Rex learned about God and his creations, and felt better for it.

Each night while Timothy slept and dreamed about future good times with his best friend, he read from the family Bible. Yes, he could read as well as talk, and he had a lot of time to leaf through the many pages of the Good Book while everybody else slept and "recharged their batteries." Many times, as the moon and stars moved across the nighttime sky, Rex would read a passage and fully decipher it. He dissected it slowly and began to realize that he was a very small piece of the puzzle in the greater overall plan, probably even more than his master knew, and it made the dog feel important.

As the two of them started on their journey, Rex would watch over Timothy and listen for any sign of life. They added a prayer to the others, asking The Lord for safe passage as they made their way across the country. In the first days of the trip it was totally quiet, and the duo wondered more than once if they were the only living souls left on Earth—a scary proposition. In the early hours of each new day Rex would listen and sniff the air for any sign of life, and in between he would read the family Bible, for that seemed very important now. Rex was right on that point.

NARRATIVE NOTES: All people who have owned various pets have gone through the emotional rollercoaster of loss. I know I have, countless times, and each time it gets harder. For me, it got to the point where I decided never to own a pet again. Now that's a hard choice to make, considering how many animals need homes. It breaks my heart to see those homeless animals shown in television commercials with looks of total despair written across their innocent faces.

One point for all to ponder: would more people adopt more animals if the costs of owning one wasn't so expensive? I think so, but the costs of owning one just seems to constantly increase as time rolls on. Veterinarians as well as other animal services really need to look at themselves in the mirror and ask if the prices they charge are too high. Could they charge less? That's a question for those professionals to answer. What I do know is if the costs of owning pets were reduced, possibly many more of them would be saved, and many more families would adopt them. As the dominos in that realm fell in that direction, wouldn't those same veterinarians then benefit from more business and greater gains in the long run? Interesting topic for discussion.

Chapter Thirty-Seven

THE CHURCH UNION

On the last weekend before the power went out, an extraordinary occurrence took place. It happened sporadically, starting Friday at noon, during Muslim prayers, continued on Saturday around Jewish synagogues, but it didn't fully blossom until Sunday morning during the first Christian church services of the day. We will visit one of those services, one in upper New York, but the same occurrence was happening everywhere across the country when all the church bells started ringing. It was on this morning, at 4:00 a.m. Eastern Standard time in the United States, that the various suns across the universe exploded all at the same time. Some were witnessed through powerful telescopes, others were too far away to be seen, but pundits talked about them constantly throughout the last Sunday of Christian worship, and the days that followed.

Most of them expressed that it was an omen, that the stars exploding across God's creation on Sunday was no coincidence. They added that it was a sign of something to come, and they were right in their assumption. Something *was* coming. This last Sabbath celebrated on planet Earth would be a very memorable one; one that would've been talked about for years, but those were years this chamber didn't have, and so it was only brought up for the next few days.

Those discussions were emotional when discussed with loved ones, friends, or even with people who didn't even know each other. Most agreed there was something brewing on the horizon; others prayed more than usual—not just before bed, but throughout the day. It seemed as if everyone felt much closer, and as a result many good deeds were carried out as the unknown day ahead approached. God seemed to be mentioned in more general conversations as Monday turned into Tuesday, and all had dreams of a better future on the last night under the stars that somehow seemed closer than normal. But let's go back to Sunday, the day of the occurrence. Read on.

Mark Foreman rang the church bell every Sunday morning at Catskill Presbyterian at 9:45 a.m. sharp. He had done so since he turned ten years of age, and he loved hearing the utter power of the bell, which could be heard for a couple of miles in each direction. He was eighteen years old now, six feet tall, and handsome with a full head of thick, wavy auburn hair. He had matured into a polished young man, ready to attend college locally, just so that he could continue to ring and hear that bell, which was a dull gold color, cracked in many places, and now over three hundred years of age. Rain or snow, hot or cold, or even if he was sick: as long as he could make it up those old wooden steps to the bell tower, Mark would manage to do his job every Sunday. It was something he was very proud of.

Mark's father Timothy, an older version of his son (they looked so much alike it was uncanny), was the church's pastor, and Mark was going to take the same path after taking a few elective classes at the community site five miles east and then going to the seminary. The plan was for him to succeed his father when he retired; and then, only then, would he relinquish his position of bell ringer for Catskill Presbyterian.

This Sunday summer morning was hotter than usual; at 8:30 a.m. it was already in the low nineties, and Pastor Foreman and his son turned all the large fans positioned around the small church on high. The structure of the religious building was two stories high; the top floor was an attic where everything not used was stored, such as Christmas tree and decorations, etc. At the front was where the large bell tower was as well, in a small enclosed room, since it was exposed to the elements. That sat five feet above the regular roof, and Mark rang it by pulling a thick rope that fell to the dusty wood floor. The church itself held fifty people comfortably, with six pews on each side, but usually only half that amount showed up each Sunday ready to praise The Lord.

The pulpit sat to the left, and the choir sat in two pews to the right, facing the pastor. A small organ was positioned next to the choir pews, facing the parishioners. A large cross hung in the middle, with two candle stands positioned below it on each side. The lighting of the candles always opened the service, and was done by one of the two ushers (usually Mark was one of them, but not on this special Sunday) designated to greet everyone as they entered the sanctuary. Two bathrooms for each sex were in the basement, along with a room for Sunday School lessons held after service for anyone interested in attending.

The complete structure outside was painted in traditional white, proudly peeling in spots while in support of The Lord, while inside all the wood was stained dark mahogany, even the pews and pulpit, which was reapplied biyearly. The church on a whole was considered cozy to most; others thought it needed more work than not, both inside and out. In reality it did, just like most other older churches, but Catskill Presbyterian's funds were below survival level at the moment. But you always had to remain positive whenever it came to praising Jesus. The Lord would see it through, father always told son during discussions of the sort. Mark believed that, just like he did in his father's various sermons. God was watching always, and He would provide, the young man thought as he dressed in his best suit on that fine sunny Sunday morning for the last time. Mark was right.

To keep the church even cooler (if that was possible without air conditioning), father told son to keep both church doors open, which was traditional, even if a few bugs dared enter into the house of The Lord. Fifty hand fans were placed just inside the front doors on the small table for added aid alongside the thirty to forty two-page programs. Service usually lasted an hour and a half, depending on congregational interaction during the question-and-answer segment, but one thing was for sure: sweat would be shared today as parishioners rubbed shoulders with each other, trying their best to weather the heat that would only get worse as the service moved along and the sun moved overhead.

The church service started as usual with John Daniels, one of the ushers, lighting the candles, and then Mark's mother Marge played the organ interlude, which she had written herself. His two parents were basically divorced, but no papers had yet been signed, and so they still lived together in the small house two blocks north. It was easier financially, it looked better that they appeared to be one happy family—in fact, the *first* family—and besides, they all had a job to do here. Father preached, mother played and directed the choir, and Mark rang the bell and helped out wherever he was needed. As a family, they were living a lie, but they prayed, asking for forgiveness to The Lord each night. Hypocritical? Maybe, but most human beings had skeletons in their closets, and people that worked directly for The Lord were no different than the congregation that walked through the front doors of the church each Sunday.

Only twenty parishioners had (counting the two ushers) entered the church that morning; less than usual, probably because of the heat, but boy did they have a tale to tell by the end of that service. Twenty-eight in total, including Pastor Foreman, Marge, Mark, and the three women and the two men that sang in the choir, witnessed what happened.

Hymns were sung and a few passages in both Testaments were read, and then as Pastor Foreman began his sermon, "Getting Along," it began to happen. During the first thirty seconds, a dove suddenly flew into the church toward the minister and landed on the edge of the pulpit, looking directly up at the elder Foreman. The pastor abruptly stopped speaking and stared shockingly back at the dove, dumbfounded. A few seconds later ten cardinals flew into the sanctuary, followed by the same number of robins. They all landed on the organ or the empty back choir pew (since they rarely needed it), and stared intently at the pastor as well.

The choir glanced around nervously at the birds that huddled behind them as time seemed to stand still, the church completely quiet except for the power fans blowing hot air throughout the interior of the religious structure. The congregation sat still as if frozen in place, and then after hearing shuffling behind them, they turned around and gasped, for animals of all kinds were entering the church. Dogs, cats, goats, squirrels, deer—you name it—walked calmly throughout the religious structure, found a place of their liking, and then sat down peacefully and stared up at the pulpit. They all basically ignored the stunned parishioners, who looked at each other in amazement. Whether they were shocked, afraid, or just completely traumatized, they just looked around constantly and never uttered a word.

A few seconds later two full grown brown bears entered the church, followed by three younger ones—their offspring, probably. They all walked down the aisle and sat down in front of the first set of pews where Mark sat by himself, staring up at the pulpit as well. One of the younger bears walked up to the younger Foreman and began lapping the boy's hand affectionately. It was a sign of peace; they had not come to harm the humans, but to join in Sunday service with them. Mark suddenly smiled and nodded up at his stunned father, who hadn't moved a muscle since the dove had flown in. Pastor Foreman slowly smiled, nodded back at his son knowingly, and then went back to his sermon as if nothing had happened.

Before we move forward, let's mention something special about the congregation. As all the animals stared intently up at the preaching minister, the parishioners became completely attuned to what Pastor Foreman was preaching. How often does a mind wander during any church sermon? Probably more so than not, but *not* on this Sunday. No, all the people that walked through Catskill Presbyterian digested every word that came out of Pastor Foreman's mouth, and they got the message he was trying to get across.

On this Sunday he had decided not to speak about any story from the Bible itself, but of just getting along with everybody and everything. It was about enjoying every moment of every day while it lasted, and relishing each breath we were thankfully allowed to take. He told them that it was a privilege and an honor to be there. Pastor Foreman had preached such a sermon before, but on this Sunday there was just a little more emotion in his message; maybe because the animals were here, maybe because there was just something in the air, but whatever it was, it hit home with his flock. Most shed tears, and many tissues were passed around. Others nodded approvingly, understanding the message acutely. Some even spoke approvingly out loud, which was out of character for this usually quiet congregation.

When the sermon was over, and they all recited The Lord's Prayer, all the animals, one by one, quietly and peacefully got up and left the church. They never looked at any of the parishioners as they went, but the people in the pews never took their disbelieving eyes off of them. The birds followed, flying overhead and then out the front doors; their wings fanning the astonished human beings below. Once they were gone, Pastor Foreman asked the congregation to pray with him, in which he thanked The Lord for this special miracle with his many creations present, and the rest of the service ran normally, if that was possible. They all walked out of the church that morning after shaking the minister's hand a different person, but as they moved into the parking lot they realized that the miracle was still happening, for the complete roof of the church was covered by birds of all kinds—many more than had been inside the church. Pastor Foreman stepped out to see the spectacle himself, shook his head in disbelief, and smiled. What unusual guests he had had today, he thought happily, shaking the hands of the rest of his flock. "The Lord works in mysteriously ways," he mused, "and today has been one of them!"

At the edge of the church property where sparse woods started, creatures of all kinds, maybe over a couple of hundred, sat staring back at the leaving congregation. The parishioners got into their cars and drove to their next destination of the day, never knowing that they would never be back. The Foreman's locked up the church, and it was only then that the animals dispersed. The birds flew like an army off the roof in every direction, and the animals by the woods walked back into the brush. Pastor Foreman shook his head yet again, took a deep breath, and then put an arm around his ex-wife and his only son. Traditionally the Foreman family always walked to church each Sunday, weather permitting, and they had so on this one as well. They spent the rest of the day thanking God for another splendid day on Earth, and were eternally grateful for what they had witnessed at the church. The minister was sure that The Lord had orchestrated the whole happening, and Mark and his mother were in no position to disagree with him.

That evening as word got around and everyone sat down for Sunday dinner, they all said a special prayer of thanks before they ate. Their tables were filled with many things, but one part of the normal meal was absent on every table for miles around, and further still: meat. There was no meat on any of the dinner tables! In its place were extra vegetables, bread, and pasta. I'm sure, and truly believe, that The Creator smiled his approval.

Churches all over the world witnessed the same miracle as the one experienced at Catskill Presbyterian. It was written about in various periodicals the next day as another work week began. Everyone was affected in one way or another, but everyone was a little kinder to everyone they encountered until the power went out three days later. The same couldn't be said for their meals. By Monday half the families had gone back to eating meat, but at least some of them hadn't; that was at least considered something, and much better than none. The Foreman's never ate another meal with meat on the menu, for they had gotten The Lord's silent message. The Creator forgave the others their weaknesses, and when the power went off, He welcomed each and every one of them Home with open arms.

None of the people *or* the animals and birds were around when the power went out, not even any of the Foreman's, as they all traveled back to The Creator together on their own spiritual journey. Catskill Presbyterian sat alone in its wake as airplanes crashed into the ground all around it. Fires from the jet fuel were put out by the thunderstorms that followed, and then the complete religious structure disappeared into thin air, replaced by flowers of all colors that grew in seconds. Nobody was around to see yet another miracle take place, but that didn't matter. It would be protected by what might follow, if anything did.

Chapter Thirty-Eight

MAGGIE WASHINGTON
AND DARKANIOUSS

*W*e now go to another dead zone realm where nothing lives. As we stare ahead of us we see what appears to be a forest of endless trees that haven't flourished in a very long time. The exterior bark of every trunk and branch are nonexistent, exposing their inner cores. Over eons of time they have hardened and cracked, leaving the dead core to fend for itself. The interior of these literal wood stalks are dark and rotted-petrified-yet this is now the exterior of what is left. They do not fall like Earth's trees after death and time; instead they stand tall and proud even though no one will ever see them.

The trunks of the trees and the ground below cannot be seen, for a dark gray, thick mist covers it, yet it doesn't move one iota since it is dead as well. These trees grow into a sky you cannot see either, for it is filled with a slightly darker cloud cover that also doesn't budge an inch. It is a lifeless horizon that seems frozen in place, devoid of any energy. No sounds are heard in any direction, and even though this place looks dark and unwelcoming, it appears peaceful in an odd sort of way. Ruins of decaying structures, or large gray rock formations, are scattered amongst the trees, some bigger than others. No one knows what they are, or what they once were—another mystery of this mysterious landscape.

Past the first few rows of endless trees we see a stationary black figure that stands about eight feet tall, wearing a black hooded robe. As we zoom inward and look inside it's hood we see that the presence has no apparent face, only a blackness that seems to have no depth, and which appears to go on forever. If there is anything inside that darkness looking outward at us, we cannot see it, and yet we *feel* it gazing out at us. At the end of the right arm of its black robe It holds what appears to be a long, thin black rod that rises two feet above its head, although no apparent hand can be seen. Looking closer, we see that its overall blackness seems to deviate in pitch, which is the only thing that changes in appearance here. There is a reason for this, for this presence must be in many different places all at one time. The more different locations it's in, the more its pitch changes. This hooded figure is another form of legion, and it has gotten a bad rap over the years, even though that reputation is unwarranted.

This dark presence's name is Darkaniouss, but you readers know its name as The Grim Reaper, the caricature Halloween creature that hovers over us in the worst of times. We think of Darkaniouss as the person that comes for us when we die, and that is true, but he is *not* there in a negative, deviant, or evil way. All these years people have said that we must travel that road after death on our own, but nothing could be farther from the truth. Darkaniouss is there to guide everything that has died onto their spiritual journeys, and then hand them off to either a loved one, a friend, or a spirit that they might not even know. Think about that for a second. Every soul that has passed on throughout time—every living thing, including plants, animals, and all those things that existed in every chamber before this one—has been led down the path to salvation, or what is referred to as the Spiritual Crossroads, but was *never* travelled alone.

At that intersection Darkaniouss has always handed them off, and then moved on to the next soul in line. The Crossroads are a junction that takes souls back to The Lord by many routes, depending on who you are and what you must experience before you reach your final destination in The Kingdom of The Creator. Sometimes this presence guides great amounts of souls down to the Crossroads at the same time, armies even, and as we look back throughout history we see where many people have died together: wars, explosions, accidents, terror attacks, etc. In those times, Darkaniouss leads a great many more than just one soul through spiritual realms. But never forget, dear reader, no soul travels alone, because of *him*, and the job he has been given.

When the power went out, He was the first guide every spirit met as they traveled back to The Creator. On that journey, the Crossroads were bypassed completely and those traveling were joined by many spirits from many different realms. Some had passed on many years before, some we have already talked about, and some we cannot talk about at this time; but make no mistake, they were led first by the death guide we have always talked about wrongly.

In this chapter we will read about one such instance that happened when The Creator called back all his children, just to prove my point. Darkaniouss is not an evil presence, nor a good one. He has no soul, no heart, nor feelings. He is just needed to do a job, just like everybody else in the realms of reflections, and he does it religiously and tirelessly. He is an angel unlike any other— just not like the one that you imagine in the tales told on planet Earth. Below is one such story, one out of many other endless ones that can fill out any wall of history past. It tells a tale that contradicts life on many fronts, including the dark force known as The Grim Reaper, better known to us now as Darkaniouss.

Margaret "Maggie" Washington sat in her normal booth at the Newport Colonial City Diner in Providence, Rhode Island—third in from the front entrance, left and opposite side from the front door. That was important, because it was *that* much further from death or injury, not that *that* mattered all that much now! You see, if a criminal entered the diner looking to stir up some killing stir-fry, then he, she, or *they* would odds on shoot people on the door side first. That's what statistics showed. Her friends, if she had any (and she *might*, because people said hello to her all the time as if they had known her all her life, yet she didn't know, or remember them), would laugh at her ideas on the subject. But it didn't matter. Why? Because Maggie Washington, eighty-five years young, alone with no family, knew she was going to die of brain cancer in the not-too-distant future.

It was a large golf-ball sized tumor on the right side, toward the back of her head. No, she hadn't been told by a doctor, for she didn't have one as far as she knew, and she didn't even feel any pain in her head; but she still knew. How, you might ask, if there were no apparent symptoms or discomfort, could she know? Because Maggie Washington had memories, that's why. No, not of the past—she remembered very little of the days she had already lived—but of the future. Maggie had memories of things that hadn't yet happened! Not too far into the future, mind you, maybe only days, or at the most weeks in advance, but it was enough for Maggie to sometimes know how certain situations would turn out. I guess you could say that Miss Washington's brain and mind thought and worked in reverse, and it had been that way for a very long time, as far as she knew, because her past disappeared very quickly, and her memories didn't live there. Not that it mattered now. Let's delve further.

Usually the memories of the future Maggie had were good ones; it was why she slowly walked from her one-room flat a block from the diner three times a day smiling, or actually *beaming*, day in and day out. She used her gift(?) to full advantage, though; for you see, Maggie could see the winning lottery numbers in those thoughts, remembering seeing them in a newspaper that had yet to be written. Most, or all people would go crazy with *that* knowledge. Greed, selfishness, and gluttony would take over, but not with Maggie. No, on most days she disregarded those memories, but once every couple of weeks, she played the numbers and won the cash needed to survive (her rent and food expenses mostly), but all of the rest went to either charities, research, needy families, or someone on the street that looked like they could use a little extra in their wallets. Those people could be homeless, jobless, hungry, or just plain depressed, but once Maggie Washington crossed their paths their lives would either change or be altered forever.

Usually (and Maggie knew none of this), the money made more money, and then strangely, the recipients of Maggie's generosities would help someone else—a classic case of paying it forward. They could be beggars, thieves, even murderers or wife beaters, but once the old lady shoved money into their empty hands (of which they told no one), they suddenly rethought their misdirected ways and directions, and magically their lives would take a 360-degree turn. Forever after then *they* would smile like Maggie did, singing a happy tune and ridding themselves of the dark and cankerous invisible tumors that had been infecting their souls. How many had she saved? Maggie certainly didn't know, but did that matter, especially now?

Another strange fact: even though Maggie Washington played the numbers and won on a semiregular basis, mysteriously *no one* remembered or recalled that she had won previously! Not once! Memories . . . they sometimes worked in strange, mysterious ways! I'm sure you're wondering: Could this be considered stealing from the rich and giving to the poor? Possibly, especially to those in power that considered all things theirs, but Maggie was also giving money to help cure diseases, help in research projects, and better society on a whole. She was changing lives for the better, and, to her, that more than balanced the books. Besides, it made her feel good in her own little world, and her soul shinned brighter with every good deed that she carried out, even though they would all fade from her mind processes quickly. Though Maggie didn't remember how long she had experienced this way of thinking, or any of her past, you, dear reader, will know in the lines printed below, because I know you're dying to find out.

Maggie Washington was an only child, born under unusual circumstances. Her mother was a prostitute who walked the streets in downtown Providence. She got pregnant, continued to sell her goods, and gave birth to a baby girl that immediately started out with much less than most reading these pages. Within hours of entering this world she was left on the doorstep of the Providence Home for Children, a foster home for unwanted young souls.

Her mother, one alias Wanda "One Time" Washington, was a shapely woman who only lived for her next high-paying trick, or the next big thrill (which was usually drinking cheap local whiskey while smoking weak pot grown in her girlfriend Sadie's parents backyard). Wanda also was "damn sure" that she was *not* cut out for raising a child, and so after giving birth to Maggie in an old shack surrounded by her associates and someone who said they knew something about delivering a baby, she staggered to the orphanage and rang the doorbell before scurrying off. A snowstorm was raging throughout the city, a powerful nor'easter in the middle of a very cold and dreary February, and poor Maggie almost froze to death in the whiteout until the door opened up for her.

Meanwhile, Wanda developed complications from her delivery and died in a lonely alleyway a few hours after giving birth to a daughter she would never know. Her story was sad in so many ways, yet when the authorities found her body curled up behind a garbage bin in a pool of blood (she had completely bled out), she had a big smile on her face. Maybe she knew what her newborn daughter would one day become—possibly Wanda saw future memories of her own—but one thing was for sure: her pain and struggle to survive in this world was thankfully over, and she could now rest in peace. Which she did. A certain tall and dark presence was there to guide her to the Crossroads, where her two sets of grandparents waited patiently, who then took her the rest of the way home to The Kingdom of The Lord. Through her many hardships spent on Planet Earth, her penance had been paid in full, and she entered into another realm which was completely covered in vast wealth and goodness. She was much more appreciative than those who had possessed more on Earth than she, and Wanda Washington's soul shined brighter than most, for she knew that The Lord had forgiven her and loved her deeply.

Once the authorities realized that the baby left off at Providence Home for Children was Wanda Washington's, they named her, keeping her last name and giving the newborn her great grandmother's first name—yes, one of the same souls that had helped her own mother find her way home.

She stayed in the orphanage for many years, growing up normally, until she was struck by lightning in her tenth year during a powerful thunderstorm. She had wandered out into the backyard of the home searching for her Raggedy Ann Doll (yes, they still made them), and was struck as she ran back to the back door. She was hospitalized and remained in a coma for three weeks, and when Maggie woke up she remembered nothing about her past and began to have memories that were yet to happen. Maggie also stopped talking, even though the doctors found nothing wrong with her vocal cords, and she never spoke another word from that day forward.

When Maggie turned fourteen, she was adopted by Norman and Carolyn Johnson, who had five children of their own. On that fateful day, while taking a wrong turn, the Johnsons drove past the orphanage, a thought hit both of them at the same time, and the rest is history. Maggie stayed with the Johnsons until all her siblings grew up and started their own families. She couldn't remember the past, but during the time they were together she saved them numerous times from having accidents. One time she stopped her oldest brother Josh from going on an airplane that eventually crashed, killing everyone on board. After that the family never doubted her premonitions.

One day they found her crying, and there was no consoling her. She could write what she couldn't speak, but she refused to type anything on her computer. A week later Norman Johnson had a fatal heart attack, and then the rest of the family knew what had disturbed her so. Even though he wasn't her biological father, she cried more than the other Johnson children, taking death a whole lot harder than the rest of the family. The good thing was she forgot the whole death experience of her adopted father, and soon after began asking (typing) why he wasn't coming home each night until she forgot him completely. Carolyn, or one of the other children would tell her that he was on a business trip and wouldn't be home that night, and that would put her at ease.

They were telling her a little white lie, but they all considered that indiscretion OK, for they were sure The Good Lord would forgive them.

How they wished at that moment that they could forget like Maggie could. They were envious, and they cried over the loss of their father while Maggie wasn't there, but they also cried tears of joy that God had seen it fit that she had come to live with them and filled their hearts and souls with so much love and happiness.

Norman had been the breadwinner of the family, Carolyn a stay at home mom, and so times became harder for the Johnsons. It was at that point that Maggie began seeing winning numbers and started playing them. The family protected Maggie by changing the story and telling her that Norman had lost his job and was looking constantly for new work in different places—another white lie they deemed necessary. When Maggie came home with her first winnings and told them what she had done, they first cried, then laughed, and then cried some more. Plans were laid out so that she would only use her gift sparingly, but as each of the children left home Maggie made sure that each was well taken care of. Her last name might be Washington, but she was a Johnson through and through. She *never* forgot that!

When Carolyn died of kidney failure Maggie cried for weeks before her mother was diagnosed and took her death just as hard as her father's. By then, all the Johnson children had moved out and were living productive lives, and so she moved into her small flat after the children sold the house. Maggie refused her share, for she didn't need it, and continued to pick numbers and collect her winnings. Eventually she forgot the Johnsons even existed, but their spirits remained in her heart even as memories of them faded away. Maggie smiled about memories she couldn't remember, but her soul knew. It shone bright, and her heart was always full of love and happiness.

Now, as Maggie sat in her booth sipping vegetable soup and thinking about her brain tumor, and death overall, she began to smile like never before. Suddenly a new brightness filled it, because a new future memory had just entered her mind. A lot of other memories made her smile, but this one was different, special. Of course, she kept it to herself, like all other new memories, for no one should learn future time passages shuffled out of order—including us readers, and so we will not know of it at this moment.

On the morning the power went out, Maggie Washington Johnson got up to go for breakfast and collapsed. She knew that she would die this day, and so she went to the floor without a fight. She closed her eyes, and when she reopened them, she smiled and spoke for the first time since she had been hit by lightning so many years before.

"Hello, Darkaniouss," she said in a voice that crackled with emotion. "I've been waiting to meet you for a while, now."

The Grim Reaper nodded and smiled inwardly (since he had no visual face), for this woman meant more to him than most. Another one of the things Darkaniouss did was watch certain people over time for certain purposes. In this case, even though he had no soul or heart, he somehow felt a special fondness for this woman who had done so much for her kind over the years. He engulfed her soul and took her past the Crossroads, for no one was waiting there for his new passenger. This he knew in advance as they both moved into unchartered territory.

Suddenly he stopped, for he was given a message from his benefactor. Without questioning the command, he turned the spirit of Maggie Washington back around, back past the Crossroads, and back into her room. He returned her soul to her body; she took a deep breath, and then Maggie returned to the land of the living.

"Thank you Darkaniouss, you are very kind," Maggie said in his head, for in her physical body she again couldn't speak outwardly. "I will forget you presently, but you will always be in my heart. I know we will meet again . . . in my memories."

She smiled warmly as he helped her to her feet. He grabbed her right hand with both sleeves of his robe, and then slowly faded away.

Maggie Washington Johnson walked down to the diner twice that day: once for breakfast, and once for lunch. After she had finished her lunch she did something out of her normal pattern. She stayed in her seat watching people come and go, nodding and smiling at them all. She never felt so uplifted, for she knew that they were going home to The Lord, the one who had given her so very much, and that made her feel so grateful. She had gladly through him shared that gift, and made him proud, but now there was more work to be done—possibly much more.

As customers came and went, unaware of what was to come, Maggie hummed a tune she had composed years before in her mind when time hit one of its many lulls. It was a religious tune that had no words, but the feeling of the notes was enough to warm the heart on the coldest day on the calendar. It was a hymn to Him, The Creator of all things. She was sure that he heard it, for her soul had brightened every time she hummed it. It was also the one memory she never forgot, because she sang it so frequently.

When the Event took place, she felt a strong breeze pass by her; the lights went out and everything became quiet. In a millisecond, all the people in the diner disappeared around her. She was instantly alone, and the Newport Colonial City Diner quickly became hot, as the air conditioners stopped working. She sat in her seat for an hour and a half, listening to various airplanes crash all around her, one very close, maybe only a few miles away, and then walked back to her flat for the last time. After looking around the room, she got down on her knees, said a prayer for all that she had been given, and then walked out into the late-day intense heat.

She walked past the diner she had eaten at over the years and smiled.

She had eaten here before, hadn't she? Maggie was sure of it. Still . . .

A Small Interruption: sometimes Maggie remembered this eatery, and on other occasions she had completely forgotten it from one meal to the next on the same day! That happened more as she got older, but it was always the first place she'd encounter whenever she got hungry. She couldn't cook her own meals, for she would forget how to make whatever she had been taught, and so by accident or by fate, she had eaten at the Newport Colonial Diner every day since she had lived alone, and silently introduce herself to the same waitresses day in and day out. They would smile and pass it off as an old lady's forgetfulness. If only they knew her whole story.

Some memories stayed with her longer than others, but none of them could be predicted. Only The Lord knew of those things, and that was the way it should be, and not questioned. Maggie protected herself, though. She wrote many notes, which she kept in her large pocketbook, and they came in handy on more than one occasion.

It *does* look familiar. And what about all of the people? Where did *they* go? It is a pickle, no doubt about it! Maggie thought as she saw smoke rise into the sky in many places. And . . . who am I?

Maggie stood stationary outside the diner, for *all* her memory had suddenly deserted her. Airplanes continued to crash, and then the powerful thunderstorms rumbled through, putting all the fires out. All during this period of time Maggie continued to stand still, as if "offline," and in a way she was.

Three days after the Event took place Darkaniouss appeared next to Maggie, put his left arm sleeve around her bony shoulders, gently touched his black rod to her wrinkled forehead with his right, and she came to. She looked up into the faceless hooded figure and smiled. She suddenly remembered all of her memories from her past, and only one from the future—a future that was now happening.

"Thank you again, Darkaniouss," Maggie said gratefully, beaming. She voiced this out loud, saying her first words since being struck by lightning so many years ago.

The Grim Reaper nodded, and then disappeared. His work was done for the time being.

Maggie Washington watched Darkaniouss disappear and smiled. He had rebooted her mind, rearranged her memory reflective lenses—something that needed to be done. Nothing during this three-day stretch had died, and so his job had been temporarily altered. That would change now, and so he returned to his home in the dead woodlands, and waited patiently like always. Memories of him faded quickly from Maggie's mind, and she shrugged her shoulders.

"There is much work to be done," she said out loud as she walked away from the Newport Colonial Diner, a place she now remembered fondly. "I don't know what that might be, but I'm actually happy about that." She smiled.

Chapter Thirty-Nine

JUSTIN FARROWS' JOURNEY

*J*ustin Farrows was homeless, and on the road traveling from town to town amongst the many cornfields throughout the state of Iowa. He planned on heading south at some point once the weather turned colder, but it was early May, in the midst of a season of new life and growth, and overall new beginnings. Justin felt those special feelings in the air, and knew it was *his* time for those things as well. Diamond dust had blown on the spiritual winds of time directly at him and had passed through every pore of his body. How did he know that? A spirit, an angel, or something else entirely had told him so through a dream he had as he slept in a church in the middle of current barren fields, ones that would soon grow new ears of corn in the next few months when the land would allow new growth of so many things.

A rebirth was happening, and another inside Justin Farrows soul was as well, and no matter how each new day would pan out no one would be able to wipe the smile off the homeless man's face. In fact, as far as Justin was concerned, he couldn't imagine himself ever frowning again. Life was good, and new beginnings were in store. He was right about those things, right as rain—right up until the power went off, and most went back to The Creator three months later, including himself. In fact, dear readers, this is a chapter where no one was left behind. Why is that relevant? Read on, and fill your soul with renewed light.

A young Justin Farrows started working on a production line in a car plant in Des Moines, Iowa. He worked his way up to fore-man, and then eventually became production manager. He was a vibrant and handsome man of six feet, thin in stature. All during his early life he was happy, popular, and full of energy. He gradu-ated from Wily High School and Trade School, and then went to work for Drive/Works.

During that time, he met and married Janus Woodrow, a pret-ty, petite blonde, and had two beautiful, healthy girls. Everything looked to be on the up and up for The Farrow family until every-thing turned upside down and hurtled it into a dark abyss that seemed to have no apparent bottom.

First, like so many in the world at this time, he lost his job along with every other employee; the car company was bought out, and the plant closed and moved north to Detroit. During his unemployment phase his oldest daughter, seven-year-old Jessica, a beautiful blonde little girl that received straight A's across the board in school and was voted most popular in her class (fol-lowing in her father's footprints), was shot dead by a disgruntled gunman named Evan Thayer. He somehow managed to shoot his way inside the school and heartlessly take twenty young innocent souls, all under the age of nine besides their teacher, leaving be-hind devastated families that were still trying to recover from that ordeal when the power went off much later.

The gun laws were still under heavy scrutiny, being fought

politically in the courts, and idiots and maniacs were still taking out their frustrations on others of all ages. All over the country, families of the victims wondered how families of nonvictims (and those who wanted gun laws to stay as they were), just didn't *get* it. Would they need to lose a loved one to understand the pain, the anguish? And would they understand it even then? To many in society, it seemed as if this gun madness might never end, and they were right. It never had a chance to fix itself, for The Event took place.

Anyway, the Farrows family fell apart after that tragedy. Justin and Janus began fighting constantly, their feelings completely raw, and their arguments, which were occurring more often, had a subconscious feel to them. You know the type, ones where true feelings come to the surface, and you don't care how much they hurt the other person when those angry, sometimes vile words surprisingly come out of your mouth. The ones that you regret later—almost *always!* These types of disagreements are commonplace after a traumatic situation is experienced, like the ones on different levels the Farrows had to deal with: a lost child, a lost job, lost income needed to help a family pay the bills.

Yes, the dominos were falling—again, falling in the wrong direction and right on top of the family foundation without reprise. You can easily understand the turmoil that was going on under the Farrows' roof—one they might not have for long. And so, after hearing many of these less than desirable arguments, and after losing her older sister, who she completely looked up to, their younger daughter, Jeannie, quite logically became depressed and despondent. She began recovery therapy, and even though the family finances were hit even harder, those sessions were deemed necessary, and they did seem to be helping.

The dominoes kept falling, though, falling *hard*, for after a few months of therapy both she and Janus were killed in a car accident on the way home from one of those therapeutic sessions. The driver of the other car, Charles Kandy, twenty-six, had just lost his job in another car factory; his job had been replaced by one of the new robot models. His state of mind was no better than that of the Farrows, and his depressive thoughts took him a million miles from where they should have been when he ran through a stop sign and hit the Farrows Toyota at seventy miles an hour—forty miles faster than the town speed limit.

He had no idea of how fast he had been traveling, or what street he was on. He was oblivious of his surroundings, and they had a fatal effect. Charles also succumbed to his head injuries a week later, never regaining consciousness. He died without much dignity, alone with his right wrist handcuffed to his hospital bed.

During Charles Kandy's unconscious realm a calm and peaceful voice spoke to him, relieving him of his burden and all of his sins. His soul returned to The Kingdom pure and free to worship The Lord and His Word. Three other souls met him at the end of his final journey, and they became inseparable forever thereafter: Janus Farrow, and her two daughters, Jessica and Jeannie.

NARRATIVE NOTES: As the population continued to grow, new car plants opened up throughout the country, creating new jobs . . . for a while. One of those plants, Drive/Works, for the most part built the new and futuristic electronically run vehicles. One of those facilities opened up just outside of Des Moines, Iowa, creating many jobs on all levels for ten years before the beginning of the fall. Two things happened. Downsizing took place, as more and more positions on the assembly lines were taken over by new robotic systems that greatly reduced costs and increased production; and the richer, more powerful companies bought out the upstarts like Drive/Works and moved their operations back to Detroit and the surrounding regions. Financial savings played a big part in these moves, but outright greed did as well.

Many jobs were promised to these displaced workers, but they never came to fruition. After spending time explaining the new mechanisms to the older, more powerful companies, employees were quickly discarded—even though some of them had already relocated expecting solid futures in Detroit. That was sinful, but that was business—heartless and uncaring as usual. The almighty dollar always came first, over all else, and let the working souls fall where they may. The souls and blood of these dominating conglomerates ran colder than the coldest, frigid winters around the Great Lakes, and many victims fell by the wayside. Justin Farrows was actually one of the luckier ones. He was just let go, and never had that nonexistent carrot dangled in front of his desperate face. Still, that didn't stop despair and depression from settling into the Farrow household, although Justin never actually took his life like many other of his fellow workers did over the following months.

Justin buried his wife and youngest daughter and fought off suicidal tendencies for months afterward. He, too, went through therapy he realistically couldn't afford, and decided to take a different route back to the living. First, he visited his church every morning and prayed to The Lord for three things that seemed out of reach. He begged for a reasoning for what had happened, the strength to go on, and finally, mercy. That last one, mercy, was a tricky one. He wanted desperately to join his wife and young daughters in heaven, for he didn't want to live without them, and he knew without a doubt that they must be there. He was severely compromised, for he didn't want to commit suicide, but wanted to go home to them.

His daily private conversations near the altar with God always ended up with tears running down his face as he quietly walked back down the aisle, head down, and out the church doors—back into the real world. The Lord never answered him during these times, but he never gave up. He couldn't and wouldn't do that. There *was* something different about being in the sanctuary of the church compared to the real world outside, and so he knew that his prayers would be answered one way or another, and so he returned again and again, day after day. He was right, but again, I'm getting ahead of myself.

Through all of this, Justin never found a job, and so he decided to sell the house just to stay out of debt. He discussed his dire situation with a real estate agent (Marilyn Roosevelt, a middle-aged, cute widower whom Justin might have taken out if he had been in the right frame of mind), left all business aspects up to her, and left all his past possessions behind. He drove his car (which was three payments in arrears) back to the dealership, handed in his keys, and started walking down the road with only his depleted checkbook, his wallet with only a few hundred dollars in cash, and the clothes on his back in his possession. Objective: He wanted to leave behind just about everything and start anew.

The future would be unknown, but that was how it should be, for only then could he be set free from all his dark and painful memories. That was the plan, the clear path: his *salvation!* The less he had, the less he would be forced to remember. He had lost so much, and now he couldn't lose anything else, only accumulate, and at this point in time he didn't want or need for much. If he was robbed, so be it. It would be God's way. If he was murdered, then he would get what he truly craved and be reunited with his family. Yes, downsizing to the smallest common denominator was the way to go—low maintenance all the way!

The homeless man slept wherever he could, usually in heavily wooded areas or scattered buildings used for shelters, some of them even churches. It was in one of them, Saint Augustine's, in which he had a dream where his prayers were finally answered and his outlook on life in general changed for the rest of his days on Earth. Seeds of new crops in the area had just been planted earlier in the day, and a light rain had begun to fall as Justin laid his head down on the third pew on the left side of the church, directly in front of the pulpit. When the homeless man closed his eyes and fell into deep slumber, in his mind he heard those newly planted seeds outside begin to grow.

For the first few moments inside Justin's dreamscape he only heard the subtle cracking of seeds separating, but then the darkness began to fade, and he found himself in a cornfield, watching cornstalks grow out of the ground and shoot ten to twenty feet into the air all around him. Rich brown dirt turned into dark green leaves of freshly growing cornstalks, and he could hear new ears of corn growing in them. He stood in-between two rows, and then they suddenly bent away from each other, opening up a wide pathway. Justin walked between the half-bent stalks until it opened up on his right.

The area was dirt covered, flat and round in shape, twenty feet in circumference, with a bright circular light illuminating in the center of it. Justin swayed slightly back and forth as he stared at it hypnotically, and then he heard a low but soothing voice, just above a whisper, coming from inside it. "Come inside," It beckoned calmly. "We have been waiting for you." Justin's body slowly tilted forward and his head moved slightly downward as his legs moved backward and upward until his feet were a foot above the ground, and then, without moving a muscle, he floated toward the light and passed through it.

At first, Justin saw speeding bolts of brightly colored speckled lights flash by at breathtaking speed, some even shooting directly through him. He traveled further until the brightness suddenly disappeared, and he witnessed *paradise!* He saw fields of green grass filled with multicolored patches of flowers, plants, and brush, perfectly positioned side by side for what seemed like hundreds, thousands, or possibly even *millions* of miles! He saw scattered trees of all types, shapes, and sizes, also multicolored, as if they were in fall-foliage mode, yet no leaves had fallen off their branches, and none were lying lifelessly on top of healthy green grass.

In fact, nothing was lifeless in this beautiful landscape; there was only vibrant life standing tall, healthy, and peacefully. In the distance on one side Justin noticed enormous tree-covered mountains that seemed to reach up to the heavens, multicolored as well. The skies above them were light blue in color, filled with white, pink, and dark blue clouds moving haphazardly in every direction. In amazement, Justin noticed at least five different suns shining brightly in various parts of the horizon, providing bright light and warmth. Different shades of blue, serene bodies of water could be seen in the distance as well, reflecting the tranquil skies above. Lakes and rivers lay to the east and west, and possibly oceans lay to the north, since water met horizon with no apparent land in sight. Deep and immense valleys lay to the south with squarish fields filled with all types of nourishment neatly lining up next to each other for as far as the eye could see.

Justin smiled broadly and breathed in the air. It felt different, easier to inhale and exhale. Purer. Uninfected. What a magnificent place this is! he amazingly thought happily, nodding approvingly.

He surveyed the whole area again and again, taking in more and more of the wonderment, and realized there weren't any dark colors in sight—no shades of grey, no dark blacks, no . . . no apparent negatives. No storm clouds or disruptions affected the perfect weather and climate in this beautiful wonderland. And then he realized the absence of other deterrents as well. There were no buildings, factories, or power plants emitting exhaust into the air, polluting it. No dark smoke filled the sky, no loud noises disrupted tranquil peace. No, this place was devoid of human error and abomination. No evil, hate, deception, carelessness, selfishness, greed, gluttony, or iniquitousness existed here. There were no wastes, no garbage or litter of any kind. Nature here was untouched, unblemished. It was shielded from dark negatives of any kind. It was life in its purist form: devoid of death.

With those positive thoughts swirling around inside Justin's mind, he suddenly saw a round, bright white and yellow light suddenly appear and move toward him from those vibrant fields that grew crops toward the south. It floated silently and effortlessly through the air, stopping just in front of him. The light slowly took on a form somewhat like a human being, about seven feet in height. It had appendages like human arms and legs, a torso, and a thin neck attached to a larger-than-average rounded head, devoid of any facial or hair covering. It hovered a foot above the ground, and sounds of calm sea waves caressing a sandy shoreline could be faintly heard inside the recesses of his mind.

"Hello Justin, I see that you have heard me and entered this special realm," the light figure said in a watery voice. "That last part was rhetorical, of course." Even though the figure had no apparent facial features, Justin knew it was smiling by the vibrating ripples he could see around its head area.

"Hello back," Justin said in the same watery voice, a voice much different than his own. "Who are you, and where am I?"

The homeless man felt no fear, for quite frankly, none was evident. Violence would be out of place in this environment, and so that negative act was quickly dismissed from Justin's thoughts and concerns. This place was something entirely different from what he had ever known; it was completely tranquil, and this presence seemed warm and friendly from its calming tone.

"I am what I appear to be, and this place has no name, and yet it has many. That is all you need to know at this time."

Justin frowned, stirring those riddle-like responses around in his head, and then he smiled, for he suddenly realized that even though he had been literally told nothing, he had been told plenty. He nodded, and said, "I understand."

"I know you do, my friend, but there is much more important information I will provide to you presently, in a timely fashion."

"You mentioned time? Isn't this my dream?"

"It was, until you moved into the light; then you willfully entered a new realm of reality." The lighted figure's complete frame vibrated, and with its right arm appendage it lightly touched Justin's chest. "Real enough for you?"

Real wasn't the word, as far as Justin was concerned! Yes, he felt the lighted entity's touch, but he felt so much more radiating through him. He experienced warmth, love, and feelings that went way beyond description—all of them positive. He suddenly was momentarily stunned, and then tears of joy streamed down his face, for he instantly knew why: he felt his wife and two daughters in this presence, as if they were connected in some way, and it was overwhelming in its knowledge.

"Did . . . did I just feel . . . ?"

"Yes, Justin, you felt your family through me," the presence answered, completing his question. "That is why I touched you: so you could feel them. And more importantly, they felt *you*."

"Oh . . . oh my!" Justin managed to say just before breaking down and crying openly. He put both hands up to his face and cried like never before. What a revelation to experience, and it was almost too much to handle. He became one overwhelming emotion, his soul shining right through his body, and he was transformed into the same light substance as the presence. His skin was shed, and his essence shinned like a beacon. The presence wrapped its upper appendages around Justin's lighted frame, and he immediately saw his wife, two daughters, and many others behind them that he didn't know lovingly smiling at him from another place, a place filled with warmth and glowing light. He smiled back, and all the hurt, grief, and missing his family left his essence, and Justin knew that his prayers had finally been answered. God, and whatever this presence was—possibly one and the same—had answered his pleas when he thought he might eternally live in agony forever.

The presence suddenly broke its embrace, and Justin quickly transformed back into his physical body, but his soul continued to shine just as brightly inside his physical form. Justin smiled knowingly at the presence, shaking his head in amazement.

"Thank you. Thank you so much!"

"You're welcome, Justin."

"How . . . how can I . . . ?"

"You can't, that's not even in the equation. You have suffered more than most, and so nothing is required of you."

"But there must be something........ "

"There is, but you will do that on your own accord, and in its own time. Now let me tell you about other things that you need to know."

And then for the next few minutes the presence spoke, and Justin listened.

When the one-way conversation was over, the presence floated with Justin back to the edge of the circular light. They said their goodbyes and Justin gingerly stepped out; then the circular light and the presence completely disappeared, leaving the homeless man alone in the massive cornfield. Justin knew many new things, information that he would keep to himself until it wouldn't matter anymore. He looked around at the growing cornstalks (they were close to thirty feet high at this point), and suddenly he felt extremely exhausted, both mentally and physically. He slowly laid down on vibrant green grass that had healthily grown in the rich soil during his time in the circular light. He closed his eyes and fell into deep slumber.

He awoke inside St. Augustine's church a new man. Yes, he was still homeless and basically penniless, but he knew deep down that he was anything but. He happily walked out of the sanctuary and continued on his spiritual journey, traveling west until the power went off, and most, him included, went back to The Creator. Once there, he was reunited with his family, and he made a choice. It was the right one.

Once Justin Farrows left St. Augustine's church after having his meeting with the lighted presence in his dreams, a great weight had been lifted, and as he headed west with no real plan in mind he enjoyed many sceneries he never would have noticed in his past depressed state. When the power went off and he went back to The Creator, he was sitting on Montara State beach, which is located just north of Montara along the San Mateo County Coast in Northern California. The beach is about a mile in length, and behind it sits sculpted sandstone cliffs that Justin fell in love with as soon as he saw them. For three days he sat either staring out at the vast Pacific Ocean meditating, or marveling at how beautiful the cliffs were, wishing his family was there to share it with him.

For him, Justin knew that this would be his final destination as he waited for The Event to happen. He didn't know exactly when that Event was going to occur, or even what it *was*, but the lighted presence had told him that something big was about to happen, so pick a place of beauty to enjoy, and just wait.

Justin smiled as he took in his beachfront surroundings, remembering his journeying days ever since leaving St. Augustine's. He had decided to travel on back roads running parallel to Route I-80 West, and so he began walking, expecting nothing out of the norm to take place, but after his interaction with the light presence how could anything be normal again? So Justin didn't seem surprised when a car pulled up beside him and an old man that looked to be in his mid-eighties wearing a Cincinnati Reds baseball cap asked him if he needed a lift. Now it had been years since hitchhiking became taboo, and Justin was about to say, "Thanks, but no thanks," when the unmistakable watery voice of the light presence suddenly whispered in his ear, "Get in." And so, he did.

The driver's name was Paul Rosen. He told Justin that he had never picked up a hitchhiker, or *anyone* else walking on the side of the road before, but something in his head told him that this person needed a ride, and so he stopped. Justin nodded, told his Good Samaritan that some things can't be explained, but he *did* appreciate the ride, and he would remember Paul in his prayers. The old man nodded, smiled warmly, and understood.

After some long, healthy conversations, and a supper in a diner that the old man refused to let Justin pay for, Paul dropped his passenger off at the Iowa/Nebraska State border. Before driving off, Paul admitted that he had only come out for a pack of cigarettes, and then instead decided to take a drive. They both laughed at that, and then Paul admitted one more thing before turning around and driving back east. He told Justin that he had smoked for over sixty years; he had tried to quit on many occasions but never could, but somehow now he felt that goal was completely possible. He admitted that he no longer had the urge to smoke, and he knew that he would never have another cancer stick again. He crushed the unopened pack in his bony pale hand, and chuckled. "It's never too late to quit!" he roared, and they both laughed again. He asked Justin to please throw the pack away for him, and he readily agreed.

Justin watched Paul drive off and honk, and then he looked down at the crushed pack in his hand. The pack had been unopened, but now the lid was ripped, and something was tucked in-between the cigarettes. Justin emptied the pack into his hand, and along with the crushed cigarettes were three folded up one-hundred-dollar bills. Tears welled up; Justin looked up into the sky and whispered, "Thank You!"

Justin had told Paul to drop him off at the corner, but the old man had insisted on pulling off at the first parking lot, for safety reasons. That went one step further, for Paul pulled into a Motel Comfort that had a diner and a corner store named Willie's, and so with that money Justin got himself a room, went to get a bite to eat, and then before turning in bought himself a couple of bottles of water for the next day ahead.

As he knelt at the side of his bed, Justin prayed to The Lord, thanking Him again for watching out for him. He also hoped for the best for his Good Samaritan, Paul Rosen. In their short amount of time together, Justin found that he liked the old man immensely and would always consider him family. Justin didn't know it, but his prayers would be answered.

Paul Rosen drove all through the night and exhaustedly fell

into deep slumber once he got home. He had lost his wife to cancer three years prior, and as he slept he was taken to the same place in his dreams as Justin, and the light presence let him not only see his wife but his two older sisters whom he loved and missed dearly as well. He woke up crying and called his only daughter, who he had been feuding with for most of their lives, and made up with her and her husband. He visited them regularly after that, and also connected and reconnected with not only his ten grandchildren, but his five great grandchildren as well.

If truth be known, Paul was with them when the power went off during his great grandchild Susan's fifth birthday party, and traveled along with them on the current back to The Creator. Since his wife had passed on he had felt such loneliness, but those last three months with his extended family were some of the happiest days of his long life.

Another Note of Interest: ever since Paul Rosen had secretly stashed those three one-hundred-dollar bills into his cigarette pack and given it to Justin to help out a new friend, he never smoked again—never even had an urge!

Next came Judy Blevins and Florence Davidson. Justin had just passed the Iowa/Nebraska border when the two twenty-year-olds suddenly pulled over one hundred yards ahead of him and got out of their cranky-sounding old Honda. They looked more like twins than best friends as Justin walked up on them. They both had shoulder-length auburn hair, cute faces, and curvy, petite bodies. Both wore flimsy tank tops and short shorts, like most of the young women were wearing these days. Paul asked them if they were having car trouble; they said no, and then proceeded to tell him that the night before they'd both had dreams telling them to pick up a walking stranger who needed a ride. Both had vividly seen Justin's face, and here he was.

With that said, Florence opened up the rear passenger side door, and Justin got in. They drove him completely across the state, had lunch in another pit-stop food court (them paying, of course), and dropped him off at the border. During that time, during endless conversations, they told him that they had both lost loved ones during the past year: Judy her mother and Florence her favorite grandmother, and so they somewhat understood his grief. Justin seemed surprised by that statement, since he hadn't told them that he had just lost his entire family. No, that information had been told to them in their dreams, they said, and that's why they had been selected to help him on his journey. Justin nodded, and teared up again. He told them both how thankful he was, and that he would pray for much happiness and joy in their lives in the future.

They dropped him off in a strip-mall parking lot and wished him well. They both got out of the car and gave him a huge hug and a kiss on the cheek, turned around, and drove off, honking the car horn repeatedly. Justin laughed as they drove out of view, and then he went over to an ice cream stand to buy a cone. Fishing into his pocket, he came out with another three hundred-dollar bills, and he shook his head in amazement. They must have stuffed it in there when they gave him that goodbye hug, he reasoned, as he stared at the crumpled-up bills.

Next to the line of stores in the strip mall was another motel, Sonny's, and Justin got a room for the night. Before turning in, he prayed to The Lord again, thanking Him and wishing the girls well. His prayers were again answered, again he didn't know they were, and again both girls dreamed of the light presence who let them see their loved ones once they feel into a deep slumber. The next evening both girls met two boys at a Cornhusker dance who quickly became their steady boyfriends. They were all inseparable and enjoying life right up until the power went off, and then they all went back to The Creator together.

The next person to pick Justin up was Chester Reeves, a thirty-five-year-old black man from Pittsburgh. He was on his way to Yellowstone National Park on a short break when he pulled off I-80 to recharge his vehicle. He saw Justin walking on the shoulder and pulled over. Why? Because a voice in his head had told him to—an insistent one—and so he did. Justin walked up alongside Chester's SUV and smiled through the open passenger window.

"Let me guess: something or someone told you to give me a lift."

Chester laughed heartily, and said, "Yep!"

Justin got in and went to Yellowstone with his new friend of the day. During their time together they talked about life in general and enjoyed the tourist attractions as if they had been life-long friends. Chester told Justin that he was an aspiring rapper, but no one would hear his material. Justin heard some of his arrangements, and even though he told his Good Samaritan of the day that he didn't really get into that type of music, he thought it was pretty good. They spent two days together, just shooting the breeze and enjoying good company. After that first day at Yellowstone, Chester drove Justin across the state of Wyoming and dropped him off at the border. After telling Justin that he wasn't crazy, the rapper told him that while he slept, a light presence had told him to drive his new friend onward, because he had someplace important to go. Justin laughed at that and just said "Thanks." They shook hands, hugged, and then he watched Chester turn around and head back east.

Again, Justin didn't know it, but Chester went back home, got inspired from their time together, recorded a song called "Gotta Be Somewhere," and finally got his long-awaited break. The right person heard it through common associates and knew a DJ in the area who took a chance and played it. Calls kept coming in from listeners, telling the disc jockey, Miles Ahead (aka Royce Rollins) that they loved it, and an employee from Wordz Music got wind of it. One thing led to another, and Chester finally got his big break. The record company was in the process of recording an album when the power went off and most went back to The Creator, and so it was never released. Up until then, "Gotta Be Somewhere" continued to be played on many radio stations, satellite included, and it would have gone all the way to number one if the world had gone on as before, but it was now spinning on a new axis, and the follow-up single "Had To Go Someplace Else" never had a chance to climb the charts.

Bachelor Robert Perrotta picked up Justin on the Utah border and drove him across the state. The homeless man saw magnificent plateaus and other marvels as they crossed the desert. They stayed over in Salt Lake City and saw the sites together. Robert, forty-five, was a recently retired veteran of the U.S. Army, spending much time overseas during his fifteen-year tenure. He witnessed death and despair almost daily, and he wore those atrocities on his sleeve. He told Justin that he woke up screaming some nights, but felt it was all worth it because he had also saved many lives as well, and was doing his part in keeping America safe. War was hell, and death was its bride, Robert told Justin like he had told many others in the past, and he wondered if that abominable marriage would ever end. Hate seemed to grow like cancer, he added, tears streaming down his cheeks. Justin realized that everyone carried a varied weight on their shoulders, and he cried along with the soldier who had made first lieutenant in his many years of service. And yet they spoke warmly of other things: family, friends, and mankind in general. They laughed about the world as it turned on its angled axis trying to keep the insanity from completely taking over.

Here the human-element factor was very strong. Robert had been driving east from Seattle, Washington, his hometown, to New York, where he had a job interview in military recruitment. The job was his if he wanted it (and he did), but as he crossed the Utah/Wyoming border he felt a strong urge to turn around for no apparent reason. He did, and after an hour saw Justin walking, and felt a spiritual light turn on inside his soul. Darkness had surrounded his life for so long, and so seeing Justin walking was like seeing a beacon shining brightly in the middle of the night. "Do the right thing," he heard a voice say in his head. He followed that thought and pulled over just in front of Justin. He knew all too well that he was about to accept a job to recruit people that very well might witness what had scarred his own mind and spirit, but he had to pick this man up first; and so he did.

After saying their goodbyes, and shedding yet even more tears, Robert headed back in the direction of his eventual destiny, feeling better about his time with Justin Farrows, and life in general. He made it to New York City, accepted the recruiting job, and touched many in his final days before the power went off and he returned to The Kingdom. Quota wasn't a priority to Robert, and so he recruited only those who actually belonged in the military

environment, not the weak-minded, lost souls he could've easily talked into joining. He didn't know it, but all of his recruits
would have gone on to defend the United States bravely and successfully if the world had gone on as usual. What he *did* know was
that after dropping Justin off, Robert never woke up screaming
again, and was able to re-enter and co-exist in the world of the
living. He met Sally Feldman, another recruiter who was dealing
with her own demons, and on the night before the power went
off he proposed to her at dinner with the silhouette of the Statue
of Liberty in the distance. She said yes!

A small tan van pulled up next to Justin next. It was com-
prised of a group of young cancer patients: six children between
the ages of eight to twelve on their way on a two-day trip to
the Hoover Dam. One child, Rollins MacMaster, a ten-year-old
who was too sick to attend, left one seat empty—one that Justin
Farrows ended up sitting in. Larry Sanderson, a forty-five-year-
old driver, doctor, and overseer, told Justin that all the children
had told him to pick him up. They had been quite insistent, and
so he had pulled over. He told the homeless man that it went
against protocol and overall compliance, but as the driver drove
past him and pulled over, a calming voice in his head told him the
children knew what they were talking about, and so he had followed the spirit of his passengers. Both men stared at each other
with tears welling up, and saw their souls shining brightly around
their frames. The children were all patients who were well enough
to make the trip, but when they were alone Larry confided to
Justin that all of them were terminal, which brought on more
tears of grief and despair.

Justin stayed with them until they left for home the next

morning, and never felt more uplifted. During their travels he was made to understand just how sick they were, yet they remained so happy and positive about everything around them, including him. They just adored him, and each one told him their stories of dealing with sickness and pain, but beamed with unrelenting hope and joy, and a love for life that most healthy children couldn't even begin to possess. Health is a gift of immense proportions, yet these children possessed a special gift that went even beyond that!

Larry told Justin that growing up he didn't believe in a higher power, but his work with terminal children over the past fifteen years had changed his views on The Lord, and His Word. Gone were his selfish, greedy, and entitled ways that he had lived by growing up, like most adolescents. Love now filled his heart, and as he lost battle after battle with his patients, they never failed to lift him up as they slowly slipped away. Every time when their little bodies began to weaken, they told him that they were headed to a better place, one without pain or sickness, and one filled with everlasting love. Larry added that he always broke down when the children told him that they were special, picked for a purpose beyond the world of the living, one handed down to them by a soothing voice that spoke to them in their dreams. The attendant told Justin that even though their bodies broke down more and more each day, their spirits always seemed to get stronger, which gave them strength for the difficult times ahead.

Justin hugged and cried with Larry when he heard these revelations. What wonders exist around us all! he thought, shaking his head and smiling through his tears. He had been through a lot, God knew he had, but these children were heading down a road that thankfully wasn't traveled by many—although one was way too often. They touched his soul, and he prayed for them every single night afterward until they all traveled on the same current back to The Kingdom.

He looked over the edge of the Hoover Dam and stared down at the water running out of the pipes and down the Colorado River. All these young cancer patients had helped Justin realize that love knew no bounds, and shined through all types of shadows and darknesses. They all demonstrated their devotion to The Lord, and their spiritual connection to Him. And lastly, they showed him that it was all right to surrender to a dark force that was too strong to defeat on this plane, yet there would be the hope of another realm waiting for them: one that was enlightening and overwhelming, where sickness could not go, one where it could not attack them in any way, shape or form. They were good lessons to learn, and it was totally amazing in Justin's mind that children so young and gravely ill were the ones teaching them!

Love. Devotion. Surrender. Those three words kept repeating over and over inside Justin's head. They meant something, something *good*, and the homeless man felt his soul brighten and expand into something even greater. It felt wonderful and exhilarating, and he felt his family's presence in the glow, feeling the same emotions he was experiencing. Justin was way beyond what he ever thought he could ever feel spiritually, and he felt honored. He thanked God for allowing him to meet these special children in the van, and their overseer and driver. He would never forget them and hoped to meet them again in the future. His hopes and prayers would eventually be answered.

Johnny Watson, Phillip Hayman, Jessica Harmon, Danielle Darwin, and William Arrington: children all, young enough to ingest new ideas, yet old enough to acquire a sickness that has won many more wars than it has lost over many eons, and created pain not even the toughest football player or heavyweight boxing champion could tolerate. And yet these young children were forced to endure the agony and destruction cancer could create; and as the doctors knew in these times, it was constantly mutating, creating new strains that the specialists had never seen before. Five young children that knew all too well that fate on this plane had betrayed them, for the cancerous cells had migrated and lived inside them from day one, slowly becoming legion, creeping throughout young tissue, muscle, arteries, blood, organs, and bone.

And still these young five patients were happy to travel to see one of the most magnificent marvels of mankind, enduring pain mixed with drugs that created chaos within a young person's physical frame. And yet still they had enough strength and energy to make Larry Sanderson (an oasis of a man stationed in the middle of a desolate, vile, and deadly desert) stop the hospital van and pick up Justin Farrows, because they had all seen him many times before. Where? In their dreams. Why him? In the dream realm they saw Justin suffer with his emotions—the loss of his family, and to a lesser extent, his job—and knew that a different kind of cancer was eating him alive, not unlike the physical cancer that was consuming them.

They had witnessed the same light presence that had visited and helped them carry on, one that had given them the strength and hope to make it through another day. They knew they could help cure this man as well, which made them happy. He was family to them, plain and simple. Oh, they had been taught by the light presence that *all* mankind was family and should be treated with the upmost respect and love, but this man shared something they knew all too well: decay. The light presence, whom they had met long before Justin had been infected with his special kind of cancer, told them to unite with him on this Hoover Dam excursion. Why? Because they needed each other—now, and in the hereafter landscape, the true realm of realms.

And so, Justin was picked up, and a righteous time had been had by all. He never knew that these five young brave souls knew who *he* was. He never knew how much they inwardly loved and cared for him so deeply. He never knew that once he saw them drive off and the cancer continued to devour their physical forms, they never felt pain again—right up until the power went off and they all traveled back to The Creator together. He never knew that he was partly responsible for that, even though he definitely was. He never knew that he had the power to do that just by spending time with them, caring for them, hugging them—loving them. He never knew. He never knew. Like all the other people that had picked him up on his spiritual journey, he . . . never . . . knew.

Jarvis Sutherland drove Justin from Hoover Dam into the heart of Las Vegas, dropping him off in front of the Paris Hotel, with the replica of the Eiffel Tower growing thirty stories into the air. Justin had always wanted to see the waterspouts of the Bellagio Hotel, and now he was here. He didn't know where he would go after this, but it would come. He was sure of that.

When Jarvis Sutherland pulled over to pick Justin up, he wondered if he had lost his mind. He was eighty-one years old, frail, and weak from a bad summer cold. He'd had it for the past two weeks, and his doctor (Dr. Rosenbaum, the family doctor for the past forty years who Jarvis highly respected) in North Phoenix had told him to stay in bed, yet here he was defying that recommendation on his way to Vegas to do a little gambling. He had made this trip during the summer every year since his wife had died ten years ago on this date, even though he didn't even like to gamble. Why? Because he won. Not much, but enough to pay on his loan for the tombstone he had bought for his beloved Susan.

Each year he would come and win just a little. He had come on other days, but on those occasions he always lost—always. Every one of 364 other days he would be a loser, but on the death date of his wife he always won. Now he was deathly ill (or at least he felt that way), and blackjack was in the cards in the Tropicana—pun intended. He'd win his measly thousand (for he knew from experience that that's all the gods would allow him to win), call it a day, and drive slowly and carefully back to Arizona.

But now he was pulling off on the shoulder, for this fella needed a ride. It wasn't just a feeling, but a *knowing!* After eighty-one years of life, he knew when to trust his instincts, and this was a strong one!

They drove into Vegas, Jarvis doing most of the talking and Justin doing most of the listening. He heard all about the old man's plans, and about how he loved his wife, and how he missed her terribly. By the time Jarvis parked his car on the Strip, he somehow felt a lot better. Justin followed his Good Samaritan into the Tropicana, and watched in disbelief as the old man won his thousand dollars in record time. During that stretch he never lost a hand, but once that amount was achieved, Jarvis gathered his chips, smiled, and cashed in his winnings. By that time his cold was almost gone, and instead of feeling like he was on his deathbed, he felt years younger than his eight decades of living.

After driving up the Strip, the two men shook hands in front of the Paris Hotel, and then Justin watched him drive off, scratching his head in utter amazement. He had never seen anything like it, but then again this walkabout had nothing normal about it.

Justin never knew that when Jarvis got back to North Phoenix, his cold was completely gone. He went to the cemetery to pay his one thousand dollars and was told that his debt had been completely paid off. When he asked who had done that, he was told that a money order had come in the mail that morning paying off whatever was left on "The Sutherland Stone." With it was a note that said "Good things happen to good people, and Jarvis Sutherland is a good man. Use this money order to pay off his debt on his wife's stone." It was signed, "from a Guardian Angel." The old man shockingly nodded, went out to visit his wife's grave, and broke down in tears.

The next day Jarvis, feeling like a million bucks, donated the one thousand dollars he had won in the Tropicana to the local animal shelter, and spent the rest of his days before the power went off trying to find homes for those animals. He was quite successful in his quest, and he even adopted three dogs and two cats for himself. Each day, even though it was hotter than blazes, he took them with him to his wife's gravesite for a spell, and each day he told her that these pets kept him from being so lonely. She heard him through different realms, and relayed through his dreams that she was happy for him.

Meanwhile, back in real time, Justin was staring at the spouts of The Bellagio Hotel in amazement when he saw a large gathering in the distance downtown, and so he headed in that direction. Ten minutes later he saw a cage holding two tigers that walked back and forth, looking disdainfully at the human onlookers, or gawkers. Justin preferred the latter term, because they seemed emotionally indifferent and were only interested in seeing a wild animal up close. That disturbed Justin on many levels, for he loved animals on a whole, and something about this scene just wasn't right. What if the tables were turned, and *they* were the ones in the cage being watched? And seriously, wasn't true animal cruelty in the cards here? Maybe, but this *was* Vegas, and they had a whole lot of different rules out here in the hot desert. Yes, it was an oasis out in the middle of nowhere, but it was extremely hot just the same. The air conditioned cages had solid roofs and walls on three sides, plus thick plexiglass on the front sections, protecting the large cats from the sun and opresive heat, but still...

Justin was about to walk back to the Paris when he saw a woman staring at the cage, crying. She carried a handkerchief in her trembling right hand, and she was constantly dabbing her tear-filled eyes with it. She looked to be in the thirty-five to forty-year range, with long brown hair that fell loosely around her shoulders. She wore a matching light blue tank top and short outfit that revealed her full figure. Others around her kept glancing over at her—not because she was crying, but because of how sensuous she looked.

All of a sudden she turned around, looked directly at him, and froze. She dabbed at her eyes one more time, and then started smiling through her tears. She waved once, and Justin pointed at himself, and mouthed, "Me?" She nodded, and started walking toward him. She had a cute tanned face, and Justin wondered if he knew her; but how could that be?

The woman stopped a foot in front of him and touched his right hand. "You're real. I dreamed of you, and now you've finally arrived."

"Dreamed of me?"

"Yes. I dreamed of taking a trip with you, and we ended up on a beach we both fell in love with."

"But why me? Why dream of me?"

"Because I had this dream of you as a little girl—as far back as I can remember. And then I dreamt of you as a teenager, and then as an adult."

"My God . . ."

"Yes, I thought the same thing when I turned around and saw you, although I kept my emotions under wraps for the most part."

"But again, why me? Why the obsession with me?"

"Because in my dream I heard a calming voice telling me that we should meet, and travel to the sea. It told me that it was written on the clouds of time, and to wait—wait for you."

"And you've been waiting here for me?"

"I've been waiting to meet you ever since I was a little girl and first saw your face in my dream. No, I didn't think I'd meet you here today. I'd kinda given up, but here you are!" And with that, she came closer, hugged him, and kissed him warmly on the cheek.

"I . . . I don't understand," Justin said, shaking his head and frowning as she smiled up at him.

"You're not supposed to. I'm not supposed to. All I know is that the voice in my dreams told me to pick you up and drive to the coast—to the ocean, I believe."

"You need to tell me what you know, because I have never dreamed of you. Please forgive me—you're beautiful and all, but this is the first time I have ever seen your face, and it's a face I surely would never forget."

The woman giggled, grabbed both his hands in hers, and nodded. "Come with me, and I'll tell you what I know."

They then walked down the Strip and went for coffee, and then this beautiful woman told him what she knew, plus about all her life before this special day.

Justin sat back in his chair and stared hypnotically at this woman who sat opposite him. She held one of his hands in hers, and he watched her take a sip of her coffee. He knew that she was special, and maybe a big part of his spiritual journey, but he was quite surprised that she knew of him. He hadn't dreamt of her, he was quite sure of that, for she was quite beautiful, and someone you wouldn't forget. She held up her free hand, smiled, and then as many people moved all around them on what otherwise was a very normal Las Vegas hot summer day, she began to speak.

"Justin, please don't talk until I'm finished, because I have a lot to tell you, and I don't want to forget any part of it." He nodded. "My name is Ruth Romano. I was born in Boston and grew up in a baseball family, rooting for the Red Sox. I was one of six children: three boys and three girls. I was the youngest, and the only one who could care less about the Red Sox, baseball, and sports in general. While the rest of the family sat around watching their beloved team, I played with Sarge, the family German shepherd mix and my best friend. My family is Roman Catholic, and we went to church every Sunday religiously. I never thought about God and Jesus Christ while I was there, because I didn't really believe in them. During conversations with my parents, I told them that I thought the Bible was nothing more than fables and distorted truths—fairytales made up to convince people that there was life after death, when there really wasn't. Death was death, and it was what it was: the end. At least that's what I thought at the time. And then I died."

Justin sat up straight with raised eyebrows.

"Yes, I died—for five minutes. I was eight. I went into cardiac arrest for no apparent reason and was revived by ambulance workers who my frantic parents called as I fell to the living room floor. It was during that five-minute period that I saw you for the first time. I saw your face through the eyes of your employer who laid you off. I saw your face as it pretty much looks now. Same age, same handsome features—"

Justin mouthed a "Thank you."

"I watched as you shakily left your boss's office in a state of shock, the light flushing out of your soul. Once you closed that office door my vision began to fade to black as the paramedics worked on me diligently, and then my heart started pumping again and I came back to life.

"Yes, I woke up in an ambulance and was driven to Boston County Hospital, where for the next week they ran every test imaginable under the sun, but they never found anything wrong with my heart or circulatory system. The specialists were confounded to say the least, and I was eventually sent home after a two-week observation stay. Life went on as normal, my incident mostly forgotten by all, until I turned twelve—and then I suddenly, without warning, died again.

"My heart stopped once more, and I went into cardiac arrest for the second time. This time I was at school, and the school nurse revived me. I again was dead for five minutes. This time I saw you sitting with your wife and young daughter in the front row in a funeral parlor. All of you were crying. Your oldest daughter had been murdered. How did I know? Because a calming, soothing voice in the mist behind you told me so. In the next few moments it told me many things—mostly things that I must keep to myself for the time being—but it also told me that I would meet you one day, and we would embark on a special journey together.

"It told me that we were spiritual twins; linked together since the beginning of the beginning. Not lovers, per se, but two people who when we finally met would love and understand each other dearly. When I was crying on the Strip looking at that caged tiger, I felt that love radiate from a distance, and that is why I turned around and saw you for the first time. It was such a powerful feeling . . ." She paused for a moment and squeezed Justin's hand.

"Anyway, once this voice spoke I knew I had gotten it all wrong. I realized that there *was* something beyond this realm.

It's never told me its name, or what it is, but I knew at that point that I believed in The Lord and Jesus Christ. I was older now, and was beginning to understand the bigger picture. Maturity played a part as well. On Sundays I began to seriously listen to the priest's sermons during church service, and they now meant something warm and special to me like they never had before. My soul shined inside and out, and I was a better person for it.

"I showed more respect for authority, my parents, brothers and sisters, friends at school, and especially for the church and the Bible. Yes, I know, I know, all my newfound beliefs in The Lord and The Word were all built on a voice in a dream, but that presence was overwhelmingly full of pure love, bliss, and positiveness. You know that as well, I'm sure." Justin nodded, knowingly. "Still, until I physically saw you on the Strip, you might have been no more than a vision in a dream that meant nothing. I didn't believe that, and I was right not to, for here you sit across from me."

Justin smiled warmly, and they both held hands across the table, feeling an electricity pass between them.

"Wow, that was stimulating! Anyway, I didn't dream of you again until I turned twenty—twenty-three years ago. Again, I went into cardiac arrest—in, of all places, Fenway Park watching the Red Sox play the Yankees. I was on a date with someone I was set up with—a one-time thing as it turned out—and I was revived by the paramedic crew in the ballpark. Again, I was unconscious for about five minutes and was taken to the local hospital, where of course they found nothing wrong. It was during that time that I saw you at your worst. Again, you were overwhelmed with loss: the deaths of your wife and youngest daughter. Even though it was in a dream, I felt your pain and grief, and I cried like never before. The voice was there with me, telling me that it was meant to be, but how could it? How could such loss—?" Ruth bit her lip as she shook her head and took a deep breath before continuing while Justin just stared at her, numb to the memory. "Anyway, the voice just replied that what must be must be, and then it told me to turn around. I did, and for the first time I saw the large circular light beaming in front of me, and I could feel the pain and dread being sucked out of my spirit, and I felt love rush in. I still felt hurt and agony for your distress, but now it was mixed with righteousness and positive vibes, making it all bearable. Even though I couldn't see the face behind the voice, I felt its presence nodding, and then I woke up on a stretcher on my way out of Fenway Park. I never found out if the Red Sox won, and I didn't care. My date came with me to the hospital, God Bless his soul, but we both knew that we had little in common and a relationship was nowhere in the cards. Once he knew I was OK, and my family arrived, he said his goodbyes, and I never saw him again. Now I don't even remember his name!

"My life in real time had its ups and downs. Even though I am talking a lot to you now, I was pretty introverted, and stayed to myself most of the time. I went to Boston College, became a veterinarian assistant, took classes at night, and eventually became a veterinarian and opened up my own practice. I loved all animals, fish, and everything in-between more than humans themselves, and helping them in all phases of their existence brought me much joy. I can thank Sarge for that. He showed me such love and true devotion, and I cried and hurt like never before when he died at the ripe old age of fifteen. German shepherds average age may not be more than ten years, but with special care I had Sarge for five more joyous years.

"On the night of his death, I dreamt of you again. I was twenty-one, and died yet again. It happened while I was studying for an exam. He had been lethargic for a few days, and I heard mom tell dad that Sarge wasn't moving. I heard that, and I knew—I knew! Most of his life Sarge always followed me around, and he always laid down at my feet whenever I was studying for a test. It was as if he knew what I was doing, giving me moral support, but now he couldn't make it up the stairs to my bedroom, and so for the past few months I had studied and slept alone. Anyway, like I said, I knew, and I ran down the stairs and ran into my father, who had tears in his eyes. I screamed bloody murder, and went into cardiac arrest once again.

"I remember falling into my father's arms as the darkness closed in around me. I recalled thinking that I wanted to die and go to heaven along with Sarge, but of course that didn't happen. Instead the darkness cleared, and I ended up in your therapist's office. You were sitting in a chair opposite his desk, dealing with your grief. I appeared behind your therapist and stared into your eyes. I could see the hurt behind them, and I remember wishing I could take it all away. I had tears in my eyes, for I still remembered that Sarge had just passed away, and I realized that I couldn't go with him. The voice was there, behind me, telling me that we were all dealing with things, and my losing Sarge was just part of balancing the books. It told me that I had work to do, much good work, and I would understand later. The voice was right. I saved many animals over the years, and if I had been allowed to go to heaven along with Sarge then most likely a lot more of my patient's lives would have been lost. The ledger of life had to balance out, I suppose." She took another long pause, and Justin nodded knowingly, tears welling up in his eyes.

"Anyway, this time I was out for about ten minutes, and came to in the ambulance—again, traveling toward another hospital stay. They kept Sarge in the freezer until I came home a week later—again, perfectly healthy—so I could say my goodbyes. I did, and wished him well in the next realm." Ruth paused and wiped her eyes before continuing.

"But let's go back a bit to when you left your therapist's office.

I stared at the door that you had just closed, and then suddenly the office became dark, and disappeared. It was then that the voice took on form, becoming the lighted presence that you eventually saw. It led me inside the circular light, and I saw the same incredible world that you did, with one difference. In it I saw Sarge running in the green grass, having fun. In his mouth he had the same green squeezable frog he had played with as a puppy. That toy had lasted half his life, and when it finally got thrown out, completely ripped apart, we couldn't find another one. My dad bought him other squeezable toys, but he didn't bother much with any of them. He missed that frog badly, and it was all that he wanted.

"No, Sarge was never quite the same after that Froggie went into the garbage can. It was as if a little part of his life was taken from him, and he knew that he could never get it back. I saw that while looking into his eyes. He'd wag his tail, and smile at me with his tongue half hanging out of his mouth, but I could see that some of the light had gone out of them, and it hurt us both to the heart. Now all of that light was back, along with his youth. He stopped at one point, as if sensing us, and looked in our direction. He nodded his head up and down, chewing on his beloved toy, and then ran off in the opposite direction. I watched him run until he was completely out of sight. Tears welled up in my eyes, for not only was Sarge happy, but he was enjoying life to the fullest. The light presence showed me that, and I was quietly thankful. The presence knew how I felt, though, and then it guided me back out of the circular light . . . and I woke up in the ambulance." Ruth smiled, remembering her vision of Sarge.

"Later, I think I was around twenty-eight or twenty-nine, I died again and ended up in the cornfields, standing next to the presence, when you appeared in-between two rows of corn. The light presence slowed down your time and sped up mine so you couldn't see me, and I bent each cornstalk in half, showing you the way to the circular light. Yes, it was me, and I stood right behind you as you walked inside it and saw the most beautiful world imaginable—the one I saw Sarge running through years before, although this time he was nowhere to be seen. I watched as the light presence put its arms around you, and then on impulse I walked over and put my arms around both of you, and saw. I saw your wife and two daughters, just like you did, but I saw even more. I also in that moment saw both my parents and two brothers, who had all recently passed on. It had been a bad few years—four funerals in as many years—and I had been reeling in grief myself. I also saw Sarge standing off to the left, green frog in mouth, wagging his tail in front of many other dogs, cats, and other animals that had passed on while I had my practice. I cried along with you at the overwhelmingness of it all, and then after breaking our spiritual embrace, retreated out of the circular light and back to our real-world time with you, just in time for another hospital stay.

"On other occasions, or deaths, I saw you on your spiritual journey after your soul was enlightened, the last being of you at the Hoover Dam. For me that was ten years ago, and I haven't dreamed of you since. About five years ago I purchased one of those new devices that they put in your chest, just under your skin, to restart your heart just in case it stops or skips a beat, but I haven't had an attack since owning it, thank God. I've heard that it has saved many thousands of lives, though, if not more. I'm glad of that, but I think that now that we have finally met, I won't need it anymore.

"Anyway, I thought our time frames might have interacted back then, and so I sold my business and moved out here as soon as you started on your spiritual journey. That was nine and a half years ago. I opened up an animal hospital just outside of town, but whenever I had free time I'd walk The Strip, hoping to run into you. That finally happened today. I was looking at that tiger, wondering how thoughtless people can be sometimes. It's a new exhibit, but it exploits the tigers on a new level entirely. It's animal cruelty, clean and simple. I was crying for the tigers, animals on a whole, the world and its many problems, and especially the frustration of not finding you, most of all. Months ago, I had pretty much given up hope, but I still kept coming back here, watching the many people walk by, hoping against hope that one of them would be you. I couldn't give up, no matter what, even though I hadn't dreamed of you in ages. The voice and the light presence had deserted me as well, and *that* bothered me on many levels. I felt so alone, and I was, but now finally you are here!

"Before you say anything, let me tell you about me in general: I never got married, or had any children. I had a few boyfriends, but none I could give my heart up to. The sick animals under my care were all the children I needed or wanted. I cared for them, and loved them all as my own, and they took up all the love I had. I knew that I loved you, but it was a different kind of love. I knew that your heart was with your wife and daughters, and so I knew that what we could share was closer to sibling love. I see you now, and I know that I feel closer to you more than anybody else I have ever met. God bless you, and thanks for listening and not interrupting."

Justin stared at Ruth for a moment, slowly got up, and then went to her. She stood up as well, and they hugged for quite some time without speaking. They then sat back down, and he filled her in on his side of the ledger. They both knew at that point that they would stay together unless circumstances dictated otherwise. Ruth agreed to travel with Justin and complete his, or *their,* spiritual journey. She made plans with her colleagues to watch over her practice until further notice. Ruth worked with two other veterinarians who would gladly take over her workload, for she told them she had no idea how long she'd be gone. After saying their goodbyes, Ruth packed up her car, and she and Justin headed north.

They talked, they laughed, sometimes they even held hands, but under no circumstances would they ever make love, even though they had strong feelings for each other. During this time neither one of them had any further interactions with the light presence, and logically they didn't expect any. They presumed that now that they were together, something that had most likely been preordained eons ago, there would be no need for any further contact or interaction. During their revelations with their pasts, they both realized how supernatural their time lapses had been. They were both shockingly amazed that Ruth had witnessed Justin's movements through life even though they hadn't actually happened yet, and they both felt spiritually overwhelmed. They both realized that they were part of something bigger than themselves, and should just let that special current take them wherever they needed to be, and so they did. They followed their intuition, and eventually ended up on Montara State Park Beach, enjoying its surroundings.

It was now, back in real time, that Justin thought about his whole spiritual journey, his time with Ruth, and his whole life on a whole. Ruth had gone to get breakfast: cottage cheese, bread, and strawberries. They both found that this was fast becoming their favorite morning meal. Before they had left Las Vegas, both had eaten like they always had, but as they moved further north they began to dislike the taste of meat, and the whole process of killing an animal for nourishment. It just wasn't right, and they became more focused on that as they drove northward. It was as if a light bulb had gone off in their heads—dim at first, and then getting progressively brighter as time went on.

Fish was discarded from their meals as well, for their feelings on eating sea life were possibly even stronger than that of animals. And here's how they knew that eating other forms of life was wrong besides just being morally wrong: they both *felt* better, and thought *clearer*. As Ruth and Justin each said a prayer before eating, they both remembered to thank The Lord for that realization. The changes in them had cleansed both their bodies and souls, and they were extremely gracious in their response.

Ruth drove up with their breakfast and kissed Justin on the cheek before sitting down next to him. They found that as time went by, they didn't need to speak to each other. They communicated through spiritual telepathy, hearing each other's thoughts clearly through their souls, which were getting brighter with each passing day. Ruth divided up their nourishment, they said grace out loud, and then ate in silence, staring out at the sea. And then waited.

That wait lasted for seven days before the power went off. They did not wait alone. Day by day they were joined by wildlife, and stray animals of all kinds. Dogs and cats mostly, but also rodents, squirrels, and others that stayed in the brush but still watched them intently. The twin spirits were aware of their presence and welcomed them all to join them in their spiritual circle, which they did. They were souls that had been discarded by society for the most part, but they all felt love here on this beach, and were drawn to Justin and Ruth like magnets.

On their last night before returning to The Creator, the stars seemed to glisten and brighten above them with more intensity, and whatever sea breeze there was calmed down, and the whole area became peaceful and still. A few minutes later the waves calmed as well, and the Pacific Ocean was quiet like never before, almost motionless. Ruth and Justin looked at each other, and knew their wait was almost over. The animals noticed the change as well and stared intently at the sea. Some whimpered or meowed, and the spiritual twins calmed them, talking soothingly to them through their newfound telepathy. They heard, and quieted. They surrounded the couple, as if shielding them from any outside forces, and went to sleep as the stars shined brightly above.

On the last day, they all awakened at sunrise. The ocean, at least on this stretch of beach, remained eerily calm for as far as the eye could see. The sun rose, and the day seemed perfect in every way. Seagulls flew overhead, more than usual, but they were all quiet, and none of them hunted their next meal. Justin and Ruth smiled knowingly and held hands. They knew. They were no longer hungry—none of them were. The time for feeding was over, and none of them ever again would feel the discomfort of hunger pains, the ache of an empty stomach, and that in itself was comforting. The birds above continued to grow in number, and many more landed on the beach, almost filling it! None of the gulls spoke, cawed, or cried. Hunger had been eliminated, and they entered a realm they had never known before. All they had ever known was hunger and survival, and now both those things were gone from their existences, and a higher form of euphoria set in. They now spent their time staring at the couple, and out at the calming sea, waiting as well. What a sight they all were! They were all one spiritual presence, sensing an Event that was fast forthcoming.

Their wait ended a little after noon, the sun high in the sky.

The sea stayed calm, but ripples began to form. The voice, or light presence, spoke inside Justin and Ruth's heads, beckoning them, beckoning them all. The words spoken to them were none they understood, and yet they completely comprehended their meaning. They stood up, held hands, and walked to the water's edge. All the animals followed close behind them, as if in a trance, and then they all walked into the ocean—or should I say *on* it. Yes, they all walked on top of the calming sea, and headed westward. The spiritual twins, all the animals and wildlife, even the gulls. They didn't float on the water like usual, but walked on top of the sea like they did on shore. About a mile off the coastline they stopped, and sea life below them swam to the surface, surrounding them. Fish of all kinds and sizes, flapping half in and half out of the water, moved around the spiritual caravan, joining them. Even sharks were in the mix, but they did not attack, for they no longer hungered either.

And then the large circular light was there, surrounding them all. They were all in the light, and felt the presence of many. The voice spoke to them, welcoming them. It spoke to Justin and Ruth, telling them that they had been in the light all the time; that they had been inside it all through their journey on their way to this place on the coast. They understood, and smiled. The light presence had never left them from the moment it first made contact with them. It had protected, nourished, and taught their souls how to become completely aware, and now they were. The circular light then disappeared, taking them all with it: the spiritual twins, the animals, and all the sea life.

And then a second later the Event happened, and the world called Earth and it's surrounding planets and solar systems inside the vast chamber changed forever.

NARRATIVE NOTES: As we near the end of this first part of *Beyond Revelations,* you might feel that my lack of information is becoming habitual, but what the lighted presence and Justin discussed cannot be explained at this time. It will eventually, though, dear reader, and the complete details of that conversation will be known to you in due time.

Justin Farrows had gone through more hardship and grief than most human beings would ever experience, yet he also discovered new and powerful emotions, and more spiritual information than *all* of us have never felt or known about in our history. Why him, and not someone else? Maybe his eventual choice would have something to do with it, and so maybe we will know the answer to that question later on down the road as well.

Now let's revisit more internal matters. It can never be talked about enough. We all miss loved ones who have passed on, along with all their memories. We would all love to see them again, know that they are all right, and in a good place. That place could be heaven, or in another peaceful place or realm. And then, in Justin's case, as well as Ruth's, to actually *see* them again, and know that they are in a better place—amazing and Earth shattering! Furthermore, that would be, for all of us, overwhelming in its smallest denomination!

Two of the spirits that Justin saw behind his family were Evan Thayer and Charles Kandy, the two men responsible for his family's deaths. He knew their faces, knew them well. They had both been implanted deep in his mind where whatever hate had resided, and so another revelation had been revealed to him. Even though on Earth in the physical realm those two men had been on the opposite side of his family's tragic demises, they were now all happily grouped together in harmony in the spiritual realm the presence had made him a witness to. The message? Forgiveness. Forgiveness had brought them all together, and so that weight of hatred (an unwarranted emotion to begin with, and one none of us should ever possess) had been lifted from his mind as well. He instantly forgave them, and the last of his heavy burdens had been unchained and released from his dark thoughts of depression.

Evan Thayer's history is an odd one. He grew up on what they referred to as "the wrong side of the tracks," living with his mother who gave birth to him at the ripe old age of fifteen. Under normal circumstances she would have been considered a handsome woman with a decent body, but life had always been hard from the moment she was born, and her features related those facts. JoLynne was one of ten children to a mother and father that couldn't support even one child comfortably, and so she began turning tricks once she turned eleven, when her body began to physically blossom prematurely. Before she went full term with Evan, JoLynne had gone through two miscarriages, and besides her various tricks, many relationships. Evan never knew his father, and began his life moving from place to place, town to town. JoLynne continued her deviant behavior, and young Evan fell asleep most nights listening to his mother's moans during her trysts with either a client or one of her many boyfriends that never seemed to stick around for long.

By the time Evan turned fourteen and his hormones began running amok, he began to have wet dreams just like any other adolescent. Literature of a sexual nature left around by his mother as long as the young boy could remember littered the apartment. Evan had read a lot of it, and his dreams reflected those sourced

tales of lust. JoLynne began hearing her adolescent son masturbate in the next room, and one night decided to seduce him.
They began having incestual sex whenever they could, with both
of them achieving many orgasms during their trysts. JoLynne
taught her son what she knew, and began to worship her. That
was his mistake, and his eventual tragic downfall.

Evan would do anything for his mom's affections, and she
knew it. Yes, JoLynne wanted him all for herself, plus to control
him mentally as well as physically. To make ends meet, she devised a deviant plan to complete that goal. She wanted him to
turn tricks, but only with men. That way she could complete two
goals at once. One, make money so that they could make ends
meet, and two, still have him all to herself. She didn't want him
to have any relationships with other women, or have a girlfriend,
otherwise her hold on him quite naturally wouldn't be as strong.
She reasoned that men as tricks didn't count as far as she was concerned, and she did know many males who wanted to have sex
with other men, or boys.

JoLynne put her plan into action. She told her current boyfriend of her deviancy, and then brought Evan into the bedroom
with the two of them. Being so young, and so open to different
sexual situations, Evan agreed to do whatever his mother wanted.
Daniel Hopkins, his mother's lover, was the first to take the young
boy, and as it was happening Evan kept telling himself that this
was all for his mother, the woman he would do anything for, but
deep down in his heart he never liked being with a man. There
was much money in it, though, and so he turned homosexual
tricks for the woman he loved.

As he got older he began to dislike it more and more, and
began to despise his mother for what she was making him do.
That, plus he realized that she was not only eating the cake, but
the icing too. She still had her boyfriends besides Evan, and began

dating a teacher named Lawrence Orwell who taught at Cornwall Elementary School. Unfortunately, one of his students was named Jessica Farrows, the daughter of Justin and Janus Farrows.

Lawrence was a good teacher by day, but a deviant sex fiend by night. At first he paid JoLynne for sex, but then it became something more, especially once he found out that her son, Evan, also turned tricks. You see, Lawrence was a closeted bisexual, and after he and JoLynne started dating and having torrid sex in her apartment at night, he confided in her his secret need to have sex with a man as well. He wanted to pay her for Evan once a week, and she readily agreed.

Lawrence was the first boyfriend JoLynne ever had that made decent money; she wanted to keep him, for he paid a lot of her bills, and so she made Evan go along with it after explaining the financial part of the equation involved. The young boy gritted his teeth and went along with it, but things went terribly wrong. Lawrence, when having conventional sex with a woman, was a normal and passionate lover; but as a homosexual lover, he was different. He was violent, and heartless. He had been a victim of rape as a young boy, being taken brutally by his uncle in his father's brother's home on more than one occasion, and now as an adult he took it out on Evan. He took the young man by force, and without care—just like he had been taken when he was raped by Uncle Ernie. He and Evan's sex became a reenactment of that horrible traumatic event, except in reverse, and though it soothed the demons in Lawrence Orwell's private hell, it created a whole new one in Evan Thayer's world. The now eighteen-year-old hated his once-a-week trysts with his mother's well-to-do boyfriend, and he told her so. JoLynne told Evan that she would talk to Lawrence, but the dark situational play didn't change, and a slow hatred and cancer began to grow inside the young man's now-tainted soul.

It all came to a head after an especially bad trick experience with the deviant teacher. Lawrence not only used Evan harshly, but berated the eighteen-year-old as well. That hurt, and Evan let that hurt burn inside his insides all through that restless night. On the morning after he again pleaded with his mother to let this sexual tryst come to an end, but his mother refused, and Evan completely lost it. He screamed at the top of his lungs as he strangled his mother slowly. As JoLynne took her last breath, she heard her only son tell her he hated her for all time. As Evan smiled down at the now-lifeless body of his mother on the bed that had been used by so many, and so often, including himself, he felt that this ending was poetic justice in the court of Evan Thayer.

Death would be her sentence, but Evan went even further. He ripped the clothes off her limp frame, turned her over onto her stomach, and viciously sodomized her repeatedly throughout that day. But that *still* wasn't the end. That happened the next morning when Evan shot his way into Cornwall Elementary and killed not only Lawrence Orwell, but little Jessica Farrows and many of her other classmates as well. By then Evan's fury had completely fogged his demented mind, and his soul became nothing more than a flicker of dim light. Evan kicked Lawrence's dead body out of his way and sat in the teacher's chair until he heard the authorities come for him. Once they entered the classroom, Evan, who knew his time was up, raised his gun in their direction, which was now empty, and was shot numerous times. He died with a smile on his face, an empty gun dangling from his limp right hand as he sat in Lawrence Orwell's chair. The gun laws were never changed, nor altered.

A Long Overdue Dedication

This past chapter was inspired by, and dedicated to, Pastor Ruth Wainwright of the Nauraushaun Presbyterian Church in Pearl River, New York. During one of her sermons, maybe all it took was the theme, or even one sentence, this story took form in my mind as I listened to her preach. Previously, there was no idea or plan to include this tale in this book, but I felt that it *had* to be added, and it fit better toward the end. If truth be known, this was the second to last Chapter written for *Beyond Revelations*, and personally, one of my favorites.

A little about Pastor Ruth. During the time of this dedication, Ruth is filling in as intern preacher, coming to Nauraushaun Presbyterian's aid until a new full-time minister can be found, but in reality Ruth and my immediate family go back much further. When my mother passed away over a decade ago, the church again was in the process of searching for a new pastor, and Ruth, in her natural spiritual way, came to our rescue. She agreed to conduct mom's funeral service in full, including traveling with us to the cemetery and leading us in spiritual guidance and prayer. Ruth will always have a special place in our thoughts, hearts, and prayers for her spiritual leadership during our time of loss. Ruth will always be considered family, and just remembering that hard time brings fresh tears, but tears of joy for her glowing presence. Ruth is a very special person who donates her time to many ventures that help others in need, and this was just one example of her heart-filled giving ways.

I, personally, have always wanted to find a way to thank her for what she did for our family when we needed her most, and this, I think, is a start. Ruth has added to my spiritual growth, as well as to many others, and I am sure she will continue to do so in the future. The light that shines brightly from her soul affects all that she meets, which makes me believe that there must be something more down the road when it comes down to my own religious beliefs, and I love her for that. People like Ruth make this world a better place, and we need many more like her. God bless Ruth and the whole Wainwright family, today, tomorrow, and forever and a day! Amen.

Chapter Forty

XTRALUNSASSA

The Rocky Mountains are a major mountain range in western North America, covering more than three thousand miles from the northernmost part of British Columbia, in western Canada, to New Mexico, in the Southwestern United States. The mountain range offers dramatic wilderness, diverse wildlife, and alpine lakes. Mount Elbert, located in Colorado, is the highest summit of the mountain range at 14,440 feet, and the second highest summit in the contiguous United States after Mount Whitney, located in California on the boundary between Inyo and Tulare Counties. The Rockies were formed more than fifty-five million years ago during the Laramide orogeny, a period of mountain building in which a number of plates began sliding underneath the North American Plate. The angle of subduction was shallow, resulting in a vast broad belt of huge mountains. Since that time, further tectonic activity and erosion by glaciers have sculpted the mountain range into dramatic peaks and valleys. During the conclusion of the last ice age, human beings began inhabiting the mountain range.

Fast forwarding, five years before the power went off and most went back to The Creator, a small crack began to form on top of the summit. It did not widen, staying only inches apart, but day by day it grew in length, going down each side of the northern and southern sides of the mountain. It wasn't detected by local hikers, but it was investigated by authorities because on radar screens the area was slightly blurred where the ground had separated and deepened. During those five years investigative teams were periodically sent up to the top of Mount Elbert to explore that blurry area, but each time that happened the actual crack appeared to close up and disappear, hiding its existence. That was only an optical illusion, playing games with the investigator's eyes, for in reality the crack was still there, continuing to grow and deepen constantly. Supernatural? More than likely, but one thing was crystal clear: something, or someone, wanted this expanding crack to stay hidden, and so it did.

We now direct our focus underneath that deepening crack, traveling miles below sea level into a small cavern-type structure with no way in or out. The outer structure surrounding the ceiling, floor, and walls were lined with rock formations that were alien in nature—material not found anywhere else on planet Earth. The cavern itself was cube shaped: twenty feet high, twenty feet squared, and full of stalagmites and stalactites, which also consisted of foreign material. In each corner there were five-foot treelike figures with many twig-like branches that were all on fire (orange and red in color), lighting the ghoulish room and keeping it warm.

Shadows from the eternal flames danced spastically to a soundless symphony that never ended on each wall, creating an "All Hallows Eve" type of atmosphere. In the center of the cavern sat a figure dressed all in black. Its head appeared to have something black covering it—a veil perhaps, hiding its face, if there was one. The figure sat in a black-framed structure the shape and size of an old telephone booth, also made out of a foreign metal not found on Earth. A glass-like material (you guessed it, foreign to normal glass) was fitted into the frame, so one could see the figure sitting inside. This booth, like the cavern, had no entrance on any side, which set up a strange situation. No way into the booth or cavern, and no way out—odd to say the least. This sitting figure didn't move at all, and so we have to slowly zoom in to get a closer look at its features.

On closer inspection we see what appears to be a woman wearing a full-length black dress. It was baggy and shapeless, and fell to the figure's ankles. A thin see-through veil covered her whole head, her straight black hair tied in a bun on top. She looked like a corpse that was sitting up; her face completely white, eyes tightly closed, with expressionless thin lips forming a straight line. She appears peaceful yet stiff, and one must wonder who she is, how old she must be, how she came to be here in this cavern of a room with no entrance, and *not* decay in the first place.

We now move forward five years to the day of the Event. The crack in Mount Elbert has by inches split the mountain in two. At the exact moment when the power went off, and most went back home to The Creator, it began to separate very quietly as if two large powerful invisible hands were gently pulling it apart slowly, inch by inch.

Meanwhile, down below in the cavern room the woman-like creature in the strange booth opened her eyes. There were no pupils, just blackness that reflected walls that were starting to crumble from the vibrations above. The figure's mouth moved and formed a large grin, and a serpent-like black tongue flicked in and out between its thin, parched lips. This strange woman opened its mouth to take in its first breaths in what seemed like ages, and yellow, square teeth could be seen behind a sadistic, wicked smile.

The figure slowly stood up, and its hair fell to its thin shoulders and changed into what appeared to be braids, but on closer inspection were actually snakelike parasites, eyeless but with mouths filled with angry, sharp black teeth that moved about on the figure's shoulder area. Two large, full breasts could now be seen underneath it's black dress, threatening to break through. Looking up, it stared at the top of the cavern and watched as cracks began to grow across it. The black booth that surrounded the figure, which we can now safely assume is a woman, began to heat up, and the black frame turned from black in color to orange red. It began to vibrate, expanding and contracting slowly, and then slowly raised steadily off the cavern floor. Large cracks in the floor appeared, split and fell inward, creating an even deeper and darker crevice in the cavern. Hot steamy air began to rise out of it, and then distant and far off rustling could be heard, echoing off the walls far below, most likely many miles down. Loud hissing noises could be heard in the abyss, and then different growling or slight roars of growing rage echoed off the newly formed walls of the separating crevice.

The figure cocked its head as it listened to those horrible sounds coming up from the dark depths below and nodded. "It is time," it said out loud in a deep baritone female voice. "It is *time!*" Disruptive and frustrated roars could be heard in response far below as the deep crevice continued to crackle and grow larger. The four treelike fire figures moved to each corner of the booth holding the figure, setting it ablaze. It dissolved quickly, and the flames curled around and caressed the black figure, and it sighed pleasingly. Above the figure's head the cracks began to separate and split upward, while above sea level Mount Elbert continued to split in two.

Eventually cracks from above and below would meet each other and begin to separate the hardcore rock foundation that had laid dormant for many, many years, but that would take time. Patience was a virtue, and so the figure waited, as it so far had, knowing that a doorway was being created for it and whatever was moving in the abyss below. The figure levitated in the flames and listened to the moving rock formations breaking up all around her. The things in the abyss scratched and clawed their way toward her, craving her caress. She knew what they were, and what they were capable of. This orbiting planet and its occupants were in for a big surprise-a very big surprise, the woman thought cunningly. In the end, it laughed to herself, they would be the last to get the joke. The figure began to cackle hysterically.

As this chapter unfolds, one wonders who this character in a booth could be, plus many other questions. I will try my best to answer them all, for keeping that information in the dark would hold no benefit from what I can see. Her name is Xtralunsassa, and she is, and has been for a very long time, the wife of the Beast. They met and coupled many chambers ago, and she is the number one demoness in the kingdom of the dark underworld, where the Beast reigns and harvests all sicknesses, sorrows, agonies, and every other negative power that keeps souls entrapped.

That kingdom is vast, and we have read about a small part of that dark realm, but because the Beast has other more important issues to deal with, Xtralunsassa, in reality, rules the roost. She has always been the most feared creature in the underworld, and decides many souls' fates—especially those who worship the Dark Lord and fail in their specialty. Yes, even those who worship the Beast are in constant fear, and could face a fate worse than those who worship The Creator. Chaos rules in the fires, and Xtralunsassa stirs that brew with an evilness that is indescribable in our languages.

When this chamber was first opened and creation inside it began, Xtralunsassa transported herself through small slits in many fractured realms, traveling over thousands of years before burying herself deep inside an ever-evolving planet, which much later would be named Earth. Putting herself in a coma-type metamorphosis, she sat in this protective booth as evolving rock formations from the underworld coupled with the materials that were forming the Earth surrounded her. As much as it tried, the foreign rock formations were pushed against the protective booth by the natural evolving planet formations, but the booth held strong. Over time, the foreign rock foundations won out; and were able to shift, or push outward, creating the small cavern-like room.

Once Xtralunsassa completed her journey (which was a dangerous one, even for her, for she could have been trapped in-between realms many times, leaving her suspended in a state for an eternity until some sort of invented help arrived, but through intensive programming in the fires that disaster had been avoided), she regained consciousness for a few minutes, and through telepathy opened one side of the booth and emptied different types of seeds on top of the rock formations that came with her. What formed from those seeds were what was moving and angrily roaring below her in the expanding crevice. Trapped and enclosed in the rock formation, they had probably known nothing but discomfort to say the least, and more likely, agony.

The wife of the Beast knew this, and surmised that the forecast called for extreme pain for the Other's Chosen Ones who still walked the surface of this forsaken planet. That was one of the reasons why she was laughing hysterically with glee as those monstrosities crept closer toward her from below.

The seeds had also produced the four tree-like structures that sat in each corner of the cavern, burning eternally. They were a different kind of creature, who would be ingested by Xtralunsassa once the doorway was complete. They would live inside the demoness until they were possibly needed, protecting her like they were presently.

Another Note Of Interest: it had been over three billion years since Xtralunsassa had laid in her dormant state. That meant she had not seen her husband in many a year, or physically ruled in the eternal fires of sorrow in a very long time. Even though she had spent the good part of those lost years in a coma-like state, Xtralunsassa had been mentally awake and aware of what was going on—not *in control*, mind you, but still different than being in a dreamlike state. From the moment she opened her eyes, she felt an evilness and viciousness grow in her darkened soul like never before. That made her extremely angry and dangerous, and somewhat mentally insane. Her husband would want her no other way.

MISCELLANEOUS
ENDING THOUGHTS

THE GRAY BETWEEN BLACK AND WHITE

As we grow up, we, as human beings, develop characteristics that define our many different personalities. While writing this first installment of *Beyond Revelations*, I discussed some ideas with a few people, some religious, and one asked incredulously, "So you're really going to go there, huh?" as if moving into that realm was sacrilegious. Well, maybe it is in a black and white world, but I live almost exclusively in the gray—that large, hazy in-between area. Why do I live there? Because that's the way the good Lord made me, and I have no choice but to be who I am. Lol! Now that's a contradiction, because that statement could be considered totally black and white. Of course, I have a choice, but I decide to be myself, and no one else. I'm human; I have all the characteristics of a one, but living in the gray is where I feel most comfortable, and so I stay there.

When approaching any situation, I try my best to look at it from every angle possible, not just one or two, or more importantly, just my own. I thank a higher power for that, and am grateful. When I meet somebody, no matter who they are or what they do, I treat them all the same. This last line is maybe the most important thought process information I have received while living in the gray—and again, I thank the Holy Father for that knowledge. I believe that's the secret for getting along with everyone, and possibly achieving world peace, which we are so far from having. Treat everybody *equally, evenly.* They state that all men (and women, of course, another gray matter) are created equal, so why not *treat* all people that way? Political leaders, religious leaders, teachers, factory workers, custodians of all kinds, servers at restaurants, sanitation workers, landscapers, etc.—they may be rated on different levels of importance, but they all should be treated with the same respect, treated the same.

If writing down thoughts from the gray is what the Lord wants, and I believe it is, then writing this book is part of His plan. It's His blueprint, His grand design, and I am just a pawn on His ever-changing game board. My creativeness can go this way or that, sideways, right size up, or upside down. It doesn't matter. All ideas come from Him, or his messengers, and so they direct what I write (I can only take partial credit). To have this idea for a book, and listen to people tell you "you *can't* write it because it's not right; you just can't go there" is living in black and white. That's rigid thinking, and I, for one, live far away from that line of thinking. I'm completely flexible in my thought processes, not afraid to write what I think is right. Under no circumstances will I be terrorized not to write what I feel. Why? Because I'm protected in the gray—in the comfort of the gray.

The gray will possess an uncertain, foggy future, and stepping into that kind of tomorrow can sometimes be risky, or even wrong, but in that blueprint you will develop a strength and confidence that no one can destroy. Living in the gray means you are not afraid to make mistakes while making up your own mind about all matters. This includes religion. I grew up in a household where religion played a big part in our upbringing, which was good. Having righteous morals to live by created a strong foundation and shaped the way I treated all other brothers and sisters. Having righteous morals made me want to share my strengths with others, and work as a good teammate. Having righteous morals made me accept people of all cultures, beliefs, religions, and *color*. I look at every topic from every angle imaginable, and then make my decision on each. Maybe I will change my mind while hearing a point of view I hadn't thought of. Maybe I will make a point that might sway someone to my way of thinking. That's living in the gray.

In religion, I can follow everything that the Good Book tells me to do, yet still not believe in a supreme being unless I spiritually find Him myself. Just believing or not believing in God, because your parents told you to, is living in black and white, and runs hollow. I feel that as a parent, you can steer your children in a certain direction, but I also believe they should make up their own minds on all issues, including believing in The Lord and the gospel. Finding out for yourself whether God exists or not is living in the gray.

Now let's flip the coin over. If you DON'T believe in God because your parents told you not to without doing due process is also living in black and white. And here's the breaking news of the day: parents, grandparents, brothers and sisters, cousins, good friends, and the most popular people in the world who do that are creating one of the biggest sins ever committed by influencing *anyone* to believe what *they* believe. That could be considered black and white, and you would be right, because everybody has to live in black and white sometimes—sometimes.

There are seven days in a week, twenty-four hours in a day, 365 days in a year except for leap year, then there are 366. I breathe air. I get sick. I will one day die! All those examples are black and white in nature. Learning facts in books, learning to read and write, learning to speak a language are all black and white, for the most part.

Let's get back to the topic concerning God. It's not that I didn't believe in God, but I did have to question His existence, because questioning all information about anything is healthy exercise. Question *everything!* Read up on it; do some research, and then make up your *own* mind. That's living in the gray. What made *me* believe that God exists happened not too long ago, even though I had been given many signals years before, in many different ways. One of those was a voice that hasn't stopped talking inside my head since I reached the age of reasoning (or thinking for myself). Back then, the word was if you heard voices in your head, you were either considered crazy or on the verge of going insane. As a child, you believe that point of view because you reason that adults know all—or at least they make you feel that way. Black and white.

I think that was the first time I took a giant leap forward into tomorrow, or ventured into the gray. The voice rebuked that reasoning, saying people of authority make up their own narratives and label them whenever they haven't any idea about what they are talking about. It happens all the time. The voice added to the argument, asking me if I *felt* crazy. Not really, I replied, but there are people who have known me all my life that would disagree with that! That might seem funny, and it is, but that's because I am who I am, and live in the gray. In reality, I have different opinions, and just think "on the edge."

Am I a rebel? That depends on what your definition of the word is. I don't think I am; I just question everything that doesn't sound or *feel* kosher, and at the end of that process I might end up with a different opinion than others. That's all it is, and nothing else. I don't disagree just to disagree. If that was the case, then even I would consider myself crazy. Anyway, the voice I hear I believe is my guardian angel, and as the years have rolled on it has come through for me time and time again. That whole story is for another time, another tale told around a different type of campfire. But let's not go off point.

A few years back, I lost my job, and within hours I heard the voice saying, "You might have to lose almost everything before you get to the promised land." What would that be, I wondered? My wife, my family, all that I had worked so hard for? I didn't know, but my future now lived in a dark, thick mist filled with question marks and uncertainty, which was unsettling at best. As the weeks and months passed by, I had a string of bad luck, and began to think I was cursed. I wondered what was happening; how could all this happen to me? (I think back on that time, and realize just how uncanny it was!)

And then, just when I thought the mist was lifting, I got sick and ended up in the hospital. Now, this health issue didn't start with my bad luck. No, it happened fifteen years prior, when I had hernia surgery. On a semi-regular basis I began to experience disruptive, painful addominal cramps weeks after that operation was performed. Years later they eventually landed me in the hospital, which produced more questions than answers.

Antibiotics helped me recover temporarily, but not even the professionals knew for sure what was wrong. Some said I had Crohn's disease, or some other digestive disorder, but none were certain, and so I was sent home with a special diet. That worked for five years, until the same symptoms came back during my "cursed" period, landing me back in the hospital for a second go around. This time, through MRIs, I found out that I had scar tissue in my intestine, attacking and weakening it. The end result produced a collapsed section of my large intestine, and I had three operations in a three-month period. They removed the infected area, and then, because lifting was a part of my job for many years, I received disability benefits. Once I won that sweepstakes, I thought back, remembering the line: "You might have to lose almost everything to get to the promised land," and realized that it was my health.

Sure, other wrenches had been thrown into the machine, but in the end if I hadn't had the operations, or if something during the procedures had gone wrong, I wouldn't be here today to write this all down. Am I a prophet? Absolutely not, I just get good advice from my guardian angel . . . who lives . . . in the gray. Think about it, though. A problem going back years, one that I had suffered with for so long, had helped me in the end. I had had a very tough time finding a new job, not to mention one that paid anything (I was outsourced), and this chip in my armor, this Achilles heel, had actually gotten me to the promised land. It also paved the way for me to write this book. In retrospect, was this fate? I think so. Justice served? Yes, for the most part, and the verdict got me to where I needed to be, and I will never forget that. Yes, God created me to think in the gray, provided me with a guardian angel, and I was rewarded. He created me to doubt even Him, and God proved to me that he was there to assist me when all looked lost. "You might have to lose almost everything to get to the promised land" was repeated over and over during those dark moments. They came out of the gray . . . the gray.

Speaking of *The Twi-Lighters*, I had always thought that when I retired I would write a book. On what, I didn't know. Well, when retirement came unexpectedly and prematurely, I began thinking in the gray more deeply, and then this title *Beyond Revelations* popped into my head. I thought further into the gray, and a beginning to this novel began to take form. Let's clarify something immediately: it's a piece of literature that doesn't happen *after* Revelations in the Bible, but *beyond* it. It could come from a parallel universe (that was never my intention), but it intertwines with actual history whenever I go back in time.

I had written other short stories back when I was young and totally inexperienced, and dated them, knowing now that that was a mistake. *Beyond Revelations* happens in the not-too-distant future—fifty years, or possibly at the end of this century. And then maybe even beyond *that!* I never mention the date of the Event, and I want it to remain timeless (or until it arrives). It's better that way, or so I've been told . . . in the depths of the gray. It's a piece of literature that's very opinionated during its many tales and storylines, and I'm sorry if I offend anyone, but by living in the gray I think I'm being fair and informative—and besides, I've got a lot to get off my chest. Not everyone will agree with the opinions I've heard in the gray, but like yours that might differ from mine, we have to respect them all.

You might also notice that I don't recite scriptures from the Bible in *The Twi-Lighters*. I won't in further volumes either. I never liked it when, while talking about a certain topic, someone will recite a verse from The Good Book to emphasize a point. If I wanted that opinion, I'd read the Bible instead of conversing with you. I want *yours*, and how *you* feel about a certain topic or situation. By reciting a passage of the Bible during a conversation, I consider that plagiarizing in a tasteless sort of way. Sorry, the gray comes at me at many different angles, which means I might be wrong, but that's just the way I feel.

I used this logic in *Beyond Revelations*. If I recited scripture in its pages, then you might as well just read the Good Book itself. I wanted to express *my* opinions on many different topics, and add *my* personality to those situations. They are what matter here, and they come straight out of the gray. Many religious leaders or historians might disagree with me on some topics, and that's what I want to stir here. Let's have a healthy conversation! I would rather be around people with different views than my own than be around people who have the same opinions as myself. How will I learn anything if everything I say people agree with or vice versa? But listening to a different angle that I didn't think about—now *that's* living in the gray at its core!

Before moving on, please allow me to be straightforward for a moment when it comes to one's point of view. Gaslighting is wrong, whether living in black and white, or in the gray, and I despise that way of communicating. That line of conversation is way out of line, and totally unacceptable under *any* circumstances. Shame on those who use this tactic, and thank God there aren't many that abuse this type of verbal bullying. Amen. (I'll leave you, dear reader, to look up the definition of that term for yourself, and decipher what it means.)

Back to positive matters . . . another topic I'd like to talk about is *how* I wrote this book. Most authors think of a theme, research it, outline it, and know the whole story before writing it. I wrote this whole book completely different—in, and *from* the gray. In other words, on the fly. I somewhat knew the core of the book when I started it (The power going off and most souls—people and all animals—going back to The Creator), but otherwise I had *no* idea where I was going! None! And that includes this part! So, I listened for the voice, and believe me, it constantly responded like never before. It spoke to me insistently at different times during the day, on different highs and lows, and I took mental notes. Sometimes I'd start writing, and I wouldn't know what the next word or sentence would say, but it always came—sometimes later rather than sooner, and so I had to leave a few stories behind before going back to complete them. Writing in the gray? Yes, I'd say so.

I related this way of cowriting with my guardian angel with musical song writers. I love music, and I have always wondered how musicians went about writing songs. Where did their ideas come from? An interesting discussion, and I would love to someday review notes with various songwriters on how they got their many different melodies and themes. Could they come from the same place as mine, or from a different realm of the gray? Could they have their own guardian angel to help them? I'm betting on it more than not. Another characteristic of a songwriter that is usually the norm, but not always the case, is that their "well of ideas" lasts only so long. Look it up, check out history. A successful songwriter will write hit after hit for five, ten, or if they're lucky, fifteen years, and then . . . nothing. No more hits, no more albums. I wondered, will that happen to me with *my* writing? I hope not, for I plan on writing for the rest of my days, but I seriously wonder if I'll be able to. Maybe I won't; and if that's the case, I better get moving before *my* creative well runs dry!

Another unusual aspect of this book is that there is very little dialogue in it. That is by design. I wanted this volume about all the characters to be told more like stories around a campfire. There's nothing creepier than a good old tale being told around a bunch of logs on a fire with friends at night, trying to scare the bejesus out of them, and I hope you believe this book has plenty of those types of stories in it. I hope you like most of them, if not all. I used dialogue only when I thought it necessary, and fought using it even then. The remaining installments will have plenty of dialogue, I can assure you of that! Different volumes are different books.

Beyond Revelations will be at least a four-part book series, more than likely five, and I plan on completing it as quickly as possible. I feel that I have something to contribute to the overall journey, and I hope to do that through this vessel. What will the other books be about? I wish I could tease you by saying "you'll just have to read them to find out," but I can't. I really don't know what will be in those novels, but the ideas will come, and I will listen intently to the voice that has helped me write *The Twi-Lighters* before typing the first word of each new chapter—in the gray. God Bless!

AUTHOR NOTE: Dear reader, you might've noticed that I capitalize some of the same words (such as Warlock/warlock) in places and don't in others, plus spell gray with an 'E' (grey), and that is because they flucuate between a realm that splits into two seperate ones before reconnecting.

I wanted to portray "The Gray Between Black And White" as a sort of sermon, not one that someone might preach in a church, per se, but to associates, friends, or loved ones. One point I'd like to make is that different churches have different rules, traditions, and rituals. That's fine, but what would all religious leaders say about letting one of their congregation conduct the sermon instead of themselves, maybe even as often as once per month? How would they feel about hearing a topic spoken from a different point of view? About what's happening in current events, maybe? I know that most churches would frown on doing such practices, and that's fine as well. You have to respect that. There are rules, regulations, and traditions to follow, and different religious sanctuaries of worship can be very strict. I prefer flexibility. I like the idea of letting someone speak their piece, as you might expect, mixing up and breaking down the old traditions. Translation: expand your mind . . . and move into the gray!

Maybe a collaboration should be added to the menu. For a religious leader, if looked at from a certain angle, this could be considered a form of mentoring to some extent. I'd like to attend a church that knows no bounds. Breakdown traditional Rituals and boundaries; knock down eternal walls. Use different formats constantly, where parishioners don't become complacent. Accept people from all ways of life, and treat them all equally. The Word must be understood by all people, and come from all sides. Unchain the restraints, so to speak, and let true and pure love, plus the spice of joy, rush in. Rejoice in different types of music from all cultures, just as long as they touch the spirit in a positive way. That's my hope for the churches of the future, one where the Gospel of the Lord lives in your heart all week long.

There is way too much goodness out there to let life get you down. Enjoy it the way you like it, and wear a smile wherever you go. Laugh and make jokes whenever life gets a little tough, and don't be afraid to ask for help from above or around you at the appropriate time. God made His presence known to me long ago, when I didn't even know He was there (it can never be repeated enough), and I'll pass his love and message on as long as I'm here. The colors of the rainbow can fill the sky without the storm, and tears of joy can reign down and wash over every soul, making it shine brighter each and every day.

Peace and love forever.

Amen.

I'M NOT DONE YET!

This endeavor of writing words on blank white background scared me more than anything else I have ever done in the past. I always knew that I wanted to write a book when I no longer had to get up each day and punch a clock, but when that time came, I put it off for as long as possible. Eventually strong thoughts and ideas kept creeping into the center of my mind from a dark closet full of terrors I tried to stay away from, but they wouldn't go away, and so I had little choice but to let them out, which became this beginning novel. Fragments of how I have felt over the years started coming together like a puzzle, and this is the final product. I wanted to develop a new style of writing, bringing my strengths and deranged personality characteristics to the forefront, and I hope you like it and find it refreshing.

As I began to layer chapter on top of chapter, I realized how much fun I was having, creating new stories and coming up with new ideas. It is extremely fulfilling, and it makes every passing moment mean more and more in every way, and I thought, "Isn't this what life should be like as retirement sets in?" I believe so, and the thought of always having something to do in the future fills me with much joy and contentment. I hope and pray that all of you dear readers find your own enjoyment in your "golden years," and true happiness. Bless you all in your future endeavors and travels.

REFLECTIONS

One of the biggest events that influenced a lot of my ideas happened on September 11, 2001. Not many horror stories unfold right in front of you in "Real Time" like what transpired on that dreadful morning. It was a day that seemed to never end, and in reality, it still hasn't, for it is still claiming victims. It had everything, though, and it brought out every emotion that we possess, and then stretched them all out. And that could be said about only the first two hours! But then something surreal happened, and the unstable balance of the day shifted.

The visual insidious events that seemed so hard to endure triggered acts of kindness, braveness, selfishlessness, and overall righteousness. Love actually began to shine through the dark storm clouds of outrage that hovered over the country and world that day. People came together and worked as one cohesive unit. Political differences were put on the back burner, and the color of one's skin, or where they came from didn't seem to matter. Tears were shed and shared with others who they might not even have known before that dreadful, fateful morning. By nightfall of that first night, heroes with large machinery began to head into lower Manhattan to help remove debris, joining the firefighters who were searching frantically for survivors, putting their own lives in peril. Later in the aftermath, hateful letters were sent out with deadly anthrax in them, to create added horror in the days that followed. Even still, the bad, the evil, and the terror—no, there was no dismissing those presences, but those entities were quickly losing their strength. Messages were sent that broadcasted narrow-minded religious ideology, which went completely against what most of society believed.

I think that was what bothered me the most later on: that narrow-mindedness, that unwillingness to agree to disagree. That not believing in the gray between black and white. It was that special kind of mental cancer rearing its ugly head again, one which has started wars and bloodshed many times in the past, and unfortunately succeeded in doing again here. At the time of this writing battles are still being fought, and the balance shifts back and forth around the world on a constant basis.

After The North Tower fell the company I worked for sent us all home, and I went directly to my son's high school and signed him out. I felt that was for the best, and he watched for himself what happened, and we talked about it, about how different people think and act, and I felt somewhat guilty about bringing someone into a world that could produce such hate and chaos.

There was one memory about getting him that I'll never forget. By the time I got to the school, policemen had already been dispatched and were guarding the front entrance. As I approached, I said that I wanted to take my son home. The officer nodded, and our eyes met. Hurt was there, although both of us managed to hold back the tears that would eventually win out. After a few heavy moments he smiled weakly, walked me through the front doors and down to the school front office. We were both in shock, going through a kamikaze flow of extreme emotions, yet still functioning. How was that possible? More food for thought.

Memoriam Note: Let us not forget the firemen, police officers, and miscellaneous other first responders who ran into The Towers while others were running out. They were our bravest heroes, and saved many lives. So many of them perished on that day, but they will never be forgotten. Ever!

It was in the days that followed where I remember for the first time crying without realizing it. I felt compelled to watch the aftermath, and as I watched people trying to find loved ones that would never come home, I cried tears like never before, but as that was happening, more and more stories kept coming in—good stories of people helping each other, and people joining together overall. I cried tears then, too, but they were different. They were for hope, hope for a better future. A light in my head came on, and I knew— *I knew!* Yes, mankind had taken a major hit, and many lives had been lost, but I knew that somehow we would make it through. On such a horrible day the light had somehow shone through the darkness! Now I know that that isn't always the case, but it was during those sad days. Good and evil, evil and good—both were there. Both had flowed through the doorway. Fragments—one step back, two forward? Maybe. Will the good always see itself through the darkness where evil lurks? No one knows, just like no one knows who will come out on top in *Beyond Revelations*—not even me. That ending hasn't been revealed to me as of yet. I have hope for the good, though—And I hope you feel the same way.

One Last Revelation: In the last few years since my life has taken a different fork in the road, I usually wake up because I've just had a bad dream, or am expecting Armageddon to take place. I don't usually remember the nightmares, and I don't know why I dread what might happen in the coming hours, but I try my best to stay prepared no matter what the future might send my way. Who knows, maybe it's just the birth of new chapters and stories ready to be typed into my computer, or maybe the true end of days is closer than we think. The answer lies in the foggy mist, that large gray area that knows no bounds.

Until we meet again, take care, and live each second as if it was your last, because you never know . . .

BEYOND REVELATIONS
BOOK ONE: THE TWI-LIGHTERS
BY DAVID ROCKEFELLER

Post Scriptum Closing Narrative Notes: When the power went off, those who were chosen to stay on Earth thought they had never missed a beat, but unbeknownst to them, they were all temporarily suspended in time. Not some—everyone. And everything. Also, in suspended animation were all life that would go back to The Creator: human beings, animals, birds, insects, reptiles, and all sea life. Suns, planets, moons , asteroids, comets, quasars, dark matter, and everything else stopped in their orbits for about sixty-two seconds as well. For billions of years movement had run rampant throughout the vastness of the chamber like heavy traffic, filling its infinite dark space, but now all things had stopped dead in their tracks without a hitch. A low hum could still be heard by the doorway, defying logic, but otherwise all was still, calm.

During that allotted time a light as strong and bright as a trillion suns traveled throughout the different universes, solar systems, quasars, and everything else in-between. That brightness surveyed the obvious magnificent beauty that the life force currents coming through the doorway had produced over many millennia. In every past chamber the creations produced had been different, but this current one had really outdone itself. No one, if asked and had witnessed every other chamber since the beginning of the inception, would dispute that.

The extreme light marveled at the magic it had produced this time around. The colors, the stars—all the moving parts were all just extraordinary! How amazing it had all turned out! Even to the brightness it was breathtaking to witness and see as it moved throughout the entire chamber in those fleeting moments before slowly dissolving into an area where no creation had yet reached.

While on its journey, though, the light spent more time examining Earth, surveying what riches the planet had produced: mountains, tree and plant life, landscapes and different rock formations. What colors they produced! And then it examined the seas and oceans, all reflecting different spectrums, depending on the mood. From the calmness of the blue, to the grayness of disruption, they portrayed the balance that had to exist in all forms throughout *everything* in the chamber! During it's short stay, the light closely studied all the occupants—the ones that would leave, and those that would stay—and was satisfied.

As the brightness moved away it maintained a calmness it had always possessed since its inception. Make no mistake, the light experienced every other emotion as well, but it's calmness always stood head and tails above the rest. And in that powerful emotion it thought confidently, "What will be will always be."

Once the bright light had completely disappeared, all things resumed movement, The Event occurred, many returned to The Creator, and those left on Earth continued onward in a different light. Pray for them, for they are our destiny.

One other note of interest, which happened exactly after the bright light disappeared and The Event took place: Earth's moon resumed movement, only it began moving and rotating in the opposite direction. Another difference, which will be mentioned in detail in future volumes, is that it also reversed *itself!* The Earth, and it's remaining Twi-lighters, now saw only the dark side (now the light side) of the bright satellite, and "the man in the moon" now faced away from the Earth, now in the dark. The significance? The answer lies in future installments, dear reader, but I *can* tell you that it will play an important part of the events that transpire in *Beyond Revelations*.

I'll be looking forward to seeing all of you in Book Two. Again, I pray for peace, love, and harmony for all of you!

THE END

Lasting thoughts to leave you with: A few of my ideas began developing in my mind while attending church service at Nauraushaun Presbyterian Church in Pearl River, New York (where my mother began taking me long before I could retain memory wavelengths). Maybe it was while listening to a sermon, listening to the choir singing a hymn, or just opening up my mind inside the Lord's house. Whatever it was, a certain door was opened between realms, and a few of those ideas started in this particular sanctuary and matured into some of the stories found inside the first installment of *Beyond Revelations*. I'm sure that will continue as I move forward into Book Two, and beyond.

If you ever have the chance to attend a church service at Nauraushaun Presbyterian, I recommend you do so. You will feel the Spirit, and possibly much more. I know I have. We have a new pastor that injects a new type of spirituality into the mix, Dr. Gregory Simpson. He is a wonderful minister who blesses us with good sermons and counsel. I hope to travel down a spiritual highway with him while creating a relationship that will last throughout future days. I consider Pastor Gregory a brother, and a friend—and isn't true friendship what we all yearn to ultimately achieve? So please feel welcomed, and join us on any given Sunday at 10:00 a.m., and become enlightened.

At the time of this writing, COVID19 is ravishing the world and church services have adapted and gone virtual. This form of activity has opened up many avenues, one being able to attend other church services. I encourage all to experience this practice. It might open up your mind, and hear The Word from a different perspective. God Bless!